EX
LIBRIS

_____

_____

_____

Romance Treasury

THE ROMANCE TREASURY ASSOCIATION

NEW YORK · TORONTO · LONDON

These stories were originally published as follows:

UNKNOWN QUEST
Copyright © 1971 by Katrina Britt
First published in London by Mills & Boon Limited in 1971

POST AT GUNDOOEE
Copyright © 1970 by Amanda Doyle
First published in London by Mills & Boon Limited in 1970

INTO A GOLDEN LAND
Copyright © 1971 by Elizabeth Hoy
First published in London by Mills & Boon Limited in 1971

ROMANCE TREASURY is published by
The Romance Treasury Association, Stratford, Ontario, Canada.

Editorial Board: A. W. Boon, Judith Burgess, Ruth Palmour,
Alice Johnson and Ilene Burgess

Dust Jacket Art by Stewart Sherwood
Story Illustrations by Gordon Raynor
Book Design by Charles Kadin
Printed by Kingsport Press Limited, Kingsport, Tennessee

Second printing May 1977

ISBN 0-919860-02-8

Printed in U.S.A.   A003

CONTENTS

UNKNOWN QUEST

UNKNOWN QUEST

Katrina Britt

Gaye Pembleton's first encounter with Lance van Eldin was explosive. She thought he was a petty bank official — stubborn and arrogant — refusing to let her overdraw her account. Then her adored father introduced him as a successful business executive, the kind of a man he would like her to marry!

Her prejudice increased, especially since Lance made no secret of his contempt for the selfish, pampered Gaye and her shallow, useless way of life. Unknowingly, Gaye had met her match.

It was a confrontation only resolved through crisis — when Gaye learned Lance's stubbornness was a strength she could rely on and his arrogance forced her to face up to a suddenly changed life and survive!

CHAPTER ONE

GAYE'S dainty heels tapped lightly on the floor of the bank. With her rosy cheeks, flawless complexion and sparkling blue eyes, every limb in perfect proportion, she was a ravishing picture of blossoming young womanhood, as delicately feminine as a flower.

Sunbeams from tall windows frolicked in her golden hair, turning it into a curtain of glittering silk as she made for a rather meek-looking little clerk who adjusted his spectacles more firmly as she approached.

Wearing a smile guaranteed to melt the heart of a more worldly man than the clerk, she focussed him with a delicious wistfulness and made her request. A slip of paper changed hands, she signed it to push it back beneath the grill. The clerk stared at it for several seconds, then pushed open a panelled door behind him and disappeared.

Gaye drummed beautifully manicured fingers impatiently on the counter and glanced at the small board bearing his name. Mr Savage. She dimpled. How hilariously funny! Anyone looking less savage she could not imagine.

He returned with an embarrassed air. 'I'm afraid your account is considerably overdrawn, Miss Pembleton,' he said, eyeing her seriously over his glasses.

She favoured him with the smile that suffers fools gladly.

'It's not the first time I've been overdrawn. Daddy will put it right. He always does.'

'Ahem!' the clerk cleared his throat nervously. 'Maybe, but this is for a rather large amount.'

Gaye moved impatiently. 'Oh, for heaven's sake stop dithering, man, and give me the money! I've told you that

11

Daddy will make it right.'

Mr Savage drew a finger around the inside of his collar. 'It's not that simple, Miss Pembleton. Could you tell me where we can contact your father?'

'No. He's abroad.'

The clerk looked suddenly hopeful. 'If you could wait a few days while we make enquiries . . .' he began.

'This is ridiculous,' Gaye cut in. 'I insist upon seeing the manager!'

Mr Savage moistened dry lips nervously. 'The manager is engaged. There is the assistant manager.'

Gaye's delicate nostrils quivered with anger. She banged a small fist on the counter and became the cynosure of all eyes. 'I insist upon seeing the manager, and at once,' she bit out.

'Is anything wrong?' drawled a deep, cultured voice.

Gaye found herself staring up at six foot two of lean, broad-shouldered masculinity in a tanned skin that materialized from the panelled doorway. Clad in a black suit of impeccable cut, he wore his arresting classical features proudly with masculine arrogance. His tall loose-knit frame moved forward lazily with the ease of a healthy, virile man who appeared to exist solely on vitamins.

Gaye was aware of fathomless dark eyes looking straight into hers with the intention of intruding into her inmost private thoughts and feelings. 'Yes, there is,' she said, coldly furious. 'I want to make a withdrawal from my account.'

Straight dark brows lifted warily. 'What's holding it up, Mr Savage?' he asked smoothly.

'The young lady's account is overdrawn.'

'I see.' Once again the dark eyes were directed towards her blue ones. 'Shall we go where we can talk?' he said, motioning her to a door in the far wall at the end of the counter.

He followed her into a room, seating her into a comfortable leather chair and offering her a cigarette from a box on the long polished table. Then, taking a lighter from his pocket, he lit it for her.

'Excuse me, won't you?' he drawled, and left the room with long economical strides.

Gaye leaned back in her chair and drew on her cigarette. Quite an eyeful, she mused, her thoughts dwelling on the teak brown curly hair which no amount of disciplined brushing could keep from falling schoolboy fashion on to his forehead. She could imagine that charm of his knocking the little girl clerks over like ninepins.

She looked around and saw a thickly-carpeted room, oak panelled with tall stained glass windows looking out on to the street. In front of her was a heavily carved table with two white phones, a large writing pad, a cigarette box and a small book rack containing manuals. On the wall to her left a large photograph of one of the founders of the bank looking down on her condescendingly.

Impishly she blew out a cloud of smoke towards his offending image, and in that moment the man returned carrying a ledger. Hitching up the knife-edged crease in his trousers, he took the seat on the opposite side of the table and opening the ledger scanned a page swiftly.

'You're certainly overdrawn,' he remarked with a professionally detached air. 'Do you require the money immediately?' Again he regarded her with his deep unfathomable gaze.

Well aware of his intent study of her face, her smile was an alluring curve of pink lips showing small pearly teeth. Deliberately, she crossed one beautiful leg over the other. 'I do.'

'Important?'

Gaye stubbed out her cigarette with a vague tremor of

uneasiness. She was getting nowhere with this infuriating creature who was eyeing her arrogantly as if she was under oath in the dock. She had the feeling that nothing short of a direct hit with a hundredweight of nutty slack would shake that calm exterior. With this in mind she decided on the pleasant approach. 'It's a private matter,' she said sweetly.

Something glittered in his eyes. 'I'm afraid you will have to be more explicit, Miss . . .' He consulted the name above the account in the ledger. 'Miss Pembleton.'

The silence that followed did not give her confidence and her eyes lowered to the long, lean hands folded loosely on the open ledger before him. Like the clear-cut strong features, his hands were those of a self-opinionated man who was never at a loss in any situation. Gaye had the distinct feeling of being unable to impress him in any way and it irritated and annoyed her profoundly. A wave of hot indignant colour flooded her clear skin. How dared he, a mere bank manager question her, Gaye Pembleton, about her private affairs! The man needed teaching a lesson. She made an effort to keep her colour down with her voice, and only partially succeeded.

'Do you know who I am?' she asked haughtily.

He leaned back in his chair, apparently unimpressed, and tossed her a narrow-eyed look that further irritated. 'Miss Pembleton,' he said firmly, 'as one of the bank's customers you will receive the same courtesy and attention as the rest. If you are in financial difficulties you have only to say and the bank will gladly advance you a loan.' Her lovely blue eyes looked at him with a faint disbelief coupled with a bewilderment that was childlike. Her lips opened slightly, then closed in her anger, and she regarded him balefully. 'You're impertinent! How dare you question me about my private affairs and insult me by offering a loan like a . . . money-lender? You'll hear more of this!'

The dark eyes, now points of steel, challenged hers. 'Are

you threatening me, Miss Pembleton?' he asked quietly.

'Threatening you?' she replied, the emphasis on the 'you' openly insulting. She rose to her feet, her small, firm bust in the cream Balenciaga suit rising and falling angrily. 'You're not that important. Thank you for nothing.'

'One moment.' The stern voice of authority halted her half way to the door and she paused, presenting him with a slim back. 'If you are in real trouble I'll loan you the money myself.'

Gaye did not even turn her head. She swept from the room as if he had not spoken, leaving a tantalizing perfume behind which reminded him that the chair facing him had never been more attractively adorned with a female form. He smiled and closed the ledger thoughtfully.

Gaye drove away still quivering with anger to find her thoughts occupied with the intricacies of London's traffic. Eventually she found herself in the vicinity of Cumberland Terrace with its dignified stone façade of columned terraced houses where the best people still resided.

The house was four-storied with lofty rooms and an imposing staircase. When Binns, her father's man, opened the door, the housekeeper was descending the stairs dressed for outdoors.

Hilda Lambert was in her early thirties with a small round face, dark hair and warm brown eyes. She had lost her husband a year ago in a car accident. Maurice Pembleton, Gaye's father, had been driving home from his club one wet evening when his car had collided with the Lamberts'. Eric Lambert had been killed instantly, but his wife, Hilda, had escaped with minor injuries.

Full of remorse that he had been a party to what the coroner had described as a tragic accident brought on by the wet, greasy surface of the road, Maurice Pembleton had offered Hilda the post of housekeeper. His former housekeeper had left to look after an invalid mother.

Hilda Lambert had accepted, deciding that anything was better than staying in the house in St John's Wood where she had been so happy with her husband. She had proved to be efficient in her job and was popular with the staff. Gaye, resenting her father's interest in the woman, had been cool in her relations with her, but Maurice Pembleton had gone out of his way to help Hilda over her tragic loss. A widower himself, he knew how shattering it could be to lose a loved one so tragically.

It was Gaye who finally nipped their friendship in the bud by confiding in her grandmother, who organized parties and cleverly kept her son too busy in his social life to pay Hilda much attention. Eventually they had drifted into their former relationship of employer and housekeeper, much to Gaye's relief.

Looking at her now neat, trim and very attractive in a tailored silk suit, Gaye wondered why she had never bothered about seeking a partner nearer her own station in life. Was she still hankering after a man who, besides holding down half a dozen directorships, was one of the wealthiest men in London? It never occurred to Gaye that her own companionship was not enough for a man like Maurice Pembleton who was young enough to enjoy life to the full.

But then it was his own fault that Gaye was so self-centred and spoiled. She had never been denied anything in her short life, never had to consider anyone but herself. She had grown up among the environment of the idle rich, savouring all the delights that money could bring from sunshine cruises to winter sports abroad.

If Hilda Lambert knew that Gaye had been the means of breaking off the friendship with her father she showed no animosity towards her. For Gaye sparkled with the inner glow of healthy youth and could be very lovable and charming when she chose. Hilda, smiling at her as she drew on her gloves in the hall, wondered how her character would develop when the cold winds of change started to blow away some of the cotton wool she had been wrapped in since birth.

'I'm glad you've arrived, Miss Pembleton,' she said pleasantly. 'Mr Van Eldin phoned to remind you that you're to lunch with him today.'

'Thanks, Mrs Lambert. I almost forgot. My account at the bank is overdrawn and I've had words with a perfectly odious manager about it.' Gaye smiled ruefully. 'It's my own fault, of course, Daddy is very generous, but the crowd I'm going around with are expensive and I lost quite a bit at the Casino the other evening.' She moved towards the staircase. 'I must dash if I'm to be ready to lunch with Teddy.'

She tripped lightly up the staircase and Hilda sighed, trying to recall her own impetuous youth, as she walked in the direction of the kitchen. She would have to tell Cook that there would be no one in to lunch. She herself was shopping in town and would lunch there.

Seated at the small table in their favourite steak house, Gaye forgot the disturbing incident at the bank that morning as she listened to Teddy Van Eldin's Boston accent.

Meeting his merry brown eyes, it occurred to her how easy it would be to become fond of him. Already on their short acquaintance friends were including them both in their invitations to parties and dinners.

Teddy Van Eldin was a slight, rangy young man who looked like a nice friendly hedgehog with his light closely cropped hair and a ready smile hovering about his mobile mouth. He was a young American of twenty who had been studying economics at London University for a year and was due to return to Boston with his mother.

Laura Van Eldin had been a widow when she chose an Englishman, Richard Van Eldin, on her second venture into marriage. Now a widow for the second time, she spent the summer at Van Eldin Towers and returned to Boston for the rest of the year.

Gaye had met Teddy at a party and had been instantly attracted to the boy with the shy demeanour. The party had been too overcrowded to be enjoyable, so they had sat on the stairs and between nibbles of sausage rolls and sips of lager they had discovered that they liked the same things.

After that they had enjoyed those things together, driving in the rain, swinging across the Heath, their lithe young bodies leaning forward together against the fresh winds, having odd meals in quaint wayside pubs and dancing to a good band.

It had seemed to Gaye that he was always ringing her up, sometimes to lunch with him like today, sometimes for a film show or a concert. There had been a pleasant platonic air about their relationship, an easy drifting quality that suited Gaye for the moment while her father was away. Yes, she thought, it would be easy to become very fond of Teddy Van Eldin.

They tucked into their thick juicy steaks with healthy young appetites with Gaye smiling at her companion's chatter until unconsciously her thoughts returned to the incident of the bank that morning. It was beastly having to wait until the end of the month for her next allowance.

Teddy looked up from his fast disappearing lunch when she gave an audible sigh. 'What's that for? Want another steak?'

Gaye looked down at her own lunch and found she had suddenly lost all appetite for it. 'No, thanks. I have more than enough here. I was miserably dwelling on the fact that I was cleaned of cash at the Casino last night. Now I'm waiting for Daddy to come home for my next allowance.'

Teddy smiled ruefully. 'I've a few pounds to spare to tide you over if you want them. Better still, we could try our luck with it at the Casino. We both lost heavily, so it's our turn to win. It would be nice to get our own back and we could split our winnings fifty-fifty then.'

Gaye laughed lightheartedly. 'I couldn't accept money from you, you idiot, but I'll go with you to the Casino. I feel like a spot of cheerful entertainment. Not that it will be very entertaining if you lose again.'

He grinned cheerfully. 'Something tells me that this is going to be my lucky day.'

'It certainly isn't mine,' she said dryly, and told him about the affair at the bank that morning.

He grimaced. 'Reminds me of my half-brother Lance. He's English, public school and all that. He's a stickler for playing the game and he can afford it. Not only did he receive the bulk of my stepfather's fortune when he died, but his godfather, who is a banker, has also made him his heir.'

'Sounds interesting,' she murmured, smiling at the waitress who brought their coffee. 'Is he in London?'

'No. The family home, Van Eldin Towers, is in Sussex. Lance inherited it from his father, but both Mother and I are free to come and go as we choose. Lance is in the States marketing a computer. He's a mathematical wizard and is raking in the shekels with an invention he's put on the market in New York.'

She wrinkled her nose. 'Sounds as dry as dust, even if it is gold dust! I bet he's one of those absent-minded geniuses who go about in odd socks leaving two more like them at home.'

Teddy dropped three lumps of sugar into his coffee with an amused grin. 'Quite the reverse. He was a gay dog in his youth.'

Gaye lifted her cup daintily. 'He sounds a mere lurch away from the family tomb. Is he so ancient?'

'He's around thirty and a bachelor—at least he was when

he wrote home a couple of weeks ago. Although he's a handsome guy, the type the girls go for, he hasn't much time for them. He's a bit of a cynic, but I like him.' Teddy said it without rancour and Gaye liked him for it.

'Well, at least he works, even if he is a future Onassis.'

He gulped down his coffee. 'Hey now, it's not my fault that I'm a student! Lance might bulldoze me into joining him when he returns. He's no time for slackers even when they've money to burn.' He looked at her thoughtfully. 'What are you doing this afternoon?'

Gaye put down her empty cup. 'Going to the grandparents to tea. Care to come?'

He shook his head regretfully. 'I'd like to, but I'm taking Mother to Sothebys. She's interested in a picture being auctioned there today.'

When they parted Gaye drove down to her grandparents' house in Greenwich. Five miles from Tower Bridge on the Surrey side, it looked across the river to the Isle of Dogs.

Rumour had it that the Isle of Dogs derived its name from King Charles the Second who kept his dogs there when he was in residence at Greenwich Palace. Gaye loved Greenwich. In the summer the pier was ablaze with tubs of geraniums and petunias and white painted seats where one could partake of refreshments while watching the river traffic go by. Many visitors never went beyond the pier and so missed the enchanting green hill of Greenwich Park with its picturesque building of the Royal Observatory set majestically on top like a crown.

Next to her own home with its secluded garden at the rear and its easy access to the West End shops, Gaye adored her grandparents' home in Greenwich. Sam Pembleton, her grandfather, had been one of the leading advocates of his day and still carried on an active retirement.

Maurice Pembleton had inherited his father's shrewd brain and ready wit both useful attributes to his success as a business tycoon and financial wizard.

Gaye found her grandmother weeding the well-planned garden which led down to the river. She looked very sweet and feminine in pastel blue. 'Hello, dear,' she said, kissing Gaye warmly. 'Your grandfather is out, but he expects to be back for tea.' She peeled off her gardening gloves as she spoke and indicated the gay furniture on the terrace. 'Let's sit on the terrace. It's much too nice to stay indoors.'

Polly Pembleton's happy married life had left her face remarkably unlined and her blue eyes mirrored the tranquillity and peace of mind of a woman who had found the perfect partner. 'Have you heard from your father?' she asked when they were seated on the terrace.

Gaye drew cigarettes and a lighter from her bag. 'Not recently. You know Daddy. He never was one for writing letters home.'

Polly watched her light a cigarette. 'I hope he's all right,' she said impressively. 'I didn't think he looked too well the last time he was here. He's working too hard.' She sighed. 'He isn't getting any younger, you know, dear.'

Gaye carefully blew out a line of smoke away from her grandmother.

'Daddy's all right,' she said carelessly. 'He's as strong as a horse and he's never ill.'

Polly looked at her as she sat daintily upright with an alertness that added to her charm. She studied the haughtiness in the delicate curve of her neck and her slender straightness, and blessed it for keeping the child above the slipshod way of living that was penetrating even the best families nowadays. She was sensible, but she had a lot to learn about life. Polly was worried, for she knew her son was not happy. He was lonely and had been since the death of his wife many years ago.

Hilda Lambert had been the only woman in whom he had shown any real interest, and Polly had thought long and often about the part she had played in parting them. She could not expect Gaye to understand. She was such a child in many ways and had been spoiled, but she thought it would be kind to drop a hint of what might happen in the near future.

'Darling,' she said gently, 'have you ever considered the possibility of your father retiring? After all, he's a very wealthy man and can afford to do so.'

Gaye laughed lightly, but her delicate face flooded with colour as she sensed a meaning underlying her grandmother's words. 'But Daddy simply lives for his work. Besides, what would he do if he retired?'

'Exactly,' Polly said meaningly.

'Oh, come off it, Gran!' Gaye spoke a trifle exasperatedly. 'What's on your mind?'

'It could mean that your father, having more time on his hands, might look around for more company.'

Gaye gave a relieved sigh. 'For the moment you had me worried. I thought you had something up your sleeve that was really going to shake me.'

Polly remarked wisely, 'I haven't, but your father might.'

Gaye crushed out her cigarette, having lost the taste for it, and her eyes grew serious. 'You mean Hilda Lambert?'

Her grandmother nodded. 'I think we were wrong in interfering between them as we did. Your father has a right to do as he pleases with his own life.'

Gaye's chin lifted militantly. 'I don't dispute it, but he has me.'

'I'm afraid you won't make any difference if he takes it in his head to draw someone closer.'

'But why should he? He has plenty of men friends with whom he goes sailing or plays golf. He could enjoy the same things when he retires as he does now.'

'But, darling, your father isn't an old man. He might fall in love.'

Gaye's reaction to this was a burst of tinkling laughter. 'Who, Daddy?'

Polly nodded quite serious. 'He's still a very attractive man.'

Gaye agreed. 'I know, but he won't marry again, not Daddy. At least not while he has me.'

'I shouldn't be so sure. Love's a powerful potent.'

'Is it?' Gaye asked, her look doubtful.

'You don't understand, my dear, because you've never been in love yourself. Isn't there one young man among your many dates who's set you off thinking of marriage?'

Gaye shook her head. 'I've met no one to come up to Daddy.'

'Darling! Don't go around looking for a father figure,' her grandmother cried in dismay. 'You need someone young and vibrantly alive, someone who will make you aware of yourself as a woman, stir you into all kinds of emotion.'

Gaye's laugh was a spontaneous ripple of mirth. 'Darling, you are delicious. I didn't know you cared.'

The older woman gave a tolerant smile. 'It's no use my saying anything, is it? You've never been in love. My dearest wish is that somewhere along your unknown quest you will find the perfect partner and enjoy the same happiness as I have.'

Her granddaughter hugged her knees and dimpled. 'You say the quaintest things, Gran. I have no quest known or otherwise that I'm aware of.'

'My dear, every girl sets out on an unknown quest without knowing it until she meets the man of her heart.'

Gaye's voice held a note of cynicism. 'Darling, you might have met the perfect mate, but it doesn't say that I shall too.'

'I know you will.' Polly smiled at her fondly. 'You have the Pembleton streak in you that won't tolerate substitutes.

You'll seek the real thing and find it. What about this boy you're going around with? The young American.'

Gaye frowned. 'You mean Teddy Van Eldin?'

'I believe that's his name. A student, is he not?'

'Yes. He's two months older than I am,' Gaye answered perversely.

Polly's eyes were a troubled blue. 'I'm not interfering, my dear, neither am I trying to rush you into marriage, but life has a habit of changing and taking you unawares. You have plenty of time to marry. At the moment you're happy and loved by your family. If you were to marry in the near future it would be because you wanted to. On the other hand if something happened in the meantime to make you feel lonely and miserable you might rush into marriage as a means of escape, and that would be a tragedy.'

Gaye wrinkled her nose. 'You're being morbid, Gran. What could happen?'

'Nothing, I hope.' The older woman smiled. 'Perhaps I am being morbid. Why not bring that young man to tea one day? I'd like to meet him.'

'Why? To look him over as a prospective suitor?'

'No. As a matter of fact I imagined you with someone a little older and more exciting as a suitor.'

Gaye sat upright. 'How do you know that Teddy isn't exciting?'

'His mother didn't give me that impression when she rang me this morning,' Polly said calmly.

Gaye stared. 'You know Mrs Van Eldin?'

'No. She rang me to say that she was very upset about her son gambling the other evening. She doesn't approve of the crowd of young people he's going around with. He must have lost heavily.'

'Sad but true,' Gaye said, unabashed. 'So did I.'

'Oh, you didn't! How naughty of you, Gaye, when you know how your father hates gambling.' Polly was mildly disapproving.

Gaye lifted slim shoulders. 'We don't make a habit of it. It was the first time for me. We all wanted something to do and the whole crowd went. Funnily enough Teddy and I were the only two who lost. The others managed to make good their losses.'

Her grandmother compressed her lips. 'I'm not sympathizing with you. I'm surprised that you hadn't more sense.'

Gaye chuckled, in no way put out by her grandmother's attitude.

'So Mrs Van Eldin thinks I'm leading her son astray? Surely Teddy is capable of looking after himself?'

'I don't think he is. I rather gathered from our conversation this morning that the boy is easily led. Probably been spoiled.' Polly twinkled. 'She continually referred to him as "my baby".'

Gaye's expression was a mixture of astonishment and mirth. 'She didn't! How perfectly priceless!'

'It's not so funny,' the older woman said wisely. 'Most mothers are inclined to spoil their sons, as you'll discover when you have sons of your own. I think I ought to tell you that Mrs Van Eldin is blaming you for her son's refusal to go home with her to Boston now that his studies are over.'

'It's the first I've heard of Teddy going home,' Gaye said indignantly. 'She sounds perfectly beastly and I hope I never meet her.'

Polly found herself agreeing. Gaye was self-willed and she could imagine matters becoming somewhat heated if they did meet.

CHAPTER TWO

IN view of what her grandmother had said that afternoon Gaye prepared for her evening out with Teddy wondering if he would come. He came smiling and optimistic. Trying to capture his mood, she snuggled down in her corner of the Jag as it roared away from the house.

The Casino held no attraction for Gaye. She had gone with the rest of the crowd for kicks, and wasn't at all happy about paying a return visit. Her father would not be pleased if he knew and she had no desire to cause trouble for Teddy.

Teddy, however, had no such thoughts. He was in great form.

'We're going to dine out before trying our luck. That Casino owes us our revenge, and I hope it's a sweet one and we win all before us. Agreed?'

He flung her a quick grin. She nodded, not altogether convinced.

'If you say so—only don't forget I've no money to help you out if you lose.'

'Stop cackling, woman. We're not going to lose. We're going to win,' he said gaily. 'What about eating at that nice Chinese place near to Marble Arch? The Pagoda.'

So the Pagoda it was where the food was excellent and they danced later to nostalgic music in the more dimly lit of the two rooms. Gaye would have been quite happy to have stayed there for the evening, but Teddy was bent on going to the Casino.

The place was full when they arrived, walking in on deep pile carpet to view the chandelier-lit scene. Most of the women at the tables were generously sprinkled with jewels.

Many of them, Gaye guessed, were keeping their diamond-adorned fingers crossed, hoping like Teddy that their luck was in.

Teddy came with his chips and because the seats were all taken, they played the first game standing. Teddy won, grinned at Gaye and placed half his chips for the next game. While the ball spun round, Gaye, scanning the faces of the other players, repelled a shudder of revulsion. Their expressions were mostly deadpan, their eyes hard, glittering pebbles fixed on the ball as it spun out their fate.

Suddenly Gaye wanted to get away. She touched Teddy's arm. 'Let's go,' she whispered.

He stared at her in amazement, but she did not care. The whole scene sickened her.

'What now?' he said. 'Just when my luck has changed?'

The ball slowed down to a stop. Teddy had won again. Several of the players now rose from the table empty-handed; their faces looked haunted. Gaye shook her head when Teddy motioned her to an empty chair.

Some of the people playing were following Teddy's lead hoping to cash in on his luck and Gaye watched the look of fascination on his face. He stood hypnotized by his luck.

'Place your bets, please,' came the voice of the croupier.

Teddy hesitated. Gaye knew instinctively that he was considering putting all his winnings on the next game, but she had reached the point when she did not care one way or the other.

'Go on!' she cried impatiently, knowing that the sooner the game was over the sooner they would be away. 'What are you waiting for?'

'That's enough, Teddy.'

At the deep voice of authority Teddy swung round to look at the speaker. 'Why, Lance, you son of a gun!' he cried in astonishment. 'When did you get back?'

Gaye turned and saw that the arrogant stranger whom

Teddy addressed as Lance was none other than the infuriating creature who had interviewed her at the bank that
morning. So he was not the bank manager after all! He
was the half-brother Teddy had told her about that afternoon at lunch. How dared he play such a practical joke on
her!

'I arrived this morning. Come on,' he said crisply.

'Wait a minute,' Teddy protested, but the other man was
adamant.

'I said come on. Your mother thought you would be here.
She isn't well and she's asking for you.'

'Oh, what the heck!' Sulkily Teddy gathered up his pile
of chips and was suddenly aware of Gaye at his side. 'Gaye,
this is my half-brother, Lance. Lance, Miss Gaye Pembleton.'

Lance gave her a cool little bow with no sign of recogni-
tion in his dark eyes and turned once again to Teddy. 'Cash
your chips and be quick about it,' he said curtly.

Teddy obeyed and left them, Gaye silent and stiff as a
rod with Lance beside her scanning the crowd with an aloof
indifference.

Gaye quivered beneath his snub as though from a direct
blow. The insufferable creature! Who did he think he was?
Her swift glance at his face was unobserved. The Casino
lights tended to darken the thick hair springing back abundantly from his well-shaped head above stern straight
brows. Even in repose the masculine line of nose and jaw
had a cruel, intimidating look. Impeccably groomed in well
fitting evening dress, he stood out from the crowd, tall, lean
and elegant. A man nevertheless, but one who appeared to
be quite indifferent to what other people, including herself,
might think about him.

To Gaye, overwhelmed with righteous indignation, there
came a curious exciting feeling in the form of a challenge,
as if the man standing beside her had thrown down the

gauntlet and dared her to pick it up.

Well, she would accept the challenge. She would show him that she was not used to being ignored. Careful, her heart whispered. Here was no ordinary adversary but an experienced man of the world who knew all the answers. Abusing or ignoring him would have no effect. Her anger had increased at his treatment of Teddy, who returned swaggering a little with his winnings. To her dismay, he offered her half the wad of notes.

Gaye's face was scarlet. 'No, thanks,' she said hastily, noting the scornful twist of his companion's lips. 'I told you I wanted none of it, Teddy.'

He grinned, shrugging off her refusal. 'Okay. We'll have a drink to celebrate then, shall we? What about it, Lance?'

'What's it to be?' Lance queried, his eyes moving swiftly from Teddy to dwell on Gaye speculatively. 'Champagne?'

The curt query shook her more because she sensed the underlying sarcasm, or was it contempt, in his voice? She could not be sure. But she was sure what Teddy lacked in character this man made up for in ruthlessness and swift decisive action. In that quivering moment she saw him as a threat to her own happy existence. With an effort she assumed a lightness she was far from feeling.

'A tomato juice for me, please. I'm not particularly fond of alcohol.'

She was not particular about a drink either, but she had no wish to spoil Teddy's evening. The stools fronting the bar were high and before she could hitch herself up on one, two hands spanned her slim waist and lifted her easily. Lance then turned to the barman and ordered two double whiskies and a tomato juice and, as silently as he had lifted her on to the stool, he passed her the drink.

She accepted it with brittle politeness, ignoring the tantalizing but cool glint in his dark eyes. The bar was filling up. Lance leaned with his back against it, having surrendered his seat to a woman in a party close by. Uneasy beneath his scrutiny, Gaye concentrated on Teddy who straddled a stool and chatted on unconcernedly beside her. Allowing the men to lead the conversation, she found herself watching the mirror at the back of the bar which reflected several of the people she had seen playing earlier at the tables. One of them, a middle-aged tubby man, caught her gaze and winked. She smiled back, feeling a little more cheerful.

'You're not drinking.' The unexpected deep tones of Lance set her teeth on edge and he was rewarded with a defiant blue gaze.

'Maybe I'm not in a drinking mood,' she said.

He held her gaze with hard eyes. 'Sorry to spoil your fun,' he drawled.

'You haven't,' Gaye bit out shortly.

'No, you haven't,' Teddy put in amiably. 'You see Gaye...'

'I'd like to go home, Teddy, if you don't mind.' She interrupted before he could explain her reluctance to visit the Casino to Lance. She had suffered more than enough of the man's hateful presence. It had nothing to do with him, in any case, and she was annoyed with Teddy for giving in to him so easily.

Gaye put down her glass and slid from her seat before Lance could help her down. One more touch of those strong lean fingers and she would have been tempted to slap that cynical look from his face.

Lance straightened lazily and put down his glass. 'I'll see Miss Pembleton home, Teddy.'

To Gaye's delight there was a sparkling glint of defiance in Teddy's eyes and he hesitated. It was the look a small boy might give an elder brother who was pushing him around. Then, as quickly as it had appeared, it went to be replaced by a resigned half-smile. 'See you, Gaye,' he said, and left them together.

Puzzled and bewildered by his behaviour, she turned wrathfully on the cause of it. 'I'm going home by taxi,' she blazed. Then, head held high, cheeks burning, she marched towards the door, remembering with a sinking heart that she had only a few shillings in her bag.

He caught her up easily with his long stride. 'I'll see you home. It's the least I can do after sending your escort away.'

She stiffened with angry pride. 'I refuse to go with you,' she said firmly.

His fingers closed over her arm and she looked up at him in pure amazement. 'But I insist,' he said softly, smiling down into her angry, flushed face.

His persistence filled her with fury as he piloted her to his car. That he dared to speak to her at all after his masquerade that morning amazed her, but then the man was capable of anything ordering poor Teddy about until he had not a leg to stand on. Fuming inwardly, she slid into the front seat keeping her distance from the infuriating figure who, tucking in his long legs, coolly took the driving seat.

They had left the car park when he said, 'I want to apologize for barging in on your evening out, but I'd like to talk to you. Would you go for a drive?'

'Yes. Home.'

'Very well, we'll talk now. Mrs Van Eldin is very upset about Teddy gambling.'

Gaye stiffened in her corner. 'Why tell me?'

'Because you appear to be encouraging him.'

Gaye nearly exploded, but restrained herself. She was giving him the advantage, but the accusation was so unexpected and unjust that she was momentarily at a loss to know how to deal with it. He had heard her urging Teddy to place his money on the last bet and had obviously drawn his own conclusions. What did she care? He could think what he liked. She listened as he continued.

'Teddy is not only easily led, he's apt to be fond of gambling. He lost a packet last year at Las Vegas when he went there for a holiday.'

She thought fleetingly of Teddy's rapt expression at the gambling table and his tractability where Lance was concerned.

'You can hardly blame me for that,' she answered, driven to getting a dig in, however slight.

'I'm not blaming you for anything. I only said that you appear to be encouraging Teddy to gamble.'

'Which is the same thing,' she took him up swiftly. 'You enjoy taking a rise out of anyone, don't you?'

'Do I?' with aggravating indifference. 'You're angry with me for fooling you as to my identity this morning, aren't you?'

'What do you care?' she retorted. 'You must have had quite a laugh at my expense.'

He neither confirmed nor denied it. 'I was at the bank to see my godfather who was at a board meeting there. I had to go to the rescue when I heard you browbeating old Savage. The man's had two heart attacks and has to avoid any excitement.'

'Very heroic,' she jeered. 'Now you're rescuing Teddy.'

'I came because Mrs Van Eldin asked me to. A friend rang her up from the Casino to say that Teddy was there.'

'So you came like a good boy.'

Instantly the indolent air vanished, but he spoke with admirable control. 'You still don't know the circumstances and I'm not going to enlighten you. What I'm going to say is, I don't think it's very wise of you to resort to gambling as a means of increasing your income.'

Her head swivelled his way and sparks appeared in her eyes.

'You're much too presumptuous, Mr Van Eldin,' she shot at him. 'What I do is entirely my own business.'

He stopped at the traffic lights and turned to look down into her face. There was a curious light in his eyes that for some reason stirred her oddly. 'I don't wish to quarrel with you,' he said quickly. 'I only want to give you a word of advice. I'm much older than you and have more knowledge of the world. A Casino is no place for a nice little girl.'

She watched the traffic lights change, her hands clasped in her lap. 'That's very magnanimous of you, but I don't need your advice.'

'Nor my company?'

'I hardly think Mrs Van Eldin would approve,' she said childishly.

'Mrs Van Eldin happens to be my stepmother. I am answerable to no one.'

Gaye knew he regarded her as young and silly and as such resented her. But he did not resent her half as much as she resented him, and she would not be sorry to see the last of the lordly Mr Van Eldin.

They reached Cumberland Terrace, and Gaye was out of the car before he could open the door for her. Flinging him a curt thanks, she did not even turn her head when the car shot away.

Gaye loved the life she led—loved waking up in a morning, taking a leisurely bath, donning an expensive dress or model suit, using exciting shades of nail varnish and experimenting with new make-up. She looked forward to the pleasant hour with her father in the evening before the guests arrived for dinner and the last-minute consultations with Cook about the well-planned meals that no one ever refused an invitation to.

It was a good life, lunching out with friends most days and enjoying the parties given by the gay young crowd she knew in between acting as hostess to her father.

She was awakened early on Sunday morning by the phone ringing beside her bed. Sleepily she reached out to pick it up. It was her friend, Dorothy Frayne.

'Hello, Gaye,' she said brightly. 'Ready for the Ban the Bomb march this morning? It looks like being a heavenly day for it.'

Gaye squinted towards the window where the sunlight streamed in between the drawn curtains. She had forgotten the march.

'Who's taking who?' she asked sleepily.

'I'm picking you up in half an hour.'

They chatted together and when Dorothy rang off on a cheerful note Gaye replaced the receiver thoughtfully. She was not too keen, but it was something to do. The crowd were going, but she doubted if Teddy would be among them after the incident at the Casino. Dorothy was leaving London, too, in the near future. Gaye had been friends with Dorothy since childhood, and now Dorothy's father, a consultant engineer, was taking his family to live in the States.

Thank goodness her father was due back soon, for life without Dorothy, Teddy and her grandparents would be pretty boring.

Dorothy arrived on time, a dark vivacious girl with the ability to squeeze every ounce of fun out of life. Her hair was a warm brown and she wore it straight with a fringe. Her laughing hazel eyes shone and she remained Gaye of an elf in her mushroom and brown dress and smart buckled shoes.

'I've a picnic basket in the boot and cans of drinks in case we get hot and thirsty,' Dorothy prattled on. 'Is Teddy coming?'

'I don't know,' Gaye answered truthfully.

Dorothy swung the car towards Trafalgar Square. 'You could ring him, or aren't you bothered?'

Gaye shrugged. 'Not really,' she answered, and was surprised to discover that she was speaking the truth. Yet during their friendship she had felt an affinity in him that could easily have been mistaken for something deeper. Now she was sure that their friendship was only the platonic kind. Annoyed that she should feel so despondent, she gave herself up to the joy of the morning and listened to Dorothy's dim chatter.

The march had been fun with some of the young men carrying banners and everything had been orderly until they returned again to Trafalgar Square. It was then that Gaye began to feel a trifle uneasy. The mounted police looked militant and the marchers were in high spirits.

She was not in the least surprised to see a sign of defiance in her companions when the police moved in to disperse them. Suddenly Gaye found herself trapped in a moving sea of humanity that separated her from her companions and threatened to engulf her. The air was filled with cries of protest amid the whinnying of horses and she was carried along like a piece of driftwood. The last thing she remembered was something striking her head before she sank into unconsciousness.

She came round to find herself in the cool spacious interior of a car. The windows were down and when her vision cleared she saw Lance Van Eldin bending over her. A quiver rippled over her face, but she controlled it.

'Take it easy. You passed out. What you were doing in a mob like that, I don't know.'

He spoke with some irritation and turned his head when a man appeared at the window of the car.

'The tea you ordered, guv'nor. It's hot and sweet the way you wanted it.'

Lance took the proffered cup. 'Thanks, you can wait for it if you will.'

He held the cup to her lips. 'Drink it,' he commanded,

and because it was less trouble to obey, she drank the hot, sweet liquid slowly.

The empty cup was passed back to the man and Lance put a hand in the pocket of his pale grey suit. 'Cigarette?' he asked, flicking open his case.

She shook her head, wondering why of all the people in London she had to meet the one she most detested. Gaye watched him return the case to his pocket and moved in protest of his intent gaze.

'Was Teddy with you in that mob?' he asked grimly.

'You know he wasn't,' she retorted. 'You also know that I haven't seen him since that night at the Casino.'

He said coldly, 'I haven't the least idea where Teddy is. I only returned from Paris this morning.' His eyes narrowed unpleasantly. 'You could have been trampled on by that mob out there. I wouldn't mind if those idiot marches did any good, but they don't. They only confuse the sensible citizens and place an intolerable burden on the police. What was your reason for going?'

Deliberately she gave him the answer she knew he expected. 'For something to do,' she said sweetly.

His face registered no surprise, although he appeared to find her reason for going incredible. 'You need a good spanking, my girl.' Leaning forward, he shifted the silken hair from the bruise on her forehead. 'You were struck by a flying shoe. Does it hurt?'

'What do you care?' she replied harshly.

'Let's say I hate to see young things hurt even when it's their own fault.'

His nearness made her nervously aware of his magnetism, taking in the well-groomed masculine fragrance and the strength of the supple brown wrist and long narrow hand that reached for her hair. The experienced look in his eyes told her that he knew the world too well and would always be one jump ahead of anyone else in consequence.

She recoiled from his touch, feeling dishevelled and less immaculate than usual. The hot tea she had drunk was oozing out of her in beads of moisture. It could have been accelerated by weakness from her unnerving experience or it could be her silly reaction to his nearness.

She looked around for her bag, found it dropped into her lap from a long arm that had reached for it from the back seat, and watched him draw forth a first-aid box from the glove compartment of the car.

Tossing back her hair, Gaye mopped her brow. She was wiping the dampness from her hands when her head was tilted back with cool fingers and a plaster placed gently on the bruise on her forehead. Gaye had closed her eyes while he was so near and opened them again to look straight into his. The colour came back swiftly into her pale face and he smiled, showing white, strong teeth.

'That's better now you have some colour in your cheeks. You had me worried. Ever fainted before?'

Gaye shook her head aware, above the hammering of her pulses of the need to get away. Impulsively she reached for the door handle.

'Thanks for everything,' she said swiftly, but before she could open the door his hand was covering hers.

'You're not going back into that mob, you little idiot. You're still not a hundred per cent fit. I'm taking you home.'

Allowing him to drag her hand away, she sank back into her seat, feeling weak and breathless. There was some truth in his words, for her whole body felt cold and clammy despite the heat of the car as it stood exposed to the morning sun.

The journey was made in silence with Gaye leaning back in her seat with closed eyes. Drawing up at her door, Lance was out in a trice to help her out. Gaye would have drawn away from his helping hand had she felt capable of making it to the house, but she was still decidedly shaky.

Binns opened the door and his welcoming smile at her appearance changed to one of concern when he saw the plaster on her forehead. His eyebrows raised sharply in approval when Lance picked her up in his arms to carry her in.

'This way, sir,' he said, leading the way up the staircase as if it was the usual procedure for Gaye to be carried to her room.

The bedroom door was opened and Lance strode in to deposit her gently on her charming divan bed.

Binns hovered in the doorway. 'Has there been an accident, sir?' he asked politely.

Lance straightened and regarded him with cool dark eyes. 'Miss Pembleton was struck with a shoe and fainted. Fortunately there was no one's foot in it at the time. I think she ought to rest for an hour or so.'

Gaye detected the satire behind the cool suggestion and fumed.

He seemed to be secretly amused and it took all her self-control not to flare up and order him from the room. To her chagrin he sat down on the bed beside her to rest a cool hand on her damp forehead.

'How do you feel?' he asked.

She stiffened beneath his touch. 'I'm perfectly all right, thanks.'

He looked down at her unabashed. 'I think you'll survive,' he drawled. 'It's quite an ordeal to be crushed in a mob, isn't it?'

Gaye could have hit him. He was so aggravatingly mocking. He might have sensed her anger and decided to add to it, for he went on with a half-smile, 'Let it be a lesson to you.'

Though it was spoken in jest, his last remark roused her indignation to boiling point. Binns was not in the doorway, but he could be lurking on the corridor. On top of which, deep within her, she knew she had behaved in an irresponsible manner. How dare he? It was none of his business. Gaye could hold her temper no longer.

'Get out!' she flared.

There was a gleam in his eyes that frightened her—a queer feeling ran through her veins, a warning that she had met her master. The next moment he was looking towards the doorway to stare at Hilda Lambert's unexpected appearance. To Gaye's surprise, he strode forward to take her hand cordially.

'Hilda! This is a pleasant surprise. How are you, and how's Eric?'

The housekeeper flushed darkly. 'Hello, Lance. Eric's dead.'

'Dead?' he echoed incredulously. 'What happened?'

Hilda shot a glance at Gaye, who sat, lips compressed in anger at being ignored.

'He was killed in a car crash a year ago.'

'I'm sorry to hear that.' The deep voice was concerned. 'It must have happened when I was in the States.' He frowned. 'What are you doing here?'

'I'm the housekeeper. Mr Pembleton has been very good to me since I lost Eric.' Hilda spared another look at Gaye. 'Has Miss Pembleton met with an accident?'

Lance turned his head in Gaye's direction as if he had forgotten her existence. 'She'll probably tell you all about it. See that she has some rest, will you?' He glanced at his watch. 'I'll have to go now. I'll take you out to dinner one evening, Hilda. I want to hear all about it. I'll give you a ring.'

When they had gone Gaye lay back thoughtfully on her bed. She had never had any occasion to think deeply about her way of life. It had flowed back along smoothly and carefree, giving her no cause to wonder where the current might lead her. It never occurred to her that her life could change until her father's affair with Hilda Lambert. She shuddered at the thought that her father could have been killed instead of Eric Lambert. Gaye could not begin to picture life without her father, and Hilda Lambert would never have him if she could help it.

The housekeeper came in at that moment with a cup of tea and two aspirins. Gaye, sitting up, accepted both politely.

'Thanks for the aspirins,' she said pleasantly. 'My head still feels woolly.'

Hilda looked at her gravely. 'You were lucky to get away so lightly. I don't think those protest marches are a good idea. They achieve so little. I know those that sponsor them have good intentions, but it's the few undesirables who slip in along the way that cause the trouble.'

Gaye shrugged and washed down the aspirins with the tea. 'One has to have something to do on Sunday. It's so dull.' Her dark blue eyes met Hilda's steadily. 'I can't understand Daddy not writing or ringing up. Have you heard from him?'

'I?' the housekeeper queried, returning her stare. 'Why should I?'

Gaye looked down into her cup. 'It was just a thought. It's so strange having no word from him.'

'His silence is nothing to worry about,' the older woman said calmly. 'We would have heard if anything had happened to him. He could be aiming to surprise you by turning up unexpectedly.'

When the housekeeper had left the room Gaye fell to thinking that she wasn't such a bad sort. Even so she could never be friends with her. As for having her for a stepmother, it didn't bear thinking about.

The shrill peal of the phone beside the bed broke her thoughts.

It was Teddy. 'I shan't be seeing you for a while, Gaye. I'm staying at a friend's house in the country with Mother. See you when I get back.'

Gaye was not surprised to hear it. Mrs Van Eldin was making sure that her son was out of the way of temptation regarding the Casino or herself. She was inclined to think it was the latter and shrugged the affair off as being of no consequence. If Teddy allowed himself to be pushed around by a possessive mother that was his business.

As she put down the phone Gaye wondered if his half-brother Lance had anything to do with it. She would not put it past him.

CHAPTER THREE

MAURICE PEMBLETON arrived home early one morning. Gaye flung herself into his arms and he looked down at her with a great tenderness.

'Well, poppet? What have you been up to while I've been away?'

'Daddy!' she exclaimed. 'What a question to greet me with!' She tip-toed to kiss his brown cheek. 'Come, have a cup of tea and tell me why you never wrote or phoned, you bad man!'

They walked to the lounge, his arm around her slim shoulders.

'Tea, please, Binns,' she said happily when he passed them on his way upstairs with her father's suitcase.

In the lounge Maurice lowered himself into his favourite chair and selected a cigar from the box his daughter picked up from the low table close by. Happily Gaye curled herself on the carpet at his feet, watching him light his cigar and lean back contentedly in his chair.

'Explain yourself,' she teased.

A tall man bordering on sandy, rake-thin with eyes very much like her own in colour, he pulled contentedly on his cigar.

'You know what it's like in the States. I've been too busy to write or phone. I thought it was better to get my business finished, then make tracks for home. I met a young man in New York whose father was my best pal at school. He was over there on business too. I told him to look me up when he comes back. I think you'll like him. He's a bachelor and a very attractive one at that.'

Gaye dimpled. 'Are you trying to get rid of me?'

'Heaven forbid,' he said. 'But I would like to see you settle down. That crowd you go around with aren't your sort. That's why I'm so strict on your allowance. I don't mind how much you spend on yourself, but you spend far too much on those hangers-on. Any hard luck story empties your purse. I'd like to bet that you're overdrawn now at the bank.'

'They're great fun really,' she said swiftly in their defence. 'And what if I am overdrawn? You don't grudge me my good times, do you?'

'You know I don't, you little imp, but I wish you would begin to look around for a nice man apart from your present class of friends. I shan't always be here, you know.'

Something in his tone made her look up quickly and grasp his hand where it lay on the arm of his chair. 'You aren't ill, are you, Daddy?' she asked anxiously.

He laughed. 'Good lord, no. Since the car accident I can't help thinking that it could have been me instead of Eric Lambert who was killed. Then where would you be? I know you could go to your grandparents, but they're two generations ahead of you and haven't your youthful slant on life.'

Gaye refused to take him seriously. 'You are being morbid, aren't you, darling? Cheer up. You'll feel better after a cup of tea.'

Maurice shook his head at her fondly. 'Still my optimistic Gaye! Pray God you'll always stay that way and let nothing get you down, because you'll find plenty of hurdles later in life.'

Gaye was puzzled. She had never known her father like this before. In some strange way he had changed.

'I don't know what's going on, but first Grandmother lectures me about settling down and now you!' she exclaimed in exasperation. 'I'm quite happy the way I am, thank you.'

Binns appeared with the tea tray which he set down impassively on the low table nearby.

Gaye poured out the tea, dropped three sugar lumps in one and passed it to her father. Her feelings were mixed when, leaning forward, she helped herself to a cigarette from a carved wooden box on the low table.

In spite of her annoyance she noticed that he looked tired and unhappy. Another thing that disturbed her was the fact that the fingers holding his cup were tobacco-stained. As a rule he was a moderate smoker.

She lit her cigarette. 'Enjoy your trip?' she asked gently.

'There were the usual setbacks, but on the whole it was successful,' he replied non-committally.

'I missed you, Daddy.'

He put down his half empty cup and patted her hand. 'I've missed you, too.' He paused uncertainly as though he found it difficult to put his next remark into words, then apparently changed his mind and looked at his watch. 'I must get to the office this morning before lunch.'

Gaye frowned, blowing out a spiral of smoke. 'You're working too hard, Daddy. Can't you relax for a day or so?'

'I'm used to being active. We can dine quietly this evening, then I can have an early night.' His smile was indulgent. 'Unless you have a date.'

'No, I haven't a date. I'll see Cook about dinner.'

Maurice stretched his legs out. 'It's good to be home. I'll take a bath, then I'll be off.'

Gaye stubbed out her cigarette and rose to her feet, impulsively leaning forward to kiss the top of his head

'It's good to have you home, darling,' she said.

Later, returning to the empty lounge, a puzzled look creased her smooth young forehead when she saw that her father had left the rest of his tea untouched. She had never known him to do that before. Normally he never had less than three cups. Thoughtfully, she rang for Binns to remove the tray.

After lunch Gaye sunbathed in the high-walled private garden at the rear of the house. The terrace was warm and sheltered even in winter. It was a pleasant retreat overlooking immaculate gardens which were full of colour for most of the year. Gaye loved the pleached lime trees and calm beauty of it all.

She lay revelling in the warm sun and thought about her father. His tired look worried her and he did not look very happy for a man returning home after a busy time abroad. The journey and working at full pressure could have tired him—or was there something else? What could there be? The more she thought about it the more she was convinced that her father loved his work too much to give it up for a less demanding life. Gradually the drowsy hum of bees and the sweet warbling of birds lulled her into taking the optimistic view that nothing was going to happen to threaten her own happy existence.

That evening she hummed happily as she dressed for dinner. Her dress was simple unadorned white that flattered her golden limbs and she applied a new shade of pale lipstick that matched the smooth lacquer of her nails.

It was around seven when she went downstairs, looking forward to a pleasant hour with her father before dinner. Suddenly she paused mid-stairs to see Binns opening the street door to admit a tall, wide-shouldered figure. Her breath halted in her throat when she looked down at the dark head of Lance Van Eldin.

He was in evening dress and looked up to where she stood unsmiling and taken aback by his sudden appearance. A wall light behind her head turned her hair into a golden halo as it clustered childishly in sweet wispy curls about her temples, her eyes were dark blue pools of consternation, and she looked absurdly young and vulnerable.

He caught her eyes and held them, his own enigmatic though slightly mocking. 'Good evening, Miss Pembleton. I trust you've recovered from your unfortunate experience.'

Before Gaye could answer, the lounge door, which had been slightly ajar, opened and her father stood there already dressed for dinner. On seeing the newcomer he strode forward with a warm welcoming smile to greet him. They clasped hands cordially while Gaye looked on in amazement.

'This is an unexpected pleasure, Lance,' her father said

'Glad to see you home, Mr Pembleton,' Lance replied.

Maurice Pembleton's eyes twinkled across to where his daughter stood stock still mid-stairs before again addressing his visitor. 'So you've already met my daughter. What's this about an unfortunate experience? Has she been in some kind of scrape or other?'

Gaye came downstairs rather hurriedly and Lance met her eyes with a challenging directness. Ignoring it, she hesitated to reassure her father.

'It was nothing, Daddy. I went on a Ban the Bomb march and when things began to get a bit rough Mr Van Eldin brought me home.'

Her glare at Lance dared him to enlarge upon her statement. For a long tantalizing moment he studied her doubtful expression, then said carelessly, 'Your daughter is a friend of my half-brother Teddy who happened to be absent that morning from the march.'

'So you came to the rescue. Thanks for taking care of my daughter. You can stay to dinner, of course?'

'I'm sorry, but it so happens that I've called to take your housekeeper out to dine,' Lance remarked, unabashed.

Gaye was suddenly shaken by the look on her father's face. She watched him recover quickly after being taken unawares, and it occurred to her shatteringly that he resented Lance taking Hilda Lambert out. A chill shuddered through her keen as an east wind. In those few revealing moments her father's feelings had been laid bare for her to see. He was in love with Hilda Lambert.

This time she knew it was useless running to her grandmother for a solution—useless raging against fate or protesting that it could not be. It was perfectly correct for him to fall in love with an unattached woman. It was only disastrous and regrettable from her own point of view.

Gaye stood with a sense of shock when a movement behind caused her to turn. Hilda Lambert, looking very attractive in a lilac evening dress covered by a lace stole, was descending the stairs. Her dark hair was neat and her face made up lightly and expertly. She looked serene, poised and in perfect control of the situation. Gaye remembered with a sense of relief that it was her evening out, consequently her father would not suggest they both stayed to dinner.

'You're early, Lance,' Hilda said with the easy familiarity of long acquaintance before addressing her employer. 'Lance insisted on calling for me, Mr Pembleton. I hope you don't mind.'

Maurice's look was guarded. 'Mind? Why should I? It's

your evening off,' he said quietly.

But Gaye knew he did mind very much. With a stricken look on his face he watched the door close behind them while Gaye trying hard to be natural linked his arm affectionately to walk with him to the lounge.

'Penny for them, Daddy,' she asked as lightly as she could.

'Eh? What did you say? I'm sorry.' He apologized quickly. 'I haven't asked how your grandparents are. Have they been well while I've been away?'

With her heart a tight cold ball of emptiness, Gaye assured him that they were quite well. When he sank into his favourite chair she poured him a drink which she placed on the low table in front of him. Then, pouring out a tomato juice for herself, she walked to the radiogram to put on one of his favourite records. The music poured forth softly and poignantly as she dropped to the floor to curl up beside his chair.

But the evening she had looked forward to was ruined. The lovely strains of an Elgar symphony washed unappreciated over her head as it was as assuredly washing over her father's. He was much too wrapped up in his thoughts to hear it, and music meant nothing to her either, not tonight. She was too choked to even enjoy a cigarette.

Maurice lit his cigar and noticed that she was not smoking.

'What, no cigarette? Have you given up smoking?' he teased.

'I don't fancy one tonight,' she answered with a heavy heart.

'Not ill, are you, my dear?'

Gaye bit her lip at the concern in his voice and clenched her hands at the thought of him leaning over Hilda with love in his eyes, herself forgotten. 'Of course not, you old silly!' She knew he expected a smile and conjured one for his benefit.

She wished with all her heart that she could throw discretion to the winds and confront him with what she had discovered. But she hadn't the courage to see the confirmation of her fears in his eyes. Instead she said on an accusing note, 'You never mentioned that you knew Lance Van Eldin.'

Her father drank from the balloon glass he held in his hand, his eyes narrowing through a haze of cigar smoke.

'I didn't know you had met him. He's the young man I told you I'd met in the States. I went to school with his father. Richard Van Eldin and I were as close as brothers when we were young. We lost touch with each other when my family moved from the district. He died not so long ago while trying to rescue a skier from an avalanche in Switzerland. He was on holiday at the time with his second wife—I think she was American.' He looked down at his daughter's thick cloud of hair and the gold-tipped lashes open fanwise on her cheeks. 'Don't you like Lance Van Eldin?'

She was leaning back against his chair with her eyes closed. 'Not much,' she admitted frankly, without opening her eyes.

'Pity,' he said regretfully. 'I was sure that you and he would like each other. I like him. He's the kind of man I'd like to think you'll choose for a husband. He's well bred, highly intelligent and would look after you better than those hairy young whipper-snappers you roam around with.' He paused. 'By the way, what happened to you at that march you went on? You know I don't like you going to those things.'

'Nothing serious. The mob got out of hand and Lance Van Eldin brought me home in his car.'

Her father frowned. 'Did Lance go on the march?'

She laughed. 'Goodness, no! I should imagine it would

be beneath his dignity. He happened to see us from his car.'

'Where was your car?'

'Dorothy gave me a lift in hers.'

'I wish you'd give that crowd up, Gaye. Dorothy is sound enough—it's the others I object to. Who is this Teddy that Lance mentioned?'

'Teddy Van Eldin? You're right about the second Mrs Van Eldin being an American. Teddy is her son and he's been studying here for a year. I met him at a party months ago. He's going back to Boston with his mother soon.'

'Do you like him?'

'Daddy!' she exclaimed in protest. 'You're trying to marry me off, aren't you?' she pouted. 'Wouldn't you mind losing me?'

'Naturally,' came the calm reply. 'But I'll be happy to see you married and settled down.'

Gaye ran her fingers around the hem of her dress nervously with the feeling that she was skating on thin ice.

'Grandmother has hinted that you could be contemplating retirement. Are you, Daddy?'

He shifted slightly beneath her lifted gaze. 'Maybe,' he replied laconically.

She shone up at him. 'Then we'll have fun when you do. Just you and I together. We'll go everywhere and do everything.'

'I'm hoping you'll be married and settled down by then.' He knocked the ash from his cigar thoughtfully. 'You didn't answer me when I asked you about Teddy Van Eldin.'

Gaye's thick lashes veiled the look in her eyes. 'Didn't I?' she prevaricated. 'We're friends, nothing more. Teddy is very young for his age. He's a few months older than I am and he's a nice boy. I could never take him seriously enough to marry him even if he wanted me to.'

'What about Lance? Why don't you like him? He's a

very attractive man. I'd like to bet that he has the choice of all the girls in his circle.'

'Not me, Daddy. In any case you're too late to pair me off with Lance Van Eldin.'

'What do you mean?' Maurice said oddly.

Gaye kept her eyes lowered and went on determinedly. 'He and Mrs Lambert are old friends. She blushed like a schoolgirl when they met the other day. When she told him about her husband being killed he said he would take her out to dinner one evening.'

Maurice emptied his glass and set it down. 'When was this?'

Gaye told him about the day Lance took her home from the Ban the Bomb march and his surprise at seeing Mrs Lambert. 'He could have been in love with her when her husband was alive.' Her father was silent for so long that she jumped to her feet, afraid of what she had deliberately implied but unwilling to rectify it. 'Come on, Daddy, let's go in to dinner,' she cried, reaching for his hands to pull him up from his chair.

He stubbed out his cigar and she saw with a pang that he seemed to have aged in the last few minutes. She pulled him to his feet and he stood looking down at her, his shoulders stooping slightly, a world of weariness on his face. She in her turn glowed up at him with a youthful defiant bearing, eager to please.

In her room that night while preparing for bed, Gaye thought of her father and Mrs Lambert until she was near to tears. It was foolish to be so upset about it, she argued, sitting at the dressing table and brushing her hair in long lethargic strokes. The thought had been too long at the back of her mind, that was the trouble. Hilda Lambert had been infintely more dangerous before her grandmother had stepped in and halted their affair than she was now.

For the first time in her life Gaye looked upon her father

with different eyes. Hitherto, she had always regarded him as a father figure. Now she was seeing him as a very attractive man who carried his years superbly—too superbly.

Silently she made a vow not to let him have one free moment when he was at home where he could contact Mrs Lambert. She had been so sure that their little affair had fizzled out and she blamed Lance Van Eldin bitterly for reviving it. His calling that evening to collect Hilda could have fanned to life the dying spark between them where her father was concerned.

Gaye pressed her lips in a spasm of fury against Lance. His entry into her life had brought nothing but trouble. Banging her hairbrush on the dressing table, she told herself that she hated him and slipped into bed.

Maurice had left for his office the following morning when Gaye went downstairs. Jenny, the little maid, who like Mrs Lambert had the previous day off duty, brought her breakfast

She was dark and plump with deep-set eyes and a voice that dissolved easily into shrieks of metallic laughter.

'Two letters for you, Miss Gaye,' she said, placing them beside her plate.

Gaye thanked her politely and picking up the first one recognized Teddy's scrawl. It was brief and to the point as if he had written it in a hurry. He said he had enjoyed the break in the country, fishing, shooting and riding, but he had missed her company and was looking forward to returning to London. He ended by saying, 'See you on Tuesday. Am motoring down. Teddy.'

Tuesday. That meant today. Gaye sighed. It was something for her to do. It would prevent her from moping. She was in no mood to meet her friend Dorothy or any member of the usual crowd. She was as restless as a leaf in the wind and felt about as defenceless. Gaye had thought of ringing up her grandmother, but she knew the old lady would not interfere with her son's affairs a second time.

She picked up the second envelope with a feeling of guilt. It bore no stamp, but she knew before the cheque dropped out that it was from her father. Gaye smiled when she saw the amount he had written on it. He really was a darling, she thought, kissing the cheque before putting it back in the envelope.

Any pangs of conscience she had during breakfast she dismissed with the airiness of youth. What if she had intimated to her father that there was something between his housekeeper and Lance Van Eldin? There was a slight possibility that there could be. She wondered if she had a split personality, because while her better half was ashamed of her conduct, her other half, fighting fiercely for her father's undivided love and attention, won hands down.

Later, after a visit to the bank to deposit her cheque, Gaye drove to the place where she was to meet Teddy for lunch. She had hardly sat down at their usual table when he appeared with his ready smile.

'Hi, beautiful,' he said, taking the seat opposite. 'Miss me?'

Gaye brightened. 'What do you think?'

'That's better,' he teased. 'You looked as though you'd lost a fortune when I came in. Not mad at me for leaving you with Lance at the Casino that night, are you?' He looked searchingly into her dark blue eyes and noted her tremulous smile.

'Of course not, silly,' she answered. 'Why should I be annoyed? We're not tied in any way. You're a free agent.'

'I wonder.' His smile was half mocking, half serious. 'I'm not so sure about that. I think you have me entangled in that lovely hair of yours.' He gazed in admiration at the sparkling golden halo around her small exquisite face. 'You're lovelier than ever.'

'Idiot!' she retorted, feeling brighter. 'You look brown

and fit. What did they do clap you in irons or throw you in the dungeons at Van Eldin Towers?'

He grinned. 'Both, and they beat me twice a day, too.' He shed the smile. 'No, seriously though, Mother worries about me. She's a good sort really and I'd like you to meet her.'

The waitress came at that moment for their order and Gaye, relieved that she need not answer, looked towards the entrance to see several of her friends coming in, headed by Dorothy. Rick Allen came next, tall, good-looking and fair. He was the Don Juan of the crowd and very aware of it, pausing at every mirror he passed to admire his handsome image. He paused now at the mirror near the entrance. Dorothy came on.

'Hello, you two,' she said gaily. 'Didn't know you were coming, or you could have bagged a table for us.'

Rick came up then with the others, saluting Gaye and Teddy as they all trooped to a nearby table.

The waitress brought their lunch and Teddy tucked in heartily, but Gaye was not hungry. She was too choked and strung up inside to eat. Normally, she would have been the gayest of them, exchanging banter with her friends, bubbling over with the joy of being with them. Now she was hardly aware of them and they might have been strangers for all the impact they had on her senses.

'Forget your ear trumpet?' Teddy hissed across the table. 'That's the second time I've spoken to you and you haven't even heard me.'

Gaye shot him a wide-eyed, startled look and suddenly relaxed.

'Sorry, I'm all bemused. Daddy came home yesterday. He met your half-brother Lance while he was in the States.'

Teddy looked up from demolishing his steak. 'Did he? Did Lance see you home all right after I'd left the Casino?'

Gaye nodded and told him about Lance rescuing her

from the Ban the Bomb march mob.

'Watch it,' he warned teasingly. 'He's a real lady-killer.'

She dimpled. 'You could be right. He's dating Mrs Lambert. She's an old friend of his.'

He stared. 'Your housekeeper?'

'Yes. He called last night to take her out to dinner.'

Teddy shrugged. 'He certainly gets around. I guess there's safety in numbers where Lance is concerned.'

Gaye said warily, 'Mrs Lambert seemed to be very attracted.'

'As long as you're not,' her companion said briefly.

No danger of that, Gaye said beneath her breath, and was tempted to confide in him about her father. She was on the brink of it when it occurred to her that he might not understand her point of view. After all, his own mother had married again. He would be sure to look at it from that angle. Men viewed life from a different angle. He would probably look on her association with her father as being unhealthy, although she knew differently.

Instead, she said thoughtfully, 'You're not staying in London because of me, are you, Teddy?'

He went a dull red and reached for his glass of water. 'What makes you ask?'

'I heard that your mother wanted you to go home to Boston and that you'd refused.'

Teddy took a long drink and put down his glass. 'Who told you, Lance?'

She shook her head, wondering if she had been wise to mention it at all. 'You know how these things get around— and don't ask me where I got it from.'

The last thing she wanted to do was to tell him about his mother ringing up her grandmother, nor did she intend to tell him about the part Lance had played in the episode at the bank. There were some things better left unsaid.

His look was honest and direct. 'I like it here, and I like

you, too.'

Gaye put down her knife and fork. 'I don't want to cause any trouble between you and your mother.' Her look across the table was as candid as his and she went on hastily, 'Your mother sent Lance to take you away from the Casino, and it seems to me that she could resent you going around with me.'

Teddy looked stubborn. 'Mother's all right. She hates me to gamble, that's all. I lost a lot of money last year in a casino in Las Vegas, and Mother's afraid it will get a hold on me.' He noticed her almost untouched plate. 'Aren't you hungry?'

'Not very.'

'What you need is some fresh air, my girl. How about taking the afternoon off and going for a run down to the coast?'

The prospect of tearing along at speed as one with the windswept road and racing clouds was something that appealed to her restless spirit until she remembered her father. She shook her head regretfully. 'Sorry, Teddy. We could be late getting back and I don't know what Daddy has arranged for tonight.'

He regarded her sympathetically. 'Have you parent trouble, too?'

She laughed. 'Goodness, no! Daddy never questions me about my activities unless he's been away for a while, like recently.'

'Have you told him about me?'

'Only in an airy kind of way. He had to know that Lance was a relation of yours. He likes your half-brother very much.'

Suddenly Rick Allen was bending over her and she felt his kiss on the top of her head, then his voice softly against her ear.

'I'm throwing a party tonight. What about it, you two?'

A long time ago Rick's nearness would have thrilled her to the tips of her toes. But that was before she had discovered how fickle and self-centred he was. Now she knew better.

'Sorry,' she said lightly. 'I've a date, but Teddy hasn't.' Rick flicked her ear lightly. 'Okay, Teddy. Eight o'clock.'

Teddy was quiet for the rest of the meal and he left her later rather abruptly. Really, she thought, young men were a bore. Thank goodness for her father!

On the way home, feeling in need of a boost to her moral, she stopped to buy an evening dress. It was in midnight blue, a colour that was infinitely flattering to blondes. It was also her father's favourite colour and she knew it would please him. When she arrived home Jenny, the maid, told her that her father had rung up to say that they would be dining out that evening. So she spent the afternoon washing her hair.

Happily, that evening, she donned the new evening dress approving the simple design and smoothing it down over her slender hips, aware that she was looking her best. Her make-up was light, a hint of colour on her eyelids, a touch of mascara on her lashes, a pale lipstick and she was ready. Her father waited for her in the lounge looking very distinguished in evening dress. As she had expected he admired her dress, enquired if it was a new one and nodded approvingly when she told him she had bought it that day.

To her relief he was quite jolly and looking forward to their evening out. As for Gaye, the fact that he was looking better added to the sense of security he gave her. He made her feel loved and protected and she wanted that more than she had ever wanted anything in her life. Being with him this evening, finding him his old self, made her forget Hilda Lambert and her threat to her own happiness.

'Where are we going?' she asked when they were on their way.

'To my club,' he answered. 'They've decided to allow visitors once a week, and about time too.'

'Lovely!' she exclaimed. 'I've often wanted to peep inside that club of yours, but there's always a commissionnaire standing on guard at the door.'

'There has to be one to keep prying females out.'

'Daddy!' she cried in protest.

Her father chuckled. 'I was only joking. I'm going to enjoy showing you off to my colleagues.'

Gaye looked up at her father to meet his teasing gaze and hugged the arm nearest to her. In the club, André the head waiter greeted them courteously, hovering to have a few words before taking them to their table.

Gaye looked round the pine-panelled walls and immaculate tables between which smart waiters moved about on thick pile carpet. Her father smiled at her wide-eyed gaze and she leaned forward to say mischievously,

'It's dreadfully hush-hush, Daddy, and one feels inclined to whisper.'

A waiter brought them drinks and she twinkled at her parent over the rim of her glass. It was then that some sixth sense alerted her unpleasantly and her gaze was drawn to the entrance of the room through which two men now appeared.

The first, a thick-set elderly man with thinning white hair, was followed by a much younger man. It was the second man on whom Gaye's eyes lingered. He sauntered in with the nonchalant air that reminded her of their first meeting. Gaye quelled a shiver at the arrogant features. The next instant she looked away, uneasily aware of the hammering of her heart. The two men were level with their table before Maurice saw them.

'Good evening, Sir Bonar. It's a while since we last met,' he exclaimed before addressing the elderly man's companion. 'I had no idea you were a member of this club,

Lance.'

'He isn't,' Sir Bonar put in smoothly. 'Says this club is always full of old fogeys. He's my godson and as it's visitors' night I persuaded him to come along.'

His light grey eyes twinkled at Gaye, who was silently rebelling against a fate that insisted upon throwing Lance Van Eldin in her path.

Maurice was saying, 'My daughter Gaye, who has already met your godson.'

Sir Bonar acknowledged the introduction with old-world courtesy and Gaye smiled in return, now fully in control of her feelings. She did not bat an eyelid when, in response to her father's invitation to join them, Lance drew up two more chairs for Sir Bonar and himself.

The lunch was excellent, but to Gaye the evening was spoiled as her companions talked business and the Stock Exchange until she could have screamed. The meal had reached the last course when André approached to say that there was dancing in the larger lounge if anyone felt inclined.

'What about it, Lance?' Maurice said. 'I know Gaye loves to dance.'

'Certainly.' Lance rose to his feet.

Gaye stood up unwillingly, ignoring the fact that she had the most attractive man in the room for her partner. There were only four couples dancing in the discreetly lit room to music from a trio, so it was quite comfortable to move about. Comfortable was not the word to describe Gaye's feelings when Lance took her in his arms. He held her easily and impersonally, and it annoyed her to find that though she was of medium height, she was a long way below his cynical mouth.

Like most athletic men, Lance danced easily and naturally. They moved around the room without exchanging word and gradually Gaye began to feel a quickening of her pulse—a strange exciting feeling, entirely new. She was discovering that there was something strangely disturbing about this man whom she had so many reasons to dislike. Her lissom young body relaxed against him and wide-eyed she studied the face that from her view looked dominated by a firm determined jaw. When suddenly he looked down and caught her gaze there was no softening in his face, neither was there in the hand that gripped her arm to detain her when the dance ended.

'Come sit down. I want to talk to you,' he said peremptorily.

She allowed him to lead her to a window seat and she sat in one corner. He took the other and half-turned to face her, offering her his cigarette case.

When she refused he merely lifted a neat brow, selected one for himself, and lit it before returning the lighter to his pocket. Then, with the cigarette between long, steady fingers, he said, 'I have reason to believe that you may have hinted about an affair between Mrs Lambert and myself. I would appreciate it if you would refrain from discussing either of us in future.'

Gaye had the sensation of having her face slapped. She shook with anger. 'What do you mean?' she said throatily.

He blew out a line of smoke coolly. 'What I say. Not only has Teddy made a few remarks concerning us, but your father has informed me that I can take his housekeeper out without his permission at any time. It seemed to me that they were both under the impression that there was something between us.'

'And you think I spread the rumour?'

'I didn't connect the story with you until I remembered something that Mrs Lambert said on the evening we dined together.'

Her tone was as icy as his. 'You object to my discussing you, yet you must have discussed me with Mrs Lambert.'

'Not exactly. Hilda said very little, but I did gather that you were jealous of her association with your father.'

Her tone was bitter. 'Mrs Lambert had designs on Daddy from the start. How do you know that she didn't start the rumour herself, to get him interested?'

His eyes narrowed at her unpleasantly. 'Because she's not the type.'

'And I am?'

'You obviously don't like her, and the reason could be jealousy.'

She picked him up quickly. 'On her part, do you mean?' she asked with acid sweetness.

'No, on yours. Did you know that your father has proposed to Hilda Lambert several times?'

Gaye went paper white. 'You don't expect me to believe that?'

'No, I don't. You don't want to. You shy away from everything that might jeopardize your easy way of life. You've been so pampered you've never had to study life's essentials.' His eyes raked her face mercilessly. 'I don't suppose it has occurred to you that your father needs other companionship than your own, that he's been lonely all these years without your mother.'

'You're not married,' she retorted. 'Would you say you were lonely?'

He tapped the long ash from his cigarette with a long finger.

'With me the question doesn't arise. I've never been married, your father has.'

'You know nothing about my father. He was perfectly content until Hilda Lambert showed up and began working on him. As for Daddy proposing to her, I'll never believe it. And I can't see why you should be so upset about having her name coupled with yours. You're single.'

She felt his sudden anger. 'I happen to want to remain

single, if you don't mind. That being so, I shall inform your father that there is nothing between Hilda and myself.'

Gaye stood up beneath his contemptuous look. She was seething with anger because there was only the weapon of words to fight him with and she could think of none strong enough to hurt.

For the rest of the evening Gaye waited uneasily for Lance to carry out his threat of putting himself in the clear to her father regarding an affair between Hilda Lambert and himself. As the evening wore on and he gave no sign of doing so she became too strung up to care.

No man had ever roused her emotions as much as this man who had declared with his keen, ruthlessly direct gaze that he had no intention of allowing any woman to share his life. Had an unfortunate love affair soured him into ruling love out of his future existence? Or was he like his godfather, who having lost the woman he had wanted preferred not to have any? Well, someone would have a good miss where Lance was concerned, for he was the kind of man who would fiendishly enjoy bending a woman to his will.

Angrily she became aware of how much the man was occupying her thoughts when her father's voice aroused her with the remark that he had spoken to her twice before she heard him. Miserably she arrived home with the bitter knowledge of another evening spoiled and an unknown dread of the future that even her father's fond goodnight kiss could not dispel.

CHAPTER FOUR

For as long as she could remember Gaye had spent the weekend at her grandparents' home in Greenwich. Occasionally, tired of the same routine, she had spent the time with her friends, leaving her father to go on his own. This Sunday, however, was rather special being in the way of a farewell dinner, for her grandparents were going away on a cruise the following day. For Gaye that weekend was a happy one, cosseted as she was by an adoring father and grandparents plus a staff who went out of their way to please.

It was natural that a gay weekend should leave her feeling flat on Monday after seeing her grandparents off on their cruise and her father to his office. Midday she went to the restaurant her friends frequented for lunch, to find Dorothy Frayne there.

'Hello, stranger,' she said. 'You missed it yesterday. We all spent the day on Rick Allen's boat on the Thames. There was dancing on deck in the evening and it was simply fab.' Perhaps Gaye did not appear to be as impressed as Dorothy would have liked her to be, for she added smugly, 'Teddy really enjoyed himself. He's taking me out tonight. Do you mind?'

Gaye shrugged slim shoulders. 'Why should I?' she answered. But she did. Teddy had not contacted her since she had refused to go out with him on the day following her father's return home. Subconsciously, she had come to the restaurant with the hope that he would be there. It was a lovely day and she would have enjoyed a quick run in his car with tea at some unexpected place along the way. Teddy was cheerful company and that was what she was

.needing right now. That he was now dating Dorothy could mean that he was hitting back at her for refusing to go out with him.

The rest of the crowd came in at that moment and, with a muted roar, welcomed her back among them. Rick Allen sat beside her and gave her shoulders a friendly squeeze. 'We've missed you,' he said, looking rather dashing in a brown suit and orange shirt.

Gaye responded to his warm greeting, countering his gay repartee with her usual wit, but her heart wasn't in it. She had lost touch with them in some way that she could not explain. Teddy did not show up, which meant that he could have been somewhere with his mother.

That evening she greeted her father with more than her usual warmth.

'Daddy, couldn't we go away somewhere? I'm bored, terribly bored.'

He looked down at her fondly. 'I wanted you to go with your grandparents on the cruise. It's not too late to catch them up. You could fly to their first port of call.'

Gaye stamped her foot angrily. 'I don't want to go with them! I told you so. I want to go with you.' She bit her lip and looked up at him near to tears. 'Please, Daddy,' she said cajolingly. 'Let's go away, just the two of us. Please!'

He quizzed her upraised sensitive face, his own suddenly very tired.

'I've some important work on at the moment, but I'll arrange something tomorrow. I think we can both do with a holiday.'

But the following morning Maurice Pembleton was too ill to go to his office. Gaye, getting up around eleven, was told by Binns on her way down to breakfast that her father was still in bed. He was flushed when she went in to see him and his breathing had lost its rhythm.

Concerned, she rang up the doctor. He was out on his

rounds and she was informed that he would be told when he came in. It was well after two in the afternoon when he finally came.

'You've been neglecting yourself, Mr Pembleton,' he said gravely on giving him a thorough examination. 'You are to stay in bed and not move out until I tell you. You have a slight touch of pneumonia and I want you to take the pills I shall prescribe until you have taken the last one.'

Maurice Pembleton was feeling much too ill to do anything, and when the doctor suggested a nurse, Gaye insisted on nursing him herself. And so began a nightmare fortnight for Gaye during which there were times when she was sure that her father was taking his last breath.

The ordeal took more out of her than she realized, but she kept stoically on, following the doctor's orders implicitly and keeping the housekeeper at bay like a dog defending a puppy. She had not wired her grandparents, hoping that the doctor was right and that the attack was not too serious, but there had been times when she wished she had done.

Then gradually he began to show some improvement, and Gaye began to relax with relief. Teddy had rung up and she had answered him briefly. Her friends, including Dorothy, had received the same treatment. Her only concern was for her father.

At the beginning of the third week he was able to take light nourishment. Her relief brought on a kind of reaction that stemmed from exhaustion. She had refused the offer of Binns to sit up with her father and give her a respite, and on Tuesday night of the third week she sought her own bed for the first time since he had been taken ill.

Gaye looked in on him several times during the night and on Wednesday morning he appeared to be much better. Weary but happy, she had a bath. Alone in the dining room, she ignored her breakfast and drank her tea thirstily.

Gaye was drinking her second cup when she heard voices in the hall and thinking it was the doctor, went to greet him.

'Good morning,' Lance Van Eldin said formally, eyeing her pallor and the blue rings of fatigue beneath her eyes. 'You look all in. How is your father?'

'Better, thank you,' she replied in a chill, small voice. 'But not well enough for visitors.'

He made an impatient gesture. 'I believe you've been flogging yourself into a state of exhaustion unnecessarily when you could have had a trained nurse to do the job more efficiently and at less cost to her health. In any case, surely Binns could have sat up with him to help you catch up on your sleep.'

Gaye was shaken with a sudden surge of resentment against this man who, while making it perfectly clear that he had a poor opinion of her, dared to thrust himself into her life uninvited and criticize her actions.

She said distantly, 'What I do is no concern of yours, and it's presumptuous of you to interfere into that which doesn't concern you. We have nothing in common, we don't even like each other, and furthermore'—viciously— 'I'd be obliged if you would stay out of my life.'

'I'm afraid it's not that easy since you've appointed yourself your father's keeper. My business happens to be with him,' he answered coldly. 'I've called to see if I can be of any help. It won't do him any good to worry aboout his business affairs.' He lifted a hand as she was about to speak. 'I've already had a word with his doctor who assured me that the danger was now over and it can do him no harm for me to spend an hour with him.'

Gaye stiffened and glared. 'We don't want your help, and if Mrs Lambert has hinted that we do she's wrong. Good day, Mr Van Eldin.'

To her chagrin he remained unmoved, regarding her contemplatively for a moment. 'I haven't seen Mrs Lambert since the night we went out to dinner. What's wrong? Afraid of her stealing your father from under your pretty nose?' There was a curious sparkling light in his eyes. 'Don't you know that fate has a gift for getting her own way in the end?'

For a brief moment or so she stared as the significance of his words seeped through to her tired brain, leaving her shaken and confused. Then anger took over. 'Get out!' she hissed between clenched teeth. She shot out an arm to indicate the door and the jerk of her muscles sent a pain through her temples like a hundred knives. She swayed as her body rebelled against lack of food and rest. She felt his arms close around her and she made a last feeble struggle before darkness claimed her.

When Gaye came to she was lying on her bed fully clothed and covered with an eiderdown. Lance was looking down at her to place a hand on her shoulder when she attempted to rise.

'Stay where you are,' he said, looking big and determined. 'You collapsed from utter exhaustion. Now go to sleep like a good girl. I'll stay with your father today and Binns can take over during the night if need be, so there's nothing to worry about.'

He drew the eiderdown back into place where she had disturbed it when she tried to rise. Her collapse had a lethal effect upon her, drugging her senses, and the look she gave him was half bemused. Strange, though, that she could trust his word when she hated him so much.

When she awoke it was to the click of the door opening to admit the maid with a covered tray. 'Had a nice sleep, Miss Gaye?' she asked brightly. 'I've brought your tea—a salad of lobster and your favourite prawns.'

Gaye sat up in dismay. 'Tea?' she echoed. 'How long have I been asleep?'

'From eleven o'clock this morning.' Gaye looked at her

watch as the maïd chatted on. 'It's now five o'clock. Cook has sent you a light tea on Mr Van Eldin's orders. "Nothing heavy," he said, "because you have to go to sleep again when you've eaten."'

Gaye eyed the tray, feeling drugged after her long sleep, and still terribly tired. She managed part of the attractively prepared meal and was thankful to relax again in her pillows before sleep claimed her once more.

Her father's convalescence was slow and she spent practically all her time with him. It was when he had progressed to leaving his bed for an hour or so each day that she left him one morning on the terrace while she went into town to do some shopping. She was making her way back to the car when Rick Allen hailed her.

'Good morning, beautiful,' he said. 'Did you know that Teddy Van Eldin is going back to Boston with his mother and that Dorothy and her family are travelling with them?' He grinned. 'Looks as if Dorothy's going to cut you out.'

Gaye concealed her surprise admirably. 'It does, doesn't it?' she said coolly.

Rick cocked a sandy brow. 'You don't look very upset. Does that mean that I have a chance?'

She dimpled mischievously. 'I didn't know you cared!'

He eyed her slim youthfulness and the parcels clasped in her arms with a gleam of admiration. 'Fibber, you know I've always cared. Can I give you a lift home?'

She shook her head. 'No, thanks, I have the car.' She looked around. 'You had better get cracking. You're in a non-parking zone.'

He winked a bold eye. 'What's a fine to drowning in those lovely blue eyes of yours? What about a date tonight now that your old man is on the mend?'

'He's still sick. Some other time.'

He started the car reluctantly. 'Give me a ring and I'll drop everything and come running.'

That was quite an admission from somebody who usually expected the girls to come running at his bidding, Gaye mused, but she was not interested in Rick. Her thoughts were circling around Teddy. She had expected him to go back to Boston, but it was a surprise to hear that Dorothy was travelling with him. Not that it mattered particularly. It was the fact that Dorothy had not told her that hurt.

As her father improved people began to call at the house, employees and business acquaintances and friends, including Lance Van Eldin. Once he had arrived with her father's secretary, a woman no longer young but obviously floored by the Van Eldin charm. At first he had been a frequent visitor, but when her father began to spend a few hours a day at the office his visits gradually dwindled down to dinner in the evening occasionally. Gaye was thankful for this. Her feelings towards him had undergone no change in spite of what he had done to help her father's business interests.

Dorothy rang up one evening when Gaye and her father were in the lounge after dinner.

'Hello, Gaye,' she said on a breathless note. 'Sorry I haven't been to see you, but I've been busy packing. We're off to America next week with Teddy and his mother. Teddy's here with me now.' Gaye heard a hurried whisper as the phone changed hands.

'Hello, Gaye.' Teddy sounded ill at ease. 'Mother has finally persuaded me to go with her to Boston. Pleased to know that your father is well on the way to recovery. Perhaps you can persuade him to bring you over with him the next time he visits the States.' He went on talking, his manner a little offhand, and Gaye knew that he had not forgotten the way she had brushed him off when her father had been so ill. Listening and answering in turn, she already had the feeling of talking to a stranger.

'That was Teddy and Dorothy,' she told her father when she sat down beside him again in the lounge. 'They're going to America next week.'

'Together?' he asked curiously.

'Teddy's mother and Dorothy's family are going too.'

'You'll miss them.' Maurice looked down at her tenderly. 'Remember telling me that you were bored and longed to go away? What do you say to a trip to Norway?'

'Are you sure you feel up to it?' Gaye scanned his face anxiously, noting that, although his features were thinner, the tiredness had gone from his eyes.

He smiled down at her. 'I feel fine. It's you I'm worried about. You look pale and you're quieter too, not a bit like yourself.'

Gaye moved with the old restlessness. 'There's nothing wrong with me. What kind of a trip is it?'

'Sir Bonar Alsager is taking some guests of his on a trip from Newcastle to Norway in his yacht for the weekend. Lance motors up there on Thursday and will take us with him. Sir Bonar is going all out to make it a real Scandinavian trip with two Norwegian girls to act as hostesses.'

Gaye hugged her knees, not finding the prospect of being in Lance Van Eldin's company very enticing. On the other hand, apart from the sea air being beneficial to her father, it would also mean that he would be away from Mrs Lambert for the weekend.

On returning from a visit to town she had found him drinking a cup of tea and talking to his housekeeper. He had looked suddenly very boyish and a spasm of jealousy had shaken her. Hilda Lambert had been laughing too, a seductive laugh, the kind that would make any man look at her twice. True, on the surface it had only appeared to be a normal conversation, but it had set her wondering if Lance had told him about there being only friendship between himself and Hilda.

Her father's voice broke in on her thoughts. 'I shall be taking Binns along, so you won't be tied down waiting on me if I happen to need it. He's to go with Sir Bonar's man and the luggage early tomorrow, if you agree to going.'

'Of course we'll go,' she said, putting her cheek against his hand as it lay on the arm of his chair, only she did wish that Sir Bonar's odious godson was not going too.

CHAPTER FIVE

LANCE called for them early on Thursday morning. Wearing a coffee-coloured lounge suit and cream shirt, he was as sleek and immaculate as the long expensive car he arrived in.

'You'd better sit by me,' he told Gaye. 'Your father needs the back seat to relax in. It's a long journey.'

That was something Gaye had not thought about, sharing the front seat with him. She also discovered that, in half turning to talk to her father, Lance was in her direct line of vision, a fact she tried to ignore. After several hours of travelling her father fell asleep and she turned to face front and edged closer to the car side. Lance was driving fast now, slowing down only in built-up areas and traffic lights. He made remarks about changes since he was last that way and cursed a hare-brained driver who, but for his own efficiency, could have caused a nasty accident.

The journey, though long, passed uneventfully and they reached Newcastle in ideal sailing weather. The sun sprayed golden rays on the sleek, black bows of the yacht as she lay at anchor—a graceful modern vessel called *Lancelot*. Sir Bonar had obviously named it after his beloved godson, Gaye thought acidly.

They were greeted on board by the two Scandinavian girls, both as blonde as Gaye and looking ravishing in their picturesque Norwegian national costumes.

'Three beautiful blondes all at once is rather overwhelming,' Lance murmured mockingly, and Maurice agreed.

The blonde hostesses were named Freda and Netta. It was Netta who escorted Gaye and her father to their respective cabins. Maurice was left in care of Binns, who was waiting for him, and Gaye was taken to her own quarters. Her cabin was a roomy single on the boat deck, luxuriously fitted and furnished with its own shower and toilet.

She unpacked her clothes, feeling rather odd, and when the yacht's sirens gave three pierceing blasts to announce her departure, Gaye wondered if she had been wise to come. Between her and her task came the disturbing vision of a virile masculine figure sitting beside her in the big car, his firm brown hands handling it expertly. The dark eyes fixed on the road ahead had not missed the fact that her father had fallen asleep in the back seat. Smooth as a whisper, he had drawn the car to a halt and reached over to tuck a rug around him before driving on. The luminous blue glance she had tossed his way had been received with an amused quirk of the well-defined mouth to which she had given no answering smile.

Gaye gave a deep sigh, wondered what it was for, and decided to wallow in a shower before slipping into a cream jersey dress. She was not impressed by the luxury of the yacht, for she had been on similar vessels, although it was nice to know that everything would run smoothly and efficiently and her wants would be attended to at the push of a button.

Her father, tired after his long journey, dined in his cabin, so Gaye made her way to the dining saloon alone. As far as she could make out the people already assembled there for dinner were mostly business associates of Sir

Bonar's. There were also two elderly couples who sat together and four naval cadets seated with the same number of teenagers at another table. Then the tall, military figure of Lance was striding towards her to lead her to Sir Bonar's table. To her dismay she found herself seated between him and his godfather and she sat down wondering what she had let herself in for.

During the meal Lance reached out a well-groomed hand for everything that happened to be beyond her reach. Yet, try as she might, her manner towards him was cool and reserved. His charm was there battering her defences, but the fact that he could be aware of his own dynamic attraction did nothing to soften her towards him. Instead it hardened her still more. His eyes mocked on occasion, resting appraisingly on her sparkling golden hair. With the rest of the party his smile was white and spontaneous, his laughter deep and pleasant. With her he was restrained and speculative, and it irritated.

Strolling through to the lounge for after-dinner coffee, Gaye found him by her side.

'Hope you enjoy the trip,' he murmured. 'There are young folk you can team up with. No need to hang around your father. He has Binns and there are no designing widows on board.'

Gaye clenched her hands. He was being deliberately provoking.

'Then you can relax, can't you?' she replied. The smile she gave him was no less brittle than his own.

'Ah, but there are quite a few distractions that could be equally dangerous. Don't you agree?'

She followed his gaze across the lounge to where the four pretty teenagers sat on a long seat drinking coffee. Serve her right! She ought to have known better and kept silent. It was the best weapon against a man who knew all the answers. He had hardly seated her when Netta was bending over her with coffee. Then they were joined by Sir Bonar and several more guests and Gaye allowed herself to be drawn in the pleasant conversation that ensued. She slipped out on deck later for a breath of night air and was pleasantly tired when she called in on her father before going to her cabin.

Gaye's first glimpse of Norway the next morning brought the sweetness of the pinewoods and the exhilarating pure mountain air of the beautiful west coast nearer. For breakfast there was Scandinavian fare consisting of cold meats, vegetables, fish, fruit salad and cheese or a full English breakfast.

Gaye chose the Scandinavian one and enjoyed it immensely. Her father joined her for lunch, looking much brighter. Lance paused at their table to ask how he was, looking very attractive in a loose-fitting cream sweater with a Fair Isle yoke and tailored white slacks. The dark lock of hair was on his forehead. Her glance travelled to the level dark brows below it and to the black lashes rimming his intent gaze. There was an attractive air of indolent grace about him as he stood regarding them.

'Glad to see you looking so well, Maurice. I don't suppose you'll want to go ashore?'

'You're right, I don't. Gaye can go. What about it, my dear? You're spending far too much time with an old man.'

'You're not an old man,' Gaye contradicted with spirit. 'I've seen Stavanger many times.'

'So have I.' Impudent lights danced in Lance's dark eyes. 'And I still think it's worth another visit.'

'I hope you enjoy it,' she said aloofly.

'No doubt about that,' was the quick reply. 'Who wouldn't with two beautiful Norwegian girls like Freda and Netta? It happens to be Freda's home town and I'm looking forward to meeting her family. Sure you won't come?'

'Yes, do go,' her father put in gently. 'I hate to think I

could be spoiling your fun.'

'You're not.' She looked at her father with steady blue eyes.

Maurice looked at Lance with a wry smile. 'It's no use, Lance. When my little girl has that look in her eyes there's no moving her.'

'So I believe,' he drawled. 'Too bad you've given in to her for so long. I'd like the handling of your daughter, Maurice, for one short month. The result might surprise you.'

Maurice laughed. But Gaye did not. His sheer effrontery dyed her cheeks scarlet. Her eyes glittered at the deliberate insult. At the same time she was conscious of a tingling sensation in her veins—a breathless kind of defiance. Her father was taking it as a joke, but then he had no idea how sometimes, even without provocation, something deep and intimately personal could flare up between her and this objectionable man who was his friend.

Well, he was no friend of hers and never would be. She answered promptly, on a slight note of triumph, 'How fortunate for me that such a thing isn't likely to happen. However,' she went on daringly, 'if you're feeling bored to that extent the two Norwegian girls are probably the stimulant you need.'

'How right you are. At least one could never be bored with them. Don't you agree?'

Gaye felt severely slapped. She was shaken with emotion —a mixture of resentment and a strange inexplicable pain. Immediately everything that was feminine in her surged up to hide her hurt.

'How should I know?' she managed lightly. 'I've never been an experienced man of the world like yourself.'

Maurice chuckled. Lance, unruffled and completely baffling, turned as Sir Bonar approached.

'Any more for sailing?' he asked banteringly. 'We're

about to go.'

The journey from Stavanger to Bergen took them between islands of marvellous scenery. Tiny dwellings nestled high up in pinewoods like eggs in green mossy nests, snow gleamed like sugar icing on mountain peaks and fishermen waved as they passed. But the climax of the trip came when they entered Bergen harbour, a fairyland of lights rivalled only by the ceiling of stars set like jewels in the purple northern sky.

Gaye had seen the same scene before, yet it never failed to fill her with delight. Bergen was a bustling expensive city with flowers everywhere. Sir Bonar accompanied his guests to one of the most selected hotels where a first-class band played for dancing and the food was excellent.

For dinner there was ptarmigan in cream sauce, nutty flavoured, dark Russian peas and cranberry jelly, salmon salad, pancakes served with fruit and ice cream and a delicious brandy sauce.

The band was one that invited the most timid of dancers to gyrate around to its wonderful rhythm. Gaye was no exception, tapping her feet as she sat with her father. Several times during the evening she had refused to dance. As she watched him it occurred to her that he was not yet a hundred per cent fit, for his head kept nodding and he was finding it difficult to stay awake.

'Tired, Daddy?' she asked gently.

'What's that?' He reared his head like a startled horse. 'It's this confounded mountain air. It's like a drug on the senses.'

'But a healthy drug. Would you like to go back to the ship?'

He answered indignantly, 'Good heavens, no! I can give Sir Bonar ten years or more and he's dancing around like a teenager.'

Gaye watched Sir Bonar dancing with Freda, one of the

Norwegian hostesses. Earlier on Lance had been dancing with her too.

Suddenly he was there staring down at her intently. 'Not dancing?' he said laconically.

She saw the excellent cut of his evening dress giving the impression that it had been moulded on to his long athletic frame. The wide shoulders made his hips look extremely narrow, but like his long hands there was a hidden latent strength about him that made her terribly aware of herself as a woman. His unexpected appearance precisely at the moment she was thinking about him sent the blood rushing to her creamy skin.

'I'm keeping Daddy company,' she answered.

He studied her high colour before spearing a meaning look at her father who was again nodding off. 'Binns is here to take your father back to the yacht. There's no sense in him overdoing it.'

'Then I shall go with him.' She rose to her feet.

'Why? Surely not to help Binns undress him?' There was a hint of devilment in his eyes and the flush his words brought on covered her whole body.

Before she could give him the cutting answer he deserved she was swung away in his arms to the musical rhythm of the band. Music is said to soothe the savage breast, but for minutes Gaye was too angry to hear it. Then gradually the magic seeped through and she gave herself up to the pure joy of dancing in the firm strong clasp of a fellow being who shared her appreciation of an excellent band. There could be nothing more to it than that, she assured herself firmly, putting the wild beating of her heart down to the extra exertion.

'So you're losing Teddy and your friend Dorothy too,' he murmured above her ear. 'I rather think that Teddy is going home to get back at you for giving him the cold shoulder.'

Gaye's pretty mouth tightened. 'I'm not upset at Teddy leaving. Not in the way you mean. I shall miss him in the same way that I shall miss Dorothy.'

'No doubt. Pity you're so determined to stick to your father. What do you intend to be eventually? Your father's chaperone through life? Don't forget that while you're warding off the amorous widows, you're also keeping your own admirers at bay.'

'Surely that's my affair?'

'Granted,' he said, swinging her clear of an approaching couple. 'I hate to see a girl going to waste, though. Why don't you like Mrs Lambert, or is it sheer jealousy on your part and you don't want your father to marry again?'

By now Gaye was becoming used to his interference and refused to be shaken by it. 'Daddy is quite happy as he is. He has no wish to marry again.'

'He hasn't the look of a happy man.'

She quivered with resentment and anger. 'It doesn't concern you in the least, and if you're pleading Mrs Lambert's cause you're wasting your time. I don't believe for one moment that Daddy ever proposed to her. He would most certainly have told me before taking such a step.'

Dancing her through an open french window on to a balcony, he released her with exasperation. 'It's time you grew up and realized that other people's happiness is as important as your own.'

Gaye could suppress her feelings no longer. He had gone too far and she had no intention of tolerating his brutal criticism. Her nostrils dilated, her eyes blazed. 'How dare you?' she stormed.

He folded his arms. 'Someone has to make you see sense before it's too late. Some day you're going to face the fact that you cost your father his chance of happiness.' He paused to observe her face, now paper-white, before going on relentlessly, 'Reading between the lines I know that

Hilda Lambert likes your father very much and she turned him down because of your attitude towards her. She doesn't want to come between you.' His mouth took on a cruel slant. 'You're nothing but a spoiled brat.'

Her hand striking his face resounded above the music coming from the room beyond. Quick as a flash his fingers curled cruelly round her slim wrists. A slow flush had crept beneath his tan and she wondered quiveringly what she had let loose. His next words fell like hailstones on the heat of her anger.

'There might have been hope for you if you'd made the gesture of accepting her, but you don't want to behave in a grown-up manner. You want to be Daddy's little girl. You have no idea of a man's needs, much less your own. Don't you know that there are other arms in which you can find love besides your father's?'

He pulled her roughly against him and fastened his mouth on her own ruthlessly. For the first time in her life Gaye came up against a passion based on anger. The kiss was never-ending. It seared right through her body, her bones felt crushed in the fury of his embrace. With a smothered cry of distress she tried vainly to move her head, but she was helpless against his brute strength. When at last he released her she staggered back, her hand against her bruised mouth.

'I wonder if that got through to you,' he said, his mouth tight, his eyes dark and smouldering. 'I doubt it.' For what seemed an age he regarded her with distaste before striding away.

Gaye stood there with her heart threatening to knock a hole in her chest. She was shaking all over with hate—and something else she could not define. The brute! Who did he think he was, interfering in things that did not concern him? She drew a long breath, composed herself, determined to go to the yacht with her father. She had barely started to cross the dance floor when she was seized around the waist and drawn into a crocodile of dancers who were weaving their way around the edge of the floor. Gaye looked round when they passed the spot where her father had been sitting, to find him gone. So it was, wedged in between two of the young cadets, she realized that she had no other option than to leave with the rest of the guests when the evening was over. She had no lack of partners, for there appeared to be a surfeit of naval officers from the ships in the harbour, but she did not enjoy herself. Her heart was not in it.

Eventually Freda and Netta rounded them up for the return to the yacht and she walked with them on the short journey to the harbour. It was a lovely evening with the mere whisper of a breeze. The surrounding hills were a myriad twinkling lights with the moon spraying a mother-of-pearl surface on the dark water. It was a sight so breath-takingly beautiful that Gaye stopped to gaze in wonder.

She gazed at the ships, silent and serene at their moor-ings in the bay, and wondered if her father was already asleep on the yacht just ahead. Inevitably she recapped what Lance had said earlier about him not looking happy. It was nonsense. His illness made him look off colour and he had come home from the trip abroad worn out with overwork. He would soon be his old self again when he grew stronger. She gave a deep sigh. She always seemed to be sighing these days and she did not know why. It was then that she was aware of being watched.

Everywhere around her was suddenly so quiet as to be almost uncanny. The rest of the guests had gone aboard the yacht and she made to follow when, with a lurch of her heart, she became conscious of a dark undefinable shape looming in front of her. For a single bewildered moment, she recognized the unsteady rolling gait of a sailor with his hat set provocatively on the back of his head. What happened next was a nightmare. She was hauled roughly in his arms and his mouth was seeking hers hungrily. He was hopelessly drunk and his drink-sodden breath turned her stomach over. Momentarily witless, she felt sick and almost hysterical with the horror of it. Then she gathered her faculties together in a desperate effort to free herself—all to no avail. Her lungs felt about to burst when rescue came.

Her attacker was suddenly jerked from her by the scruff of his neck and given a well-aimed uppercut. He went down silently as a log and Gaye saw that he was quite young when his hat rolled off and Lance dragged his unconscious form to a sitting position against the capstan on the quay.

Almost reeling with deep gasps of thankfulness that the nightmare was over, she was aware—in a curious detached fashion—of a pair of concerned dark eyes gazing down at her in the moonlight. She felt him grasp her arms and wondered if he knew how fiercely he was gripping.

'Not hurt, are you?'

His voice sounded strangely hoarse and she shook her head dumbly. It was only by sheer will-power that she managed to keep standing on her trembling legs. In the half light his eyes glittered down at her oddly, sending a queer sensation through her veins. Gaye felt his controlled anger and numbly watched him draw a handkerchief from his pocket to wipe her lips gently. It was his very gentleness that aroused her slumbering resentment against him.

She said a trifle shakily, 'This needn't have happened if you hadn't stopped me from returning to the yacht earlier with Daddy.'

He regarded her for a moment in silence, then returned the handkerchief lazily to his pocket. 'My dear child, you left the hotel in the company of Freda and Netta. Had you continued with them to the yacht you would now be safe and sound in your cabin. But no, you had to dawdle on the docks of a strange country late at night, an easy prey for drunken sailors. I dread to think what might have happened if by chance we'd sailed without you.'

He spoke softly as one would to a wayward child, and the fact that he regarded her as such roused her anger still further. Moreover, there was logic in what he said.

'Perhaps it was my own fault,' she shot at him fiercely. 'Even so, that sailor behaved no worse than you did earlier on this evening, and he had an excuse for his actions. He was drunk.' A flush stained her paleness at the memory of his kisses and the unabashed smile he now favoured her with. The urge to shake him made her tremble. 'You're the most despicable man I've ever met! You saved me from an unpleasant experience. I'm grateful for that, although you're no better than ... than that sailor lying there!'

The amusement deepened in his voice. 'You mean sitting there, don't you?' With an ironical lift of dark brows he glanced towards the sailor, still propped up against the capstan his head lolling on one side sublimely unaware of them. 'So I'm no better than he is.' His eyes met hers with challenging directness. 'Maybe you would prefer his company to mine.'

Gaye's show of bravery suddenly deserted her. As he made to leave her she swallowed on a dismayed gasp and with a quick lithe movement sprang past him towards the yacht. She could still hear his amused laughter in her ears when she arrived breathless in her cabin to shoot the bolt on her door decisively in its socket.

On the Monday evening following the cruise, Rick Allen gave a farewell party at his flat for Teddy and Dorothy. Gaye arrived to find the party in full swing and was greeted hilariously by her friends all wearing silly paper hats. Teddy and Dorothy waved to her from across the room and someone shoved a glass and plate in her hand. It was at a party given by Rick in this same flat that she had met

Teddy months ago. Now they were about to say goodbye.

Rick rose from a bevy of girls and came to sit beside her, and it was not until much later when he was called to the record player that Gaye found Teddy at her elbow.

Her smile was warm and friendly. 'So you're going home, Teddy,' she said.

'Yep,' he said offhandedly, his mouth strangely set. 'We leave the day after tomorrow.'

Gaye bit her lip, already feeling the barrier between them, 'We haven't had much time together just lately, have we? I shall miss you. Looking forward to going home?'

'You know I'm not.' He took her hand between both his. 'I wish you'd come to Boston for a visit, Gaye. We'd take care of you.'

'I'm sure you would. Thanks for asking me. Perhaps when Daddy is stronger we might pay you a flying visit, but I don't want to leave him until he is.'

He caressed her hand thoughtfully. 'Think you could tear yourself away for the day tomorrow? We could lunch in town and drive down to Van Eldin Towers. You've never been and I think you'll enjoy it.' He looked at her appealingly, adding quickly when he saw her hesitate,

'Mother and Lance won't be there. They'll both be out.'

Impulsively, she squeezed his hand. 'I'd love to come,' she said, and meant it.

The morning was swathed in a warm mist, the kind heralding a nice day, when Teddy called to collect her in his Jaguar. Gaye ran from the house on elegant golden legs, her model coat in bronze, coral and white flying open to reveal a white, tailored dress beneath. His wolf whistle was as sharp as his eyes caressing her trim waist and slim, streamlined figure.

'Phew!' He passed a hand in an unnecessary smoothing motion over his short cropped hair. 'You look wonderful. An outfit like that calls for lunch at the Carlton Tower.'

Gaye slid into her old seat beside him feeling brighter than she had done for weeks. 'We'll go Dutch, shall we?'

Teddy cleared his throat in a mock stern manner. 'No, you won't, honey. What kind of a guy do you take me for to ask you out to lunch then let you foot the bill?'

In the Chelsea Room at the Carlton Tower they had eaten their share of an excellent lunch, each evading any mention of future parting. It was Teddy who first got down to it. They were lingering over fragrant coffee and looking down through a sunlit window on to Cadogan Place slumbering peacefully in the sun.

'I'm going to miss all this,' he said morosely.

Gaye caught the sadness in his eyes, knowing that the memory of it would always give her a piercing sweet pain.

'You'll come back,' she said, losing a little of her new-found lightness.

'Will you be waiting for me?'

She answered evasively, hating to hurt him. 'I'll still be with Daddy, I hope.'

She felt his disappointment and watched him move, thoroughly out of humour.

'Come on, let's go. The day will be over soon enough.'

Van Eldin Towers lay at the end of a long drive between immaculate trees and shrubs. The grounds had an Edwardian air about them with innumerable flowers and neatly planted borders of roses and colourful plants. Teddy pulled up at the charming entrance, having regained his sense of humour. He explained that the place had been in the family for generations, the gardens being set out in the first place by a royal gardener.

Gaye, looking up at the noble growth of ivy on the mellowed stone façade, was enchanted by its quiet graciousness. The atmosphere inside was one of harmonious beauty with the cream Regency striped curtains and pelmets at the tall windows matching the elegant furniture.

Gaye enjoyed herself immensely exploring the house and would have liked to linger in some of the charmingly furnished rooms where exquisite cabinets containing china and objets d'art caught her eye. The gun room was the only one she hurried through. Apart from the fact that she hated guns there were too many reminders of the absent Lance, cups he had won in all kinds of sport and several remarkably lifelike photographs of him in action on polo ponies.

They had tea at the end of it in an elaborate patio-styled garden with wrought iron and baroque columns made enchanting by a luxuriant profusion of flowers and antique garden furniture.

As they turned out of the drive on their return journey, a big car waited for them to clear the entrance before turning in. Lance lifted a negligent hand, showing an immaculate cuff as he passed.

Gaye, hastily averting her eyes, had only a glimpse of his companion.

'That was Mother and Lance,' Teddy said. 'Like to go back to meet her?'

'No, thanks,' she replied quickly. 'I don't think she would be interested.'

'Why not? Mother enjoys meeting people.'

'But not me. I'm the girl who went gambling with you. Remember?'

Teddy laughed. 'So what? One look at you and Mother would be as captivated as I am.' He slowed the car down to study her slender fairness. Her face was innocent of make-up and her skin tanned to a silken, smooth golden brown. 'You know I like you very much, I like everything about you—your warm glowing vitality, your femininity and gentle voice, the sparkle of laughter in your blue eyes, and above all your utter lack of contempt.'

Gaye was touched—who wouldn't be when a man professed his admiration in so charming a way? But he was on dangerous ground and she made an attempt to steer him off it.

'Your half-brother Lance would hardly agree with you. You know that Daddy and I spent the weekend on Sir Bonar Alsager's yacht.'

'Yes. Mother and I were invited, but we had already accepted an invitation to stay with friends.'

Because I was going, Gaye thought wryly, but did not say so. They parted at her door, where he looked down at her as though imprinting her image on his mind for all time.

'I'll be gone before you're up tomorrow,' he said with a crooked smile. 'Take care of yourself and don't forget me. I'll write.'

Then he was gone and Gaye went indoors with the feeling of having lost a limb. Her lips quivered from the imprint of his kiss

Jenny opened the door and informed her that Miss Dorothy Frayne had called while she was out and was ringing her up later. Gaye thanked her and looked at her watch surprised to find that it was seven o'clock. She had no idea it was so late.

'Is Daddy home, Jenny?' she asked.

'He's in the lounge, miss.'

Gaye hurried to her room for a quick change and a wash. In ten minutes she was tripping lightly downstairs to join her father. He was pouring out what she guessed was his second glass of brandy and he looked up quickly as she entered the lounge.

'Caught you tippling in secret!' she teased, and kissed his cheek.

'One has to do something when you're out,' he said, smiling at her fondly. 'Had a nice day?'

'Lovely.' She dropped at his feet in her favourite position by his chair and told him about her day with Teddy. She was half way through when the phone rang in the hall.

'Sorry to find you out,' Dorothy said. 'As you know, we leave early tomorrow and I called to say goodbye.' There was a queer little break in her voice before she went on, 'Funny, isn't it? When Daddy first suggested our going to the States I was terribly keen. Now the actual time has come I don't want to go.' Another pause during which Gaye was sure she was wiping her eyes, then, 'I'll miss you, Gaye. The crowd too.'

'I'll miss you,' Gaye said unhappily. 'You must write.'

They talked for quite a while, each trying to cheer up the other. When Gaye finally put down the phone to return to the lounge she found her father asleep. In her keyed-up state there seemed to be a queer hush about the house and restlessly she opened the french window for a comforting breath of cool night air. Walking slowly along the path in the now silent garden, Gaye felt terribly lonely and depressed. With her grandparents away and Teddy on the point of leaving with Dorothy the future loomed ahead with empty spaces she would have to fill. Thank heaven Daddy was taking her away on a holiday when he had settled all his business commitments. He had promised they would be away within a month. To Gaye, who was eager for action, it was eternity.

Mechanically, she made for a small recess at the end of the garden. Here the wall was hollowed out to contain a rose arbour and a seat. Sitting down, she breathed in the garden scents with the uneasy conviction that her life was changing. Her happy existence was being undermined in a way she found incomprehensible. Her father had not been the same man since his illness. He was quiet and withdrawn and there were times when she could not get near him. Quite often his interest in what she was saying flagged and he had been quick to apologize. Gaye had been both irritated and hurt. She glanced at her watch—another ten minutes to go before dinner. He could sleep until then. Neither of them were very cheerful company for each other at the moment. Maybe she was becoming too emotional. They were both below par in health, her father from his illness and herself through nursing him. They needed a holiday.

The sound of firm footsteps coming towards her told her that he had wakened and had come to look for her. Eagerly she dashed from her seat, rounding the corner into masculine arms. Her arms were around him, her cheek pressed against his chest before she realized that there was something strangely unfamiliar about him. He was leaner and more supple, too supple for her father.

'My, my, what a welcome! How long have you cared?' drawled a deep mocking voice.

Her heart became an uncontrollable leaping thing when, breath suspended in her lungs, she looked up dazedly into the dark, smiling face of Lance before thrusting him away from her.

'What are you doing here?' she said frigidly.

'Your father asked me to dinner. Did he not tell you?'

Momentarily she stood and stared, a dull flush creeping beneath her clear skin. Ignoring the charming smile, she willed her heartbeat back to normal, calling on her pride to cover her embarrassment at having embraced him.

'No, he didn't,' she said quickly, taking small, light steps towards the house.

He followed casually, keeping up easily with his long, lazy stride.

'He's asleep. Is he finding his work at the office too wearing?' he asked companionably as if they were the best of friends.

'Not really,' she answered briefly. 'He doesn't go until ten in the morning and leaves at half past four.'

'I believe he's planning to go away on holiday. Going

with him?'

'Of course.' Her tone implied it to be a silly question.

'Stubborn little cuss, aren't you?'

'I haven't the least idea what you are talking about,' she said sweetly. 'Anyway, here's Daddy.' She smiled at her father who was standing on the terrace. 'Had a nice sleep, darling?'

'Yes. I don't know what our guest thinks about me inviting him to dinner to find me asleep. Come in, Lance,' he said cordially. 'There's still time for a drink before dinner.'

For the rest of the evening Gaye set herself out to be as pleasant as possible under the circumstances. Really, it was too bad of Daddy not to tell her that Lance was coming. With mixed feelings she listened while her father guided the conversation which, with their coming holiday in mind, was mostly about travel.

'I like Scotland for a holiday myself. It has everything a man could wish for,' he said. 'The strong mountain air is conducive to a good night's rest and a good appetite. Not that I was ever a hearty eater, neither is Gaye, for that matter. She's eating nothing these days.' He smiled across at his daughter. The light played on her hair turning it into a halo of golden silk. Beneath it her small, fine-boned face was ethereally lovely. 'I think she's spending too much time with her old man.'

'You could be right there.' Lance's dark eyes held a devilish glint. 'I think Teddy is disappointed at not being able to take her to see his home in Boston.'

Her father showed intense surprise. 'Is that so? Why didn't you say, my dear? You know you could have gone with my blessing. You need young company.'

Gaye shot Lance a look fit to kill. 'I'd much rather be with you, Daddy. You know that.'

'That's not the point, my dear. I'm very grateful for what you've done for me, but you're young and need a break. I'm a generation ahead of you.'

Lance, leaning across the table to light his host's cigar before his own, said maliciously, 'You've allowed her too much of her own way, Maurice. You'll have to get her married off.'

Maurice chuckled. 'Exactly what her grandmother and I have been telling her.'

'Daddy!' Gaye admonished, her expression stormy.

'Lance is right. It's time you looked around for someone.' '

Gaye's eyes were drawn across the table to where Lance was watching her intently, noting her thinned nostrils and face pale with anger.

'Our guest doesn't practise what he preaches. I don't see him diving down the aisle,' she retorted.

Lance drew on his cigar leaning back in his chair, quite unruffled.

'It's different for a man. A woman needs the protection and security of marriage.'

'In other words, look what she's missing in ignoring the great male of the species,' Gaye said with a curl of the lip.

'Exactly,' drawled Lance.

Maurice looked from one to the other. 'I think you've met your match this time, my dear,' he said jocularly.

Gaye made no answer. She could not without being rude to their guest.

CHAPTER SIX

SINCE her grandparents had left on their cruise Gaye had missed them terribly—missed her grandmother's reassurance and her grandfather's teasing. There had been postcards from every port. It was Wednesday when the cablegram came from Tangier. Binns was out and Mrs Lambert and Jenny were off duty too.

Gaye opened it with trembling fingers to read: 'Maurice, Father had slight seizure—In hospital here—Imperative he should not be moved—No immediate danger—Will write —Mother.'

Gaye's first thought was to contact her father at once. Her watch said two-thirty when she rang his office to be informed by his secretary that he had not yet returned from lunch. Gaye had one or two purchases to make in town for their holiday, so she decided to do some shopping, calling in on her father later.

It was four o'clock when she reached his office. His secretary looked up with a smile when she entered. 'Your father has returned, Miss Pembleton,' she said, 'but he's engaged.'

Gaye walked to the door of her father's office and, without the slightest presentiment, opened the door quietly and peeped in. What she saw rooted her to the spot. Maurice Pembleton and Hilda Lambert were in other's arms and he was kissing her between murmured endearments that stabbed Gaye to the heart. They were oblivious of everything but their love for each other. She stared at them for what seemed an age in silence, unable to move or take in what she saw. Finally she closed the door silently, to slink away like a wounded animal, thankful that his secretary was too busy taking down a phone call to see her go. Lightheaded with shock, the cablegram forgotten, Gaye found herself out on the street and closed her eyes. Already her vivid imagination was trying feverishly to visualize herself taking second place in her father's affections. She couldn't. Gaye swayed with jealousy when she thought of the woman who had taken first place in his heart. In that same tortured instant there came a flashback of Lance, lean-faced, dark-eyed, saying, 'Hilda Lambert loves your father, but she has no wish to come between you.'

But she had. Gaye bit her lips, bordering on hysteria. She did not even think of her reason for calling at the office to see her father. All she could think of was losing the comradeship of the one being she had loved and trusted above all else in the world. She stumbled into her car to sit ashen-faced and trembling. She would never accept Hilda Lambert in her mother's place. Neither would she tolerate being pushed in the background by their complete absorption in each other.

Her shaking fingers reached out to start the car with the one idea in mind—to get away from it all. Recklessly, she shot in and out of the traffic, hardly conscious of a taxi driver's rude remarks when she missed him by inches. Built-up areas were tossed aside with the speedometer rising when she hit the motorway. On she drove like one possessed, the breeze through the open car window lifting her hair to send silken strands across her face, momentarily obscuring her vision. She cleared them with an impatient hand and saw the sudden curve in the road ahead too late to do anything about it. It seemed to Gaye that in the next few minutes all hell was let loose as she made a last frantic attempt to clear the bend. The air was rent with the shrieking of brakes followed by the sound of tortured, twisting metal and the terrible impact of splintering glass. Gaye was flung violently into space, to fall with a sickening thud on soft earth. There was an agonizing pain in her back, followed by an aching numbness that filled her with fear.

Bordering on the fringe of unconsciousness, she lay quite still listening to the slamming of car doors and footsteps approaching. It would be Lance who bent over her, she thought weakly.

'Good God, Gaye!' he cried hoarsely, pale beneath his tan. 'No, don't touch her,' this as someone bent over her. 'My place is just down the road—the big house on the left among the trees. Will someone go to phone for an ambulance, and for God's sake be quick about it!'

Gaye opened her eyes to a strange world of blurred faces and blinding lights where hands prodded her ruthlessly and grave masculine voices were accompanied from time to time by cool feminine ones. The smell of antiseptic was everywhere. There were times when her whole body felt on fire and her tongue too big for her mouth—times when she struggled vainly to rise, only to sink back again when sharp agonizing pain took over the slim, protesting body.

Days and nights fused together in a time of agony as more white-clad figures stood over her deep in consultation. Then she was left alone in a desert of pain where a masculine hand above a white cuff held a drink to her parched lips. It was that same hand that held her own firmly and reassuringly, pulling her back from a darkness that beckoned unceasingly.

Gradually the hand won and she awoke one morning with a steady gaze and clear eyes to find Lance beside her. He looked tired and drawn, not a bit like his usual self. A half-smile softened his rather grim expression. 'Hello,' he said.

Her blue eyes fastened on to him, questioning his reason for being there. Her smooth young forehead puckered as she remembered his presence at the time of her accident. It was all coming back to her now like a nightmare from which she had awakened in the sweat of fear. The shock of seeing her father and Hilda Lambert together and, later, her own wild driving of the car culminating in the accident.

'Did you bring me here?' she asked weakly, finding it an effort to talk.

'Sort of. How do you feel?'

She closed her eyes and shook her head in an attempt to stop the tears. 'I don't feel anything. Have you been here since they brought me in?'

'On and off.'

She wished her brain wasn't so woolly. 'On and off?' she echoed.

'You've been ill for two weeks.'

Gaye heard him dimly, remembering the hand that had clasped hers, making her hold on to life when all she wanted was to sink into oblivion.

'Poor Daddy! He must be awfully tired sitting and holding my hand all that time. Where is he now?'

He regarded her silently for a few moments. 'I don't want to confuse you, but can you remember what happened prior to your accident?'

Gaye began to tremble. She found herself going through it all again—her surreptitious opening of the office door—her entrance ...

'Please, I don't want to talk about it,' she moaned.

'Not even what you were doing so far from home on the motorway?' he prompted gently.

Her lips quivered. 'I was unhappy.'

'Unhappy?' he probed. 'What about?'

She went on reluctantly. 'There was a cablegram from Grandmother. Grandfather had been taken ill in Tangier.' She paused then went on hurriedly, her voice growing stronger, 'That's where Daddy is, isn't it? He's gone to see Grandfather. Is he very ill?'

He leaned forward to place a hand on her forehead, his eyes keen. Then he straightened. 'He has to stay in bed for a while like you.'

'I shan't stay in bed long. I feel much better. I can't feel my legs, though. They must be numb with me lying here.'

He shook his head, a pained smile hovering around his mouth.

'You'll have to be very brave. It's something you have to face up to. Better to tell you now before you find out for yourself, which you're sure to do pretty soon.'

Every scrap of colour left her face and her blue eyes were

tragic pools. He meant her father and Mrs Lambert, of course. He was going to tell her about them. Gaye clenched her hands and her lips quivered. She wanted to stop him, tell him she did not want to know. Then something he said pinned her attention. He was talking about her car accident.

'When you were thrown clear from your car you injured your spine in the fall. The membrane protecting the spinal cord was bruised and this caused the nerves of your back to become inflamed, giving you a high fever.'

Her voice was a choked whisper. 'What are you trying to tell me?'

'You have a temporary paralysis in your legs which only time will heal.' He had taken her hand in his and spoken softly as if to soften the blow.

Gaye couldn't take it in. She stared and went on staring at his brown strong hand holding her small white one. Her thoughts were as scattered as a flock of sheep and her brain as woolly. She lay there limply and as the gist of what he had said got through to her she pulled her hand away, her eyes widening in horror.

'You mean that I can't walk? That I'll have to lie in bed perhaps for years?' Her voice rose in her panic. 'I don't believe it. You're trying to frighten me. Go away, I hate you! Do you hear? I hate you!'

Gaye turned her face into her pillow and cried weakly. Sister came bustling in and when Gaye had composed herself Lance had gone.

'Is it true?' she asked dully, as Sister straightened her bed covers efficiently. 'Am I really paralysed?'

'I'm afraid so.' Sister tucked in the sheets. 'There's no reason why the use shouldn't come back given time. I know it's a shock, but that was no way to treat Mr Van Eldin. You were sure to find out soon and he thought it kinder to explain that the condition is only temporary before you discovered it for yourself and feared the worst.' Her tone became slightly reprimanding. 'The poor man has been sitting up with you day and night for two weeks, leaving you only to have a wash and a meal. So no more crying, please. Be a sensible girl and you'll soon be on your feet again.'

Gaye stifled a sob. 'You're right. I'm going to be well enough to go home when Daddy comes. I don't suppose you know where he is?' she asked hopefully.

Sister shook her head and turned blindly away. How many times had she to remind herself that emotional women were no good as nurses? Yet once again her emotions surfaced despite all efforts to subdue them.

Lance did not call again that day, but Gaye heard Sister answering his enquiry as to her condition on the phone in the corridor. Only then did it occur to her that he had not answered her question concerning the whereabouts of her father.

Gaye slept fitfully that night, awakening to the early morning sound of voices and trolleys on the corridor outside her room. Her door was slightly ajar and the young clear voices of the student nurses was distinguishable from Sister's austere tones.

'Nurse,' Sister was saying in the low tones of authority, 'no newspapers are to find their way into ward six today. The inquest on the victims of the plane crash is in all the papers this morning. Miss Pembleton's father was among them.'

'Poor girl!' the nurse exclaimed, borrowing her superior's low tones. 'I wouldn't like to be the one to tell her. Wasn't he going away on his honeymoon?'

'I believe so.' Sister's tone did not encourage further discussion. 'No more talking on the corridor, please, and remember, no papers.'

Gaye lay with closed eyes. Oh, God, it wasn't true! It was someone else they had been talking about. It had to be. Daddy wouldn't die like that. She began to tremble as with an ague. Her whole body was on fire, yet the beads of moisture on her forehead were cold and clammy. By the time the two student nurses came in to attend to her she was in a state of shock.

For the next three days she was not allowed visitors. She lay under sedation on doctor's orders. On the fourth day she was much better and mid-morning Sister came in from the phone in the corridor.

'Mr Van Eldin will not be coming in to see you for a day or so. He has to go away on business.'

Gaye told herself she did not care, but she missed him all the same. Her friends came to see her. Sister did not allow them to stay long and no one mentioned her father.

Lance came two days later, immaculately groomed and minus the tired look he had worn. His perusal of her pale face was keen, his smile enigmatic.

'Daddy's dead, isn't he?' she said before he could sit down.

Quickly he hitched his trousers by the knife-edged crease and sat on the chair beside her bed. 'So you know. I was hoping to keep it from you until your grandmother could come and give you her shoulder to cry on. Who told you?' he asked grimly.

'No one,' she answered truthfully through a welter of pain and anguish. 'It was you who held my hand when I was so ill, wasn't it, pulling me back into a world that I had no further use for now that Daddy has gone?'

His eyes narrowed at the bitterness in hers. 'You're talking nonsense,' he said firmly. 'You haven't begun to live yet.' His regard was shrewd. 'When did you first know about your father?'

She traced the pattern on the bed cover with her finger. 'While you were away.'

'How did you hear? Come on, I want to know,' he persisted.

'I overheard someone discussing it on the corridor. It was in the morning paper.'

'That was why you had a recurrence of the fever. Fortunately it was only a mild attack. Feeling better?' He quirked a dark brow.

'What do you think?' Gaye knew she was being rude, but she could not help it. She would like to have shaken him, he was so aggravatingly dictatorial.

A swift look of restraint passed over his lean features.

'I think you're feeling much better,' he said, an odd gleam in his eyes. 'You wouldn't have answered me like that if you weren't.' He leaned forward, his arms across his knees. 'You were very lucky to escape without more serious injury when your car crashed. Had the car door not opened for you to sail through you could have been smashed up beyond repair.'

'How do you know that I'm not now?'

'You know you're not. There's no reason why, with time, you shouldn't be as good as new.'

'Twelve months?' she echoed bitterly. 'Staring up at the ceiling until I go round the bend? No, thank you!' Her mouth set stubbornly. 'I shan't make any attempt to get well. I've nothing to live for now that Daddy has gone. Can't you see that?'

'All I see is a spoilt child wallowing in her own misfortunes, so self-centred that she isn't even interested in the way her father died.'

She swallowed on a mound of pain in her throat. 'He's dead, isn't he? Mrs Lambert too. If she isn't she ought to be. She killed him!' Gaye bit out viciously.

Lance sat back in his chair. 'Your father and Mrs Lambert were very much in love. They had been meeting without your knowledge. On the day of your car accident they were married in the morning by special licence, and intended taking an evening plane to Paris for their honeymoon. Your father rang me up saying that he had spent sleepless nights wondering at the best way to break the news to you. He couldn't bear the thought of writing you a letter. He wanted someone to be with you when you were told, he asked me to break the news to you personally. I was to take you to Boston to stay with Teddy and his mother until your father returned from his honeymoon.' He saw her wince and his voice softened. 'Unfortunately, I was delayed by an American friend who had flown over from the States specially to see me. I had left the house and was starting on my way to see you when I heard your car crash. I went to help and found you.'

Gaye did not speak. She closed her eyes wearily, wishing with all her heart that she could die too.

'There is one consolation,' he went on in level tones. 'Your father didn't suffer. The plane crashed at take-off and there were no survivors. Death must have been instantaneous.'

Gaye shuddered. Why couldn't she have gone with him instead of Mrs Lambert? Then through a veil of suffering she guiltily spared a thought for her grandmother. Poor Polly! Her husband's collapse must have been a blow to her, but the death of her only son must have been shattering.

As though he was aware of what she was thinking, Lance said,

'Your grandmother is coming to see you as soon as possible. I don't know if she has written to you.'

She shook her head. Polly hated writing letters and always left the chore to her husband.

'Poor Gran,' she said huskily.

'You were saying about a cablegram.'

Gaye moistened dry lips and told him stumblingly of receiving the cable and taking it to her father. Her voice trembled when she told him about finding Mrs Lambert in his arms.

'And you drove away with the intention of smashing yourself up. Well, you nearly succeeded,' he commented dryly.

'I didn't do it intentionally. I was speeding and lost control of the car.'

He ma··· a small scoffing sound. 'Quite a girl, aren't you? What about using some of that spirit of yours in resolving to get well? It's up to you how soon you get on your feet.'

The dictatorial note was again in his voice, rousing all her latent resentment.

'You make it sound so easy. Then you haven't to lie flat on your back perhaps for years.' Her voice hardened. 'You don't have to come to see me every day either. You can forget all about me from now on and leave me alone.'

'It isn't that simple,' he said, holding her gaze with his own. 'Your father put you in my care and asked me to look after you until he returned. Normally your grandparents could have taken over, but they're away. Your grandmother also has enough on her hands already with an invalid husband, so you'll have to put up with me and like it.'

Gaye's spirit disintegrated at his words. What did it matter who had charge of her? Someone had to in her present state. Wearily she closed her eyes. Lance went on talking about her father's affairs, but she heard only half of what he was saying. When he left she was already asleep.

Days passed, each one like the last. Gaye sank into a kind of inertia and remained oblivious of life going on around her. Her ward overflowed with flowers and gifts, but she never looked at them. She lay for hours gazing up at the ceiling, her feelings as numb as her legs. The pain had left her back and only recurred when she sat up too long. It was quite a relief to sit up without feeling sick and giddy, but the fact remained that she was unable to stand, much less walk alone. Her legs were heavy and useless and she lay like a puppet flung there carelessly by fate.

Her friends breezed in and out regularly with sympathetic looks, determined to cheer her up with arms full of flowers and gifts. Their company shortened her day, but she was relieved when they left. Life to Gaye was not the joyous thing it used to be. Nights of pain had sharpened the contours of her face and her eyes were shadowed with a deep sadness.

Lance continued to visit her each day with his satirical smile and they grew no closer. Then one morning he did not appear and the time dragged in consequence. Her grandmother arrived unexpectedly in the afternoon, thinner and deeply tanned. She embraced Gaye warmly, asked her how she was and said she was hoping her husband would soon be well enough to be moved.

She looked older and appeared to have shrunk as she told Gaye that she had booked in at a hotel nearby in order to spend as much time with her as possible. She had a message from Lance. He had not called in to see her that morning because he did not want to tire her out for her grandmother's visit in the afternoon. He stayed away for two days obviously giving them time to talk together.

On the third morning he strode in, meticulously groomed as usual, his eyes luminescent beneath the tantalizing lock of hair on his forehead. It was his glittering eyes that had fascinated Gaye at their first meeting and were now sending all the nurses dreamy-eyed about him. It was impossible not to notice the extra attention she received from them when he was there and the number of times they glided past the half-open door of her ward on some pretext or other to gaze in at him.

Unaware of the havoc he was causing in their feminine breasts, he crossed long legs, leaned back in his chair and said conversationally,

'I took your grandmother out to dinner last evening.

She's very concerned about you. She's talking about getting permission to bring your grandfather home so that she can look after you.' He paused, waiting for her to comment. When she did not do so, he continued, 'Personally, I don't think it will be fair to saddle her with two invalids. She's no longer young and would probably find it a great strain.'

Gaye lifted a clear steady gaze. 'What do you suggest?' she asked sarcastically. 'Dropping me in the Thames?'

His eyes narrowed on the glitter in them. 'It might do the trick and shake you out of that melancholy state you're in. Someone has to help you find your feet again without the cotton wool wrapping your grandmother would be all in favour of.'

'Perhaps we could consult that computer of yours,' she said acidly.

He regarded her with admirable self-restraint. 'You're coming on! The accident certainly hasn't dulled your wit.' A movement at the door drew his attention as Sister appeared bearing fragrant cups of coffee on a tray.

'Coffee, Mr Van Eldin?' she said.

She was rewarded with a charming smile. 'Please,' he drawled in his attractive voice.

Gaye's coffee was put beside her and the pillows placed more comfortably at her back before Sister left the room. Lance drank his coffee, but Gaye ignored hers, wishing that he would not insist on reminding her about the future. She did not want to know. At the same time she knew she would miss his visits if he were to stop coming. She was unhappy in his presence and unhappy in his absence. The situaton recalled an incident to her mind in her primary school days.

One of the small boys in her class had sent her a note which read:

'Dear Gaye, I like you. Do you like me? John.'

To which she had replied, 'Dear John, I half like you and

I half don't like you, but I think I half don't like you most. Gaye.'

'Drink your coffee.'

The brusque command shook her out of her thoughts.

Automatically, she reached for her coffee, quivering beneath his curtness. She drank part of it and put down her cup. 'You see, you have me well trained already. At least you won't have to order me to sit. I shall be doing plenty of that.'

His mouth quirked at the corners. 'It's a good beginning for when I take you in hand.' He folded his arms. 'You see, I'm taking on the job of looking after you. Your father would have wished it.'

Gaye was bereft of words. The last thing she wanted was an enforced indebtedness towards him. All he had done for her—all he would do—was for the sake of her father. 'You?' Her face flooded with colour. 'You just be joking!'

'On the contrary, I was never more serious. You're going to Van Eldin Towers to recuperate.'

A pinched look came around her nostrils and she stared at him defiantly. 'I want neither your help nor your pity. I suppose I ought to be grateful for what you've done for me. Maybe I am, but you don't have a duty to me in any way. Daddy would have wished me to go to my grandparents and that's where I'm going.'

'If you were the only one to be considered that would be the solution, but there are other people involved.' Lance spoke with a grim significance in his voice. 'The doctors have told your grandmother that your grandfather must have no worry. With you around utterly dependent on them he's sure to worry. They both will.'

Her lips tightened. 'I can go home. Binns and Jenny can look after me. I could have a nurse too if I needed one.'

'That's out. Your house is up for sale. No sense in leaving it to deteriorate.' There was an added edge to his voice. 'There's no alternative. You're going to learn to live without being cosseted. First you're going to walk again. Keep thinking that and you will.'

Hate and anger flared, rasping her breath in her throat. 'Thanks for the pep talk! What do you propose to do? Beat me and lock me up in the cellars of Van Eldin Towers if I don't do as I'm told?'

His laugh was a flash of white teeth. 'As a matter of fact you will regard what I have in mind as being equally as drastic. I'm taking you to Van Eldin towers as my wife.'

Her blue eyes widened to their fullest extent. 'You're crazy if you think for one moment that I would marry you! Why, we don't even like each other!'

The satirical look was back again on his face. 'It's essential for us to have a temporary marriage to stop the gossips, otherwise you would have to have a chaperone.' His eyes narrowed. 'That would interfere with my plans for you. I want a free hand where you're concerned. The same can be said of your father's estate. Everything will go through much quicker with a man on the job.'

He held her look with his own. He was making it quite clear that he did not care whether he had her approval or consent. No one had ever treated her like this before. She had always been the one who called the tune. Gaye stared at him dumbly, remembering the night he had come to dinner and her father's words spoken lightly at the time but which now held a wealth of meaning.

'It looks as if you've met your match,' he had said.

That he would go all out to get his own way, she had no doubt. It was there in the firm strong lines of his face and the challenging directness of his keen dark eyes. Whether he would do so was another matter. When, at last, she spoke her voice had the husky quality of having taken part in a verbal slanging battle of words.

'Marry me,' she said, 'and I'll give you hell.'

He gave a short laugh. 'Even hell can be bearable with company,' he answered softly.

CHAPTER SEVEN

THEY were married before Mrs Pembleton rejoined her husband in Tangier. Everything was planned and carried out with the speed of Lance behind it. He was to take Gaye from the hospital dressed for her wedding, which was to be at Van Eldin Towers. Her grandmother was arranging the small wedding reception there, so it was Sister who helped Gaye into a long romantic dress of Tricelon moss crêpe in white with soft cape sleeves and a V-neckline. Lance had given her a diamond pendant as a wedding gift. A circlet of gold held it in place around her slender young throat and the high Empire bodice of her dress emphasized the slim lines of her slender young figure. Her golden hair had been shampooed into a glittering halo and she looked young and ethereally lovely.

'For luck,' Sister said on a sentimental note, thrusting a small object into her hand.

It was a small tube of padded brown leather to which eyes, nose, mouth and small hands and feet had been added realistically. It was topped by a fuzzy mop of brown hair standing out like a mop, and the result was a rather grotesque little creature with a lovable grin. Gaye adored it on sight. She was taken to the door of the hospital in a wheel chair and, with the good wishes of Sister and her staff ringing in her ears, Lance carried her to his car.

She had awakened that morning as she had every morning since her accident, with no interest in her surroundings.

Her first show of any feeling had been the smile of thanks she had flickered at Sister for the small gift which she held in her hand. Lance had awakened no response when, as he came quite close to fasten on the diamond pendant, his teeth had flashed down at her in a quick smile.

The moment Lance placed her in the front seat of the car she began to tremble with fear. When he put on speed after leaving London she was terrified. Sweat clung damply to her temples and she found herself going through the torture of nightmare moments before her car crashed. Gaye tried not to check the speed as panic rose inside her and her hands clenched until her nails bit into her flesh, causing an ache which spread painfully to her shoulder muscles and neck.

'Relax,' Lance said gently when she cringed as they neared a bend. 'You're in no danger. I'm not aiming to break the sound barrier.'

Impossible to tell him that she was not reassured—that the terrifying sound of breaking glass and twisting metal still gave her nightmares. To her mortification weak tears spilled from her eyes and she found she could not stop shaking. She saw the concern on Lance's face before he stopped the car. Suddenly his arms were around her, holding her close, cradling her head in the comforting hollow of his shoulder. She crumpled against him.

Presently she grew calmer, accepted the handkerchief he offered and blew her nose.

He eyed her candidly with a pained smile. 'Fortunately a bride is expected to cry on her wedding day, and you're one of those lucky people whose nose doesn't go red afterwards.'

The banality of his tones steadied her as nothing else could. A strange new emotion banished her fear and caused her heart to beat in thick strokes. She had found his concern more than comforting. Yet it was all part of the job he had set out to do. To him she was a spoiled child and the sooner she was well the sooner he would have her off his hands. He would do the job thoroughly with all the cool calculation he was capable of. He was looking down at her appraisingly, his stern mouth curved into a smile. 'I should add that crying becomes you. Your eyes have become soft and melting and you have that untouched look that a man likes to see in his bride. Better now?'

She nodded, thankful that she had used no make-up.

'We'll go, then, shall we?'

She assented and he drove on at a moderate speed, sparing her a glance from time to time, teasing her out of her weepy state. But when the car pulled up at Van Eldin Towers the sick dread of a long and weary future ahead blurred her vision.

Lance carried her into a tastefully furnished room with light wood panelling and thickly patterned carpet. It was sun-warmed and welcoming, the ultimate in sophisticated wealth.

Sir Bonar, her grandmother and the vicar were there. The vicar, a worried-looking spare little man, rose from a champagne-coloured chair to watch Lance lower Gaye down gently on to a luxurious matching sofa.

The wedding service was brief, with Gaye's look of frailty thrown into sharp contrast by Lance, strong and vibrant with health, beside her. She had sat through it all like a pale little ghost. She felt nothing. From her waist down there was a dead numbness that seemed to spread to her brain and mind.

Her grandmother shed a few tears. She was obviously thrilled with her beloved granddaughter's marriage. It was so romantic, the kind she had wished for her, with a husband who would cherish and love her as she deserved to be loved. The child was not looking very happy, but that was only to be expected. She had not recovered from her accident and her father's tragic death. He would have been delighted with the match. Tears welled anew in her eyes at the thought of her son. His tragic end had been a terrible shock and one from which she would never fully recover. The only consolation was that he had gone with the woman he loved. He had been lonely for so long.

There was a small wedding reception in the dining room after the ceremony. A toast was drunk with Sir Bonar making the usual light remarks a wedding merited. Mrs Pembleton beamed her approval and Lance was his calm unruffled self.

Later, Lance carried Gaye to her own suite of rooms specially prepared with a wheelchair in mind. She was exhausted by the time he laid her on the bed. The long unaccustomed sitting and being carried had jarred her back into an agonizing ache. It had taken all her will power to fight off the sickly feeling of faintness that threatened to engulf her. She closed her eyes to open them again when Lance pressed a bell beside her bed to bring a nurse, cool and efficient, in navy and white.

Nurse Russell was well-made, ginger-haired and around thirty. Gaye, encountering the direct gaze of light blue eyes, decided she was bearable.

Lance introduced them with a charming smile. 'I hope you'll be very happy together,' he said. 'But I may as well tell you, nurse, that I hope your stay with us will be a short one. I want my wife to walk again as soon as possible.' Gaye looked away from his half-teasing, half-serious smile. He could not wish for it more than she did, and for the end of their so-called marriage. The faintness was now coming over her in waves. She felt Lance bending over her and she was lifted just enough to take a sip or two of the brandy he held to her lips. It made her cough, but the warm trickle inside her chased away the faintness and her colour returned. Her grandmother came in all concern and with a swift kiss on the top of her scented hair, he left her with the two women.

Gaye awoke the next morning to a charming, sophisticated yet lively room. The accent was on white with a shaggy white carpet, Buckingham bed with tweed upholstery, white dressing table, coffee table, and white tweed papered walls with curtains and lampshades to match. Transparent vinyl drapes covered two tall windows and a spacious bay looking out on the garden. The overall white effect was subtly contrasted with a beige-covered chaise-longue, caramel, coffee, brown and orange cushions, several flower arrangements in chocolate brown urns and the blazing autumn tints of an abstract painting on the wall. Everything was there for an invalid's comfort, from the pile of glossy magazines to a record player and the latest discs.

But Gaye found no pleasure in her surroundings. Her only emotion was an aching loneliness somewhere in the half aliveness of her body and an inertia that increased when she remembered that her grandmother was leaving that morning for Tangier.

She was sitting up in bed wondering how she was ever going to survive one day, much less a year of being a semi-invalid under Lance's roof, when he strode in after taking her grandmother to the plane. He was wearing a smart, blue striped city-going suit with pink lime-striped silk shirt and tie. He brought with him a fresh breeze of morning air and his vitality made her feel inadequate to deal with him.

He stood looking down at her small shadowed face and the blue smudges beneath her eyes. This morning there was a faint pink in her cheeks and it deepened beneath his scrutiny.

'You're a better colour this morning,' he said. 'Sleep well?'

'Yes, thanks,' she replied, her eyes on the letters he held in his hand.

He tossed them on the bed. 'Letters from Teddy and

Dorothy, I presume,' he commented without much expression.

Gaye looked down to see that the envelopes had been slit open neatly and shot him a surprised stare.

His eyebrows lifted mockingly. 'Yes, I opened them for you. I haven't read them.' Lazily, he drew a cigarette case from his pocket. 'Cigarette?' Without waiting for her answer, he lit one and placed it in her mouth. Then lighting one for himself, he lowered his long length into a chair near the bed. The small novelty Sister had given her caught his attention from the dressing table and he reached out a long arm to pick it up and study it with some amusement.

Gaye, uneasy in his presence, drew on her cigarette and, looking down at the letters on the bed deliberately shut him out of her thoughts. The top one she recognized as Teddy's and felt guilty that she had thought about him so little since her accident. Now she was remembering the light clasp of his hand as they walked across the downs. His jacket had been flung carelessly over a shoulder and they were singing a rollicking sea song, happy in the perfect intransigence of youth, living for the moment. Now there were no moments to live for. Not for her.

She felt Lance's narrowed gaze, saw that he had replaced the novelty on the table and was giving her his undivided attention.

Gaye knocked the ash from her cigarette. 'Did Gran go off all right?' she said tonelessly.

'Yes. She was worried about you. She sends her love and hopes you will soon walk again.'

'Have I really walked?' Her tone was bitter. 'I feel as though I never have. What's more I don't think I shall ever walk again.'

'Of course you'll walk again,' he said, narrowed eyes concentrating on her through the haze of smoke he exhaled. 'There's a specialist coming to see you today. If his verdict is the same as the others, we'll get cracking on building you up. Then we'll try exercises. You're naturally slim—the kind that has plenty of energy to burn.' His smile was suddenly white. 'I remember you fairly sparkling with it.'

Gaye sat wordless, wanting him to go and wishing that he would not keep alluding to the past. It was as painful as her empty future. But nothing appeared to be further from his mind. He sat there cool and detached with so little understanding of how she was feeling that she had to air her resentment against him.

'I refuse to see another of your miracle men,' she said, tense and dark-eyed. 'I'm sick of being prodded and examined as if I was some kind of prize heifer. I suppose you mean well. Even so, you needn't have married me or gone to all the trouble you have to make things easier for me. You're making yourself a lot of hard work for nothing.'

He leaned forward to crush out his cigarette in an ashtray on the coffee table nearby. Gaye had the feeling that he would have liked to do the same with her.

'I'm the best judge of that,' he said, slightly belligerent. 'Had your father lived you would have lost him to another woman and would have had to adjust your own life accordingly. You still have to adjust your life, but in a different way—a much harder way because it involves physical suffering whereas the other would have been purely mental. You're bewildered, miserable and unhappy, but it will pass.'

Suddenly she was shaking, her lips quivering sensitively. 'Can't you understand? I don't want to live in a world that, to me, has become strange and empty.' The ash from her cigarette fell on the pretty counterpane and she brushed it off impatiently. 'All I want is to be left alone.'

'I'm disappointed in you. You fought hard enough to save your father when he was so ill. I know you did it mostly for yourself because you were afraid of losing him.

However, the challenge to battle against overwhelming odds was there. You accepted it and you won. You can do it again.'

Her smile was bitter. 'But it was all in vain, wasn't it? He died just the same. Well, I'm dead too. At least half of me is.'

She had to look down to hide the sudden rush of tears.

He said slowly and deliberately, his eyes on her down-bent head,

'That's the half we're going to bring to life again, and the other half will come to life with it.'

Gaye raised a strained white face, her eyes luminous with unshed tears. She was too bound up in her own misery for anything he said to get through. 'That isn't the way I see it and I'd be obliged if you would leave me alone. I'm not seeing your specialist. I'm not seeing anyone. Just leave me alone!'

But she did. He came in the afternoon, a tall, proud man with a high intelligent forehead and clever hands. His examination was thorough and convincing.

'Time and patience, Mrs Van Eldin,' he said with a smile. 'This time next year there's no reason why you shouldn't be walking around normally, even starting a family.'

Gaye, flushing to the roots of her hair, was tempted to throw something at him. Lance did not move a muscle. Anyone would think from his behaviour that they were a happily married couple.

The visit of the specialist started off a period in which Gaye felt she would go mad. There were endless days of lying there staring in turn at the ceiling or through the windows into the garden. The drapes had been taken down to give her a better view and at times her gaze would rest on the vase of rosebuds placed where she could see them and smell their fragrance. They were fresh every day and as varied as the vitamin-packed meals served to her so attractively on a pretty tray.

She ate them because it was something to do and less trouble than refusing. Her grandfather was well enough to write and she looked forward to his letters and the unexpected small gift slipped in the same post by her grandmother, small mementoes from abroad, a gay silk pyjama suit, quaint containers filled with the mysterious perfume of healing herbs, a small wood carving deliciously lifelike. All around her were echoes of her grandparents' love and thoughtfulness.

She wrote to Dorothy and Teddy after reading their letters of congratulation on her marriage. Teddy had not replied, and she had not expected him to. He had been appalled at her accident and Gaye wondered if he had felt the same about her marriage to Lance.

Dorothy was having a hectic time with more dates than she could handle. She begged Gaye to come over and visit her when she was better, which she hoped was soon.

Sir Bonar had become a frequent visitor, calling to take tea with her in the afternoon and sometimes dining with Lance at night. Gaye, with a better understanding since she lost her father, sensed his loneliness. On one of the occasions when he had paid her a visit he had told her the reason why he had never married. He had loved Lance's mother too well to be satisfied with anyone else.

'She chose Richard Van Eldin,' he said with a sigh. 'Not that I blamed her. He was like Lance, handsome and dashing, a fine man.'

Sir Bonar was not handsome by any means, but he was attractive in a well-groomed way. One by one his features were not outstanding, but together they made an intelligent and kindly face. Gaye liked him. He reminded her of her father in the way that he could be charming to old and young alike, receiving the same warm response.

'I'm waiting patiently for you both to use my wedding present,' he said one day over tea, his eyes twinkling.

'Your wedding present?' Gaye had echoed blankly.

'Yes, didn't Lance tell you? It's a honeymoon anywhere you wish when you're well enough to enjoy it.'

Gaye had blinked. 'That's awfully sweet of you,' she had answered, wondering what he would have said if he had known there would be no honeymoon.

Good food and constant attention gradually built up her health. A wheelchair was provided which she soon managed to manipulate expertly.

'That's what I was afraid of,' said Lance, striding out to her in the garden one day after standing on the terrace watching her cutting flowers and moving as though she and the chair were one. 'You'll become so attached to that thing that you won't make the effort to walk.'

When her back was well enough for her to be carried without pain Lance swept her up in his arms and bore her in to dinner. They seldom dined alone. Usually it was business associates, accountants, solicitors and people connected with her father's estate, or friends. Consequently they grew no closer. Since he had discovered her liking for Sir Bonar he dined with them more or less every evening. It appeared to Gaye that Lance was as anxious as she was for them not to get close.

Each evening at half past nine Lance delivered her promptly to her room. One evening he placed her on her bed and said with determination,

'Nurse is getting you up at half past seven in the morning. We're going for a swim in the outdoor pool. The weather is still warm enough—besides, the pool is heated.' He looked down into her amazed face.

'Your general health has improved enough for you to begin the fight back on your own two feet.'

'Why?' she asked sarcastically

'Wait and see,' was the cool response.

So it began with a swim in the pool before breakfast. Gaye did everything with the same ill grace that she had accepted the wheelchair. She hated having to obey Lance even though she knew it was for her own good. Most of all she hated to have to put her arms around his neck—hated her utter dependence on him, when he carried her about.

They clashed often, Gaye with a mutinous look and a stubbornness that Lance always overcame by the iron hand in the velvet glove like the morning she refused to get up early for their usual bathe.

She had never been an early riser in the past mainly because she had kept so many late nights. Now she had not that excuse, for Lance insisted upon her going to bed at half past nine, religiously getting her up at half past seven the next morning for their swim.

He had entered her room one morning well after half past seven to find her still in bed.

'Not well?' he asked, giving her a keen glance.

Gaye looked up at him like a tousled kitten, her creamy shoulders rising above the frothy neck of her night attire. 'Go to blazes!' she exclaimed with deliberate rudeness. 'I'm not getting up this morning!'

Lance folded his arms, big and forbidding in his bath robe, and consulted his wrist watch. 'You have exactly ten minutes to get into your swim suit. I'm sending Nurse in to you and if you're not ready when I come back I'll put you into it myself.'

As always she became aware of that queer frightening feeling when ever she was alone with him in a world where he was master. The pounding of her heart increased a new and undefinable fear.

Watching her, Lance refused to be affected by the dislike and shrinking fear in her blue eyes. Why should he when she was the kind of girl he most despised—the kind that was spoiled sick into taking everything as her right and giving nothing in return?

She had never known what it was to love someone better than herself. Yet there was something about her that stirred his sense of adventure—a challenge he had accepted from their first meeting. It wasn't her fault that she had been spoiled from birth with the kind of suffocating attention that stunts the growth of a worthwhile character. He was only human and fully aware of the fascination of delicate bones, lovely brows, the perfection of a small straight nose and the alluring softness of her mouth. He had seen sadness deepen the beauty of her face, but it was sadness for her own plight. He wasn't aware that her character had undergone any change since she lost her father. Was he reaching down for something inside her that wasn't there? Perhaps he had been wrong to marry her. With his close knowledge of her over the past few months he knew she was in no way ready for marriage. Acquaintances of his, much older men than he, had married young girls because they were lovely and decorative, but he was too intelligent to be satisfied with so little.

'Ten minutes,' he repeated on a frown of annoyance, and left her.

When he returned later to sweep her up in his arms she avoided the gleaming eyes that always held a quizzical look in their depths whenever they encountered hers. Despite her hatred she was becoming more aware of his charm and sometimes found herself wondering what his eyes would be like softened by love.

As the days passed into weeks Gaye had not the slightest inclination to walk. She had grown afraid of the outside world and was content to stay within her own four walls. There was no denying that she was looking better, thanks to Lance filling her days with activity. Her golden hair regained its lustre, gleaming like spun silk above deep blue eyes bright and clear with health. But the old Gaye with the sunny temperament had gone. She was morose and unco-operative, with days when she was openly rude to the staff and Lance in particular.

In her more thoughtful moments she wondered at his endless patience, at the same time not wishing to come up against his anger. But the day came when she did. It happened on the morning Lance travelled early to London in connection with her father's estate. The time of stress had gradually built up inside her until the let up of her daily routine with him acted as the last straw.

The day had begun with Nurse coming in to rouse her at half past seven for her usual swim and Gaye had sent her packing under a shower of books, magazines and everything that she could lay her hands on to throw in her temper. She had lain in bed all the morning smoking and wallowing in a well of depression and refusing to eat or see anyone. The room was in a shambles with most of the stuff she had thrown, including fruit, lying near the door.

In the afternoon she had fallen into an uneasy sleep and was awakened by the door opening abruptly. Her heart jerked as Lance strode in and stooped to pick something up from beneath his foot. It was Sister's small parting gift. In dead silence he gazed around to find that he was standing in utter chaos. The room was a shambles with fruit, books, magazines, chocolates, even the vase of roses lying where Gaye had flung them in her temper. He quirked a brow that could have meant that he wasn't in the least surprised, but Gaye knew by the sudden set of his face that he was blazingly angry. She watched him walk towards her and quivered as he stopped tongue in cheek to say with a dangerous softness, 'Been having fun? What's the idea refusing your meals and throwing things at all and sundry?'

'Oh, go away!' she shot at him swiftly. The upheaval inside her at his unexpected appearance was subsiding, her anger rising to meet his when he looked down at her after placing Sister's gift on the table beside the mound of cigarette ends. 'I'm sick of you and your get-well tactics. Where have they got me? Nowhere. I can't walk. I'll never walk, so leave me alone. I hate everybody and most of all I hate you carrying me—touching me!'

His mouth became thin and cruel and his dark eyes compelled her flinching ones to meet them. Deliberately he sat down on the bed facing her and leaning forward, planted a hand firmly on each side of her slender form.

'Still very much the spoiled brat, aren't you? Did you know that all spoiled brats have to be chastized if they're to be made at all likeable?'

Her breath caught in her throat and she shrank back in her pillows when his face came nearer. She saw the dark glittering eyes between thick springy lashes, the slight flaring of his nostrils, and panicked.

'Touch me and I'll scream,' she threatened.

His eyes narrowed on a sudden gleam. 'You hate me touching you, don't you?' he said maliciously.

Before she could realize his intention he was pinning down her arms to brutally crush her lips with his own. For what to Gaye seemed an endless space of time he proceeded to punish her with draining, merciless kisses, sliding his mouth down her neck to softer flesh before returning again to her lips. When, at last, he lifted his head she had to draw in long shuddering gasps to replenish her lungs.

He was breathing rather heavily himself when he finally released her and rose to his feet, the stray lock of hair falling across his forehead. 'Misbehave again and you'll be punished. Be as rude to me as you wish, but I will not tolerate you ill-using the staff. They're only doing their job. Understand?' He gave a second glance at the mound of cigarette ends. 'And cut out that chain smoking or I'll cut your supply. No wonder you're off your food!'

The click of the door followed and all was quiet. Gaye lay quivering with humiliation and hate. Most of all she was afraid of the situation she was in—helpless and dependent on a man who disliked her as much as she disliked him—a man who was determined to alter her until she did not recognize herself.

She thought feverishly of past delights when each day dawned with yet another whim gratified by a doting parent, when she had been the happiest and most carefree of persons. Why had her father had to die? Hot tears forced their way beneath her lids and she found herself crying for her father, for her own hopeless future and for the way fate was working against her.

Bitterly she built up a hate of Lance, blaming him for taking away her joy in living and her freedom to do as she liked, even her identity. He had made her more vulnerable to hurt and more unhappy than she had ever been in her life.

As she lay there it gradually dawned on her that there was no point in carrying on the way she was. She had to get away, give herself a new start, and to do that she had to learn to walk again. Reaching a definite decision helped to calm her. It was the catharsis she needed. Hitherto her life had centred entirely around herself with no thought to count her blessings. Now she had to win back one of the most precious—the gift to walk again in the sun, to battle against the winds and to glory in the soft rain falling on her face.

For a week Lance left her severely alone. Since she had told him that she hated his touch he had Nurse wheeling her into the dining room in her chair. Before their guests he was the charming and attentive husband, but on the few occasions they dined alone he assumed a chilly politeness. If her behaviour and his chastisement had erected a barrier between them Lance showed her he had no intention of surmounting it.

Evidently he was waiting for her apology and his own would automatically follow. Since she had no intention of doing so her only alternative was to show an airy indifference. Her only vulnerable point where he was concerned was her pride. She hated the way he looked at her with no particular expression save one of cool neutrality. Sir Bonar had chosen that week to go to Paris on business and Gaye missed his cheerful company. So the days dragged on, but at least they gave her the opportunity to try to walk when Nurse was not about. She began by easing herself up from her chair to put her weight on her legs and when each time she fell back defeated, she tried again.

CHAPTER EIGHT

On Friday morning a letter from her grandfather added to her depression. He had written to say that on the advice of his doctor, he had decided to spend the winter in Tangier, so they would not be returning home until the spring.

On a wave of acute disappointment Gaye clenched the letter into a ball in her hand and flung it into the waste paper basket. Damn them all, she thought viciously. No one cared about her, but she would show them!

Gripping the arms of her wheelchair determinedly, she pushed herself up on to her feet. To her utter amazement and delight she stood for a full minute before falling back into her chair incredulously. Trembling, she tried again, but she was shaking too much in her excitement to keep her balance and fell into her chair.

On Saturday morning Nurse awoke her at half past seven on Lance's orders. So the old routine started again, filling her day with activity, this time with a difference. Determined to walk whatever the cost, she gave in meekly to Lance and Nurse. If either were surprised at her docileness they did not comment. Lance, she knew, would take it that she had decided to behave herself rather than run the risk of a reprisal in the form of his hateful kisses.

That evening they dined alone. Several times during the meal Gaye caught Lance studying her thoughtfully. She was sublimely unaware that she was looking particularly lovely in a beautifully made dress of singing yellow in a dull-shiny material with a belt of silver blazer buttons cleverly contrasting with the material to give it an exclusive air. Her golden hair shimmered in the light and her eyes were as blue and guileless as the night sky.

She knew he was puzzled by her unusual air of meekness and was much too smart to be hoodwinked, as she discovered when he wheeled her later to her room.

Resting his hands on the arms of her chair, he looked down into her face. 'Like to try to walk?' he asked softly.

She looked up startled and suspicious. He couldn't know. He was merely guessing. 'Yes ... yes, I would,' she said with such meekness that he lifted a brow.

'Put your arms around my neck and I'll lift you up, then lower you on to your feet.'

Blindly she obeyed, to find to her dismay that her legs buckled under her. Trembling, she clung to him, inwardly reeling from the blow that her legs had not responded as they had done the previous day.

Lance, however, treated the whole thing lightheartedly and Gaye felt a swift kiss on her hair. 'Never mind, you tried. Better luck next time. Any pain?'

Only the pain of anguished disappointment, but he was not to know why. She shook her head, hating to have to cling to him. He held her silently for a moment before picking her up to place her on the bed. Her face looked pinched and her eyes bright with unshed tears.

He put on a wry smile. 'You've been thinking about it too much. We could give the daily routine a rest for a bit, but days off don't agree with you.'

She knew he was referring to the day she went berserk and the old dislike flared. 'I'll manage,' she said shortly.

He straightened abruptly. 'Maybe it was the wrong time of the day to try. You're tired.' He placed a fist playfully beneath her chin. 'There'll be other days.'

But Gaye could not respond to his bantering and when Nurse came in answer to his ring he left them together. As Nurse prepared her for bed Gaye wondered hollowly what she thought of a newly married couple who did not share the same room and never appeared to be eager for each other's company.

Outwardly, Lance appeared to be satisfied with things as they were. His visits to London were rare and he carried on most of his business from the library of Van Eldin Towers, putting in long-distance calls to the States regarding his computer.

There were long-distance calls to his stepmother too. Gaye heard him speaking to her one morning as she sat in her wheelchair on the terrace. It was near to the open french window of the library. She wondered what she had thought when Lance told her of his marriage. Gaye could imagine she would not be very pleased.

Her head turned at a movement behind her. Lance was leaning against the frame of the french window watching her. He was wearing a brown jacket, brown velvet trousers and a brown moiré polo-necked shirt. The colour deepened his eyes, giving them an amber glow in their depths.

He straightened and strolled towards her, slanting his head to look down at the book unopened in her lap.

'Not interested, or just bored?' he asked with a quirk of a friendly brow, his eyes scanning the youthful contours of her face and her shadowed eyes.

'A bit of both,' she admitted noncommittally.

'Like a drive?'

Her eyes appeared to be eager, but she showed no enthusiasm. 'Now? Like this?' She looked down at her navy and white trouser suit.

His gaze roved over her appreciatively. 'Why not? I'll bring the car round.'

She watched him go, wishing she could take off from her tired body and leave behind for ever the stranger she was fast becoming to herself. With all the time in the world for retrospection Gaye knew she had changed a great deal in the last few months. She felt years older since her accident and more mature. Could this be how all grown up people felt, this cold detachment from a world no longer one of fantasy but real and grasping? Had she to go on paying for what the world had given her so unstintingly in the past?

'Where are we going?' she asked when they were driving along in his big roomy car.

'Some place you've never been before.'

'How do you know?'

'I don't.' She heard the grin in his voice. 'I'm only guessing.'

They crested a hill and she looked across unspoilt country where silent hills under cobalt blue skies made her long to walk beneath the golden shade of beech trees in nearby woodland glades. A soft breeze through the open car window caressed her hair with no thoughts of the car crash to spoil her enjoyment. Lance had cured her of that with smooth steady drives and picnics on the downs.

'Here we are,' he said at last, swinging the car off the road to take a side one, unmade and bumpy, leading to a delightful black and white timbered house called The Doggery.

Two white gates were opened for them to pass through

obviously operated from the house, for when they drew up at the door a woman came out surrounded by a litter of small dogs. She was tall and slim in her thirties with smooth brown hair, a ready smile and brown eyes.

'Hello, Lance!' She beamed with pleasure when she saw him.

Her look at Gaye was friendly but not curious when Lance unfolded his long length from the car, leaving her seated.

'What about it, Gaye?'

Lance had walked round to where she sat and bent in to look at her. But Gaye was already peering down at the white and gold pekinese puppies milling around their owner's feet. The woman, whom Lance had introduced as Kay Foster, scooped one up and handed it to Gaye.

'My favourite,' she said with a smile. 'She's well behaved, obedient, doesn't snap, and besides being thoroughly healthy, she's a real lady.'

Lance grinned. 'Sounds like a perfect description of the ideal wife!'

Gaye fondled the struggling, silky little body. 'She's lovely. Can I really have her?'

Lance looked mockingly at Kay Foster. 'Shall we let her have it?'

Mrs Foster laughed. 'I think the puppy has already adopted her,' she said, watching it snuggle down contentedly against Gaye's neck.

'What are you going to call it?' Lance asked. They were on their way home after buying a dog basket.

Gaye looked down at the small dog asleep on her knee. 'Misty,' she said, seeing it through a mist of tears.

'Rather a comedown after all those names on her pedigree sheet,' he scoffed. A short silence followed before he said coolly, 'I have to go to the States quite unexpectedly. Stepmother wants my advice on a business problem. I leave early tomorrow morning.'

Gaye felt relief and regret merging oddly together. She had come to rely on him in a way that puzzled as well as frightened her. Maybe it was just as well that they were parting for a while.

It was this close proximity with him, his small kindnesses that made her forget he was merely carrying out his duty. He had promised her father to look after her and he was doing just that. It also occurred to her that she owed him a good deal. He had stressed the impermanence of their marriage, yet he had looked after her as a husband would.

With his usual imperturbability he went on talking, not appearing to notice her silence as he told her he would be back as soon as he could.

He left early the next morning and in the days that followed she put all she had into learning to walk. Holding tightly to her wheelchair, she managed to stand for a few moments, the time lengthening into minutes as she gained confidence. At last she was able to stand without the aid of her chair.

Her progress was slow—walking a step at a time, pushing the wheelchair in front of her like a child learning to walk with a push-chair. Misty followed her progress with delight. Thinking it part of a game, she ran around her in circles, stopping to look up at her from time to time with barks of appreciation. Her yapping brought Nurse to see what all the noise was about and she was equally delighted to see her patient on her feet. Rather tentatively she mentioned the possibility of being able to take a few days off to go to see her mother when Gaye's progress was more assured. Her mother was not well, she said, and she was worried about her.

Gaye did not hesitate, but told her to go as she was now quite able to look after herself; besides, there was an excellent staff to help if needed. Flushed with victory, Gaye wondered around her rooms touching everything and looking at her reflection in the big mirror. The picture was one of a slim girl whose small pale face beneath the cloud of bright hair was saddened by eloquent blue eyes. Her whole bearing had changed. The sparkle had gone, leaving an air of tiredness tinged with bitterness. The miracle of walking again had lifted her from the depths and with a defiant quirk at fate she was determined to enjoy the respite.

She revelled now in the joy of early rising when before the mere thought of it had made her shudder. She loved the early sky flushed over her newly minted day. The fact that she owed it to Lance made her hatred of him diminish. She who had blamed him for all her misfortunes now magnanimously decided that it was not his fault after all. He had taught her things she would never forget.

Gaye always remembered the first morning she ventured into the garden on her own two feet. Her watch said seven o'clock when, uncaring that her slippers were wet, she walked across the lawns leaving dark green imprints on the silver dew-sprayed grass. At last, with her wrap feeling damp about her legs, she arrived triumphantly at the goldfish pond to sit down on the stone edge.

Closing her eyes, she knew that the exhilaration and wonder at being able to walk in the fresh air would not last. Her ability to walk again opened all kinds of problems to be faced, the most important being her marriage. There would be no reason for it to go on. It was over almost before it had begun, with no regret on her part. Days ago she had been afraid to leave the sanctuary of her four walls. Now it held no terror. The thought no longer overwhelmed her or made her shrink from the outcome of it. In the midst of her appalling helplessness and misery the use of her legs had opened the door of her prison. She was free to spread her wings and fly away, but where could she fly?

Gaye must have sat there for a long time searching for an answer to the problem of what to do with her life when a sneeze made her conscious of wet ankles and she set off laboriously back to the house.

Flushed with the exertion of walking, she reached her room to sink into a breuer chair. The house was very quiet. She missed Nurse, but she missed Lance more. She missed the early morning swim, the exercises on the rowing machine and the deep breathing yoga-fashion in the gym. He had laughed at her first feeble efforts until she had hated the flash of his white smile. Goaded by it, she had gone on from strength to strength until finally she had regained the use of her legs.

When he strode in after an impatient tap on her door she could not believe it, and stared as she would at a ghost.

He smiled. 'Surprised?' he asked in his deep familiar tones.

Surprised put it mildly. Her whole being was singing as her heart lurched before doing a positive jig. Much to her amazement she found herself gazing up hungrily into his dark sardonic expression. Was he thinner or did the extra tan make his face appear leaner than she remembered? Whatever it was seemed unimportant before the wave of feeling that engulfed her and threatened to propel her out of her chair into his arms.

'Very,' she replied faintly, shaken to the depths at his unexpected return.

He moved nearer in that easy way of his that caught at her heart.

'How are you feeling, or were before I came in?' This time an odd little smile lurked around his mouth.

So he had noticed her sudden drawing in of the emotion he had aroused and put it down to revulsion on her part! 'Fine,' she answered, trying to play it cool. 'I missed you.'

The three words had tumbled out without her being

aware of them.

Her admission seemed to surprise him. 'I missed you too, or rather our sparring. I found it very refreshing.'

He gave the laugh of a man happy to be home, and in that instant the reason for the queer goings-on inside her became cataclysmically clear. She loved him passionately and hopelessly. It was the most stupendous feeling she had ever known. It dwarfed everything else. It was like a blood transfusion giving her a new exciting vitality, a palpitating awareness of the world around her, making her part of it.

'How does it feel to walk again?'

He had reached her chair to place his hands on the arms. As he leaned over her, his face with the dark lock of hair on his forehead was very near.

Her eyes widened. 'You know?' she managed weakly.

'I know everything. That fact that I neither wrote nor phoned doesn't mean that I haven't kept in touch. Nurse has provided me, at my request, with a daily bulletin of your progress.'

She quivered inwardly. Never a step out of place as usual! He was doing his job down to the last detail, like that computer of his. Gaye wanted to go all regal and cold, an impossible feat with him so near.

Words tumbled from her lips as if someone else was speaking them.

'It's wonderful, isn't it? I suppose you're pleased about it, too,' she croaked inanely.

'Pleased?' he echoed with the intonation that it was the understatement of the year. 'I'm delighted.'

Of course he was. His obligations to her were almost at an end. The annulment of their marriage could go through with a mere rustle of paper. But that would not stop her loving him. Nothing would. It was then that her heart quivered beneath the blow that fate dealt her. She had fallen in love at the eleventh hour with a man who had no feelings for her at all in that direction. He would only be too pleased to be rid of her when the time came. She shivered in her chair. His nearness was now intolerable not because she hated him but because she loved him as one loves once in a lifetime.

'You're pale. Are you cold?' Swiftly he bent down to feel the hem of her wrap and slippers. 'You've been out walking in the damp grass, you little idiot. Your feet and ankles are wet.' He straightened, his eyes glittering at her. 'Come on, let me see you walk, then it's a hot bath for you before you take a chill.'

He backed across the room for her to follow him, which she did mechanically with a breathless pulsing in her throat. The urge to fling herself into his arms and breathe in his comforting masculine fragrance was more than she could bear. Then she was smiling up at him tremulously, thrilling to the hands that reached out to clasp her shoulders. An expression that she was in no state to analyse smouldered for an instant in his eyes before it was quickly banished.

It was Misty who broke the spell. She came dashing in out of the garden yapping up at him indignantly, her round eyes daring him to touch her beloved mistress.

He chuckled. 'Misty thinks I'm going to hurt you.' He raised a tantalizing brow. 'I wonder what she would do if I kissed you? Yap with jealousy, I'm afraid.' He did not kiss her. Instead he bent down to scoop the small writhing creature up and hand her to Gaye. 'Shut up, you little pest!' he said, chuckling. The dog gave him a last defiant yap accompanied by a withering look from her large round eyes and he brought a playful feint with his fist to her tiny jaw. 'I'll send someone to run your bath. Take it nice and hot. Can you make it for breakfast in half an hour?' She nodded. 'Good. I've a surprise for you.'

Gaye forgot his last words as she revelled in a bath before stepping under the cold shower to emerge fresh and tingling. She was still bemused by her love for Lance. She could think of nothing save that he was home again under the same roof and she would see him soon. She began to sober up when slipping on an attractive trouser suit in a warm apricot. In the past her coolness towards him had sprung from her genuine dislike of him. Now it had to be assumed like the wearing of a cloak to cover up her love, though heaven knew how long she would be able to do so with Lance in daily proximity.

Gaye ached for yet dreaded the end of their association, knowing it would be kinder to herself in the long run to end it as soon as possible. Leaving Misty asleep in her basket, she made her way to the dining room, pausing outside the lounge on her way at the sound of voices from within.

Lance was leaning against the mantelpiece looking down on two women sitting on the champagne-coloured sofa. Their heads turned as she entered and Lance strode across to take her arm and draw her to where the women sat. So this was his surprise, she thought, hollowly finding the older of the two women vaguely familiar.

'My stepmother, Mrs Laura Van Eldin, and her niece, Miss Judith Main. My wife, Gaye,' Lance said smoothly.

To Gaye's surprise Mrs Van Eldin was nothing like she had imagined. She had pictured someone tall, elegant and dictatorial. This woman was the exact opposite. She was small, neat and attractive with Teddy's colouring and even a few freckles sprinkled across her pretty nose. Her eyes, so like Teddy's, held a sadness in their depths, but her friendliness radiated the warmth of the sun.

'Why, she's lovely, Lance! Don't you agree, Judith?' She turned to her niece with a pleasant laugh.

The tall girl who had risen slightly behind her lifted beautifully groomed brows. 'But so young,' she murmured.

Laura Van Eldin laughed again with the same pleasant laugh as before.

'But how wonderful to be described as "so young",' she said, the warmth of her greeting taking the sting out of her companion's remark. Leaning forward, she kissed Gaye warmly on her cheek. 'I've been longing to meet you, partly because I feel I owe you an apology.'

'An apology?' Gaye repeated, her genuine interest intensified now that she saw how very charming Teddy's mother really was.

Laura Van Eldin nodded seriously. 'I thought you were a bad influence on Teddy when I was told you went gambling with him. Teddy has told me since how you hated him gambling and wanted him to leave the night I sent Lance to fetch him home.'

Gaye twinkled. 'Maybe I owe you an apology too. Gran told me about you ringing her up, and I'm afraid I pictured you as being entirely different from what you are.'

'You must tell me about it some time. I think we'd better go in to breakfast. Poor Lance must be starving.'

Lance evidently was, for he had already made for the dining room with Judith.

Quite unperturbed, Laura thrust her arm in Gaye's and walked with her to the dining room. 'I was so thrilled to hear that you could walk again after that appalling accident. I think you've been very brave. I'm an awful coward myself over the smallest ailment.'

She chatted on delightfully during breakfast which had been made interesting by the addition of several American dishes—a clear indication that she was popular with the staff of Van Eldin Towers.

Lance was fond of her. It showed in the teasing look which came into play often in his eyes when they talked. There was nothing cynical or mocking in his manner towards her.

Gaye liked her, and wished it was as easy to like her niece. Eyeing the girl's perfectly manicured, ringless hands she wondered about her being unattached. Most men could be intrigued by her disdainful air and good looks. She looked around twenty-five, with eyes as green and cool as the sea—until she gazed provocatively at Lance.

With his image mirrored in her eyes she scintillated as she gave him news of people they both knew in the States. Gaye, exploring the strange new pangs of love, also discovered that the pangs of jealousy were intermingled in their depths. The feeling was a definite pain somewhere near her heart as she watched them laughing over an amusing incident they had shared at some time or another.

Breakfast over, the two women confessed to a tiredness after their long journey and were content to rest for most of the day. Lance, ever energetic, tackled the mountain of paper work awaiting him in the library.

The three women were having afternoon tea when he came in to say that they had been invited out to dinner that evening by Sir Bonar, who had returned from Paris.

The arrival of their guests was something she had not anticipated, and Gaye, taking Misty out into the garden before she changed for dinner that evening, thought about the complications it could bring. Though there would be compensations too, the most important being less opportunity for her and Lance to be alone together. The problem of them occupying separate rooms would be dealt with by Lance in his usual competent fashion, for she was confident that he had no desire for anything intimate to develop between them. From the start when he had announced so coolly that they were to be married in order to give him a free hand in her affairs his manner had shown without the need for words that there could never be anything between him and Gaye Pembleton. She fell to considering the possibility of his bringing his stepmother on a visit to widen the breach between them with her enchanting presence. If that was so she would play along and look for something definite to do with her life when the break between them finally came. With this thought in mind, unhappy though it was, she had to be content.

Her dress for the evening was a Boussac printed soft material in rich shades of cinnamon on a creamy ground. It fell in folds from her slim figure, soft, romantic and graceful, a perfect foil for her golden hair.

When she entered the lounge Judith was there, striking in green and silver. Lance, tall and wide-shouldered in evening dress, was in the act of lighting her cigarette from a lighter he held in long steady fingers. Gaye paused on the threshold, feeling like an intruder, and watched him light his own cigarette and return the lighter to his pocket. His expression did not alter when he saw her standing there and she walked to the sofa, aware of his narrowed gaze as she sat down.

'Cigarette, Mrs Van Eldin?' he asked banteringly, and was rewarded by a cool shake of her head.

Amazing how one could sizzle inside yet maintain an outside layer of cool dignity, she thought tremulously, feeling how unfair it was for love to be so soul-destroying. Far better if it made itself known from the start instead of disclosing its presence when it was too deep rooted to be dislodged. It was a relief to see Laura appear looking very sweet and feminine in petunia velvet.

It was half an hour's run to Sir Bonar's residence. Gaye shared the back seat in the car with Laura at her request. From where she sat Lance's lean, dark face was very close to Judith's when he turned his head her way several times as they talked.

The lights of Sir Bonar's charming house blazed a welcome when they arrived. He was there to greet them, taking Gaye aside to say how happy he was that she could walk again. Then they were seated in the lounge with a drink before dinner, apparently the only guests.

As she admired the elegantly furnished room, Gaye felt the absence of the feminine touch as something tangible. Van Eldin Towers had it because Laura Van Eldin had resided there with her husband, and left behind the homely touch. Here in this charming room it was absent. It was not so much the magnificent blooms in their Ming vases conforming coldly to pattern, the touch lacking was more subtle. Gaye was trying to make up her mind what it was when they all trooped in to dinner.

She found herself seated at the top end of the left-hand side of the table with Sir Bonar at the head and Lance sitting facing her. Their glasses were filled and to her surprise Sir Bonar rose, obviously with the intention of making a speech.

He began, 'As you all know, Gaye excepted, this dinner is being given in her honour. To see her walking again is too wonderful for words. Not that I ever doubted she would walk again. She's a Pembleton, and I can say with true conviction from my knowledge of her grandfather over the years that you can't keep a Pembleton down.' He raised his glass. 'To Gaye and her wonderful recovery.'

'To Gaye,' was the swift response, and with a sinking heart she knew the short silence that followed was hers to fill. In a moment of panic she looked swiftly across the table to the mocking gaze of Lance. Was it a shade malicious? She was in no state to be sure.

She knew he was watching the colour surge up into her face with ironical eyes and it woke all her latent courage. Avoiding his eyes, she said in a small clear voice, 'Thank you, Sir Bonar, everyone. It's very sweet of you all, but I can't take all the credit. My hus ... Lance had a lot to do with it. It's a wonder I haven't muscles like footballs the way he put me through my paces!'

Her colour had deepened when she had shied away from referring to Lance as her husband. She could not refer to him as belonging to her when he was in no way connected other than by the signing of a certificate.

In the midst of her confusion she heard his deep familiar tones, awakening her every nerve into pulsing action.

'What my wife means is that I literally hounded her into walking. Don't believe it. She learned to walk all by herself while I was in the States.'

As usual he was unruffled, speaking with the ease of the arrogant male. He had no such qualms about referring to her as his wife. The way he had emphasized it meant he had noticed her shying away from admitting their obvious relationship. Well, let him think what he chose. She avoided his glance during dinner, thankful that Sir Bonar was an excellent host and an entertaining one, giving an enjoyable account of his stay in Paris. It was during coffee later in the lounge when Sir Bonar asked Gaye under cover of the music to accompany him to the library.

Mystified as to his intention, she sat down and watched him go to a wall safe to take out a small case. Holding it almost reverently, he said, 'Years ago I bought a present for the girl I loved. On the night I was going to give it to her she told me of her engagement to Richard Van Eldin.' His smile was sad. 'She was Lance's mother. I kept it with the idea of giving it to her daughter, but she did not have a daughter, only a son, Lance. So I decided to save it to give to his daughter when he had one. Now since knowing you I want you to have it.'

The diamond bracelet he released from the case flashed with the purity of rare and valuable stones. Gaye, staring at it, realized it must have cost a small fortune.

'Please,' she said almost pleadingly as he would have fastened it on her arm, 'I would rather you kept it for Lance's daughter.'

'But, my dear, I want you to have it.'

Gaye shook her head, hating to hurt him. 'Please save it.'

She smiled up into his perplexed expression. 'I have a feeling that it will only be one of many presents you'll shower on his children.'

She was more thankful than she could say when Lance entered after tapping lightly on the door.

Sir Bonar turned. 'Ah, Lance, you're just in time to persuade this rather stubborn wife of yours to accept a little present from me, as a token of my esteem and admiration. She has refused it.'

Lance strolled lazily across the room to favour her a look that warned her of trouble and he gave her a chilling little smile.

Quickly she said in explanation, 'I refused it on the grounds that Sir Bonar had been saving it to give to someone else.' Frantically she searched around for an excuse to back up her refusal still more, and found one of sorts. 'I'm sorry, Sir Bonar, but I should always have the feeling that it didn't belong to me.'

'Nonsense,' he replied. 'You could keep it and give it later to your daughter if that's how you feel about it. After all, she'll be Lance's daughter too.'

Gaye felt the hot tide of colour sweep over her face and neck. She felt near to tears in her resolve not to accept the bracelet.

'You must try to persuade her to accept it some other time when she's feeling less tired,' Lance put in smoothly. 'She's evidently scared of accepting so expensive a gift and would worry at the responsibility of keeping it. She's tired, and I came in with the intention of taking her home.'

'I understand.' Sir Bonar replaced the bracelet in its case and returned it to the safe.

In her room preparing for bed that night Gaye came to the conclusion that the distressing incident with Sir Bonar could be the forerunner of many if she stayed with Lance. She had slipped on her nightdress when a tap came on her door and she reached for a wrap and went to open it. It was Lance, still in evening dress. She backed as he walked in.

'Come, sit down. I want to talk to you.'

Gaye sat down in the chair he drew up for her. With heart beating in thick strokes she waited with bated breath while he lodged on her dressing table and planted his hands on either side of him.

'Why did you refuse Sir Bonar's gift? You knew you had hurt him.'

She hesitated, wondering if he knew the whole story of the bracelet. If he did not, it was not her place to tell him. 'I couldn't possibly accept it under the circumstances,' she said firmly.

'Under what circumstances?' he probed mercilessly.

'You know what I mean. Sir Bonar thinks our marriage is real and was giving me the present under that impression.'

'The marriage is perfectly legal.'

'On paper, yes. But you know as well as I do that it's only temporary.' Her sinews tightened under a spasm of pain. For the life of her she could not speak about Sir Bonar expecting them to have children. She stole a peep at his dark brooding face from beneath her lashes. 'It wouldn't have been honest to accept it knowing we were deceiving him.'

He gave an unpleasant smile. 'You're improving. I seem to recall a time when you were not so honest when it suited your purpose.'

Her face paled. He was referring to the time she deliberately suggested that there was something between him and Hilda Lambert to her father.

'Aren't you doing much the same thing in deceiving Sir Bonar about your marriage?' she asked bitingly.

'I've kept him happy, which is more than you did your father. There was no reason why you couldn't have accepted the bracelet. You could have returned it later if you wished.'

Tears came in her eyes after hovering at the first mention of her father. 'That's a rotten thing to say!' she blazed. 'And furthermore, since I can walk your obligations to me are at an end. You can get our marriage annulled.'

'Your father's estate isn't settled yet. You'll have to be patient. Ending the marriage now would only complicate matters further.'

'I can't see how it can,' she protested.

'Your father made a will. Did you know?'

She stared wide-eyed. 'No. He never mentioned one.'

'He made it a few weeks after the accident in which Eric Lambert was killed. He was worried in case something should happen. Your father blamed himself for Eric's death.'

'It wasn't his fault,' she picked him up quickly in defence of her father. 'The road was greasy with the rain and the car skidded.'

'I can quite believe that. However, it wasn't the only worry your father had.'

'You mean Mrs Lambert?' Her lips shrank from shaping the words.

'No, you. He didn't like the crowd you were associating with. Apparently they were taking advantage of your good nature and borrowing money from you which they never repaid.'

She moved uneasily under his scrutiny, remembering the day at the bank when he had questioned her on her need for the withdrawal from her account. He must have known then that she was in the habit of helping out her friends.

'Daddy didn't mind. He knew it made me happy to be in a position to help them out.'

'According to your father they weren't the kind of people who deserved help. They were spongers.'

Gaye felt the flush of anger, knowing that there was some truth in what he said. Since her accident many things had appeared in their true perspective. Her sense of values had changed and she had found herself viewing life from different angles. The old crowd she had gone around with weren't fundamentally bad but ruined by too easy a life, as she had been. Gaye could not sit in judgement on them because she had been one of them herself until she had learned differently. Probably they never would, but this man sitting in judgement on them would never understand. He had no such weaknesses. Those long lithe limbs of his covered a hidden strength of muscle and character, some of which he owed to the way he had disciplined himself.

'They were my friends,' she said. 'Had I been in trouble they would have helped me.'

'Your father didn't think so. You don't inherit any of his money until you're twenty-five. Your allowance will continue, of course.'

Gaye clenched her quivering hands together in her lap, her face paper white. 'But that's unfair! I can't believe Daddy would do such a thing.'

'He was only safeguarding your interests. He reckoned that if you married before that age your husband would be only too happy to keep you.' His voice held a cynical note. 'Your father was making sure you wouldn't be married for your money. There were always your grandparents at hand with whom you could live comfortably on your allowance if you chose. By the way, have you let them know you can walk again?'

'Yes. I've also told them I may pay them a visit.'

'Plenty of time for that,' he said smoothly.

Gaye felt as though she was battling against a brick wall. One by one he was knocking down her defences like a game of ten-pin bowling. But he had had his way long enough. It was her turn.

'I've told them I'll let them know when I've booked a passage and that it would be soon. There's nothing to keep me here.'

His voice had a metallic hardness. 'I appreciate you wanting to see your grandparents, but I was hoping you would be content to stay here for a while until you're completely fit. You appear to get on well with my stepmother.'

She sat silent, pulled two ways. While the urge to be with him was overwhelming she could not forget what it would entail. There were two women in the house now who would not miss anything that went on—their having separate apartments in the house for one thing.

'I don't think I should enjoy it. Your guests will certainly think it odd, for one thing, that we have separate rooms.' Her flush was very becoming. In her mind she was already standing the pins up for him to knock down again, and he did just that so blandly that if there had been anything handy to throw at him she would have let fly.

'That can soon be dealt with. I can tell them that you're not quite sure enough of yourself yet to take the stairs. You'll be free to do as you wish. I sent Nurse Russell a cheque and she won't be back.'

Gaye could hear him knocking down the pins expertly and neatly, but she tried again. 'There are too many complications for either of us to be happy the way things are. Sir Bonar said something about a wedding gift.'

Gaye did not mention the honeymoon his godfather had promised him in so many words. She could not without betraying her feeling for him. His dark eyes were too keen. He wouldn't miss a thing—her tremulous lips and unsteady hands plus the inability to look him in the eye.

He gave his odd little smile. 'You mean the honeymoon wherever we wish? There again I could say you weren't really fit for it.' His look was one of sardonic sharpness. 'Mrs Van Eldin will be very disappointed if you leave now.

Her plans include a party to celebrate your recovery.'

A sudden smile hovered around his clear-cut lips, a smile she rarely encountered. It transformed the granite lines of his face, making him infinitely dear. His charm was leading her on dangerous ground. At this rate how long would it be before he discovered her feelings for him? She gathered her scattered wits and spoke at random.

'How long is Mrs Van Eldin staying?'

'My stepmother always comes for Christmas. Teddy usually comes too, but he's gone on an expedition of sorts so he won't be here.'

'Christmas doesn't mean a thing to me now, but it does to my grandparents. I'm going to spend it with them.'

'I see. Now we're back to the spoilt child who wants to run to grandparents who will only be too pleased to go on spoiling her. If you're afraid of my wanting to make something of our marriage I can clear your mind on that score. You're in no danger as far as I'm concerned.' The smile had left his face and his eyes glittered. 'In any case it's only common courtesy on your part to stay until your guests have gone.'

'Your guests, you mean,' she picked him up swiftly, smarting under his brutal frankness. All he cared about was her playing the game as he had planned it. So he had not brought his stepmother with him to help keep their marriage non-existent beneath the surface. He did not need that kind of help. He was quite capable of dealing with any emergency himself. It was no use her pitting her strength against his, the only solution was for her to go away before she got bruised by his subtle yet cruel handling.

Her own hurt was too deep to want to hurt him in return. She felt like an injured puppy wanting the sanctuary of her room to lick her wounds. 'I'm sorry, but I've made up my mind to go to my grandparents,' she said quietly.

He was silent for a moment and when he eventually

spoke his voice had an edge to it that told her she would get her own way.

'If that's what you want I won't stop you.' He straightened as though the discussion was at an end and for some strange reason Gaye felt the air alive with electric currents. In moving he had knocked over the little present Sister had given her on leaving hospital. Setting it upright, he said with a dangerous quietness, 'You're afraid of me, aren't you, Gaye? I wonder why?' He had turned now to look at her speculatively.

She met his eyes steadily. 'Because I want to spend Christmas with my grandparents,' she said, now in complete command of her feelings.

'Instead of the person you hate.' His lips tilted mockingly. 'I hardly think that's the reason for you wanting to go so suddenly. Christmas is still a distance away and all your friends are here.' He pushed his hands into his pockets. 'I'm disappointed in you. You went through a bad patch surprisingly well, losing that "little girl" image I'd become familiar with. Now it's back again and you're bleating like a scared lamb for your family.'

She lifted her chin. 'That's what you think,' she retorted. 'Surely the obvious reason is that I want to get away from your . . . your arrangement of my life.'

'You mean you're afraid of our acquaintance growing into something deeper?'

Gaye felt the heat of anger in her throat at his cool implication that she could be growing fond of him. Fond was hardly the word for the aching yearning inside her that increased shatteringly at his nearness. 'I don't see there's any risk of us becoming matey. You've made it perfectly clear that you intended to steer clear of any entanglement from the beginning.'

'So there's not even a hint of friendship left between us after all this time.'

'There never was anything fundamental between us. We disliked each other from the start—and now, if you'll excuse me, I'm tired.'

He drew a bunch of keys from his pocket and placed them on the dressing table. 'The keys to the cars in the garage. You may use any of them except mine. I'll see about booking your passage. Meanwhile I expect you to behave normally to my guests until you leave for Tangier.'

She raised her eyes to meet his and their shared glance set every nerve in her body quivering. Stay with him until in his indomitable way he had learned her secret? Never! The thought that he might have learned it already did nothing to comfort her.

She slipped into bed feeling utterly weary. A collision with Lance was an exhausting business. Leaving him with a formidable barrier of thousands of miles between them was the best solution, but it did nothing to heal her bruised heart. If her going to Tangier infuriated him because it disrupted his plans he could find solace in the company of Judith Main.

She had scored her first victory over him, but she felt no elation and sleep eluded her long after she had switched off the light.

CHAPTER NINE

At dinner one evening Lance told Gaye he had booked her flight to Tangier.

'You'll be flying three weeks from today. I saw no sense in your going sooner. You should be perfectly fit to stand the journey by then.'

Gaye took his news without demur. The idea of booking

her own flight, a much earlier one, had been in her mind, but he was quite capable of cancelling it if he felt that way. So she had left it to him. After all, three weeks was not an eternity. She had expected much more opposition and had been surprised and a little hurt at his attitude. He could not have discussed it with his stepmother, for she looked up in surprise at his words.

'Surely you aren't going away for Christmas, Gaye?' she exclaimed in dismay.

'Gaye wants to spend Christmas with her grandparents,' Lance put in smoothly. 'The change will be good for her.'

Laura's smile at Gaye was warm with kindly charm. 'I suppose it will. You're looking a bit peaky and in need of the sun and I can understand Lance wanting you to get really fit again. You've had no married life to speak of.'

Gaye flushed, lowering her eyes from Lance's taunting smile. She felt Judith's regard keenly, knowing that she was eyeing her in a knowledgeable way. As a columnist on a newspaper, she was adept at putting two and two together and would weigh up their marriage as being distinctly odd. Maybe her job was in a way responsible for her looking at one as if under a microscope. Laura was indifferent. She never probed.

'I'm awfully sorry, dear, that you're going away,' she was saying. 'I was depending on you to help me out with the thousand and one jobs I let myself in for at Christmas. You know the kind of thing—presiding over bazaars, parties for the village children and visiting the hospital. But I mustn't be selfish. You are, no doubt, anxious to see your grandparents.' Gaye smiled at her, thinking what a dear she was even if she was saying all the wrong things. Laura went on, 'I love Tangier. All that lovely sun!' Her glance at her stepson was roguish. 'Surely you're not letting Gaye go on her own, Lance? Why, it's a gorgeous place for a honeymoon. Just imagine nothing to do all day but make love in the comforting, cosy sense of *laissez-faire*.'

Judith's laugh was light. 'You missed your vocation, Aunt Laura,' she scoffed. 'You would have done well in my job, adding your light romantic touch to the more sordid reports. It has been said, you know, that Tangier is the easiest place in which to slip into hell.'

Laura's eyes misted with bitter-sweet memories. 'It can also be the easiest way to heaven if you're in love,' she answered reminiscently.

Lance grinned. 'I think you would have done better running a column as Aunty. Letters to the lovelorn and that sort of thing.'

His stepmother looked serious. 'I've always wanted to do something like that.'

They all laughed and Gaye began to breathe freely again when Lance ingeniously guided the conversation into other channels encouraging Judith to talk of past assignments for her newspaper.

In the days that followed, Laura fitted into her own little niche in the household with barely a whisper. During her stay at Van Eldin Towers, Gaye had discovered Lance taking on the role of Squire in his handling of the estate. Laura entertained and accepted invitations frequently never interfering with Gaye, but her friendliness and concern for her welfare was heart-warming. Consequently Gaye was left to do whatever she wished, taking casual strolls which gradually lengthened into long walks with Misty as she grew accustomed to walking again. Sometimes there were picnics, a favourite with Laura, when all three women went motoring, stopping at a beauty spot to eat and revel in the scenery. The three weeks' respite Gaye had been given before her flight to Tangier went on wings and, with only a week to go, she found herself shopping for last-minute purchases.

Of Lance she saw very little. He had taken them to

several shows and to dinner occasionally, but most of his time was spent in conferring with Sir Bonar and business associates. He would listen with tender amusement at some query of Laura's when handing out advice on one of her many activities and answer her tolerantly. Laura would give him a butterfly kiss on his tanned cheek and say how dim she was not to have found the answer herself.

His nearness became a gnawing ache to Gaye. Her face grew thinner and more sharply defined as she became more vulnerable where he was concerned.

Apart from him looking at her speculatively from time to time, there was no perceptible change in him. He was the same as ever, cool and so non-committal, that she longed to shake him by doing something completely outrageous. As the time for her departure drew nearer she began to feel depressed and unsure of herself. The thought that she was walking out of his life never to return filled her with misery. There would be no more quickened heartbeats at the sound of his firm footsteps, no more absurd feelings of happiness when she heard his deep, pleasant voice. How to go through life without him was something she could not bear to think about.

The first time she drove up to London on the longest venture she had made since her accident it had seemed like coming home. But the feeling had not lasted, for she saw none of her friends. Already the tang of autumn smote the air with a chilly hand. On the way the leaves dropped forlornly from the trees, scattering a grim warning of long, dark nights ahead with illuminated shops lighting their way through a dark, unpredictable winter. Gaye parked her car and walked through select shops with a feeling of not belonging. New faces replaced those of her favourite assistants who had probably been promoted or left to get married.

It was the same at the old rendezvous her friends had

used for lunch. As usual it was full when she made her way through a sea of strange faces for a vacant seat. Their favourite table was now filled with an alien crowd with none of the familiar faces. Disappointed, she acknowledged one or two vaguely familiar ones whom she felt she ought to know but could not place and tried to whip up an appetite for lunch.

She left later with a last look towards the table the alien crowd occupied as if her longing to see the old faces had by some miracle brought them back again. The lunch, what she had eaten of it, had not filled the cold emptiness inside her. It was a hollow feeling of not belonging anywhere in the strangeness about her. Aimlessly she strolled along, seeing no one she knew and making a vain attempt to fit her mood into the atmosphere of the town. She passed Rick Allen's flat and wondered if any of the old crowd were there with him, but decided against calling to see.

The thought of Rick was suddenly warming. Gaye had never loved him. The girlish crush she had once had on him had never been the soul-shattering love she felt for Lance. Nevertheless the good times they had shared brought about a sick yearning for a last party at his flat where the warm wave of greeting from her friends washed over her when she entered.

In the end she had slipped into her car to drive in the direction of her old home. There was a long blue American car parked outside and the windows had new drapes. Gaye wished she knew who they were so she could pay them a visit and found herself resenting whoever lived there.

On the evening before she left for Tangier she dined alone with Lance. Laura and Judith were dining out with friends over from the States. Gaye had bought some really beautiful dresses for her trip to Tangier and with a last defiant gesture, she decided to wear one for dinner. It was in a floppy white Dacron and cotton with an exquisitely embroidered border around the neck, sleeves and skirt. Lance, seating her at the table, gave her an admiring look. With eyebrows raised charmingly, he said equably, 'The lass with the delicate air. Nice dress.'

'Glad you like it,' she replied flippantly. 'It was described as being cloud-soft with harem seductiveness. I thought it would go down well in Tangier.'

'You surprise me. I thought for a moment that you'd put it on for my benefit.'

Her look was wide-eyed and innocent. 'Why should I do that?'

'As a final assault on my defences.'

'I'm afraid it would take a battering ram with outsize horns to make any impression there,' she said sweetly. 'In any case it might not be worth the effort.'

An expression came into his eyes that set her heart racing. Funny that she could both love and dislike him too. She disliked him now for his arrogant assumption that she was setting her cap at him.

'Why not try it and see?' he said lazily. 'Life's full of surprises.'

She flickered a smile. 'No, thanks, I won't bother. I'll let you know what results I have in Tangier if you like.'

He uncorked the wine pouring it out with a steady hand. 'I hope you don't intend to seduce one or two sheiks. They go for English girls in a big way, especially if they have golden hair. But I doubt whether you would be foolish enough to try that caper.'

'I might if things get as dull as they are here,' she shot at him, stung by his obvious indifference.

'So it's dull. I could liven things up for you if that's what you want, only I don't think you would enjoy the way I'd do it.'

Gaye sobered suddenly beneath his challenging gaze. There was no passion or lively interest in his tone. He spoke as he would have done to a child who would regard a word of warning as sufficient. She moved uneasily, aware of a sense of strangeness in the room, a kind of dynamic atmosphere with a subtle undercurrent. If he was conscious of it he gave no sign, although his mood was rather unusual. The lighthearted mood he had greeted her with had changed to one of glittering devilment in his eyes.

He went on without waiting for a reply. 'After all, the setting is right for it,' he murmured. 'Nice of our guests to leave us on our own. Even the staff have done their best to make our last evening together. . . .' he paused, the gleam in his eyes visible between narrowed lids . . . 'shall we say something to remember?'

With fast beating heart Gaye knew he was referring to the soft rosy glow from the red candles placed strategically to give intimate lighting. There was only one way to fight him, and that was to match his coolness with the same reserve.

With an effort she managed to assume a conventional air. 'You don't mind my going to Tangier?'

'Not if it means you coming back fighting fit.' His features appeared hard in the subdued lighting, his eyes enigmatic, giving no clue to his thoughts. A short silence vibrated between them, then he said quietly, 'Don't go wandering in strange places alone while you're there, will you?'

Her chin lifted. 'I can take care of myself. I've been abroad scores of times.'

He held her blue gaze with sardonic dark eyes. 'Not in the state you're in at the moment. You're passing through a very unhappy phase and that mood of not caring could be dangerous.' He paused before continuing in the clipped tones of ramming every word home, 'It's time you began to mature. All your life you've clung to your father like a limpet, not giving yourself the chance to mature or use your own initiative apart from making demands for what he could give you. Now he's gone, and left you lost and afraid.'

'I'm not,' she contradicted. 'I just don't care any more.'

'That's the usual reaction of someone who has never known real trouble before. They can't take it when it comes. Facing up to life's hard knocks cuts them down to size. The time will come when you'll speak of your father without the trembling lips and misty eyes and you can bring it nearer by thinking only of the happy times you shared together. When you go to Tangier you will probably find your grandparents speaking of him constantly, even though his death has been as shattering to them as it has to you.'

She gave him a pale, unhappy stare. 'Strange as it may seem to you I love my grandparents deeply and I think I understand better than anyone how they feel. You don't give me credit for any feeling, do you?'

'You have feeling all right, but it's been mostly for yourself. For instance, you haven't thought what your going away will mean to others.'

'You surely can't mean yourself?' she said with a curl of her lip.

'I meant Misty. What's going to happen to her while you're away? Do you want her sent back to Mrs Foster?'

Her look was tragic and she felt his rebuke like a stinging slap. She had thought of Misty and the idea of leaving her had been added anguish. But she would not tell him so. He was determined to think the worst of her. Well, let him! What did she care? But she did. She cared that much that she was near to tears. Dispassionately she wondered at her calmness in answering him.

'I'd like her to stay here if it's all right with you,' she said bleakly.

He smiled. 'This is her home. Drink your wine.'

'You know I don't drink.'

'Drink it. It will give you an appetite for dinner.'

'That's rich,' she said caustically. 'You kill my appetite with your worldly cynicism, then order me to drink wine to restore it.'

'I didn't intend to, but I do intend to see you eat at dinner. If you don't there's no flight to Tangier for you tomorrow.'

Gaye shot him a blue gaze of frozen incredulity. 'Charming man, aren't you? You couldn't have given me a better incentive.'

Even as she spoke Gaye knew it would need more than an incentive to make her eat. Her recent encounter with him had left her in a bruised and battered state of nerves. Her eyes stung with unshed tears and she was thankful of the dim lighting. The dinner was not elaborate and her portion slid down remarkably well despite the fact that her throat felt too constricted to swallow. The atmosphere did nothing to help, for it was too charged with tension. She wondered if he felt it too. Most of the time she kept her gaze lowered, but she knew his eyes were often on her face as though he was conscious of her nearness.

Dinner was inevitably followed by coffee taken in the lounge and silently Gaye vowed to leave after it on the excuse of finishing her packing. In the lounge the lights were full on and very revealing after the soft dimness of the dining room. Lance dispensed it, handing Gaye her cup before strolling over to the radiogram to put on some music.

She had seated herself in one corner of the champagne sofa and watched uneasily as Lance took the other corner, stretching out long legs before drinking his coffee. The record was a musical selection from a popular show enjoying a long run in London. Lance had taken the three of them to see it and Gaye had enjoyed the lilting music and romantic theme. Listening to it now, she was untouched by its former charm. All she could think of was tomorrow and her parting with Lance, perhaps for ever.

He drank his coffee and putting down his cup leaned forward with his arms along his knees to listen. A swift sidelong glance revealed the springy tendrils of dark curly hair at the nape of his neck and she longed to put out a hand to touch them.

They listened in constrained silence and when he rose at the end to put on another record she put down her cup. Suddenly her intention to flee was halted by the unexpected sound of familiar music. It broke over her in poignant waves, washing the lounge out of focus as another took its place. She was with her father in their lounge at home listening to the same piece, an Elgar symphony and his favourite. She bit on a trembling lip, but the parting from Lance and Misty plus the tender memories of her father proved too much for her new-found courage. With a strangled sob she ran from the room. Lance called after her, but she did not stop until she reached the sanctuary of her own quarters.

CHAPTER TEN

TANGIER greeted Gaye like a bouquet of exotic blooms giving off strange, exciting scents. Her grandmother was waiting for her and her eyes misted as Gaye flung young, eager arms around her.

'It's wonderful to see you walking again, dear, but you're still too thin,' she said, eyeing the slender figure, pale face and shadowed eyes.

Gaye smiled, immeasurably comforted by her grandmother's warm greeting. 'I've been taking long walks since I regained the use of my legs.' She took the blue, silk-clad arm. 'How's Grandfather?'

'Improving. We've moved to the house of a friend, a Colonel Sheard. He's retired from the Indian Army and has a delightful villa up on the old mountain. It's much cooler than where we were living near the Casbah.'

Outside the airport a car waited and a soldierly-looking middle-aged man, smart in white drill, slid from behind the wheel when they approached. Her grandmother introduced them and Gaye looked up into shrewd grey eyes in a face tanned by tropical sun. The small moustache he wore was part of his military bearing and a smile softened his rather stern features.

'Delighted to meet you, Mrs Van Eldin. I hope you enjoy your stay in Tangier. You're a deuced pretty girl to be coming to Tangier on your own, if I may say so. What's that husband of yours doing letting you come alone?'

'Yes, Gaye,' Polly said with a puzzled frown. 'I did think Lance would have come too. You could have had a honeymoon here.'

Gaye slid into the back seat of the car beside her grandmother, thankful that neither of them could see her face.

'Lance was unable to come. His stepmother is paying her usual visit there for Christmas. She's not at all as I imagined. She's absolutely charming.' Gaye went on to tell a surprised Polly about Laura and her niece Judith until the Colonel pulled up at the post office for her to wire home of her safe arrival.

Her wire dispatched, they left the town centre behind and drove towards the old mountain. Traffic was light on the road and the view far below was of yellow beaches stretching for miles. There were numerous delightful small bays and coves and the view across the Atlantic was as enjoyable as the fresh breeze coming in through the car window.

The Villa Sheard was one of several small, enchanting villas decorating the mountain. It was a white, immaculate building with dome-shaped doorways and windows and elegant archways. Gaye loved the courtyard, built as an octagonal patio open to the sky, with a swimming pool in the centre. It was lined with colourful tiles of Moorish design and the blue water looked cool and inviting.

Gaye's grandfather awaited them in the salon where brilliant white walls contrasted charmingly with the dazzling blue of the sea through the dome-shaped windows. Wearing white drill and looking tanned and fit, he rose from a nest of Thai silk cushions on the long window seat to greet her.

'How's my Gaye?' he said teasingly when she reached up to kiss his thin cheek. 'I suppose there'll be no holding you down now you've found your feet again.'

'Fine now I've seen you. I've missed you both terribly and I loved your letters. Are you really quite well now, Grandfather?'

Gaye's eyes scanned his face anxiously, noting that on closer inspection his skin had a delicate look.

'Well enough apart from tiring easily, but then I'm not as young as I was. Come, sit down and tell me all about this husband of yours.'

He drew her down beside him on the long window seat and as the Colonel left them together, Polly discarded her white, wide-brimmed hat and left the room to return with a daintily laid tray from which she dispensed tea.

'How is Lance?' she asked, passing Gaye a cup.

'Fine as usual. He sends his regards to you both.' Gaye tried to speak lightly as a little of the anguish she had felt at their parting returned.

Lance had driven her to the airport and dutifully seen her off with the usual supply of magazines, cigarettes and chocolates. At the last moment he had taken her chin between his hard fingers and bestowed a kiss on her lips which, Gaye thought bitterly, was all part of the service of being taken care of by the imperturbable Lance Van Eldin. Then the plane was winging her out of his life. Through a blur of tears she had looked down at the magazines in her lap and her bruised feelings had frozen into a hard substance spreading to encase her heart. The joy of being reunited with her grandparents had dispelled her unhappiness. It was later in the solitude of her room that the torture began again.

Her room was lofty to give the maximum coolness with blue walls and a canopied bed resting on an inlaid tiled floor of Moorish design. White sheepskin rugs cuddled her feet and Gaye saw a wardrobe, table, several chairs and a bedside lamp. Venetian blinds kept out the sun in the bedroom and bathroom which had a sunken bath in black and green and a shower.

Gaye unpacked, bathed and put on a wrap. As she brushed her hair she thought of Van Eldin Towers where soon the north winds could bring snow and a white Christmas. She saw Lance hatless with the snow glistening on his dark hair, that white smile of his dazzling Judith who would be elegantly wrapped in furs and smiling at him provocatively. Gaye Pembleton would only be remembered when Laura mentioned her or when he scribbled one of his polite notes.

After a surprisingly restful night a tap on her door awakened her. Her sleepy eyes focussed on a slimly built man of medium height. He had thin nondescript hair sleeked back from a thin face and twinkling, grey eyes. Wearing a white jacket, he carried a tray and appeared to be in his forties.

'Good morning, Mrs Van Eldin,' he said politely. 'I was out yesterday when you arrived, so you won't know me. I've brought you a cuppa and the name's Bert Roach. I used to be the Colonel's batman. Now I'm general dogsbody.' He smiled as if he thoroughly enjoyed the role. 'Mrs Pembleton would like to know if you would care to have breakfast with her or here in your room. Mr Pembleton stays in bed until eleven and the Colonel is out riding.' He placed the tray on the bedside table. 'And call me Bill.'

Gaye smiled. 'Thanks, Bill. Will you tell Gran that I'll be having breakfast with her as soon as I'm up and dressed?'

The dining room was a corner of the patio and was protected from the sun by a latticed reed roof supported by white pillars. Blue, red and white cushions lined a wall couch and Bertoia chairs were placed round a Saarinen table. Polly was already there, cool in a sleeveless dress and thrilled to be having a companion for breakfast, which she usually ate on her own.

They spent the morning at the swimming pool with Gaye revelling in the cool, blue water while Polly relaxed on a hammock seat.

There they were joined by Gaye's grandfather and the Colonel, back from his morning ride. At the Colonel's suggestion they went for lunchtime cocktails to the Yacht Club. As a number of British residents were members he thought it was a good idea for Gaye to meet them and so contact some of the young people. Driving to the docks, they were admitted past the policeman at the gates and made their way along the road to the Clubhouse where Gaye enrolled as a temporary member. Over cocktail canapés and a variety of drinks Gaye was overwhelmed with invitations to all kinds of sport and parties. It was a relief to know that she could fill her days and so obliterate the image of Lance from her mind.

The real Tangier to Gaye was the ancient Arab world within the Casbah a life apart from the modern bustle outside. Most of the houses built inside the city walls were of seventeenth-century origin with enchanting Moorish and

Portuguese design which Gaye found more absorbing than the world outside.

She loved the markets with their piles of aubergines, pepper, fish and fruit, making shopping a delight. The shops where one changed money for Tangian currency were numerous and opened all day. She went often to the Rue Amrah, which the residents claimed was the coolest place during the heat of the day and looked out through the Door of the Sea. This was an opening cut in the city wall to give the residents a view of the sea. It led out to a walk with a stone balustrade from which one could obtain a marvellous view of the bay.

A friend of the Colonel's loaned her a horse and Gaye began to take an early morning ride along with the Colonel. He was an interesting companion, taking her to places on horseback that were not so easily accessible by car. His interest was balm to her bruised heart and a means of shutting out her memories of Lance.

The distance between them increased her longing to see him again. Each time he wrote to her, enclosing her letters from friends or a polite note enquiring how she was, her heart would twist painfully, her fingers trembling when she slit open the envelope bearing his masculine hand.

Her behaviour did not go unnoticed by her grandmother. Polly was worried about her tenseness and her growing friendship with the Colonel. Not that she did not trust him. She knew he was too fond of his own way of life to want to change it. Also he was a man's man. If he had felt any leaning in the past towards the opposite sex he had outlived it long ago. The Army had been his one and only love, but he was a prominent figure in Tangier and people talked.

As for Gaye, one could see she was far from happy. Several times Polly had probed gently, a thing she hated, with no success. Gaye had given nothing away. Could she still be pining for her father and was clinging to the Colonel as a father figure? Gradually Polly worked herself up into an unhappy frame of mind where her granddaughter was concerned. After all, she was responsible for her while she was in Tangier.

With this thought in mind she tackled her about it one morning at breakfast. Colonel Sheard had gone on a weekend cruise with a friend from the Yacht Club. Gaye had been invited, but a bad cold had kept her indoors. On the Sunday morning she appeared to be much better and was looking particularly bewitching in a blue and white sunsuit. As she looked at her beautifully smooth, honey gold limbs it occurred to the older woman that she was lovely enough to make even the Colonel think twice about his single state. Breakfast over, they sat with a last cup of tea enjoying the pleasant coolness before the sun intruded to higher the temperature.

'Don't you think, my dear,' Polly began rather tentatively, her eyes on a sunbeam spraying gold dust through the reed roof on to her granddaughter's golden hair. 'Don't you think you are being a little unwise to go about with the Colonel so much?'

'Unwise?' Gaye's look clearly indicated that her grandmother was slowly going out of her mind. She frowned. 'In what way, Gran? He's hardly the seducing type, and I am married.'

'Exactly,' Polly said dryly.

Gaye's laugh held no mirth in it. 'Gran! I thought you were broadminded.'

'I am. Some of the residents of Tangier are not, unfortunately.'

Gaye stared down into her cup, avoiding her grandmother's searching eyes. 'I see no wrong in going about with Colonel Sheard. You can't go around much in the heat and grandfather has to take it easy. There are the people from the Yacht Club, but they are also the Colonel's friends.

I can't very well avoid his company. Besides, I enjoy going with him.'

'Because he's a substitute for your father?'

Gaye's eyes flashed sparks. 'No one can take Daddy's place. No one.'

Polly, seeing her blue eyes near to tears, said gently, 'I agree, darling. Is that why you're so unhappy these days? You're missing him?'

Gaye shook her head. 'Maybe it's because I'm growing up.'

Polly winced. 'You've changed, Gaye. You sound quite hard.'

'Do I? It could be the heat getting me down. Forget it, Gran.'

But Polly could not. This tight-lipped stranger was not the impish child she knew. 'Would it help me to talk about it?' she asked gently.

When Gaye did not answer she thought it wise to say no more. She had made her point and would wait with hope for it to bring results. The next few days found her busy preparing for Gaye's twenty-first birthday.

In order to save the Colonel any inconvenience, Polly decided to hire a room at one of the best hotels in Tangier for the occasion.

Gaye felt none of the enthusiasm she used to at an approaching birthday party. It would be the first one without her father and she dreaded it. Her dress for the occasion was orange, lemon and almond green silk jersey. It fitted her slenderness like a glove and her sandals were designed to match the golden filigree belt around her small waist.

'You look a very sweet twenty-one, my dear,' Polly said fondly, looking very nice herself in navy lace.

The room booked for the party was prettily decorated with exotic blooms down the centre of the table and in several urns around the room. Gaye received her guests with a smile, trying not to think about the absence of her father, greeting people she had already met and a few she hadn't. With her mind a blank she did not see the tall figure who held out a well-kept hand until its clasp sent an electric sense of shock through her whole system.

'Lance!' her heart cried, sending the echo through her lips.

The dark eyes glittered down into her startled blue ones. 'Surprised?' drawled the deep, beloved voice. 'Many happy returns.'

Surprised? Her happiness at his nearness took away her speech.

'Why didn't you tell me about your birthday?' He smiled down at her, every bit as attractive as she remembered.

Aware that she must have been looking up at him like an infatuated schoolgirl, Gaye welcomed her grandmother's approach.

'Glad you made it, Lance. My husband is dying to meet you,' she said, kissing his tanned cheek before she led him to where her husband and Colonel Sheard were sharing a drink with friends.

So her grandmother had sent for him and he had come in the line of duty. Fiercely Gaye wished he had stayed away, hating him for awakening her slumbering emotions. She almost wished she had told her grandmother the truth about their marriage, but she knew she could not have endured to see the disappointment on her sweet face.

Lance sat beside her at the head of the table with her grandparents on either side. Somehow, Gaye smiled her way through the evening, acknowledging the toast and making the usual little speech of thanks. There was one moment when she faltered. She had blown out the candles on her cake and was finding it hard to cut when Lance covered her hand with his to drive the knife through.

In the dancing which followed later in an adjoining room Gaye was claimed for every dance. Whirling round the room, she deliberately avoided looking towards the spot where Lance sat talking to her grandparents who appeared to be getting on with him remarkably well.

It was nearing the end of the party when he came to her. The dance number had ended and before she could be claimed by another partner he was bending over her suavely.

'Don't you think it's time I had a dance?' he said quietly.

Gaye had been preparing herself all evening for further encounter with him, to no avail. He had only to come near to start the ripple of feeling coursing through her veins. She trembled. To dance with him, to feel his arms about her and breathe in his own particular fragrance would be the last straw.

'I think I'm beginning to feel tired,' she said, flushing when she remembered her last dance had finished, leaving her laughing and clinging to her partner after a heady whirl.

He raised an ironic brow. 'Then perhaps we can take a short stroll along the terrace. It's heated, so you won't need a wrap.'

They walked silently side by side out of the room and along the terrace with Gaye stealing a glance at the set of his broad shoulders and the proud tilt of his dark head embodying all the characteristics of his masculine charm and good looks. What use was it wishing he had stayed away when she was so unhappy without him? It might be torture to be with him, but it was sweet torture she could bear.

At the end of the terrace Lance leaned against the corner of the wall and offered his cigarette case. When she refused he lit one for himself and looked away from her across the bay. It was a heavenly night, with a dark, blue ceiling of sky twinkling with a myriad stars above the moonlit bay. The perfume from a nearby datura tree drifted and mingled with the scent of his cigarette. Gaye felt she would remember it for the rest of her life.

She drifted to the stone balustrade, trying to calm the riot of emotion clouding her mind, determined to be as cool, calm and collected as he. It occurred to her numbly that he was looking very fit and had obviously not lost any sleep where she was concerned. Suddenly she had to speak to subdue the wave of pain.

'How is Misty?' she asked in a voice narrowly missing a quiver.

He took his time in answering, blowing out a line of smoke lazily and watching it disintegrate slowly before replying.

'Misty is fine, although she missed you until my stepmother took her in hand.' He looked down at her standing a little way from him showing the enchanting curve of her cheek and the treacherous blinking of the thick fringe of lashes. His concentrated stare sufficed to send the blood rushing to her cheeks and she turned her face away, hoping he would not notice it in the dim lighting of the terrace. Apparently he had not, for he addressed her in his familiar imperturbable manner.

'My stepmother sends her love. You've made quite a hit with her.'

But not with you, she thought hollowly. Aloud, she said, 'I like her very much. I hope she's well.'

'Perfectly.' She felt the pause to be as disturbing as his brooding look. 'No query as to how I am?'

So he had noticed her assumed indifference to his own wellbeing, sublimely unaware what it cost her not to ask after him. She answered without turning, her hands gripping the stone balustrade as she would a lifeline.

'You appear to be as fit as ever.'

'Do I? That makes two of us, for you're looking very fit yourself. May I say how lovely you look tonight and congratulate you on carrying the evening off so well. You make a charming hostess.'

'I ought to. I've been brought up that way. My life has been a continual round of parties. As you once remarked, I've been a spoiled brat,' she reminded him acidly.

'Yes, you have, haven't you?' he said in a voice she did not care for. It was smooth and dangerous, indicating a change of mood.

She felt him glowering down at her. 'How long are you staying?' she asked abruptly.

'Isn't that rather precipitate seeing I've only just arrived? You haven't had my present yet.'

He straightened from the corner of the wall and Gaye concentrated on a lighthouse in the far distance flashing its light reassuringly across the water.

'If you think for one moment that I shall accept a present from you you're very much mistaken.'

'This is from my stepmother,' he went on as if she had not spoken and taking a small case from his pocket. 'I'm pleased you get on so well together. She's a lovely person and has had her share of unhappiness. Her first husband drank and gambled and treated her atrociously.' He offered her the case. 'Go on, take it and open it.'

Gaye took the case and opened it to gaze upon a pair of diamond ear-rings. 'They're lovely,' she murmured, a lump blocking her throat when she thought of how she had misjudged Teddy's mother.

He tossed his cigarette away and, slipping a hand inside his jacket, drew out a small oblong case. It occurred ro her idiotically that he had kept his own present over his heart—which could only be coincidence, of course.

'And now mine. I shall have to insist you accept it for the

sake of appearances.' But she could do anything about it he had taken an exquisite gold wrist watch from the case and fastened it on her wrist. 'I noticed you'd smashed yours in the car crash and took the liberty of replacing it.' Putting her wrist to his ear, he listened to the movement and compared the time with his own watch. With all her nerves haywire at his touch, she watched him turn her wrist and breathe in the perfume she had applied. 'Nice perfume,' he drawled. 'What is it? Let me guess. It's French and exclusive.' He lifted an eyebrow. 'Present from a boy-friend?'

Gaye would have liked to say it was, but she spoke the truth.

'My father bought it on his last trip to Paris,' she said, and winced to recall that he was going to Paris when he was killed.

His lips touched her wrist and she wondered if he was consoling her or responding to the beauty of the evening. When his lips moved a fraction higher she waited breathlessly for him to follow it up with more kisses up her arm. She closed her eyes, her heart beating heavily in her chest. The moment passed and she could almost feel his sudden withdrawal as he straightened abruptly away from her.

'Come on,' he said, releasing her wrist. 'Your guests will be missing you.'

Gaye was shattered. For one magical moment she had been sure her love had reached out to him and brought a brief response. Now she knew with a heartbroken gasp that there was no love in him to respond where she was concerned.

She turned away blindly and in her hurry to get away caught her shoulder against the corner of the wall where he had been leaning only a few minutes before. The impact flung her off balance and instantly his arms whipped round her.

'Gaye!' he said, turning her round in his arms to look

down into her face with concern. 'Are you hurt?'

Never had she blessed a dim light so much as blinking away the tears she shook her head. For what seemed an age he stared down into her face anxiously until his arms began to tighten, his head lowered and gradually towards hers. Nearer he came, his lips seeking hers, his warm breath reaching her mouth, but before their lips could meet he drew back with an almost inaudible exclamation. His hold slackened, leaving her still within the circle of arms and expressing neither tenderness or passion. Apart from a muscle flickering in his cheek, his expression was unread-able. It was his voice with those familiar mocking tones that whipped her back to sanity.

'Great guns! That perfume is certainly powerful stuff. It goes to show one should never underrate its potency in romantic surroundings. Don't you agree?'

Complete silence followed, with Gaye inwardly reeling from the snub like a mortal blow. Being an experienced man of the world he understood the insidious effect of a glamorous night. To him it was false enchantment because he felt no love for her. Had it been some other woman he might have accepted what the night offered with no thought of the consequences. As it was she was still part of the job he had set himself out to finish with no more complications than he could help to hinder its completion.

Gaye was shaken with confused emotion, half resent-ment, half pain, brought on by his brutal frankness. It acted as a spur, urging everything feminine in her to hide her hurt. She even managed a husky chuckle and lightly disen-gaged herself from his arms.

'It must be some perfume to rock you on your pedestal!'

He flickered a swift look of admiration over her slender form, an impersonal admiration of the kind a man might narrow at a woman passing by whose appearance gave him pleasure to gaze upon. Gaye felt murderous. How she would have loved to shatter his cool air of detachment, tear his emotions apart and watch him suffer as she was from callous treatment! Then as swiftly as it had arisen her feeling of hostility melted beneath the fire of her love for him. It was far too great to foster any mean or petty thoughts of revenge.

If she had needed further proof that she meant nothing to him it was here plain as a pikestaff. Had he felt a shred of love for her he could not have been so cruel as he had been tonight. With this bitter thought in mind to speed her on she hurried ahead to join her guests, hoping desperately to lose herself among the gay chattering throng.

It was not until after the party that Gaye managed to shed part of her grief and misery. Colonel Sheard's car only held four people comfortably, so Lance had refused to accompany them afterwards for a last drink at the villa. It was only at the last moment when he stood tall and remote on the steps of the hotel that Gaye discovered he was staying there.

Unhappy though she was, Gaye refused to allow her grief to mar what otherwise had been a successful and delightful party. In her seat beside her grandmother she hugged her arm and placed her head against the comforting warmth of the older woman's shoulder.

'Thanks for the party, Gran. It was lovely.'

Polly looked down on her fondly. 'Yes, everything went off well, didn't it? I was pleased when Lance came. He wrote to ask me if you had replaced your wrist watch because he wanted it to be a surprise. I told him you hadn't. It's very pretty.'

She lifted Gaye's wrist to admire it, wondering at the child's reserve. Silently the older woman chided herself for being too observant. Young people today are much more casual about their marriages than they were in her day. Her darling was a child no longer but a married woman with all the poise and confidence that marriage brings. All the same, she regretted the loss of her impishness which now only peeped out on rare occasions. Of course, the loss of her father could account for that. Poor Maurice! He would have been upset at what his beloved child had gone through. Thank heaven she had married a good man.

Then Gaye was smiling up at her. 'I must remember to thank Grandfather for his cheque. It's very sweet of you both, but I didn't expect it. After all, you gave me the party.'

Polly returned her smile. 'I'm glad you weren't disappointed. You haven't got your man with you, though.' She made sure that her husband and the Colonel seated in the front of the car were deep in conversation before she went on, 'I don't like the thought of Lance staying in a hotel and you being at the villa. You could join him at his hotel. Your grandfather and I would understand.'

Gaye fought down a rising panic. 'Lance doesn't mind,' she said quickly.

'Has he said so?' Polly probed, looking worried.

'Not in so many words,' Gaye answered truthfully. 'I think he's only too happy to see me getting really fit and well again.'

Which was the truth, she told herself fiercely. He was probably making plans already for when she was off his hands for good. It was indeed fortunate that her bed at the villa was only a single one and there were no more rooms vacant at the villa. She wondered how Lance would have reacted if on arrival he had found himself sharing a bedroom with her at the villa. He would have wriggled out of it somehow with his usual slickness. The mere thought of being held passionately in his arms started her blood careering madly through her veins, until she realized the utter futility of thinking along such lines.

She gave her grandfather an extra hug before going to

bed that night. She thought he looked tired and not too well.

'I like your husband, Gaye,' he said when she kissed him goodnight. 'He's the kind of man who will make you happy.'

Gaye went to bed appalled by the position she was in. Her break with Lance was going to be more difficult than she realized. But there was no alternative. The end had to come and she had to have the courage to face it. She would get a job, fill her days with work.

She would show Lance that she could battle through on her own. A spoilt brat, he had called her. With accumulated wretchedness she recalled his merciless kisses and his arrogant assumption that he would make something of her when he had finished. She had been immature, a child to be bent to his will, and he had succeeded more than he would ever know. Hating him so much in the past made it seem so wildly impossible for her to love him as she did now to distraction.

Lying back wearily against her pillows, Gaye knew, despite all her worrying, that Lance would finally sever the bond of marriage between them in his own good time. Lance, who had from their first meeting played havoc with her emotions, destroying her happy existence, mocking, punishing and being brutally realistic. She could imagine him congratulating himself on a job well done even whistling softly at his subtle handling of the situation where he could so easily become involved.

One thing was certain. There was no returning to Van Eldin Towers for her nor to her grandparents' home at Greenwich. There was no reason why she should not stay in Tangier and train for a nurse at the English hospital. With her future part solved, Gaye tried to sleep.

CHAPTER ELEVEN

GAYE slept fitfully during the night of her birthday party, to wake unrefreshed and restless. Her watch said seven o'clock. In a few hours she would be meeting Lance again, and her heart sank. She needed time to think and plan what to do, for it was impossible for her to go on as she was after last night.

The villa was quiet with no one yet astir. The Colonel would be the first to rise for his morning ride. Pity she could not go with him this morning. A ride in the fresh morning air would refresh her mind and put her on her mettle for her encounter with Lance. It was out, of course. Lance always breakfasted early and would be at the villa soon afterwards. However, there was no reason why she should not go for a short ride on her own. If she hurried she could be gone before the Colonel was up.

She dressed swiftly, moving like a slim shadow through the silent villa and meeting no one. Fortunately the Colonel's Arab stallion was stabled several boxes away from her pony, so he would have no idea she was out. Gaye rode along the mountain road, welcoming the cool, fresh breeze blowing in from the sea. As she neared the Casbah the air became invaded with the smells of the East—an exciting mixture of sweat, smoke, spices, camels and exotic perfumes. Already there were a number of beggars sitting yoga-fashion in the dust, for the Arab sees no loss of face in begging. To him it is a humbling of himself to Allah, regarding his poverty as something holy.

With the thought of curtailing her ride Gaye wheeled right from the road leading to the beach to pass an excavated site beloved of archaeologists. She passed olive-crushing pits and the remains of arches set on tiled floors of what had once been Roman steam baths and spared a thought for Teddy. He would have enjoyed prowling round the diggings. She wondered about the expedition he was on and if he had gone for an excuse not to go to Van Eldin Towers for Christmas because she would be there.

His companionship had meant a great deal during their short but memorable acquaintance. She had loved their walks in sunlit parks, the hours spent in conversation over hot chocolate in their favourite milk bar and dancing together in dimly lit rooms. There had been an air of enchantment about it at the time. Now, thanks to Lance, it was a pleasant memory, a way of growing up in a boy-and-girl affair. If Lance had not intervened she might even have drifted into marriage with Teddy, not realizing that the affection she had for Teddy could be dwarfed by the passion and need lying dormant in her. It had taken Lance to awaken her. She had run away this morning because she was afraid of meeting him, afraid of the havoc to her senses his appearance invariably brought.

What a blessing he had no idea of her trembling limbs each time his deep, warm tones came within hearing distance. Love had come to her entirely unbidden, a thing apart from any youthful infatuation of the kind she had once felt for Rick Allen. Her love for Lance was so great that it swamped the love she had for her father.

Tears welled in her eyes at the thought of him. If only he were here with his wise counsel to help and guide her! The cut-off feeling of having no one to confide in created an urge to be away before it became any worse. With her grandfather not yet fit Gaye felt it to be unfair to burden her grandmother with her troubles. Her sense of loneliness became more acute. Her world lay in ruins around her and she stood alone, even now unable to take in the appalling sense of loss and the emptiness of her future.

Deep in unhappy thought, Gaye had allowed her pony to wander on, not heeding the direction in which they were going, when the sound of the dull thudding of hooves brought her back to reality. The next instant she was whipped from her saddle and hauled against flowing robes. Her cries were muffled, her heart thudding with the awareness of the straining of the big beast beneath her as the rider held her close, riding for all he was worth. Her breath halted in her lungs from sheer fright, but it was impossible to free her face or even move in the iron arm pinning her down.

After what seemed like hours of riding the horse was wheeled to a sudden halt with a shuddering of its coat. Gaye was lowered to her feet. The rider dropped beside her, throwing his robe over his shoulder to cover his face, leaving only his dark eyes visible. She struggled vainly against his cruel grip on her arm.

'How dare you? Let me go at once! At once! Do you hear?' she cried, trying to stop the quiver in her voice.

The Arab ignored her and jerked her forward. With the despairing thought that there was little likelihood of being understood by this hard man of the desert, Gaye looked up at a Moroccan palace with sombre walls and heavy doors studded with spikes. They were evidently expected, for a smaller door inset in the larger one suddenly opened and she was thrust unceremoniously forward into a courtyard. The door swung to behind her and she was alone.

Bewildered and still unable to grasp that she had been abducted, Gaye looked around a pleasant courtyard. The palace was obviously occupied, for she could hear voices and the laughter of children. It appeared to be two-storeyed with a huge verandah built in marble, Arabesque trellis-work. The laughter came from an inner courtyard visible through a picturesque archway.

Gingerly, Gaye approached it to see children splashing about in a fountain watched by a woman in a long robe. Her face was partly veiled and when Gaye entered the courtyard she regarded her levelly with dark eyes before moving forward gracefully to meet her.

Her carriage was proud and seductively feminine, her long robe opening to reveal slim legs visible through the black chiffon caftan dress. When she drew nearer Gaye saw she was quite young with hennaed finger and toenails and absurdly long eyelashes veiling lustrous dark eyes. Her regard was friendly and Gaye breathed a sigh of relief.

'Why have I been brought here?' she demanded.

The girl shook her head and motioned her to follow. Side by side they walked across the courtyard, and the children paused in their play to focus her with big, round dark eyes.

At the entrance to the palace, the girl slipped off her shoes, motioning to Gaye to do likewise. She obeyed, knowing it was the custom to enter an Arab dwelling minus one's shoes. They entered a very long, high-ceilinged room with a wall of dome-shaped narrow windows down one side and an opposite wall covered from floor to ceiling with Oriental rugs. The colourful mosaic floor was covered by Persian rugs, very little furniture and lots of cushions in various shapes and sizes.

The girl led Gaye to a divan covered in rich brocade and took a large cushion herself nearby on the floor. Gaye sat down uneasily, sick inside in case she was late home and her grandparents started worrying. Strangely enough her own plight did not worry her unduly. It could be the laughter of the children outside ruling out anything sinister about her being there.

She looked down at the girl, who was studying her curiously. She had clasped her knees, showing numerous jewelled bangles up her arms and heavily ringed hands. She had necklets and a girdle around her slim waist of precious stones, giving the impression that she was someone of rank in the household. That being so, it was possible that she spoke English.

Gaye tried again. 'Please, if you can understand what I say, tell me why I have been brought here?'

The girl smiled. 'Perhaps it is because you have hair the gold of the sunset and eyes as blue as desert skies. Who knows?'

She spoke in excellent English, then clapped her hands and spoke quickly in Arabic to a very young girl of around twelve who appeared through a curtained doorway at the far end of the room. Gaye recognized the word '*Gawa*' as meaning coffee, but she could not understand the rest. Her eyes were drawn towards the curtained doorway through which the servant girl had disappeared and her companion drew her own conclusion.

'You will find it impossible to leave the palace without my father's permission. It is not for me to question the Sheikh's actions. I am to entertain you like a dutiful daughter until he comes.'

'But I can't stay here,' Gaye cried in dismay. 'My people will worry if I don't return. When do you expect your father?'

Her companion lifted slim shoulders. 'He comes and goes as he pleases. I hope he is a long time, for I want to talk to you of many things. Not that I am ignorant of the outside world. I have travelled much with my father, the Sheikh, but I spend most of my time here because I have everything I want.'

The serving girl returned with a tray on which were two bowls. One was passed to her and Gaye looked down on to a kind of curd probably made from goat's or camel's milk. She ate it and found it quite palatable. She had no appetite for any of the luscious fruits and watched the serving girl pour black coffee from a silver pot into delicate handless cups. As she drank it, she mused rather hollowly on the last evening at Van Eldin Towers when she had dined with Lance wearing the dress created to give an air of harem seductiveness. He had warned her of the Sheikh's appetite for blondes, little knowing she would come up against it. She became aware of her hostess speaking again when the serving girl cleared away the remains of the meal.

'Is this the first time you have entered a sheikh's palace?' she asked politely.

Gaye nodded, choking back the retort that it would also be the last where she was concerned. Then the strangest thing happened and Gaye was sure she heard the ringing of a phone from the curtained doorway.

'Excuse me,' her companion said politely, making her way swiftly towards it. A few minutes later she was back, smiling. 'That was a call from my father, the Sheikh. He will be here very soon.'

Gaye stared incredulously. 'You have a phone?' she asked, wildly hopeful.

'Of course. We are not far from Tangier.'

Suddenly everything seemed so easy. She could phone Lance at his hotel. But how could she tell him exactly where she was? She hadn't a clue. Perhaps if she learned the girl's name it would help. She could be known in Tangier.

'What is your name?' she asked.

'Aisha,' she replied. 'And yours?'

'Gaye—Gaye Van Eldin. Look, Aisha, my husband will be very angry when he learns about this. Won't you let me phone him? He might be persuaded to forget the whole incident if you allowed him to fetch me home.' Her chin lifted determinedly. 'Your father could get into serious trouble with the authorities.'

Aisha shook her head. 'I dare not interfere in my father's

affairs. Do not be alarmed. You are in no danger.'

She clapped her hands again and a bevy of dancing girls drifted in clad in gossamer attire to the accompaniment of music from the curtained doorway. It was the kind of piercing yet bewitching sound to which the dancers, decked out in lots of jewellery, swirled, gyrated and bent their apparently boneless young bodies enchantingly.

The dance over, three girl acrobats replaced them. But Gaye was in no mood to be entertained. She was pondering on the seriousness of being unable to let her grandparents know where she was. She would be missed at breakfast. If the Colonel was late returning from his morning ride they would assume that she was with him. Lance would be furious, thinking she had done it deliberately to slight him for last night, and her grandmother would take a dim view of her riding with another man and leaving her own husband to wait their return.

She had seen no men about the palace apart from the one who had brought her, but it was sure to be well guarded. The acrobats finished their act and Aisha showed her the Oriental rugs adorning the walls, explaining that most of them were prayer rugs. More coffee was brought and Aisha questioned her on her own way of life. As she listened and answered mechanically, Gaye had the despairing conviction that she could be there all day. She had reached the pitch when she was seriously considering making a dash for the phone when it rang again.

Aisha answered it to return and say, 'You are to come with me to the door of the palace.'

After the friendly shade of the room the sudden glare of the sun blinded. Gaye closed her eyes against its fierceness, feeling the ground hot beneath her feet. She opened them again to a deserted courtyard. The children had gone and Aisha was putting on her shoes. Hurriedly, Gaye put on her own and they walked to the outer door of the palace. The small door was opened as before and Gaye found herself outside with the palace door closing to behind her. She was free.

To Gaye the relief was so overwhelming that she had to quell a rush of tears.

'Mrs Van Eldin? Are you all right? I'm sorry this had to happen.'

The Colonel was hurrying towards her to place a fatherly arm around her shoulders with deep concern.

Apart from being slightly hysterical, she thought, blinking up at him unbelievingly. 'How did you know I was here?'

'I didn't. I guessed after seeing your pony heading riderless from this direction while on my morning ride. But let's not stop here. The sun is gaining heat and it's going to be very hot soon.' He led her to where the horses were tethered to a clump of date palms and when they were on their way he explained.

'Sheikh Ednim is a friend of mine and I happened to · know he admired you. That was why I was so relieved to have you ride with me instead of you going alone. The Sheikh has a weakness for English women. When he sees one he likes he arranges to have her kidnapped and taken to his palace. But his motives are quite harmless. He asks nothing more than that she dines with him, after which he sends her back to her home with one or two costly pieces of jewellery. It didn't take long to put two and two together and discover that you were his latest victim.'

'But how did you get in touch with him so quickly? He wasn't at the palace,' Gaye asked curiously.

'There was nothing clever about it. You're not the first pretty woman I've rescued from the old rascal. He has a house in the Casbah. I called to see him there after rounding up your pony. I told him of the seriousness of causing any anxiety to your grandparents on your behalf, and he finally agreed to ring through to his palace telling them to release you.'

'Which they did. As simple as that,' Gaye marvelled. 'Don't his activities get him into trouble?'

The Colonel laughed. 'They haven't up to now. He's a disarming old rascal and one can't help liking him. Funnily enough the women he abducts are usually quite happy to dine with him when once they're convinced that they have nothing to fear. The costly gift he presents them with in return for a few hours of their company more than makes up for any inconvenience caused.'

She chuckled. 'He sounds a real character. What about his wives? I presume he has a harem.'

'And dozens of children. You probably saw some of them playing in the palace.'

Gaye thought of the children in the courtyard. 'And Aisha? Where does she come in?' she asked curiously.

'Aisha is his favourite daughter. She accompanies him on his travels abroad with several of his wives. She's fifteen and already betrothed to some wealthy sheikh.' He went on to tell her one or two amusing exploits of the Sheikh. When they reached the villa, he said,

'I won't be coming in. I'm leaving directly I've put the horses away. Meeting an old Army friend off the plane. I'll just about make it.'

Impulsively she reached up to kiss his cheek. 'Thanks for rescuing me. Would you mind if we said nothing to my grandparents about it? I'd like to save them any unnecessary worry.'

He frowned thoughtfully. 'Very well, but I should tell your husband what's happened. Likely as not he's already here kicking his heels wondering where the devil you are.'

'I'll explain,' she promised, hoping Lance had not yet put in an appearance.

He had, of course, which was not surprising, seeing that

it was not far from eleven o'clock by her watch. He was there in the picturesque courtyard doorway, looking thunderous. Her heart somersaulted as she met his smouldering gaze.

'So you're back,' he said sarcastically. 'Enjoy your ride?'

Gaye drew in a silent breath ready to explain exactly what had happened, but he was not in the mood to listen to a detailed account. He was taking it for granted that she had gone riding with the Colonel in spite of the fact of his coming to the villa to see her.

She halted a few paces from him, perturbed and vaguely uneasy of the silence. Usually Bert, the Colonel's handyman, was whistling about the place and going about his duties cheerfully. Pushing back her bright hair, she focussed him with a deep blue gaze.

'I'm sorry ...' she began.

'Don't apologize for something you did deliberately knowing your grandparents might worry if you were late returning,' he interrupted swiftly. 'Or didn't it matter as long as you showed me how little you cared about my visit?'

Gaye knew she looked as pale and forlorn as she felt, but there was no softening in him. A wave of misery engulfed her when she held his gaze numbly, seeing the blaze of anger fade to leave his eyes cold and merciless. He stared as if he hated her and she could not speak for the life of her.

'You might have finished your kissing before reaching the villa—or didn't that matter either?' he went on, each word acting as a whiplash to her bruised feelings.

Her eyes widened. It had not occurred to her that he could have seen the kiss of gratitude she had given the Colonel. Was he deliberately provoking her into a final blow-up in order to end the impossible situation between them? As far as she was concerned their association was already at an end.

'I don't think anything matters where you're concerned, does it?' she asked wearily. 'You haven't even given me a chance to explain.'

'Explain?' He glared down at her. 'What is there to explain?'

'Nothing,' she said, her anger rising to meet his own. 'You probably wouldn't believe me. You're far too angry to be even reasonable.'

He gave a short bitter laugh. 'Angry is hardly the word I'd use. Disgust would be more appropriate.' His cold sneer put her teeth on edge. 'So you've found another sugar daddy at last. I might have known it wouldn't be long before you did. Well, I wish you joy of him.'

'Thanks,' she said huskily. 'At least he's human, which is more than I can say of you.'

'Is that your idea of being human? An old fool who'll pander to your every whim?'

Gaye lifted her chin. 'Is it any business of yours what my ideas are?'

'No, I don't suppose it is now. At least he'll be able to comfort you.'

His mood had changed suddenly and he stood aside for her to enter the villa. They had entered the salon when she turned to look up at his uncompromising gaze. What she saw there made her heart beat in thick ponderous strokes and her skin went clammy.

'What is it you have to tell me?' she asked tremulously.

His hand touched her arm and she drew away. 'You'd better sit down,' he said.

Gaye drew herself up. 'I'd rather stand.'

'Just as you like.' He paused as though reluctant to go on. 'Then, 'While you were out gallivanting with the Colonel your grandfather had a stroke.'

Gaye went white to the lips. 'Did he know I was out?'

'Neither of them did. Apparently he was all right when your grandmother got up at eight. When she returned with a cup of tea he was unconscious. An ambulance was called, but he was dead on arrival at the hospital.'

Gaye covered her face with a trembling hand and felt him guiding her to the long window seat from where her grandfather had greeted her on the day she arrived. She sank down and he pushed cushions behind her back. Gaye closed hot dry eyes, trying vainly to take it in. Numbly she heard the clink of a glass, then Lance was sitting beside her and the smell of brandy drifted to her pale nostrils. She drew back, but his arm was around her compelling her to drink. She sipped and the liquid coursed through her veins like fire. Her cheeks burned and gradually her whole body, but her heart lay a dead thing in her breast.

When Lance put down the glass and drew her into his arms she felt no reaction to his nearness. She couldn't even cry, although something like a dry sob escaped her.

'It's funny,' she said almost to herself. 'I thought he was looking very tired after the party last night and I gave him an extra hug.' Another dry sob escaped her in spite of her determination to keep up a brave front. Trying hard to regain her poise, she switched her thoughts to her grandmother.

'Poor Gran! Where is she?'

'Lying down with a sedative in her room under doctor's orders.'

The first initial shock was wearing off and she was suddenly achingly aware of his nearness. Hastily she drew away from the circle of his arm.

'I must go to her,' she said.

'She's asleep. I looked in not long ago.' His voice was gentle, but his manner was as chilly as the night wind. She ached for him to go and leave her instead of sitting contemplating her as if she was some kind of problem he had to solve. 'I'm sorry I had to break the news so quickly, but there's no time to be lost,' he said at last. 'It's your grandmother's wish for your grandfather to be buried at Greenwich. That means we have to go back as soon as possible. I've already enquired at the airport for an early plane and they're going to call me back. I want you to pack your things and those of your grandparents' too. Bert will give you a hand.' His head swivelled towards the door as the Colonel's handyman appeared carrying a covered tray to place it on a low table nearby.

He shot a look of sympathy at Gaye. 'I'm sorry, Mrs Van Eldin, about your bereavement. If there's anything I can do...'

'There is,' Lance cut in smoothly. 'Everything will have to be packed and ready to leave. Perhaps you can help Mrs Van Eldin. Mrs Pembleton won't be in much of a state to do anything. So in case I'm not back until the last moment I'd like you to see that they have lunch and possibly tea later. I'm hoping we shall be away by early evening.'

'I'll do that, Mr Van Eldin. The Colonel will be upset when he knows.'

With a sad smile Bert left the room and Lance drew the table nearer to where Gaye sat on the window seat.

'I believe you've missed breakfast,' he said, taking the white cloth covering the tray. 'I asked Bert to bring it when you arrived, although I don't suppose you'll feel much like eating.' She watched him pour out two cups of tea with a steady hand and pass her one. 'Drink it. It will steady your nerves. Cigarette?'

He made a put to take out his case, but dropped his hand when she refused. It occurred to her that he might not have had breakfast himself, but she dared not ask him. The easy friendliness with which he had addressed Bert had gone. He was as cool and remote as a stranger. She hardly glanced at the food on the tray knowing she could not swallow a morsel of it. The tea was good, though, easing the choked feeling in her throat.

'Another cup?' he queried, putting down his empty cup. When she refused he did not insist. 'No breakfast either?' he asked.

She shook her head.

'Try to eat some lunch, won't you, and persuade your grandmother to do the same?' He stood looking down at her bent head and the small hands dovetailed in her lap. 'You and I will have things to talk over when we get back home.' He drew a deep breath and she wondered if it was one of relief. 'I take it that things are serious between you and the Colonel. Where is he, by the way?'

Gaye spoke without lifting her head.

'He's meeting an old Army pal off the plane.'

His laugh was short and bitter. 'Don't tell me he's roping in the best man already!'

Gaye bit her lip. If he sought to shake her out of her apathy he was succeeding. But he was doctoring her with a dose of hate. He did not want her himself, yet he was attacking the Colonel whom he imagined was taking her off his hands.

'The Colonel isn't that kind of man,' she said, aware of using the man unfairly in giving the impression that there was something between them.

Had it been anyone else but Lance she would not have done it. He would be so pleased to see the last of her that he was unlikely to tackle the Colonel about it. In fact she doubted if he would have tackled him in any case. Had he wanted her for himself he would have made her his, Colonel or no Colonel.

When he spoke his voice was clipped with distaste.

'So you've eventually decided on a father-figure to comfort that small, frightened heart of yours. Well, well, I expected better of you. I'd even go so far as to say that, with my knowledge of you through the last twelve months, you needed someone with a bit more to give than the Colonel—and I don't mean money.' Gaye felt her face colour and shot him a malevolent glance. His eyes had narrowed cruelly, his drawl insulting. 'There's a saying that the Colonel's lady and Judy O'Grady are sisters under the skin. Remember that when he's making his tepid love to you.'

He was tearing strips off her and would have gone on doing so had not the phone rang. He strode to answer it.

'The airport? Yes, speaking.... You can? Splendid.... No, that will be fine.... Thank you very much.'

Gaye listened with the conviction that the girl on the other end of the line had been probably bowled over by his deep charming voice and had gone all out to get him what he asked for. She would like to bet that the same girl would make it her business to be there when they arrived for the plane to see if his looks matched his voice. There being no doubt about that, she would envy his wife for all she was worth, little knowing he had about as much regard for Gaye as he had for herself.

When he came back the anger had gone from his face, leaving a metallic hardness that reached his eyes.

'We fly out at six this evening. The doctor is calling after lunch to see your grandmother. I'll be back as soon as I can.'

The Colonel arrived home for lunch and was shocked to hear of Sam Pembleton's death. He went with them to the plane with Gaye lingering to thank him for all he had done to make her grandfather's last months happy. She left him with the feeling of saying goodbye to a real friend and lifted her hand sadly when the plane taxied along the runway, an action not missed by Lance, who had managed to make his farewell gestures very brief in that quarter.

The house at Greenwich had been prepared for their arrival by a Mr and Mrs Bennett, kindly neighbours who had been taking care of it and keeping it aired while they were away. It was natural that Gaye should stay with her grandmother in her present state, for Polly, still numbed with the shock of her husband, had eaten nothing since his death.

Laura Van Eldin and her niece called, bringing Misty along with them. Gaye was touched by the small dog's welcome. Laura welcomed her home warmly too and Gaye thanked her for the birthday present of the ear-rings.

CHAPTER TWELVE

IT was a cold blustery day a week before Christmas when Sam Pembleton was laid to rest in the shadow of the little church where he had worshipped as a boy and later married.

Lance, Sir Bonar, Laura and Judith went along with his former colleagues and many friends. Polly insisted on going, although she did not look up to it. Gaye was worried about her. Since losing her husband she had eaten little or nothing. That night she looked really ill and Gaye, helping her to bed, decided to send for the doctor.

It was delayed shock, he said, plus a chill. He left capsules to be given at regular intervals and she was to stay in bed until he called again. The night passed with Gaye, too worried to sleep, dozing in a chair by her grandmother's room between giving her the capsules and warm drinks.

The next morning the vague look had left her eyes and her face was no longer flushed. The doctor was pleased when he called. Gaye was to continue giving her the capsules and light meals. To her intense relief Polly had a better night and was much better on the second morning. Dazed from lack of sleep, Gaye went downstairs to make a cup of tea for them both and draw the bolts on the door for the daily woman when she arrived. She returned to find her grandmother eager for her cup of tea and scanning her granddaughter's shadowed eyes critically.

'I'm awfully sorry, dear, for keeping you away from Lance and giving you all this trouble into the bargain,' she said as they drank their tea. 'You look very tired.'

Lance thought so too when he arrived around eleven as the doctor was leaving and followed Gaye into the kitchen.

His look was thunderous. 'Why on earth didn't you let me know that your grandmother was ill instead of bearing the brunt of it yourself? You look as if you'd spent the night on the tiles,' he said irritably.

She lifted tired shoulders. 'I'll get over it. She's much better and the doctor says she can get up today.'

He had leaned against the kitchen door and it took one glance at his dark brooding face to start off the usual feeling of helplessness. Self-discipline and all the rigid control she was capable of did not prevent his nearness from sending her emotions haywire. Her hands trembled as she heated milk in a pan and mixed the foundation of a nourishing drink for her grandmother in a pretty beaker.

'Your grandmother's illness was only what could be expected. They were a devoted couple,' he said conversationally. 'I had to go to London yesterday and while I was there I ran into your friend the Colonel.' He paused before continuing maliciously, 'Or should I have said your intended? I suppose you know an aunt of his has left him the bulk of her money. He's in London to see her lawyers.'

It was a surprise to Gaye, but she did not comment upon it. When the pan of milk was ready she poured it into the beaker, stirred it and placed it on a tray.

'No comment?' he queried aggravatingly. 'I hope I

haven't put my foot in it. Did you know he was coming, or is he aiming to surprise you?'

She turned on him furiously. 'Why didn't you ask him?' Trembling, she went to pick up the tray, to be forestalled by long arms.

'I'll take that. You'll be spilling it all over the place.'

He picked up the tray and she stalked out of the kitchen to lead the way upstairs, keeping ahead of him to avoid further conversation.

Polly was sitting up in bed wearing a blue bedjacket the colour of her eyes. Unlike Gaye she was pleased to see Lance.

'Hello, Lance,' she said. 'How nice to see you. I'm afraid you'll think I'm being very tiresome.'

'Nothing of the kind,' he contradicted in his deep charming voice, setting the tray down on the bedside table and pushing his hands in his pockets to smile down at her. 'I think you've done remarkably well. How are you feeling?'

'Much better. I must apologize for keeping Gaye away from you for so long.'

'Don't worry about that. I only wish you'd let me know then I could have helped. Gaye looks tired out.'

'Yes, she does, poor darling. She's been grand. The doctor says I can get up, so I'll ask Mrs Baker our daily woman to cook the meals today then Gaye can have a rest.' Her look at Lance was sweetly apologetic. 'I've got over the worst. It was the shock, you see. He ... he went so suddenly and the swift journey home made it all part of a nightmare from which I'm only just awakening.'

Lance's regard was tender as he put a hand on her shoulder. 'I understand. You were very close, but time is a great healer. I have a few papers that need your signature when you feel up to it.'

Polly placed a trembling hand over his as it rested on her shoulder. 'It's so kind of you to do all the running about and seeing to everything for me. I do appreciate it.'

'It's the least I can do.' He watched Gaye pass her the drink thoughtfully. 'We're hoping you will both be able to spend Christmas with us at Van Eldin Towers.'

'It's only two days off,' Gaye put in bleakly. 'Think you'll feel up to it, Gran?'

She had moved to the other side of the bed and avoided looking across at Lance as she spoke. Polly looked at them in turn over her beaker.

'We could go in the car for Christmas Day if that's all right, Lance. I think a day will be enough to start with. I would like to come home to my own bed.'

He shrugged wide shoulders. 'If that's what you want. I was hoping you would stay over Christmas. It's my stepmother's birthday on Christmas Eve and she's giving a small party.'

'Is it really? And you never told us, you naughty boy,' Polly exclaimed cheerfully. 'We'll come on Christmas Eve, then. Gaye can drive us up in the car.'

After Lance's visit Polly perked up wonderfully well and she appeared to be looking forward to going to Laura's birthday party. Gaye motored up to London to buy the birthday presents, a very feminine housecoat in pastel colours from herself and a set of nightdress and negligée from her grandmother.

On Christmas Eve morning Gaye awoke to swirling snowflakes attaching themselves prettily to her bedroom window. Her heart lifted with hope, for if the snow persisted the roads would become impassable and they would be unable to go to Van Eldin Towers. Their short visit would bring no complications, but Gaye was apprehensive about their going. She knew things could not continue much longer as they were, but at the same time she wanted her grandmother to get well before anything was settled.

The sun came out when they were having breakfast, turning the fall of snow into a glittering white blanket. By lunch-time the sky was a smiling blue and the snow started to melt away except in places where it lay in thick drifts.

At five o'clock they were ready with their coats on hand and Gaye was picking up the car keys when she halted in her tracks at the sound of a car. The fluttering inside her told her it could only be Lance. It was. He walked in heart-breakingly attractive in evening dress, his smile white. Gaye's fluttering verged on panic and it was left to Polly to greet him, which she did on a surprised but happy note.

'Why, Lance!' she cried. 'Gaye could have run us up without bothering you.'

Lazily, he picked up her wrap from the back of a chair and dropped it around her thin shoulders. 'Thought you'd be more comfortable in a bigger car,' he said, offering her his arm gallantly.

He was back to pick up the gift parcels in their pretty wrappings, scooping up Misty beneath his other arm, with Gaye avoiding his eyes to follow him to the car. Misty and the presents were put in the back seat and Gaye sank in beside them, closing her eyes wearily as the car moved away. Some time during the evening she must pluck up courage from somewhere to tackle him regarding fixing a date for the annulment of their marriage. Worrying over her grandmother had shelved it for the time being, but his sudden appearance and the havoc it brought to her placid existence convinced Gaye she had stood enough. She was determined to break free of the torment.

They arrived to find Van Eldin Towers in a Christmas-card setting. The house was etched in snow and Laura stood in the lighted open doorway against a background of a huge illuminated Christmas tree in the hall to greet them. She kissed them warmly, accepting their presents graci-ously and giving her pleasant little laugh when Misty barked on recognizing her. Taking their coats, she asked

Polly if she was better and ushered them into the lounge to meet the other guests.

They were introduced to an American couple, friends of Laura's who were talking to Sir Bonar and Judith when Lance pushed a drink in their hand and they were joined by Laura. At dinner Gaye found herself seated by Lance with Laura and Judith on his right. Her grandmother sat on her other side with Sir Bonar. During the meal she hid her feelings beneath a friendly smile and pleasant manner, even managing to appear natural to Lance on the few occasions he addressed her.

Later in the lounge she was careful to avoid contact with him, in spite of the fact that she was aware of his every move, laughing at some joke with Judith, teasing her grandmother and now smoking as he talked with Sir Bonar and the American couple. When he suddenly strode from the room to fetch something her eyes were pinned to the door waiting for his return. A spasm of pain crossed her face as the thought occurred that he still regarded her as a spoilt brat who preferred a father figure to pander to her every need. He had tried hard, lashing her with his tongue unmercifully when she was quivering over the loss of her grandfather in a last endeavour to bring out the best in her. His indifference since had told her that it had been his final attempt, for he had appeared to be no whit put out at her avoidance of him.

He came back carrying some papers and when his eyes met hers across the room hers were the first to drop. The evening wore on with Sir Bonar and Polly getting on very well together. Pleased that she appeared to be enjoying herself, Gaye looked around for Misty to take her for a little break in the garden. To her dismay she could not find her in the room, although she could have sworn to seeing her moments before.

'Try the library,' Laura suggested. 'She could have followed Lance when he went out not so long ago.'

Gaye entered the library and switched on the light to see no sign of the little dog. Closing the door, she searched the room, and gave a stifled gasp when someone uncurled their long length from a chair with its back to her.

'Looking for someone?' Lance asked lazily.

Her heart somersaulted in her breast. 'How you frightened me!' she said shakily.

'My appearance usually does,' he said watchfully. 'I wonder why.'

Without appearing to have moved he was between her and the door with the smouldering intenseness of a watchdog ready to pounce if she put a step forward. Panic scattered her wits at the feeling of something strange in the air and to her dismay she found herself backing away from him.

'You may well back away, my girl,' he said ominously. 'What do you mean by letting me think you were serious about the Colonel?'

Still backing, she shook her head. 'I didn't. You assumed it was true.'

With a fast beating heart she watched him slowly coming nearer, his long strides swallowing up the space she was leaving between them with the despairing thought that she had not even got Misty to bark in her defence.

'You also let me believe that you'd been out gallivanting with him when you'd gone for a ride on your own and been picked up by some sheikh.'

'You were in no mood to believe anything,' she said, feeling the solidness of the wall behind her.

When he stopped he was very near, glowering down at her in the old familiar way.

'That wasn't the only reason. There was another. What was it?'

Gaye drew in a tremulous breath. 'It was an easy way for

you to be rid of me. Why not leave it at that?'

He stared down at her for a long moment before saying very quietly,

'Who said I wanted to be rid of you?'

'You do. You know you do,' she blazed. 'Just as I want to be rid of you!'

Gaye was shaking now in every limb, past caring whether he saw it or not.

'I couldn't be rid of you however much I tried. You're too deep down under my skin. I did want to be rid of the old Gaye who wanted everything her own way, even to putting her own selfish wants before her father's happiness. She was so self-centred and shallow that I had to find out if there was anything worth while underneath.'

'And you found there wasn't.'

He placed his hands each side of her on the wall, imprisoning her between them, and went on as if she had not spoken.

'I wanted to see sadness and compassion deepen the beauty of your eyes. I wanted to see your face reflect the tragedies that for you had existed outside your own little world. At the same time I found the thought of your being hurt insupportable.' His hands moved to grip her slender shoulders and his eyes riveted on her face. 'From our first meeting you roused the hunter in me. You possessed everything that makes a man pursue a woman on the surface, but there had to be something more fundamental to make it worth the chase. So I used the rapier-like thrust of words with the cynical approach, and there were moments when I glimpsed what I had been looking for. It wasn't until I heard the rumours of you and the Colonel and came to the villa that morning for you to let me believe they were true that I felt I had failed utterly.'

Suddenly it was all too much for Gaye, his sudden softening, his hands gripping her shoulders and the torture of his nearness.

'So you failed. Now for heaven's sake leave me alone,' she cried, pushing at his chest furiously. 'I want our marriage annulled.'

She might as well have pushed at the wall behind her for all the impression she made. He stood firm before lifting her chin with hard fingers.

'Is that what you really want?' he demanded, looking down into her face searchingly. 'Can you look me in the eyes and say it?'

She made a pitiful attempt, but her eyes blurred with tears as her gaze fell before his. The next moment his arms were around her, drawing her to him.

'You can no more let me go than I can you,' he said thickly. 'The chemical reaction that flares between us when we meet has forged a link binding us together for all time.'

He continued to hold her very close until her trembling stopped and she relaxed against him to swoon in the heaven of his nearness, trying to believe that he loved her. Seconds later she was convinced when, with a half-smile wonderfully tender, he bent his head to take her lips. The kiss that followed wiped out all the bitterness and tears and it seemed to Gaye that she passed out of a long tunnel into the light. This was what her grandmother meant, what every girl gropes for, through different ways, by different routes along her unknown quest. When he lifted his head he looked down at her in the way she had so achingly yearned for. She wanted to weep for joy and gratitude at being chosen from the crowd for the gift of true love. All the deep emotion he had hoped to see on her face was there as she clasped her arms around his neck to meet his incredibly hungry kisses.

When at last he lifted his head to allow her to draw breath his mouth wandered to her neck, drinking in her sweetness like a man parched with thirst. It was much later when Gaye remembered Misty.

'Have you seen Misty?' she said, her face flushed from his kisses.

His grin answered her. 'You hid her, didn't you?' she accused him.

He laughed and gave her a quick hug. 'I had to get you away from the others. She's upstairs in your grandmother's room.'

'Gran's room? But we're going home tonight. You know what she said about wanting her own bed.'

'If I know my stepmother your gran is already being tucked up in her bed upstairs. I've waited long enough for my wife.'

She thrilled at the passion in her voice and said mischievously,

'Am I to have my old room on the ground floor?'

'No, by heaven, you're not, Mrs Van Eldin. You're sharing mine from now on.' He consulted his watch. 'I'd say another two hours before we can retire without making it too obvious. I'll try to bear it.'

Gaye was surprised to see the time. 'Hadn't we better join your guests? They'll be wondering what's happened to us.'

He smiled ruefully. 'Roll on bedtime,' he said with a look that made her heart race. 'Not scared of me now, are you?'

How could anyone so blissfully happy be scared? she thought, shaking her head and lifting her face for his kiss before joining their guests.

POST AT GUNDOOEE

Post at Gundooee

Amanda Doyle

Lindsay, for the first time in her life, was on her own, independent. Escape from the expensive flat where she had lived with her selfish, demanding cousin, Carleen, brought sweet relief on her long journey to the Australian outback.

Overwhelmed by her good fortune, she almost forgot about the one small detail she had left out on her application for the post of bookkeeper at the sheep and cattle ranch.

Only when she was met at Gundooee Station by Rod Bennett, the station manager, was she reminded in no uncertain terms that the piece of personal information should not have been omitted. She should have stated quite clearly that Lindsay Dutten was a woman!

CHAPTER 1

LINDSAY DUTTEN pushed a tendril of brown hair back from her forehead, and sighed.

It was straight hair of an unremarkable colour—brown, mouse—and inclined to be difficult in the humid summer heat of Sydney. She was resigned to its contrariness, though, in much the same way that she was resigned to the fact of her orphaned status in life, and her unwelcome but unavoidable dependence upon her cousin Carleen, with whom she shared this unit.

Her sigh, just then, carried a burden of resignation for almost *everything*, Lindsay acknowledged wryly to herself in a spurt of self-honesty. She was one of the doormats of this world, she supposed. There were the givers and the takers in life, and in the same way there were the doormats and those who walked upon them, without sparing a thought that, in cushioning their own feet, they might be trampling a fellow-mortal, more sensitive and inarticulate than they.

Lindsay wondered, as she carefully spooned small mounds of caviar on to the canapés she was preparing for Carleen's party tonight, if it were possible to be a doormat *and* a taker at one and the same time. Lindsay didn't think such a combination either likely or frequent. In her experience, the doormats were destined to give—sometimes unstintingly— while the takers took as though it were their right, and often stepped heavily upon the doormats' fingers even as they clutched greedily at the offerings which were being proffered.

Lindsay's lips were pursed in a suddenly uncharacteristically mutinous manner, as she pushed her recalcitrant hair back again, and surveyed the trays of dainty and exotic bouchées which she had prepared. About two dozen people, Carleen had said. That meant there weren't enough yet.

'Make them attractive, but as substantial as possible, will you, darling. I hate stingy eats.' Carleen's cool, commanding voice rang in her cousin's ears, and Lindsay did her best to shut out the memory, as she began to fill tiny vol-au-vent cases with a mixture of creamy smoked blue-cod.

Carleen hated stinginess, enjoyed luxury, to such an extent that her demands upon Lindsay's own monetary contribution to the weekly budget had increased out of all proportion to her own just lately.

'After all, it's my flat, Lindsay,' Carleen had pointed out reasonably, with that peculiarly one-sided reasoning of which she was sometimes all too capable, 'and it's only out of a sense of duty to Mother and Father that I'm letting you share. They'd have worried about you on your own, and goodness knows, you've been enough of a bother to them one way and another, without stringing yourself around their necks all your life. I know you didn't *ask* for your parents to dump you in this world all alone,' she added judicially, aware of Lindsay's uncomfortable flush. 'Car accidents can happen to anyone. But it was quite decent of Mum to take you in, considering you were only her cousin's child—and not even her favourite cousin, at that. Anyway, I do think you could contribute more than you do to the running of this place, I really do!'

'But, Carleen, I already give you nearly two-thirds of my salary. Shorthand-typists don't get as much as models, remember! With what I give you, I'm only left with a few dollars for clothes and things.' She gestured vaguely. 'Why can't we be a bit less extravagant when you—when we entertain?' she suggested with some temerity. 'You didn't *have* to have oyster cocktails to start with the other night, when that photographer came. I could have done it far more cheaply for you, and just as nicely, with some iced consommé and——'

'Darling, that photographer, as you call him, happens to be the best in the game in this whole city at the moment,' Carleen interrupted coldly. 'He's the entrée to the big time, so far as I'm concerned, and if I say you'll give him oysters, then you'll *give* him oysters, do you hear?'

'Yes, Carleen.'

Her cousin studied her nails critically. They were long nails, beautifully kept, oval, perfect—so perfect that Lindsay suspected that the critical, annoyed appraisal they were receiving was not meant for them at all, but for Lindsay herself!

'I'll need another three dollars at least from you, Lindsay.'

'Three dollars!'

'At least. I ought to make it four. You haven't got half the incidental expenses that I have myself. In my profession one can't afford to let appearances slide, whereas nobody notices a nondescript little typist to-ing and fro-ing, you must admit. Why, you don't even need to go to the hairdresser, or anything, do you? They'd only tell you that that dead-straight mouse of yours is best kept clean and brushed, and you can do that just as well yourself at home. You're lucky.'

Lindsay had fingered the 'dead-straight mouse' doubtfully.

'I've never thought myself particularly *lucky*,' she stated dubiously.

'Then it's time you started counting your blessings,' Carleen replied tartly. 'In the first place, you were lucky that Mum and Dad took you in at all, and I personally think you've fallen on your feet being able to share a unit like this with me. You could have ended up alone, couldn't you, in some crappy boarding place?'

Lindsay scraped the last of the New Zealand blue-cod from the bowl, and placed the last lid, with some finality, on the last vol-au-vent. Blindly she stared out of the window as she rinsed her hands under the kitchen taps and dried her fingers absently.

Carleen's unit, high up on Dover Heights, had a breath-taking view of the harbour. The water today was green rather than blue, choppy with the salt-spumed restlessness of foamy 'white horses' that broke before the stiff sea breeze. Yachts of all descriptions scudded about. Sails of many colours darted and dipped, hoist by every type of craft, from the jauntily weaving dinghies to the thrusting eighteen-footers and the more stately twelve metres leaning into the wind. The headlands loomed above, jutting like stone-struck warriors on guard, impressively aloof from the dizzy gaiety enacted by the myriad craft in the sparkling water below, impervious to the suck and swell of the Pacific breakers that pounded hungrily against their feet.

Lindsay was oblivious to the splendour of the scene.

Her eyes—large, luminous green eyes that were her one singular claim to beauty—were misted and suddenly dreamy. Her mouth—generous and expressive, but too wide and vulnerable altogether—softened into a gentle curve of nostalgia, the mutiny gone. Her tip-tilted nose wrinkled under its scattering of freckles.

Almost she imagined that she could smell the bush!

Not the Sydney bush. Not the harbour fringe of eucalypt, nor the mangrove of the northern inlets, nor the banksia and bottlebrush of Kuringai. Not any of those, no.

What Lindsay imagined for a moment that she could smell was the scent of the *real* bush—the country place where she had been born. She had only been six years old when her parents had met with that fatal accident and she had been taken away to the city by her mother's dutiful cousin, but still she could remember those warm, earthy, country smells. There had been a grove of citrus trees at the side of the house, oily and pungent when the leaves were wetted by rain; sweet-perfumed wattle on dark-trunked, blue-foliaged boughs, all fuzzed with clusters of golden-yellow balls; delicate gum-blossom, creamy and fragile. The orchards had been riotous with scented blooms, cerise and pink and white, and after that there had been the fruit, clinging lavishly to sagging branches—apples, peaches, nectarines, apricots, warm to the hand, juicy and luscious—and after those, the plums and winter pears.

Her recollections, dimmed by her youth and the passage of time, had taken on a Utopian quality. Her childhood now seemed to her to have been one of happiness, of super-abundance.

It was difficult to know exactly which of her memories were real, which imagined. She was almost certain that she could remember a pony, a squat little skewbald fellow called Taffy. There had been several dogs, too, living in kennels under the trees at the back of the house. She had been secretly afraid of their bouncing enthusiasm when they ran up to lick her. She could remember tractors, gay with bright paint, droning monotonously over the paddocks as their ploughs churned the soil to a rich tilth, and she still carried in her mind the vague image of a man called Bill, who had allowed her to ride on the footplate as he ploughed, and who had given her boiled sweets from his pocket.

Lindsay could not recall a single jarring note in that secure life in the country. If there had been any unhappy moments, they had been confined to mere trivialities, such as her secret fear of the dogs.

Her real unhappiness had come later.

Mulling it over, she could only conclude, in fairness, that no one was to blame—certainly not the cousins whom she now called Uncle and Aunt, and to whom she would always feel a measure of gratitude for the way in which they had stepped into the breach. They had never actually complained about the additional commitment her presence represented, and it was almost certainly unintentional that they had made Lindsay conscious that she was a nuisance from the very outset. They had placed her in a boarding-school—not the exclusive establishment to which they had sent their own daughter, Carleen, but a quite adequate institution which gave her a proper education, and attended to her physical well-being and development while conveniently ignoring the spiritual wilderness into which a small, lonely child had been plunged.

Even at school, Lindsay reflected, she had been a doormat. Shyness, uncertainty, and a total lack of affection at her aunt's house, had all combined to render her withdrawn and self-effacing. She was demonstrative and warm-hearted by nature, but soon learned to curb and suppress these qualities in herself, for fear of a rebuff. She had been unremarkable on the sports field, average in the classroom. In her final year, the headmistress had advised a business course, as Lindsay would be expected to support herself at the earliest opportunity—the uncle and aunt had made this clear in an interview relating to vocational guidance, and Lindsay, who had no particular strong bent in any direction, had been glad to avail herself of her senior's advice. She had worked diligently, yearning for the time when she could regard herself as independent, no longer a burden upon her relatives. She had followed up her school commercial course with a year of advanced tuition at a special college, and when she passed out, she was proficient not only at shorthand and typing, but also at book-keeping and elementary accountancy.

The position which she held at present called for neither of these latter qualifications. Perhaps, if she had had a more positive personality, she might have projected herself better at all those interviews, she thought now, wistfully. Instead, she had been miserably shy and over-anxious, terrified that she would be turned down, that those other, more confident applicants would be accepted in her stead.

They were, of course!

Lindsay was learning the hard way!

She knew she had only herself to blame. She had gone home in a mood of bitter self-reproach, and in a fit of reckless despair had blued her entire savings on a natty little linen suit—the sort which her rivals had been wearing at those interviews! It was a basic suit of uncluttered simplicity and excellent cut, and Lindsay was surprised at its improving effect, not only upon her physical aspect, but upon her morale. Gazing at her reflection in the mirror, she had seen a slender, well-proportioned figure, of medium height, dressed in a subtle shade of muted olive that livened the green in her wide, beautiful eyes. Her fly-away hair was flattened submissively against her ears. Her legs, encased in pretty, honey-coloured nylons, seemed depressingly long and coltish to her critical appraisal, but quite neat, nevertheless, and she had lightened her old shoes with a new sand colour to match her cotton gloves.

The overall effect pleased Lindsay. Her wide mouth curved into an approving smile. Perhaps a touch of lipstick? Those other g..ls had! Carefully she rouged her lips with a soft peach colour and went, almost gaily, to her next interview.

Half an hour later, her gaiety had subsided, but an aura of confidence remained. Lindsay knew it was that pretty suit!

She also knew that, when she took it off and placed it back on its hanger, the new-found poise would probably get hung up along with the suit. But who cared? For the moment—and *that* was what mattered!—she knew that she felt good and looked good.

Another half-hour, and Lindsay had acquired a passable job as a stenographer with a respectable firm, and when she took off the olive linen that night, she smoothed it out with careful affection before putting it away, because she knew that its magic had procured her her independence.

At least, she had *thought* her independence was assured—but her uncle and aunt had had other ideas.

'That's nice for you, Lindsay,' they had said when she told them. 'Now that you can support yourself, you will be able to move in with Carleen. What a good thing she has that extra room!'

'With—*Carleen?* But I thought——'

Lindsay was dismayed. Carleen, five years her senior, had never treated Lindsay with anything but scant civility, or in her kinder moments, amused patronage. Her beauty, poise, and assurance served only to highlight Lindsay's own feelings of inadequacy, and since she had become established in the top flight of models, she had scarcely bothered with the younger cousin who, to use her own frequent description, had been 'foisted' on them.

'What did you think?'

'Well'—Lindsay hesitated, striving for tact—'I thought that at last I would be able to strike out on my own, and relieve you of your responsibility for me. You've both been wonderful, and I'm enormously grateful, Aunt, but you have your own lives to lead, things you both want to do, and I just thought I'd like to be—well—self-supporting as soon as possible.'

'You *will* be self-supporting.' Aunt Evelyn sounded impatient. 'Naturally you will contribute to the upkeep of the flat. It will be far more economical for Carleen to run it on two salaries than one, and a great comfort to us to know that you are there to do things for her. A model's life is extraordinarily demanding, and you know how hopeless that dear child has always been at anything domestic. In her position, she has to entertain a great deal—one has to keep up appearances, you know, and you will be able to relieve her of some of the more mundane tasks in the flat. You're much better at them than she is.'

Lindsay stared soberly at the woman who had taken her into her home so readily. (Where might she be otherwise? An orphanage?)

'I do think you might be more gracious about it, Lindsay,' pursued Aunt Evelyn crisply. 'After all we've done for you, surely it's little enough to expect of you? You need not mix with Carleen's friends—in fact, I'm sure she would prefer you to keep in the background. You're hardly their type, and you've always liked to efface yourself whenever possible, so it should suit you both very well. Your uncle and I have this cruise to Japan coming up shortly, too, if you remember. I shall shut up the house, and go away with a peaceful mind. Surely that's not too much to ask for? A little peace of mind, after all we've done for you? If you *are* enormously grateful, as you say you are, then now is your chance to prove it.'

'Very well, Aunt,' Lindsay had replied quietly. 'Does Carleen know? When shall I move my things?'

'Yes, she knows. We've discussed it with her, and she agrees that you share with her, so long as you do your bit. Remember, not many young girls are able to go to their very first job from a luxury flat, so it's to your advantage, too.'

'I'll do my best,' she had been assured with all the sincerity at Linday's command.

And I *have* done my best, Lindsay told herself now, wearily surveying the trays of food which she. had come home early to prepare, Carleen having warned that she herself would be late because of a hair appointment.

She *had* done her best, but she was not quite sure how much longer she would be capable of carrying on like this.

Life with Carleen was anything but easy. It was a time-consuming job on its own, without trying to combine it with an office situation. After more than a year of it, Lindsay felt tired to her very bones, and she knew that her work was suffering. Often she dragged herself home through the peak-hour bustle, only to have to whisk around the unit, tidying up Carleen's clothes, ironing garments which her cousin had left laid out with a note pinned to them—'Be a darling, Lindsay', those notes always pleaded disarmingly—hurriedly preparing innumerable dinners *à deux,* from which she knew she was expected to efface herself with some tactful excuse when Carleen's swain of the moment should appear, or more frequently, like tonight, assembling an array of food and cocktails for 'some of the crowd'. Here again, Lindsay was discouraged from putting in an appearance.

'That's marvellous!' Carleen could be generous with her praise. 'They look perfectly delicious, Lindsay! Now, don't you bother hanging around. You don't really hear much noise from your room, do you, sweet? A good thing it's furthest from the lounge. See you in the morning, then— *if* I'm awake before you leave for the office. Or would you like me to bring you a coffee later—we'll be making some, I'm sure?'

'No, don't bother, Carleen. Goodnight.'

Lying in her bed, listening to the hubbub of voices, the laughter that sometimes reached screaming point, and which kept her awake far into the night, Lindsay often felt like screaming herself—only it would not have been a scream of merriment, but of sheer hysteria and desperation! She would try to close her mind to those disturbing sounds. Endeavouring to coax herself into that evasive state of sleep, she would conjure up childhood memories of peaceful country life—of lucerne plots with fat sheep grazing, willows trailing their green fronds in the slow-running creek, the lonely cry of a mopoke in the still bush dawn.

It was always the same after one of Carleen's parties. Lindsay's alarm would rouse her, and, heavy-eyed, she would crawl from the sheets, dress hurriedly, and attack the mountain of washing-up which Carleen had stacked in the kitchenette. Before she left for work, she generally managed to empty the ash-trays, put away the spare glasses, and marvel at the way in which Carleen contrived to sleep through the din. How lovely she looked, with her long blonde tresses spread around her, one arm outflung—like a sleeping Princess, Lindsay thought wryly, except for the scattering of dainty, brief undergarments flung carelessly on to the foot of the bed. A Princess would doubtless have had a servant to remove them and tidy the bed-chamber, but Lindsay herself had no intention of going as far as that!

This evening, Lindsay found herself asking the same old question. How much longer could she go on? Carleen had been more demanding of late, and was not slow, when Lindsay tried to make her see how much she already had to do, in reminding her of her debt to her own parents. It was the cruellest form of moral blackmail, but Carleen did not hesitate to apply it whenever it suited her to do so.

Tonight, more than ever before, Lindsay experienced a quiet sense of despair, of longing to escape. As she stared bleakly from the window, up there on Dover Heights, watching the yachts returning to their moorings in the gathering darkness without really seeing them at all, a poem which she had always loved came unbidden to her mind:

> '*In my wild erratic fancy, visions come to me of Clancy*
>   *Gone a-droving down the Cooper where the Western*
>   *drovers go;*
>   *As the stock are slowly stringing, Clancy rides behind*
>   *them singing,*
>   *For the drover's life has pleasures that the townsfolk*
>   *never know.*'

Lindsay spoke the next verse aloud, savouring each line.

> '*And the bush has friends to meet him, and their*
>   *kindly voices greet him*
> *In the murmur of the breezes and the river on its*
>   *bars,*
> '*And he sees the vision splendid of the sunlit plains*
>   *extended,*
> '*And at night the wondrous glory of the everlasting*
>   *stars.*'

Preoccupied as she was with her 'vision splendid', she had

not heard Carleen's key in the lock, and was unaware of her presence until a prolonged sigh of exasperation sounded from the kitchen doorway.

'Lindsay, what *are* you doing? Have you got everything ready? They'll be here soon, you know.' Carleen's voice was sharp.

'Yes, I know.' Lindsay came out of her trance.

'Well, stop standing there spouting Banjo Paterson—if you've nothing better to do, you may press my blouse. And for the love of God, don't moon around quoting poetry in front of my friends, will you? They'll think you're odder than they already do—and in any case, Paterson's positively old hat, or didn't you know?'

Without waiting for an answer, Carleen took the garment to which she had referred from the laundry basket, handed it to her cousin, and disappeared. Moments later, Lindsay could hear the shower running, and Carleen's voice humming the latest hit as she turned herself beneath the spray.

Abstractedly, Lindsay switched on the iron, pulled the board down from its wall supports.

How had the rest of the poem gone? She couldn't remember the next few verses.

'And something, something, something—something, something, la, dee, da,' she muttered, spreading the blouse over the board.

Yes, that was it!

> *'And I somehow rather fancy that I'd like to change*
> *with Clancy,*
> *Like to take a turn at droving, where the seasons*
> *come and go,*
> *While he faced the round eternal of the cash-book and*
> *the journal—*
> *But I doubt he'd suit the office, Clancy of the Over-*
> *flow.'*

Lindsay's generous mouth curved a little bitterly.
No, he wouldn't have suited the office, any more than she

did herself. She was a misfit, just as Clancy would have been if he had had to forsake the freedom of the plains for her sort of nine-to-five employment in the city.

> *'And I sometimes rather fancy that I'd like to change with Clancy.'*

Oh, *how* she would like to change! Only Lindsay herself knew how trapped she felt, here in this unit with Carleen. She was just a cypher, really—a pair of hands that did things which were useful to her cousin, uncomplainingly, unquestioningly, because of that debt. *Always* there was that debt! Lindsay was asking herself now how long it took to pay off a debt of such magnitude. All of your life, maybe?

She shuddered at the prospect. She could imagine herself as an old, bent woman, still stooped over this very ironing-board, saying, 'Yes, Carleen,' 'No, Carleen.'

'Haven't you finished?' Her cousin spoke from the doorway, wafting a cloud of French perfume into the small kitchen.

Carleen's hair was still confined in a shower-cap, and there was cream on her face, but standing there in her quilted housecoat and swansdown-trimmed mules, she managed to look as glamorous as though she were posing for some perfumerie commercial.

'Thanks'—as Lindsay handed her the blouse—'Have you put those pastry things in the oven? Well, switch it on, for goodness' sake! Another few minutes, and they'll be starting to arrive. What *has* got into you tonight?'

Lindsay was wondering the very same thing. Whatever had possessed her to go into a dream world like that, when there was so much yet to be done? How could she possibly have forgotten to switch on the oven? Oh dear! She'd be caught now, most probably!

In feverish haste, she took glasses from the sideboard, assembled bottles together, carried through the plates of savouries, and put olives and mixed nuts into small bowls which she dotted about the lounge. After that, she got ice from the refrigerator, crushed it, and placed it in its own thermally-protected container.

She was in the act of carrying this through when the door-bell rang.

'Drat! Someone's early!' Carleen's voice, muffled and an-noyed, came from her bedroom. 'Answer that, will you, Lindsay. I'll be out in a couple of minutes.'

Lindsay glanced from her apron down to her old shoes. Then, with a shrug, half humorous, half despairing, she went to the front door.

Carleen's photographer—the one for whom Lindsay had made the oyster cocktail a few evenings ago—took in her shabby appearance with one comprehensive sweep of his light-blue eyes, and then averted them politely.

They were quite nice eyes, really, and his smiling mouth was pleasant, if not exactly strong. Lindsay decided that Carleen had sometimes done a lot worse!

'Good evening. Am I too early?'

'No, not at all. Won't you please come in, and I'll give you a drink while you wait. Carleen won't be long, and I dare say some of the others will arrive soon, too.'

He followed her along the hall to the sitting-room.

'You must be the little cousin,' he observed quite kindly. 'The one who hates parties and people.'

'Yes, that's right.' Lindsay forced a stilted smile. Was that what Carleen told them? Oh well, what did it matter? There was nothing to be gained by defending herself to this man. It was pure chance that she had not managed to escape before he arrived, and his definition of her, while strangely hurtful, was of no real consequence, after all.

'Martini? Or would you prefer something here?' She indi-cated the bottles on the sideboard.

'Martini would be very nice. Dry, please.' He watched with interest as she speared an olive, and laid it deftly across the filled glass. 'Tell me,' accepting his drink, 'what have you got against people? Or parties either, for that matter? You seemed to do that with the efficiency of long experience.'

Lindsay flushed.

'N-nothing. Nothing, of course,' she declared with hasty politeness.

'Then why not honour us with your presence this evening—just for once? I don't mind being left alone while you go and change—not that you aren't perfectly charming as you are,' he added, with what to Lindsay appeared to be spontaneous gallantry.

'Oh no, I couldn't! I mean——'

'What *do* you mean?' He was studying her closely.

'Well, I mean, I just couldn't. I've—er—things to do.'

'Don't you want to?'

'N-not particularly. I don't know any of Carleen's friends,' she pointed out lamely.

'Has anyone ever told you that you have an interesting face, little cousin?' His abrupt change of topic took her by surprise. 'That bone-structure would photograph well.'

Lindsay smiled. What a line! All Carleen's friends had a line, one way or another. You expected it of them. They were given to extravagant statements and exaggerated phrases, and their conversation was usually quite generously spattered with 'darlings' and 'sweethearts'.

Knowing this, she simply smiled, making no attempt to reply.

'There has to be first time, doesn't there?' he persisted. 'What are you smiling at? You look as enigmatic as the Mona Lisa! Why not come tonight—with my support, of course! I've helped launch countless young lovelies into society, you know.'

'Lindsay can't possibly come.' Carleen's voice came sweetly from behind them. 'Such a pity! She has other things to do, haven't you, pet? Now, do let her go, John. It's not fair to the poor girl to let her get caught by the others looking like that, is it? You, of all people, should know women's little vanities by now. We hate to be discovered without our *face* on, darling.' She gave a tinkling laugh.

'Some faces can stand it.' Lindsay caught his words as she fled from the room, thankful to take the opportunity to escape, but her cousin's reply was lost in the chinking of ice as Carleen helped herself to a drink.

Soon after that, the bell rang again, and for some time the front door remained open while 'the crowd' poured in.

The same old routine followed. As the party gathered momentum, the hum of conversation caused the flat to literally vibrate with the buzz of human voices. The sounds of speech and laughter, the clink of glasses, the beat of the record-player, chased each other in and out of Lindsay's brain as she moved about her room, and finally went to bed.

Her clock showed her that it was two o'clock before the noise began to diminish. She could hear goodbyes being called every now and then, and the bang of the front door as people departed.

Soon there were only two voices left—Carleen's and the photographer's.

'Coffee, John? Let's make some in the kitchen, now that we're alone.'

'Sounds cosy,' the deeper voice agreed.

They were there for quite some time, and Lindsay relaxed. The low exchange of talk had an almost soporific effect on her after the previous abandoned din, and she was on the very brink of sleep when Carleen and the man passed her door again on the way to the lobby.

'—wonderful evening, sweet.' His voice. 'Make it by twelve-thirty if you can, tomorrow, will you, Carleen?'

'I'll try, darling. I hope I wake up. I mustn't be late if Sarino himself is to be there, must I? It's my big chance!'

'Wrong, my pet. I'm your big chance, and don't you forget it! Although I'll admit Sarino's handy with a lens.' A pause. 'Why don't you bring that little cousin along with you when you come? She's got a challenging face—a sort of *undiscovered* quality, quite appealing—and those green eyes are remarkable. Green as the sea itself. In fact, that's what I see her as—a seascape. One of those *gran turismo* poster backgrounds, if you like—you know, the cliff road winding away, and in the foreground the sophisticates, watched from a distance by this green-eyed water-nymph in the briefest little bikini you ever saw—all big green eyes and green sea spray——'

'Darling, you've gone quite, quite mad. It must be the champagne.' Carleen's voice was dry, amused. 'She'd be utterly hopeless. She would freeze at the mere thought, and you'd embarrass her. She's full of inhibitions, you know.'

'She didn't strike me as quite that.'

'Well, she is. In fact, she's as dull as ditchwater. Quite the dreariest flat-mate possible.' There was a bite in that cool, floating tone. Lindsay, now sitting upright in her thin cotton pyjamas, listened with a sort of awestruck compulsion, shivered. She wished she hadn't begun to listen, because now, to her horror, she found she couldn't stop. Even in her humiliation, something drove her to it!

'Don't you like her? Why have her, then? Why not get someone else to share—someone who *isn't* as dull as ditchwater?'

'Oh, John, I'd love to, you know that, but she—well—Carleen's voice became honeyed, almost, one might say, *sacrificial*—'I can't let her down, John, the poor child. Do you know, she actually *begged* me to take her in, and what was I to do? My parents had had her for years, and I couldn't let them do it for ever, could I—limit their lives in that tedious way? No, I decided that it was my turn to offer her a roof, even though she cramps my style, too, just the teeniest little bit. I told her that she could stay here for just as long as she needed me,' Carleen finished on a positively magnanimous note.

John's voice came.

'Or you needed her.'

'*What* did you say?'

There was a rich, amused chuckle—the man's.

'You heard me, darling,' he said smoothly. 'I said, for as long as *you* need *her*. Oh, come off it, Carleen, be honest! We're birds of a feather, and I can read you like a book. We're both unscrupulous, and we both *use* people, so why not admit it? We're even going to *use* Sarino tomorrow, aren't we? You're using your dull little cousin for all the nasty little domesticities that you yourself can't bear, and so long as she copes with the sordid, everyday domestic routine, you'll keep her. Well, I want to use her, too—or her eyes, at any rate. That's all I want, sweetie, just her eyes, so you needn't worry that she'll spoil things for us.' He adopted a more persuasive tone. 'You have my word, Carleen—from one rogue to another! So take that jealous look off your pretty face, you little spitfire. Of course, I'll have to play her along just a little bit at first, to get her co-operation. You and I will both know it doesn't mean a thing, and it shouldn't be too difficult. I don't think your little cousin has ever had much attention from the male of the species, and I can be quite devastating when I like. *You* should know that! And remember, my interest is solely professional. If you don't bring her along, I'll be really disappointed.'

'She'll be working. How do you expect me to get round that?' Carleen's voice was sullen.

'You'll get round it, sweet, just as you get your way in other things.'

'And if I don't?'

'Then *I'll* get round Sarino.'

'You wouldn't!'

'I would. If I'm to be disappointed, then I'll make certain that you are, too.'

'Then I'm afraid you'll just have to *be* disappointed, *both* of you,' came Lindsay's strangled interruption from the doorway.

She had meant to sound calm, even sarcastic, but instead her voice was husky with hurt, as she stood there confronting them, heedless of the ridiculous figure she must present in her checked cotton pyjamas, with bare feet and ruffled hair. Her whole body was shaking with outrage and humiliation. It was no use trying to carry the thing off with elaborate sophistication—such a measure was quite beyond Lindsay just then!

'Lindsay!' Carleen uttered shrilly, then, collecting herself—'Darling, did we wake you up, you poor sweet?'

Lindsay threw back her head and met her cousin's eyes. There was about her a curious air of dignity, as if some hidden force had taken possession of her and was guiding her actions, telling her just what must be done, what must be said.

'No,' she returned evenly, 'you did not wake me up, and I am not your sweet. I am merely your dull flat-mate, whom you told could stay here just as long as I needed you—wasn't that how you put it? Well, it will be a relief to you to know that I *don't* need you any longer, Carleen, so you can start looking for someone else to share straight away. I shall be out of here by the end of next week.'

'But, *darling*——'

'As for you'—Lindsay addressed herself now to the man—'there is just one thing that I would like you to know. You were quite right in thinking that I've had little attention from the male of the species, and having just heard your own sickening revelations, I count myself lucky to have been spared. Goodnight!'

'Well done, Green Eyes! I guessed there was a bit of hidden spirit under that submissive little exterior. How about that, Carleen!'

'Shut up, John!' Carleen snapped. 'You keep out of this, you'll only make things worse.' She advanced towards Lindsay, arms outstretched placatingly. 'Lindsay darling, you don't really mean that. You're tired and a bit put out. I'm sorry we were so noisy. You've every reason to feel irritable, but you can't be serious.'

'I'm perfectly serious, Carleen. I'm leaving in a week.'

'Dear, don't be *silly*. Where would you go?'

'I don't know yet, but I'll find somewhere,' Lindsay retorted hardily.

'I think Green Eyes really *is* serious, sweetie! Could be you have a problem on your hands.'

'John, for heaven's sake, go, if all you can do is to stand there being clever!'

'Don't hurry away because of me,' Lindsay told him politely, although inside she felt quite numb with shock, 'because I'm going back to bed in any case.'

Not waiting even to observe his reaction, she went blindly in the direction of her bedroom, and once within its sanctuary, turned the key in the lock and huddled miserably between the sheets.

Her heart was racing at a threatening pace, and tears, unshed, stung her eyelids. When Carleen banged and rattled on the door some minutes later, she was thankful that she could pretend to be asleep.

CHAPTER 2

NEXT morning it was no surprise to Lindsay to find that she looked as dreadful as she felt!

That beastly photographer would not give twopence for her green eyes today, she decided grimly, observing their puffed lids and reddened rims in the mirror as she dragged on her clothes.

Her eyes! That was all he had wanted—to *use* her, or a part of her, just as Carleen did!

And she had actually been foolish enough to be warmed by his evidence of sincerity, had thought him quite charming when she had shown him in last night. She had permitted herself to be flattered by his complimentary phrases, only to discover that he had not meant them—or, at least, not in the way she had supposed. There was no kindness in him after all, only ambition and selfishness.

Lindsay patted her face with a cold, damp flannel, and shivered at the extent of her own gullibility. What an idiot she had been! And how pathetically little she knew about men! Familiar as she was with Carleen's spiteful ways and catty remarks about her fellow-creatures, she had stupidly thought that men were above such feline artifices, that those were confined to a woman's world alone. Now she knew better! She had been far too ready to be deceived, because nobody had ever praised her in such a warm fashion before. She had even been stupid enough to believe the man had wanted her at the party because he had found her attractive. Even though she had refused, it had been encouraging that a sophisticated friend of Carleen's had actually begged her to stay—that he had sought her out because he found her own particular brand of shy charm irresistible.

Something inside Lindsay shrank with humiliation as she recalled the extent of her disillusion. She had responded as a flower might to the promise of sunshine, unfurling its petals tentatively to those warming rays, only to find itself drenched and frayed by a sudden douche of icy rain. For Lindsay, the effect was as bracing and astringent as a slap on the face.

Her longing for independence had hardened into resolution to actually achieve her freedom from Carleen and her kind. Bitterness was useless, a corroding emotion if ever there was one. Distrust, though, was harder to eradicate. It would be a long time, if ever, before Lindsay would believe in other people, but right now it was supremely necessary to believe in *herself*.

The realisation of that need enabled her to face Carleen's ensuing pleas and tantrums with an equanimity she was far from feeling. The other girl begged, cajoled, and finally theatened, but Lindsay remained adamant. After a prolonged bout of sulks and silence, Carleen resorted to sarcasm.

'Who'd want you, anyway? You won't find it easy to get someone to share with you. It's like living with a saintly dormouse, heaven knows!'

'I'll find a place,' returned Lindsay imperturbably, pleased to find her newly acquired courage a foil for Carleen's venom.

'I'm not so sure.' Carleen smiled rather waspishly. 'Word has sort of got around that as a flat-mate you're a dead loss, darling. The general impression seems to be that I've finally turned you out.'

'But'—Lindsay blinked in bewilderment—'that's not true! You know it's not, and so do I. And so does Mr—er—what was his name, the photographer?'

'John?' Her cousin's laugh was brittle, taunting. 'He's forgotten all about the other night. I asked him to, and he agreed, so long as I do things his way professionally. Why should that bother me? He's the tops, after all.' She shrugged. 'Haven't you ever heard of honour among thieves, pet? It's very convenient at times.'

'Sydney's a big place.' Lindsay tried to appear sanguine, to stop the flutterings of apprehension inside herself. 'It's ridiculous to suggest that you can influence a whole city against me, Carleen.'

'Maybe.' The other lifted her shoulders again, lit a cigarette and leaned back in her chair, blowing a thoughtful
smoke ring. 'On the other hand, most people will ask where
you've been living before, won't they, and with whom?'

'I can live alone.'

Sitting in the bus later, wedged between a hard-faced
businessman immersed in the financial pages and a plump
housewife who smelt strongly of onions, Lindsay prided
herself upon the dignity of her reply. It had been an effective
exit line, at any rate, she thought, recalling with a sudden
spurt of fun the expressions that had chased themselves
across her cousin's lovely face as she picked up her handbag
and walked to the door. Dislike, frustration, helpless rage
had distorted Carleen's classic features, and yet she managed,
as always, to appear incredibly beautiful in a quite frightening way. She had usually succeeded in getting her own
wishes met in everything, simply because of that ineradicable
beauty, and she had been none too pleased at having her way
challenged by Lindsay, of all people.

It was stuffy in the bus, although a welcome shaft of air
from the platform fanned the long rear seat into which
Lindsay had squeezed herself.

They jolted down into Double Bay, with its gay boutiques
and pavements alive with shoppers, and then up the hill
towards Edgecliff. At the Cross the housewife got out, and
her place was immediately taken by another of the standing
passengers. The businessman never raised his eyes from his
paper, dedicating his entire attention to it in the way that
regular commuters do, oblivious to his surroundings, in-
curious as to his fellow-travellers. No doubt a sort of built-in
radar would tell him when his own destination was near, and
he would fold up his newspaper with automatic precision,
preparatory to leaving the bus, without even bothering to
glance about him.

He had finished the financial columns now, and had
turned another page, folding the paper back upon itself to
render it more manageable in the confined space.

Lindsay's eyes wandered over the newsprint only vaguely,

her mind absorbed in her own problems.

Advertisements, he was at now.

Registered teacher. Works Superintendent. Cost Accountant. Salesman with Ambition. Deputy Director of Public
Relations. The next advertisement was enclosed in a neat
black square, and printed in heavier type.

Somewhere in Lindsay's inattentive brain, a little bell
rang. It was an unexpected little bell, but it rang loudly
enough to bring her eyes, already passing on to Stationery
Representative and District Midwife, back to the message
inside the neat black square. The message was to the effect
that Gundooee Station was needing a book-keeper, experienced, single preferred, salary negotiable on appointment. It
also told the reader how many sheep and cattle and sub-bores
Gundooee Station had—the first two were in thousands, the
last in single figures. Sub-bores, whatever *they* were, came a
poor third on Gundooee Station, decided Lindsay whimsically.

She read on.

'Airstrip eighty miles west of Emmadanda. The successful
applicant will be responsible to the station manager, but personal initiative rewarded. Enclose qualifications, own hand-
writing. All communications answered.'

Well, Lindsay asked the little bell reprovingly, what is
there to ring about in that? It was, after all, just another
advertisement, like the Cost Accountant and the Salesman
with Ambition.

The bus groaned on, and the businessman turned to sport.
Races, mostly.

Gundooee.

What a strange name! Lindsay wondered what it meant.
Perhaps it did not have a meaning at all. Maybe it was just a
name, but it had a nice friendly sound. Emmadanda, too,
was pretty and quaint. Lindsay thought she could imagine
the sort of place Emmadanda would be. It would be tiny and
clean, with narrow streets lined with jacaranda trees, all
mauve and drooping, a pretty country town held in the arm
of a willow-fringed river.

Lindsay's green eyes became soft and misty.

Even sitting here, she could smell the cool, wet willow smell of that river, could hear the shallow singing of the rippling water, feel the caressing tree-clad shade of its peaceful bends. There would be orchards and lucerne plots and a neat, red-roofed house somewhere nearby, and that house would be Gundooee. At least, it would be *quite* near. Eighty miles, the advertisement had said, but it had implied that Emmadanda was desirably close, hadn't it?

Lindsay sighed.

Gun-doo-ee. What a pretty, friendly name! A 'bush' name, with a 'bush' sound of friendship and welcome.

> *'And the bush has friends to meet him, and their*
> *kindly voices greet him.'*

She pushed the haunting words to the back of her mind and stood up as her own stop came in sight. Other alighting passengers jostled, propelling her forward, as she made her way rather dreamily to the exit.

All along the street, that refrain seemed to echo, her own footsteps keeping time with it. It was a lilting measure, that one of Banjo Paterson's, easy to walk to. *Too* easy! At lunchtime, it was still with her, when she bought coffee and a sandwich, and carried her paper cup and packet to the park bench in the gardens opposite the office block in which she worked.

'Emma-danda, Emma-danda,' trilled a bird in the bushes behind her seat. 'Gun-doo-ee, Gun-doo-ee,' whispered the lapping water at the base of the near-by fountain.

Some madness seemed to have taken possession of Lindsay. I'm crazy, she thought, even as she was buying a copy of that newspaper and stuffing it into her hold-all.

They'll want a man, anyway, she was telling herself all the way home on the bus. It's meant for a man, quite obviously, although they don't say.

But why should it matter, to *them*? coaxed a tiny, persuasive voice within, as she walked towards the lift. So long as the 'someone' can keep books, why should *they* mind?

With a name like Lindsay, it could be either, couldn't it?

suggested the small, persistent devil inside her again, as she pushed the button and swept upwards to the top of the Dover Heights unit-block.

Lindsay Hallingham Dutten. There was definitely a masculine ring to that name, especially if you couldn't see the luminous green eyes, sensitively curving mouth, fly-away brown hair, and fragilely coltish limbs of its indubitably feminine possessor!

Thank goodness for Grandfather Hallingham! breathed Lindsay, as she fitted her key in the Yale lock and let herself into the flat. There had been times when she'd hankered for a 'Jane', or 'Margaret', even 'Adelaide' or 'Euphemia', but now there was a satisfyingly nondescript sound about her middle name that gave her cause for gratitude. If anything, it leaned slightly to a suggestion of male ownership rather than complete sexlessness, she decided, and for her present purpose that was all to the good!

Lindsay made herself a cup of tea to still the fluttering unease within herself at the boldness of her intention. It was difficult to sit in the kitchenette, perched up there on the heights above the harbour, watching the yachts and ferries and hydrofoils in the sea below, when already you could feel the peace and stillness of the bush about you, smell the gum-trees, see the paddocks full of sheep in the country sunshine.

Presently she got up, rinsed her cup and saucer, and went to the bureau in the lounge. It was gratifying to find that all but one of her certificates made no mention of her actual sex.

She put the offending one aside, and studied the others thoughtfully.

'This is to certify that the bearer Lindsay H. Dutten has satisfied the Board of Examiners——'

'that Lindsay Hallingham Dutten has passed with merit the required examination in Advanced Book-keeping——'

'A Pass with Credit has been awarded to Lindsay Hallingham Dutten by the Examining Board of the College——'

She was sitting on the floor, with the certificates still spread out around her, when her cousin came in.

'Don't tell me they've sacked you from the office as *well*?'

Carleen spoke almost with relish as she took in the scene.

'No, but—Carleen, I'm going to try for another post. Look!' In her enthusiasm and excitement, Lindsay could not sustain her own antagonism, even in the face of Carleen's unfriendliness. She opened the newspaper, and pointed out the advertisement. 'See that? I'm going to try for it, Carleen. A job in the country—just what I've always longed for!'

The other girl read the item, handed it back.

'You must be out of your tiny mind, Lindsay. That's obviously a man's position; you twit! Why don't you look in the Governess column if you're determined on country life——' She yawned. 'Boring as it is, it might just suit you down to the ground.'

Lindsay flushed, half defiant, half guilty.

'It doesn't *say* it's for a man, Carleen. It just says it's for a book-keeper, doesn't it?'

'Darling, you know perfectly well it's for a man,' drawled Carleen. 'Why pretend? For heaven's sake, come down to earth.'

'But they don't *say*, do they? And I need never have realised, need I? If I could land it, they wouldn't know until I got there that I wasn't a man, and once they saw that my work is efficient, they wouldn't mind, I'm *sure*. All they want is a book-keeper, and with a name like Lindsay, I could be either, couldn't I, anyway?'

Carleen raised one eyebrow. It was a very expressive eyebrow, neatly shaped, and she lifted it quite beautifully, in a way that suggested scepticism, amusement, and a certain element of surprise.

'Well, *well*! What duplicity, from a saintly dormouse! I didn't think you were capable of such deception. Don't tell me you're human, after all? You can hardly accuse John and me after this little revelation, can you?'

'It's not really deception,' mumbled Lindsay damply, red-cheeked and a bit miserable now. 'I mean, they don't *say*——'

Carleen studied her uncertain face, shook her own head.

'You aren't likely to get it, anyway, so why waste time talking about it? By the end of the week, you'll doubtless have come to your senses, and will realise what a good wicket you're on here with me. I'll be quite prepared to overlook your quite atrocious and embarrassing behaviour of the other evening, Lindsay, and we'll just go on as before, so long as you pull your weight about the place.'

With this magnanimous utterance, Carleen went to her bedroom, leaving Lindsay more unhappy, apprehensive, indignant, and determined than she had been before.

'I can't bear it,' she muttered to herself. 'Not another week!'

A few minutes later she was writing with desperation.

'Credentials are enclosed herewith. I am accustomed to positions demanding trust and initiative, and furthermore am free to take up the post immediately. Salary is not of paramount importance, providing employment and surroundings are congenial, and I should be prepared initially to accept the minimum award of remuneration as per scale at present pertaining. I have former experience of, and a marked preference for, country life, and trust that you will seriously and favourably consider my application.

Yours faithfully,
Lindsay H. Dutten.'

She signed her name with a flourish, and addressed an envelope to The Manager, Gundooee Station, Via Emmadanda.

Her step was swift and assured as she walked along to the local Post Office and slipped the letter through the slot. It was something to manage a spring in your step, when your palms were actually moist with fright and your heart thudding like a bongo drum!

A week later, Lindsay was walking the same route, but without quite such a spring. She was walking the same route because it was not only the way to the Post Office, but to the taxi stance as well, and the lack of spring was partly because of the weight of the suitcase she carried, but also because of Carleen's farewell scene.

Lindsay's knees trembled as she recalled it.

Her petulant cousin had been unbelievably nasty in every way. Her final reprisal had been the taking back of any clothes which she had bestowed on Lindsay over the past eighteen months. Even though they had been given in a spirit of patronisation, Lindsay had been grateful for them, and had spent a good deal of time shortening hems, mending seams, and sewing on buttons, to make them fashionable and presentable. They had comprised the better part of her wardrobe, and it had been something of a shock to find Carleen snatching them all from their hangers and dumping them on her own bed in a fit of rage when she saw that Lindsay was really serious about leaving.

'I—I thought you'd given them to me,' she had protested rather stupidly, aghast at her cousin's malicious action.

'I *loaned* them to you, which is a very different thing,' Carleen had retorted coldly. 'If you choose to go, you forfeit them, naturally. They'll probably come in handy for my next flat-mate. I shall make sure they go to someone who *appreciates* them, at any rate!'

Lindsay had swallowed her dismay, resumed her packing.

There had not been very much, after that, to put into her cases, and by dint of some rather ruthless cramming, she had been able to fit all her possessions into the one bulging suitcase which she now carried. At least Carleen had saved her the burden of a lot of luggage, she told herself as she panted on her way, smiling half grimly. And if the manager of Gundooee Station was really expecting a male book-keeper in trousers, it could hardly matter to him if the female one who turned up instead had only the suit she stood up in, one cotton sun-dress, and a faded denim skirt to her name! Just so long as she was the perfect *book-keeper*, it couldn't matter at all!

Because it was so early in the morning, there was a taxi waiting at the rank. The city was scarcely astir, the streets almost empty. The rising sun cast long-fingered shadows upon the great columns of sky-scrapers, and the air was warm, gently suffused with the pink light that foretold another hot humid day.

'The station, please—Central.'

Lindsay heaved her case into the taxi-driver's hands and collapsed thankfully into the back seat.

'Central Station,' the driver echoed nasally, and let in the clutch.

Lindsay sat holding her fingers tightly together to stop herself from trembling. She was on her way! This was the final, irrevocable step!

Away down to her right, the harbour could be glimpsed from time to time, calm tracts of sparkling water today, ink-blue, with passing views of jetties and boat-houses, and occasionally a peep at the majestic grey arch of the famous Bridge, now challenged for pride of place among Sydney's landmarks by the petal-shaped domes of the Opera House.

She sank back against the worn leather upholstery and marvelled anew at the miracle of having been chosen, recalling her wonder upon opening her own self-addressed envelope and discovering, not only her returned certificates, but a memo which told her that she had been engaged, and giving travelling instructions as well. It had been signed in a pretty, feminine hand—Vera E. Manning (Mrs.).

Lindsay supposed that Mrs. Manning must be the manager's wife. Perhaps, with the temporary absence of a proper book-keeper, she had been handling his correspondence for him. In that case, they would be very glad to see Lindsay! For her, the fact that it had been Mrs. Manning who had replied was an added guarantee of her own welcome.

'Thank you.'

She paid the driver, and picked up her case again, made her way to the ticket office.

'The end of the line, eh?' the clerk grinned as he punched the date on to her ticket and handed it over.

She was aware of his curious, good-natured scrutiny. Perhaps her hair was flying away again, although it had been smooth when she left the unit. She had kept the window open in the taxi all the way to the station, though, so it was probably in a mess.

She hoped this pretty linen-textured suit would create the same good impression upon Mr. and Mrs. Manning as it had upon her last employer. She would have to take care not to spill anything on it in the train, since it was now the only decent article in her wardrobe! Luckily it was virtually non-crushable, and the muted olive colour was at once cool and practical for travelling. She had wrapped her sand-coloured gloves in a piece of tissue and tucked them into the side pocket of her hold-all. They had been washed last night for the occasion, and Lindsay intended to put them on at the very last minute, just as she arrived at Gundooee, so that they would add to her feeling of neatness and poise.

The train was crowded. By noon the carriage was sweltering and stuffy, in spite of the open window and draught from the corridor. Smuts and flies, sticky paper, children crying with heat and exhaustion, a wedge of sunlight across one's face and knee, so fiercely penetrating through the glass that it was sheer relief each time the train changed direction and the burning wedge momentarily disappeared.

Lindsay stared out of the window, determinedly directing her concentration to the passing landscape.

They were over the Great Dividing Range now, the Blue Mountains with their magnificent, plunging gorges and majestic peaks, the ochre-crusted escarpments and impenetrable, eucalypt-choked gullies were behind them.

Memory stirred, painfully, uncertainly, in Lindsay, as they traversed the lower slopes of the west side. Her childhood hovered, half imagined, half recognised. The creeks, the poplars, small lush paddocks, lucerne, orchards, lanes. The same, yet not the same. Familiar enough, though, to imbue in the fragile-limbed girl, looking eagerly out of the window, an almost exquisite sense of homecoming. Her green eyes shone with warmth and expectancy.

Some hours and a couple of hundred miles later, the same green eyes were shining no longer. They were strained with fatigue, wide with dismay, and just the tiniest bit alarmed, too. Lindsay had found her childhood—and lost it again! It was away back there—*hours* and *hours, miles* and *miles*, back there—and the distance between her and it was increasing with every minute that she was being tossed from side to side, alone now in a compartment that swayed with speed as the train seemed suddenly to gather urgency, as if it, too, was wishing the journey over.

And who could blame it? Not Lindsay, certainly!

She closed her dust-rimmed eyes against the blatant glare of the endless wastes outside the window. No more friendly hills and little creeks, warm soils and shining kurrajongs. No more pretty green willows and elegant, slim poplars, lively townships, and well-stocked paddocks.

Here, there was nothing but flat, hard plain, and to Lindsay's apprehensive eyes, it appeared devoid of vegetation and life, except for the odd patch of twisted scrub, and those funny little dumpy bushes that looked desiccated and unattractively steely in colour.

Once her heart was gladdened by the sight of a profusely blooming sea of golden mulga blossom, but for the most part the landscape seemed to her desolate and monotonous and awesomely lonely. The occasional austere railway siding, and sometimes a fettler's hut or high-banked ground tank and windmill were the sole indication of possible human habitation. The few sheep she saw were depressingly lean and wrinkled, with prominent shoulder bones, starved necks and drooping flanks, quite unlike the plump-quartered lambs she thought she could remember.

Once, at a distance, she caught sight of a larger mob, moving slowly along in a cloud of dust, with a drover's plant bringing up the rear, and as the carriages clanked noisily over the sleepers—lickety-split, lickety-split, lickety-split—a kangaroo raised his head, on the alert, and rubbed his furry stomach with his fore-paws.

As the light faded, Lindsay evidenced the strangest metamorphosis in the scene about her. The sky became scorched with flame, seared with gold and scarlet, as the sun sank lower on the ever-distant horizon. The sky colours were harsh in their clarity, but the reflection on the plains was incredibly, wonderfully soft and misty, lending the stretches of gibber and grotesque, stunted trees a rosy dimension of breathtaking beauty.

Lindsay was entranced. Her spirits lifted a little. This could almost be Clancy's 'vision splendid', she thought, wiping the gathering beads of perspiration from her forehead with a handkerchief which in the morning had been crisp and white, but was now as limp and dusty as its owner. She must be nearing journey's end, too. Emmadanda could not be far now.

Emmadanda. That pretty, *pretty* name! Soon she would arrive there, and then there was just a little hop to Gundooee, and then she would be among the friends and kindly voices of the bush, just like the poem had said.

The thought of a long, cold drink, perhaps a salad, and a refreshing bath, almost made Lindsay groan aloud with pleasant anticipation.

With the lowering of the sun, the air became alive with birds—great flocks of brightly coloured parrots, banking clouds of pink and grey galahs, chains of wild duck, all were returning with the coming of night from their daytime feeding grounds to their resting places at the water-holes. In the gathering dusk, a couple of emus, startled by the noise of the train, went pelting off into the scrub with a queer, ungainly, rocking gait, their long legs splaying out in all directions like puppet attachments to their big, plumaged bodies.

At last the pace slackened. When the train finally stopped, Lindsay took down her case, collected her handbag and holdall, and climbed stiffly down on to the platform.

Not Emmadanda's platform. Lindsay found herself gazing blankly at a completely unfamiliar name.

'Emmadanda?' The man she asked was one of two who had got out of the next carriage. They seemed to be the only other people left on the train besides herself. 'Emmadanda?' He stroked his unshaven chin, peered at her curiously. 'Yer gotta take the motor-train to Emmadanda. It's the end of the line, see. You arst that bloke over there when 'e's leavin'. It's generally about 'arf an hour, once 'e transfers 'is supplies, see.'

'Oh, I see.' Lindsay forced her lips to smile. 'Thank you.'

'Any time.' Her informant spat neatly into the space between the siding and the train, and sauntered after his mate. 'Say, Herb,' she heard him call to the man already busy loading crates and boxes into a single-carriaged motorised affair, 'you gotta passenger fer Emma—a sheila, too, yer lucky coot!'

'That right? You want to swop?' They exchanged grins in the half dark, but Lindsay's own presence now precluded a further exchange. The second man threw a couple of canvas bags into his little motor-train, and then turned to Lindsay.

'*You* wouldn't be L. H. Dutten, I reckon,' he stated tentatively.

'That's right. Lindsay Dutten.'

'Dinkum?'—sceptically. 'Then, in that case, this message is for you.' He fished in the breast pocket of his soiled khaki shirt. 'There's more light up in the cab if you can't see it too good.'

'Er—thanks.' She took the scrap of paper, unfolded it, read the message, her eagerness wilting.

It had no beginning. No end. It simply said—

'Stay at pub in Emma overnight. Mail-plane leaves for Gundooee 10 a.m. Don't miss it.'

'Message received and understood?' The driver slung her case into the rear van compartment, slammed the door.

'Yes, thank you. Understood,' Lindsay mumbled. She felt numb with tiredness, unable to think of anything except this terrible sense of anti-climax. It was, after all, a very crude note, she excused herself.

'Good-oh! It seemed quite clear when I took it over the transceiver, and then I began to wonder who in tarnation to give it to. I reckon I was lookin' out for a man—not that they *said*, one way or the other,' he added quickly, taking in Lindsay's quick flush and arrested expression.

'Is it far?'

'Eh?'

'Emmadanda? Is it far?' If it is, I'll never make it, she was thinking desperately. If it's far, I can't go on, even if it means missing that wretched mail-plane in the morning.

' 'Bout forty minutes, that's all. You must've come all the way, eh? Reckon you look plain tuckered out.'

She smiled wanly.

'Yes, I think I must be—er—tuckered out. I'm glad it's no further than that.'

'Hop in, then. Sit there near the window, and you'll get all the breeze that's goin'.'

'Do you live in Emmadanda?' she asked, above the noise of the motor.

'Gawd, no! I come back here tonight. My missus and the kids is here, see. I just do this Emma run twice a week—to oblige the authorities, like.' He gave her his pleasant grin once more, and after smiling back politely, Lindsay relapsed into silence. Her legs were stiff, cramped, her brain somehow paralysed.

Never mind, she told herself bracingly, if you aren't at Gundooee tonight, with its friendly bush greeting and kindly voices, at least you'll be at Emmadanda. Just forty minutes to that pretty little town with the quaintly pretty name, nestling in the bend of a cool, green river. There might not be jacarandas lining the streets—because Lindsay realised that this was hardly jacaranda country—but there would be a real bush welcome waiting for her at Emmadanda.

> *'And the bush has friends to meet him, and their*
> *   kindly voices greet him*
> *In the murmur of the breezes, and the river on its*
> *   bars.*
> *And he sees the vision splendid of the sunlit plans*
> *   extended——'*

Lindsay had seen the sunlit plains—desolate, awesomely lonely, she had been reluctantly forced to acknowledge their splendour in the light of the setting sun. Now the sunlit plains were behind her, and around her—out there in the dark, was only the solitariness of the great Australian bush, but Emmadanda lay ahead.

She eased her weary shoulders, lifted her cheek to the breeze from the window, and took a steadying breath of anticipation. Dear, quaint little Emmadanda was just around the corner—or rather, dead ahead, since there appeared to be no corners on these wide expanses of plain.

'Here we are, then.' The driver drew up without warning, hauling on the brakes, and there was an answering squeal of protest from almost every mechanised part of the motor. He opened the door, waved a hand vaguely into the darkness, and said grandly, 'Emma! There she is!'

'Thank you so much,' Lindsay breathed, to his retreating back, because he had already started to unload his cargo.

She stepped down, looked about her, blinked! Then she looked—and blinked—again. Disbelievingly.

'Is—is *this* Emmadanda?' Her voice was husky, but she managed, somehow, to take her case when the man passed it out to her.

'Mm?' He was totally preoccupied.

'The—the hotel?' she suggested, almost fearfully.

A jerk of the head. 'That's her—the pub. Hardly grand enough to be called a *hotel*, I reckon.'

Or even a *pub*, thought Lindsay bleakly, eyeing the long outline of a tin-roofed shack with misgiving.

'D-do I just go in?' She could scarcely whisper.

'Well, there ain't a commissionaire, if that's what you're waiting for,' came the laconic retort.

'G-goodnight. Goodbye.'

'So long, miss.'

Lindsay picked up her case, looked up and down the street. There was only one, so wide that it wasn't even a thoroughfare, really—just a bit of the hard-baked plain, with a few houses scattered about. They all had the same corrugated iron roofs, shining ghostly in the thin moonlight. One had a window full of tins. Lindsay could see the columns of stacked groceries in the building right next to her. Further down was a shed with two petrol bowsers close beside it.

The hotel, the pub, was in between. It was the only dwelling with a balcony, a hideous skirting of wrought iron, peeling and rusty, ludicrously Victorian in this setting. It sat on raised blocks to elevate it from its less important neighbours, which squatted disconsolately in the dust. Over the top was a long board with faded lettering. The word 'Welcome' stood out in black capitals, and underneath, in smaller print, Lindsay could discern 'Harry Meehan, Prop.'

She swallowed, lifted her case, went up the steps, along the veranda, past a window beyond which flickered a kerosene lamp, and into a narrow hall.

What followed was mercifully vague. Not that Harry Meehan and his wife weren't kind—they *were*! They welcomed her with interest, even excitement, since they did not get many visitors out here in Emma—'Plenty of boozers, but not *residents*,' Harry had explained. They plied her with tucker, because she looked dead beat—'Fancy a sheila, such a young slip of a one at that, comin' out here on 'er own, eh! Now you get some of that into you, and a good strong cup of tea, and you'll soon be jake.'

Lindsay found that her appetite had mysteriously fled. She made a gallant attack on the salt beef and fresh damper, but finally had to admit defeat. The tea was heaven-sent, and fortified her sufficiently to enable her to reach the room they pointed out, and to follow Mrs. Meehan on a conducted tour of the plumbing facilities.

'You stand under and pull on that rope and the water'll come down when the bucket tips, see,' Mrs. Meehan obligingly demonstrated the shower. 'Don't worry if the colour's queer, the tank's a bit low, that's all. We don't have it piped to the showers. Some of them blokes in the bar would be standing under it all day long to revive themselves after a bender if we did, and it's our scarcest commodity out here. Don't *you* worry, though—*you* just use what you want,' she told Lindsay generously.

At the door of Lindsay's room, she giggled.

'Don't forget to soap yourself before you up-end the bucket—it's a common mistake with beginners.'

'I won't. Goodnight, and thank you, Mrs. Meehan.'

By the time Lindsay had manipulated the strange shower, cleaned her teeth in the brackish water, drawn on her pyjamas, and crawled miserably beneath the mosquito net that graced her lumpy stretcher, she couldn't think at all.

Which was maybe a good thing!

CHAPTER 3

MORNING brought the birds back. They flew overhead, calling raucously, piercing deep into Lindsay's unconscious state. Plumbing the depths of her exhausted slumber, their sounds were like anguished screams from an avian Underworld.

She threw off the sheet and crawled out from beneath the mosquito net, poured water from an aluminium pitcher into the shallow pan on the washstand, and splashed her face. Then she dressed with care, paying more than her usual attention to her make-up. Whatever happened, she intended to meet her fate with outward composure, even though the leaden ball of anticlimax still rolled around slowly inside her stomach.

Gundooee could hardly be worse than this! From the small window in the dining-room, the view offered nothing more than the now hideously familiar brown distances, broken by a single clump of shade-trees near the pub, from which came the dismal and recurring carr-carr-carr of the crows that festooned the upper branches.

'They don't go away to feed like the others,' explained Mrs. Meehan, passing her a cornflake packet and a jug of reconstituted milk. 'Hang about 'ere all day, that lot will, waitin' for scraps from the garbage. Git out of 'ere, youse black scavengers, you!' she yelled, flinging the window wide and hurling one of the small stones that lined the sill, presumably left there for just such a purpose.

The birds lifted themselves out of range with harsh screeching cries, spread their wings and closed them again, sinking back on to their scrawny perches and eyeing the building patiently.

'See,' repeated Mrs. Meehan triumphantly, 'nothink'll move 'em!'

Lindsay guessed that the whole thing had become something of a ritual between the hotel proprietress and the crows, and that Mrs. Meehan would have been surprised and disappointed if her onslaught had had any other result than the one it habitually did. It was probably one small amusement with which to relieve the monotony of another day in Emmadanda, Lindsay thought, with a twinge of sympathy for the thin, sun-browned woman at her side.

'How often does the mail-plane come?' she asked presently, taking a piece of damper, now a good bit harder than it had been last night, and spreading it with tinned butter and home-made marmalade.

'It don't really call 'ere at all, as a rule. We're the end of the line, see. We connect twice a week with the rail junction, so we don't need a plane. It's only for the folks outback.'

Outback! Lindsay tried not to look at the desolate landscape, concentrated instead on the red and white checks of the shabby gingham tablecloth.

'You mean, it's calling specially for me?'

Mrs. Meehan shrugged.

'Reckon it is. They must 'ave arst 'im to, out at Gundooee, because they couldn't get in for you themselves. Better be ready, eh? 'E don't do it for everybody, but Gundooee's different.'

Lindsay longed to ask in what way Gundooee differed, but she could not bring herself to the point of speech on that particular topic. She was inquisitive, but now too fearful of what the answer might reveal to ever put the question. She could not make up her mind between those two contradictory proverbs—'Ignorance is bliss' or 'Better the Devil you know than the one you don't'—and in the final event, cowardice prevailed. She settled for ignorance!

Harry Meehan took her case out for her and left her there to await the plane. She stood beneath the shade trees, in a world that was hot and bright and suddenly very lonely now that even Harry had deserted her. Perspiration oozed from her pores, even in the shadow. The birds rustled and cawed above her head, cocking their heads at her cheekily. They were hard blobs of jet against a sky that was blatantly blue and cloudless.

By the time the little silver plane came droning out of the blueness, the heat waves had set the whole landscape swimming with movement, and Lindsay was sagging against the mottled tree-trunk, wondering how she could bear to walk out into the direct rays of that relentless sun.

She was helped aboard, and they were off. The pilot, having bestowed upon her a surprised first glance and a laconic greeting, was obviously longing to be airborne again, and Lindsay, with a disembodied feeling of fatalism, was also anxious to be gone. Even though she had never flown before, it was something, at least, to be leaving Emmadanda!

The little plane rocked and bucked, plummeting every now and then with a suddenness that brought Lindsay's heart into her mouth. The pilot seemed to sense her tautness. He turned and grinned reassuringly.

'Sorry,' he said. 'Air-pockets. The heat's the trouble, flying this low. It's hardly worth getting above them when we've only eighty to go. Not too uncomfortable, are you?'

'No, no.' She smiled, but it was a pretty sickly effort, she knew.

'First time up?' He sounded kind.

Lindsay nodded.

'I see.' He pointed a thumb downwards. 'How's that for a panorama, then? A real bird's-eye view, eh!'

She peeped down, glad to take her mind off the bucking aircraft.

'What are those marks? They look like—sort of—pools.'

'Clay-pans,' he told her, 'not pools. We're still on the rim of the artesian basin here. The water's underneath, and you have to go down to get it. That's why you see so many bores. They tap the water down below and pump it up into the tanks with windmills—or engines, if there's no wind. There's one down there, you see. The bore drains take the flow—you can see the pattern they make, fanning out from the bore. Without these man-made watering places, the stock would die out in these parts. The finding of artesian water has been a key to development out here.'

'They look awfully thin—the sheep, I mean—coming out

on the train,' Lindsay offered diffidently.

'Ah well, they would be. They've had a bad go back there at Emma. Didn't get the rains that they got up this end. It's a nasty feeling, watching the storms skirting the horizon and giving you a miss, when you know other places, quite near, are getting a decent fall.'

Lindsay pondered over what he had told her. She was appalled at her own ignorance, at the cruelty, the irrevocability, the *challenge*, of the sort of country that she was seeing. She had never dreamed such tracts as this existed. It wasn't a bit like the 'bush' of her childhood dreams! This was a harsh reality that made her want to cry, because in its own way it was a moving experience just to see the enormity of it from above, like this. It was also humbling and frightening, because she didn't understand it.

There was not another bore for ages. Now that she knew what they were, she realised why, in the advertisement, the sheep and cattle on Gundooee had numbered thousands, and the sub-bores less than the fingers of her two hands.

Away to the west, she could see what she thought were hills—or was it all a mirage? There were plenty of those around, because of the wavering heat reflections, and they created weird and incredibly realistic images of water-filled lakes and shimmering seas.

No, this time they really were hills, the pilot told her. They were rough hulks of red and buff, thrown crudely upwards millions of years ago, when beyond the sandhills on the other side had been a great inland sea. Now there were only dried-up salt lakes for most of the year, and fossilised remains that told of the prehistoric animal and fish life that had once inhabited the central vastness of the Australian continent before the gigantic upheaval which had altered its entire geological and physical nature.

The awesome, rearing shapes remained distant, and the next time Lindsay blinked, they had disappeared altogether, and the plain was back. The shimmer of saltbush and bluebush, mulga and gibber, ever-changing in its effects, was behind them now, and below was a seemingly kinder landscape, grassed with coarse herbage, dotted with sturdier specimens of trees—ironbark, box and bloodwood.

The little plane banked low, circled over what looked like a small village, and descended gently towards an airstrip on the fringe. As they touched down, lifted, touched again, and ran smoothly along between the markers, Lindsay was aware of small knots of waiting people, and a variety of vehicles. There were jeeps, Blitzes, shabby utilities, all parked haphazardly around. Her heart fluttered nervously. A reception committee? Oh—no!

'Mail-day,' grinned the pilot. 'There's my mates, all waiting for me as usual. The most popular cove this side of the Alice, that's me!'

Lindsay expelled her pent-up breath. Of course, that was it! They were waiting for the mail-plane, not for Lindsay herself. How stupid of her!

No doubt the arrival of mail-day must be quite an occasion out here—such an occasion, indeed, that it might even be possible for Lindsay Hallingham Dutten, newly engaged book-keeper at Gundooee Station, to slip into her new role almost incognito, without anyone even noticing that the 'him' was after all a 'her'. There were enough folk around, goodness knows! It should not be hard to become one of the crowd, to identify with the knots of expectant people lining the strip with eyes only for their mail and supplies. Afterwards, when they dispersed, she would seek out Mr. Manning, and announce herself with the minimum of fuss.

Afterwards, Lindsay was to ask herself despairingly many time, how *could* she have known? Who would have thought that all those people—yes, every last one of them, with their Blitzes and jeeps and old tin trucks—belonged to Gundooee Station itself—that the whole village that she had spied from the air and upon which she and the pilot had swooped in the little silver plane was Gundooee homestead, and not a town at all.

How could she have guessed that all had come to meet the mail-plane, from their outcamps and boundary-riders' huts and well-sinkers' sites and from the village that was Gundooee homestead itself—all had come to collect their mail and supplies, and all appeared to know that a book-keeper was expected along with the mail!

As Lindsay stepped out, she was first of all aware of the intense glare of light. She had to screw up her eyes to ward off the reflection of the sun on the galvanised roof of the hangar directly behind the waiting groups.

The next thing that struck her, quite forcibly, was that, apart from three lubras standing there flaunting gaudy cotton dresses, there wasn't a single other woman on that airstrip except Lindsay herself! They were all men, every one of them, save for Lindsay and the lubras. And what a collection they seemed to her astonished eyes!

They were as varied as a bag of liquorice allsorts.

A couple of young men, mid-twentyish, were scantily clad in khaki shorts, their bare brown chests glistening with sweat and rippling muscle. The older ones appeared to favour khaki trousers and yellowing singlets, while the dark-skinned members—the Aborigines—wore faded shirts of indeterminate colour, braces, and wide, sagging trousers, felted with grease, dust, and perspiration from themselves and their horses. The trousers, indeed, might well have stood up alone, without the aid of those tired braces! thought Lindsay fastidiously to herself.

The hats were much the same all round the group. They were wide-brimmed felts, depending for individuality upon the angle at which they were worn and the amount of battering they had suffered.

So were the boots alike. Pair after pair, all the same. Tanned leather stock boots, with elastic sides and defined heels, covered with fine yellow dust. All the same.

And so were the eyes, in one respect, at least. They all carried a certain gleam, apart from unconcealed astonishment, that was indefinable to Lindsay, but which made her feel every bit as uncomfortable as did the sudden, complete silence which ensued the moment she stepped down into their midst.

Only one man's eyes did not hold that peculiar gleam. Lindsay, registering the fact, found her own drawn back irresistibly to his. They were a clear, steady grey, this man's eyes, well-set beneath beetling brows in a lean, tanned face

that was saved from narrowness by the width and strength of
its clean-cut jaw. A rocklike physique, too, that went with
the jaw. A six-footer, at least, with powerful shoulders and
narrow hips, long agile limbs.

Lindsay. peeping shyly, saw now that there were several
other things that were different about this particular man,
things she had not noticed at first. Not only were his eyes
narrowed upon her without any significant expression at all,
when all those other eyes carried that discomfiting gleam, but
she was aware that his clothes, too, were subtly different in a
minor sort of way—narrow-legged moleskins, a many-poc-
keted bush shirt, a kangaroo-hide belt at the hips. His hat
was just like the rest, but he was alone in raising it.

He did this with an unselfconscious brevity, a purely reflex
action. Then he stepped towards her and said politely,

'May I be of any help? You look a bit lost.'

Lindsay was grateful. At last someone had spoken, breaking that sudden, oddly oppressive silence! She was so grateful that she summoned up courage to smile at the man who
had taken the initiative, and her green eyes softened, reflect-
ing the warm and friendly gratitude she was feeling.

'Oh, thank you, I wonder if you could? Help, I mean. I'm
looking for Mr. Manning, the manager of Gundooee Station.
This is Gundooee, isn't it?' How silly that sounded, out here
in the middle of nowhere!

The men were all grinning, as if they were enjoying themselves, all except the big man to whom Lindsay had addressed herself.

'That's right'—his quiet voice was deep, abrupt. Puzzlement had crept into the clear grey gaze. 'But there's no Mr.
Manning here, I'm afraid.'

'Oh, I see.' Lindsay fumbled, because she didn't see at all.
'I—I had a letter from—from Mrs. Manning, just last week,
and I naturally thought——'

She tailed off, because the beetling brows were lower now,
and they were drawing together in an irritable way. The
man's voice, however, was still carefully polite.

'I am the manager, here at Gundooee. My name is Bennett, Rod Bennett. If I can help at all, Miss—er——'

'Dutten,' Lindsay supplied, rather breathlessly. 'Lindsay Dutten.'

'*Dutten!* You can't mean——?'

Oh yes, I can, said Lindsay under her breath, crossing her fingers in their nice, clean, sand-coloured gloves. That's just what I *can*, and *do*, mean.

'I'm Lindsay Hallingham Dutten,' she announced clearly and sweetly, with a confidence that belied the apprehension gathering within her, 'and I've been engaged as a book-keeper for Gundooee Station. And—and here I am,' she concluded less certainly.

The effect of this rather obvious pronouncement upon the entire group was prodigious. Jaws dropped, mouths fell open, eyes protruded—flabbergasted!

'Skin the rakin' lizards! A *sheila!*'

A man somewhere to her left, a man in a shabby singlet with a hole near the shoulder, bared his yellow teeth and spoke, seemingly for all, while another let out a high-spirited sort of cowboy yodel of unmistakable enthusiasm. Out of the corner of her eye, Lindsay saw his elbow come jabbing sharply into the ribs of the man beside him.

'Grey Eyes', alias Mr. Rod Bennett, must have spotted the gesture too, although Lindsay could have sworn his gaze had not shifted for one second from her own face.

'That'll do, Art.' The deep voice held a ring of authority. 'Get your mail and tobacco, all of you, and anything else you want. I'll take the homestead bag, Mac, and Mannie will give you tea up at the house as usual'—this to the pilot. 'Now,' he turned to Lindsay, '*you* come with *me*.'

How grim he seemed, yet curiously urbane. Lindsay quailed. There was something positively unnerving about Mr. Bennett's patient politeness in the face of his very evident displeasure.

'My—my things?' she squeaked.

'Bring them up to the side veranda, Mickie, will you?'

'Sure thing, Rod.' One of the young, brown-chested men stepped forward with alacrity.

As she turned to follow the manager, Lindsay heard whispering, quite distinctly, coming from the huddle of men who had immediately surrounded the one with her suitcase.

'No jumpin' the gun, now, Mickie, just 'cos you got a head start'—'We all start the same, mind'—'Odds or evens?'—'A fiver in, an' winner take all.'

'Cut it, all of you!' The big man ahead of her stopped so abruptly that Lindsay almost cannoned right into him. He thundered the words, and this time he really did seem very angry.

'We wasn't doin' nothink, boss—not 'ere.' Art sounded injured.

'Not here, not *anywhere*. Understand?'

'O.K., Rod.' The chorus was resigned.

The little group made way for Mickie and the suitcase, and gave their attention instead to the mail-plane and its cargo, and Lindsay turned once more in the wake of the big, brown, square-jawed man who was already striding away ahead of her over the bare, hot ground.

She had to run to catch up, and for a moment she tried to match her step with his in order to keep alongside of him. It was no use. The powerful strides were taking him away again, and he didn't even look around, or attempt to wait for her. He might at least have slowed down a little, she thought resentfully, finding herself almost running now to keep abreast of him.

'Were they—were they doing something wrong, your—er—the men?' she asked curiously, as she puffed along at his side.

He shot her a quick, incredulous look.

'Didn't you understand what they were doing?' he countered, in a carefully expressionless voice.

Lindsay shook her head.

'No,' she panted. 'Did you?'

'My God!'

The man lengthened his stride, and Lindsay broke into a trot.

What an odd creature! she was thinking. That was no sort of an answer at all, and her question had been perfectly civil. Whatever had she said to annoy him so much? Or was it only those men who had angered him? There was no way of telling, really.

Soon he was slowing down, lifting the catch on the white wicket gate that was set in a pretty white paling fence, standing aside and indicating that she should precede him.

Lindsay did, and was instantly enchanted. It was like stepping into another world. Cool, green, buffalo lawns swept before her, close-cropped, still damp from the sprinklers that had been rotating over them. Bougainvillea tumbled rampant along the fence, and unfamiliar but attractive shrubs lined the borders around the house—mimosas, acacias, oleander, several species of palm. The house itself—the 'homestead', he had called it as he led the way once again—was vast, a low, rambling building with gauzed verandas running right around it. It had a white roof that dipped away at different angles in all directions, indicating its extensive and wandering interior, and in several corners were big round rainwater tanks, set up on stands, with cone-shaped lids and a tap at the bottom.

Mr. Bennett took the steps to the veranda in a couple of bounds, and held open the fly-screen door. Lindsay, exhausted, stumbled inside.

Out of the sun it was cool and dim. Oh, this blessed shade! she thought, leaning against a veranda column and savouring it. She felt on the point of collapse. All that standing about in the heat, under the shade trees at Emmadanda, waiting for the mail-plane, seemed to have sapped her customary energy. And out here at the Gundooee airstrip there hadn't even been a tree!

The man beckoned her to follow, and Lindsay dragged herself away from the support of the veranda-post and obeyed.

Perhaps he would offer her some tea, as he had done to the pilot. 'Tea as usual,' he had said, and, 'Mannie will give it.'

Lindsay's parched throat was crying out for moisture. She could think of nothing more acceptable, right now, than a good cup of tea. She could drink a whole pot full!

'In here, please. Sit down there.' He indicated a leather chair, placed his broad-brimmed hat on a wide, flat-topped desk, and began to pace about on the other side of the room, as if collecting his thoughts for some sort of verbal battle to come.

Lindsay wilted into the chair, hardly caring where she was, and not minding in the least if he never fired the opening volley, since she had a fair idea of what was coming. Her face felt pale and sticky, and her olive linen suit clung to her thighs and shoulder-blades, limply and unappealingly. She closed her eyes, and the pacing stopped immediately.

'Aren't you well?' How abrupt, unsympathetic, he was! A *brute* of a man!

'Of course I'm well,' she defended herself indignantly, wishing he would stop peering at her like that. 'But you must surely admit that it's quite—quite *warm*.'

As soon as she had uttered them, Lindsay wished the words unsaid. You could tell by the quick frown, the repressed line of his mouth, that book-keepers, whether male or female, were not expected to complain of the heat the moment they arrived.

Rod Bennett, leaning over her with one hand on the tooled leather top of his office desk, opened his mouth to speak, apparently changed his mind, and left the room. Lindsay heard his heavy steps fading away along the veranda and closed her eyes thankfully again. Oh, for a cup of Mannie's tea, whoever Mannie was!

'Take these.' A curt command. The manager was back. He passed her a couple of pills and a pannikin of water. 'Go on, they won't hurt you, they're only salt tablets.'

Salt! Lindsay wasn't feeling like salt just now. She could think of nothing more thirst-making than salt! She screwed up her nose.

'Do I have to?' she asked doubtfully—and that was her second mistake.

The broad shoulders shrugged. 'No, you don't have to.' The deep voice was uncaring. 'I *could* leave you to die in your tracks, but I intend to get some answers first. Now, *drink up*!' A whiplash command suddenly supplanted the man's formerly lazy speech.

Lindsay did—hastily.

When she had finished the water, he took the empty mug

and said, 'Only an idiot, or someone completely inexperienced, would travel out in these parts without a hat.'

Lindsay flushed, patted her perspiring brow with her handkerchief, and decided to let that remark pass.

'You don't look altogether an idiot, so that leaves us with inexperience, doesn't it?' He hitched his moleskins, took the swivel chair on the opposite side of the desk, and placed his hands, palms down, on the leather top, eyeing her intently.

Lindsay quivered with nervousness. His eyes were unblinking. They were the most unswerving eyes she had ever come across, and they seemed to bore right into her, unwavering, relentless. His whole attitude was akin to the concentration of a tiger about to spring.

'Well?'

'Well.' She licked her dry lips.

'Let's have the story,' he said quietly. 'Why did you do it?'

'D-do what?'

'You know perfectly well *what*. Why did you apply for the book-keeper post here?'

Lindsay essayed a surprised smile.

'Because the post was advertised, and I happen to be a book-keeper,' she returned with commendable confidence. 'N-needing a p-post,' she added with something of a wobble, spoiling the whole effect. Oh, Lindsay, you ass!

'You were aware that the position required a man.' That wasn't even a question. The way Rod Bennett said it, it was simply a statement of fact.

It would take all her powers of persuasion to carry this off, Lindsay could see that.

'A—a *man*? Good *gracious*!' Now, *that* sounded convincing! She wondered whether to beat her brow in the best theatrical tradition, decided against it.

'You knew.' Again the statement.

'It—it didn't *say*,' she pointed out archly.

'It *implied*.'

'If it did, I'm afraid I wasn't aware of the implications.'

'And *still* aren't aware of them, by all appearances,' came the enigmatic murmur.

'How do you mean?' Lindsay gazed at him innocently.

He shot her that quick, incredulous look—the one he had given her outside. Then he passed his hand over his tanned, clean-shaven jaw, and paused. The pause lengthened.

Lindsay began to fidget. A pity that granite face was so unreadable. It would have helped, just then, to know what the man was thinking. As it was, she had no idea at all as to whether she was winning or losing.

Finally, Rod Bennett sat back, opened a drawer and took out a letter. He placed it carefully on the desk in front of him.

'As you can see, your own correspondence in the matter,' he told her, eyeing her with judicial sternness, as though she were a prisoner at the bar. He read—' "I am accustomed to positions demanding trust and initiative." How old are you, Miss—er—Dutten?'

'I'm twenty-one. Why?'

'An incredibly tender age to be so accustomed to positions of trust, don't you think?' he pointed out dryly.

Lindsay blushed.

'I don't know,' she muttered lamely, looking down at her hands. 'I'm completely trust-*worthy*,' she added, almost inaudibly.

'It's a different thing,' he asserted unkindly. Her adversary was giving no quarter. 'Now, let's see. Yes, here we are. "I have former experience of, and a marked preference for, country life." ' He looked up. 'And you came out here—*without* even a hat—to a position which anyone with one shred of prior experience would have known was intended for a man?'

He eyed her sceptically, and Lindsay wriggled in her chair.

'I—I was *born* in the bush,' she told him. Torn between indignation and despair, the words came tumbling out. 'I was *born* in it, I tell you, and I do have a preference for it. I love it—I always have. I've been longing for ages and ages to get away from that horrid city. You can be so lonely there—lonely, lonely, even in all the crowds of people. I—I longed to escape, and that's what the advertisement was, an escape. Oh, can't you see? It was all because of Clancy, anyway.'

'*Who?*'

'Clancy. *You* know. "The bush has friends to meet him, and their kindly voices greet him"—*that* Clancy. I wanted the f-friends and the k-kindly voices.'

She faltered to a halt, ashamed to find that her throat was suddenly choked with threatening tears. She gazed at him helplessly with huge, wet-lashed eyes that were misty with pleading.

He appeared totally unmoved.

'Where were you born?'

'Near Batlow. It's down——'

'I know it. Orchard country.' His tone was contemptuous. 'How long were you there?'

'Six years.'

'And then?'

'My parents were killed, both of them.'

'And after that?'

'I went to the city, to a—a sort of aunt.'

'And?'

'How do you mean—*and*? I mean, I've *told* you. I hated the city. I've never liked it. I always longed for the bush again, for freedom. And then I saw——'

'Are *you* telling *me*'—Rod Bennett interrupted in calculated tones of sheer, cold, forbidding, incredulous fury—'that you remained in the city after you were six years old? That that was your sole encounter with the "bush", as you are pleased to call it? That on the strength of a few childhood years in a fertile, climatically equable, civilised area like Batlow—*Batlow!*—you had the presumption to apply as a book-keeper for Gundooee Station, eighty miles out from Emmadanda, beyond the Black Stump, at the back of nowhere, where the crows fly backwards to keep the dust out of their eyes? That you have the temerity to say, in addition, that you were experienced in station life?'

'C-*country* life, I said,' she corrected him fearfully.

He was standing now. He had left his chair and he had come right around the desk to tower over her. Colour had risen angrily beneath his heavy tan, and his grey eyes were dark, sparking with rage.

Lindsay was terrified.

'I've got all the qualifications, Mr. Bennett. Truly I have. If you'll give me a trial. Mrs. Manning seemed to th-think that my qualifications were acceptable.'

'Mannie can't be blamed for this! You misled her! She's in her seventies—an old family retainer. Unfortunately I had to visit another of our properties at short notice, and I instructed Mannie to choose an applicant on my behalf. She's not accustomed to engaging staff, but she'd have made a better job of it if you'd been on the level.'

'I was on the level, Mr. Bennett. My certificates are all in order. I can't see that experience really matters all that much—what I mean—' she qualified hastily, quailing at his deepening expression of grimness. 'What I mean *is*, book-keeping is book-keeping, and that's all that's to it. It's the same anywhere.'

'Is it?' The words were jaded. So were the lines about his mouth—jaded and cynical, as he sought in one of the flap pockets of his khaki shirt for the makings, and began to roll a cigarette, with calm, experienced, square-tipped fingers. Lindsay found her eyes fastened upon those steady fingers, mesmerized, as they tipped tobacco deftly, fashioned a neat cylinder.

Rod Bennett licked the edges of his smoke carefully, neatened the ends.

'Is it?' he repeated tiredly, as if he had had enough of the whole question. 'Have you ever stocked a station store, Miss Dutten, to cover the needs of a large and varied complement of men? All and every possible need, remember, since we have no shops around the corner out here! Have *you* ever been responsible for expensive and explosive fuels, and spirits that must be signed for? Handed out discretionary 'finger money' to black stockmen? Kept a check on the numbered drugs and replacements in a station medical chest? Relayed messages and orders over a transceiver? Helped men to write letters and fill in forms when they've forgotten what it's like even to read? Acted as general factotum, adviser, confidante, counter-hand, peacemaker, court-of-appeal, ombudsman over gambling debts and personal difficulties—I could go on *ad infinitum*, Miss Dutten, and all *that* is before you even get out the cash book.'

Lindsay swallowed. Her hands were clutching themselves together, and her assurance had slipped, right down to her pretty sand-coloured shoes. She was badly shaken.

'I can *try*,' she whispered persuasively, willing her hope-lessness not to show. 'I can try, if you'll only give me a chance. I'm here, aren't I, s-so you may as well. I'll do my best, I really will.'

He seemed not to have even heard her.

'And added to that, you're a *woman*,' he intoned bitterly. 'Not even a woman, a mere girl! That's the biggest complication of the whole damn lot, and heaven knows what I've done to deserve to be saddled with it!'

'But I can look after myself, I always have. I've done it for years,' she assured him eagerly. 'I won't be at all a bother, I promise.'

'A *bother*?' He ground out his cigarette end impatiently.

Lindsay took that as the signal to stand up. She felt positively frayed as a result of this unpleasant skirmish. All she prayed for now was that it would end quickly, whatever the outcome.

When she stood up, her action somehow brought her closer to him. Lindsay felt dwarfed beside that powerful, masculine frame. Not daring to speak, she nevertheless found herself forced to look up, right into the stern grey eyes that were so near, above her. For a long moment their gazes held, locked in challenge.

Impossible to tell what was going on behind that grim mask. Somewhere near the man's jaw a small muscle flickered, the merest ripple in his sunseamed cheek. Lindsay watched it, fascinated—took in, too, the crisp dark hair that sprang away from his temple, the imperious aquilinity of the nose and fine chiselling of the lips. She gulped, audibly, in an effort to clear the sudden nervous constriction in her throat.

The man appeared to come to a decision at last.

'I'll give you a trial, Miss Dutten, since you've come such a long way.' The words were deeply gruff, grudging, one might have said. 'You will receive the minimum rate, but on

the other hand I shall not expect—or indeed encourage—
you, a woman, to perform *all* the duties I listed a moment
ago. Your tasks and the area of your authority will be strictly
limited, and under my constant surveillance. Do I make myself perfectly clear?'

Lindsay nodded.

'Perfectly clear,' she hastened to agree huskily.

Rod Bennett turned, walked to the door and opened it,
standing aside to let her pass.

'Just one more thing.' A hand came down on her shoulder,
arresting her passage.

'Yes?'

'Just get one thing quite clear in your mind, Miss Dutten.
If I thought for one moment that you had *intentionally* deceived me as to your sex'—the manager paused significantly
—'I would pack you out of here in my own aircraft before
you could even say Ned Kelly. Do you understand that?'

Once again, grey eyes locked with green. It was the green
ones which wavered, slid down to stare instead at the man's
dusty stock-boots, planted there so near.

Lindsay couldn't trust herself to speak just then. She had
the feeling that words—*any* words—might be the wrong
ones, might alter the delicate balance of a danger-fraught
situation and plunge her over the brink towards instant
dismissal, back to the airstrip, back to Emmadanda, back to
that railway junction whose name she couldn't even remember, back to Sydney itself.

At the mere thought, Lindsay's head went up and down
several times, very smartly, to let the man know that she
understood.

She understood very well indeed, and she was anything
but sanguine about the outcome of her own incredible folly!

CHAPTER 4

LINDSAY followed the Gundooee manager back along the veranda, through the gauze door, and down the steps into the grilling sun once more.

Sitting on the white paling fence beside the wicket gate, swinging his legs idly against the rails, was Mickie, and planted in the dust beside the fence was her solitary suitcase. When Rod Bennett approached, the young man slid down nimbly and picked up the case, grinning openly at the flushed-faced girl who came panting back down the path in the manager's wake.

'Thanks, Mick,' the older man said briefly, picked up the case himself, and turned to Lindsay. 'Come with me. I'll show you to your cottage.'

'My cottage! Do you mean one of my very *own*?' she asked, intrigued.

'The *book-keeper's* cottage, Miss Dutten,' he elucidated repressively. 'It's down near the store, for convenience, you understand. The book-keeper sleeps and works there, but takes his meals at the homestead.'

'Oh. I see.'

He was walking briskly as he spoke, and again she found herself almost running in an effort to keep up.

They were taking a different direction this time. The airstrip and hangar were now on the other side of the big sprawling homestead, and Lindsay and the manager were walking away from it, passing an assortment of sheds and buildings which from the air had made her think that this was a clustered village, but which were in reality spaced quite a distance apart from each other when you were actually walking among them. She saw engine sheds, a power-house, station-hands' quarters with a row of open-sided shower cubicles at one end, feed stores, a blacksmith's shop, a harness room, a fowl-yard, and in the distance a long, low shearing-shed with yards and races surrounding it.

'Just around this corner.'

Rod Bennett rounded the corner of the station store and pulled up short in front of a neat pink weatherboard cottage with a small canvas awning over its cement porch.

He stopped so abruptly that, this time, Lindsay *did* bump into him.

A hard hand gripped her painfully above the elbow, restored her balance, and let go. He hadn't even looked her way, because his eyes were already busy elsewhere. They were taking in the scene around the little weatherboard building.

It seemed to Lindsay that there were almost as many people standing around it as there had been down at the airstrip to await that plane.

The black stockmen weren't there, it was true, and neither were the lubras in their bright cotton dresses—they had all gone back to their humpies over at the creek, and even from here, one could hear the yapping of their mangy dogs, the crying of the piccanins, and the laughter of the women, underneath the distant line of shade trees.

The aboriginal members of Gundooee Station had apparently taken their supplies and gone, but most, or all, of the others now seemed to be gathered about the precincts of the book-keeper's cottage, busying themselves in a number of ways. To her astonishment Lindsay registered the fact that even Mickie was present. He must have taken an alternative route after he had handed over her suitcase—a quicker route, because he had reached the cottage before they did themselves, and Mr. Bennett had certainly set a spanking pace.

Mickie was apparently absorbed in lowering the striped sun-blind to a more effective angle over the front steps. From the attention Mickie was devoting to his task, it appeared to be a tricky and absorbing operation.

A couple of the men were realigning the whitewashed stones which flanked the path, while others made half-hearted attacks on the weeds inside the old motor-tyres which served to enclose small shrubs and saplings—the only gesture towards any sort of garden that the cottage possessed. Further off, a singleted figure stooped to pick up a tin that glinted with metallic viciousness in the harsh noon light. To the left, yet another began to kick at a burr with the heel of his boot. One or two, unable to find some reasonable excuse for occupation, simply stood and scuffed at the dust.

Rod Bennett surveyed these activities in silence for a moment. Then—

'What's going on here?' he asked severely.

All the men stopped what they were doing, and the ones who were not doing anything stopped that, too, and regarded him somewhat sheepishly. Then they looked at each other, at Lindsay, at Rod, at each other. No one seemed to know how to reply, and therefore no one spoke at all.

'Well? What's going on?' Rod Bennett sounded stern. 'Mail-day's as good as over, didn't you know? Bluey, I thought you had a fence to ride?'

'Most certainly, boss,' mumbled a gaunt individual with an unruly thatch of bright red hair spiking from beneath his slouch hat. 'I just reckoned these stones could do with a bit of a shift, see. *You* know, they was kind of untidy, see.'

'I see more than you think! Barney? The number five bore?'

'Sure thing, Rod. I've got the casin' in the jeep. We just thought, I mean, these weeds 'ere are gettin' downright cheeky, they're comin' up that quick.'

'—just spotted this tin on me way to the quarters, Rod. Thought one of them blinkin' 'orses might shy at it if I didn't pick it up.'

'Collectin' up a bit of wire, I was——'

'Prickly little bastards, these burrs, eh, Rod?'

'We got the supplies up in the Blitz, Rod. I mean, you couldn't expect for a sheila ter be carryin' all them heavy packin' cases, could yer, now?'

'Quite, Herb,' agreed the man at Lindsay's side equably. 'From now on that can be your own job on mail-days. Part of the drill.'

Herb, a thickset man with a four-day stubble and a singular lack of teeth, received this news with some evidence of bewilderment.

'Yer don't mean *every* time, do yer, Rod?' he enquired in dismay.

'That's just what I do mean, Herb. *Every* time.' Rod Bennett smiled pleasantly at Herb's toothless gape. 'And you, Artie, can get a hoe, and cut burrs the *proper* way for the rest of the day. The horse paddock's getting pretty thick with them.'

'Aw, cripes, boss! Yer mean, all them burrs in the 'orse paddock? Stone the crows! There's acres of 'em!'

'That's right, Art. It's time they were done.' He turned his attention to the men kneeling beside the motor-tyres. 'You might as well weed all those beds, while you're at it. Even if the cottage is to remain empty in the meantime, it's as well to keep the place tidy, I reckon.'

'Empty?' The wail was a chorused protest, unanimous, heartfelt. To a man, they all stopped what they had been doing again, and blinked at Rod.

'Yes, that's right—empty. I was simply showing Miss Dutten the layout, the whereabouts of the store, and the place where the book-keeper used to stay.' His voice was deeply calm, utterly convincing—so convincing that for a moment Lindsay could almost have believed him to be serious. But hadn't he just *said* that she could have a cottage of her very own? That the book-keeper always slept and worked in his own cottage near the store? And it was such a dear little cottage, too!

Lindsay peeped at his set face. He appeared to be in deadly earnest. Very hesitantly, she plucked at his khaki shirt-sleeve.

'Excuse me, Mr. Bennett, but you just said a moment ago that——'

'Never mind what I said a moment ago.' Rod Bennett scowled down at her, as if her fingers on his arm were an unwelcome reminder of a presence that irritated almost beyond endurance. 'You can come with me,' he added, in the same sort of voice he had used at the airstrip, and which seemed to Lindsay to be loaded with forbearance. Then he picked up her case again and swung on his heel.

'But I thought——' gasped Lindsay, catching up with him around the corner of the store.

'Then don't. *Don't* think,' he rasped out briefly.

'But my cottage?' she panted. 'That dear little cottage? Aren't I going to have it, like the book-keeper always does?'

'No, Miss Dutten, you are not!'

'*Why* not? The other book-keeepers always did, so why not me?'

'Because you are not like the other book-keepers,' he told her curtly, opening the wicket gate and almost pushing her through in front of him.

'But you haven't tried me out yet,' protested Lindsay hotly, 'so how can you possibly know that I'm not like the others?'

Rod Bennett seized her elbow in a grasp that hurt, and practically lifted her up the steps and through the gauze door. Inside, he let her go, dumped her case down on the wooden veranda boards, pushed back his hat, and looked at her.

Lindsay gazed back, aware of the exasperation lurking in the grey depths of his eyes, the small white strip near his hairline where the suntan stopped, the glint of a couple of grey strands among the dark, clipped hairs at his temple, the brown strength of his throat in the open-necked shirt, the grim set of his mouth as he closed his lips upon whatever words he had been about to utter.

Lindsay's stare was limpid, green, and clear, and tinged with uncontrolled curiosity. She had never met a man of this type before—she hadn't, for that matter, met many men of *any* type!—and she found him both interesting and—well—*fascinating*, in a rather frightening sort of way. No wonder all those other men down there had positively jumped to do his bidding! He wasn't the sort of person to brook an argument when he issued orders, of that much one could be sure.

Rod Bennett's own stare was grey, candid, and uncomfortably penetrating. It seemed to search right into her own brain, to where her puzzlement and weariness and curiosity were mingling bewilderingly.

Lindsay watched the exasperation giving way to a tiny glimmer of some other, warmer emotion that she was unable to identify. Although he now looked slightly less dangerous, his mouth was still unyielding, however, as he stated positively,

'The others were different.'

'How do you mean?'

'The others were men.'

'Oh-h-h!' Lindsay's own lips pursed soundlessly. 'Does it m-matter?' she added after a moment, wishing that he didn't have to be quite so grim about it.

'It matters, yes.' He sent his broad-brimmed hat spinning into a deckchair impatiently. 'For two pins, I'd send you back. I *ought* to send you back.'

'But *why*?'

Brown fingers raked through his hair in a gesture of pure indecision. 'Those men——' he muttered.

'I thought they were being perfectly sweet,' Lindsay felt bound to defend them. 'After all, they were only trying to make things nice for me, weren't they? They meant to be friendly. My new bush friends.' She gazed out through the gauze at the sun-drenched lawn and shrubs, shimmering in a haze of heat, then brought her eyes back to his. 'They were the friends, the kindly voices—like in the poem.'

'The poem?'

'I *told* you. Like in Clancy.'

'Of the Overflow,' she felt bound to tack on, seeing his blank look.

'Ah yes. Clancy.' Rod Bennett's grey eyes flickered with amused irony. He fingered his chin. 'I don't suppose I could send you back, after that, could I? Not without a trial.'

'You *promised*, Mr. Bennett.'

He straightened up, sighed.

'That's right, I promised.' He picked up the case, for what seemed to Lindsay the hundredth time since her arrival. 'I'll show you to your room, and you can have a wash and join us for lunch. The dining-room is around that corner of the veranda. Mannie will get you some sheets and stuff afterwards, and you can make up a bed.'

'Thank *you*, Mr. Bennett. I really do mean that!'

He indicated a doorway, placed her luggage in what she hoped would now be its final resting-place, on the foot of the bed.

'I must be mad,' he grumbled deeply.

'I beg your pardon?'

'Lunch will be in a quarter of an hour.' Rod Bennett spoke abruptly. 'Please be punctual. Unpunctuality fouls up the cogs in a station's efficiency machine quicker than almost anything else.'

'Yes, Mr. Bennett,' she assured the broad, retreating back, sinking down weakly on to the bed beside her case, and listening to the beat of his heavy boots fading out along the veranda.

Phew! It looked as though she had made it, Lindsay reflected with relief. But only just!

For a while it had been touch and go out there, but now she felt that the first ditch had been safely negotiated. She was here, and she could stay, even if it was only on trial. She had bought herself a little time in which to prove to that strange, tough man that one's sex had no relevance whatever when it came to book-keeping. Once Rod Bennett saw what a neat, methodical set of books she could turn out, he would forget all about that one little drawback—the fact that she happened to be a girl.

Having become acquainted with the layout of the homestead precincts, Lindsay could not see that being a girl mattered even the tiniest little bit. She could soon learn to do all those other things too, the general factotum things that he had reeled off so blightingly.

Lindsay gave an involuntary shiver as she remembered the manager's eyes, how cold they had gone, when he said that bit about deceiving him. His eyes, indeed, had almost disappeared into cold, nasty, grey slits, and you'd have said there was a real hint of threat in his voice—

'If I thought for one moment that you had *intentionally* deceived me——'

Lindsay gulped. It was better not to recall how he had looked when he had said that. It made her feel apprehensive and uncomfortable, all over again, just when she was beginning to recover her equilibrium. She thrust the recollection from her, and surveyed her surroundings with returning interest.

The room was pleasant—not as nice as the dear little cottage would have been, but gracious and spacious and homely-looking, with high, cool white ceilings and heavy Victorian furniture, a brass bedstead, floral curtains. The quilt she was sitting on was of white cotton, heavily fringed, and the mattress felt soft and springy. Lindsay would have liked to lie down on it right now, and drift off to sleep. She would like to forget all about Gundooee Station and its manager, just for the present, but Rod Bennett had said she must come for lunch, so she had better get ready.

She found the bathroom, washed her face and hands, came back to the bedroom and took off her pretty olive suit, hanging it up with care in the big wardrobe. Her mouth curled at the sight of its cavernous interior, and the rows of empty coat-hangers. Her suit and denim skirt and cotton sun-dress would not take up much of that room. Alas for all the pretty things which Carleen had snatched back so spitefully at the last moment! They would have gone some way, at least, towards filling up this generous space.

Lindsay put on the denim skirt now, buttoned her white cotton shirt, brushed her hair. Then she walked somewhat hesitantly across the hall to the dining-room.

Rod Bennett was there waiting for her. He made the fact that he was waiting obvious by looking pointedly at the watch strapped to one hairy brown wrist, and then he introduced her to the woman she knew must be Mannie, before putting her into her chair.

Mannie was already seated. She was thin and elderly, with wispy white hair and a complexion that was parched and drawn by the sun into a criss-cross pattern of wrinkles. They scored her cheeks, fanned about her eyes, corrugated her brow, lined her mouth. When she smiled they all changed direction, like miniature railway lines whose points had been changed. She smiled at Lindsay just now, and her beady brown eyes were alert, but also welcoming and kind.

Rod Bennett waved a hand between the woman and the girl.

'This is Miss Dutten, Mannie,' he told the old woman on his right. Then, to Lindsay, 'Mrs. Manning, or Mannie, as she prefers to be called.' He took his place at the head of the table. 'I have already prepared Mannie to expect a *Miss* Dutten instead of a Mister—isn't that so, Mannie?'

'Please just call me Lindsay. I'm not used to being called Miss.'

'Perhaps that is why you omitted it from your correspondence?' came the quick, sarcastic reply, and Lindsay felt quick colour tinting her cheeks.

'Now, Rod my dear, don't go on about it any more,' begged the old lady, unexpectedly coming to the girl's defence. 'As Miss Dutten—as Lindsay—is here, it's a *fait accompli*, isn't it, however vexed you may feel, so let's just make the best of it. In any case'—she twinkled deliberately—'it will be nice for me to have some feminine company apart from Sibbie and Bella, with all their skylarks.'

'Sibbie and Bella?' Lindsay was loth to speak at all in the face of Rod Bennett's own preoccupied silence as he got on with his meal, but as Mannie appeared to be in a more friendly and talkative mood, it seemed churlish not to join in.

'Yes, my dear. The lubras.'

'Do—do they work in the house?'

Lindsay had wondered about that. While she had been sitting on her bed, she had heard shrieks and giggles coming from somewhere at the back of the veranda, and the accompanying clatter and clash of cutlery and crockery told her that the sounds probably emanated from the kitchen.

'They do help—and hinder too,' smiled the old woman. 'I don't let them handle the food, and so I do all the cooking myself, but they do wash the dishes and peel the vegetables, and they turn the housework into a sort of fun session that can become quite riotous at times. You'll hear them soon, if you haven't already. They're apt to regard everything as a joke, which makes them the pleasantest possible people to have around one—when they *are* around.'

'Aren't they always?' Lindsay was moved to enquire politely, stealing another furtive glance at the stern figure on her right. He was eating with an abstracted expression on his face. Obviously his thoughts were engaged elsewhere, and he was quite oblivious of the women's conversational exchange.

'No, not always,' replied Mannie with a sigh. 'That's the one drawback. They can be somewhat irresponsible about turning up. One just has to be thankful when they do. They are a people of superstition, the aborigines, and a certain amount of religious rite and ceremony interferes with the living of their lives as the white man lives it. Things are changing gradually, of course, and not before time. I'm afraid we've done very badly by the people from whom the white settlers took Australia, and have, as a nation, realised our culpability rather late. Up till now, their fortunes have depended to a great extent on the sympathy or otherwise of the individuals who employ them, although recently the Government has taken a hand, and of course there are the Missions, which do an enormous amount of helpful work. Out here they still have cultural sessions of one sort or another, singing ceremonies, corroborees to celebrate spiritual events, and all kinds of ritual to do with their Dreamtime beliefs. Sometimes, too'—she laughed—'they just go walkabout for no apparent reason.'

'Walkabout?'

'They just move away, Lindsay—into the night, you might say. After being apparently quite settled and happy, they suddenly get the urge to wander, and they leave their gunyahs or humpies, the bark huts they make, and they just seem to disappear into nowhere. It's part of their inherent tendency to nomadism. But of course you'll know all this, anyway'—Mannie waved a deprecating hand apologetically —'I was forgetting that you have had previous experience of Outback ways.'

'Miss Dutten's previous experience has unfortunately been confined to the Batlow area,' put in Rod Bennett cuttingly. (So he *had* been listening, after all!)

'Batlow?' Mannie blinked. 'Goodness, isn't that the place where those lovely apples come from? Pears, too, I think.'

'Quite.' The manager succeeded in bringing a wealth of derision to that word.

'Yes, well'—the old woman glanced tactfully away from Lindsay's scarlet cheeks—'you'll have to tell me all about it some time, dear. Such pretty country, so I've heard. Will you be in for tea, Rod, or shall I pack you something? We're usually not so late as this on mail-days, you see, Lindsay. The men are almost always out for lunch, but with a new book-keeper coming—well, that's different.'

'It was certainly different today, anyway,' agreed the big man at the head of the table, holding Lindsay's eye as if delighting in her agonised expression. 'A few scones in my saddle-bag would be welcome, Mannie, thank you. I left it on the dresser in the kitchen.'

Rod Bennett got to his feet, smiled down and laid a kindly hand under Mannie's arm, helping her from her chair—not that Mannie was decrepit or in real need of such help. It was more a gesture of true affection and gallantry, Lindsay perceived with amazement, and the man's eyes were soft, considerate and fond, not remote and cool and disapproving like they were when they rested on *her.* Lindsay thought wistfully that it must be pleasant to have a difficult man like that on your side instead of against you, and to be the recipient of such a gentle, respectful look from those wide-set, expressive grey eyes.

It wasn't very likely to happen to her, though!

She cleared her throat.

'Er—thank you for meeting me at the plane, Mr. Bennett,' she mumbled. 'I'm sorry to have interrupted your day.'

'Not at all, Miss Dutten. It is usual, as Mannie has already said, for me to be on hand to meet a new employee, I assure you,' he returned formally.

'Don't you think it would be more friendly to say Lindsay, Rod?' interpolated Mannie with what seemed to Lindsay an awesome show of courage. *'I'm* going to—and you just call me Mannie, my dear. We all use Christian names out here.'

'I find the name Lindsay too equivocal in the circumstances, thank you, Mannie, to wish to use it,' stated Rod Bennett coldly. Scowling brows descended, turned the grey eyes into those nasty slits again. The slits were narrowed accusingly upon the girl who hesitantly started to collect plates, as the housekeeper was already doing. 'In any case, repeated use of her proper status might remind *Miss* Dutten that there are certain occasions when it is unforgivably remiss to omit the use of it with accuracy.'

Upon which quelling statement he strode from the room.

'Now what did he mean by that?' asked Mannie good-humouredly. 'It's not as if you did it on *purpose.*'

She continued her task with every impression of unruffled calm. Obviously Rod Bennett did not present the fearsome figure to her that he did to Lindsay, who now licked her dry lips tremulously and carried a pile of plates to the trolley with hands that trembled a tiny bit.

'I—I think perhaps he's still very angry, all the same. It's because I'm a girl, he's made that quite clear. Doesn't he like women?' She gazed apprehensively at the tall, retreating, slouch-hatted figure that crossed the yard outside the window with long, purposeful strides.

'Who? Rod? Of *course* he likes women—and they *adore* him!' averred the old lady indignantly, as though Lindsay had been guilty of casting some sort of aspersion upon her beloved employer. 'Why, he's got those lovely Brisbane belles eating out of his hand. They just fall over themselves to go out with him—he's *very* eligible, you know. It's a wonder he hasn't settled down with one of them before now, because some of them have been quite gorgeous. They sometimes come out here to stay, when the Races are on. He can pick and choose, really, Lindsay, a man like *him*, but I must say he's taking quite a time making up his mind. There hasn't been a single girl who has come out to stay at Gundooee who wasn't quite irresistibly beautiful and charming,' stated Mannie with pride.

Then it must be *her* that he didn't like, thought Lindsay sadly. Her, in particular, if it wasn't all women.

She sighed inwardly. Life was not going to be very easy if her employer had taken a dislike to her at the outset! Things weren't going to be easy in any respect, come to that. Lindsay was just beginning to realise how abysmally ignorant she was of all things pertaining to station life. This heat, for instance, when it was only just spring in Sydney. How much hotter would, or could, it get, when the summer really developed? Already her cotton shirt was clinging to her shoulders as she pushed the laden trolley through a long passage, across a narrow covered-way, to the kitchen block; through another gauze door, and into a large, surprisingly modern kitchen, warm in spite of the big whirring fans and the hum of an air-conditioning unit.

Sibbie and Bella were there already, chattering like magpies in the laundry off the far end of the room, giggling together as they washed the cotton overalls they had been wearing yesterday, and squeezed the soapsuds into amusing shapes with artful black fingers.

Every morning, when they came up to the homestead, Mannie would give them a clean overall to put on, and while they were waiting for the lunch dishes, they would wash the garments they had worn on the previous day. Then they would hang them out on the line, where the hot sun soon dried them, drawing out the bright, treasured colour in the process. When the colours became disappointingly faded from the constant washings, Sibbie and Bella would lose interest in the washing of their overalls, and become careless. Then Mannie would have to send them to the store for some new ones.

'This youngfella missus name belonga Lindsay,' Mannie was telling them now, and they clutched the wrung-out washing to their drooping bosoms, screeching with mirth as though Lindsay was quite the funniest name on earth. Their smiles were wide and beautifully white and unmistakably friendly, and Lindsay found her own mouth curving into a warm, answering greeting before following Mannie back into the kitchen.

'Shall I help with the washing-up?' she asked shyly.

'No, my dear, I wouldn't start that if I were you. It's best to leave them to the things they can do well, I find, and believe me, you'll have plenty to occupy your time once you settle in. I'm just going to get Rod's scones ready for his tucker-bag, and if I were you I'd unpack your things, and then go down to the store and check-in today's supplies.'

'Yes, of course. Just one thing, Mannie. I'd like to let my—er—cousin know that I've arrived safely, if that's possible.' Lindsay couldn't help sounding as dubious as she felt about that.

Gundooee seemed like the end of the world—or the deserted centre of it!—and short of sending a message by one of the crows that cawed hardily on the tankstand outside, there seemed little prospect of communication.

The city, and her life there, had already taken on the fragile substance of a dream. The present was the only reality —the drumming heat, the sweltering outbuildings, the rambling homestead with its green lawns, dim, air-conditioned interior, gauzed verandas; the brown, smiling, wrinkled face of the dear old lady here beside her; the suppressed giggling of Sibbie and Bella in the laundry beyond; the disapproving assessment of Rod Bennett's critical, unfriendly eyes—all these were real, involving her in a need for present thought and action.

The aunt and uncle, the spiteful Carleen, that hypocritical photographer, (whatever Rod Bennett might think of her, at least he wasn't hypocritical enough to *pretend*!) had all become faint, distant figures in her shadowed, unhappy past. Already she was finding that the miles that now lay between them had caused a subtle alteration in her relationship with those people. No longer had they the power to hurt her, as they formerly had. Almost, she could feel sorry for them, and the motives which drove them, and coloured their associations with their fellows. The jealousies, the comparisons, the petty quarrels that resulted, were washed into nothingness by the great blue vastness of the sky outside the window of the Gundooee kitchen. That sky seemed to dome itself right over its own world, shutting it off from the 'elsewhere'. It was a world that was inhabited by a comparative handful of people, forced by their very intimacy with each other to live by a different standard altogether, because the horizon they shared was frighteningly vast, lonely, humbling in its very magnitude.

'I don't suppose it's possible to send a message?' she said

again.

Mannie turned in surprise, laughing with genuine amusement.

'Of course it's possible!' she told Lindsay. 'We're very much in touch here, really, you know. You just write out what you want to say, and I'll send a telegram for you over the transceiver—that's what we call the modern form of pedal wireless, Lindsay, because they hardly ever use pedal sets any more. I don't suppose you needed them at Batlow, did you? Ah well, here we depend on them for almost everything—telegrams and messages, and to summon the Flying Doctor or the Air Ambulance, and of course we have the galah session, and the school of the air.'

'School? You mean, proper lessons?' Lindsay looked her surprise.

'Oh yes, proper lessons, just the same as if the children were in class together. Each pupil has his own call-sign, you see, and one by one the children are called in by the School-of-the-Air teacher. They participate in discussions, have questions and answers just as in a normal class—they even learn poetry and do plays. They have correspondence lessons by post, too, of course.'

'But that's marvellous!' Lindsay was impressed. 'And the galah session? Was that what you called it?'

'Yes, the galah—or sometimes it's termed the magpie. Now that's different again, and mostly for adults—housewives, in fact. They have an open session at a certain time each day, and all the women from near and far join in, swapping gossip and bits of news. There's nothing private about the Outback, Lindsay, even when you're miles from your nearest neighbour! Everyone knows what everyone else is doing, and the galah session is largely responsible. We call it that after those flocks of chattering pink and grey parrots, and believe me, the noise of human voices, the static, the calling-in of the signs, can sometimes be as noisy as any flock of birds! Even the tiniest detail can seem a meaty piece of gossip on the galah. It's the true bush telegraph!'

'They—they won't have heard about *me*?' asked Lindsay diffidently.

Poor Lindsay! Her ideas about bush life were being shattered every minute.

'Oh yes, they will—if not today, then tomorrow. Everyone knew that Gundooee was getting a new book-keeper. And very soon they will know that not only did the new book-keeper arrive, but that he turned out to be a girl instead of a man.' Mannie chuckled irrepressibly. '*That* should set them by the ears!'

Lindsay shuddered.

'W-will they know that Mr. Bennett was very angry when he found out?' she asked somewhat dismally.

Mannie's wrinkled face was still creased with humour.

'*Was* he angry?' she countered mildly. 'I don't think so. Rod is a very controlled person, and doesn't give away his feelings very easily. He has to be controlled, Lindsay, being in charge of a large number of people of such varying types, you see. It's a position of great responsibility, Rod's. He's got to know how to do everything he expects his men to do, and be able to do it better, so that they respect him. And he's got to be a bit of a psychologist, too. He often says it's part of his job to know what his men are thinking, almost before they know it themselves, and that way he can keep the path smooth, anticipating little troubles, and ironing them out before they can grow into big ones. I must say he's very good at doing that—almost uncanny, in fact—but on the other hand, it's very difficult to tell what's going on in his own mind. He's adept at concealing his feelings, and that gives him an immediate advantage in dealing with the grievances of others. All his men respect him, and depend upon his judgment to a greater or lesser extent, and his own temperament gives them encouragement to confide in him. I'd be very surprised to hear that he was angry—and in front of a mere girl, too!'

Mannie's paragon could apparently do no wrong in *her* eyes!

Lindsay swallowed, remembering.

'He was angry, all right,' she asserted feelingly.

'You were probably tired and a little overwrought, and imagined it,' Mannie told her comfortingly. 'In any case, although *you* will have been mentioned on the galah, nobody would dare to discuss Rod or his affairs so frivolously. They have far too much respect for him to do such a thing. They'll only have heard that Mr. Dutten turned out to be a Miss, and after all, what harm is there in them hearing that? It was a most unfortunate misunderstanding, nothing more.'

'Er—yes—most unfortunate.'

Lindsay moved her slender shoulders as if thereby she could ease her miserable load of guilt. If only Mannie knew! If only Mannie could guess how little misunderstanding there had really been! If only she could know how calculated had been Lindsay's deception from the outset! And if *he* should ever suspect—well, he'd pack her out of here on his very own plane before she could even say 'Ned Kelly', and it didn't take very long to say *that*!

'The message, dear?' came Mannie's gentle interruption to her thoughts. 'And you can follow it up with a more detailed letter on mail-day. Right?'

'Yes, thank you, Mannie.'

What a kind and helpful person Mannie was, reflected Lindsay to herself as she completed the unpacking of her meagre wardrobe later.

Mannie had told her that she used once to be governess to the Bennett family when they were small. Rod had been the youngest of three brothers, and when his parents died he had invited Mannie, who was by then widowed and struggling to maintain herself on a small pension, to return to Gundooee to act as his housekeeper. She had been grateful to accept. The old days spent at the station held happy memories for her, and now that she was in real need of a home and companionship, she could think of no place she would rather be.

There was little enough that she could do for Rod in return, she had confided to Lindsay, but he never allowed her to feel beholden in any way. Indeed, the reverse was the case. He acted as though Mannie herself was doing him a great favour in just being there, making her own quiet contribution to the running of the property. He had actually *wanted* Mannie to return to Gundooee, thought Lindsay wanly, even though she happened to be a woman. He had wanted—and invited—her.

He hadn't wanted Lindsay though. He hadn't exactly invited her, either, she had to admit. In a way she had invited herself, Lindsay supposed. She had gone into this with her eyes open, except that she had imagined that all country places were the same. *That* had been her big mistake. She had been thankful to leave the city behind her, had revelled in the scenery over the Mountains and through the Central West, had actually enjoyed herself until the train angled off into the 'never-never', (or what seemed to Lindsay's inexperienced observation to be the 'never-never'!) and at the end of that frightening and lonely journey, Emmadanda had been a surprise, and not a pleasant one.

Gundooee now seemed like an oasis in the desert of her hopes. She knew instinctively that she could be happy here the very moment she stepped out of that plane. Even the peculiar gleam in the eyes of all those men couldn't detract from the welcome in their smiles, could it? They had been the bush friends, about to greet her with their kindly voices, only something had spoilt it all, something had prevented them. Some*one*. The man who hadn't had a smile for her. The man whose grey eyes had held no strange gleam. Rod Bennett himself. And he had turned out to be the Boss.

Lindsay placed her nylon tights carefully in one of the big mahogany drawers, and mourned her luck. Why had she to run into such a man as he? Things could have been so different, except for him. Instead of a new, happy, 'bush' atmosphere, he made her feel virtually stateless, unwanted. She had cut the other ties that bound in order to come to Gundooee, and now the manager was going to try to freeze her out with his cold words of censure, his chilly grey gaze, his thoroughly unfriendly attitude, his *Miss* Dutten! Why, he had already refused even to let her have that dear little cottage that the book-keeper had always had. And it wasn't because she was a woman, whatever he liked to pretend. Hadn't Mannie told her that he *liked* girls, as a rule? All those lovely Brisbane belles—he must like those girls, mustn't he, to invite them out here to Gundooee for the Races just as he must like Mannie to have asked her to live here.

He liked those other girls, and he liked Mannie, too. It was Lindsay he *didn't* like! His antipathy was almost a living thing between them, and there was little that Lindsay could do about that.

She stood up, smoothed down her denim skirt and walked over to the mirror, gazed wistfully at her reflection.

What she saw was strangely depressing—a slender, girlish figure in a white shirt, a schoolgirl outfit!—guileless green eyes, wounded and apprehensive; coltish bare legs and arms too skinny to ever be seductive; an innocent mouth; bright brown, unmanageable hair that refused to be coaxed into a more elegant coiffure.

No, she certainly was no belle, but an ugly duckling for sure. And as for those clothes——! Clothes didn't make a beauty, but they certainly must help! If only she still had some of Carleen's, they might have helped a little bit towards a more sophisticated image.

She had so wanted to be liked, to find herself among friends. She *had* found some, too—Mannie, with her wrinkled, gentle face, Sibbie and Bella with their watermelon smiles and gay giggles, all those men who had surrounded her when she stepped out of the plane.

All except for one person alone.

Slumping disconsolately down upon the bed, unable to understand herself or the reason for her own misery, Lindsay admitted to her chagrin how unkind Fate could be— admitted that the very person whose friendship she would *really* like to have was the man whose antagonism was so chillingly obvious.

Rod Bennett.

CHAPTER 5

LINDSAY got up early next morning, mainly because she could not sleep. Depression gripped her, but she could also admit to an underlying determination to make a good impression on her boss at the first opportunity.

Sun-up was preluded by the whining and whimpering of the dogs in the settlement down at the creek. Their barking reached Lindsay's ears even before the first traditional crowing of the cock in the fowl-run or the shrill chattering of the birds which nested in the shrubs and saplings outside the window. She slipped from her bed and padded quietly out on to the veranda.

The birds' noise seemed to be concentrated around the banks of the big ground-tank beyond the garden. In the first faint light, Lindsay could not see the birds themselves, only the raised edges of the tank and the silhouette of the windmill that towered at one end. The sails were stirring lazily in the breath of dawn. The shaft of warm air from the plains could hardly be called a breeze, and was not sufficiently strong to blow the sails into revolutions, and the pump-rod groaned every now and then—a deep, baritone interruption to the trilling and cheeping of the birds—as though frustrated by its own inactivity.

A splash at the far end of the tank sent the birds chittering away into the trees. Lindsay pressed her nose against the gauze and peered out curiously.

Someone was swimming in the tank.

She could just discern a dark head moving, arms cleaving the water with long, easy, powerful strokes that scarcely disturbed the surface. That head, and the foot-splash, told her that whoever the swimmer was, he was certainly moving fast, up to one end, then back, then up again, without apparent effort.

268

After a time the figure stopped swimming, climbed out of the water and towelled itself perfunctorily. Then it came towards the house.

Lindsay waited only long enough to perceive that the dawn swimmer was none other than Rod Bennett himself, clad in brief black trunks, his tanned body glistening with wetness, the towel that had only half performed its task slung carelessly around his neck.

As he approached, she turned quietly and hastened back to her room. It would be awful if he caught her spying on him!

After she had dressed, she walked down towards the store. In the pocket of her denim skirt she carried the keys of both the store and the little cottage. The manager had given them to her the previous afternoon with an off-hand suggestion that she had better 'get started', and Lindsay had wondered, as she eyed the rows of unfamiliar bottles, cans, packs, and tins, the assortment of clothing and bedding, the drugs and chemicals, just where one *did* start, and how!

She had locked the store again hastily, and had gone instead to the cottage, relieved to find herself in the more familiar world of accounts, receipts, and statements.

Today she planned an early assault on the problem of that store. There was little to be gained by putting off the evil moment any longer. After all, it was possible that someone might ask for something at any time, and she would feel very stupid if she had not at least familiarised herself with the layout.

Lindsay hummed under her breath as she walked, her depression gone. There was something about this fresh, Outback morning that induced optimism, banished apprehension. As she neared the station-hands' quarters, she caught the sound of whistling, and several varieties of singing, together with the splash and splutter of noisy ablutions, and as she passed the building, she realised that these sounds all emanated from the row of shower cubicles. She was relieved to note that whereas yesterday the showers had been open for all to see, pieces of sacking had now been nailed roughly to the bottom half of each cubicle, secured by hooks of fencing wire, so that the lower portion of the ablutionist's anatomy was effectively screened.

Even so, Lindsay went scarlet with embarrassment as, too late, she realised that she had walked right into the men's bathing session. Head down, she scuttled along the row, obtaining, as she ran, a cineramic impression of flailing arms, dripping heads, muscular shoulders, grunts, splutters, whistles.

A sidelong glimpse of a freckled back and thatch of red hair that could only belong to Bluey—Mickie's face grinning cheekily over the hessian—Herb's toothless mouth agape as she scudded past—Artie's baritone from the final cubicle—

'I been chasin' sheilas for more than half me life, but seldom have I found one I'd ask ter be me wife,' Artie was rumbling enthusiastically as she flew past.

'*Don't* you try ter leave me, *don't* you try ter run——'

The united chorus of the refrain reached Lindsey's ears as she panted round the far corner. The occupants of all the cubicles had joined in for that bit, and the subsequent laughter followed her as she plunged her hand into her skirt-pocket and brought out the key of the store.

Inside, she slammed the door and stood for a moment, slightly shaken by her experience, then, after recovering her breath, she began to check over all the things that were in the room.

Lindsay had no idea what some of the articles were. After gazing around with a certain amount of self-exasperation at her own ignorance, she decided that the only system she could adopt which would make for sensible handling would be to regroup all the supplies which she did know along one lot of shelves, and place all the ones which were unfamiliar at the other end of the place. She would then be able to surreptitiously to enlist the aid of one of the men, and by the time Rod Bennett turned up, she would be *au fait* with her domain. There was a hope in Lindsay's mind that he never *would* turn up! After all, that was what he hired a book-keeper for, wasn't it? Maybe he would just leave her to do things in her own way, and with the men's help she would manage to bungle along somehow. Lindsay found herself praying fervently that this was the way it would be!

She had piled the heaps of khaki clothing together in a corner, sorted blankets and bolts of bright cotton materials, and was in the process of dragging a couple of rolled leather machinery-belts across the floor—they were surprisingly heavy, and covered with a grease preservative which added to their slippery state—when the door opened and a shadow darkened the entrance. Lindsay straightened, turned to face the bow-legged, lounging figure that now sauntered inside.

Artie's grin was faintly self-conscious. He cleared his throat noisily.

'G'day, Lindsay. A beaut mornin', eh?'

'Er—good morning. Artie, isn't it? I'm just beginning to put the right names to the right faces, I think.'

'Bang on, this time, then. Artie's me monicker, true enough. Williams is the other bit. Artie Williams.'

Lindsay paused uncertainly. She had not been properly introduced to any of the men yet, and now that one of them was actually here, announcing himself, perhaps she should shake hands. *Did* one shake hands out here in the Outback, or didn't one? They all seemed such casual, friendly people that Lindsay could not be sure. It was better not to take chances, anyway—better not to risk offending.

She wiped her hand down the side of her denim skirt, leaving a disastrous trail of belt-grease, and held it out in Artie's direction.

'How do you do,' said Lindsay formally.

Artie blinked, but only for a moment, before he gripped her hand in a crushing grasp and shook it vigorously.

'Reckon I'm O.K.,' he told her on a note of surprise that this slender, rather lost-looking sheila could possibly be concerned as to his present state of health. 'How about you?' he added, with commendable presence of mind.

'I'm O.K. too.'

Lindsay smiled, and Art smiled, and then they both laughed, quite uproariously.

'That's that, then,' observed Artie with some relief. 'Yer gone and got grease on yer skirt now, Lindsay.' He poked a gnarled finger in the direction of the smear.

'Oh dear, so I have!' she wailed. 'It's my only skirt, too.'

'Reckon there's somethink 'ere for that, though. There's somethink 'ere for *everythink*, supposed to be.' The station-hand began to go through the assortment of bottles on the shelf. 'Yep, 'ere we are—Kum-Kleen—I reckon that'll shift it.'

He handed her a stoppered bottle with a red and white label.

'Yer shouldn't of 'ad it *there*, though, Lindsay. Not right beside that belly-ache mixture. And look where yer've got the strychnine for them dingo baits! Good Gawd Almighty! If Rod sees any of them things mixed up with the stummick stuff, 'e'll 'ave yer hide, I'm tellin' yer! 'E can't afford fer folk ter be swallerin' the wrong stuff away out 'ere, yer know, Lindsay. The Flyin' Doctor ain't a ruddy miracle man, quick though 'e is when we need 'im.'

'*I* didn't put them there,' Lindsay hastened to point out in self-defence. 'I was just beginning to sort things out, Artie, and I haven't touched the bottles yet.'

'Well, they ought ter be locked up, and clocked in on that chart, see. It must've been that Lowney feller then—the last bloke. 'E was on the booze somethink awful this last while.'

'Oh, I see.' Lindsay had wondered about the previous book-keeper. 'Was he—er—dismissed?'

Artie shook his head.

' 'E would of been,' he asserted darkly, 'only 'e ran off with a well-sinker's wife first. Kind of took Rod on the 'op.'

'Oh.' Fancy anyone managing to take the psychic Rod Bennett on the hop! Lindsay was aware of a tiny thrust of respect for her predecessor, booze and all. 'Surely he must have been very upset—the well-sinker, I mean?'

' 'E was flamin' crazy at first'—Art spoke with retrospective relish—'but 'e soon got sort of used to it. 'E's got 'is sights set on a little filly out at Peperina since then. 'Ere, give me that cloth and I'll rub it for yer.'

Before she could reply, Artie had taken the cleaning fluid from her, splashed it liberally on to some wadding, and rubbed clumsily at her skirt with blunt-fingered, awkward hands. He appeared absorbed in his task, completely unabashed at his necessary proximity.

'There y'are! That's fixed it.' He handed back the Kum-Kleen, dropped the wadding in the rubbish tin, and grinned engagingly. Lindsay smiled back, then retreated quickly to the other side of the counter at the answering gleam in his eye. It was the self-same gleam that had been present in all those eyes that morning—was it only two mornings ago?—when she had alighted from the plane. All eyes but one pair, that is.

'Er—thank you, Artie. I'm very grateful,' she said from her place of instinctive sanctuary. 'Now, is there something I can do for you? Something you came in to get?'

Lindsay's direct question produced quite an astounding effect upon Art. The gleam in his eye faded instantly, to be replaced by a look of acute embarrassment. Colour gathered slowly under his rugged tan, deepening to such a rich plum shade that Lindsay wondered, in quick alarm, if the man was sickening for some sort of physical fit. He took off his wide, battered felt hat, wiped his forehead with a rough palm, scratched his ear uncomfortably, shifted his feet in their heavy boots, slammed the hat on again, and turned to her with a sudden show of iron determination.

'I reckon I never came for somethink in the store, Lindsay,' he muttered doggedly.

'For what, then, Artie?' Lindsay asked, intrigued.

'I came to get a kiss, that's what.'

The admission was delivered in such a strangled, choking, but determined tone that Lindsay was asking herself if she could possibly have heard aright.

'Did you say—you did say—a *kiss*?' she repeated, half startled, half incredulous.

'Yeah—a kiss,' Artie reiterated with a slight indication of returning courage.

'Yes, that's what I th-thought you said.' Lindsay's voice was weak. She sat down heavily on the pile of blankets.

There was silence for a moment, broken only by the sound of Art's still-restricted breathing processes.

'Well—will yer?' he asked, diffidently.

'I—I don't think—no, Artie, I'm afraid not,' returned

Lindsay firmly.

'*Please*, Lindsay. Just one.'

'No, Artie, not one. Couldn't you go over to—to Peperina, maybe? Like the—er—the well-sinker?' she suggested helpfully, touched by the man's air of defeat.

Artie shook his head dejectedly.

'It ain't the same,' he said dismally. 'Yer see, Lindsay'—he gave her a direct, pleading look—'it's gotter be *you*. Nobody else will do.'

'Me?' Her eyes rounded. 'But why *me*?'

Artie scuffed self-consciously at the floor-boards with the toe of his boot.

' 'Cos we're bettin' on it, see, Lindsay.'

Lindsay's eyes, round before, were now like saucers.

'*Betting* on it! Do you mean, betting on—er—on *me*?'

'Yeah, that's right.'

'Good gracious!' Her mind was racing, implications jostling with one another for pride of place.

'First bloke home collects the kitty,' Artie explained now, earnestly. 'I reckoned this was me chance, Lindsay, when I seen yer comin' in 'ere. I didn't mean ter startle yer, honest. I wasn't goin' ter *pounce* on yer, or anythink like that. Even now, if yer won't do it, well, yer won't, and that's me out. I'd most certainly 'ave liked ter collect, all the same.' His deep voice was wistful.

'And if it isn't you, will one of the others try?'

'You bet yer, Lindsay, they'll try. I don't know how or when or where, but they'll *try*—Herb and Mickie and Blue and Shorty.'

'And if *you* get a kiss, then they'll stop trying?' Lindsay was assembling her thoughts.

'That's it.'

'If *you* get a kiss, that will be the end of it?'

'That'll be the end of it.'

'Once and for ever?'

'Once an' fer all, Lindsay—you can bet on that!'

'I don't think so, Artie. I think there's enough betting going on around here without me starting,' Lindsay was driven to point out smilingly.

Artie grinned, unabashed. 'Gee, Lindsay, you're a little beaut! Does that mean you'll do it?'

'I'll do it, Artie. I don't think I have much choice.'

'Except who *with*,' he elucidated with some humility.

'I'd like you to be the one,' said Lindsay gently.

Artie scratched his ear, caught once more in a transfixing agony of embarrassment.

'I ain't much of a hand,' he mumbled apologetically.

'Never mind,' comforted Lindsay. 'I'll do all I can to help. But how will the others know? Will they just take your word for it?'

'Not them. That's the other thing. That's why I reckoned on this bein' a good time ter take the bull by the 'orns,' Artie was explaining. 'Cook's gettin' breakfast, and they're all out there waitin' around fer the tucker-bell, so if we was ter go outside——'

'I see. Let's get it over, then, Artie, shall we?'

Lindsay got off the bale of blankets and walked to the door with resolution in her step.

'I'll go yer splits, Lindsay, if yer like? How about that?'

'No, thank you, Art,' she declined with dignity. 'I don't wish to make off the deal, only to end it. It's as much for my sake as yours.'

'You're a beaut, a little beaut.' He pulled the door shut behind him, locked it, passed her the key. 'Not a word, though, eh, Lindsay? Not to Mannie, or to Rod? Rod, most of all. 'E'd skin us alive if 'e knew.'

'Not a word to anyone,' Lindsay found herself promising with due solemnity and a sense of complete unreality, as she and Artie walked together over the bare, smooth ground in the warm, early hush of that Outback dawn, until they were within sight and range of the clinking sounds of the hut-cook's breakfast pans, and in full view of the men who were hanging about waiting to eat that breakfast.

Lindsay and Artie stopped and faced each other.

'I ain't much,' warned Artie once more. He was very red indeed.

'If it's only for a bet, it doesn't matter, does it,' Lindsay reminded him encouragingly, 'just as long as it's a kiss.'

Strange that she should not mind! Strange that she should be the one to impart confidence and consolation to this big, awkward, inarticulate bushman! But then perhaps it was because she could sense in Artie a fundamental kindness, a basic decency, a hesitant humility and honesty that were oddly endearing qualities in a work-roughened, tough-living 'outbacker', that she didn't mind him being the *one*. Artie was nice, and Artie was on the level. If Lindsay hadn't agreed, he'd have been willing to leave it at that.

She sent him a warm smile.

'You're a decent kid, Lindsay.'

He put his hands on her shoulders, and gave her a quick peck on the cheek, and Lindsay, suddenly afraid that the gesture had not even been noticed by the men lounging around near the cook-house, found herself putting her arms right around Art's sun-seamed neck and squeezing hard.

They might as well do the thing properly, she told herself. It was better to leave no doubt at all in those other men's minds that a kiss had been exchanged, because she did not want to be pestered any more over this wretched bet! She wanted it settled, once and for all, as Artie had promised it would be, and that was why she hugged Art just as hard as she could, and even gave him a return kiss near the side of his stubbled chin.

That should do it! she told herself, noting with a sense of satisfaction that the men outside the cook-house were now standing immobile in their tracks, as though turned to stone by the unexpected scene they had witnessed. The conversation had ceased. The silence was so complete that it seemed to Lindsay as though the very birds had ceased to sing. Even the cook, who had stopped clattering his tin plates and pannikins about inside the cook-house and had come to stand in the doorway, suddenly stopped wiping his hands on the front of his butcher's apron and left his fingers dangling stupidly in mid-air.

Yes, thought Lindsay with gratification, *that* should finish the whole silly affair! The effect on the bystanders had been dramatic indeed.

She opened her mouth to say something light-hearted to

Artie—she *felt* light-hearted, as though she had successfully disposed of a potentially unpleasant business—and then she closed her lips again, because Artie's eyes weren't looking at her at all. They were centred on something right behind her, a little to her left, and they held an oddly riveted expression, every bit as dramatic in its intensity as the silent tableau down beside the cook-house.

Lindsay turned to see what could possibly have captured Artie's attention so completely, and stiffened as visibly as though she had been Lot's wife turning into a pillar of salt.

Rod Bennett was standing not far away, his feet in their heeled stockman's boots planted a little apart on the dusty ground, his brown hands linked casually into the plaited hide belt that held up his moleskins. That was the *only* casual thing about him, that stance!

Lindsay felt the impact of his shrewd grey gaze rake her with a force that was almost physical. She took an involuntary step backwards, bumped into the transfixed Artie, who seemed to recover his senses at the contact and shambled off towards the cook-house as fast as he could.

Rod Bennett ground his heel in the dust with a curious sort of savagery, turned without a word, and went the other way. Lindsay, still encased in her own immobility, stared after him until he was out of sight. Then she forced her tottering limbs in the direction of the homestead.

Breakfast tasted like sawdust that morning! Lindsay chewed her way through chop and egg with wooden concentration, aware of the relish with which her employer, to her right, disposed of his own much larger helping. She swallowed hot tea automatically, folded her napkin thankfully when the meal was at an end.

She might have known, of course, that a man like Rod Bennett would not allow such a facile escape!

'I wish to see you in my office, please, Miss Dutten,' he announced firmly when they finally left the table.

'Certainly, Mr. Bennett.' Lindsay tried to match his calmness, but failed miserably. She actually felt sick with dread. She could see her dismissal looming up to meet her, and felt powerless to prevent it.

If only she could explain! If only he could be made to understand what a light-hearted, meaningless, *silly* little act it had all been. Like a schoolgirl dare, almost. But Rod Bennett didn't look the sort who would have any patience with schoolgirls or their dares, just as he hadn't with his own men's inveterate inclination to gamble on any and every incident that presented itself. 'He'd skin us alive,' Artie had said, and Lindsay had promised not to tell. If she told, she would maybe be able to make Rod Bennett understand the harmlessness of that one little kiss, but in doing so she would forfeit her friendship with all the men, and in her capacity as store-keeper she would be coming into contact with them a good deal more than with the aloof and unfriendly Mr. Bennett.

No, to tell would be unthinkable. And yet *not* to tell meant the permanent banishment of all those things for which Lindsay found herself wistfully longing—the warmth of a grey-eyed welcome, the fond glance of respect, the caressing comfort of a true affection that was reserved exclusively for Mannie. Lindsay longed for the contribution she intended to make to Gundooee to be recognised in the same way. She wanted to be *wanted*, longed to be able to call Gundooee her home, the way Mannie could. Lindsay knew, as she followed the big, loping figure in the direction of his office, that this man was capable of all those endearing qualities that so attracted her, because he gave them all, unstintingly, to Mannie. How nice to bask in the sunshine of his approval, the way the old lady did, thought Lindsay enviously. If she, Lindsay, could just enjoy that approval, too, she would not ask for more. After all, she wasn't one of those lovely, sophisticated Brisbane Belles, with pretty clothes and loads of poise and a fund of amusing repartee. She was only simple Lindsay Dutten, longing for a home and a welcome, and that was as much as one could expect when one had flyaway hair, gangling limbs, an uncertain manner, and a skirt that still reeked of Artie's Kum-Kleen!

The interview only took a few minutes. Just a few, measly minutes, Lindsay told herself as she reeled down the passage and out on to the veranda. A few measly minutes to condemn you out of hand and shred your hopes into little pieces.

'I have no intention of discussing in detail the unsavoury scene I witnessed earlier, Miss Dutten. It did not come as any great surprise to me, however.' A jaded sigh. 'Like women in the shearing-sheds, I knew you added up to a packet of trouble the minute you stepped off that plane. And yet I hoped—I thought——' He was pacing angrily, visibly put out.

'*What* did you think, hope, Mr. Bennett?' Lindsay had asked humbly. There was something faintly encouraging in that slight hesitation in a man who was obviously not given to hesitations of any sort.

'Never mind what I thought,' he growled deeply. 'It seems I was wrong, anyway. But'—a disgusted glance—'on your *second* day—so short a time——'

'It wasn't like that, Mr. Bennett, truly it wasn't!' How awful to have to suffer like this, not even to be able to *say*, to have to go on letting him think—oh!

'I saw with my own eyes how it was, thank you, Miss Dutten. Explanations would be futile, in the circumstances.' How cold those grey eyes, how chilly that disdainful mouth! It seemed an effort for him even to speak to her, as though the sight of her was unbearably distasteful. He forced himself to proceed. 'Obviously, there is one thing, and one thing only, which as an employer I must ascertain. You were an agreeable party, Miss Dutten? A willing and agreeable party?'

Lindsay could only stare, mesmerised. Inside, she was hollow, unable to think.

'Come now, Miss Dutten, you can surely see that this is something I have to know? If you were coerced, compromised in any way, then it's up to me to discipline my men.'

'I was willing, Mr. Bennett.' Lindsay heard her own voice dully, echoing in a vacuum of despair.

'Yes, I thought so. That's how it appeared to me, too.' For some reason, his broad shoulders appeared to slump. Just for a moment, his eyes were a different sort of grey—wounded, vulnerable almost. And then the chill, the self-discipline, were back.

He doesn't like being wrong, thought Lindsay shrewdly to herself. He doesn't like to be wrong about anything, and his pride is hurt, and that's why he looked sort of *defeated* a moment ago.

'In that case I shall of course leave the matter where it is. But as for *you*—I shall have to have your categoric assurance that such a thing will not occur again. If it does, you'll go!'

'Oh, it won't, it *won't*, Mr. Bennett, honestly. It was only once—I mean—I wish I could explain——'

'Useless, in any case, when I have the evidence of my own eyes,' he reminded her quellingly. 'You may go, Miss Dutten.'

'Yes, Mr. Bennett. I'd just like to say——'

'You may *go*, Miss Dutten,' he repeated impatiently. 'I don't intend to waste more time talking about it. Just see that you keep out of the men's way as much as possible—and mine, too,' he added forcibly. 'It's as bad as having women in the sheds, damn it!' He was still muttering gruffly to himself as she scuttled for the door.

Lindsay saw little of him, indeed, after that. Certainly he was courteous when he came in for meals, but there was that way he had of being distantly polite that told Lindsay she was stateless, unaccepted, still very much of an intruder, who had brought with her nothing but unwelcome complications in his eyes.

Rod Bennett always made breakfast as brief an affair as possible. Hair still wet from his morning swim, brown throat exposed in his open-necked khaki shirt, he would favour Mannie with his warm, grey, affectionate regard, help her into her chair with a tanned, capable hand that could be curiously gentle, and give her that slow, endearing smile. Then he would turn to Lindsay, and the warm light would fade from his eyes, leaving them cold and, somehow, *careful*.

'Good morning, Miss Dutten,' was what she always got, accompanied by the merest curl of the mouth, a grimace that couldn't even be called a half smile.

With the other men, things were different. They were instantly and openly friendly, beguiling in their rough, outspoken way. She liked them for their cheerful, casual grins that lit their weathered faces whenever she appeared; their teasing, and their fun.

They reorganised the store for her; showed her how to work the transceiver; how to make a fly-veil with bobbing corks to keep those buzzing little pests at bay while she worked; how to tell when it might rain because the birds were flying low, or what the morrow would be like by the sunset. They taught her about the wild life around her, the bush mice, the marsupials, the eagles nesting in the mulga, the rabbits in their sandy, many-holed burrows, the honey-eaters seeking out the scrub blossoms, the path of the wild bees.

She learned that Sibbie and Bella had husbands, down there at the creek. They were the two aboriginal stockmen who had been at the plane the day she arrived, and their names were Jimmy and Tommo. Down at the gunyahs, she befriended the merry little children who ran about, fat-tummied and skinny-limbed, laughing widely whenever she appeared. They wore wispy rags, sometimes not even those, and the smell of dogs and goanna fat hung about them as they played down by the creek baiting yabbies, or dug for grubs under the bark of the trees, or simply ran about, pelting each other with quandongs, skipping with an old rope in the shade of a spotted gum, or throwing their home-made bubberas, warming the boomerangs first with all the earnestness and concentration of their forebears.

When their parents yelled 'All-about, quickfella, youse lot!' they would drop their playthings and run to get their tucker—civilised, station tucker, with plentiful meat and damper and johnny-cakes made with the white man's flour, now an accepted part of their life, just as were the fragments of white man's clothing which they wore, and the much-prized cheap ornamental combs which they stuck in their oiled hair.

Lindsay discovered that perfume of any sort was a very quick way to these simple people's hearts, and that their spending money—or 'finger' money as they sometimes called it—was often spent on hair-oil, highly scented shaving lotions (which Lindsay suspected found its way to their heads also!), and the ubiquitous combs and beads. Josie, one of the young teenage girls who sometimes came to help her mother in the house, had shown Lindsay a whole dillybag full of such treasures and trinkets. Laying them reverently on the ground between them, she had uncorked the stoppers on the small bottles of oils and lotions, sniffing with a properly ceremonial dignity, and explaining to Lindsay that this was the way to keep him 'smellum plenty strongfella, eh!', whereas the scent would soon 'go walkabout' if used in the traditional manner. Reeling from the heady, concentrated reek that assailed her nostrils, Lindsay conceded the point, and could only conclude that the cheap perfume had undergone some sort of horrid chemical metamorphosis through Josie's frequent exposures to the air and heat—or perhaps through sheer old age!

As stockmen, Jimmy and Tommo were a valued part of the Gundooee work-out, and their superb native horsemanship was evident even to Lindsay's unknowledgeable eye as they cut out steers at the dusty yards to which Mickie had obligingly driven her in the station jeep, expressly to watch the show. She marvelled at the control they displayed, both of the cattle and of their own mounts, because they made such exceedingly careless pictures in the saddle. Their bodies seemed to sag nervelessly in their faded shirts and felted trousers, battered hats crammed down on black glistening foreheads, Jimmy's broad nose and grizzled beard jutting beneath the brim, Tommo, with his filthy but ever-present pipe clenched unlit in his teeth. Even when the stock-horses whirled without warning in the wake of a scrubber, their bodies remained limp and uncaring, but tenaciously glued to that saddle, as though they and the horses were acting through the medium of a single mind.

'They make it look so *easy*,' breathed Lindsay, who had not ridden a horse since the podgy Taffy of her tender years.

'Well, it's not,' Mickie assured her laughingly. 'This is my third year here as a jackaroo—Shorty's, too—and they can still run rings around us, and most of the other men. Rod's the only one on the place who can rival them at that game— not surprising, really, since Jimmy's own father taught him all his horsemanship almost as soon as he could walk.'

'Jimmy's father? I hadn't realised that Jimmy had been here all his life. I thought, from what Mannie has told me, that the aborigines came and went on walkabouts, and never stayed as long as a whole generation in one place.'

'It's difficult to generalise, Lindsay, because there are so many different types among them, and a great many these days are of mixed blood, and adopt varying genetic attributes of both sides of such assimilations. Jimmy's great-grand-father was supposed to be an Afghan, one of the camel-drivers from further out, in the days before the Bitumen and the railway. He married a full-blooded aboriginal girl, and Jimmy's father, in his turn, married the half-caste daughter of a local storeman, so there was a bit of a mix-up all round.'

'And so they put down roots? No more wanderlust?'

Mickie nodded. 'You could say that I suppose. As de-velopment spread, and the seasonal ebb and flow of nature's bounty is counteracted by regular supplies of food and clothing from the stations' stores, there isn't the same need to go chasing off on a survival course from time to time, either.'

'No, I see what you mean. Which reminds me, talking of stores, tomorrow must be mail-day again, isn't it?'

'That's right.' Mickie slid off the tail-board of the jeep where he had been perching to drink a pannikin of tea, threw the dregs in the dust, and tucked his own mug, along with Lindsay's, into a corner among the assortment of junk that littered the back of the vehicle. He grinned, hitched his trousers, and jerked a thumb in the direction of the drafting-out operations. 'Smoko is over, then, Lindsay. Shorty will take you back, the lucky blighter. Rod said I was to take his place, and send him home with you. O.K.?'

'Yes, of course. And thanks for arranging it, Mickie. I *have* enjoyed watching!'

'Don't thank me, thank Rod. It was his idea, after all,' returned her escort surprisingly. 'Said he didn't suppose you'd had much chance to see cattle being cut out, where you came from.'

Yes, she could her him saying that, all right, thought Lindsay. She could imagine the ironic look in his eye, the sarcastic lift to his mouth. Batlow, he'd been thinking. *Batlow!*

Remembering the derision with which he'd referred to her beloved Utopian childhood home, Lindsay felt her first instinctive flame of gratitude to Rod for his thoughtfulness flicker, and then snuff out. It hadn't really been for her that he'd arranged this outing. He had merely wanted Mickie to change places with Shorty, that was all.

'Don't look so gloomy, Lindsay. What's there to be gloomy about in a mail-day? Unless, of course, you've been expecting a letter that didn't come? A *love*-letter, maybe?'

'Don't be a dope, Mickie,' Lindsay laughed, dragging her thoughts back unwillingly to what her young escort was saying.

'No love-letter, then?'

'Of course not.'

'No bloke down there in the Big Smoke, wilting away for lack of his Lindsay?' Mickie's blue eyes were teasing.

'No. No bloke.'

'No bloke *anywhere*?'

'Not anywhere.' She jumped down from the jeep, bare brown limbs flying as she leapt, a girlish figure in the white shirt, faded blue skirt and sandshoes which had seen her through her final schooldays.

'There's hope for me yet, then, eh!' Mickie gave her a playful chuck under the chin. 'I'm glad you aren't expecting a letter on that mail-plane, Lindsay girl.'

He gave her a two-fingered salute, jammed his hat down more firmly on his perspiring brow, and sauntered off in the direction of the dust-cloud of pounding hooves and wheeling horses.

Lindsay settled the fly-veil down over her own hat again. Then she took a sugar-bag from the back of the jeep and sat down in the small patch of shade on its off-side to await the appearance of Shorty.

No bloke anywhere. Not *anywhere*. That's what she'd said

to Mickie, and of course it was true. There was no man in Lindsay's life, there never had been, and there wasn't likely to be. No man whose letters she breathlessly awaited off that mail-plane with a fond yearning of the heart; no man to put his arms around her and tell her not to worry about all the things she didn't know; no man to kiss away the confused doubts that tortured her about her future here and all its uncertainties; no man whose broad frame she could lean on, whose shoulder she could cry on, whose love could make a little 'ugly duckling' believe herself, almost, to be a beautiful, sophisticated, needed, *wanted* swan.

No, there was no bloke in her life, no one at all.

But sitting there on that dusty sugar-bag in the small square of shade with the flies buzzing in a small, persistent cloud, and the grunts and shouts of stockmen and beasts undulating towards her on the swimming waves of heat, Lindsay knew that, if there *had* been such a bloke, she could picture almost exactly how she would like that bloke to be.

He would be tall and sunburnt, with lean, tanned cheeks, and an endearing sort of groove that ran from nose to mouth. The mouth would be firm, a strong but flexible sort of mouth that kept you guessing between tenderness and severity. His hair would be a crisp, blacky-brown, springing away from a wide, intelligent forehead with a tiny white sun-strip at the top where his wide hat protected it, and maybe there would be one or two little grey hairs glinting just near the ear, because this bloke wasn't exactly a youth, like Mickie and Shorty, he was experienced and responsible, inclined very often to be grave and serious and—sometimes—cen-sorious. But he wouldn't be like that to Lindsay, of course. For Lindsay, he would smile, with the slow, careful smile that showed the uneven whiteness of his teeth against the brownness of his face; a sweet, reluctant sort of smile that lit his keen grey eyes with a warmth and kindness that came right into his deep, stern voice, too, whenever he said things like, 'Good morning, Mannie,' and 'Thank you, Mannie.'

Oh, *Lindsay*! Whatever are you *thinking*? Lindsay, shaking with the horror of self-discovery, got tremblingly to her feet, and walked slowly around to the passenger side of the jeep as Shorty approached.

Rod Bennett's image, exquisite, painful, torturing in its proximity and reality, receded, resolved itself into a shimmering, tree-dotted plain, a shouting, whirling mob of men, horses, and cattle, and a clean-shaven square-built young jackaroo, who scrambled into the jeep beside her, slapped her bare knee in a matey fashion and said, 'O.K., Lindsay, let's go!'

'Oh yes, Shorty. Yes!'

Lindsay would have gone anywhere, just then, to escape from the pain and wonder of that dream!

CHAPTER 6

A LETTER on mail-day?

Lindsay had not been expecting one, but she received one all the same. From Carleen. She recognised the slanted, forceful capitals just as soon as she saw them.

It was Lindsay's task to sort out the letters, taking Rod's to his desk, and collecting the outgoing ones he had left there to be put in the returning mail-bag. This she could do at leisure, since the pilot usually spent the best part of an hour drinking his tea and chatting to Mannie about 'local' happenings that took place maybe a hundred miles away. While she was dealing with the post, Herb and Artie carried her supplies up to the store for her.

Today Lindsay put her own letter carefully to one side, and took it to her bedroom. What on earth had caused Carleen to write?

She was soon to find out!

'Mummy was pleased to hear that you had arrived safely at Gundooee, and that you have settled in. It sounds a terribly out-of-the-way place, but my dear, you must surely have realised by now just who Rod Bennett is? It's incredible, Lindsay, it really is, that you haven't heard of him. I mean, he's one of *the* Bennetts, you silly child, not just a manager on a property. As well as Gundooee, they own a whole string of other places, *and* he's an international swimmer, into the bargain. I can forgive you for not knowing that, as you'd have been too young when he represented Australia, but the rest——! Poor sweet, it's that dull little life you've always persisted in carving out for yourself that's responsible for your sublime ignorance, no doubt, but he's the *toast* of Brisbane society, that man, and as yet he seems to have eluded marriage, *don't* ask me how! Actually, I'm not working at the moment. John has just finished the promised series with Sarino, and a great success, very exhausting, though, and I've said I'll only consider some more later if he agrees to do things my way. He's beginning to bore me, actually—I think we've got to know each other too well, no mystery left, that sort of thing, and it occurs to me that you might invite me up to stay at Gundooee for a while. I've missed you, Lindsay, I truly have, and I've felt awful about some of the things I said. I didn't mean them, pet—*you* know *me*. Fix it with your employer, will you? Just say that you've a cousin who is worried about you away out there, and who wants to come and see for herself that you're all right. I know he has oodles of Queensland girls to stay at Races time, and anyway, when he sees me he won't mind a bit that you did it. Write by return, will you, and let me know when to come. Yours ever, Carleen.'

Lindsay sank down on the bed in a confusion of surprise and bewilderment. One of *the* Bennetts! Lindsay had no idea who *the* Bennetts were, but if he was one of them, she supposed that that must account for his air of undisputed authority and the frequent trips to other properties in that graceful red-and-silver plane of his.

As for the swimming—well, she shouldn't be surprised at that, either. Recalling the grace, speed, and power of the dawn performer whom she still secretly watched sometimes she could only think what an inappropriate exercising pool for a swimmer of international calibre was that muddy, high-banked ground tank, with its brackish water and makeshift springboard. Lindsay couldn't remember *any* names in that connection. Not being good at sport herself, she had had only a minimal interest in its various spheres, and it would have been a few years ago, anyway, because from all she had read about the big-time, one retired early from that particular level of competition. Why, by about twenty-six years of age one was almost regarded as passé! She'd have been a mere schoolgirl when Rod Bennett was at the peak in his field!

Not that she had reason to doubt anything which Carleen had said. Even that bit about Rod's being the toast of Brisbane society was synonymous with what Mannie had already told her.

But Carleen *here*? Something inside Lindsay went cold at the mere thought. She had found herself a haven of peace on this great, lonely station. Away from the hateful hurly-burly of the city, she could feel her cramped personality slowly emerging like a butterfly from a chrysalis. Tentatively at first, more securely now, Lindsay was beginning to regard herself as a part of Gundooee. Her relationship with the men was a warming one, full of fun and joking. Forthright criticisms, outspoken comments, gruff compliments were meted out to her in turn, all part and parcel of these big, spare-talking, easy-going station-hands, who had taken this particular 'blinkin' *lost*-lookin' little sheila' to their hearts, showing her the ropes, and protecting her from Rod's possible ire when the need arose. They cunningly cushioned her mistakes, concealed her ignorance to the best of their not inconsiderable, and sometimes downright ingenious ability.

Carleen *here*? Oh, no, she couldn't possibly. It would all be spoilt, the whole precariously satisfactory situation!

Lindsay got up off the bed, sat down instead at her dressing-table, and wrote quickly, with determination.

'Dear Carleen, Thank you for you letter. I'm so glad that your modelling series with Sarino was such a success. Congratulations! You must have worked very hard to deserve that result from such a demanding creature! I'm afraid you would find life very dull out here. There is really nothing exciting to do, as I'm busy most of the time (I have to do a lot of other things besides the actual keeping of the books, as it turns out!) I wouldn't be able to be with you very much at all. In any case, I feel my employer would regard it as something of an impertinence and an imposition to ask one of my relatives to stay, when I've been here such a very short space of time myself. I'm sure you'll understand. Please give my love to Aunt and Uncle.

As always, Lindsay.'

She sealed the envelope, addressed and stamped it, and took the mail-bag back to the pilot in the kitchen.

' 'Day, Lindsay.' It was the same man who had brought her here from Emmadanda all those weeks ago. 'How's tricks?'

'Not too bad, Mac, thank you. And you?'

'Mannie and I are catching up on all the gossip, you might say.' He sipped cautiously at his steaming mug of tea, twinkled from the old woman to the young girl. 'I was just telling her you can expect company tomorrow, probably. Margie Lockwith from over at Dinewan was telling me she might drop in tomorrow to see Rod.'

'Who is Margie Lockwith?'

'The Dinewan Lockwiths. My last call before here. A real nice kid, Margie. You'll like her. A lot of people reckon that she and Rod might make a go of it yet.'

'Now, Mac!' Mannie's voice was reproving. 'That's idle gossip, and you know it!'

'Maybe. But where there's smoke there's often fire. Anyway, he couldn't get anyone more suitable, could he, Mannie, you'll have to admit that? There's nothing that Margie can't do—rides like a native, swims like a fish, sews, paints. You name it, Margie does it! To my mind, she'd make the ideal wife for some lucky cove, and with Rod around, no other blighter gets a look-in. As for her cooking—wow!'

'She's a capable lass,' conceded Mannie, 'and a very nice person, too.'

'That's what I mean. That's what I'm *saying*.' Mac stood up, slung the mail-bag over his shoulder. 'She's a real nice girl. She'll make a good friend for Lindsay here, too. That's all I mean. You don't mind, but I told her all about Lindsay being here, just a pint-sizer, I said, and all on her own. You'll like Margie, Lindsay.'

And when Margie arrived, Lindsay found that she did like her, just as the mail-pilot had predicted.

Margie dropped in, next day, quite literally. It seemed that as well as all those other wonderful things she was able to do, she could also fly a plane. She brought it down with a show of feminine skill on the station airstrip, and came to meet Lindsay, who had run out of the store at the unexpected droning noise low overhead.

A small, neat girl, she was, and therefore something of a shock to Lindsay, who had visualised a frighteningly capable-looking creature of Amazonian proportions. She had flaxen hair, bleached into oddly attractive streaks by the sun, a complexion as smooth and gold as a ripening peach, lazy blue eyes, and a good-natured mouth. When she smiled, Lindsay thought she had never seen such beautiful, white, even, pearly teeth as Margie's. They were perhaps her best feature, and as she smiled very often, one was constantly reminded of their particular fascination.

Instead of shaking hands, Margie put both of her own hands on Lindsay's shoulders, and gave the other girl something between a shake and a hug. The general message this greeting conveyed was one of open and unaffected friendli-ness, and Lindsay found herself instantly drawn to this pretty young woman who had flown in on that aeroplane as though it were the easiest thing in the world, and who still twirled a large pair of glare-goggles on one finger.

'Hullo! You must be Lindsay. I knew the moment I saw you! Mac has told me all about you, you see.'

Lindsay smiled. 'I heard you were coming,' she confessed. 'But I never dreamed you'd come down right out of the sky like that!'

Margie laughed, shrugged. 'Why not? It's the quickest way, after all. It takes ages to go round by Peperina, and the roads are practically non-existent. I wouldn't see nearly so many people if I hadn't learned to get myself around that way—not the ones I *want* to see, anyway!'

'Does that apply to me, by any chance, along with all those other lucky ones?' Rod Bennett's deep chuckle startled Lindsay. He was right behind her, but she had been unaware of his approach.

'You *know* it does! That's why I came on Sunday, to make sure I'd find you about the homestead somewhere. How are you, Rod?'

Lindsay saw him gather the other girl against him with a muscular brown arm, hug her in a casual, almost brotherly manner, and let her go, grinning lazily.

Pretty fit, thanks. It's good see you, Margie. Have you met—er—Miss Dutten?'

Margie raised a shapely eyebrow in surprise.

'*Miss* Dutten? Good gracious, Rod, what a horrid, unfriendly sound that has! I suppose you must mean Lindsay?' She was teasing him.

'That's right.'

'Then why call her by that other fearsome title? It sounds too formal for words! Don't tell me that he *always* says it that way, does he, Lindsay?'

'Well——' Lindsay was scarlet.

'Rod, I think that's unkind! He *can* be, when he wants to, you know, Lindsay. The old lord-and-master routine. He's probably still mad at you for being a girl, when he was expecting a man to replace that awful Bob Lowney. We heard all about it on the galah next day. Are you, Rod? Still mad?'

Rod Bennett linked Margie's arm in his, and turned her towards the house. He didn't seem angry or perturbed, merely amused.

'Just leave me to run my own station in my own way, will you, Margie? My little meddlesome Margie?' There was genuine affection in the look he bent on the girl now walking at his side—a patient, caressing, indulgent sort of look, Lindsay couldn't help noticing.

Margie smiled up at him, engagingly, because of those beautiful pearly teeth. There was laughter in her own eyes, persuasion, too.

'Well, I'm not coming ten steps further until you promise to say Lindsay, like the rest of us. Poor girl, what will she think of us? You told me when you engaged him—her, I mean—that the new book-keeper had had a good deal of experience of Outback life, and I'll bet this is the first Outback property she's ever been on where she was called *Miss* Dutten.'

'I'm prepared to bet on *that*, too!' Rod's deep voice was dry. He lifted a satiric eyebrow tellingly at Lindsay to let her know just what he meant. Then he seemed to take pity on her guilt-ridden expression, and capitulated with sudden, quite devastating charm. It appeared that he would do a lot for Margie! 'Very well, then—Lindsay. Leave your work at the cottage just now, and come up to the house with us, will you? It will be an opportunity for you to get to know another of your own sex in this wilderness of men you've landed among. There have no doubt been times since your arrival when you may have longed for the company of a girl of your own age. I'm sure Margie will be delighted to oblige.'

Margie giggled. 'Said with all the superiority of his thirty years! Come on, then, Lindsay. Let's conduct this tottering ancient up to his homestead, shall we?'

The conversation at the table was animated that day. Margie kept up a non-stop flow, and although it was mostly about people whom Lindsay had never met, it was nevertheless entertaining and amusing. Rod Bennett smiled a lot more than he usually did when there were just Mannie and herself present, Lindsay couldn't help noticing, and when he did, it was in that slow, endearing way that lifted his mouth at the corners and spread a warm light into his eyes. There was no doubt at all that he was uncharacteristically well-disposed towards the enchanting, gentle Margie!

When she was leaving, she kissed Rod, then Mannie, then Lindsay, one after the other, without favour. It was a heart-warming gesture that brought Lindsay into the circle. She found herself beaming with pleasure, but if Rod had even noticed, his expression remained unreadable.

'We must introduce Lindsay around, Rod. Maybe I could bring some of the others over to play tennis, if the court is in working order.'

'That would be nice for Lindsay, Margie. I don't think the court has been rolled or marked for some time, but I'm sure Mickie and Shortie will be delighted to oblige if it means the chance of a game with some other young folk.'

'*And* you? You'll play?' Margie looked expectant, cajoling.

Rod grimaced.

'Probably not, I think, Margie. Not this time. I've rather a lot on hand just now.'

It's because of me, thought Lindsay miserably. He usually plays, but not this time, not when I'm included. He's never going to approve of me being here, never, *never*.

Margie remained cheerfully unconvinced.

'We'll see,' she temporised. 'But you tell them to get the court ready, anyway, will you, Lindsay, and I'll round up a few of the folk one day. If we don't make our own entertainment out here, nothing ever happens in the social line, and I know there are heaps of people dying to meet you—especially after all the speculation that's been going on over the galah!'

'You women and your galah,' Rod chided, grinning suddenly. 'Get going now, Margie, before the light beats you. And give your parents my regards.'

'I will, and they sent theirs, of course. 'Bye, Mannie. 'Bye, Lindsay. I'll be seeing you.'

Lindsay watched the man and the girl walking companionably together back to the airstrip. She was bending over her files in the cottage when the little plane took off again, and from the window she could see Rod Bennett waving his hat as it banked once around the homestead and then soared off out of sight.

Several times during the following week, Lindsay found herself thinking about Margie's visit—wondering, too, about Carleen, and how she would take the news that her proposal had been turned down. Knowing well how much her cousin liked to get her own way without dispute, Lindsay could only feel thankful that she would not be present when Carleen opened her note. She could well imagine the sulky pout on that pretty mouth, the thwarted snapping of those lovely eyes!

It was towards the end of the week that Herb sidled up to the veranda next to Rod's office. Lindsay was busy checking over the numbered bottles in the station medical box, which was kept on a wall-fixture on the veranda, she supposed because it was a readily accessible place for all and sundry in an emergency, although only she, Rod, and Mannie were in possession of a key.

Shorty had cut his arm rather badly only two days before, and Lindsay had had her first experience of applying first-aid on the directions of the Flying Doctor over the transceiver. It was a nasty wound, and both she and Shorty had been several shades paler by the time she had finished cleaning and binding the arm and dispensing antibiotic tablets from one of the numbered containers. She felt that she had acquitted herself not too badly for a beginner, and had had an unexpected reward in Rod's quiet 'Well done, Lindsay,' when he heard about it that evening. Artie, who had shepherded the injured Shorty to the homestead and had been present at the performance, cancelled that out by exclaiming,

'Well *done*, boss? Crikey, yer should've *been* there! She was shakin' like a rakin' jelly! I near bust me sides at the look on Shorty's face—Nursie here was that white around the gills we reckoned she might cough up any time!'

'Artie!'

'That'll do, Art.' Rod's voice held reproof, but there was a smile lurking in his eye. 'Maybe she did even better than I thought,' he added kindly, and Lindsay felt quick colour coming into her cheeks at such unexpected praise.

She had dressed the arm successfully each day since then, and had boiled and re-rolled the used bandages. She laid them in their place now, and turned at Herb's approach.

'Hullo, Herb.'

'G'day, Lindsay. Are yer busy?'

'Not too busy to help if I can. What's up?'

Herb took off his hat, and twirled it self-consciously between his fingers. Then he put it on the small wicker table and pulled a crumpled piece of paper from his pocket. It was soiled and thumbed, as though it had been folded and unfolded a good many times by Herb's own leathery hands.

He coughed apologetically.

'I was thinkin', Lindsay. It's like this, see. I been tryin' ter write a letter fer about six years now, and I sort of reckoned —well, now that *you're* here—that maybe between us we could 'ave a go. That's if you ain't too busy?'

'Not at all, Herb. I'll help if I can,' she reiterated.

Herb gave a grunt.

'That's great! I reckoned yer might. It takes a feller a long time on 'is own, yer know,' he confessed candidly. 'I s'pose that's 'ow I ain't never got round ter doin' it fer a year or two. I thought I'd better make the most of you while we got yer, Lindsay. Yer see, we all know Rod don't 'old with wimmen book-keepers, so I reckon yer won't be 'ere for *ever*. Not that *we* don't want yer!' he added hastily, as if he sensed the surge of distress in his listener. 'We'll cover up for yer just as long as we can, yer can bet on that! But—well, *you* know Rod.'

I'm beginning to, thought Lindsay sadly. That's the whole trouble. I'm beginning to, and I don't *want* to go away.

'Would you like me to write it for you, Herb, and you can sign it? Or I could type it out for you, down at the cottage?'

'Maybe if we was ter get it wrote first——' Herb dithered. 'It's ter me wife, actually.'

'Your wife?' Lindsay tried to conceal her surprise. 'I didn't know you were married, Herb.'

'I done it years ago, Lindsay,' Herb responded glumly. 'But I didn't go much on it, not fer long. I reckon I was as blind as a coot at the time. Shearin' out on the Barwon, we was. We was laid off a while between sheds, and the beer was runnin' a ruddy banker that night. There was this dame, see, and—well, I got in tow with 'er, somehow, and between 'er and this binge I was on, when I come ter me senses, blimey if she 'adn't got the parson, and the weddin' bells was ringin' and the lot! Nell, 'er name was.'

He sighed reminiscently, opened up the paper, and spread it out beside his hat on the little cane table.

'This is what I've wrote so far, Lindsay. Dear Nell, I 'ope you are well.' A gruff chuckle. 'That's poetry, ain't it? *Nell* and *well*. Reckon she never knew she'd married a blinkin' 'Enry Lawson! 'Ave yer got any ideas, Lindsay, as ter what we can put now?'

'It's difficult when you haven't—er—seen her for a while,' Lindsay replied tactfully. 'How long is it, Herb?'

'Must be about ten or twelve years, I reckon. She's livin' at Toowoomba, see. 'Er ma's got a café there, but I ain't been ter see 'er for years, see. There ain't been nothink ter take me over Toowoomba way, 'as there?' reasoned Herb mildly. 'What I mean is, why should *I* want ter to go to a place like Toowoomba?'

'Yes, quite,' murmured Lindsay delicately.

Oh dear! Poor Herb! And poor Lindsay. This was obviously one of the more challenging assignments that came the way of the Gundooee book-keeper!

Lindsay did her best. Between them they concocted quite the strangest epistle it had ever been her privilege to witness, mainly because of Herb's readiness to take instant offence if she did not adopt his own somewhat couthy suggestions. Ah well. He knew the distant Nell much better than Lindsay did herself, so who was she to argue?

She typed out the resulting letter, watched Herb scrawl his name painstakingly at the bottom, and addressed the envelope. By the time it was all done, and Herb had bidden her a satisfied goodnight, she felt quite limp and exhausted, as though all her natural creativeness had been drained out of her.

It was something, at least, that Herb was so pleased! He had dusted off his hat with the triumphant air of one who has achieved a difficult goal, and had gone sauntering off into the night whistling breathily through his naked gums.

Lindsay found that she was smiling to herself as she included Herb's letter in the out-going bundle on mail-day, wondering idly what Nell's reaction would be when she got it. There had been no suggestion on her husband's part that he missed her to any great extent! Indeed, apart from one or two meaty reminiscences unblushingly recounted by the prosaic Herb, the letter was innocuous in the extreme, and not by any stretch of imagination could it have been termed a passionate document. Lindsay could only hope that Nell, whose bridal bliss had been so short-lived, would not be disappointed!

The mail-bag contained a second letter from Carleen. What a week for letters, one way and another, thought Lindsay, slitting it open forthwith. She took the single sheet of paper from its tissue-lined envelope, and found herself beginning to tremble so violently that she had to sit down quite quickly.

Her face felt drained of colour and her breath came in funny little shallow gasps.

Disbelievingly, she read it again.

'How typical of you, Lindsay, to refuse me even a tiny little favour after all Mummy and Daddy have done for you. It would have been so easy for you to invite a relative out there for a while, but that was too much to hope for, wasn't it? Or did you start getting silly ideas of your own when I told you who Rod Bennett is? I hope not, because, my dear, you wouldn't stand a chance, and you know it. But that's no reason to be a dog-in-the-manger about him, is it. Anyway, it doesn't really matter, and in the end perhaps it's even to the good that he doesn't know we're even distantly related. I mean, with you on the payroll there, I prefer to have a separate identity altogether, so I have got Matt Standley, who is a friend of the Bennetts, to get me an invitation to Gundooee, and will be arriving shortly. As I shall be a guest, while you are in the category of an employee, I don't think our paths will cross much at all. Should you be tempted to let it be known that we're related, or in fact have ever seen each other before, then my advice is, *don't do it*, Lindsay. It would be too bad if Rod Bennett got to find out that you came there under false pretences, wouldn't it, pretending that you didn't know the post was for a man, when you and I both know you did? I gather he's the sort who'd hate to be made a fool of by any woman, least of all a minor employee. Matt tells me that he was quite furious about the mix-up over some woman book-keeper at the time, and that you're only there on sufferance because you didn't seem to have anywhere to go, so I shouldn't think you'd last a minute if he knew how you'd bluffed him. Well, Lindsay, all the best, and I shall look forward to seeing you soon—as a *complete* stranger, of course. Yours in haste, Carleen.'

Lindsay crumpled up the note and put it in the wastepaper basket, as if by simply throwing it away she could dispense with the whole problem.

It was not as easy as that, though! When Carleen set her mind on something, she always got it. Always! She had made up her mind to come to Gundooee, and so she was coming, with or without her cousin's connivance. Lindsay's imagination baulked at the reason behind Carleen's decision. It was too dreadful, too blatant, even to think about!

How had she managed it, though? How did Carleen ever manage to do all the things she wanted to do? By twisting the truth just the teeniest bit, Lindsay surmised. By a little artful pretence, a few well-chosen prevarications, a pathetic smile, a calculated and well-timed sigh.

But how, *this* time? How?

Lindsay knew that she would have to wait, and even then, perhaps she might never know. She was not in a position to mention Carleen's name, or the fact that she had heard from her, or had forewarning of her coming. She had no idea when, or how, Carleen intended to come. All she had said was that it would be 'soon'. She wasn't the kind to procrastinate, once her mind was made up, so Lindsay could only suppose that 'soon' might even mean next week!

Only a few more days, perhaps, and then—Carleen. The thought was almost unbearable, but Lindsay knew that the reality itself would be worse! Gone the peace, the tranquillity, the fun with the jackaroos and station-hands. Even the status quo of her relationship with Rod Bennett would be bound to change. Just now, there was a state of truce, precarious, *precious*. A word of praise could bring a glow to Lindsay's heart, a slow smile could transform her day. It was dangerous to become so—so—*fond* of someone, that the mere fact of being noticed by him could turn a mundane moment into a memorable one. Dangerous, and stupid. Lindsay, in her deepest self, knew that she was guilty of just such folly! She couldn't help herself, although she knew it was a hopeless situation, a quite fruitless expenditure of this soul-searing emotion, made even more impossible by the mere fact that Rod was who he was.

All this was hard enough to contend with, and now—Carleen!

Lindsay found herself talking to the pilot and Mannie with strangely wooden effort. Even her smile felt stiff and strained, as though her cheeks would crack, and it was difficult to concentrate on what they were saying.

'Margie was telling me she met you, Lindsay. She was full

of plans about brightening things up for you here.'

They'd soon be brightened up all right, thought Lindsay bitterly, but not by Margie!

'She's nice, Mac. She was really sweet and friendly, just like you said. She's going to bring some others over one day, and we're going to play tennis, it seems.'

'That's Margie! Always on for a bit of action. She can handle that plane O.K., too. She'll be trying to rope Rod in for a game, I expect.'

'He's busy these days.' Mannie spoke from her position behind the tea-pot. 'But he'll be glad of some company for Lindsay. We do worry a little bit about you, dear. I'm not as young as I was, or I'd do more to make life exciting, and Rod has been convinced from the beginning that this was no post for a girl. Too lonely.'

'But I love it, Mannie. I love it. The peace, the plains. I've got into the way of loving it all, just the way it is.'

I don't *want* it to change. I don't *want* it to be different, she wailed silently inside herself. But it will be, very soon. It's bound to be different, with Carleen.

Mannie did not appear to know anything at all about Carleen coming. If she had, Lindsay was certain that she would have mentioned it then, right there in the kitchen in front of the pilot. That was the way Mannie was—gentle, but forthright, in the candid Outback tradition. There was no pretence in Mannie, no hypocrisy, although of course she possessed a certain tact which was entirely lacking in the blunt-spoken, casual station-hands. Lindsay was now more amused than hurt by their frank criticisms, to which she had at first been much too sensitive. Their motives were ones of true kindness, and the inclination to help along a 'new chum' engendered most of their forthright offers of advice. Once one fully understood that fact, one could be grateful for the basic honesty of their approach. One always knew how one stood with them, and in a more subtle way, one did with Mannie also.

No, if Mannie had heard anything at all about a visitor coming—especially a female visitor—she would have been sure to mention it just now. That meant that Rod had not told her about it, yet. He had not told anyone.

Lindsey was aware of her own tense expectancy each time there was a pause in the conversation after that. During even the most momentary silence, she would find her eyes fastened anxiously upon Rod's stern, deeply tanned face, waiting, waiting, for that announcement. It was like waiting for the judge to don the black cap, thought Lindsay to herself, with a grim attempt at a humour she was far from feeling.

When he finally imparted the information, he did it, as Rod always did everything, unpredictably—in his own time, in his own fashion, and at his own pace.

He didn't just work it into the conversation. He came specially out of his office to where Mannie and Lindsay were sitting comfortably in semi-darkness, and he came, she supposed, for that express purpose. They always sat there, she and Mannie, in the deck-chairs, looking out through the gauze to where the garden outlines were merging so rapidly into the night, chatting idly when they had something to say, lapsing into companionable silence when they hadn't. Rod generally retired to his study, working, reading, until the rest of the household had gone to bed.

Tonight, he was the one with something to say. Lindsay watched him switch off his office light, close the door, and come towards them along the veranda, a tall broad figure in pale drill trousers, a dazzlingly white shirt with uprolled sleeves, and the tie he always put on when he changed in the evening knotted neatly at his throat. His hair was damp from the shower, still smatted down tidily against his forehead, and as he drew up a third chair and took his place quite near, Lindsay could smell the faint, masculine aroma of cigarettes and shave-lotion.

Rod sat there for some moments, then stretched his legs out more comfortably in front of him and reached into his pocket for the makings. In the dimness his bare forearms were mahogany-coloured against the whiteness of his shirt. Lindsay caught the whiff of tobacco, knew that he was rubbing it around between his palms. A rustle of paper, the rasp of a match. Then smoke rising above his head—a tranquil plume that drifted peacefully away along the veranda.

When he had drawn on his cigarette in silence for a minute or two, he announced pleasantly,

'I have a surprise up my sleeve for you, Mannie—for you and Lindsay.'

'Yes, Rod?' That was Mannie, immediately interested.

'Yes. We're going to have a visitor.'

'Are we?' The old lady showed no surprise. After all, Rod often had visitors at Gundooee, so why should she?

'We are. I thought it would be a good thing for Lindsay, a little company about her own age, or at least, very little older. Another *girl*, at any rate.' He stressed his point delicately.

'Oh, that *will* be nice!' Mannie was enthusiastic now. 'Who is it, Rod? Someone who's been before?'

'No, she hasn't been before, Mannie. In fact, I don't even know her myself yet. She's a friend of Matt Standley's, and a very nice girl, he says. She's been working too hard, it seems, and has had a particularly nasty bout of bronchitis—she's prone to it, apparently. Did you say something, Lindsay?'

What Lindsay had actually said was 'Piffle!'—under her breath, of course, but she *had* made a tiny sound unintentionally.

'No, nothing, Rod.'

'I beg your pardon, I thought you did. Well, anyway, her doctor has advised a dry inland climate for a while, plus peace and rest, and when Matt asked me to have her, I was naturally very glad to agree—for Lindsay's sake. *Did* you say something, Lindsay?'

'No, nothing at all. I thought I'd swallowed a mosquito, just for a moment. I'm sure there's one buzzing about, and my throat suddenly went all tickly.'

'One rarely *swallows* a mosquito,' Rod pointed out, leaning towards her in the gloom, and treating her to a suspiciously probing inspection. 'Anyway, as I was saying, Matt said she's been under considerable stress lately, and the combination of dry heat, rest and a bit of peace and quiet immediately made him think of Gundooee. I'm very glad he did, and it will be very nice for you to have another girl around, Lindsay. I often think you're out with those men far more than is strictly necessary. It doesn't seem right. This way, there will at least be two of you, and I'm sure you'll become good friends in a very short time. I've said that she's to stay just as long as she pleases. She's a model, apparently, and has no more assignments in the immediate offing. Very wisely she deferred them until she's quite well again, so I hope she may even stay for some months. I think the east room, don't you, Mannie? It's the coolest.'

'Sibbie will make up the bed tomorrow. When is she coming, Rod, and how?'

'On Thursday, in the early afternoon, I think. She's chartering a flight direct from Sydney.'

She would! Trust Carleen to miss out on those interminable hours of train-ride, toiling through desolate wastes, and changing at a junction which should have been Emmadanda, only Emmadanda was a whole forty minutes further on, and then finding out that Emmadanda wasn't a pretty little jacaranda-lined town but a one-horse outpost with two dogs and some crows and a rusty bucket shower, and waiting in grilling sunshine all alone for a plane you had been warned curtly *not* to miss, and coming down at Gundooee to find you weren't as welcome as you had hoped because you happened to be a girl, and that you were, in fact, downright *unwelcome* in one person's eyes, and that was the most dreadful thing of all, because they happened to be nice, expressive grey eyes, too, the sort you really wanted to have a welcome in. Trust Carleen to miss out on *that*!

A charter flight, direct from Sydney. And when she arrived, they'd know she was going to be a girl, because that's what Rod had arranged for, and that's what Rod would be expecting. A girl, both welcome and wanted.

'Her name, by the way, is Carleen Vincent.'

Oh, Rod! I could have told you that! thought Lindsay sadly.

'It's a pretty name, Carleen,' said Rod.

CHAPTER 7

WHEN Carleen arrived she stepped daintily down from the aircraft, taking Rod's extended hand to help her to the ground.

People always extended their hand to help Carleen—especially men! There was something about her fragile build, willowy slenderness and elegantly languid movements that called for such gestures. She had come to regard them as her prerogative, and was seldom disappointed.

Not today, anyway. You could tell by the way she peeped coyly up into Rod Bennett's tough, brown face, and the way her mouth curved into a tiny, oblique smile, that Carleen was anything but disappointed. And you'd have said, by the way Rod's lip curled faintly at the corner and his grey eyes kindled with surprised admiration, that *he* wasn't disappointed, either.

Of course, Carleen, looking as she did today, would have merited such a glance from even a confirmed misogynist, and Rod Bennett certainly was not that. He *liked* girls, Mannie had stressed that often. Especially tall, sophisticated, pretty girls who vamped him with an openly flirtatious eye, invited him with the pursing of their soft, rouged mouths, who kept hold of his hand for just that extra, lingering moment, as Carleen was doing now.

'Mr. Bennett?' Rod?' Her voice was attractively husky, with just the right degree of shy hesitation. 'Oh, I'm so glad to be here! Matt has told me all about you, and I just knew that Gundooee was the very place to help me recover my strength and get quite well again. And this is Mannie—I've heard about you, too. And I suppose you must be Lindsay, the little book-keeper?' Carleen's eye sought Lindsay's coolly. 'How odd to find a woman occupying a post of that sort, isn't it? Away out here one just naturally assumes that a man would be infinitely more suitable, somehow.'

'Lindsay is making a surprisingly successful attempt at it'—Rod was watching Lindsay herself as he spoke, smiling quite kindly—'although it certainly isn't a usual position for a girl to find herself in. As you say, Carleen—I may call you that?—we do normally confine the position to the masculine field.'

'I would have thought so, naturally, although I expect as a temporary measure, that it works well enough. Would you mind carrying these for me, Lindsay? You can go ahead with them to my room if you like. I suppose you must know where it is?'

'Yes—er—of course.'

Lindsay stepped forward quickly, took the vanity-case and handbag which were being held out imperiously.

Carleen smiled up at Rod with faint apology.

'I still get a little bit tired, I'm afraid,' Lindsay heard her telling him sweetly as she left them, 'but I know I'm going to pick up very quickly now that I'm here. Do you have many other servants, Rod, to help you in the house? It looks quite enormous from here.'

His deep-toned reply was lost to Lindsay, who found that her teeth were clenched so firmly together that her jaw positively ached, and her fingers gripped the handles of Carleen's bags so tightly that her knuckles showed white under the pressure.

She dumped the bags unceremoniously on a chair in the east bedroom, and turned to discover Carleen coming through the doorway with Rod just behind her.

'I say, do be careful of that case, will you, Lindsay, and don't go hurling it around like that? I'm not accustomed to having others treat my possessions so carelessly. I trust you aren't so lackadaisical about *everything*, my dear?' She put her hand to her forehead. Her beautifully-kept and mani-cured fingers were spread out in a touchingly weary gesture. 'My goodness, it *is* warm, isn't it, out here? Or perhaps it's just that I'm still not quite myself.' An apologetic smile in Rod's direction. 'I'm perfectly strong, *really*, but you must forgive me if I don't appear so just now. It's all very frustrating when one is unaccustomed to having been ill.'

'Not at all, Carleen,' Rod's voice held a concern that must have gratified the girl who had sunk on to the bed with a gracefulness calculated to show those long, shapely legs and curvaceous hips to their best advantage. 'You must take care, and only do just as much or as little as you feel able to. It's much hotter here than in Sydney, of course, but once you're acclimatized, you'll probably find the dry heat easier to withstand than the humidity of the coast. Perhaps you should rest just now.'

'I think I will, if you don't mind. There's cologne in my cosmetic case there, Lindsay. Perhaps you would be kind enough to fix me a nice cold pad—you *do* have iced water, I'm sure?—and I shall put it on my forehead and close my eyes for a while.'

'Yes, do that. I'll leave you to Lindsay's ministrations, then, Carleen. Just remember that you're very welcome here, and make yourself at home.'

'You are sweet, Rod. So considerate. And I don't wonder that Matt immediately thought of Gundooee as the very place for my convalescence. What a charming and delightfully modern homestead it is! I've always adored the country, and I know already that I'm going to love it here. You've given me such a warm welcome already.'

He had, too! thought Lindsay grimly to herself, as Rod's heavy step faded away through the hall. No salt tablets thrown carelessly at her with a kitchen mug half full of water—not for Carleen! Oh no! For Carleen there had been a kind concern, a gentle indulgence, a lingeringly warm regard, tinged with admiration and considerateness—a very male, protective sort of look, it had been.

When the sound of those heeled stockman's boots had quite gone, Carleen opened her eyes again and looked straight at Lindsay.

'You can get the iced water if you like. Some in a bowl, and a jug for drinking would be nice. I wasn't pretending when I said just now that my head is aching. They gave me a whale of a send-off party at the Club last night. You'd have thought I was going to the Never-Never, the way they went on.' She looked about her. 'It almost is, actually, isn't it?'

'Is what?'

'The Never-Never. What a ghastly stretch of country to fly over! All that peculiar tufty desert, and those stones thrown around all over the place. I must say it's a relief to find such an attractively civilised human being at the end of it. He's even more handsome than I'd remembered from his photos.' She gazed at Lindsay's flushed, indignant expression with malicious curiosity. 'Do you find him handsome, I wonder, Lindsay?'

'Who?'

'Rod, of course—who else?'

'I haven't really thought about it,' Lindsay replied coldly.

'Then don't begin to, darling, will you, and it will be much much pleasanter all round. Tell me, are there many other women on the scene at the moment? Any since you've been here? Ones of *consequence*, I mean.'

'I really couldn't say.'

'Come, darling, you must know. You're only human, after all, and you can't fool me, either. I can see that you're alive to Rod Bennett's attractions as a man. I saw the way you looked at him just now—a sort of awareness that you never had in Sydney—and in certain aspects I can also see that you've matured quite surprisingly since I saw you last. However, it's not *you* I'm talking about at the moment. Has he had any other members of the fair sex coasting around lately?'

Lindsay gave her cousin a look of unconcealed disdain.

'What a ruthless, calculating creature you are, aren't you, Carleen, to even ask such a thing when you've only just arrived.'

The other shrugged, laughed huskily and without shame.

'Well, one does like to know the military strength of one's opponents, darling, after all. If you want to be cagey and uncooperative, go ahead by all means. It won't worry me! I shall ask that old governess or whatever she is. What's her name? Mannie? I shall ask Mannie, and she'll tell me all I want to know without even guessing she's been catechised. I can be quite subtle when necessary, you know, Lindsay.'

'Carleen, if you expect me to stand by while you cold-bloodedly——'

'Wait!' Carleen interrupted, waving an imperious hand for silence. Then she leaned up on one elbow off the pillow and looked Lindsay over with eyes that glittered oddly. There was something a little bit frightening in the pale, menacing measure of that look. 'Let's just be clear on one point, Lindsay, shall we—although I thought I'd made the position clear in my letter, actually. The only thing I expect of *you* is silence, do you understand? I'm not asking you to do anything, or say anything. Your role is simply one of abstention, and that should be right up your negative little street, shouldn't it? But don't you dare presume to moralise, or to judge, will you, Lindsay? That would be presumptuous of you, my dear, and I should make you very, very sorry if you did. Do you understand?'

'I've always *understood* you, Carleen.'

'Good. Then there's no need to underline the situation any further, is there? Go and get that iced water for me now, will you, Lindsay? Oh, and by the way——'

'Yes?' Lindsay paused woodenly in the doorway.

'Now that we've discussed things'—Carleen smiled sweetly and appeasingly—'there's no need to refer to them again. There's always the possibility that we might be overheard, and in any case, I don't intend to fraternise with the employees at Gundooee to the extent of long, intimate dicussions closeted in my bedroom. From now on, just remember your own position here, and the fact that I'm a guest in your employer's household, and I'm sure we shall get along perfectly, Lindsay.'

'Yes, Carleen.' Lindsay felt the words clotting in her throat. In fact, it was all she could do to speak at all just then, so overwhelmed was she by disgust and misery.

At tea that night it was almost worse! To have to sit there, watching it all, and saying nothing, took all the strength of will that Lindsay could muster. She had left it too late now, in any case, to do a thing about it. Carleen was here, an ever-present threat to Lindsay's own security, and Carleen was enjoying the situation enormously. She had spent the afternoon resting on her bed with the veranda-blinds pulled down outside to screen off the glare and heat. Lindsay had heard the shower running in the bathroom she shared with Carleen at just about the same time as she heard Rod turning on the spray in his own private shower-recess off his own room. After Carleen came out, the whole hall was pervaded by the tantalising scent of her expensive eau de toilette. If Rod had by any chance forgotten that they now had a new, and very feminine, addition to the household, he must most certainly have been reminded of the fact by that enchanting, pervasive perfume.

Tonight Carleen was wearing a filmy dress of printed chiffon, with long transparent sleeves and a softly pleated skirt that did wonderful things for her beautiful legs. Encased in clover-pink nylons, they seemed incredibly long and shapely. Her shoes were of a deeper, toning shade, with delicate silvered heels and matching silver buckles. She had swept her long golden tresses into an elaborate coil on top of her head, to reveal the pretty set of her small, neat ears and the gentle curve of her neck above the frilled throat of her frock. The effect was at once as tender as a petunia, as dramatic as an orchid.

Lindsay was very much aware of the contrast they must make. She had put on the skirt of her linen suit, and her 'other' white blouse, and was even now regretting her bare brown legs and the old-fashioned shoes which she had successfully renovated with an application of honey-toned colour before she came to Gundooee. Up till this moment, she had been satisfied enough with these things, but tonight, her few possessions seemed duller, more inadequate, than ever before. In her bedroom she had taken extra care with her make-up, feathering her brows into pretty arches, adding a touch of mascara to her long, curling lashes, brushing her hair until it shone in a nut-brown obedient curtain.

Lindsay had then gazed at herself in the mirror, staring critically back at the wide green innocence of those eyes in the glass with a feeling of self-reproach. Why was she going to this extra trouble tonight? Because of Carleen? Because of Rod? Or just because she felt so miserably overburdened by the present untenable situation into which she had been precipitated?

Lindsay couldn't answer any of those questions honestly. Not tonight. Her mind was a welter of confused ideas, chaotic thinking and muddled emotions. All she *did* know, as she surveyed her girlishly simple reflection in the mirror, was that fine feathers *did* make fine birds—or, at any rate, they certainly helped! And Lindsay didn't possess any feathers at all, only a white 'other blouse', just slightly better than her everyday cotton shirt, and a skirt that was admittedly an improvement on her faded denim one, and a pair of shoes which looked just a little nicer in their present sand colour than they had in their previous scuffed white shabbiness.

Carleen was being put into her chair, quite tenderly, by Rod. As he bent a little to push the chair into place, his head, behind the girl's own fair one, appeared darkly swarthy, almost saturnine. In his crisply laundered shirt and narrow trousers, he looked carelessly, urbanely handsome.

When Carleen put her head back and smiled her acknowledgement of his thoughtful gesture, his white teeth glinted momentarily, and his eyes darkened inexplicably. Like that, they were almost black, unfathomable, tantalisingly unreadable.

'You're feeling better, Carleen? You certainly *look* very decorative and charming, I can assure you, but outward appearances can be misleading, and of course you did have an unpleasantly tiring trip to get here, I'm afraid.'

Tiring? Huh! And what about poor Lindsay's own unpleasantly tiring trip? There had been no sympathetic enquiries for her, no tender, darkening glances. Just a brief injunction *not* to miss Mac's plane, and when she got here, a reproving glare when she dared to comment on the heat, a couple of salt tablets, and a scarifying lecture on the importance of stating one's sex when one applied for the post of book-keeper on Gundooee Station.

'Oh, *so* much better, thank you, Rod! In fact, I'm feeling quite refreshed—my old self, almost. I'm longing to take part in all your country activities again.' She leaned towards him.

'I've brought my riding clothes, of course,' she confided eagerly. 'I suppose you have some good horses here—hacks, I mean—as well as those funny nondescript stock-horses. I really appreciate good horseflesh, you know!'

'Do you, indeed? I'm sure we can supply you with a suitable mount, in that case. I've a very sweet little mare, part Arab, that should be the very thing, I think. In fact'—a flattering appraisal of Carleen's deliciously appealing profile —'I should think that you and Chalita will make a very well-matched pair.'

'May I ride with *you*? What I mean is'—Carleen hesitated delicately—'all those *men*——'

'Yes, of course. I shall take you whenever I can, if you really like that sort of thing—whenever it is suitable, that is,' Rod promised agreeably.

'Such a pity that you won't be able to accompany us, too, Lindsay. You *did* tell me you couldn't ride, I think?'

Lindsay hadn't told her anything of the sort! She hadn't needed to, because Carleen already knew it. She knew perfectly well that the functional boarding-school to which her younger relation had been sent had not provided extra frills in the form of expensive riding lessons, as her own school had done.

'We gotter *do* somethink about it,' muttered Artie indignantly, some two weeks later. 'Ain't we, Mick? We gotter *do* somethink. She's in fer the knockout stakes, that dame is, Lindsay—any mutt can see that. She's makin' rings around yer, that's what! She's been out with Rod on them perishin' 'orses every day this week, givin' 'erself airs, preenin' them fine feathers, and never missin' a single trick in the knockout stakes.'

'What are they, Art? The—er—knockout stakes?' Lindsay felt moved to enquire. Artie's indignation was of a quite ferocious nature.

'Never *you* mind what they are, Lindsay. You don't know dames like we know dames,' he told her darkly. 'That's not surprisin', either, 'cos you ain't a dame yourself—not like *'er*. You're just a decent little slip of a dinkum little sheila, that's what you are, and that's what she's not. She ain't dinkum, she ain't on the level, she's just a *dame*, and me and the other blokes ain't goin' ter let a dame run rings around our Lindsay, are we, see? We ain't goin' ter stand by and let a spoofer like 'er get one-up on you in the knockout stakes. What'll we do, though, Mick, eh?'

Mickie grinned. 'We could teach her to ride, for a start.'

'Stone the blinkin' crows, so we could! Why didn't I think of that before? We teach 'er ter ride, and then she can go out with 'em, too. And that makes three of 'em, don't it, instead of just them two.' Artie chuckled exultantly. 'By crikey, that'll shift the odds a bit, eh!'

Lindsay smiled innocently from one man to the other, touched at their concern. It was nice to be a dinkum little sheila, and not just a dame! It made you feel warm and soft inside, and it made you not mind quite so much about the handsome couple Rod and Carleen made, riding off together on those lovely horses.

It was true, what Artie had said. They had been out together every single day this week, at one end of the day or the other. Carleen looked superb in her tailored riding pants, polished boots and open-necked shirt of deepest blue silk. The part-Arab mare, Chalita, was a delicate-stepping creature, the prettiest dappled grey, and, as Rod had predicted, the horse and rider were perfectly matched in elegance, style, and beauty of movement. His own mount was the bay stallion he always used, an intelligent, rather mettlesome animal that he rode on a curb and martingale. Looking after them enviously as they went off across the plain, Lindsay could not stop herself thinking how wonderful it must be to ride at Rod's side like that, in close companionship—just you and Rod and the horses and the plain.

'Would yer *like* ter ride, Lindsay girl?' asked Artie now. 'Would yer like if we learned yer?'

'I'd love it, Artie,' she replied promptly, with enthusiasm. If she could ride, then perhaps Rod might ask her, some time, to ride with him over the plain, the way he was doing now with Carleen. She would leave the competition stuff to them, if they wished to enter for some races, which was what these stakes must be. She would not aspire to those heights, but if she could attain a certain proficiency, why then, some day he might ask Lindsay herself to go with him—perhaps when Carleen had gone back to Sydney.

'I'd just love it!' she repeated breathlessly, her eyes shining.

Shorty looked her over critically.

'You can't wear that skirt, though, Lindsay. That won't do.'

'I have my shorts.'

'Shorts ain't no use,' Artie told her bluntly. 'The stirrup leathers'll pinch yer legs, see. Ain't yer got any strides?'

'Strides?'

'You know. Duds.'

'No jeans, or anything?' suggested Mickie.

Lindsay thought of Carleen's beautifully cut jodhpurs. She had noticed two pairs in Carleen's room when she had been making the bed one day.

'No. No jeans,' she admitted forlornly.

'Why not use some of them khaki duds in the store?' Herb said. 'There's 'eaps of 'em there, ain't there, an' if the book-keeper can't lay 'er 'ands on 'em, then I don't know who can!'

Herb's idea was unanimously adopted in lieu of any better one being proposed, and that was how Lindsay began her riding lessons—clad in a pair of khaki trousers which were the smallest size she could find in the pile. As they happened to have a thirty-two-inch waist measurement, it was necessary to wear a belt (happily the store could provide that, too!), beneath which the khaki cloth bulged in uneasy lumps and folds right down to the place where she had rolled the turn-ups over an extra couple of times to enable her shabby sandshoes to peep out the bottom.

They brought in a horse called Dusty on which to teach her. Dusty was an angular beast, all drooping limbs and bony protuberances. He had a large, deceptively unintelligent head, a sleepy eye, and a tendency to help his rider into the saddle by dint of a well-aimed nip. Lindsay was terrified of him.

'He's so—*tall*,' she said dubiously, eyeing the distance between the saddle and the ground with some misgiving.

'It ain't 'im that's tall, it's you that's small, see, Lindsay. It's a different thing altogether, that.'

'It amounts to the same thing, surely, Artie?'

'No, it don't! Where's yer spirit, eh? Come on, Lindsay, once we get you up there, yer'll be O.K,' he assured her bracingly. 'Up yer go, now!'

Willing hands pushed and lifted, and Lindsay felt herself borne through the air, willy-nilly. Then she was somehow in the saddle, fumbling for the reins with nervous fingers.

'Git yer feet in the stirrups first.' Artie.

'Don't hold the reins *and* that monkey-grip, Lindsay. He's not energetic enough to buck, anyway.' Mickie.

'Straighten out yer legs, Lindsay. The way you're crouchin' up there, yer'd think you was perchin' on a flamin' ant-hill.' Herb.

'Just relax, now, Lindsay, and give him a little kick.' Shorty.

'Gently does it!'

They all yelled advice. Dusty edged forward reluctantly. His limbs appeared to be quite rusty with disuse, and upon that encouraging supposition, she kicked a little harder and he walked gingerly around the saddling-yard. It was comforting to discover that Dusty was even less enthusiastic than she was herself!

The first lesson was pronounced a success by all who contributed, and after that, the procedure was repeated every evening just before sundown, when the men had ridden in, unsaddled, watered, and fed their own horses, with varying degrees of progress on the pupil's part.

'Yer better get good quick, Lindsay,' Artie urged her one day, watching the two specks that were Carleen and Rod coming through the shade trees along the creek on their horses. 'We want yer ter be real good, quick, Lindsay— quicker than wot you are, see.'

'I can't see any need to hurry, Artie,' she replied mildly. 'Surely it's better to be slow and steady, and learn thoroughly while I'm about it?'

'There ain't time for that,' retorted Artie obscurely, and it seemed that the others were in agreement with him.

'I think we'll take you for a longer ride tomorrow, Lindsay,' Shorty told her. 'Mickie and I will come back early. What you need is a longer spell in the saddle, to get the proper feel of it. This way, we're stopping and starting too much.'

'Very well, if you think it will help.'

Lindsay was amenable to any suggestion that might be of benefit. She was actually enjoying her riding lessons, and it was thrilling to be past that tedious stage of having to be led once she was outside the yard. She was certainly beginning to acquire more confidence, and was well content with her own advancement. However, the men had all been so kind, had put so much time and effort into her initiation, that she was willing to please them in any way she could.

She came back from that expedition so stiff and sore that she could hardly move when she finally slid from the saddle. Her nose was sunburnt because her hat had kept sliding back when Dusty trotted or cantered, and her face was scarlet with effort, beaded with a fine dew of perspiration, and smeared by several trails of grime where she had been swiping at the wayward flies which got under her veil.

She was going to be late for tea! Lindsay quickened her pace, awkwardly because of the stiffness of her limbs, the soreness of her racked muscles. She slammed the wicket gate in the white fence, and raced up the path, head down—smack into Rod Bennett.

'Hold on there!'

He gripped her arm, steadied her, and then stepped back a little. He was already changed, into a blue shirt tonight, with a cravat at his neck instead of a tie. The effect was one of rakish charm. As dark as the devil, thought Lindsay, and with the same dangerous fascination! Her heart was pounding, and a pulse beat in her throat. The breathlessness she was experiencing had little to do with the fact that she had been hurrying.

'Oh, I'm sorry. I just wasn't thinking where I was going, I'm afraid.'

She looked up to find Rod's eyes crinkling at the corners

as he inspected her state of dusty dishevelment. When his eyes reached her trousers, he had to grin, quite openly. His teeth glinted in the half light.

'I must say you're a ball of fashion, Lindsay. Have you been having some more riding lessons?'

'How did you know about my riding lessons?' she asked in surprise. He had never put in an appearance at them, and the only glimpses of him that she had caught were of a distant figure, usually in the company of another distant figure—Carleen, of course.

'It's my business to know what goes on on my own station, Lindsay,' he reminded her with a strangely quizzical expression. 'How are you coming on, by the way?'

'Not very fast, it appears,' she admitted humbly. '*I* am quite pleased with my progress, but the men don't seem to be. They say I'll never win the—er—knockout stakes at this rate.'

Rod's grey gaze sharpened. His eyes narrowed with a keenness that made her feel uncomfortably self-conscious all of a sudden.

'Do they, by George! So that's what they say, eh?' He stroked his chin with a brown, square-tipped finger. 'I've noticed them all there, putting you and Dusty through your paces every night, and I reckoned they must be up to something.'

'Yes, they've all been so kind. They want me to learn—and of course I want it, too. I had a pony once, long ago, at—er—at Batlow.' She paused uncertainly, wishing she hadn't said that. She waited for the quick frown that the mention of her childhood home usually brought, but surprisingly, it did not come. Rod was still stroking his chin. He appeared deep in thought.

'Did you, Lindsay?' was all he replied, abstractedly.

'Yes, a dear little coloured one, brown and white.' She hesitated, then—'What is it, Rod, this knockout stakes? Something to do with the Races at Peperina?'

'No, not at Peperina, Lindsay.'

'But a race?'

'I suppose you *could* call it that,' he murmured gravely. 'A race, but with no set time or place for the finish.'

Lindsay wiped her palm over her moist forehead in a sudden, worried gesture, carrying the dusty smear near one eyebrow right across to her temple.

'Oh dear!' she exclaimed nervously, 'I do hope they aren't expecting me to enter for it. I'd never be good enough.'

Rod caught her hand on its way back from making the new dust-streak, and said sharply,

'Good God, Lindsay! What have you done here?'

He turned her palm upwards and inspected it more closely. Her hand in his looked strangely pale and small.

'They're blisters,' she told him simply. 'I went for a long, *long* ride today. I keep wanting to use both hands on the reins, but they all say I've got to learn to control the horse with just one hand, because of opening gates and carrying things. They say that everyone out here can ride with only one hand, so I did it the whole time today. That's why I've got blisters.'

'I see.' He released his grasp. 'You'd better put something on them. Are you feeling stiff?'

'A bit.'

'Have a good hot bath instead of a shower tonight, Lindsay. Take your time, and soak. It will help the stiffness to go away, and it doesn't matter if you're late for tea, just once.'

'I will, Rod. Thank you.'

'Lindsay.'

'Yes?'

He looked down at her, his sternness softening visibly.

'Don't worry about the knockout stakes too much,' he advised her kindly. 'If the men happen to mention them again, just say that Rod says there would be no point in you entering for them in any case. Have you got that? *Rod says.*'

She sighed relievedly.

'I'm glad. I won't worry any more, then, Rod.' She turned to go.

'That's right. There's no necessity to worry. And— Lindsay?'

'Yes?' She turned back.

'About not being *good* enough'—he put a hand beneath her chin, tilted her face gently, looked right into her eyes with a quite unfamiliar expression in his own steady grey ones—'I think that sometimes, Lindsay, you're inclined to underestimate yourself.'

A rustle sounded through the gauze near by. Then the veranda door swung open, and Carleen appeared.

'Oh, there you are, Rod! How nice of you to suggest a walk in the garden before tea. I'm sorry to have kept you waiting. Good gracious, Lindsay, you aren't even changed yet. You'll be late for tea if you don't hurry.'

'I'm—just going,' Lindsay whispered huskily.

'Take your time,' Rod reminded her as she went. 'It doesn't matter at all if tea is late tonight.'

Lindsay did not suppose that it did! Not tonight! With a heart that ached unbearably, she watched Carleen link her arm through Rod's and wander down the path at his side in a drift of French perfume. It obviously mattered to neither of them that supper might be late! Lindsay went stiffly to her room, peeled off her dusty clothes, and soaked. She felt curiously depressed—so much so, indeed, that she did not even bother to put on her 'best' skirt and blouse for the meal. Her faded blue one matched her own faded blue mood, and so on it went, along with several dabs of cold cream to the tip of her sunburnt nose and forehead. Her skin would probably peel, she realised gloomily, and peering into the mirror she could discern a thickening crop of freckles. *Freckles!* Lindsay powdered them despairingly, and made her way to the dining-room.

Rod appeared to be in an unusually benign mood tonight. He smiled a lot, and adopted a leisurely, bantering tone with Carleen, who as always centred the conversation upon herself as much as possible. When Rod was in one of these teasing moods of his, he suddenly seemed much younger—carefree— as if he had purposely shelved his many responsibilities for the evening with the express intention of enjoying himself. This was the way he had been with Margie, and now he was the same with Carleen. There was something about both of these young women that appealed to Rod, without a doubt.

With Lindsay, he was different.

Reserved? Inscrutable? Lindsay sought in her mind for the correct definition, failed to find it.

What else could she expect, in all honesty? She was simply the book-keeper—the unforgivably *female* book-keeper—and as such she received the somewhat distant consideration of a courteous employer who was indubitably a very busy man, with lots of more important things about which to think than his personal approach to the more sensitive among his employees.

Watching covertly as he engaged in a bout of diverting repartee with Carleen, his mouth curving in a cynically attractive manner, his eyes glinting appreciatively as she leaned towards him, Lindsay remembered that moment outside this evening with a curious little pang. Just for one second, as he gazed down at her in the gloaming with that darkening expression, it had seemed to Lindsay as though he was seeing her, for the very first time, in a human light. She could still feel the warmth and firmness of his hand as he took hers, the strength of his fingers, the kindness beneath his lazy amusement over her khaki store trousers with their bulging bottom and rolled-up cuffs.

Just for one second, out there in the garden, it had seemed to Lindsay as though some hidden, unbidden magic had drawn herself and Rod together in its spell. Something quite intangible had been happening, something that had set Lindsay's nerves deliciously aquiver.

And then the gauze door had creaked on its hinges. With Carleen's appearance, the magic moment had fled—probably for ever.

Lindsay could not imagine any girl being lucky enough to have a moment such as that one with Rod twice in any lifetime!

CHAPTER 8

THE following week Margie brought a party of young people over to play tennis.

Shorty and Mick, the two jackaroos, joined in, and together with Carleen and Lindsay, made up a party of eight. The boys worked hard for a couple of evenings beforehand, sprinkling the court with water, rolling it, and marking out new white lines with lime. Lindsay did all she could to help, carrying water, moving the strings that they had stretched out as a guide to straightness, and bringing them mugs of tea or beer at intervals. Carleen was conspicuous by her absence, although she did appear once or twice, simulating interest in their progress, but at the same time taking care not to linger sufficiently long to be given something to do.

The visitors who walked up from the plane with Margie all had on crisp white tennis clothes, and even Mickie and Shorty, when they came whistling up from their quarters, looked unfamiliarly smart in their white shorts and shirts, socks, and whitened tennis shoes, their muscular limbs appearing more brown and sinewy than ever in contrast.

Lindsay knew that her own shorts and shirt were, as always, a compromise, but she was proud of her sandshoes, which the boys had whitened for her when they were doing their own, and which had come up like new. She found herself looking forward to the afternoon enormously.

She played a passable game of tennis, and once she learned that Rod himself had opted out on the pretext of doing some work in his office, felt her self-consciousness slipping away. He would 'be around', he assured them, and would certainly attend the barbecue lunch on the lawn, and would come out from time to time to cheer them on and see who was winning. Even Carleen's own pleas could not persuade him to change his mind about playing, and when she discovered his intention not to take part, she immediately said that in that case, she wouldn't either. She was sure he could do with some company, and she'd promise not to distract him if his work was really as important as all that.

Only Margie's diplomatic intervention saved the numbers from being thrown out by having one girl too few. With an ungracious shrug, Carleen finally agreed to take part.

'Not the easiest of visitors to have around, I should imagine,' Margie murmured softly, looking after Carleen as she strolled away. 'How do you get on with her, Lindsay, I wonder?'

Lindsay, too, watched the elegant blonde girl as she stopped to chat to the people in Margie's party. She ignored Mick and Shorty, just as she ignored all the other employees on Gundooee, hardly deigning to pass the time of day with them. As for Sibbie and Bella and those other loyal and friendly aborigines from the gunyahs down on the creek, she avoided these with a noticeable fastidiousness that almost amounted to mysophobia.

Today Carleen had on a sleeveless tennis dress with a brief, pleated skirt that swung in a pretty, kilted effect about her long, slender legs. Her hair was tied back with a broad red ribbon that matched the little scarlet motif on her pocket. She was laughing in that familiarly husky, attractive way at something one of the men was saying to her, spinning her racket carelessly with one hand as she replied.

'I don't see very much of her, Margie,' Lindsay admitted, shrugging briefly. 'None of us do, really, except for Rod.'

'I see.' The other girl looked thoughtful, and just a little bit puzzled. 'Is she staying for very long, do you know, Lindsay?'

'Until she's quite better—I'm quoting Rod now. She's had—er—bronchitis, or something, I believe.' Lindsay was vague.

Margie raised an eyebrow, smiled openly, that pretty, candid smile that showed her pearly, even teeth.

'She looks as strong as an ox, if you ask me—disgustingly healthy, in fact. Oh well, come on, Lindsay. Shall we go and help Mannie and Rod start the barbecue?'

Following Margie over the lawn, Lindsay found herself hoping that Margie's own feelings had not been hurt by her revelation that Rod and Carleen were so frequently in each other's company. There had been such an odd look in her eye for a fleeting second, and Lindsay wondered if Margie, for all her gaiety and undiscriminating friendliness towards everyone, might not be vulnerable where Rod himself was concerned. That was what Mac had hinted in the kitchen one day, and it was all too possible that he could be right. People like Margie were better than most at concealing the depth of their emotions, and Lindsay hoped, quite fervently, that Carleen would not in some way inflict a hurt on this friendly girl whom she was beginning to like so much. Margie was worth ten of Carleen, she thought fiercely. How blind men could be, if they were dazzled by that lovely, shallow façade!

The barbecue was a success, by any standards. Large succulent steaks from the station's cold-room were grilled over the open fire, and accompanied by an assortment of salads and fruits prepared by Mannie and Lindsay. Rod was turning the steaks, doling out potatoes which he had buried in their jackets in the hot ashes to cook. He handled the operation with the dexterity born of many years of preparing meals in the great outdoors with a minimum of culinary equipment.

Margie and her crowd had brought cold desserts as their contribution to the lunch, and after that Rod boiled the billy, in the traditional country way, placing a small, sappy eucalypt bough carefully across the top to disperse the smoke, and tapping the blackened billy all round when he had brewed-up, to sink the tea-leaves to the bottom. They drank the tea scalding hot. It was a refreshing finish to what for Lindsay had been an excitingly unusual meal, although the others, even Carleen, were obviously well versed in the barbecue art.

Afterwards they all lay around for a while to recover, in the plots of shade on the lawn, talking idly, smoking, exchanging views and stories. Then the first doubles players tossed for service, and wandered over to the court, and Lindsay,

Margie, Shorty, and Mick began to clear up the remains of the picnic and carry things into the house, insisting that Mannie should leave everything to them, and go to lie down on her bed for her afternoon sleep, as she was accustomed to doing each day.

By the time they returned, Rod had dealt with the dying embers of his fire and had strolled across to watch the tennis in progress. When they approached he stood up, moved to one end of the long wooden garden seat to make room for them all, and then they all sat down again. Lindsay, at the other end of the bench, hoped that he would soon tire of looking on, and that he would have gone back to his office before her own turn came.

He didn't, of course. When Carleen and the others came off, he passed around the beer and iced fruit juice from the table just behind him, and chatted to his visitors.

'You play a very neat game, Carleen.' She heard his deep voice among the others. 'That's quite a backhand you have, and you obviously use that pretty little head in tennis, as in everything else. That lob of yours broke deadlock, and then you were home and dry.'

'How nice of you, Rod, to notice. I do wish *you* would play, too, though. Won't you change your mind?'

'Not today, I think. I might give you a game of singles some time, if you like, now that the boys have the court in order. I don't promise to spare you, though, just because you happen to look so delectably feminine. I'll be out to win, I assure you.'

She gave a small, secretive smile.

'Darling, you never do spare me, do you? I thrive on it, Rod, that masterful touch! And remember—*I* am out to win, too, so that should be interesting, shouldn't it?' she murmured.

Lindsay looked away. They were talking in riddles which she did not understand, but the smug, complacent expression on Carleen's face sent little shivers down her spine, for no particular reason.

Her eyes met Margie's, and what Margie did then surprised her. She closed one eye, and winked at Lindsay, quite solemnly—and Lindsay knew that she, too, had heard that snippet of conversation.

Lindsay never made up her mind, afterwards, whether it was that upsetting morsel of conversation, or Rod's own presence on the sidelines, which was responsible for her lack of concentration, but whatever it was, Shorty must have cursed his inept partner soundly more than once under his breath. Apart from one or two miraculous recoveries, she had never played such appalling tennis in her life. She slammed, whacked, hooked, hesitated—all with disastrous consequences. And then a singing ball from Mick put an end to it all.

In other circumstances, Lindsay might have been grateful for such an abrupt finish when she was acquitting herself so badly, but just now it was difficult to feel gratitude, to feel anything, indeed, but that searing pain in her left eye, that peculiar knocking in her head, that distant woolliness in her legs.

She could only stand rooted to the spot, her racket at her feet, her hand clapped hard against the injured eye, while its companion watered in sympathy.

'Gosh, Lindsay, I'm *sorry*!' Mickie had hurdled the net and come quickly to her side. Voices gabbled all about her.

And then someone spoke a little louder. Lindsay recognised that tone of brusque authority even though she was unable to see its owner.

'All right, everyone, I'll take care of it. There's no need to break up the party, that game was a foregone conclusion anyway. You others have another set now, and I'll look after Lindsay.' She felt a firm grasp on her upper arm, leading her away. 'Come with me,' said the voice near her ear, in very much the same tone as it had done on her very first day— that forbearing, polite, no-nonsense tone that had bidden her, '*You* come with *me*.'

Lindsay permitted herself to be led into the house. Rod took her straight to the bathroom, pushed her gently but firmly into the cane chair there, and flicked on the overhead light. Then he pulled her fingers away from her streaming eye, and cupped her face in his hands.

'Let me see, Lindsay, please. Look up. Look down.'

He was completely impersonal in his efficient inspection. Finally he squeezed out a cloth in cold water, formed it into a neat, square pad, and placed it against her eye, putting her own fingers back over it.

'Just hold that there for a while, and I'll get some iced water from the kitchen for the next round.'

'W-will it be all right?'

Rod grinned.

'You're going to have a corker of a black eye, I should think, but in all other respects it's fortunately unharmed. You must have shut it instinctively as you turned to avoid the ball. One's reflexes can be surprisingly quick and effective under those circumstances.'

Lindsay derived cold comfort from his words.

'A *black* eye? Oh no! You mean, the kind that then goes purple and yellow by turns?' she asked in dismay.

'That's the kind I mean, exactly. A pity, I grant you—I prefer them green and soft, myself, just as you do. Green and soft, like a mist on a lily-pond.'

Rod was saying *that*, about *her* eyes? He couldn't be! She bit her lip in vexation that the lily-pond greenness, in one of them, at least, was evidently gone for some time if his diagnosis was to be trusted.

'Maybe a piece of steak——' she suggested timidly. 'I've heard that it sometimes works.'

He chuckled.

'Haven't you had enough steak for today?' he asked whimsically, then, shrugging, 'Very well, Lindsay, I'll get some. There was plenty left over from lunch—but I'm afraid your optimism will go unrewarded. *Nothing* is going to prevent that eye from turning black.'

When he returned, he took her out on to the veranda and adjusted one of the deck-chairs near his office door into a reclining position.

'Sit down there, Lindsay, and lean right back. You'll be more comfortable and cool here. Does your head ache at all?'

'Only a tiny bit. It's nothing.'

Rod drew up a chair close beside hers, and leaned over her,

putting the piece of steak he had brought gently in place. He was devastatingly near. Even the faintly nauseating odour of uncooked meat right next to her nose did little to inhibit the emotion that Lindsay felt go surging through her at his proximity.

'Close the other eye, too, Lindsay. I'll hold it in place for a while, and then I must do some work. I shall be very near in my office, though, so you must call me if you want me at all.'

Lindsay obediently shut both eyes. She was glad to, because she couldn't have gone on looking at Rod's square jaw-line, brown column of throat, and wide shoulders much longer, and since his chest across her line of vision rendered any other view virtually impossible, it seemed prudent to obey.

She sighed.

'I'm sorry I messed up the afternoon for everyone. I can't think how I did it.'

'Never mind about it now. These things happen; although' —she could detect the smile in his voice—'I must say you're a glutton for punishment, aren't you, little one?'

A light touch brushed over her brow—just the barest suggestion of a hand's caressing movement. Lindsay must have imagined it. She kept her eyes shut tightly because she did not want to discover that she had been wrong.

'So *there* you are! I've been searching for you everywhere!'

Lindsay opened her eyes abruptly, struggling to a sitting position and said, slightly breathlessly, because she had been startled by the other girl's silent approach, 'I—I'll take it now, Rod. There's no need for you to hold it, any more. Th-thank you for all you did.'

'How is she, anyway?' Carleen did not bother to address herself to Lindsay. 'We've had another set, and now the other three are having to play cut-throat.'

There was a waspishly accusing note in that statement that was not lost upon Lindsay, although it appeared to escape the man beside her.

He stood up, stretched in a leisurely fashion, and said

equably,

'She'll live, I think, Carleen. Did you have a good set? Who won this time—you and Barry?'

'Of course, darling. I always win—if it's at all possible.' A pretty, deprecating smile took the boastfulness out of her reply. 'I was just telling Lindsay that the other day, wasn't I, Lindsay? I suppose some of us are born to win, others to be defeated—it's probably all a matter of destiny. So far, I've been lucky.' She yawned complacently. 'I'd love a cool drink, Rod. Could I have one, do you think? And then we could carry some more out to the lawn for the others, couldn't we?'

'You may prefer to stay there and rest for a while, Lindsay,' Rod suggested kindly, as he turned to accompany Carleen along the veranda.

'I—yes—I think I shall, if you don't mind,' she mumbled confusedly. Anything to be spared the sight of that slender hand resting possessively on his bare brown forearm, those guileless eyes turned up to his, the inviting intimacy of that smile that effectively shut out the rest of the world, and left just two people—Rod and Carleen.

By evening Lindsay's eye was swollen and darkening, and when she got up next morning she saw that the entire area was puffy and discoloured. Alas! As Rod had forecast, no measures known to man could have prevented her from ending up with a black eye that would have made many a prize-fighter's battle scars look pale in comparison.

She was down in the store later on when Carleen approached, looking elegant and appropriately cool in a sleeveless turquoise tabard over matching shorts. She clucked sympathetically at the sight of Lindsay bent over her log book at the far end of the room.

'Hello,' she greeted her amicably. 'You appeared so miserable at breakfast this morning that I thought I'd come down and offer my services. Don't look so surprised, Lindsay. I really was sorry for you yesterday, but there didn't seem much point in not going on with the party. I'm sure you'd have only felt worse if we'd all stopped, anyway.'

'Oh, I would!' Lindsay assured her eagerly, warmed at this

unexpected *volte-face* on the other's part. 'I'd have felt
dreadful if everyone had stopped playing just because of me.
And Rod was really awfully kind.'

'*Wasn't* he! I thought so, too, I must say. With him there
to administer first-aid and comfort, there was really no need
for anyone else, was there?' Carleen surveyed the store with
idle interest. 'What are you doing now, Lindsay? What are
all these things, for goodness' sake?'

She picked up one of an assortment of unfamiliar objects
from the pile on the counter and turned it between her
fingers.

'Those are machinery spares—windmill ones there, and
those are for the bores. This pile is mainly electrical, and that
lot are for Rod's plane.'

'Goodness, aren't you clever, knowing which ones are
which!' Carleen's voice held genuine admiration.

Lindsay flushed.

'I didn't at first,' she admitted humbly. 'I got into some
awful muddles, but the men rallied round and helped, so
that Rod wouldn't find out how ignorant I was. They taught
me how to identify them, and there are some illustrated cata-
logues—look, these ones here, all numbered, you see—and I
still refer to these any time I'm in doubt.'

'And after you tick them there? What then?'

'Then they go to the machinery shop or the blacksmith's
shop, and the men just take them when they need them. All
I'm doing here is checking them against the invoices to make
sure that everything has arrived that was ordered.'

'Oh, I *see*.' Carleen ran her hand along the counter
thoughtfully, inspected her fingers, and wrinkled her pretty
nose at the dust she had gathered on them. 'Rather a depressing place, isn't it? And so is the whole homestead, if one
never had a break, I should think. Of course, once Rod is
married, I don't suppose for a moment he'd want to live
away out here in the back-blocks—he'd probably just visit
occasionally in his plane.' She bent down to inspect the
shelves under the counter. 'Heavens, what stuff! And what's
in those cupboards there? The locked ones?'

Lindsay showed her, explained that these were not drugs

in the medical sense, but simply potentially dangerous fluids, for which the men had to sign if they received them.

'And of course the people down at the creek aren't allowed them even if they *could* sign for them—which of course they can't.'

'You mean, the blacks?'

'Yes, the aborigines.'

'Why ever not? They could always put an identification mark in the book, surely? You know, a cross or something in the way of an individual squiggle.'

Lindsay shook her head.

'Rod says not. He says there's no reason for them to need any of those things anyway, not in the course of their particular work, he meant.'

Carleen folded her arms, smiling faintly.

'What an archaic set-up, isn't it!' She gazed out of the window, with which the saddling-yard was aligned. There were only two horses remaining, reins looped over the rail, heads dropped close together, as though they were exchanging whispered horse-talk in the heat while they waited. At this time of day the men were usually all away, but evidently there must still be a couple of them about the place, still to ride out. 'And do the blacks ever come and bother you to give them things?'

Lindsay ticked off an item in her book, and put it into its correct pile.

'No, never. At least, one did just once. He pointed to some bottle or other—I forget what—and said he wanted it to clean harness with. But when I said he couldn't have it, he just laughed and went away.'

'Here, let me do some of that with you.'

Carleen was in such a pleasantly friendly mood that Lindsay would have felt churlish had she refused.

Together they listed all the spares on the bench, Carleen reading them out and ticking off the quantities while Lindsay identified them and put them into the correct pile. It was a laborious business, and it was not difficult to guess that the transparent Carleen was very soon utterly bored by the monotony of it all. Her attention was inclined to wander, but she resolutely struck to her post, and the two girls had actually completed the task, and were preparing to go back to the homestead, when the door opened and Artie and Tommo came in.

Artie appeared quite taken aback to discover that Lindsay was not alone, and even more surprised that her companion was none other than the stand-offish young woman whom he had disdainfully classified as a dame, and who up till now had been in the habit of treating him as if he didn't exist at all.

He touched his hat, and became very red.

'G'day,' he mumbled, his eyes shifting back to Lindsay as quickly as possible. 'I wonder if them galvanised staples 'ave come in yet, Lindsay, the ones we was waitin' for last week?'

'They'll be here somewhere, Artie.' She eyed the un-opened packages still to be checked. 'It will take me a while to find them, though, I'm afraid. Could you come back, maybe?'

Artie prodded the boards with the toe of his dusty boot, undecided.

'I'm supposed ter be out with 'Erb right now, mendin' a fence, see. 'E's goin' ter think I've lost me bloomin' way in the scrub, ain't 'e, I'm that late. I've got everythink else we're needin' ter take out except fer them rakin' staples.' He hesitated, brightened. 'Tell yer what, Lindsay. When you come across 'em, you leave 'em out on the counter, and Tommo 'ere'll bring 'em after me, see. 'E's ridin' that stretch anyway, this arvo, and I reckon maybe we'll 'ave enough ter keep us goin' till 'e comes. You leave 'em out and 'e'll get 'em. 'E can go down 'ome fer some grub in the meantime. O.K?'

Tommo rolled his eyes and nodded sagely to show that it was O.K. by him, too, and then he and Artie disappeared together, leaving Lindsay and Carleen to start sorting fran-tically through packages and parcels once more.

'Drat those men! I thought we'd finished.' Carleen's good humour had evidently been tried too far. She helped half-heartedly after that, impatient to be gone, and heaved a sigh of relief when at last the carton had been unearthed and put conspicuously on the bench-top above the shelves.

As they went out together, Lindsay reached up to the nail above the door and retrieved her bunch of keys.

'I never dare to leave them in my pocket,' she explained, 'in case they drop out when I'm bending down somewhere and I lose them. I've made a point of hanging them up when I come in, and the same in my own room up at the house. Funny how things get to be a habit. You soon find yourself doing them automatically.'

'Aren't you going to lock just now?'

'No, because Tommo will have to come back for those things. I'll just take the keys with me, though. It's only for an hour or so, in any case, while we have lunch.'

The two girls had their meal with Mannie—just the three of them. When Rod was out all day, there did not seem much point in preparing anything elaborate. Carleen was a light, selective eater in any event, always preoccupied with her figure, and Mannie had the elderly person's dislike of anything too heavy or substantial, so they usually settled for salad, or a simple snack of eggs.

After lunch was over, Carleen asked Lindsay to come to her own bedroom, and once there she stood for a moment, hesitating, before asking the younger girl, with a noticeable display of diffidence, if she could possibly do her a favour. The customary demanding note was quite absent from Carleen's voice just now, and as she made her request she smiled with unfamiliar warmth, and Lindsay found herself responding. What else could she do but comply, in view of Carleen's amiable overtures and her help in the store that morning?

'It's this, Lindsay. The hem of this frock. I must have caught it on something—look!—and I've ripped some of the stitching out. Quite a lot of it, I'm afraid.'

Lindsay inspected the garment. It was of fine lawn, a rather lovely tobacco brown print.

'I'll do it for you this evening, if you like.'

Carleen's lips pursed with disappointment.

'Oh dear, I'd hoped to *wear* it this evening,' she murmured plaintively. 'It's so hot today, and my other dresses all have sleeves. Couldn't you be a dear and do it now? How long

332

would it take? I'd do it myself, but you know how hopeless I am with things like that, and it's such very fine material, I'd be certain to make a hash of it.'

Lindsay glanced from her watch to her cousin's hopeful countenance, and gave in.

'Sit in my window-seat, here, then, Lindsay, and I'll get Mannie's work-box for you. I saw some thread there exactly this colour the other day. The light will be at your back there.' She darted off eagerly, brought back the sewing kit and thanked Lindsay prettily once more.

'I'll leave you to it,' she said from the doorway. 'Just put it on the bed when you've finished, and I shall hang it up later.'

Carleen wore the dress that night. It had been a painstaking task to make all those tiny unseen stitches, but one would never have known that anything had been wrong with it at all. Indeed, its wearer had seldom looked lovelier, decided Lindsay impartially. There was a certain glow about Carleen this evening, a translucent beauty in her classic features, an unusual serenity in her sometimes discontented blue eyes.

Rod himself seemed aware of her in a different way tonight, too. Gone was the bantering, teasing tone he so often adopted, the sophisticated sparring and amused cynicism which he and Carleen so often employed in their verbal jousting. Tonight he was responding to this new, serene Carleen with a flatteringly serious and masculine interest which the recipient evidently found inordinately pleasing. Her thoughtfulness to Mannie, her inclusion of Lindsay in the conversation, reflected a mysterious but by no means unwelcome change in her attitude, and after dinner she even helped to carry out the dishes before joining Rod in his office for a cigarette.

Whether it was that Carleen's newly acquired good humour rubbed off on everyone else, or whether it was the fact that it induced an answering affability in Rod in particular, Lindsay could not have said. Whatever was responsible, there was a subtle alteration in the atmosphere at Gundooee homestead over the next couple of days, and Lindsay basked in the change. No undercurrents of uncertainty, jealousy, or sarcasm were there to disrupt the pleasant state of existing harmony. Carleen was noticeably kindly disposed to all and sundry, Rod was less watchful and critical, and Mannie almost purred with satisfaction that life was now as pleasantly peaceful as it had been when she and Rod were alone.

Indeed, if anything, it was even nicer now, she confided to Lindsay in the kitchen. It did Rod good to have the girls around. An old lady was no fit company for a young man of thirty, who should be thinking about marriage and a family of his own. Mannie had strong views on the subject, and did not hesitate to air them when she felt inclined.

'I wouldn't be surprised if those two have come to some sort of private understanding,' she observed when she and Lindsay were alone one day. 'I've never known Rod to be quite like he is just now, not even with Margie. He's more relaxed and happy, somehow, than ever before. As for Carleen—well, I must admit I've been quite wrong about her. I didn't take to her at first, but she's been so different lately, thoughtful and kind, I can only think that perhaps the poor child's recent illness made her narky, and that she's feeling better now. I know what it can be like, trying to appear normal, and be pleasant, when you aren't feeling too well. It's all a bit of a bother, but one has to pretend, to save a fuss.'

A knife had twisted in Lindsay's heart, a knife that caused a pain of bitterness to flood through her whole being.

Carleen, who had come with blatant calculation to annex Rod Bennett for herself, looked like succeeding, if Mannie's observations were accurate. And as for Rod, he had never seemed happier, as if he had suddenly found something for which he had been searching for a very long time. Lindsay had herself sensed the very thing that Mannie had put into words!

You were supposed to be *glad* when a person you loved found happiness, Lindsay reminded herself fiercely. You were supposed to be glad in an unselfish, basic sort of way. Easier said than done, that, but she'd have to try! And she'd have to be glad for Carleen too. It really did appear that

Carleen had fallen properly in love with Rod—with Rod as a person, and not just as a wealthy, athletic, eligible symbol whom she had come intentionally to pursue. What else but love could account for such a devastating change in someone's nature, could bring about that amiability and softness which had previously not existed?

Lindsay put these thoughts firmly to the back of her mind, and concentrated on Mannie's last sentence. It was, to Lindsay, a revealing one, although she was certain that Mannie was totally unaware of that fact. It confirmed something of what Lindsay had actually suspected for some time now, and that was that the old lady was far from well. Just lately, Lindsay couldn't help noticing that Mannie spent much more time resting in her room, and when she reappeared, she did not seem refreshed. Often, too, when she rose from her chair on the veranda, she would stand quite still for a while, as if the effort of getting up had been almost too much for her, as if she had to give herself a minute or two to readjust.

Observing these signs, Lindsay had taken over some of Mannie's tasks in the house as unobtrusively as possible—so unobtrusively, indeed, that the old woman seemed hardly aware of it—and lately she had made a point of coming up from the book-keeper's cottage or the store in plenty of time to help Mannie prepare the evening meal. In the mornings, too, it was as often as not Lindsay herself who cut thick hunks of cold meat and sandwiched them with pickles and butter between bread-slices for Rod's saddle-bag, and who turned out a tray of puffy golden scones to cool in time to accompany those sandwiches.

Mannie had perhaps noticed, but if she did, she made no comment. Maybe she was too weary and languid to bother remarking on the fact, but more than likely she refrained because, as she had said just now, one did not welcome a fuss.

On that realisation, Lindsay closed her lips upon what she had been about to say. She would respect Mannie's wish for privacy, but the sight of those tiredly circled eyes and the lines of suffering about the old lady's mouth did nothing to make her decision to keep silence an easier one.

It was the one discordant note in a presently idyllic world, that secret which Lindsay was convinced that she shared without Mannie's knowledge.

Before dinner-time came round that evening, Lindsay was able to display the lemon pie she had made while Mannie was having her rest, and the casserole already cooking slowly in the oven. Sibbie and Bella had peeled and prepared all manner of vegetables for her to put in it, and it smelt unbelievably appetising as Lindsay lifted the lid and showed Mannie what she had done. Her reward, if she had sought one at all, was in the gentle glow of appreciation in Mannie's tired eyes as she had thanked her.

After dinner, she and Mannie drew up their deck-chairs and talked desultorily. Further along the veranda, from Rod's study, came the soft buzz of voices in conversation—Carleen's light, fluted tone, and Rod's own deep one. Lindsay steeled herself not to listen to the muffled sounds of that intimate, after-dinner chat.

The air tonight was laden with perfume. It came from the border of stocks just outside the gauze screen in front of the place where they sat, and from the bed of geraniums in the centre of the lawn. Beyond, the trees were ghostly shapes, lifting a tangle of silvered branches to the moon that floated timelessly above it in its sea of stars.

Lindsay lay back, contemplating the peaceful scene, loth to disturb the soothing silence by speech or any other means, when it was rudely broken by the sound of running feet. They thudded over the hard, bare moon-bathed ground—nearer, nearer. Then the wicket-gate slammed at the bottom of the garden, and Jimmy pounded along the path, up the steps, through the swing-door.

'Boss! Boss!' he was yelling urgently. 'You come quick-fella, Boss, allasame that cheekyfella water burn-up, burn-up, in bingie belonga Tommo!' Rod was out of his study in a flash, flicking on the veranda light.

'What did you say, Jimmy?' he asked sternly. 'Better you talk clear, eh—not gabble-gabble allasame nobody savvy. Clear, Jimmy. Slow, eh? Now, what is it?'

Jimmy's dark, glistening chest was heaving. All he had on was a pair of khaki trousers. His feet were bare, and it was the first time that Lindsay had ever seen him without the beloved pipe which was usually clenched in his strong white teeth.

'That proper badfella water Tommo drink out of that bottle, Boss. Him get plurry mad, bin chase them lubras and piccaninnies—pokem! pokem!—alonga that big stick——' Jimmy's wiry black arms jabbed out savagely in all directions to illustrate his point.

'Where is he now?' Rod asked abruptly.

'Him bin lie on ground now, Boss. Them others hold 'im down while I get Boss, plenty quickfella, see.'

The others had gathered around Rod and Jimmy.

'Wh-what does he mean, Rod? What's he saying?' Carleen put an anxious hand on Rod's arm.

'It sounds as though he's drunk,' was the terse reply.

'Drunk! But where could he get drink, away out *here*? And what could he possibly get drunk *on*?'

'The only place he could get it'—Rod sought and held Lindsay's eye—'would be the store. As for what it *is*, that I intend to find out.'

His eyes were dark with anger. Lindsay's own were fastened on his face, as though mesmerised with foreboding. All the colour had left her cheeks, so that the bruised place around her eye stood out in liverish relief.

'You come, Boss, eh? That proper cheekyfella water, make Tommo crawl oneside alonga that ground allasame him plurry carpet-snake with 'is back broke, see. That badfella stuff *killum* Tommo, Boss!'

'Oh no!' The words escaped Lindsay's numbed lips in an agonised protest. She swayed on her feet.

Rod's hand steadied her. In fact, his fingers bit brutally into her soft flesh as he shook her slightly and said with grim emphasis,

'Not *kill*, you little idiot. He means *hurt*. By the sound of things, he's a long way from dead!'

Without another word he followed Jimmy through the gauze door and down the steps. Seconds later, the little gate clicked back into place, and the two figures disappeared in the night.

'Goodness, what a thing to happen!' Carleen sounded shocked.

Lindsay sank down into the nearest chair. She dared not think, could not *let* herself think, how such a thing could have come about. The only certainy was that it *had*!

Down at the gunyahs came the shrill barking of dogs, the almost hysterical crying of children, and at one point a blood-curdling yell.

'I think I shall go to bed.' Mannie got up stiffly, gave Lindsay's arm a tiny, comforting squeeze, under cover of the semi-darkness, and tactfully withdrew.

A match rasped as Carleen lit a cigarette and stretched her legs.

'I'll stay with you, if you like,' she volunteered. 'I doubt if I could get to sleep with all that racket going on, in any event.'

Lindsay swallowed, unable to trust herself to speak. A strange fear had her in its grip, a sort of guilt that *wasn't* guilt. How could it be, when she knew perfectly well that she had always been so careful of all those fluids and poisons at the store, ever since Artie had warned her on her very first day? Rod will have your hide, he'd said. Remembering, Lindsay shivered. It was a shiver of shock, of dread, of this guilt that wasn't, of an odd, instinctive hopelessness.

It seemed an interminable time before things were quiet once more down at the settlement. One by one the noises abated, until, with the last plaintive whimper of the last dog, there was finally silence.

Shortly after that, Rod came back. He came treading purposefully along the veranda with a curiously set face, hitched around a chair with the toe of his shoe, sat down, and commenced to roll himself a smoke. The fact that he hadn't uttered a single word unnerved Lindsay completely. Anything would seem preferable to this ominous silence!

Carleen spoke first. 'Is he all right, Rod?' she asked, half fearfully.

'He'll do,' Rod replied shortly. He took a long pull on the

cigarette between his fingers, and exhaled as though he were expelling a weary sigh at the same time.

'Was it—was he drunk?'

'Yes, Carleen, I'm afraid he was drunk. Very drunk. And what he was drunk *on*'—a significant pause—'was methylated spirits.'

'Did he tell you that that's what it was?'

'He didn't have to tell me,' Rod pointed out tersely. 'The poor beggar was stinking with it.'

'Oh.' Carleen pursed her lips in concern. 'How awful for you!'

'But worse for him,' he observed tritely. 'He'll have a blinder of a hangover in the morning, and probably won't be fit for days.' Another pause. 'He got the meths from the store, by all accounts. I won't say *stole* it—these people aren't strong on the moral issues.' Rod turned to Lindsay, addressed himself to her exclusively, holding her in a direct penetrating regard. 'If you have an explanation, Lindsay, I'd certainly like to hear it,' he said quietly, although he didn't sound as if he'd really *like* to hear anything she might have to say, at all!

Lindsay licked her lips.

'I'm terribly sorry, Rod, truly I am, but I honestly can't see how I could be to blame. I mean, I've always been so careful, ever since you said. I—I always keep the store locked, and I just don't see how he could have got it.'

'Always? Without fail?'

'Yes, always. *Truly.*'

Carleen's dress rustled as she uncrossed her legs, reached forward to stub out her cigarette.

'Not *quite* always, Lindsay.' She seemed reluctant to speak. 'I mean, do forgive me, my dear, for pointing it out, but you didn't the other day, for instance, did you? That day at lunch-time, remember? You said it wouldn't matter for an hour or two.' She waved a manicured hand apologetically. 'I don't want to interfere, of course. I'm not *meaning* anything, but just in the cause of accuracy——' Her voice tailed off uncertainly.

'*Did* you leave it unlocked one day over the lunch period,

Lindsay?' Rod's voice had a depth of grimness that made her flinch.

'Yes, but——'

'And yet you've just told me that you always lock up, without fail?'

'Yes, well, I do.' She floundered unhappily. 'I mean, there was a reason, that day. The men had staples to collect. I left them on the counter for them. But everything else was locked. I swear it was!'

'You mean you *think* it was,' he corrected her mercilessly.

'No, truly. All the cupboards were locked, every one of them, although the main door was open.'

'It was from the cupboard that he got the stuff, Lindsay. The second on the right.' Rod's voice was oddly bleak. 'Far from being locked, that cupboard door wasn't even shut. It was wide open, so he just took it.'

'Rod, you *must* believe me. Please?' Lindsay was begging him in her distress.

'Why should I believe you, Lindsay—much as I would like to? You have already made one false statement. Why not another?'

Lindsay could only gaze at him in nightmarish disbelief at what he was saying. Through a mist of horror she heard Carleen's voice saying silkily,

'Darling, you're only *human*, I mean, aren't we *all*? Anyone can make a mistake.'

Rod Bennett got to his feet, looked down to where Lindsay sat, nursing her knees in hunched-up misery.

'Some mistakes are redeemable, others are not,' he said harshly. 'I find it very difficult to forgive a mistake that is caused by arrant carelessness and not an error of judgement. I'm deeply disappointed in you, Lindsay. That's all I'll trust myself to say on the matter tonight.'

Without waiting for a further reply, he went into his office and shut the door.

Carleen stirred in her canvas chair.

'Poor Lindsay,' she said sympathetically into the darkness. 'It does look as though you may have cooked your goose, doesn't it?'

CHAPTER 9

For Lindsay, the days that followed were unbearably lonely. She could confide her thoughts and fears to no one, so she was forced to exist in this awful vacuum of solitariness, just Lindsay and her suspicions. They were uneasy thoughts to live with. It was bad enough to even think such things, but to be unable to unburden herself to anybody made the situation even more unpleasant.

Whom, after all, could she tell? Not Rod, with this new barrier of reserve and aloofness between them. He was absolutely unapproachable these days!

Mannie? Yes, perhaps, if she hadn't known that Mannie already had enough with which to concern herself, in her fight against failing health.

Carleen? No, most of all, not Carleen!

Lindsay shied from the thought of a direct confrontation with anyone who could be capable of the dastardly deed of which she suspected her distant cousin. Carleen had demonstrated to Lindsay that she would stop at very little to gain her ends! She had shown that she could be completely and utterly ruthless—clever, too. She had somehow managed to unlock that cupboard at the store, had actually left the door ajar in order to tempt poor old Tommo beyond endurance, and—cleverest of all—had succeeded in locking it again and returning Lindsay's keys to her room without coming under the slightest suspicion from anybody.

When could she have done it?

Lindsay, tossing and turning in sleepless torment, could only suppose that it must have been that day at lunch-time, when they had been together at the store. Carleen would have had time to run back with the keys and unlock the cupboard while Lindsay had been helping Mannie with the lunch. And? After lunch? Lindsay hated herself for thinking this way, but the whole thing added up, didn't it?

Carleen had prevailed upon her to do that hem before going back to the store. She had seen to it that Lindsay sat in her window-seat, from which the route to the store was invisible, and she had taken the keys from Lindsay's own bedroom and relocked the cupboard. That peculiar serenity—*smugness*, Lindsay could call it now, in the light of what she knew!—had stemmed from the fact that Carleen realised, almost immediately, that her plan had half succeeded already. Doubtless she had inspected the contents of that cupboard to make sure there was nothing really lethal in it when she opened it, and when she returned, had noted the disappearance of the large purple flagon.

It only remained to be patient, to wait. In time, her action was almost certain to rebound in the only possible quarter where blame could logically be laid—upon Lindsay herself!

When morning came, Lindsay was thankful. She crawled out of bed, walked softly out on to the veranda—a wistful, unhappy figure in her thin cotton pyjamas.

From the tank came a splash in the half light, and the birds rose screeching and chittering from its banks and settled in the garden trees, shuffling their wings resentfully. Rod was having his morning bathe. Lindsay watched the dark head moving in the water through eyes that were suddenly misted over, so that the outline of the swimmer became blurred and wavy. They were out of sympathy now, she and that swimmer. They were poles apart in every way. Carleen had successfully seen to that!

Lindsay returned to her room, pulled on her clothes, and went to breakfast, helped Mannie to clear the table, made her own and Carleen's beds—Carleen refused to allow Sibbie and Bella into her room—and then took down her keys and started off for the cottage.

Before she came around the corner near the blacksmith's shop, Lindsay could hear the animated conversation that was taking place. As there was a certain amount of intermittent hammering and clanking going on as well, the talk almost amounted to a forthright exchange of shouts, so that Lindsay could not possibly have failed to hear it, even had she wished. And as she took in what was being said, she *did* wish—very much indeed! Artie and Mickie were the participants, and she didn't like the gist of that conversation at all!

'I'm tellin' yer, Mick, it won't do. *She's* goin' around like a cat wot's got all the cream, and our little kitten ain't even got scraps!'

'You're right, Artie, so help me, you are. But what can we do about it?'

'Well, you ain't done much ter shorten them odds, and that's a dinkum fact. What in ruddy 'ell you was at, near doin' 'er in altogether with a rakin' tennis-ball in the eye, I can't think. Why can't yer play tennis more gentle, for Pete's sake?'

'It was purely a case of rotten luck, Artie, that's all.' Mick's voice was conciliatory. 'She just didn't seem to see the ball, and wham! I must say, she wasn't playing all that well, in any case.'

'I 'eard as much from Shorty. I wouldn't put me money on 'er against a blinkin' mosquito, with a tennis racquet. But this other—well, I reckon we 'ad a good chance, Mickie, until this latest flummoxer. I got me own ideas about *that*, too,' Artie added mysteriously.

'There's not much hope at the moment, Art, I grant you, but maybe we can do something to tip the scales a bit. You leave it with me.'

'Well, if yer don't do better than yer did on the tennis-court, 'eaven 'elp us! Our Lindsay's goin' around lookin' about as fetchin' as a flippin' pirate, with that yeller patch all round 'er eye!'

'You leave it with me,' shouted Mickie again above the hammering. 'I'll think of something. Oh, hullo, Lindsay. A beaut morning, isn't it?'

He grinned at her from his post at the head of the restive horse which his companion was busy shoeing.

Artie looked up, too, rather sheepishly. He had a home-rolled cigarette and two shoeing nails stuck moistly between his lips, and the horse's near front hoof between his legs. To Lindsay it was miraculous that he had been able to speak at all in his present state of occupation, let alone speak so loudly.

'Hullo,' she replied, with a friendly smile. 'A nice day, yes.'

'We was just talkin' about yer, wasn't we, Mick?' Artie informed her now, quite unnecessarily.

'About me, Art?'

'Yeah, Lindsay, that's right. Tell me, 'ow's yer blinker comin' on?'

'If you mean my eye, you can see for yourself,' returned Lindsay unhelpfully.

Artie did. He placed the horse's forefoot carefully back on the ground, returned his bent back to an upright position, and inspected her critically.

'Jeez!' he gloomed. 'If you arst me, it was nicer purple. It's gone a kind of a mustard yeller, ain't it?'

'That means it's getting better. It will go on fading all the time now, and it's not a bit sore any more, so that's a relief. Soon it will be back to normal, I'm sure.'

Back to its lily-pond green—only Rod never noticed any more, not these days.

'Maybe not soon enough,' Artie sighed almost under his breath.

'Soon enough for *what*?'

Better have this out here and now, Lindsay decided. In view of that disquieting exchange she had just heard, there was no time like the present to bring things out into the open. Whatever the men were up to—and it was obvious that they were up to something—Lindsay had no desire to be involved in any way. She was in enough trouble without them engineering any more!

'For what?' she insisted, determinedly.

Artie scratched his ear bewilderedly, while Mickie stroked the velvet nose of the animal he was holding.

'Aw, nothin', really, Lindsay. Skip it.'

'No, Artie, I won't skip it—not this time.'

'It ain't nothin', honest,' he assured her with a gaze as blank and innocent as a lamb's.

Lindsay hesitated. He certainly appeared convincingly

truthful, but——

'Look here, you two,' she said firmly, 'I'm not going to ask if you don't want to tell me, but there's just one thing I think you should know. If it's anything to do with the—er—the knockout stakes, you can forget about it. As a matter of fact, I mentioned it to Rod, and——'

'You *what*?' Mickie's hand jerked the horse's head unintentionally.

'Slit me gizzard! Yer *never*?' exclaimed Artie in disbelief. 'What did 'e say?'

'He said'—Lindsay told them very clearly and slowly—'that there was absolutely no use in my even thinking of competing in it. *That's* what he said.'

She marched off, leaving the men staring at each other in consternation.

'Maybe 'e's bluffin', of course, Mick. I reckon it's still worth a try.'

Artie's considered comment, which just reached her ears as she disappeared, dispelled any satisfaction Lindsay was feeling that she had at last put a stop to their undisclosed machinations.

She was finding out, the hard way, that there is no one so obstinate, determined, persistent, *conniving*, as a big, tough, casual, stubble-chinned outback station-hand with something to lose! She only wished she knew what Artie was conniving at. You'd think he and Mickie could see for themselves that, even with the aid of those riding lessons they had given her, she would never be good enough on a horse to enter an actual race.

And the knockout stakes! It sounded like a very fast and very professional elimination race, that—not at all the sort of thing that Lindsay, who could do little more than cling precariously to Dusty's long, bony back when he chose to trot, might ever win. Not *ever*!

'My progress seems to be at a standstill, somehow,' she confessed to Mick that evening. Like everything else in life at the moment, she could have added forlornly, but of course she didn't. That was something one had to suffer in silence, just as one had to accept Rod's distant courtesy, Carleen's smug air of triumph, and the kindly, unspoken sympathy of the station-hands themselves, which in itself was enough to tell her that even they believed that she had been careless about that cupboard, and were sorry for her because she had incurred the Boss's wrath.

'Never mind, Lindsay,' the young jackaroo replied comfortingly. 'If you can just hang on for a couple of weeks, till we get the Dinewan block mustered, we'll give you a really intensive course when we come back. That's all you're needing, you know—practice.'

'Dinewan? Isn't that Margie's home? The Lockwith property?'

'That's correct. It's right next their boundary, which is why it's called that. It isn't the furthest outcamp on the place by any means, but it's the least accessible, in rougher country, with a river-bed between us and it. That's why Margie finds it easier to pop over in her little plane.'

'I see. And do you *all* go?'

It would be almost a relief to be without Rod for a while, thought Lindsay mournfully. The old Rod was gone, and in his place was a tense-jawed, curt-tongued, bleak-eyed stranger whom Lindsay could well do without. If only Rod was going, the interval would give Lindsay time to condition herself, as best she could, to these new circumstances that prevailed here at the homestead. When he came back, he might even have forgotten about the lapse for which he believed her responsible, or, if not forgotten, at least forgiven!

'Yes, we'll all be out.' She heard Mick's answer with unmitigated relief. 'It usually takes us a week or ten days out there, the rounding-up and branding. It's scrubby, difficult country to work. Oh, hello there, Carleen, I was looking for you, as it happens. That's what I came up to the house for.'

Carleen raised an indifferent eyebrow, posed herself carefully in her chair to make the most of her lovely figure in the emerald shift she wore tonight.

'Were you?' she said with noticeable lack of enthusiasm, crossing her legs daintily and plucking a cigarette from her monogrammed gold case.

'Yes. I'll tell you what it is.' Mick did not allow himself to be put off by her disinterest. 'Tomorrow we're going to be dropping dingo-baits from the air, and I wondered if you'd like to come too? It's an exhilarating experience, one I'm sure you'd enjoy.'

'Oh!' Lindsay leaned forward eagerly. 'Could I come too, Mick, do you think? I'd be so interested to see what you do.'

'Sorry, Lindsay,' he told her regretfully, 'but there wouldn't be room for you both. I'll be handing the baits, and'—a pause—'Rod himself will be the pilot, as always. It calls for quite skilled flying, you know.'

'If Carleen isn't keen——' Lindsay glanced hopefully to where the other girl lounged back in her chair, smoking.

'Who said I wasn't keen?' Carleen smiled rather snubbingly. 'Of course I'd love to go. Rod's been promising to take me for a ride in his plane for ages.'

'It will be around ten o'clock, then. You come down to the strip.'

'I'll be there,' she promised airily, and even waved a friendly hand as Mick took his departure. 'Perhaps, next time, you will get a turn, Lindsay,' she said patronisingly, and as always, when Carleen looked like that, Lindsay found her fingers clenching tight against her palms in sheer irritation.

The Carleen who stepped out on to the airstrip that morning was an elegant Carleen in beautiful separates of matching rose shantung. The open-necked shirt, the divided culotte-skirt into which it was tucked, the wide belt cinching her tiny waist, were appropriately casual and sporty—just the thing in which to do a stint of aerial dingo-baiting.

The Carleen who returned was a different Carleen altogether. This Carleen was an abject Carleen, a depleted Carleen, a very sick Carleen, and judging by the glitter in her baleful blue eye as Mickie led her tenderly up the path, an angry Carleen, too, although at the moment she didn't appear to have the energy with which to show it. She leaned heavily on Mickie's arm as she wobbled along at his side. Her cheeks were verging on what could only be described as chartreuse, her forehead moist and streaked with perspiration, her hair lank and unattractive, her pretty shantung outfit all limp and crushed and stained.

'How *dared* you!' Lindsay, standing speechlessly behind the gauze, heard Carleen almost spit the words out, albeit weakly. 'To make a fool of me like that in front of Rod—oh! —how *dare* you?'

'I'm sorry, Carleen.' There was solicitude in Mick's tone as he supported her along the path. 'But how was I to know you wouldn't be an exactly happy passenger?'

'*Happy?* Ugh! *You* knew.'

'Of course I didn't, or I wouldn't have dreamed of asking you, would I? I was very sorry for you up there, believe me, especially when Rod got so angry. You mustn't take his impatience too much to heart, though. As I said, low flying like that calls for a great deal of skill and judgement, and a chap has to give it all his concentration for every single second— even when someone's being sick right there beside him, and begging him to stop.' Mickie looked down at the wilting figure pityingly. 'If only you hadn't kept clutching at his sleeve, he wouldn't have got so furious,' he pointed out reasonably.

'Well, *you* did nothing to help, I must say,' she replied, with pure loathing in her voice.

'I couldn't very well, could I? I mean, I was so busy putting those baits down the shute on each run. It's the low flying, you know, in this climate, that sometimes makes it just a little bit bumpy. The heat comes up off the ground to meet the aircraft—boom, boom, boom. That's why one has to go fast when it gets rocky——'

'Will you *stop* it?'

'I'm sorry, Carleen. I was only explaining why the—are you going to be sick again?'

'My room—hurry!'

'The east one, isn't it? We'll go in the other door, then. It's quicker. Never mind, Carleen, you'll soon feel better. And don't be too upset about Rod. It's difficult for any man to pilot a small plane successfully at such a low altitude with a hysterical female clutching at him all the time, as I've already said. And then to be sick in the *cockpit*——'

Mickie's reproachful voice disappeared around the corner with Carleen. A few moments later, he passed by again, and Lindsay saw him cram his wide felt hat on his head at a triumphant angle and step jauntily down the path. On his face was much the same smug, self-satisfied, victorious sort of smirk that Carleen herself sometimes wore when—oh!

Lindsay stared after Mickie with widening eyes and open mouth. Then she walked quietly to Carleen's room.

'Can I do anything for you?' she asked timidly, in genuine sympathy.

'Oh, go *away*.' The muffled reply was so discouraging that Lindsay obeyed it—and went.

She and Mannie had lunch alone that day. Carleen's door was shut, and the blinds on the French window that gave on to the veranda were pulled down, too. Lindsay knocked gently, but receiving no reply, she and the old lady decided that it would be best to leave things as they were.

Lindsay had gone back to her office in the little pink weatherboard cottage, and was adding up bank accounts for the aboriginal employees' trusts, when a plane droned overhead and banked around the homestead before coming down. She had supposed it to be Rod, coming in from another expedition, but then she remembered that he hadn't been about for lunch, so it couldn't be Rod after all.

It was Margie. Even as she came walking up from the strip, tugging off her goggles, Lindsay was aware of something different about her—a certain suppressed excitement, an aura of sunshine and happiness that was a reflection of the shine in her calm, blue eyes, the gleam in her pearly smile, the bloom on her peach-soft cheeks.

'Oh, *Lindsay*!' She hugged the other girl as if she were attempting thereby to transmit some of her own special secret, blissful wonder. 'Oh, *Lindsay*. I just had to come and tell you—share it with someone! I just couldn't wait! Lindsay, *look*. Isn't it the most beautiful, gorgeous, dreamy thing you ever saw?'

She held out her small, capable, sun-browned hand for her companion to inspect the band of three winking diamonds—a big one in the middle and smaller sisters on either side.

So that was it! Lindsay should have guessed. What else could have given Margie this extra special glow? What but betrothal to the man she loved and longed for gave *any* girl that extra special glow, come to that? And Rod—that's why he had not come in for lunch. He hadn't gone dropping dingo-baits or riding the run or any of those things at all— not *this* afternoon.

This afternoon he had gone over to Dinewan. He was probably there, even now, waiting impatiently for Margie to come back again.

'Margie!' Lindsay's voice was husky with feeling, and her eyes were a little bit sort of moist—just with surprise, she told herself, even though she had really been expecting it!— but the hug she gave Margie in return was warm-hearted and generous and sincere.

'I'm so very happy for you, Margie, and as for Rod—well, I've always thought he deserved the very b-best, and he could not have chosen a nicer, more wonderful person than you. I hope you'll be marvellously happy.'

Margie stared.

'Rod?' She giggled. 'Whatever has Rod got to do with it? Lindsay, are you all right?' she added anxiously.

Lindsay ran a hand across her brow as though it hurt.

'I—don't know,' she said stupidly. 'I—am I mixed up, or something?'

The other girl laughed merrily.

'Or something? I should just think so! My dear, that ring on my finger was put there by Mac, *not* Rod. Isn't it the prettiest little ring?' She twirled her hand for the sun to catch the stones.

Lindsay swallowed.

'*Mac?* But I thought—I mean—we all thought——'

'I know.' Margie nodded serenely. 'Even Mac thought it, too, the idiot, although I did my level best to show him where my feelings lay. Short of knocking him on the head and dragging him to the altar, I couldn't have done much more in the way of chasing that man without losing my self-respect altogether. Heavens, even the reason I took my first flying lessons was because of Mac—you know, a shared experience, a bond in common. But it all went right over his head!' She shook her own head in mock despair.

'It's wonderful news you've brought, Margie,' Mannie enthused over the tea-pot in the great, long kitchen, which was somehow the spot where all the gossipy conclaves at Gundooee homestead always seemed to take place. 'Where will you live, my dear? Mac's people are from further north, aren't they?'

'Yes, his brother runs the family place, and he's been looking around for something suitable for ages. He took on this contract for the mail-run to fill in time until he found exactly what he wanted. It gave him a marvellous opportunity to see all sorts of properties, and with the kitchen cuppa and the gossip thrown in along the route, to hear of anything that might be coming on the market. Now he's bought the Emerton place on the other side of Peperina, so I'll be very near home, really. It's all so wonderful!' Her eyes were shining with merriment. 'I had to hint like anything when he told me he'd bought the property,' she continued in a spate which simply couldn't stop. 'You know, I kept saying how marvellous, and would he be going to live there very soon, and how I supposed he'd be thinking of getting married, and—oh, the shameless things I had to *say* before the penny dropped! And then the silly darling duffer just suddenly looked at me in the queerest way and said, look here, Margie, you can't possibly mean, and I said that's just what I *do* mean and do I have to spell it out in words of one syllable, and then he just sort of sighed and grabbed me and nearly squashed the life out of me. Do you know this, he hadn't ever even kissed me before, not once, and—oh, Mannie, I'm in the seventh heaven! Isn't that really the most gorgeous little ring you ever did see? Do look.'

'It's sweet, Margie. And how nice of you to fly straight over and tell us before it gets out over the galah! Once that happens, the whole of Australia will know! I'm sure Rod will be enormously happy for you, too, just as we are.'

In the hall on her way out again, Margie stopped and put her hand on Lindsay's arm to detain her. Her eyes, now, were oddly serious—not alive with dancing excitement as they had been in the kitchen, but soberly sincere.

'It's true, Lindsay,' she assured her softly, 'what Mannie said just now. About Rod, I mean. He *will* be pleased for me.' She paused again, then—'Lindsay, there's just one thing I'd like you to know, about all this. Rod has never, ever, thought about me in the way you may have supposed, nor I about him. He's always been to me like the older brother I never had, and I—well, you could say he's regarded me as a sister, that's all—sometimes even a little nuisance of a sister, I dare say! I've always recognised that fact, never expected or wanted anything different. I suppose that's the reason why we've always got on so well together, and had such fun. He's one of three brothers, you see. There are no girls in Rod's family at all.'

Lindsay's eyes were exploring Margie's earnest face.

'Margie, why are you telling me this?' she asked slowly.

She couldn't stop herself asking that. It was something she felt compelled to know.

Margie gave her a direct look. It was a look of extra-ordinary understanding and kindness.

'Because,' she replied simply, 'you're in love with him, aren't you? I just felt I wanted you to know.'

Lindsay's eyes were full of tears which she utterly refused to shed. She turned her head away, gazed blankly at the picture on the wall beside her, not really seeing anything at all.

'It—doesn't really matter, Margie,' she told the other girl in a choked voice. 'It won't make any difference—none at all. But it was nice of you, anyway. Thanks.'

Margie gave her hand a sympathetic squeeze.

'Where is she today, anyhow?'

Lindsay did not have to ask to whom Margie referred. They both knew *that*!

'She's asleep in her room, I think. She—er—isn't very well today.'

'Lindsay, I'm *sorry*,' Margie said, before she left her there in the dimness of the hall and went back alone to her little plane—and Lindsay knew, from the compassion in Margie's gentle blue eyes as she spoke those words, that this time they

352

did not refer to Carleen!

She did not see Carleen again until tea-time that night. She was still pale and heavy-eyed, but in a way even more feminine because of it, in an appealing sort of way.

Rod seemed to think so, anyway! As he brought her a brandy and lemonade from the drinks cabinet in the sitting-room and leaned over her in her chair, he was more solicitous than Lindsay had ever seen him before.

'Drink it, Carleen, please. It will do you good, I think.' He smiled with charming persuasiveness.

Carleen put back her head and gazed up at him, her lustrous eyes eloquent with apology. She laid that ever-possessive hand on his arm, and said softly, 'Rod, darling, I'm *so* sorry about this morning. What fools we girls can be sometimes, can't we! We're so—so weak, and you men are so strong—you really do show us up to our great discredit sometimes, you know. It isn't kind.'

Rod passed her the glass he held, regarded her with a certain grave deference.

'My dear, it's I who should apologise. I behaved like a boorish brute, and to a guest in my own house, at that. It was unforgivable of me, I know, but perhaps you'll be generous and try to forget, hm?'

The way she was gazing at him, she'd have forgiven him if he'd chopped off her head, thought Lindsay to herself with uncharacteristic waspishness.

'But of *course*! I've done that already, where you're concerned. After all, it wasn't you who invited me on such a ghastly expedition, and I must admit, looking back, that you *did* look a little surprised and put-out when I insisted on coming.' She smiled appealingly. 'I was so terrified, but do you know, I've learned something, too, Rod, from the experience. I've learned that we women aren't designed for such tough and frightening assignments at all. We're too delicate and easily alarmed—at least, I know *I* am. In future, I shall know my place as a member of the weaker sex, and leave those things to men. To *you*, Rod.'

'I'm glad to hear it, Carleen.' He patted her shoulder comfortingly with a large brown hand. 'You're much too fragile and lovely to enjoy such things as that this morning, especially when you've been ill lately, too. I dare say Mickie only meant to be kind, but I'm sure most men would agree with me that your role in their world should be in the nature of a decorative one.'

'Why, Rod! How gallant of you!'

Carleen sipped her brandy, obviously mollified.

Later, when Rod invited her to come for a ride with him on the following afternoon, she appeared keener than usual, but her eyelids drooped suddenly and her pretty mouth took on a slightly petulant pout when he added, carelessly,

'Perhaps you'd like to join us, too, this time, Lindsay—you and Dusty?'

Lindsay flushed.

'Oh, I don't think—I mean——'

He glanced at her, took in her dubious expression, and his jaw tightened.

'It's an order, if you prefer things that way,' he said more firmly. 'I want to make sure that you're safe on the horse my men have allotted you, and also to check your progress. Presumably, after all those tedious lessons, you must have learned a little, surely?'

She pressed her lips together.

'Very well,' she answered, somewhat ungraciously, aware of the superior gleam in Carleen's eye. 'If you insist.'

'I do insist.' Rod was adamant. 'After tomorrow, I and the rest of the men will be away for possibly more than a week, and you three women will be here at the homestead alone. I have no qualms whatever about Carleen's own superb horsemanship, but I certainly don't want *you* tinkering around in my absence on some animal which you have possibly little or no idea how to control. I shall see for myself tomorrow, so please be ready to accompany us.'

'Very well, Rod.'

She refused to look Carleen's way this time, but she knew that the other girl, well aware of her shortcomings on horseback, was secretly amused at the prospect of the morrow's ride.

Lindsay arrived at the saddling yard punctually next day

to find Dusty tied to the sliprail, waiting for her. Carleen was already mounted on the daintily prancing Chalita, and she was immediately aware of just how wide a margin there was between both the proficiency and the sartorial appearance of Rod's two equestrienne companions! Lindsay looked down ruefully at her bagging khaki trousers, whose excessive width had pleated itself neatly out over the belt around her middle like a frill around a leg of ham. Oh well—— She shrugged resignedly, observing Rod's striding figure approaching from the region of the near-by power-house. It was too late, now, to do anything about those trousers even had there been an alternative. It was too late to do anything about anything!

Rod helped her into the saddle, handed her the reins, and let down the sliprail before mounting his own snorting stallion and following her out of the yard.

For Lindsay, that ride represented a gruelling experience that she would never care to repeat. Mostly it was because Dusty's stubborn gait was somehow unmatched to that of his more active equine mates, she decided regretfully, as she jogged along behind the others in an uncomfortably bumpy trot.

It seemed to Lindsay that she trotted for miles that afternoon, without respite. Miles and miles. The other horses ambled along at a fast, lively walk, ears up, eyes alert, necks straining to be given their heads, while, in the rear, Dusty trotted and trotted, urged on by the thud of Lindsay's sandshoes digging ineffectively into his foaming flanks.

Lindsay slowed down to a walk, savouring the brief moment of respite, but as the distance between herself and the others appeared to be widening at an alarming rate, she was soon forced to urge him into that monotonous trot once more.

Carleen seemed to have purposely set out to capture Rod's entire attention on that ride. She talked animatedly, every now and then gesturing with graceful eloquence to illustrate a point she was making. There wasn't a doubt that Rod was being entertained to the fullest of Carleen's not inconsiderable ability, and all the time Lindsay trotted and trotted a little to the rear.

The miles went by—or, at least, Lindsay found herself hoping that they were going by. You could hardly go on trotting at this maddeningly frustrating pace without some distance being covered, could you? The only trouble was, there was distance everywhere, out here. So much distance. Flat, brown, plains sort of distance. Muted, hazy, *distant* distance. Outback, relentless, *interminable* distance.

It seemed to Lindsay, as Dusty followed those others at this tireless jog of his, that he and she were trotting along on an actual treadmill of distance!

When the stitch that had developed in her side became almost unbearable, she managed to release a furtive groan under cover of Carleen's tinkling laugh, and when, presently, a sound started up deep in the region of Dusty's sagging middle, she thought that perhaps he had developed a stitch in sympathy. The sound inside him was like a heavy boot stepping on a creaking board, and it came with montonous regularity, every time his bony carcase vibrated to his own trot.

Rod must have heard it, too, the creaking board sound. He stopped, came back, took in her set face and twisted mouth with instant concern.

'What is it? A stitch? Can't you spur this old nag on a bit, Lindsay?' He smiled kindly. 'I remember what it can be like—as a boy, jogging along on a pony behind the men's horses, having trouble keeping up. Won't Dusty go a little faster for you?'

She shook her head. 'I'm sorry, Rod. I can't get him to go faster, or even slower, unless he walks—and he takes his time about that, too. He just has a mind of his own, that's all. I suppose, at his age, one does! If we can only stand still a minute, the pain in my side will go.' There was pleading in her voice. It was wonderful to be standing here, and not trot-trotting on into the distance.

Rod pushed back his hat, considered her thoughtfully for a moment, and then said apologetically,

'I'm sorry, Lindsay. I thought you were handling him quite well, actually. I'll tell you what we'll do. You take Chalita for a little while. Carleen has ridden most of the steam out of her anyway. Carleen can easily cope with Martian, and I'll relieve you of old Dusty for a while. He'll perhaps go better for me. Some of these old horses can be sinfully cunning when it suits them. They need a firm hand, and a rider who's up to their tricks. Do you mind, Carleen?'

'Of course not.'

Carleen looked pleased at the idea of riding Martian. She mounted him with ease, laughing as he sidled around with arching neck and rolling eye, disapproving openly of his unfamiliar rider. It was a challenge, and she handled it beautifully.

There was admiration still lurking in Rod's eye as he turned now to Lindsay and held Chalita firmly while she clambered awkwardly into the saddle.

Straight away, things seemed to go wrong. The little mare shied suddenly away, jerking the reins from Rod's grasp before Lindsay had secured them properly in her nervous fingers. She leaned forward frantically, missed the reins altogether, flung her arms instead around Chalita's dappled neck, and the animal promptly went mad. She plunged and reared away over the ground, and Lindsay didn't quite know what happened next.

There was a distinct curse as Rod threw himself on to the surprised Dusty and dug in a brutal heel in hot pursuit. Pounding hooves sounded deafeningly close to Lindsay's ears, and then as Rod came alongside, Chalita propped on all four feet, as if mischievously aware that the game was up. Lindsay, by this time too confused to know what she was doing or why, went sailing through the air in a neat arc and landed with a resounding thud in the dust not far away.

It only seemed a matter of seconds after she hit the ground before she was being scooped up into a pair of powerful arms and crushed against a khaki-shirted chest.

'Lindsay! Lindsay? Thank God——' as she opened her eyes she saw his set face above her, pale with remorse, tense with anxiety.

Lindsay smiled, rather sleepily. She still couldn't quite think how she had got here, close against Rod's broad chest, cushioned in his muscular hold.

'I'm all right,' she assured him, almost happily.

'Thank heaven for that!' His deep voice was oddly harsh in its relief. 'I should never have tried it, Lindsay. It was all my fault. You aren't quite ready for Chalita, I'm afraid. Can you walk? Sure? Let me see you do it. I'm sorry, Lindsay, but there seems no alternative to Dusty, after all, does there?' He gave her the ghost of a grin, still pale beneath his heavy tan.

'We'll *all* walk, this time—very slowly,' said Rod quite tenderly, as he put her into Dusty's saddle once more. 'If necessary, I'll lead him.'

And that was how they returned to the homestead, with Carleen on Chalita prancing skittishly in front, and Rod on his impatient stallion, pulling a recalcitrant and by now extremely weary Dusty behind him.

'Gawd'l'mighty! Look at that!' Herb poked Artie sharply in the ribs and indicated the approaching trio. 'What d'yer make of that, now, Art?'

His companion screwed up his eyes against the setting sun, and squinted with critical interest at the horses and riders. Then he cupped his hands over his wrinkled forehead to make quite sure he was seeing right before replying gloomily,

'Nothink very good, by the look of it, 'Erb. That's *'er* in the lead, I reckon, as natty as yer please. Cor, she can ride, that dame! And there's Lindsay comin' up be'ind, only why's Rod leadin' 'er, for Pete's sake? We learned 'er 'ow ter ride, didn't we? Why d'yer suppose 'e's leadin' 'er?'

Lindsay saw the two figures drift tactfully out of view behind the tankstand, but she was too weary and worn to even wonder who they were or why they were there.

Rod seemed aware of her exhaustion, too.

'You go up to the house, Lindsay. Carleen and I will turn the horses out for the night.'

Carleen and I.

It was dismissal, but Lindsay was past feeling hurt or rebuffed. Three's a crowd, she reminded herself dismally, especially when the third one can't even ride properly!

'Pst! 'Ere! Lindsay?'

She had passed the tankstand now, to be confronted by Herb and Artie. They were idling casually in her path with their hands in their pockets. Herb coughed.

''Ullo, Lindsay!' he greeted her, on a note of surprised discovery, as if she was the very last person he expected to see passing behind this tankstand, albeit it was right on the recognised route to the homestead from the yard. ''Ave yer been out fer a ride, then, eh? With Rod and *'er*, was it? 'Ow did yer get on, Lindsay?'

Not even Herb's sublime approach could hide the anxiety behind his question. Artie, too, was standing waiting for her reply with bow-legged curiosity.

'I didn't get on. I got off.' She attempted a smile that was somehow not very successful.

'*Stone* the crows! Yer mean—yer don't mean yer fell off?' Art shook his grizzled head incredulously.

'I didn't fall off. I was thrown off.' She felt her tender places gingerly. 'I was *hurled* off,' she confessed, with a fleeting, urchin grin, but just the slightest tremor in her voice all the same.

Lindsay pushed past them, making for the house. She was not in a mood for further conversation right then.

'Well, I'll be danged!' Herb looked after her, and Artie, too, knocked back his hat and gazed after that small, hurrying figure. His angular bow-legged body had slumped into a curiously dejected arc.

'It don't seem too good, I must admit.' Artie cleared his throat noisily, and looked his mate squarely in the eye. 'I reckon the knockout stakes might soon be over, 'Erb, an' it'll be Bluey and Cook collectin', worst luck—not us.'

'Maybe not, Art, old cobber.' A spark of returning optimism gleamed in Herb's beady eye. 'We could win out yet if we play things right, yer know, Artie. Maybe Mick'll 'ave another of them bright ideas.'

'Bright ideas? Jeeze!' Artie spat neatly to one side to register his disgust. 'Them brain-waves of Mick's is about as subtle as a man-eatin' crocodile sittin' on a mudbank.'

'Ah well,' Herb said on a sigh, 'while there's life there's

'ope, Artie. Ain't that what they say? While there's life there's 'ope.'

But you could tell, from the way he said it, that not even Herb believed it, really. Not now.

CHAPTER 10

THE men rode out next morning.

Lindsay pressed her nose to the gauze and watched them
until they were out of sight. Blue and Shorty and Cook had
gone ahead earlier, and now the others followed, Rod riding
in front with Jimmy and Tommo. Artie, Herb, and Mickie
bringing up the rear. They all rode the same way, these men,
legs thrust out long in the stirrups, wide hat pulled down,
body angled in a carelessly relaxed position in a saddle that
was cluttered with saddle-bag, water-bag, ropes, pint-pot,
and various other impedimenta to fulfil their present needs.
A couple of horses without anyone on their backs loped
along beside Herb, but there were other spares, too, already
out at the Dinewan Block. Hughes, a boundary rider, lived
in a hut out that way and could provide extra mounts, as
could his mate Jenison from the Billabong outcamp.

Lindsay had only seen these men to nod to on mail-days,
and even then they did not always bother to come in to the
homestead. She knew approximately where they lived,
though, and others like them at the other huts and outposts.
Each place was identified on the wall-map in Rod's study by
a neat cross. Beside the crosses were names like Billabong,
Goofgap, Rainbow, Loophole, Force Eight, Blue Lady, Dog-
leg Plains, or simply, in one particular instance, Fawcett's
Place.

That cross with 'Fawcett's Place' printed beside it was the
most outlying one of all, and Fawcett himself had never been
in for a single mail-day since Lindsay's arrival.

When she mentioned this phenomenon to Artie, he had
laughed and replied,

' 'E's a kind of 'ermit, see, Lindsay. Old Fawcett don't take
ter company. Yer'd be lucky ter see 'im as often as yer see

Santa Claus 'imself, and that's the truth. Sometimes 'e don't come in fer a whole year, and then it's only because 'is rakin' beard's beginning' ter trip 'is feet up and 'is shears is blunt.'

Lindsay didn't quite believe Artie, but all the same, whenever she looked at that far-away little cross that was Fawcett's Place, she envisaged a bearded recluse, an independent, fierce yet lonely old man, a mysterious and strangely poignant figure.

The knot of riders that she watched until they were a mere dust-ball in the distance weren't going anywhere near Fawcett's Place today. They were heading west and then tracking along the dry creek-bed until they got to the Dinewan Block's camp. Rod had shown her on the map when she asked him to, a brow raised briefly in surprise that she should evince an interest. The truth was that Lindsay's imagination was captured by the immensity of space represented on that map—the spread of 'the Bush', as she privately called it. She had had to learn, very quickly, that 'the Bush' meant not only the pretty, lush area where she herself had been born and spent those first six Utopian years, but many other things as well. 'The Bush' had hundreds of different forms—endless mutations, depending upon which part of it you happened to be in! And now Mickie had told her that 'the Bush' where they were now going to muster was a different Bush again from the homestead and its environs.

The idea held a peculiar fascination for Lindsay, and so she pressed her nose to the gauze and viewed their departure with as much awe as if they had been John the Baptist departing for the Wilderness.

When there was not even a dust-ball left, she gave a little sigh, and went to find Mannie. The old lady was in the kitchen, sorting through some articles for Sibbie and Bella to wash. She had delayed the laundry this week until Rod had left, so that she could include his things at the last minute.

Lindsay noted her pallor and the blueness around her mouth with misgiving.

'Let me do that for you, Mannie dear,' she said quickly, hiding the rush of sympathy she couldn't help feeling, 'and I'll do the lunch, too, today. Why don't you go and lie down for a while? We might as well make the most of the men's absence, don't you think, and we can eat very lightly while Rod's away, can't we?'

Mannie smiled wearily.

'Perhaps I will. Thank you, Lindsay.'

She was more than usually quiescent—a disquieting sign, Lindsay could not help feeling, with a strange sense of foreboding, but Carleen, in whom she later confided, merely shrugged and pointed out,

'She's old, Lindsay, isn't she? I mean, what do you expect, at her age, out here in this wretched climate? It's a wonder to me that Rod bothers to keep her on. An old people's home would be more suitable, and she'd be comfortable there, with no responsibilities. He's probably just putting it off until he gets married. In my opinion, there certainly would not be room for both that old woman *and* a wife here at Gundooee, and I shan't hesitate to say so when the moment is right.'

Lindsay could only stare, quite horrified at Carleen's callousness. What was more, the way she had spoken, it seemed as if Mannie had been right about that private understanding. 'I shan't hesitate'— 'when the moment is right'.

A chill shiver ran through Lindsay. Carleen had spoken as if she was almost the mistress of Gundooee homestead already.

'It's always a mistake,' continued Carleen reflectively, as if completely unaware of the effect her casual words were having upon her listener. 'It's been proved time and again that two women in the same house can be a fatal mistake.'

'But surely an old lady, a dear, elderly person like Mannie could hardly make any difference, and when Rod is so—so fond——'

'Too fond. Such sentimentality can cause friction, just as much as could the presence of a younger woman.' Her eyes narrowed suddenly upon Lindsay, as she amended, softly, 'Even younger women employees. Book-keepers, for instance.'

'Carleen, please don't talk like that to Mannie, will you, not yet—even if you're thinking and feeling that way. If you could just help me to persuade her to take things a little easier, I'll fill in for her. That's all I want. I—I shan't expect *you* to have to do anything extra.'

'It would be presumptuous of you if you did, darling. Just remember that I'm here as a visitor,' Carleen pointed out silkily.

In the end, persuasion was not required to induce Mannie to ease up a little. Fate took a hand instead, in the form of a collapse from which it was quite difficult to bring the old lady round. Carleen helped to carry her into her room and lay her on her bed, but it was Lindsay who later assisted her to undress, comforted her, and brought her a reviving cup of warm, sweet tea.

'I think I should call up the doctor, Mannie,' she suggested worriedly.

'No, please don't do that, Lindsay—not while Rod's off. I'll be all right if I rest. That's all I need, my dear—a good rest in bed.'

'But just to *ask* him?'

'No, Lindsay, please don't do that. I'd hate all the fuss.'

Lindsay hesitated, but finally allowed herself to be dissuaded.

The next few days were dreary ones. Lindsay missed Mannie's company about the house, and soon came to realise that she had somehow acted as a buffer between herself and Carleen, who were beginning to get on each other's nerves. Lindsay was normally able to conceal, or at least control, the irritation which Carleen's behaviour frequently induced. Often, when she felt her fingers clenching into her palms with hurt or annoyance, she had simply walked away to see what Mannie might be doing. And Mannie, like as not, would start to tell her something, to talk about some entirely different topic, and Lindsay's ire would begin to fade.

Now she could not do that. There was no escape from Carleen's baiting, and you would almost have said that the other girl was aware of that fact, perhaps even trading on it. She was not in a pleasant mood at all these days. Lindsay supposed it could only mean that she missed Rod's company and masculine attentions.

When, at the beginning of the next week, the rain started, the situation deteriorated even further. The dark, low-hang-

ing clouds were a reflection of Carleen's black mood, and the
rain that drenched and drizzled by turns kept time with
Lindsay's own fits of depression and malaise. She took care
to stay out of Carleen's way as much as she possibly could,
and derived a curious sense of comfort from going to Rod's
study, and looking at the wall map which hung there.

It was comforting to be able to put one's finger on the
exact spot where those men were, comforting to know that
their work must be almost done, out there at that little cross
that was the Dinewan Block camp, comforting to think that
they would soon be back at the homestead, and then this
miserable phase would be over. Soon Carleen's overbearing
presence would be diluted once more by the banter and teasing of the jackaroos and station-hands, even if, at the same
time, she must also witness the strengthening of the other
girl's association with Rod himself.

'I wonder why you do it, Lindsay?'

Carleen's voice, cool and composed, made her jump.

'D-do what?'

'I wonder why you come in here—into Rod's own office—
and stand there looking at his map all the time? What do
you get out of it, Lindsay?' There was a sarcastic glitter in
her eye.

'Why, nothing. I mean, I only come to look. Just to see
where they are, sort of thing.'

'You mean where Rod is, don't you?'

'I—didn't say that.' She tried to pass, but Carleen put a
hand across the doorway and blocked her path with a deliberate movement. 'Please let me go, Carleen. I have to get
the breakfast.'

'No, *you* didn't say it, Lindsay'—Carleen ignored her request—'It's *I* who am saying it. You haven't the guts to say
it, have you? You'd rather just sneak in here and look at his
things, at that map.' She smiled nastily. 'Tell me, Lindsay,
what else do you do?' she asked with cynical curiosity. 'Do
you stroke his possessions and moon in his chair, as well as
gaze at his map? Perhaps you even go to his bedroom, and
worship there in silence.'

Lindsay stared.

'Well, do you?'

Lindsay felt the first faint quiver of alarm. She had never, ever, seen Carleen in quite this mood before. It was somehow rather frightening. It quite made one's blood congeal.

'Carleen, don't be stupid! You don't know what you're saying!'

There was a secretive smile hovering on those lovely lips, a smile quite without amusement.

'Oh yes, I do. I know more than you think, my dear Lindsay. I've watched you, the way you look at him and leap to do his bidding. I've seen you come mooning in here since he's been gone, too. I've even heard you confess that you're in love with him. You are, aren't you?'

'Carleen. *Please!*'

'Oh yes, you are. I heard with my own ears. You didn't deny it to Margie, did you, out there in the hall? You didn't deny it to her as you're doing to me.' Carleen's eyes were ice-pale. 'I've known ever since I overheard you talking that day. I only suspected before, but then I knew. And if I hadn't, the drooling way you looked into Rod's eyes when he picked you up the other day was enough to tell me. Enough to tell *him*, too.' She looked at Lindsay with naked dislike. 'I believe you fell off that horse on purpose. All that nonsense about a stitch in your side——'

'Carleen, you must be mad!' Lindsay's mouth was dry, her eyes wide with dismay.

Carleen gave a laugh that was oddly shrill and chilling.

'Mad? No. But I will be if things carry on like this much longer, you little snake in the grass! How *dare* you stand there pretending that butter wouldn't melt in your mouth, that you don't understand a word I'm saying, that *you* don't want him, too. Well'—a shrug—'you aren't going to have the chance, Lindsay. You're going, do you hear? Things were fine until you started all this "poor little girl" business—those blistered hands, your eye, that fall off Chalita. You can give up trying to draw attention to yourself all the time, and *go*.'

'Wh-where would I go?' Lindsay stammered, stupefied.

'I don't know and I don't care, but you'll leave here, that's the one sure thing! You'll *get out*! If you don't'—she passed a hand over her trembling mouth—'if you don't, I'll tell Rod what a deceitful little creature you are, and he'll *make* you go. Wouldn't you rather leave of your own free will than under a cloud?'

Lindsay squared her shoulders. Doormat! Doormat! chided a tiny voice inside her—and it seemed to be *that* voice which spoke just now, not her own one at all.

'I don't intend to leave, Carleen, of my own will or yours. If you tell Rod about my initial deception, I'll tell him that you unlocked that cupboard and let Tommo get at that stuff, on purpose.'

Carleen smirked.

'I thought you might say that,' she nodded calmly. 'You haven't the slightest hope of proving it, though, have you? It would simply be my word against yours, wouldn't it, and if you lied in order to get this job in the first place, you could soon lie again, couldn't you? As Rod said to you at that time, anyone who makes one false statement can always be expected to make another. Why should he believe you?'

Lindsay's shoulders sagged, but she would not admit defeat. She licked her lips.

'Carleen, I—I've no intention of letting you bully me any longer. You've done it all your life and got away with it, but not any more. And I can tell you this—*I* am going to speak to Rod when he comes back. I'm going to confess everything, as I should have long ago. I know he'll send me away, but not before he knows about you, too—how you schemed to get here, how you made me promise not to tell, and the reason why. He'll loathe the pair of us, and we deserve it.' She lifted her head, and looked the other girl soberly in the face. 'I'll admit to you now that I love Rod. I know he doesn't even see me, doesn't even know I exist, but I love him and I'm not ashamed of it. In fact, I'm proud of it! And because I do love him, I'm not going to stand by and see him go into marriage without his knowing the whole story, and then he can judge for himself. If I confess, you're going to be exposed, too! You don't love Rod, Carleen. You don't love anyone. You've never cared for anyone except yourself in your whole life. Just yourself.'

Carleen's face was aflame with temper. She almost looked as though she was going to hit Lindsay. Indeed she raised her hand, palm open, and Lindsay found herself cowering away.

'Shut up, will you. Shut up! I won't listen! You aren't going to spoil things for me, Lindsay, not now, not after going so far. I *will* have my way, I will, I will! I *hate* you, do you hear?'

Her voice had risen to a scream. The colour had drained from her face, leaving it parchment-white, contorted with pure fury into an ugly mask. Carleen put her hands up to her face with a frustrated little moan and flounced away.

Seconds later, from the living-room, there came a tinkling sound, the crash of breaking glass. Typically, Carleen must have taken out her rage and venom on some ornament! At almost the same moment, Lindsay heard a tiny noise from Mannie's bedroom—a strange, lingering little sigh that broke the sudden silence following that crash.

Still numbed and shaking from her confrontation with her cousin, she raced into the room, sick with dread, knowing instinctively that something was very far wrong. Then she stumbled back to the door, trying to rally her common sense for this new emergency.

'Carleen! Carleen, come quickly. *Please*. Mannie's ill, terribly ill. I think she—she may even be dying. Please come, Carleen—quickly!'

To her credit, Carleen came, the tears of rage still wet on her cheeks.

Together they lifted Mannie's unconscious form, covered her with blankets, noted the heavy breathing, that strange blueness in her face.

'We'll have to call up the doctor, won't we, Carleen? The Flying Doctor. We'll have to get him here as quickly as possible.'

She looked across to Carleen for support, for help, and was surprised to see the expression that came over her cousin's beautiful, classic features. An indescribable expression, it was, calm and bitter and desperate all at once.

And then Carleen shook her head. Kneeling there on the

other side of the bed, with her face all pale and pinched and strained, and the tears drying rapidly beneath her eyes, she simply looked back at Lindsay—back and *beyond* her—and shook her head.

'Lindsay, we can't,' she said in a curiously dead, shocked voice. 'We can't call up anyone. I've broken the transceiver.'

Lindsay's own heart seemed to stop for one terrifying, suffocating second.

'You've *what*?'

'I've broken it, Lindsay—the set. I didn't mean it—that alabaster vase, the big figurine, I was so furious—you know what my temper's like.' Carleen's voice was no more than a whisper, with a note of pleading and despair in it that Lindsay had never thought to hear. She was moved to instant compassion at the other's overwhelming air of shame and remorse.

'What shall we do?' she asked stupidly. Her brain seemed to have stopped functioning, events had crowded in so fast.

Carleen wiped her eyes.

'I didn't mean to,' she said hoarsely. 'You do believe that, Lindsay? I didn't aim on purpose, it just seemed to fly out of my hand, it's so heavy. And you haven't ordered batteries for the other one, have you—the set that needs recharging, down at the store?'

'I was going to. Next mail-day.' Lindsay's tone was bleak.

Between them, Mannie lay without moving. Still that laboured breathing, that dreadful blueness in her face.

'You'll have to go for help, Lindsay.' Carleen stood up, smoothed down her skirt with sudden decision.

'Help? How?'

'You'll have to go out and get Rod. You'll need to ride out.'

Lindsay looked askance.

'Ride? Away out there? I'd never manage to do that, I'd never make it. *You* could, though, Carleen. It's our only hope. If you could get to Rod and tell him, he could fly Mannie out to the Base hospital in his plane.'

Carleen shook her head. Her normal colour was returning—and so was her normal voice!

'Why should *I* go, for heaven's sake? It's not my place to do that, is it?'

Lindsay stared. 'But you can ride, and I can't. You *know* that! And anyway, it was you who broke the transceiver, the wretched thing.' Her patience was beginning to give way under the spell of the old, taunting look with which Carleen was favouring her.

'And *you* forgot to order spares for the battery-set in the store,' Carleen returned evenly. 'You admitted as much last mail-day. It's you who is the employee, after all, Lindsay, isn't it, and your duty is clear. I'm merely a guest in this house, remember. Anyway'—she lifted her shoulders somewhat fatalistically—'why should it really worry me whether Mannie lives or dies? She's old, after all, and she might not like that Old Folks' Home much, might she, in the end?'

'You—oh!'

'You hurry and put on your trousers, Lindsay, and I'll catch and saddle your horse for you.' As Lindsay turned blindly to the door, she heard Carleen add, 'You'll know where you're making for better than I, anyway. You've certainly studied that map often enough!'

Lindsay dragged on the baggy trousers she had borrowed from the store, crammed her hat with its bobbing fly-veil on her head. Then she filled one of the canvas water-bags that hung out on the veranda and ran down to the saddling yard —down through the deserted village of outbuildings that were all part of Gundooee homestead—past the little pink weatherboard cottage, past the store, enmeshed in a nightmare that this could really be happening to her.

'Where's Dusty?'

Carleen looked up from the strap she was tightening around Chalita's girth, and shrugged.

'Not in, it seems. This is the only horse that's handy.'

Lindsay was aghast.

'But I'll never get there on Chalita, Carleen. Wh-what if she bolts?'

'Just see to it that she bolts in the right direction, and you'll get there all the quicker, won't you?' Carleen retorted tartly. 'For goodness' sake, Lindsay, be realistic. Even if Dusty was around for me to catch, you'd never get there on *him*—not all that distance, when it's all you can do to even make him trot. Here, give me your water-bag.'

'Carleen, *wouldn't* you go?'

'You know the answer to that, so why ask?'

Lindsay pressed her lips together so that the wicked things she wanted to say just couldn't get out to turn into actual words. Then she crossed her fingers, muttered a brief and silent prayer.

'Hold her for me, won't you, Carleen?' she whispered fearfully. 'Don't let go too soon, like Rod did.'

Carleen gave her a searing look of scorn, but nevertheless she did hang on to the cheek-strap quite tightly until Lindsay was in the saddle, and waited until she saw the reins firmly in her grasp before letting go.

'Keep looking in case Mannie comes to, and frets, won't you, Carleen?'

'Don't saw her mouth like that, Lindsay—that's why she's tossing her head.'

'Look after Mannie.'

'I will—and good luck!' There was a curious twist to Carleen's mouth as she said that. Then she turned away towards the house, not even taking time to wave.

Perhaps that was as well, as it might have startled Chalita, who was behaving in a very fractious manner as it was!

Lindsay was secretly terrified. She had read somewhere that a horse has a built-in communications system that tells it when its rider is frightened, and she was doing her best to stifle her fear in case Chalita might discover it.

Several times during that lonely morning journey, Lindsay thought Chalita *had* found out. She had several isolated moments of sheer panic—once when the highly strung mare shied suddenly at a tiny snake that wriggled in the dust quite near her hoof, and once when for no apparent reason at all she reared up on her hind legs and snorted. Somehow, on both occasions, Lindsay managed to keep her seat, and to refrain from putting her arms around Chalita's neck again. Instead, she reached frantically for the monkey-grip on the pommel and clung to both it and the reins with almost hysterical strength.

These experiences appeared to unsettle Chalita as much as they did her rider. There was a faint quivering right through her body, a pricking of her ears, that told Lindsay her own fright had been communicated. Her palms were sweaty with it, her forehead beaded with it, and her shirt, too, clung to her back with the very stickiness of pure, uncontrollable fear.

By noon she had reached the point in the dingo fence where she knew she must leave its guiding ribbon and break away to the west. Lindsay was loth to leave that comforting landmark behind. Ahead of her was more rugged country, with stunted scrub that sometimes screened her way. The rain had stopped, but the ground was treacherously soft in places, and the horse blew through her nostrils in terror as her hooves sank in the ridges of sand which must be traversed.

Lindsay's mouth was parched. She would have liked to stop and have a drink from her water-bag, but Chalita seemed sensitive to even the slightest touch on her rump, and Lindsay was afraid that if she once got off she would never manage to mount again on her own. If she could only stay in the saddle, she must be getting near that camp, surely, judging by her watch and the position of the sun.

Now Chalita was pushing nervously through a belt of scrub. The sickly smell of gidyea was all about them, and in the distance was a disquieting and unidentifiable sound, a peculiar, sighing sort of sound that Lindsay found it impossible to place. Like grit rushing in the wind, if there had been a wind. The little mare did not seem too happy about that sound, either. Her fits of quivering started again, and she blew gently through dilated nostrils, rolled her eye, and walked sideways.

When they breasted the next ridge, Lindsay's eyes rolled too. They almost rolled right out of her head, and she thought she might be going to cry. With frustration. With disappointment.

After all, it was a terrible anticlimax to have endured what she already had, to have managed to stay aboard Chalita through that long, hot, lonely morning, with the sun sucking back the moisture from the plain in a greedy steam, and her fear drying up her mouth, and not being able to get to that water-bag, and the gidyea exuding this nauseating smell, and her own perspiration running into her eyes, to find herself thwarted by a dried-up creek-bed that wasn't dry any longer.

Lindsay eyed the widespread stream of muddy water with a sinking frustration. The trees that represented the edges of the creek-bed were a depressingly long way out into the stream, even though the water only lapped their trunks at the base. Bubbling eddies of froth moved lazily away into the main current from where the slow-moving stream was disturbed by those trees in its midst. She could only survey the flood that stretched in front of her with an indecision that she knew was cowardly, while the mare shook beneath her.

Away on the other side of the water, a bell sounded distantly. A bell? Yes, there it was again, the faintest tinkle. To Lindsay, the tinkle was like an angel sound from heaven, beckoning her to come. Surely a bell must mean a human habitation. The camp?

She leaned forward, shivering every bit as uncontrollably as Chalita, and together they went into the water, slipping and splashing towards the other side.

Lindsay was more than half-way across when the water first touched her sandshoes, causing her to hunch her knees into a sort of jockey position. By the time her rolled-up trouser cuffs were soaking, Chalita had started to swim.

Lindsay's mouth went slack with horror when she realised what that rhythmic, floating sensation beneath her meant. She clung limpet-like to the saddle, but when the water broke over that, too, and eddied around her waist, she knew that she would have to swim as well. But how did you swim, in an outback, swollen, rushing creek, with all your clothes on and your hat with its bobbing-cork fly-veil sitting on your head?

The hat was tossed recklessly into the current, and Lindsay saw it bobbing away from her, corks and all. Her shirt, too? Oh, no! Not with all those men at the outcamp, away ahead where the bell had tinkled. Too late, now, anyway.

Chalita's gallant little head, thrusting forward, was all that remained above water.

Thoughts galloped through Lindsay's brain at alarming speed. What did you do? What did you *do*?

Well, first of all you had to keep contact with your horse, hadn't you? You got off carefully, and you kept hold of the saddle and you sort of swam along too. But did you get off on the upstream side or the downstream side? Upstream, you had the current to contend with, pushing you close against the horse, and that might not please Chalita. Downstream, you might be carried away altogether, to the Gulf of Carpentaria or Lake Eyre or wherever this particular creek was running to. Or you could get off backwards and hang on to the tail, couldn't you? Lindsay was sure she had read that somewhere in a book once, in the library at school. The Indians did it, in South America.

At least that was a middle course—the tail.

You just kicked your feet out of the stirrups, like this. No, like *this*! Try again, Lindsay—perhaps the Indians didn't use saddles. And then you worked your way backwards, slowly, because the current didn't want you to do that, and tried to snatch you away. And then you slid down over the rump and grabbed your horse's tail. Her tail? Her *tail*? Oh, there it was! Lindsay's fingers entwined themselves in its coarse, comforting, floating strands and hung on grimly right near the tip.

The water took all force out of the horse's flailing hind-feet, so that although they were quite near her they were powerless to harm. Discovering this, Lindsay's confidence returned. She kept her head above the water quite easily as they passed the second line of trees, and Chalita began to flounder into quieter waters.

And then a voice yelled from the approaching bank.

Lindsay was so surprised to hear a voice—a *human* voice, at a time like this!—that she almost forgot to listen to what it was saying. Even when she concentrated, the words made little sense.

'Leggo, missus! Leggo that tail, quickfella, missus, alla-same them hooves belonga Chalita proper killum you! Leggo quickfella, missus. They mebbe killum you *finish*!'

It was the way that raucous voice yelled *finish* that
prompted Lindsay to let go. She was reluctant to part
company with Chalita—this creek had forged an extraordinary bond between them—but when the word 'finish'
was yelled at you in that sort of voice, it had a horribly final
sound.

Her fingers slackened and the tail floated away. She heard
Chalita's feet clattering through the shallows, but when her
own feet sought for a hold, she banged her knee on a stone—
floundered. Then the pull of the current was snatching her
back, and her head went under.

Lindsay choked and struggled, with her mouth full of the
swirling brown water. It sang in her ears, and twined itself
around her limbs, so that her efforts became feeble and in-
effectual. So feeble—just that singing in her head, blotting
out thought.

When Tommo dragged her up the bank he flipped her
over like a codfish, and pressed the water out of her lungs,
and when she had recovered from her fit of coughing he
turned her back the other way, helped her to a sitting position and grinned.

Lindsay didn't grin back. She didn't feel much like grinning.

'You nearly drowned me,' she accused him croakily.

'O.K., missus. All good-oh now, eh?'

'Not good-oh, Tommo,' she whispered plaintively. 'I've
just been d-drowned.'

Tommo's white teeth flashed in an ear-splitting smile.

'You proper sillyfella missus, not get back alonga dat
saddle quick. You wait till water bin shallow, dem cheekyfella hoof they pokum you allasame they killum you, eh,
missus? Maybe killum you finish! Kick you to glory!'

Lindsay stared silently into those laughing dark eyes.

'You want Tommo take you alonga that camp, missus?
Two, mebbee three mile? Eh?'

'Yes, please, Tommo,' she begged. 'Take me to the camp.'
And then she fainted.

Lindsay was thankful afterwards that she hadn't known

much about that ride to the camp. When she came to her senses, it was to find herself slung ignominiously across Tommo's saddle like an ailing sheep. Her head dangled and her legs dangled and her middle felt as though it was being sawn in two.

When Tommo clattered into the camp and unloaded her with a singular lack of ceremony into Rod's arms she passed out again, but this time, when she regained consciousness, she was surprisingly still in them, but wrapped in a blanket, wet clothes and all.

Lindsay looked up into Rod's anxious grey eyes and then she put her head against his shirt and cried. She couldn't seem to stop crying, even though he was holding her so comfortingly and stroking the damp hair away from her eyes and saying over and over in a tender sort of voice, 'Don't cry, Lindsay, you're all right now, darling, don't cry, Lindsay,' and she began to think that so much crying must have made her delirious.

It was only when he said more severely, 'Why did you do it, Lindsay? Why have you come?' that she remembered, with a sudden shock that effectively banished her hysteria, just why she had set out in the first place. Through chattering teeth she told him about Mannie, about the transceiver being broken accidentally.

All the time she was speaking, Rod listened attentively in silence, grave-faced, patient. Only when she mentioned the transceiver did he interrupt.

'Couldn't you have used the other set, Lindsay? The one at the store?'

She shook her head miserably, began to shake uncontrollably.

'I c-couldn't. I meant to order b-batteries. I was g-*going* to, but I h-hadn't *done* it.'

'I see.'

He put her down gently, flat on the ground, and went away, and when he came back again, it was with neat spirits in a tin pannikin.

'Drink it, Lindsay.' He raised her up in his arms again, held the mug against her lips. 'Just drink it up. It won't matter if it makes you sick. Maybe you've still got some of that river water inside you.'

He gave the ghost of a grin as he tilted the contents carefully down her throat. Then he laid her back, stood up, and said from that incredible height,

'Now, don't worry, Lindsay. I'm going to contact Dinewan on my transmitter. It hasn't the range of the transceivers, you see, but the Lockwiths' place isn't far from here at all, and they can then contact Base for me.'

He went away again, and Lindsay closed her eyes, feeling the raw spirit coursing through her, bringing with it a warming glow. Her nausea was diminishing.

When he came back this time, Rod's face held a puzzled expression. He put a blanket-roll he had brought underneath her head, and looked at her strangely. When he had sat down beside her, he said, almost carelessly,

'Funny thing, that. When Margie got through, they said they'd received the Gundooee call over the morning session, and that Mannie has been taken in. She's safely at the hospital right now.'

Lindsay's gaze was blank. Even Rod's face swam a little out of focus.

'But—received a call? They couldn't have!' she protested weakly. 'The transceiver was broken, *smashed*. At least, Carleen said——' Her voice died away as realisation dawned.

'What did Carleen say?'

'She said—she said—I thought—— It doesn't matter really.'

Lindsay was feeling sick again.

'It matters to *me*.' Rod spoke with quiet emphasis. He was silent for a moment. 'I'll tell you what Carleen is saying now, and that may help you to remember.'

'Saying *now*?' she repeated, incredulous.

'Well, a few minutes ago, to be exact. When Margie contacted the homestead on the set that was working.' He paused, continued without expression. 'Carleen says now that you got completely hysterical when Mannie collapsed, and went haring off on horseback before she could stop you. I must say'—he looked at her critically—'you did seem extraordinarily overwrought.'

Rod's face wavered again. It came and went in a kind of vacuum of weakness, a fantasy feeling that this couldn't possibly be happening.

'In fact, you're still overwrought, I think, Lindsay.'

He gathered her shaking frame in his arms again, but this time Lindsay clawed at his hands, pushed him from her even though a spasm of that dreadful weakness assailed her.

'Don't touch me, not if you don't believe. You—don't believe me, d-do you? You don't trust me, Rod.'

'Hush, darling.' He resisted her fumbling attempts to push him away, and held her firmly. 'Of course I believe you!'

Suddenly she went limp in his arms. What was real, what was false, in this swaying, reeling world? It must be the aftermath, the shock. You couldn't get almost drowned, and not suffer some sort of momentary ill effect.

'Well, you shouldn't,' she mumbled wearily against him. 'You shouldn't trust me, do you hear me, Rod? I've deceived you s-since the very beginning.'

'Shh! I know.'

'You *c-can't* know.' She moved her wet head irritably, closed her eyes. 'How can you know, when I'm only j-just telling you? I pretended.'

'Yes, I know, pet, I know.' His deep voice was humouring her, as if she were a petulant child. 'You pretended to be a man, or rather, you omitted to state that you were a girl. A woman.' His arms tightened about her. 'I've known it all along.'

Lindsay's eyes opened again.

'How could you know?'

'It's what's called passive deceit.' He smiled faintly. 'You didn't even put *Miss* Lindsay Dutten on the stamped and self-addressed envelope which you enclosed for a reply. I checked with Mannie afterwards, and as I suspected, you'd just put L. H. Dutten—most unusual, that. Even people who accidentally leave it out before a signature almost always remember to put it on an envelope.'

She gazed at him incredulously. 'You knew from the beginning?'

'From the beginning,' he agreed calmly.

'Then why didn't you send me away?' she asked suspiciously.

Rod's grey eyes twinkled with sudden amusement.

'Because of Clancy,' he replied with a solemnity that was belied by the laughter in his eyes.

'Clancy?'

'Yes, Clancy. Remember? Clancy of the Overflow? I didn't think he'd like it.'

'Like what?'

'I thought he'd be disappointed if, having come all that way, your bush friends didn't greet you with those kindly voices, the way you expected them to. It would have been letting old Clancy down a bit, if I'd sent you away.'

'Oh.' Her eyes fell before his. 'Your voice wasn't very kind,' she mumbled, gazing at his middle shirt button.

He grinned. 'No, it wasn't, just at first, was it? I reckoned you were making plenty of bush friends for the time being, and hearing plenty of kindly voices without mine. Getting kisses, too.'

'Oh, Rod! You mean Artie?' She looked up again, dimpling. 'Rod, that was only for a bet.'

'Yes, I realised that—a good bit later.' A pause. 'Do you only give away kisses when a bet is involved?' he asked in an odd sort of voice, bringing his head down very near to catch her reply.

Colour washed over Lindsay's pale cheeks.

'No—yes—I mean—of course not!' she said weakly. His face was really terribly close, so close that it was difficult to think what she was saying. His grey eyes, smouldering darkly, were within inches of hers. And his mouth, that firm-lipped mouth—so close——

'Then we don't have to bet on it, do we,' he stated calmly, before he bent his head just that little bit more and covered her mouth with his.

Lindsay returned that kiss with a heady sensation of utter and unprecedented bliss. Half-way through she even managed to disentangle her damp arms from the blanket and put them around his neck, with the result that Rod seemed to go on kissing, only this time with a mounting passion that left her breathless.

Finally, he held her away from him and said indistinctly,

'Dear heaven, Lindsay, how I've wanted to do that! When you're my wife, I'll kiss you just as often as I please,' he told her with a return to his normal, masterful tone.

'My—your——? What did you say? Just then, Rod?' She spoke rather feebly, because she was still recovering her breath.

'You heard me, Lindsay, my own sweet darling. I'm warning you of my intention to marry you, that's all.' He smiled down at her, the passion still blazing in his eyes at war with the gruff matter-of-factness in his voice.

'Oh, Rod!' Lindsay breathed his name ecstatically, flung her arms around his neck again, half laughing, half crying, with a mixture of delight and sheer physical weakness.

He kissed her gently, as if sensing that she was almost at the limit of her strength, and then he took her hands from behind his head.

'I'm only telling you now,' he told her with mischievous candour. 'I can choose a better time and place for *asking* you, Lindsay. The men will be in soon, and your shirt's still wet. You'll have to get out of those clothes, and I'll dry them by the fire here. I'll give you this blanket to wrap around you till you get them back, and I'll dry that blanket, too. Can you manage, do you think? Could a prospective husband help in any way?'

Her cheeks were aflame.

'I—I'll manage, thank you,' she said hastily.

Rod chuckled softly.

'Over by that tree, then.' He helped her to her feet, handed her the second blanket. 'Tonight we'll light a second fire, a little bit away, so that the sound of the ringers changing places won't disturb you. You'll hear the ringer out there in the darkness singing his cattle to soothe them and stop any other night noises from alarming the mob.' A smile crept into his voice. 'I'll make sure Artie's not one of them tonight. His singing is of a rather unrestful quality, and his repertoire of songs is pretty border-line, too. You can have my saddle

for a pillow, and you should sleep all right. Tomorrow we'll
ride back in together.'

Lindsay paused on her somewhat wobbly course to the
tree.

'Goodness!' she exclaimed. 'I forgot all about Chalita!
She ran off when I let go her tail. What shall I ride back
on?'

'You mean Dusty, of course,' he said abruptly, striding
after her and putting a hand on her forehead. 'You aren't
still shocked, are you, Lindsay?' he added, with a sudden
return of anxiety.

'Chalita,' she repeated firmly. 'Dusty wasn't around, so I
came on Chalita, but she ran away when I—when I was in
the w-water.'

The memory of that drowning sensation made her shiver.

'I see. Well, she'll come in during the night, probably,' he
told her evenly. 'Don't worry about it, Lindsay. She'll hear
the bells on the tailer's horses—she knows the sound well.
She'll come sniffing around, and we'll catch her.'

Lindsay wriggled her way out of her wet clothes and came
back wrapped in the second blanket, handed Rod her other
things. She felt incredibly slack and weary, but wonderfully
happy and content, too.

Rod accepted the clothes. The firelight was at his back in
the rapidly descending dusk, so that she couldn't see his
expression clearly, but when he spoke his voice was angry,
heavy with control.

'*You* couldn't have caught Chalita, Lindsay, never in a
million years. You couldn't have saddled her either. And
when I think of you *riding* her——' He broke off, swallowed
audibly. 'Both Chalita and Dusty were in when I rode out
here, Lindsay—not in the saddling yard itself, but in the horse
paddock, close at hand,' he informed her bleakly.

Then he waited.

It seemed to Lindsay, from the patient stance of those
dusty, elastic-sided boots planted there in the dust, that Rod
might be prepared to wait there for ever till he got a reply.
There was a certain relentlessness about him that told her he
was in one of his 'I expect and intend to get an answer' moods.

She rubbed her hand over her brow, looked up at him with misty green eyes that were hollow pools in her white face.

'Do we have to talk about it?' she asked, pleading.

'No, darling, we do not.' He patted her shoulder with unexpected kindness. 'We don't need to talk about it for a long, long time—not until it's just a memory. Just one little thing, though, Lindsay. Carleen knew about your own pretence from the beginning, didn't she?' His grey glance was probing.

Lindsay nodded dumbly.

'O.K.' Surprisingly, Rod smiled. It was that slow, caressing smile that just curled the corners of his mouth. 'I'll talk to her when we get back. There'll be absolutely no unpleasantness, but I don't think you'll see her much again. I'm sure she won't want to stay, in fact, once she hears we're getting married.'

Lindsay smiled tremulously. She couldn't voice her gratitude. Some day, she would tell Rod everything. Not just now, though. It didn't matter right now.

She went over and sat in her blanket beside the fire which Rod had got going for her, and watched the evening routine in the camp. When he came back with her dry clothes she put them on again, over by the same tree.

The men straggled in, in twos and threes, turning their horses loose with bell and hobbles to pick up what they could, carrying their saddles back to put them where Rod directed, under the gums, and then making for their own swag and quart-pot to brew up that ever welcome mug of tea. Jimmy and Tommo came in then, leading three fresh horses which they tied up under a couple of near-by saplings before making their way to their own fire, laying down their battered felt hats beside their swags, and getting out their quart-pots like everyone else was doing.

As they passed her, they gave Lindsay a puzzled glance, but showed their even white teeth in their customary friendly smiles.

The other men, too, kept looking over at Lindsay. She could see their eyes darting her way under cover of their smoko operations, but if Rod was aware of those furtive, peeping looks or the bouts of whispering that accompanied them, he gave no sign. He was obviously content not to notice. He seemed to be waiting for something.

When all the men had come into camp for the night, except for the horse-tailer out there with the cattle until the first ringer had had his meal and could take his place, and the steaks were beginning to sizzle and spit on the three different fires, Rod stepped into the clearing between the fires and called to Lindsay.

'Come here for a moment, please, Lindsay,' he said, with that old, familiar ring of authority. 'I wish to say something.'

Lindsay stood up and obeyed, just like everyone always did when Rod used that stern, commanding tone. She walked out of her own warm firelit circle, and into the clearing.

'Come here, Lindsay. Right here to me.'

All eyes were watching. Curiously, the quart-pots and pannikins ceased their chinking, and even the steaks seemed to sizzle more quietly than before, as she and Rod stood there together in the little pool of silence.

Then, with the eyes still gazing and the bush all about them, Rod took off his hat, tilted up her chin with steady fingers, and kissed her with a slow, deliberate tenderness, right on her lips. Then he put his hat under his arm, and turned to the firelight where Artie and Herb were kneeling on one knee over the steaks.

'*Now*, Artie,' he murmured deeply, 'you go and collect on the knockout stakes, eh!'

Rod took Lindsay's hand and led her gently back to her own little fire away from the rest, and as their feet crunched softly over the fallen gumleaves, they heard Art's voice, breathless with stupefaction—

'Well! If that don't beat all!'

Lindsay gazed at Rod.

'You knew?' she said wonderingly.

'I told you there'd be no point in you competing, didn't I? You were home and dry already, you see.'

'All *along*?' she whispered incredulously.

Just for one brief moment, Rod's teeth glinted in the firelight.

'It's up to every man to know what goes on on his own station, Lindsay,' he muttered huskily, before he gave her that second kiss.

INTO A GOLDEN LAND

into a golden land

Elizabeth Hoy

The opportunity to accompany her ecologist
father on a mission to Algiers had been too good
to miss. The little oasis town of Sidi Bou Kef
promised to be everything Alison had hoped
for—golden sun, sand, romance—until she
discovered that Brett Meredith was there too!

And just as there had been no explanation for the
way he had walked out of her life in England,
there seemed to be no reason for his present
treatment of her. Alison knew now, however, that
whatever new distractions were there to fascinate
her, they meant nothing without Brett's love.

CHAPTER ONE

It was the sunlight, warm as a caress on her closed lids, that awakened her. She lay bemused, her glance travelling slowly round the strange bedroom. Sharply cut strips of brilliance coming through the opened slats of the louvred blinds lay across the tiled floor in bars of brazen gold. African gold. And only yesterday she had walked across the tarmac at London Airport in the cold February rain.

Surfacing slowly from her long deep sleep, Alison thought briefly of the flight, a boring interlude when time and the great jet plane seemed to stand still in a world of grey cloud. Once she had caught a glimpse of snow-capped mountain peaks. The Alps? Or would it be the Pyrenees? Her father, dozing at her side, was not to be disturbed by the question. More endless plateaux of grey clouds, breaking to reveal a dark blue sea. Then, losing height, there was more sea, miles of it, and finally Algiers, a town of blinding white in a blaze of sunlight. Disappointingly, the airport was much like any airport, but the Sheik Achmed al Raschid himself had met them, a tall, powerful old man in traditional Arab dress, his shrewd but kindly dark eyes looking out from beneath grizzled brows.

Touching his palms together in the Islamic salute, he had greeted them. 'Professor Warrender ... I am honoured! And your charming daughter.' His courtly bow in her direction made Alison feel like royalty. Ought she to respond with a dropped curtsey? How was one supposed to behave towards a sheik? A ruler in his own land, a man of wealth and power.

A vintage Rolls-Royce awaited them, a slim Arab chauffeur at the wheel. Alighting to open the doors of the car, he too had bowed low to the distinguished guests, stealing a respectful glance at the great professor who was coming to make the desert blossom like a rose.

Alison wished they might have stayed a while in the city of Algiers, the snatched glimpse of its outskirts beyond the airport was tantalising as the car hurried them along an excellent motorway under the reddening evening sky. Dusk had fallen rapidly. In the fading light there had been unexpectedly green farmlands and white Arab villages. Then the headlights had taken over as they passed through the deep gorges which pierce the Atlas mountains, sombre corridors of jagged rock where shadows lurk and water drips. After that night had fallen rapidly, and there was only the swathe of light cut by the car as it travelled on. The motor road had long been left behind, the track became rough. Alison, beginning to feel travel-worn, and shaken, listened drowsily to the voices of the Sheik and her father. The Sheik's English was good. He had, it emerged, in the long-distant past spent several youthful years at a famous English public school. 'My father was Anglophile,' he explained, 'resisting the influence of our French overlords.'

'And now there are no longer any French overlords,' the Professor prompted.

'For some years past,' the Sheik agreed, 'we have regained our independence. But we are still busy rescuing our ancient culture from the Gallic trappings imposed by a foreign power. And for me there are many good ideas from England.' He read several English newspapers, he told them, and regularly listened to English broadcasting on his radio receiver. It was from a B.B.C. news-cast that he had heard extracts from a lecture on reafforestation that Professor Warrender had given to an august body of experts at a recent meeting of the World Forestry Congress.

'I knew then that you must come to me, that I must enlist your services,' the old man said imperiously.

They talked of the ever-present danger of the encroaching desert sand. Everywhere in North Africa, the good land was threatened by the insidiously moving golden dunes. Hence the need for trees, thousands of them, to bind the shifting soil and create what the Professor called a 'micro climate' ... a density of atmosphere sufficient to induce humidity and encourage rainfall. And never could trees be produced quickly enough. It was to be John Warrender's mission this spring to supervise the planting of precious seedlings in the Sheik's domain, an operation which took place at the end of the February rainy season. There had been many failures in the past through lack of expertise.

'But this year you will guide us!' the Sheik exulted. With the garrulousness of age he rambled on as the car bumped and lurched through the darkne . But all that he said was interesting even to the t .vel-weary Alison. Imperious he might be, as befitting a ruler, but his heart was kind and large and he was genuinely anxious to make his little kingdom in the wilderness a place of humanity and progress. He was not, he told them, rich as sheiks go, having no oil interests. What income he had must be maintained by successful horticulture, through which he hoped to bring employment and prosperity to his people. But it was slow work. The spectres of poverty and ignorance still lingered.

'You will help me to banish these spectres, my dear Professor,' he ended. 'It was with great hope I invited you to join me here.'

An invitation that had come, as it happened, at a particularly opportune moment when the Professor, run down after a bad attack of flu, was glad to have the chance of a few weeks in the Algerian warmth and sunshine. It had not been difficult for him to obtain a term's leave from the provincial university where he taught, and the Sheik had hospitably welcomed the idea that he should bring with him his eldest daughter, to keep house for him in the villa allotted to them in the palace grounds.

And here they were, in the oasis town of Sidi bou Kef! Jumping out of bed, Alison stepped on to a leopardskin rug which felt curiously alive under her bare feet. It was too early to disturb her father, or to expect the cup of tea with which Lalla, the sloe-eyed maid, had promised to waken her. There would be time to explore a little before the day proper began. Last night she had been glad enough to go to bed immediately after the meal served to them in the rather bare but pleasant pink-walled dining-room.

'The Villa Fleurie is not luxurious,' the Sheik had apologised, 'but I hope you will find it adequate.'

A hurried survey last night had been reassuring. There were three comfortably furnished bedrooms, a well-fitted kitchen, a living-room opening on to a covered verandah, and an excellent bathroom with an electrical water heater and shower. The electricity—generated on the estate—was, she was to discover, a little erratic. But it was wonderful to have a bathroom at all in the middle of the waterless Sahara. And the third bedroom would do beautifully for Fiona, her seventeen-year-old sister, when she joined them later on for her Easter holiday. A diffident mention of this possibility last night had brought a flood of hospitable assurances from the Sheik. 'My dear Professor,' he had declared expansively, 'the villa is yours to use as you wish. Please accommodate any member of your family within its all too humble walls. I shall be honoured by their presence!'

It was all quite unbelievable, Alison thought as she took a quick, rather chilly, shower—the horticultural problems of a remote North African sheik uprooting them from their humdrum Sussex home and transporting them to this strange romantic spot. For of course it was romantic. No doubt the poverty the Sheik had spoken of existed beneath the surface, but no matter how poor you were in Algeria you had for most of the time a gorgeous climate; sun and warmth to laze in instead of the perpetual rain and fogs of wintery England.

Back in her bedroom she slipped on a pair of fawn slacks and a rose cashmere sweater. Were trousered females permitted in this part of the world? Or did women still go about shrouded and veiled? Last night, passing through the villages, she had glimpsed white-robed figures scuttling from the headlights, shapeless as bundles of laundry. Men or women? It hadn't been clear. In cities like Tunis or Algiers there would be plenty of European fashion, but she wasn't sure of the customs out here in the wilds of the Sahara.

'You'd better watch your step,' Fiona had warned her. 'If you go about Sidi bou Kef in shorts or suchlike you'll probably be pounced upon by some Arab warrior, who'll throw you over the back of his fiery steed and carry you off to his harem.'

'Gosh!' she had continued yearningly, 'I can't wait to see those pure-bred Arabs—the horses, I mean, not the men. Do you think the Sheik will let me do some riding?'

Fiona since her sixth year had been a devoted horsewoman, and was now the owner of a Welsh cob, oddly named Dora, who grew fat and lazy in the paddock behind the Warrenders' Downland home during Fiona's absences at boarding school. This was to be her last term and apart from her interest in horses her future was something of a problem. She wasn't attracted to nursing—a hard life but a rewarding one, Alison told her. Though Alison herself had been glad enough to leave St Clare's soon after taking her Finals to keep house for their father. Since the death of their mother when Fiona was twelve he had suffered at the hands of a series of unsatisfactory domestic helps. Now Alison enjoyed running the big old house, entertaining academics and students. Sometimes she wondered if she would ever do anything else. She hadn't meant to give up nursing altogether, but her father had become dependent upon her and it was difficult to break away.

At the moment, however, these problems seemed distant. A whole new world lay just beyond the glass doors which led to the verandah. With a last look in the mirror at her freshly scrubbed, wholesome young face, Alison tied her thick chestnut gold hair into a ponytail and went out into the shining morning. Standing on the top steps of the short flight which led from the verandah to the garden, she caught her breath. It was all so beautiful! Flower beds descended in a series of terraces to a vividly blue lily pond. There were archways covered with roses, borders gay with geraniums, the inevitable purple clouds of bougain-villea. Where the garden ended date palms stood like grey-green feather dusters against the blue sky. Beyond their naked boles citrus groves flourished, the orange and lemon trees in bloom, their fragrance sharp as spice on the crisp morning air.

Following a path which led through these fruit orchards, Alison came to an olive grove and then to a plantation of gnarled old fig trees, already laden with small green figs. She found it difficult to accept this far-reaching lush growth as an 'oasis', a word which hither-to had conjured up for her the vision of a few palm trees grouped round a solitary well in the midst of a waste of desert sands. But the whole of the district of Sidi bou Kef, she had discovered, was known as an oasis, its cultivated land covering many square miles. And somewhere in the vicinity of the Villa Fleurie and its garden the Sheik's palace was hidden. Would she and her father ever be invited into this sanctum? Alison wondered. Did the Sheik keep a harem, or was polygamy one of the things which had vanished with an obsolete past? Dancing girls and concubines ... somehow she couldn't imagine the dignified Sheik bothering his grey head with such frivolities.

The path petered out as she left the trees behind her, coming out on to a trackless stretch of rough grass, thorn bushes and rocks. Was this the beginning of the authentic desert? The fringe of the great Sahara itself? Climbing a hillock, she looked out over miles of sand, tawny as the hide of a lion, fashioned into fantastic mounds and hollows by the wind. It was breathlessly quiet. A small lizard scuttled almost over her bare sandalled feet, making a metallic sound as it went. She

shrank back. Ought she to go any further? People so
easily got lost in the trackless desert. She thought of the
grim stories of luckless travellers dying of thirst. But as
long as she kept the trees in sight she would be all
right. Pressing on, she was conscious of a mounting
excitement, the sand slipping beneath her feet. Sometimes she was high on the top of a dune, then she
would slide down into a sheltered hollow where the
morning sun already gathered heat. How empty it
was! Not a blade of grass now, or a living creature to
be seen.

How long she wandered on she did not know, but
turning at last, she looked behind her—and the reassuring treeline which marked the Al Raschid estate
had vanished, the contours of the land blotting them
out. There was nothing but sand all round her, before
and behind; wherever she looked sand and more sand.
The sun was gaining strength. The sky, a molten blue,
seemed to close her in like an immense bowl, shutting
her down into the featureless landscape. Once she
turned, then again, and realised she had no idea of her
direction. Panic possessed her; how silly it was of her to
have come so far! She began to run in a futile way,
stumbling and slipping in the loose sand. Her heart
pounded, the blood drummed in her ears.

Blundering over a final hillock, she found herself on
a rough road, blessedly stable under her feet. It must
lead somewhere—but which way should she go? The
drumming in her ears grew louder, swelling to a
mighty rushing sound. She had barely time to throw
herself out of the way as a band of Arab horsemen swept
down upon her, rounding a corner in the road. Waving
rifles above their heads, they thundered past, their
savage screams bursting upon the desert quietness like

all hell let loose. On the sandy verge of the road where she had flung herself Alison lay too stunned as yet to be thankful that she had not been trampled to death. Had she been caught in the middle of some tribal battle? But against whom were the Arabs screaming and waving their rifles? There did not appear to be any opposing force in the offing, the sand once more stretching away in empty innocence, having swallowed up the horsemen and their mounts. Only the faint sound of the retreating hooves could still be heard. Then suddenly there was the swish of approaching car tyres, and round the corner came a great white car, American by the look of it, with yards of chassis fore and aft.

Scrambling to her feet, Alison pressed herself against the stony ridge which bounded the road, wondering if the huge bit of hardware could edge past her. Having been saved from the hooves of wild horses, was she now to be crushed by this juggernaut of a car? She was almost too distraught to care.

The car stopped. She was vaguely aware that the young man at the wheel was dark-haired, amber-eyed and unusually good-looking. The amber eyes showed concern. 'Are you in some kind of trouble?' the young man asked. He had seen her scrambling to her feet, looking no doubt as dishevelled as she felt.

'I've come rather further than I meant to,' she began. 'Lost my way. Can you tell me how to get back to Sidi bou Kef?'

He opened the offside door of the car. 'The best way to get to Sidi would be to jump right in here beside me. That's where I'm heading for.' The amber eyes now held a glint of amusement. Or was it mischief? She padded round the incredibly long car, wondering if she were inviting some kind of hideous adventure, getting into this lush vehicle with a strange young man in the middle of nowhere. But at least he spoke English, though he didn't give an altogether English impression. There was a touch of the exotic about him; the carefully trimmed curls, the classic profile, the gold bangle on one elegant wrist. His silk polo-necked sweater was the colour of buttercups, his dusty-pink trousers perfectly pressed, and as she took her seat at his side Alison caught a whiff of expensive skin lotion. Hands languidly draped on the wheel, he turned and smiled at her. There was no mistake about the amusement.

I expect I look a sight, she thought ruefully. There was sand all over her rose-coloured cardigan, sand on her hands and in her hair, which had come adrift from its fastening and tumbled in a coppery cascade about her face.

With a well-behaved purr the outsize car, a Cadillac, got into action. It had the sort of springs that could cope with a desert track, and the upholstery was seductive. Leaning back against the soft red leather, Alison relaxed, hardly caring if she were being abducted. She had walked a long way over the slippery sand and she was desperately hungry. She ought not to have come all this way without breakfast. She ought not to have come at all.

The young man at her side seemed to be thinking much the same thing. 'How is it that you're wandering about the Sahara all alone at this hour of the morning?' he asked.

She shook the hair out of her eyes. 'I just came to have a look round before breakfast. At least that's what I meant to do, then I got fascinated with the wild scenery, went further than I intended ... and lost my bearings. There's a certain sameness about miles and miles of sand...'

'There sure is!' he laughed. 'Are you staying at Sidi? On a tour, perhaps? I haven't noticed you around the one and only hotel.'

'I'm with my father at the Villa Fleurie. We're the guests of the Sheik al Raschid.'

'Good heavens, that old Tartar! I didn't know he went in for English house parties.'

'This isn't a house party,' Alison explained. 'My father, who is a professor of ecology, has come to advise the Sheik on reafforestation.'

The young man shook his head. 'Ecology? What on earth is that?'

'A science that deals with the conservation of life and plants,' Alison provided primly.

The smile which was never far from the well-cut lips widened. 'I'll take your word for it. And were you looking for life and plants in the sandy wastes?'

'No,' Alison returned shortly. 'I was just having a walk, exploring a bit. We only arrived after dark last night and it's all such a change from Sussex.'

This time the young man threw back his head and roared with laughter. 'I'll say it is! So your nice English walk before breakfast ... so healthy, my dear! ... turned into a scramble in the sand. When I saw you lying at the track-side against the rocks I thought you were hurt.'

'I was more or less knocked off my feet by a band of howling dervishes,' Alison explained. 'Arabs on horseback screaming and waving their rifles.'

'Oh, my lot,' the young man said in a matter-of-fact tone. 'I'm sorry they scared you. What you saw was a run through for a sequence we shall be filming later in the day. Your screaming dervishes were a bunch of extras. And incidentally, dervishes don't ride horses, they dance. Religious dances.'

But Alison wasn't interested in technical accuracies. 'Film extras!' she gasped. 'And I thought I'd been caught in the middle of some desert battle.'

'No. It was just a scene from *Hills of Sand*, a picture I'm directing on location for an American–French set-up with its headquarters in Paris, where I live, when I'm not in New York. Your friend the Sheik has given us more or less grudging permission to use Sidi bou Kef as our headquarters. I'm staying with the members of my company at the Hotel Regence.' He half turned from the wheel to give her a slight bow. 'My name, in case it interests you, is Everton, Paul Everton.'

'And mine is Alison Warrender,' Alison contributed.

The amber eyes flashed. 'Miss Warrender—Alison! I'm delighted to meet you on a golden spring morning in the wastes of the Sahara. What could be more romantic? Can I tempt you to come along to the hotel and have breakfast with me?'

'No, thank you,' Alison's voice was firm. This smooth young film director was a fast worker! 'But I'll be most grateful to you if you would drop me off at the Villa Fleurie. That is, if it's not out of your way.'

'What if it is? It's my pleasure to serve you.'

'You're very kind.'

All this gallantry at eight o'clock in the morning! Alison couldn't resist giving him a sardonic glance. But there were trees on the narrowing horizon now. They were nearly home. The Villa, she told him, should be somewhere behind those olive groves to the left.

He gave a theatrical sigh. 'So soon! And you won't

have breakfast with me. Can I offer you something more exciting ... dinner this evening, for instance? At the Regence. You could meet some of my crowd. It's going to be a bit dull for you, isn't it, at the Villa Fleurie while your father and the old Sheik hobnob over their trees?'

He could be right, Alison agreed privately. Fast worker or not, there was something likeable about this young man. An American–French film director who lived in Paris—a type entirely out of her orbit. Most of the men she had met so far had been young doctors or medical students at St Clare's, and more recently the rather prosaic academic friends of her father, with an occasional undergraduate thrown in to liven things up. Not that she had had much time for dating undergraduates during the last two years. Nor had she wanted dates, having been badly hurt during her last year in hospital by a catastrophic love affair with one of the registrars. The thought of him could still hurt horribly. His abrupt ending to their friendship had been so unfair, so inexplicable. She thrust the painful memory aside. But, obscurely, it made it easier for her to accept Paul Everton's invitation.

'Thank you,' she said. 'I'd like to have dinner with you and your friends this evening.' That it wasn't to be entirely *tête-à-tête* was somehow reassuring.

'Fine!' He looked pleased. 'I'll pick you up at the main gate of the Sheik's estate about eight o'clock.'

'Won't you make it a little earlier, and come to the Villa and have a drink?'

'And meet Papa?' he grinned. 'Okay, if that's how you want it. But I'm afraid I can't get away much before eight.'

She nodded. 'I'll expect you at eight, then.'

They had reached the great Moorish doorway which was apparently the entrance to the Al Raschid estate. It was set in a high wall over which curtains of wistaria cascaded. Paul Everton stopped the car, and Alison, feeling a little doubtful, got out. The Villa, she supposed, would be some yards further down the tree-lined lane, but she didn't like to ask Paul to take her there. He had already come a couple of miles out of his way. If she could get through this iron-studded and rather grim door she would easily find her way home.

'Thank you very much for the lift,' she said.

'Thank *you*,' he returned, with a flourish, 'for a delightful interlude.' He began to back the car along the narrow way, calling, '*À tout à l'heure*, then! See you this evening.'

She watched him turning the mammoth car skilfully, and when it had vanished with a roar of acceleration, she pulled the bell handle at the side of the dark doorway. The ringing echoed away as if down a hollow passage, a rather spooky sound. And spooky indeed was the ancient manservant who answered the summons. Small, stooped and shrivelled within the usual sheet-like garment which enveloped him, he peered suspiciously at the stranger.

'My name is Warrender,' she said, speaking in French, which she had found was the language spoken by most of the Sheik's servants.

Illumination dawned on the wrinkled countenance. 'Ah, the so honourable *anglaise*! Guests of our noble lord.' He flung the door wide and turning led the way down a passageway which was as long and uninviting as the echoing bell had hinted.

There was sunshine at the end of it, however, and a courtyard flanked on its four sides by a two-storey building with latticed windows looking on to an ornate balcony. The pillars supporting the balcony were twined with climbing roses, honeysuckle and bougainvillea. A shallow staircase led from the courtyard to the balcony. When they reached it the old man halted. Would the young lady like to see the women of the Sheik? he asked, pointing upwards. *'Là-haut, l'appartement des dames.'*

The harem! Feeling foolishly startled, Alison said hurriedly, *'Plus tard, monsieur.* Another time. It is necesary now that I return to the Villa.'

'Bien,' the old man nodded, and hobbled on. But as Alison made to follow him an eager young voice called, 'Miss Warrender!'

Turning, Alison saw a young girl about Fiona's age running along the balcony and down the stairs. In her small pale face her dark eyes were enormous, her whole air one of breathless excitement. She was dressed in a long green dress of stiff silk, caught at the waist by a wide gold belt. Heavy earrings of gold hung from her ears and bangles jingled upon her wrists. Alison saw as she drew near that her eyes were outlined with kohl. In spite of this she had the innocent prettiness of a kitten.

'Bo'jour, mees. I am Haidie. I spik English. The Sheik is my grandfather. Yes?'

Alison smiled up into the rapt lovely little face. 'How nice of you to come and greet me! My name is Alison.' She held out her hand. Haidie, after looking at it a moment shyly, took it briefly. Perhaps shaking hands wasn't an Arab custom.

'Will you come with me and meet my mother, my aunts and my grandmother, who is the wife of the Sheik? She is wishing to welcome you.'

A harem full of grandmothers and mothers and

aunts! Somehow this was not quite what Alison had expected. 'May I come later in the day?' she asked. 'I have been for a long walk and my father will be wondering where I am.'

Haidie nodded, though she looked a little disappointed. 'You come as soon as you can, Mees Alison. *Cet après-midi*, perhaps.' Her great eyes widened and she clasped her hands together in a little gesture of rapture. 'We make you the English five o'clock tea. Yes?'

Alison smiled. 'I'd love to come to tea. Thank you very much. But now I must go.' She turned to the patiently waiting guide, and following him across the courtyard thought that she was not doing too badly on her first day in Sidi bou Kef—a dinner invitation with a film director, and now an invitation to a harem tea party!

The door through which the old man guided her led into a large dimly lit passageway with heavily latticed windows. Curlicues of Moorish script embellished the walls. At the far end a beautiful archway led to a wilderness of garden.

Here the old man halted. If the *mademoiselle* would take the path through this garden, he indicated, she would find the gateway to the Villa Fleurie at the pathway's end. Perhaps he had come with her as far as his beat covered. Could he be the keeper of the women's quarters ... the harem? Alison speculated.

It was an orderly wilderness through which she walked, though the massive rose beds could have done with a little judicious pruning.

Soon she was back at the Villa, where the Professor was just finishing his breakfast on the verandah.

'You've been out early. Have you had a nice walk,

my dear?' he greeted her absently. It did not seem to occur to him that she had been away for the best part of two hours, but no doubt he had slept late, and where domestic matters were involved he was incurably casual. At all events he had not missed her.

Too hungry to be hurt by his nonchalance, Alison poured herself a cup of coffee from the silver coffee pot. There was cream to go with it, and brown cane sugar— a French-style breakfast, no bacon or eggs, Alison saw a little regretfully. But the Swedish crispbread was all that crispbread should be. So was the cereal, the dish of fresh apricot compôte, the honey, the Normandy farm butter. When Alison exclaimed at the butter her father told her it came from a large importing firm in Algiers. 'All the Sheik's groceries, he told me last night as we drove here, are brought out from the capital once a week, and in a place like Algiers there would be almost the same wide choice as one would find in Paris. So we shan't starve.'

'I wondered about the milk and the cream,' he ended. 'Cows must be at a premium in this pastureless wilderness. But milk too, it seems, comes by air from the South of France to Algiers, and there are very good brands to be had in tins.'

While she ate Alison related her morning's adventures—film actors on location, screaming Arab warriors on horseback all but trampling her into the sand, the young film director who had come to her rescue and invited her to dinner. 'How's that for fast work?' she ended.

Before her father had time to comment there was a rustling among the rose bushes and the Sheik appeared, full of ceremonial morning greetings. Had they slept well? Was all as it should be at the Villa?

Was Lalla looking after them?

These courtesies out of the way, he launched into what was obviously the real purpose of his early morning visit—a survey of the work upon which the Professor could perhaps start right away. It was diffidently put, but his eagerness was apparent, and as John Warrender was equally eager a lively discussion on the merits of the various new trees followed. Aneure, cyanophylla, pucanantha; precious seedlings of these rarer species were ready and waiting to be planted. As well as the more usual cupressus, there were eucalyptus and good-tempered acacia. The strips of ploughed land between the trees as well as acting as fire-breaks could be sown with wheat and barley and millet. 'Food for the humans as well as the marauding camels and goats,' the Sheik said. To deal with these animals more barbed-wire fences must be erected.

After about half an hour of this the Sheik seemed to become aware of the patiently listening Alison. 'All this must be pretty boring for you, Miss Warrender,' he offered. 'Unless you share your father's enthusiasm for ecology.'

'I'm afraid I don't understand a great deal about it,' Alison admitted. 'I'm not really a bit clever, or scientific. I keep house for my father.'

'Which is a waste of her skills,' the Professor put in loyally. 'I ought not to let her sacrifice her career for my sake—but I'm afraid we just drift on.' He made a small helpless gesture.'

'Your career?' the Sheik asked Alison with interest.

'I trained to become a hospital nurse,' she explained.

The Sheik sat bolt upright in his wicker lounge chair. 'A nurse?' he echoed, his busy eyebrows bristling with excitement. There was a small hospital in Sidi bou Kef, it emerged, the apple of his eye. He had started it a few years ago, financing it out of his own pocket—just thirty beds and an operating theatre, as well as an outpatient department. It would give him the greatest pleasure to show Miss Warrender over it one day, and to have her opinion of its working.

'I'd love to see over your hospital, Sheik,' Alison agreed, 'but I'm afraid my opinion wouldn't have much value. I'd only just qualified when I left my hospital two years ago.'

'But you will not have forgotten all you have learned. Perhaps some time you could give a talk to my student nurses. It has been uphill work forming my staff and we have had many what you call teething troubles. In the beginning it was difficult. The older folk in this part of the world are inclined to be fatalists where illness is concerned, believing in the will of Allah rather than in medical skill.'

But gradually, he added, Western influences were permeating.

'There is,' he went on, 'an American ship with the euphoric name of *Hope*, permanently anchored now in a Tunisian harbour. Young American doctors come to it for two or three months at a time, nurses for a longer spell of duty. The ship is equipped to treat a large number of patients, and the doctors, learning about Eastern disease, in their turn help to teach Arab medical students the Western ways. It is an excellent arrangement.' He sighed and shrugged. 'But alas, we have no harbour here to attract a wealthy American ship with all the latest scientific devices for dealing with disease. Greatly daring, I began advertising in the London medical journals for even one doctor who would come and help us. Response was slow, but at last someone took pity on us and some eighteen months ago an English doctor agreed to join us for a time—an able young man. You must meet him...'

Alison, listening rather hazily to all this, gazed out over the sunny garden, watching the fountain that played in a small lily pond among the roses. Gushing up into the air in a silver stream, it sent droplets to sparkle on the petals of the surrounding flowers. The scent of wet roses floated on the air. High in the branches of the flowering fruit trees doves crooned. Hospitals and doctors and little Arab girls learning to be nurses. It was difficult to imagine sickness and misery in this beautiful sun-drenched land. But of course they existed.

An English doctor, the Sheik had said. What kind of man would come out here in answer to an advertisement in a medical journal from some obscure and distant sheik? A crank, she thought, or a saint. And neither category particularly appealed to her. Not that it could possibly matter. But it would be interesting to see the Sheik's little hospital. One way and another life in the desert was promising quite a number of diversions.

CHAPTER TWO

AFTER some more conversation about trees the Sheik departed. The Professor, it had been arranged, should drive round the tree plantations in an estate car which had been allotted to him. 'Ahmed, the gardening boy, brought it round before breakfast,' he told Alison. 'It's in the lane just outside the gate.'

'Why not come with me?' he suggested as he rose from the table.

'Why not?' she echoed dreamily. In this tranced and sunlit moment nothing seemed quite real. He looked into the wide grey eyes that could never hide their owner's feelings—candid eyes, lit with an honesty he had lived with and loved for the happiest years of his life. There were times when Alison reminded him disturbingly of her mother. She had her mother's eyes.

'What was it you were telling me about Arab tribesmen when the Sheik interrupted us?' he asked as they walked through the terraced garden.

'Oh, that!' Alison laughed. 'They weren't Arab tribesmen after all, but film extras.' She told him again about Paul Everton, and of her promise to dine with him.

'A film director,' he murmured a little doubtfully. 'A total stranger. I suppose it will be all right.'

'He's coming here at eight o'clock this evening to pick me up. You can meet him then, give him the once-over.'

John Warrender grimaced. 'In this day and age parents don't give their children's friends the once-over. You have sense enough to look after yourself. At all events he'll be a change from our Sussex academics.' He gave her a searching glance. 'I hope this trip isn't going to be tedious for you, stuck out here in the wilds with no one of your own kind to hobnob with.'

She told him of Haidie's invitation to tea. 'In the harem,' she ended impressively. 'It seems to be full of grandmothers and aunts and cousins.'

He laughed. 'So much for the glamorous Orient! But it will be an experience.' And after a moment while he paused to light a post-breakfast pipe, 'This hospital of the Sheik's ... that might turn out to be quite an interest for you. And a young English doctor. We must make his acquaintance.' His glance mocked her a little through the thin haze of pipe smoke. 'He might be a more suitable companion for you than this exotic-sounding film director with the come-hither tactics.'

For the next two hours they bumped over narrow tracks between rows of trees, most of them mature and well established. In a date grove they stopped to watch boys shinning up the long stems of the palms, mysteriously busy with the fronds of blossom half hidden among the leafy tops.

'Pollinating by hand,' John Warrender explained. 'Cross-fertilising—an archaic method, but it seems to yield good results.' Water ran in a criss-cross of little channels everywhere. Saucer-like hollows surrounded many of the trees. They needed the fierce heat of the sun on their foliage and moisture at their roots to ensure the best results, the Professor went on. 'Just now, after the rainy season, the water supply is fairly easily maintained, but one of my problems is to ensure that we can overcome the drought conditions which will set in later on ...'

He took her through olive groves, through fig and apricot orchards and to the place where the land was being prepared for the seedlings he would be planting.

Their homeward route lay through the town centre, a larger town than Alison had expected, its buildings blindingly white in the blaze of the noonday sun. They cruised down a wide main thoroughfare, from which she glimpsed networks of narrow side streets, lined with a fascinating assortment of open-fronted shops. Many of these streets were covered by latticed roofs, through which the light spilled down like golden coins. In the main street animals and humanity jostled in a never-ending vociferous stream. The noise was deafening. White-robed Arabs driving donkeys before them, or balancing grotesquely on the tiny creatures' backs, cried *'Balak! Balak!'* in lordly, imperious tones. 'Make way! Make way!' A camel came loping along with a supercilious air, a picturesquely dressed Bedouin perched on its back. Its reins were of scarlet leather, silver bells hung from its harness. John Warrender slowed the estate car to let it pass, giving Alison plenty of time to marvel at its long languorous eyelashes and thick sneering lips. It was a bad-tempered-looking creature, but with a certain built-in dignity, bred for countless centuries to fetch and carry submissively across the trackless sands of the Sahara.

Presently the street widened to a square, dominated by a mosque, its minaret rising in slender beauty against the cobalt sky. Here were the larger, more European buildings; a cinema, a police station, the Hotel Regence where Paul Everton and his cast were staying. Where was the hospital? Alison wondered.

'Would you like a drink?' John Warrender asked, slowing up outside the hotel. But Alison, for some indefinable reason, didn't want to risk running into Paul Everton just now. Time enough to see him again tonight.

'Why don't we go to one of the native cafés?' she suggested, 'and sample the famous mint tea?'

Turning into a side street, they stopped at a shady terrace, where the tin-topped tables stood under a striped awning. The customers, exclusively male, were dressed in a fascinating assortment of colourful flowing garments. And the mint tea was unexpectedly refreshing. It was while they were drinking that a resounding voice came from the top of the minaret, calling the faithful to prayer. '*Alla il Allah* ... There is one God and Mahomed is his prophet.' All the tea drinkers in the little café instantly left their tables, and throwing themselves face downward on the hot pavement, quite without self-consciousness, joined in the wave of prayer. Hundreds of voices all over the little town lifted up to God in the quiet noonday heat. It was a moving moment.

Back at the Villa lunch was awaiting them: couscous, a sort of savoury semolina mixed with young green vegetables, herbs and small pieces of deliciously tender lamb. This was followed by a large bowl of sweet yoghurt and a platter of fruit—orange, apricots, dates, bananas and grapes, all brought to the table by the smiling Lalla. Her housekeeping, Alison could see, was going to be made fairly simple. No meals to plan, unless she wanted to, no cleaning to see to. Lalla had made it clear that all this was her province. Just as well there was a hospital in the background where she might sometimes make herself useful, Alison thought.

But after lunch she was glad to be idle, tired after her long morning in the sun, and her early adventures with their moments of alarm and anxiety. Stretched on a cane lounge chair, she leafed through a pile of French magazines she had found in the living-room, obviously put there for her diversion. Glancing through a copy of *Paris Match* the title *Hills of Sand* caught her eye, and there was an article about Paul Everton and the film he was making at Sidi bou Kef. It was clear he was highly thought of in the world of French cinema. There was a photograph of him, looking strikingly handsome in a trendy dinner jacket and frilled white shirt. Darienne Chevasse, a French actress, the film's leading lady, was by his side, a tall and sultry beauty with great liquid eyes and dark flowing hair, well cast for the part of heroine in the story. A brief outline of the plot was given. It all sounded a little obvious and dated, but no doubt Paul Everton would be capable of giving a new twist to old material, and there was always a public for romances dealing with life in the remoter towns of the Sahara desert. Sidi bou Kef was, in fact, the perfect setting.

The magazine slipped from her grasp. Overcome with sunshine and after-lunch drowsiness, she dozed off. She did not know how long she slept when approaching footsteps awakened her. Still half asleep, she turned in her chair.

'I'm sorry to have disturbed you,' a polite English voice offered, 'but I'm looking for the Sheik and thought he might be here at the Villa...'

'I'm afraid he's not——' Alison began, then her heart turned a violent somersault. She shaded her eyes with her hand, peering up through the dazzle of sunlight. 'Brett!' she whispered faintly. 'Brett Meredith!' Shrinking back into the shelter of the chair's canopy, she felt quite sick with shock. The hospital, she thought wildly. The young English doctor. And it had to be Brett! In a dazed way she gazed up at the blurred figure of the young man standing over her, as stricken with astonishment as herself.

'Alison!' he was saying. 'Alison Warrender, by all that's wonderful!' He passed a hand over his eyes. 'Or are you her double?'

Sitting up, she let the chestnut hair fall over her face, shielding her a little from those direct blue eyes that at times could be so cold, so impenetrable. At the moment they were merely flabbergasted.

'No, it's me all right,' she said, ignoring niceties of grammar.

His laughter was a little shaky, more an expression of uncertainty than of pleasure.

'When the Sheik told us there was an English doctor at his hospital I never dreamed it could be you.' She tried to keep the wonder out of her voice, the sheer heart-shaking joy.

'But this is extraordinary!' He sat down on a canvas chair beside her. She could focus him a little more clearly now. If only she didn't feel so tousled and hot ... just awakened out of sleep. And her heart was still thumping uncomfortably, making her feel silly and breathless. He was just the same as ever, she thought with a ridiculous pang of relief. The same thatch of unruly blond hair, the fair skin, tanned by the Algerian sunshine. And those oddly hypnotic eyes— alight now with pleasure at the sight of her—no doubt because he was a little lonely in this outpost of the Sahara and she was a familiar face from home.

'What in heaven's name are you doing here?' he asked. 'You're the last person I would have expected to find in Achmed al Raschid's little kingdom.'

'I'm not a newly recruited member of his harem, if that's what you're thinking,' she said, and instantly felt it to be a tasteless quip. Trust her at a moment like this to say all the wrong things!

'I'm here with my father, Professor Warrender,' she began again with more dignity.

'The ecologist! So that's it! I've heard so much about him during the past couple of weeks from the Sheik, but even though I knew his name was War-render, I didn't connect him with you.'

'There was no reason why you should,' she said. A name that had no doubt slid out from his memory long ago with the trivia of lost years.

'What happened to your nursing career?' he was asking. 'I'd imagined you ruling over the wards by now in some lucky hospital ... one of our more brilliant young Sisters. Either that or marriage.'

'Thank you, kind sir!' She tossed the hair out of her eyes, longing fruitlessly for a brief private session with comb and pocket mirror. She felt unkempt and sticky, all wrong for this earth-shaking conversation. Doves crooned in the almond trees, the little fountain sparkled and splashed, roses swooned, pouring out their perfume in the afternoon heat.

She said, 'I shouldn't have thought you would have time to imagine anything about me ... or even remember my existence.'

'Wouldn't you?' It was softly spoken and he was looking at her in a way which made her feel stupid and gauche. Oh, it was crazy to be so churned up by his reappearance, after more than two years and one of the most unmistakable brush-offs a girl could suffer. Where was her pride?

She said, 'After I qualified I went home to keep house for my father.'

'I'm sorry you've given up nursing. You're too good to lose.' He smiled at her. His smiles that were so rare, so irresistible, lighting his whole rather too controlled young face with warmth and light. 'I've got a hospital here ... perhaps the Sheik told you? It's one of his pet enterprises. Maybe you'll come and have a look round it one of these days.' He stood up. 'Well, it's very nice to have seen you again, young Warrender.' He held out his hand and she felt her fingers clasped briefly, firmly in his own.

'And now I really must track down the Sheik. We're having a spot of bother at the hospital with the electrical generator. A ramshackle affair that is for ever going wrong.' He shrugged and grinned.

'Ali!' he called to the gardening boy who was squatting over a distant flower bed. 'Do you know where I can find the Sheik?'

'Where they plant the new trees,' Ali supplied, and added importantly, 'I take you to him.' All too glad to leave his weeding, he sprang to his feet.

When they had gone off together Alison went to her room for a belated freshening-up. She would have to hurry to keep her appointment with Haidie, but for the moment she could only stand and stare blankly at her shocked face in the mirror. Brett here in Sidi bou Kef! The sight of him had thrown her so completely off balance that she hardly knew what she had said to him. She pressed her hand against her heart as though to ease an actual physical pain, while sickeningly the past returned to mock her.

That other spring when she and Brett had been so much together, snatching what chances they could from their crowded working hours. Trips to the country in his shabby little car, theatre dates on hospital complimentary tickets, cups of coffee late at night in the little café outside the hospital gates, where Brett could still be 'on call'. He had planned for these meetings as eagerly as she had. Or so she had thought.

And she had fallen wholly, unguardedly in love with him.

Then suddenly it was all over. On the evening of the hospital annual ball he had let her down flat. She had waited for him as arranged in the foyer of the hotel where the dance was being held. If he had been delayed by an emergency he could have got a message to her, surely! But there had been no message. After almost two hours Simon Frayne, a young houseman, had found her sitting disconsolately by the reception desk watching the swing doors. 'Give him up, whoever he is,' he had advised lightly, 'and come and dance with me.'

She had spent what was left of the evening in his company. He was amusing, companionable; one of the many housemen she had gone out with before she became serious about Brett. The next day she expected some explanation from Brett, but none was forthcoming. She hadn't seen him then for more than a week, apart from glimpses of him at work, and gradually, painfully it dawned on her that he was deliberately avoiding her. When she did at last encounter him face to face in one of the corridors she had asked him point-blank what was the matter. He looked surprised and seemed to have difficulty in throwing his mind back to the night of the ball when she reminded him about it. Then he had remembered. He had had a call to Casualty, he said, and had been too rushed to get in touch with her and tell her so. 'I'm sure you weren't lacking partners,' he had ended in a wholly uninterested tone. The verdict was plain enough. He was through with her. Soon after that he had left St Clare's for a senior appointment in another hospital. And she hadn't set eyes on him, until today in this improbable Algerian garden.

So what? For a brief springtime he had cultivated her friendship, then he had cooled off. There could have been half a dozen reasons, or no reason at all. He had been working hard for one of his numerous exams. But whatever competition she was up against she hadn't succeeded in holding his interest—which she had probably exaggerated, making too much out of too little. And she had paid for her mistake with a heart-ache which still crazily persisted.

For heaven's sake forget it! she upbraided herself. She put her hands to her head and her eyes, looking back at her from the mirror, were wide and wild. Blast Brett Meredith! She wasn't going to let him spoil this wonderful holiday in North Africa. Let life be all fresh and new, she urged herself, not cluttered up with the stale mistakes of the past. She was glad she was going out with Paul Everton tonight, meeting film people. And right now there was the tea party waiting for her in the harem.

Fresh and cool presently in a crisp cotton frock, she ran into the garden and through the Moorish doorway into the secret domain beyond. Instantly the little old man was at her side, like a faithful watchdog. Nobody, she guessed, came or went in this guarded area without his knowledge. Though many of the taboos connected with the cloistering of well-born women might be vanishing in theory, custom dies hard, especially among the old, and the tottering custodian would not take kindly to change.

'Salaam!' he greeted Alison with dignity, then went before her to the foot of the wrought-iron staircase. Haidie was waiting expectantly at the top, still wearing her gay green frock and jingling bangles.

'We are full of joy that you come to see us!' she cried as Alison mounted the stairs. 'My grandmother, my mother ... all the family await you. We have prepared for you the real English tea.'

She had been to a French boarding school in Algiers, she went on, as she led the way through a long lofty room. 'It was there I learned of the English "five o'clock"; the special tea-drinking ceremony in the afternoon. In France too they have it now in *chic* circles.'

Alison looked about her with interest, though the room was not very well lit. What light there was came in splinters of sunshine through the latticed windows, revealing walls hung with rich silks and engraved with Arabic script. There was a mosaic floor in the centre of which a fountain dripped into a large marble bowl. Round the walls ran a low seat, cushioned with red velvet, and at one end of the room a great throne-like chair stood on a raised dais. Just above this an elaborately carved and closely shuttered balcony protruded.

'It is behind that balcony we have our apartments,' Haidie explained, as Alison stood still to gaze up at it. 'It is here in this room that my grandfather gives the banquets. Sometimes we are permitted to join his guests. At other times we just peep through the chinks in the latticed shutters of the balcony. Do you not think it is a beautiful salon?'

'Very beautiful,' Alison agreed, glancing at the empty space before her. 'But where do people sit when there is a party ... what do you use for a dining table?'

'The fountain is covered over,' Haidie explained, 'and a great table stands in the centre of the room. That is for when we entertain European visitors. For our own people there are cushions on the floor and low tables shared by small groups.'

They walked on over priceless prayer rugs and leopardskins to a distant door.

'*Voilà!* Haidie exclaimed, throwing the door open.

It led into a large pleasant sunny room, full of small, gaily clad women. Violet, magenta, bright yellow, cerise; the colours of their voluminous dresses were as bright as the flowers in the Villa garden. Round every neck hung layers of heavy necklaces—gold, silver, and semi-precious stones. A cloying oriental perfume floated on the air. At the entrance of the two girls a twitter of voices fell silent. Tiny girl-children dressed in exactly the same way as their elders, even to the necklaces, hid their faces in the flowing skirts of mothers and aunts.

Haidie embarked on a confused round of introductions, beginning with a formidable and incredibly ancient old lady in magenta satin, whose pouched and hooded eyes held a snake-like vigilance. 'Fatima, the great-grandmother of us all,' Haidie presented her.

'*Marhaba!*' the old lady murmured the Arabic greeting. 'Allah be with you.'

'She is *bien agée*,' Haidie boasted. 'Nearly a hundred years old. Maybe more, nobody quite knows.'

After that, Halide, the Sheik's wife, seemed young in comparison, though she must have been well into her seventies. Then came Haidie's mother, Kaira, and the aunts—a whole bevy of them, whose names Alison didn't even try to remember. There were cousins too, of every degree.

The little girls, having been dragged from the protective folds of skirts and presented one by one to the distinguished stranger, Alison was invited to sit down upon a pile of cushions close to the low divan upon which old Fatima squatted, cross-legged. Tea was brought in by a procession of smiling serving maids, who eyed Alison with frank curiosity. The Queen Anne silver tea service was as English as Haidie had promised, but the tea was to be served in glass tumblers. Cubes of sugar having been given to the children, they were taken away by the maids, 'To play in the courtyard until it is time for them to go to bed,' Haidie said. Alison was rather sorry to see them go. Their small alert faces and bright dark eyes attracted her. She would have liked to make friends with them. The courtyard, Haidie explained, was an inner one, well away from the ordinary comings and goings of the palace. 'It has shade and it has sun,' she said, 'and a pool for the children to play in. We often sit there with our embroidery in the cool of the evening. Later I will take you there. I hope you will come and share it with us from time to time.'

'And now I pour you the real English tea,' Kaira announced proudly. Alison found it weak and not very hot, but gave it the praise she knew would be expected. Small sweet cakes made of honey and almonds were pressed upon her, and even more cloying sweetmeats of Turkish delight, marzipan and various other unrecognisable confections. Regretting her substantial lunch, Alison sampled them all. She knew enough of the Arab laws of hospitality to not refuse anything put before her. Rejection of proffered food could be looked upon as a deadly insult. But her dinner with Paul Everton loomed. Another day she must arrange her gastronomical engagements a little more carefully.

Conversation too was proving difficult. 'Only my mother and I and my younger cousins who have been to school in Algiers speak English, and that not very well,' Haidie apologised.

'And my French is not all that wonderful,' Alison admitted. But as the meal progressed it somehow became a little easier, the language difficulty being mysteriously overcome—as is so often the case—by the warm sympathy of those who are trying to make contact. Only the older aunts kept silent, breaking now and then into fits of irrepressible giggles.

'It is because they do not understand what we say,' Haidie excused them. 'And they are not accustomed to English visitors.' She turned to the aunts and spoke to them for a moment in rapid Arabic. They nodded, smiled in Alison's direction, their fluttering hands making small apologetic gestures. It was obvious they had been scolded for a lapse in good manners. There must be no more giggling!

After that Alison did her best to include them in the conversation, speaking to them in her careful, if halting, schoolgirl French. Almost too overcome with shyness to respond, they gazed at her in awe, until one of them remarked that her fair hair was so beautiful. 'Can it truly be real?' she whispered.

'They are hopeless!' Kaira sighed. 'Making such personal remarks! They just don't know how to behave.' Clearly she was ashamed of her older relatives. 'But we are so shut away here in Sidi bou Kef,' she went on. 'Only on our radio sets do we learn how the world is opening up to women. Here we are to a certain extent still segregated.' She brought the big word out proudly. 'It is not my father's fault. He is in favour of progress in every way and would like us to learn many new things. But opportunities are scarce. If,' she ended diffidently, 'you could come here now and then and speak with us in English, telling us about the customs of your country, or reading to us from English books . . .'

'I'd love to do that,' Alison agreed quickly, and found that she meant it. There was something very appealing about this group of cheerful little women, more or less cut off from the world by their wealth and position. If they were lonely, so was she. It would be a pleasure to visit them from time to time.

It was amazing how quickly the afternoon went by, and presently Alison stood up from her pile of cushions, which she had found unexpectedly comfortable. She had stayed too long, she apologised, and was overwhelmed with hospitable reassurances. It was impossible that she could ever wear out her welcome, they urged as they crowded around her to say goodbye, pressing her for promises of another visit very soon.

More ceremoniously the great-grandmother, like a goddess on her divan-throne, bowed over her clasped hands and wished the departing stranger, '*Neharak sa'id!*'

The early twilight was falling as Alison ran back to the villa through the palace grounds. Doves made their amorous calls from the red-tiled walls, and in the lily pond the frogs had already begun their nightly chorus. A heavy dew distilled the scents from flowers and trees.

You can actually *taste* the perfume of the lemon blossom, Alison marvelled. Standing still a moment, she savoured the peace of the African evening. It was all so poignantly beautiful, an empty Eden. Heartbreak returned. If only Brett were here with her in this enchanted garden ... the Brett she had once known, or thought she knew. The Brett she had trusted.

Impatiently she shook the thought away and hurried up the path to the verandah. It was growing late and she must be ready for her date with Paul Everton.

CHAPTER THREE

THE Hotel Regence, on the outskirts of the town's main square, stood surrounded by its own small but lush garden, shaded by palm trees. Entering its grilled gateway one left behind the narrow streets, the dust and turmoil of Sidi bou Kef. Here was luxury and peace and order. In the marble-paved foyer Alison peered for reassurance at her reflection in a convenient wall mirror. The lighting from a crystal chandelier was golden and kindly. She looked, she decided, 'all right', at least as far as face and hair-do were concerned. Her frock wasn't exactly dramatic. Coming to the Sahara, which she had visualised as a remote and uncivilised place, she hadn't brought anything very much in the way of evening wear. The frock she wore now was straight and white and absolutely plain, relieved only by the silver and blue medallion which hung from her neck on a heavy chain. For coolness' sake she had gathered her chestnut hair into a knot at the crown of her head, combing it severely from her brow. Eye make-up was the only exotic touch she had allowed herself.

'You're adorable,' Paul had told her when he called for her at the Villa. And then, with a soft laugh, 'Can anyone in this day and age be as innocent and untouched as you look? If it wasn't for those magnificent, exciting eyes...'

'You don't have to chat me up so feverishly,' she had cut him short.

'Feverish is about right,' he had returned undaunted. 'You've sent my temperature up a hundred degrees!'

Fortunately her father had joined them at that point, and over an introductory sherry Paul had played up to the older man with just the right degree of charm and deference.

Your tact is showing, Alison had wanted to mock him, but suppressed the impulse. She mustn't be so bitchy, she scolded herself. But there was something about Paul Everton which put her on her guard. With his striking good looks, his perpetual good humour, his flow of charm, he was just about too good to be true.

As though sensing her unspoken judgement of him he had behaved with grave courtesy on the brief drive to the hotel, treating her with a gently respectful air. She might have been his maiden aunt, she thought with amusement, as he handed her carefully out of the car. And now in the hotel lounge he was introducing her with smooth efficiency to the various members of the cast of *Hills of Sand*.

Darienne Chevasse was not quite so perfect in the flesh as she had appeared in the *Paris Match* photograph. For one thing she was much less ethereal; everything from her vital statistics to her wide-mouthed smile was on a generous scale. She didn't look as if she took Paul Everton or anybody else very seriously, not even her work. Her laughter rang out again and again as the drinks circulated. Alison liked her, and was fascinated at the easy way she handled the male lead, Pierre Jamelle, who was obviously head over heels in love with her.

Drinking a sharp, iced Campari, Alison tried to sort out the others who were milling around her, secondary role people, bit part players, camera men, two unidentified girls who might have been 'continuity', and even a middle-aged wardrobe mistress. She would never remember all their names, but it didn't greatly matter. She wasn't likely to see very much of them, nor were they particularly interested in the stray newcomer whom Paul had presented dramatically as 'la belle anglaise', whom he had found lost in the desert at dawn.

'But Paul finds girls everywhere,' somebody laughed. 'Put him down in the middle of Siberia and he'll come up with a Tartar beauty queen. L'homme fatal!'

'Idiot!' Paul growled, but his white teeth flashed in his perfectly tanned face, obviously pleased with this tribute to his prowess.

Wasn't it all just a bit obvious and ... unsubtle? Alison thought with an odd world-weariness which surprised her. She ought to be thrilled at meeting all these film people, but somehow they didn't represent what she had come to the Sahara to find. The mysterious Orient ... a primitive society, something utterly different from the twentieth-century world she had left behind.

A little later Paul was leading her to the dining-room where, after all, they were to dine tête-à-tête, the Hills of Sand company tactfully withdrawing to leave them alone. The table Paul had booked was in a secluded alcove, half hidden by potted palms. The candles on the white cloth had rose-coloured shades. Somewhere in the background a Moorish orchestra played strange music, sad and wild as the winds that blow over the endless sand-dunes when the moon is white and cold.

'Don't let's have native dishes,' Paul advised. 'The French cuisine here is good, like so much else the French left behind when their colonising days came to an end.'

So they ate delicious hors d'oeuvres, grilled fresh trout lifted straight from the reserve at the bottom of the hotel garden, some sort of game served with a sharp sauce. Paul said they were quails which ran freely through the desert scrub, and were caught by Arab boys who crawled after them, trapping the birds in their bare hands. A Provençal dish of mixed spring vegetables followed, then a crisp salad with the classic dressing, and finally a golden sweet soufflé, light as a cloud, that melted in the mouth—all this with thé appropriate wines. And Alison, with a healthy young appetite, enjoyed every stage of the long repast. Although there were moments when a faint uneasiness at its lavishness assailed her. It made her feel uncomfortably in Paul's debt. But he was being the perfect host, warm and friendly without being too personal, talking mostly about his film.

'We've got to avoid Beau Geste and the sands of the desert growing cold, and all that dated stuff. The whole story revolves around Darienne, daughter of a *colon* ... that is, one of the French settlers who ran this part of the world before liberation. Returning as a tourist, Darienne meets her childhood sweetheart, a young Arab nobleman, who had once been her playmate. Now he is a Caid, ruling over a large tract of desert land and several small towns like Sidi bou Kef. There's a native festival with dancing, competitions, horse-racing, torchlight processions, and it's in this setting that Darienne meets her young man again, and completely loses her heart to him.'

'It all sounds very exciting,' Alison said politely.

Paul shrugged. 'It could be frightfully old hat, but we're giving it an original twist in our treatment of the love story, ruthlessly abandoning the romantic angle for a slab of harsh realism. Oh, Hassan is in love with Claudine all right—that's Darienne's name in the film —but he turns her down flat. Hassan, you see, has political ambitions; wants to be a leader in his emerging country. Marrying Claudine, he thinks, might hinder his career, not because they happen to be of different nationalities, or because she's the daughter of a one-time colonist, but because she's comparatively poor, with a background that would give him no political leverage, and he's already more or less committed to the daughter of a rich powerful oil-well sheik. It's the old story of man's universal struggle for wealth and power, with love coming off a bad second best.'

'So no happy endings?' Alison said.

Paul shook his head. 'No happy endings.' He looked suitably grave for a moment, then brightened up. 'We've got an unexpected bonus in the festival sequences. I didn't realise it when we picked this location, but we couldn't have chosen a better time. There actually *is* a festival in the offing here in Sidi bou Kef, with all the trappings I could have wished: snake charmers, native dancers, mock battles. That's where my Arab warriors come in ... the local boys I was working in the desert this morning.' He turned to her with a rueful air. 'Poor Alison! They did scare you, didn't they? It was a nasty moment when they almost ran you down. I would never have forgiven myself if any harm had come to you.'

Sitting beside her on the banquette, he covered her hand with his own. It was his first lapse into the sentimental mood which she had dreaded, and she moved uneasily under his touch.

'Happy endings,' he said softly. 'Life is too short to worry about such things when happy beginnings are such bliss. You're adorable, Alison.' His voice dropped to a whisper. 'All white and gold, like the orange blossom in the Oasis orchards. If you knew what you do to me...'

She drew her hand away from him sharply. 'Look, Paul, if we're going to be friends it's got to be on a sensible basis.'

'Sensible!' he moaned.

'Can't two people enjoy one another's company without a lot of ... silliness?'

'If you think love is silly...'

'I don't think the sort of thing we're talking about has anything to do with love. I mean real love.'

Leaning his elbows on the table, Paul propped his chin on his hands and looked at her sadly. 'Heaven help us! A girl with ideals. My poor child, don't you know that ideals went out with crinolines?'

Alison said firmly, 'I don't know anything of the sort.' And all unbidden her thoughts flew to Brett. Did Brett believe in ideals? What was it that had brought him here to the wilderness, turning his back on the rat-race of modern life?

She heard Paul's exaggerated sigh. 'A sad case of arrested development,' he teased her. 'You'll grow up, my dear. Which is rather a pity ... you're tantalisingly sweet the way you are now.'

'Why did you ask me to dinner this evening?' Alison demanded bluntly.

Paul seemed mildly startled. 'A question that ought never to be asked. But since you've asked it, the answer is that I asked you out to dinner because you intrigue me. I find you refreshing, and a little mysterious. As I said before, nobody could possibly be as innocent and transparent as you look. Also, our dawn encounter this morning held a hint of romance, don't you think? And now perhaps you'll tell me why you accepted my invitation?'

'*Touchée!*' Alison laughed. 'And I don't find it easy to answer your question. I just don't know.' She pondered a moment. 'I find myself in a new, exciting environment ... and you're a part of it all. I was grateful to you for coming to my rescue this morning, though I don't suppose I was as lost as I imagined. And...' once more she hesitated, 'I suppose I was tempted by the prospect of seeing a bit of Sidi bou Kef night life.'

Paul grinned. 'As honest a reply as I would have expected. And see some night life you shall.'

'Oh, I didn't mean anything special,' Alison corrected hastily. 'Having dinner with you and meeting the cast of your film ... all that's quite enough.'

'But that's only the beginning,' Paul said, standing up and stretching out his hand to her. 'Now we're going to see the Ouled Naïls, the dancing girls I've imported from Casablanca as extras for one of the sequences in the film. They're giving a performance in the cinema near by. They only arrived yesterday and I haven't yet seen them dance—so this is in the nature of an audition.'

Which somehow put the whole thing on a business footing. An evening's entertainment which was part of Paul's work surely redeemed it from the too personal implications she might have feared. And Darienne Chevasse added further assurance by joining them as they were leaving the dining-room, taking Paul's arm in a matter-of-fact manner.

'Are we going to see the dancing?' she asked, including herself in his plans so confidently that Alison was more than ever put at ease. With a girl on either arm

Paul strolled across the foyer.

'Did hè give you a good dinner?' Darienne was asking Alison, in the tone of a mother who might be enquiring if her child had been behaving himself. (What was her relationship to her director?)

'Dinner was perfect,' Alison said, and Paul, drawing her closer, gave her arm a little squeeze. As if aware of his movement Darienne laughed. 'If there is anything Paul likes better than having one beautiful woman to escort, it is having two beautiful women!'

'Who told you you were beautiful, Funny Face?' Paul teased her.

'You did,' Darienne returned pertly. 'And many another beside you. Also, I have a mirror.'

'And an endless supply of self-conceit.'

'Of course,' Darienne agreed, unruffled. 'Without conceit one could not face the all-seeing eye of the great cameras, to say nothing of the cynical eyes of the man who makes the film and for whom one dances like a puppet on a string.'

'Don't listen to her, Alison,' Paul warned. 'Anything less like a puppet on a string...'

But they had reached the centre of the little square by now and the lighted doorway of the cinema was before them. They entered a foyer thronged with members of the filming team, and a sprinkling of Arabs in their colourful robes. Men exclusively. Arab women in this little town, Alison guessed, did not appear in public places of amusement.

Presently they were seated in the auditorium, Paul choosing the front row of the stalls, with Darienne and Alison on either side of him, though at the moment he paid scant attention to either of them, busy with technical asides to the various hovering members of his staff. There were cameras set up in the rear of the building. The dancing Alison gathered was not only to be an audition, but a film test.

After a lot of discussion and camera manipulation the house lights were dimmed and the curtains went up to reveal an ornate stage on which the dancers awaited in a semicircular row: young girls, scantily attired in richly coloured silks, their midriffs uncovered. They wore the usual tangle of beads about their slender necks. Headdresses studded with pearls bound the veils which hung down their backs. Gold bangles tinkled on ankles and wrists. Like ballet dancers their eyes were slanted and enlarged with generous applications of black make-up. It gave to their small pointed faces a rather pathetic appeal. How old would they be? Alison wondered; scarcely more than children. Which made the dancing which followed all the more incongruous, the boneless undulations, interspersed with the frank contortions and twitchings of the belly-dancer. Alison found it frankly repellent. And it went on and on, to the reedy music of the native orchestra. It was all rather monotonous, she thought, and not particularly seductive.

'They're all right,' she heard Paul say to Darienne as the performance ended, 'but they want pepping up a bit, and this drum and flute orchestra won't do at all. We've got to put a lot more zing into the whole act— have you up there on the stage in the centre of the group.'

'Oh, Paul, I couldn't!' Darienne protested.

'Yes, you could, my love. You told me when I cast you for the part that you would be able to tackle the odd spot of belly-dancing.'

'But not like these Ouled Naïls!'

'So much the better. They look as if they were doing it in their sleep, zombies. You'll bring the right hint of shrinking self-consciousness, boldness mixed with reluctance, the sophisticated approach. And you've got a figure that will put these skinny little kids in the shade.'

'Paul, you're horrible!' Darienne groaned. But she looked pleased and flattered.

Seeing the gratification on her lovely face, Alison felt an odd pity for her. It must be awful, she thought, to be a film actress, at the mercy of any director's whims, whether his ideas were in good taste or bad. Neither body nor soul could be your own. Her own years of hospital training and her subsequent job as housekeeper to her father might be dull at times, but at least they were occupations that left her her dignity.

A few minutes later they had followed the small audience out of the cinema. 'Are you and Alison coming back to the hotel?' Darienne was asking. 'There's late-night dancing tonight, and a floor show at midnight.'

'I ought to be getting back to the Villa,' Alison said urgently. It was almost midnight already and she didn't want to go dancing with Paul Everton. So far the evening had been manageable—and quite pleasant. But there was a certain gleam in Paul's eyes when he fixed them on her that put her on her guard. 'I really must go home,' she insisted.

'I'll take you, then, if you won't be persuaded,' Paul agreed with a shrug.

'I'll go along to the hotel and corner a ringside table,' Darienne said. 'Don't be long, Paul,' she called over her shoulder as she hurried away. 'I don't want you to miss the floor show. It includes that sword-swallower you thought you might use in the film.'

There was a familiar, almost brother and sister air about their attitude towards one another. Was it because they worked together? Yet Alison couldn't imagine Paul really feeling brotherly towards the glamorous Darienne.

They were standing on the cinema steps in a blaze of light. Paul turned to say a few words to the doorman, while Alison looked down at the animated scene in the little boulevard below. Palm trees at intervals lined the sidewalks. There were pavement cafés doing a roaring trade in spite of the lateness of the hour; Arabs wrapped in their enveloping burnouses, drinking mint tea, fingering their conversation beads, playing mysterious games with cards and checkers. In the roadway young bloods strolled. There was even one belated sleepy camel led on a crimson rein by an important small boy.

'Let's watch it all for a moment before we go,' Alison begged when Paul came back to her. A sudden chill wind blew straight from the desert, ruffling the palm trees that bordered the square. In her thin sleeveless dress Alison shivered. Paul put an arm about her. 'You're cold. Hasn't anyone warned you about the icy wind which sweeps over the sand after dark in these parts?' His arm tightened about her and his handsome face held a whimsical tenderness.

'You need someone to take care of you.' Taking off his velvet dinner jacket, he wrapped it around her with such an exaggerated air of solicitude that she wanted to laugh. Ham acting, she thought. A man of the theatre with grease-paint in his veins instead of blood. Did anyone ever get at the real Paul behind the facade? she wondered. And if so, would it be worth the effort? Yet there was something likeable about him. And the velvet jacket was unexpectedly welcome. Warm from the contact with his body, she snuggled into it gratefully. Taking the lapels in either hand, he pulled them up about her neck, and stooping, dropped a light kiss on her brow. It was nothing ... a casual caress given on the impulse of the moment. But glancing over his shoulder at that moment Alison met Brett Meredith's stony gaze. He was coming out of the hotel garden opposite and his astonishment at the sight of her in Paul's embrace was so obvious that it was comical.

But it didn't make her want to laugh. Her heart felt small and cold, as she moved away from Paul, and risking the loss of the velvet jacket raised her hand in salute. Unsmilingly, Brett returned the gesture, his blue eyes steely. Then he went on his way walking towards a small shabby car parked in the square.

'A friend of mine,' she explained, in some confusion. But Paul either hadn't noticed the momentary encounter or wasn't interested.

'Sure you won't change your mind and stay for the floor show?'

She shook her head, thanking him. 'It's late and I've had a long day.' Suddenly she was tired. Whatever zest there had been had gone out of the evening.

Paul did not try to persuade her. Perhaps he too was tired ... of the evening, and of her. She hoped she hadn't been an unappreciative guest and said so, thanking him and telling him how much she had enjoyed herself.

'You don't have to make polite speeches,' he told her, sounding a little hurt. 'If I'm not coaxing you to come dancing with me it's because I have to be up at the crack of dawn and out on location with those damned Arab warriors. The rushes of this morning's shots were hopeless.' He talked technicalities until they reached his car.

It was warm in its luxurious interior, and handing him back his jacket, Alison leaned against the seductive upholstery and thought about steely blue eyes. It just would happen, she thought bitterly; Brett walking out of the hotel to see her in a clinch with the flashy young film director. For of course Brett would know who Paul was. In the small desert town he would be a public character from the moment of his arrival. And it was clear that Brett disapproved of him. At least there had been no doubt about his disapproval of that unfortunate kiss—the glacial look he had given her. Though it was hardly any business of his. Yet, passionately, she wished it had not happened.

The night was dry and cool. Paul drove slowly out of the town and down the winding lane that led to the Villa. About half way along he pulled into the side under a grove of lemon trees. Somewhere a nightingale was pouring out its song. It was the only sound in the starlit silence. Once more it was all too beautiful. Alison felt a lump rise in her throat.

She said, 'That nightingale! Even the frogs have stopped their croaking to listen to it.'

But it wasn't like that, Paul told her. 'The frogs always stop their little concert on the stroke of midnight. Maybe they have a frogs' musicians' union which controls the hours they work.'

They laughed together at the whimsical idea, and, turning, Paul took Alison purposefully in his arms.

'The inevitable goodnight smooch,' she sighed resignedly as his lips touched the cheek she had hurriedly turned aside. 'I suppose it's only to be expected after the marvellous dinner you gave me.'

She knew it was a dreadful thing to have said the moment it was out. He released her abruptly, his face a thundercloud as he set the car in motion once more.

'I'm sorry, Paul!' she offered meekly. 'I ought not to have said that ... it's only that ...'

'I was trampling on your precious ideals,' he finished for her. 'Let me tell you, my child, those same ideals are going to cause you a lot more hurt than a few stray kisses.'

How right he was! she thought grimly.

They drove on in silence until they stopped before the gate of the Villa. He did not offer to walk with her up to the house. His goodnight was cool and curt, and when she thanked him again for a pleasant evening he made a sardonic noise. Then, as if suddenly relenting, he got out of the car and opened the lattice gate for her with a gallant air. 'Sorry if I snapped just now,' he apologised. 'It's just that you're a novel experience in my life. Film directors aren't usually given the brush-off by the dollies they take out.'

'I'm hardly a dolly,' Alison pointed out coldly.

'I'll say you're not!' he laughed, his good humour restored. 'That's what intrigues me. I hope you'll come out with me again before too long ... if I promise to behave myself.'

He sounded so chastened that she relented. 'You're very forgiving,' she said.

He shook his head. 'Just persevering.'

They stood for a moment in the scented darkness. In the distance the nightingale still sang.

'Well, I won't push my luck just now,' Paul said

softly. 'But I'll keep in touch.'

She watched him get into his car and drive away and walked slowly towards the house, her thoughts, the moment she was alone, flying to Brett. All the evening she had kept him resolutely out of her mind, determined to enjoy herself with Paul. But his appearance outside the cinema had thrown her into a ridiculous state of confusion. If only he hadn't seen her kissing Paul! But why should she care? Hadn't he shown her only too clearly how little she mattered to him—not only in the past, but today? He had greeted her with natural surprise; no more. 'Nice to have seen you again, young Warrender.' She couldn't echo his sentiments. Seeing Brett Meredith again here in Sidi bou Kef was the last thing she would have wanted. What had brought him to this out-of-the-way North African hospital? Ambitious, hard-working, eager for a consultancy—surely he would have been better off remaining in London! It was all very puzzling, and maddeningly annoying. But she wasn't going to let him spoil her Algerian adventure. He had hurt her enough already.

CHAPTER FOUR

THE next few days passed uneventfully. Interesting herself in her father's work, Alison went with him each morning on his rounds of the various plantations in the Oasis. In the hot sunshine they walked or drove down the aisles of established trees, mostly eucalyptus and acacias, planted in serried ranks to keep back the encroaching sand.

Sometimes the Sheik came with them. Alison found herself enjoying his company more and more. He had a lively intelligence and quick sense of humour. The Sahara, he reminded them, had once been a region of forests—destroyed, it was said, by the invading Romans. Water still lurked beneath the surface. But how to get at this water was one of the problems facing the Professor and his fellow scientists. Meanwhile, irrigation was the most pressing problem. Catchments dug for the winter rains would soon dry up, and the wadis, or river valleys, were rapidly emptying. Fortunately there were several good wells on the Sheik's land, and an endless supply of willing workers to wheel the heavy watering tanks from place to place.

'At least,' the Sheik qualified one morning when the three of them sat drinking mid-morning coffee on the Villa verandah, 'I usually have more workers than I need. But just now a couple of score of my best young men have rushed off to join up with the film people who are setting my township by the ears.' He shrugged regretfully. 'I doubt if I should have given them permission to use my territory for their film if I had realised all it would entail. So many of my young people are being pressed into service as what they call "extras", earning weekly pay packets beyond their wildest dreams—and incidentally, picking up some of the less desirable ideas that pervade Western civilisation. This is not the sort of so-called progress I want for them.' He sighed and shook his grey head. 'I ought to have been more cautious, but the young director who came to see me had a glib tongue and a persuasive manner. Paul Everton ... he tells me he is half French and half American, and it would seem he has an international reputation as a Nouveau Art film-maker.'

She had met Paul Everton, Alison disclosed, and told the Sheik of her adventure with the rough-riding Arab warriors on her first morning in Sidi bou Kef, and how Paul had come to her rescue. 'He invited me to dinner at the Regence the same evening, and introduced me to some of the actors and actresses he has working for him. It was interesting.' Her voice trailed away as she met the Sheik's sharp glance at this last piece of information. His beetling brows positively bristled with disapproval.

'You meet this stranger once, by chance, and then accept an invitation to dine with him? Do you mean alone! Without a chaperone, unaccompanied by your parent?' His tone held more of puzzlement than condemnation.

'We allow our daughters more freedom, I expect, than is customary in this part of the world,' John Warrender put in quickly.

The Sheik nodded. 'No doubt that is so. Perhaps it is you who are wise. I read much in your English journals of the advancement of women in all parts of the globe. In India and Israel now there are even women Prime Ministers.' He shook his grizzled head with a sort of bewilderment, and turned to Alison. 'Do you think my womenfolk are happy?' he demanded with disconcerting bluntness. 'It is difficult to break the habits of generations—the tendency of the older members of my family to cling to their seclusion.'

'It's perhaps a little hard on the younger women,' Alison offered diffidently. Especially Kaira and Haidie ... Haidie often speaks longingly of her years at boarding school in Algiers.'

'I hear you have been with them several afternoons,

reading your English books to them. It is kind of you.'
The old man inclined his head with a courtly air.

'It's not kind at all,' Alison said. 'I enjoy the readings
and the things we talk about afterwards. The trouble
is that I have so few books with me, only one or two
Brontë novels and an anthology of poetry.'

'I think I know where I can find you some more,' the
Sheik said, his eyebrows waving like antennae. They
always became agitated, she had noticed, when he was
excited; and this discussion about his womenfolk had
somehow touched him on the raw. He longed to be
'modern', do the right thing by them, but isolated in
this remote community he wasn't quite sure how best
to achieve the changes which might be necessary.

'Young Dr. Meredith,' he went on, 'has quite a library. I am sure he would lend you whatever you wanted
for your sessions with Kaira and Haidie. You must
meet him, and see our hospital. I will arrange it.'

'That will be nice,' Alison murmured inadequately.
For some reason she couldn't bring herself to tell the
Sheik that she had already encountered Brett Meredith, and that he was in fact a figure from her hospital
past. She had, she reflected, come rather a cropper in
disclosing her association with Paul. The old man
would begin to think she did nothing but run round
Sidi bou Kef picking up boy-friends. And, it occurred
to her, she hadn't yet mentioned her unexpected meeting with Brett to her father. Not that there was any
particular reason for keeping it secret, but it hurt to
talk about him, hurt to remember his cold-eyed glance
as she stood on the steps of the cinema with Paul Everton's arms about her.

'I will ask him to dinner,' the Sheik said. 'Tomorrow
evening. We will open the banqueting room, prepare

for you the traditional Arab delicacies, summon the musicians . . .'

'My wife, Halide, will join us,' he went on with growing enthusiasm. 'Kairi, my daughter-in-law, Haidie my granddaughter.' He stood up, a tall impressive figure in his colourful robe and flowing headdress. 'I will go now and give instructions to my household, and send a messenger to our doctor friend—whom, incidentally, I have not seen for almost a week. Usually he visits me constantly.'

Was he keeping away from the palace because of her presence here? Alison wondered, and dismissed the suspicion as self-important nonsense. He was probably busy with his work. She remembered that he had said he hoped she would visit him in his hospital. But it had all been very vague and so far no specific invitation had materialised.

But tomorrow night he would be coming to dinner.

She wished she had something to wear more attractive than the plain white frock. All these social engagements! She hadn't dreamed it would be like this when she packed to come away—picturing herself living in slacks and shorts in the middle of a sandy wilderness. Not that Brett would care what she looked like tomorrow evening. It was for her own sake, she assured herself, that she wanted something more striking than one of her last summer's plainer little numbers. The al Raschid women would, no doubt, be magnificent in coloured silks, dripping with jewellery and Oriental glamour, while she in her simple dress would look like an English house sparrow among a flock of rainbow parakeets.

So after lunch she set out on foot for Sidi bou Kef, hoping against hope that she would find some sort of

dress shop there. If not she could fall back on the
Regence. She had noticed the other evening a small
boutique in a corner of the foyer which called itself 'La
Petite Couturière' and displayed in its single window
one vast black ostrich feather fan and a pair of long
mauve suede gloves. But she wouldn't go to the Regence if she could help. She didn't particularly want to
run into Paul Everton again, having found herself
slightly nettled that his, 'Be seeing you,' and promise to
'Keep in touch' had so far come to nothing. It wasn't
that she wanted to be involved with him. But she
hadn't been very polite to him during their evening
together and she hoped he wasn't offended or hurt.
Was there something about her that scared men off?
she wondered, thinking again of Brett.

It was stiflingly hot in the main street of Sidi, with
sun-blinds down and shopkeepers sitting on stools by
their doors catching whatever breath of air might be
going. Of course there wasn't anything that looked re-
motely like a dress shop. She peered in a discouraged
way down one or two side streets, which were even
more hopeless. Jewellers' shops, silk shops, goldsmiths,
small cavernous food shops, their windowless fronts
crammed with every imaginable culinary commodity
from spice cakes to olive oil in great rose-coloured jars.
But no dress shops. And she was hot and thirsty beyond
belief.

So the Regence it must be. As she passed through the
swing doors of the entrance the rush of air-conditioned
coolness that met her was very welcome, and the foyer,
marble-paved, green with potted palms, offered a blissful refuge from the heat. The tinkle of a fountain
added to the general air of freshness and tranquillity.
Hopefully she looked at the display in the little bouti-

que window. Still the same black fan on view. Maybe they didn't have anything else. She couldn't, she thought lightheadedly, go to the Sheik's party clad only in an outsize black ostrich feather fan and a pair of elbow-length gloves!

'Hi-ya!' a cheery voice greeted her, and turning from the boutique window she found herself face to face with Darienne Chevasse, 'You interested in our little Rue de la Paix effort?' she asked.

'I've been hunting all over the town for a dress shop,' Alison began.

'What a hope!' Darienne laughed. 'There are silk shops which would run you up a frock of sorts in a few hours, but you couldn't possibly wear it. Gorgeous colours, but no style ... make you look like a sack tied in the middle. You would do much better here—if Madame Despard who runs the boutique is around. Let's go upstairs and see. Her studio, as she calls it, is on the first floor.'

'Aren't you filming today?' Alison enquired as they went up in the gilded lift.

'No. We are having a few days of very welcome rest. Paul has had to go to Paris to straighten out some complications which have arisen over making *Hills of Sand*. For one thing we're over-running the time schedule. It's all budgeted beforehand, you see, to the last franc and the last half hour. But Paul will fix it ... talk the backers round. Paul,' she added with an oddly possessive air of pride, 'always fixes everything.'

And he was in Paris. Alison breathed a sigh of relief. With him safely out of the way she could enjoy herself for half an hour with Darienne, who seemed genuinely glad of her company. Her advice over the frock too was useful. With her knowledgeable help Alison bought a filmy black chiffon, high-necked, long-skirted and with lots of frills.

'Pile your lovely corn-coloured hair on top of your head,' she counselled, 'and you'll look a million.' She had already found out the sort of occasion for which the frock was being purchased, and was frankly jealous. 'A party at the Sheik's palace! How super!' she sighed. 'All those divinely handsome Arabs ... probably you'll be the only woman present.'

'Oh no,' Alison corrected. 'The Sheik's wife and daughter-in-law and granddaughter are coming. Nor will the men all be Arab. The English doctor from the local hospital has been invited.'

'Dr Meredith,' Darienne put in, rather surprisingly. 'He's a honey. You'll like him. I had a touch of fever when I first got here and he treated me. A bit on the strong silent side perhaps, but none the worse for that. He's probably soft as putty underneath. That sort usually are. I bet the black chiffon frock will throw him.'

Alison's laughter was a little hollow; she didn't reveal the fact that she already knew Dr Meredith and that the likelihood of his being thrown by anything as frivolous as a frock was indeed remote.

Nevertheless she carried the box containing the black chiffon down to the lounge where they had tea, with a distinct feeling of triumph. It was the kind of frock she would never have had the courage to buy without Darienne's moral support.

After tea Darienne insisted upon driving her back to the Villa. 'Come and see me again some time,' she invited as Alison got out of the car.

'I'd like to,' Alison returned warmly. 'I've enjoyed this afternoon. Thank you very much for your help with the frock.'

Darienne peered a little wistfully at the pretty little house among its flowers beyond the latticed gateway. 'I wish the Sheik would invite some of *us* to his parties,' she sighed. 'But I don't think he likes us. I've got a feeling that we're tolerated rather than welcomed by the high-ups in this burg. That Dr Meredith certainly gave me the impression that we're looked upon as a bit of a disaster. Not me, personally. He was sweet to *me*. But after he'd seen me he had a drink with Paul in the bar and hinted that we're an unsettling influence to the locals we're using as extras. They're beginning to imagine themselves as world-famous film stars, well on the way to making easy fortunes. They don't want to work in the orchards as long as we're here to offer them more amusing employment, such as riding round the desert staging mock battles.'

Alison remembered that the Sheik had said very much the same thing.

'Put in a good word for us with the old man,' Darienne called over her shoulder as she turned the car, and drove off, saving Alison from the awkwardness of making the kind of promise it would be very difficult to fulfil, since her sympathies were all with the Sheik, who might well find a bunch of malcontents on his hands when the film company departed leaving Sidi bou Kef to sink back into its age-old tranquillity.

It was mild and starlit when Alison and her father walked across the gardens to the palace the following evening, with a hint of moonrise in the eastern sky behind the tree-tops. Alison, wishing she had a more glamorous wrap, had thrown her everyday camel coat about her shoulders. It rather spoiled the effect of the diaphanous black frock, but she was soon able to lay it aside, handing it to the servant who bowed them into the banqueting-room, which had been transformed for the occasion. Warmed with glowing charcoal stoves, the not very powerful electric lights in the chandeliers were helped out by numerous tall candles in wrought silver candlesticks. The soft light brought out the rich colours of the silken wall hangings and the prayer rugs scattered about the mosaic floor.

A large oval walnut table covered the hidden fountain. It was laid with an impressive array of silver and glass and great bowls of fruit. Latticed windows and doorways had been thrown open, revealing the wide balcony beyond hung with fairy lights. In the court-yard below there were more fairy lights and an array of small tables flanked by wicker chairs and rustic seats. It looked romantic and inviting, Alison thought. But for the moment sociabilities were being confined to the banqueting-room, where the Sheik, resplendent in scarlet and purple, presented the guests of honour. Half a dozen of his henchmen bowed over their joined palms to Alison and the Professor. Then the Sheik was introducing Hussein Joujima, his son, and Hamed, his grandson, Haidie's brother. He had the same quick dark eyes and delicately cut features.

'The Doctor Meredith,' the old man was announc-ing, and Alison turned to face Brett, her heart missing missing a beat. 'He tells me you and he are already acquainted,' the Sheik went on, 'that you have worked together in his London hospital. This is good, very good. Now perhaps you will at times give him your support in the work he undertakes for my people in Sidi bou Kef.'

Alison, only half listening, held Brett's hand, meeting his disconcertingly direct blue eyes. 'You're looking very lovely tonight,' he said in an undertone that brought the quick warmth to her cheeks. Brett didn't usually pay compliments. But he seemed to be in a genial mood this evening, leading her presently to a wide divan-like seat where they sat side by side in nests of vividly coloured cushions, a perfect foil for her black chiffon. And she had been right about the women of the household; seated together on the raised dais at the end of the room they were clad in every imaginable hue from magenta to emerald green.

High above in a little gallery native musicians were playing soft, wandering melodies, that sounded like the dripping of far-off water, the cool, reedy music of flutes.

Brett looked about him at the exotic scene with an incredulous headshake. 'You and I landing up in this oriental set-up, young Warrender! I just can't believe it. The long arm of coincidence stretching to breaking point.'

'It is rather extraordinary,' Alison agreed drily.

'And very pleasant,' Brett added, just a little too glibly—a polite cliché.

A servant in voluminous scarlet trousers, with a dagger at his waist, stood before them with glasses of wine on a tray, a light white wine, dry and cold and very refreshing. Another servant followed with a platter of savouries. 'The Arab version of cocktail snippets,' Brett explained. 'They're called *kibbehs* and are made of brown bread, pulped raw meat, mixed with cracked wheat, herbs, spices and—of all things—grated orange peel.'

But they tasted delicious when Alison sampled one of them.

'I should go easy on them if I were you,' Brett advised. 'For they're pretty substantial and the main meal is sure to be lavish. It's considered very bad manners in Arab circles not to eat all that's put before you.' He was wearing a pale tussore dinner jacket and looked unusually spruce, his thatch of blond hair newly trimmed and slicked down for the occasion.

Only the non-Arabs, Alison noticed, were drinking the wine. The Sheik, Brett told her, was a stickler for the Moslem law, which forbade the use of alcohol, and though the wine was scarcely more than lightly fermented grape juice it would be taboo.

Listening to him Alison felt suddenly happy and at ease. Once more the novelty of the situation overwhelmed her. To be with Brett here in a Sheik's banqueting hall, drinking wine that tasted as if it were made of all the perfumes in the sleeping African gardens. Surely it was a dream! And Brett relaxed now and smiling down at her, apparently having forgotten his disapproval of the little scene on the steps of the cinema the other night. Or was it that he didn't think enough of her to disapprove? She thrust the edge of disillusion away from her. Nothing must spoil this fabulous party!

It was a little disappointing when they moved to the dining table to find she had been placed as the lady guest of honour beside the Sheik, with Hamed on her other side. Her father was on the Sheik's left, with Kaira beside him, and sitting opposite her Brett squired Haidie. Madame Halide, the Sheik's ageing wife, had refused to come to the central table, remaining sitting on cushions on her dais, her meal being served to her on a low brass coffee table.

The conversation was lively, and mostly in French. As

the Sheik and the Professor inevitably began to talk shop to one another Alison was left with Hamed. He had, it emerged, spent two years in Paris at the Sorbonne, and during that time had visited England on several occasions, making week-end trips with groups of fellow students to the Sussex coast. Brighton seemed to be his idea of heaven. 'The freedom, the gaiety, the singing!' he yearned nostalgically.

Alison had seen them often enough ... the little bands of students from across the Channel wandering along the front with their guitars and outlandish gear.

Across the table Haidie and Brett were chattering with animation, their heads close together. Haidie's beauty tonight was arresting. She seemed all made of dark gold fire, with her jewels and bangles, her coloured silks and cascade of black curls. Alison tried not to watch them, concentrating on Hamed and his stories. And the menu was novel enough and exacting enough to keep her busy—kebab cooked barbecue fashion on the charcoal stoves, omelettes stuffed with lamb's liver and onion, great flapping rounds of unleavened bread. The main dish was a whole roast sheep, from which portions were cut by the servants with the daggers they carried. There were delicious green vegetables to go with it, and sauces and salads, fruits of every kind, sweet and natural yoghurt, dishes of sweetmeats.

Endlessly the meal went on, and Alison was glad when the coffee stage was reached and they were able to move freely about the long and now overheated room. Escaping from Hamed, obviously attracted and inclined to stick, she went and sat on the cushions beside old Madame Halide. They talked for a while in snatches of French, English and even in Arabic, for this was the language in which the old lady was most at home and Alison had managed to pick up a few words of it during her afternoon sessions in the harem. But it was all rather a strain and her heart gave a great foolish leap when she saw Brett approaching them with a purposeful air.

'May I rob you of your companion for a little while, Madame?' he asked the old lady, with a bow.

The old lady smiled and shrugged. '*C'est normal, monsieur!* Youth must seek youth, *n'est-ce pas?*'

He held out a hand to Alison. 'Would you like to come down into the courtyard for a breath of fresh air?'

'I'd adore it, Brett!' She jumped up from the dais with an eagerness she couldn't conceal. Putting a light hand under her elbow, he led her out on to the balcony, and into the courtyard below, where they found a seat almost concealed by a grove of potted palms beside a lily pond.

'Marvellous meal,' Brett said. 'But the lingering odours of whole roast sheep were beginning to get a bit overpowering.' He turned to her with his serious air. 'I hope you won't be cold in your thin frock.'

'Oh, I'm quite warm, thanks,' she assured him.

He said, 'I wanted to talk to you.'

Her breath came shallowly and she was suddenly tinglingly aware of him on the seat beside her—so small a seat that their shoulders were almost touching. There was a hint of jasmine scent in the air. Fairy-light reflections danced in the lily pond, where a great fat frog sat on a lily pad, staring at them with protruberant eyes. Its throat pulsed and it began its raucous croaking. A chill little breeze, springing up from nowhere, stirred the palm fronds. 'I ought not to have

brought you out of that overheated room,' Brett reproached himself. Then he laughed softly. 'Sorry I
haven't got a velvet jacket to wrap you in!'

So that was it! He hadn't forgotten the scene outside
the cinema and had brought her out here to taunt her
with it. She said with what dignity she could muster,
ignoring the snide allusion, 'I don't need a jacket.'

He slid an arm along the back of the seat. 'A protective arm perhaps, then?' The mockery in his tone this
time was unmistakable.

She was suddenly angry. 'What is it, Brett? What are
you getting at?'

He took his arm away and shrugged. 'I'm merely
marvelling at your ability to pick up good-looking boy-
friends even in the depths of the Sahara.'

'Paul Everton is hardly a boy-friend. Nor did I "pick
him up", as you so inelegantly put it. The first morning I was here I went for an early morning walk in the
desert, going further than I meant to. Paul came along
in his car and offered me a welcome lift back home,
that's all.' The bit about the Arab warriors on horseback would, she thought, sound over-dramatic, and
she was too annoyed for long explanations.

'And the consequence was ...' Brett parodied the old
parlour game, 'you went out to dinner with him the
very same evening and kissed him on the steps of the
cinema for all the world to see.'

'Does it matter to you if I did?' she cried, goaded.

'Of course it doesn't,' he said with an almost exaggerated carelessness. The moon that was well up above
the tree-tops by now threw a silvery light on his fair
hair. He fingered the buttonhole in his lapel. Jasmine.
So that was where the scent had been coming from.
Had Haidie given it to him? She had been wearing a

sprig in her hair...

'It's just,' he was saying, 'that it was a little reminiscent of another similar scene that I chanced upon one night at St Clare's.'

She turned to him, wide-eyed. 'Brett, what on earth are you talking about?'

'You and your following of medicos at St Clare's. You were always pretty popular with the housemen...'

'Was that a crime?' she broke in with growing uneasiness.

'Of course not. You enjoyed your off-duty time ... and good luck to you.' There was a small significant pause, the blue eyes fixing her. 'Especially occasions like the annual hospital ball.'

Now what was in his mind? Her heart turned over. Was she at last going to hear the answer to a question which had puzzled her for so long? 'If you mean that last annual ball before you left St Clare's,' she said. 'You promised to take me to it, and then let me down flat—with never a word of explanation afterwards.'

'I know. I'm sorry. But I got caught up with an emergency in Casualty and couldn't get a message to you. In the early hours of the morning, when at last I was free, I scribbled a note to you, explaining what had happened. I was on my way to drop it in the letter box of the Nurses' Home when I saw you in the open doorway with the light behind you, very much as it was the other night at the cinema. You and young Simon Frayne were exchanging a pretty thorough goodnight kiss. I realised you had had an escort after all—a far more efficient one than myself probably, and apologies were redundant. So I put the note in my pocket and trotted off to my digs.'

There was a long moment's silence. Then Alison

said in a small voice, 'Was that why you dropped me cold?'

He turned to her with a blank look. 'Did I drop you cold? I wasn't aware of it.'

If he had slapped her face, it couldn't have been a more direct repudiation of that halcyon springtime friendship. She felt her cheeks flame in the darkness. 'We had been seeing a good deal of each other,' she brought out uncertainly.

'Ah yes!' He appeared to mull it over, as if searching his memory. 'Those drives into the country. It was a particularly beautiful May and June that year, I remember, and there was a lull in my rota of exams...'

'And I was accessible,' Alison said bitterly.

'Charmingly so. But I didn't dream of serious competition with your more amusing boy-friends. And the exams soon caught up with me again.' He sighed, pushing back a lock of moon-silvered hair. 'I'm a dull dog, I'm afraid, Alison, almost wholly absorbed in becoming a competent diagnostician and surgeon—something that takes, I should think, just about a lifetime. It was on that level, I fancy, that you and I made the most satisfactory contact. You were always one of my best theatre nurses. In fact...' he paused a moment to give her a long earnest look, 'it was to talk to you about that I lured you out here just now. I don't know how we got sidetracked with your love life.' He laughed lightly. 'Not that I'm claiming any part in it. I wouldn't presume!'

Alison, her hands clasped tightly on her lap, felt her palms grow wet. Was he being deliberately cruel? Or was it all as casual as he was making it sound? Her reason told her he was handing her no more than the simple truth. The weeks of friendship upon which she had foolishly built so much had meant little to him. But hadn't she known this for long enough? Why come up with a reaction of shocked surprise at this juncture? Because meeting Brett here in Sidi bou Kef had thrown her off balance, robbed her of the defence of indifference she had been building up slowly and painfully through the intervening years. She would have to pull herself together, recover her cool.

'You wanted to tell me about your hospital,' she invited him.

She could feel him coming to life—all eagerness and interest now, his arm once more along the back of the seat. 'I was wondering if you would care to come along tomorrow morning to see a session in my little theatre. There isn't anything very exciting on, but it will give you an idea of the difficulties I'm up against and how we're coping. It's eye work tomorrow. A strabismuth and an enucleation of lens. How about it? I could send a car for you about nine.'

'That will be fine, Brett. I shall enjoy a glimpse of the theatre again.'

'I hoped you'd say that. You're far too good to abandon your nursing altogether.' He stood up, bringing their moonlit interlude to an end. Oh, wasted moonlight!

It wasn't the chill breeze that made her shiver, but the ice in her heart.

'You *are* cold,' he said with concern. And then with a laugh, 'I really must take to wearing velvet jackets! Let's get you back to the charcoal stoves and the candlelight.'

His arm about her shoulder was light and impersonal as they walked back to the banqueting-room. Haidie and Hamed were waiting for them, Haidie with her big brown eyes fastening hungrily on Brett; Hamed putting out an eager hand to Alison. 'I hoped I would have been the one to show you the courtyard,' he said.

But the evening was nearly over, the party breaking up.

CHAPTER FIVE

IT was barely nine the next morning when Brett's promised car drew up at the Villa gate; the shabby little Citröen Alison had noticed outside the hotel the night she had dined with Paul. It was driven by an Arab boy, who got out of the car to bow to her as she approached. As they drove along the sandy lane under the trees, he told her that his name was Mahomed, and that he longed to go to London and train to be a doctor, like Dr Ali ben Hassan his brother, who had lived and worked in a London hospital, St Jude's, where he had met Dr Meredith, to whom he was now assistant.

Alison asked him about his schooling; what exams he had passed, and it emerged that he had been to school in Algiers and achieved his Baccalauréat, which is the French equivalent of an advanced G.C.E. 'It was my brother who persuaded Dr Meredith to come here,' he volunteered, answering one of the questions which had teased Alison's thoughts as she lay awake last night, too strung up after the party to sleep. Usually she slept as soon as her head touched the pillow, but last night she had tossed and turned, going over and over her conversation with Brett in the courtyard, recalling his every look and intonation. But no matter how diligently she added it all up, it always came out with the same answer. Brett had never been anything more than mildly interested in her. But hadn't she known that all along? Why this belated heartache about it? A weak-minded reaction to their unexpected encounter here in Sidi bou Kef. Once more she told herself she'd just have to snap out of it.

The hospital, a one-storey building, lay on the far side of the town, a small domed building, with a depressed-looking clump of palm trees to one side of it. Like most native dwellings, it was built round a courtyard, which seemed alarmingly full as Alison crossed it. Women with babies in their arms sat patiently on the bare ground, others crowded into the shelter of any shadow thrown by the surrounding walls. Some of the women were veiled, some in shabby European dress, faded cotton frocks, or shapeless sweaters and skirts. These were mostly the younger women. There was a sprinkling of men—old and young. Many of the waiting patients seemed to be suffering from eye trouble.

A young nurse in hospital apron and Arab headdress showed her into the surgery, where Brett, almost at the end of his morning clinic, greeted her shortly, inviting her to stand by his side while he dealt with the last few cases, a whooping-cough baby, a garage mechanic with a neck carbuncle and a girl with red, weeping eyelids—conjunctivitis.

'A universal complaint,' Brett enlarged in an aside to Alison. 'Eye trouble is very prevalent here, partly because of the sun's glare, or injury through sand-storms, or genetic traits. Lack of hygiene is also a frequent cause of disease, especially in new-born babies. Most of them are delivered in unfavourable conditions by some local "handywoman". But I'm hoping to combat all that in time, when I can persuade the Sheik to build an additional ward we can use exclusively for gynaecological cases.'

All pretty small beer for an ambitious young surgeon, Alison thought, and wondered once more what exactly had brought him out here.

While he talked to her in quick asides, he dealt with his patients, swiftly, efficiently, his blue eyes hard, missing nothing. He sent the carbuncle man into an annexe to be treated by Dr Ali ben Hassan, and spent five precious minutes trying to persuade the conjunctivitis girl to wear dark glasses. With the whooping-cough baby and its mother he was smiling and gentle, and when the baby smiled back at him, he seemed foolishly pleased. Instantly, of course, Alison's heart warmed to him. Seeing him in his clinic brought back the past so vividly. Her first contact with him in St Clare's had been when she had stood by his side through the long hours in the outpatient department.

When the last of this morning's patients had been disposed of, he took her into the adjoining room and introduced her to Dr Hassan.

'We worked together at Jude's in London,' Brett explained. Ali ben Hassan, tall for an Arab, had a quiet and competent air. He didn't bow to Alison over folded palms, but took her hand in a firm grip of greeting.

'I'll show you round the hospital later on,' Brett promised when they had left Ali. 'Just now I want to snatch a cup of coffee before we go into the theatre. You are coming to watch, aren't you?'

'Of course, Brett, that's why I'm here.'

Hurrying her through the still crowded courtyard,

he led the way through an arched gateway into a narrow back street.

'Are all these people waiting to see you?' Alison had to ask.

He gave a small shrug of resignation. 'They congregate there for hours. There's nothing I can do about it. Appointment times mean nothing to them. Lots of those waiting this morning won't be seen until evening surgery, others sit there because some relative is in the wards, others ... just sit.'

He pushed open a doorway in one of a row of tall blank-walled native style houses. 'This is my pad. Definitely the wrong side of the tracks, but conveniently close to the hospital.' She followed him up a bare cement staircase into a square room, lit by a large window which opened on to the inevitable courtyard. There were armchairs, book-lined walls, Bedouin rugs on the clean tiled floor, and a central table, littered with letters, papers and medical journals. Beyond it was a surprisingly well-kept kitchen with an electric cooker, formica working-tops over adequate cupboards and a gleamingly clean sink.

'Who keeps all this so beautifully?' Alison couldn't refrain from asking, as Brett switched on the kettle and proceeded to find cups and saucers.

He laughed, sounding pleased with himself. 'Oh, I've found myself a treasure, a dear old grannie called Dalia, all earrings and bangles and floating draperies, but she works like a piston engine. Comes every day at the crack of dawn to get my breakfast. Then she cleans through, and returns in the evening if I want her and makes my evening meal. I'd be lost without her. I've even trained her to boil all the drinking water. We keep it in those exquisite pots.' He pointed to a couple of jars beneath the sink, rosy ochre in colour and beautifully shaped, marked with intricate designs.

When Alison admired them, he told her they came from Delma, a village about ten miles away, famous for its potteries. 'I'll take you there some time,' he promised carelessly.

The coffee was excellent. They drank it sitting at the kitchen table. Brett spoke again of the extra wards he needed for the hospital.

'It sounds as if you're pretty settled here,' Alison probed. And then, coming right out with it, 'What made you come here, Brett ... I mean apart from Ali's persuasiveness?'

'Who told you Ali persuaded me to come?' Brett asked sharply.

'Mohamed, when he fetched me in the car this morning.'

Brett looked faintly annoyed. 'I didn't need much persuading. I'd seen old Sheik al Raschid's advert in the *Lancet*. I showed it to Ali who hadn't yet spotted it. He was keen straight away; liked the idea of getting back here. Local boy makes good and so on, and I imagine he was a bit homesick. Anyway we decided to have a bash at it together.'

'Because you thought you could do some good in Algeria?'

'No,' Brett returned flatly. 'Because I needed the money. Old man Raschid was offering a pretty generous salary, and I was sick of working for the chicken feed, which is all that young doctors can pick up in England.'

Alison felt a pang of disappointment. What had she expected? A flow of idealistic sentiments? But Brett was apparently no altruist.

'The experience is all to the good, too,' he was saying. 'I've always been interested in eye work—in fact I was specialising in it at St Jude's. And I've picked up a lot of know-how with out-of-the-way eye diseases since I came here. Had an infant with oblique muscular atrophy the other day.' He broke off abruptly. 'But we'd better get back on the job.'

During the two hours in the theatre Alison went into a kind of trance, past and present mixing inextricably. She felt as if she were back at St Clare's; the voluminous green overall which enveloped her, the mask over her nose and mouth, the cap imprisoning her bright hair ... it was all so reminiscent. And Brett, clad like herself in sterile covering, worked with a skill it was a joy to watch, Ali acting as his anaesthetist. Zeena, the chief nurse, scrubbed up and sterile, presided over the instrument trolley, passing the necessary probes and scalpels.

'Another time you shall be my scrubbed nurse,' Brett had promised Alison before they started work, as though he was offering her the greatest honour in the world. But today her role was onlooker. It was very hot in the little theatre, and absolutely silent save for the faint hissing of the autoclave, the tinkle of instruments being replaced on the glass top of the trolley, and the stertorous breathing of the unconscious patient. Alison felt as if she too were asleep on her feet, dreaming the whole thing. Only Brett's hands were alive, moving delicately, skilfully about their work.

Later, as he drove her home, she told him how absorbing it had all been. Theatre work—she had always loved it.

'Then come and help me, whenever you can. I'll be very glad of you,' he assured her. 'I have only two fully trained nurses on my staff, the rest are trainees. So we're a bit tight on schedule, and not only in the theatre. You wouldn't like to drop in and give me your moral support at afternoon surgery, I suppose?' he added.

'Today, do you mean?' Alison shook her head. 'I'm afraid I can't manage it. I'll come to surgery in the morning.' She told him about her reading sessions with Haidie and Kaira, in the women's quarters of the palace. 'They'll be so disappointed if I don't turn up. And incidentally, may I borrow one or two of the English books I saw on the shelves in your house?'

'Take whatever you like,' he agreed expansively. 'Just walk up the stairs and help yourself if I'm not at home. The street door is kept on the latch and you'll always be welcome.'

When they halted at the Villa gateway he turned to her impulsively, putting a hand on her arm. 'Thank you for coming to the hospital this morning.' His blue eyes had lost their frostiness as he smiled. 'You're a good kid, Alison, I'm glad you've come to Sidi bou Kef. That's a bonus I hardly expected.'

She went up the Villa pathway feeling ridiculously lighthearted. The whole morning now lay behind her in a rosy glow. Working with Brett again was going to be marvellous, more than marvellous. He wasn't the only one who had found an unexpected bonus in Sidi bou Kef.

Over the lunch table her father announced that he was going into Algiers that afternoon to pick up a batch of seedlings, which were coming by air from the famous seed nursery at Blida. 'Why don't you come with me?' he suggested.

'I've got a date with Haidie ... one of our reading sessions,' Alison said a little regretfully.

'You can read with Haidie any time,' John Warrender pointed out. 'Tell her you'll make up for it another day. The trip into town would do you good. Perhaps there's some shopping you would like to do?'

One or two more frocks, Alison thought. Something a little more attractive than the serviceable cottons she had brought with her. It was tempting. While she hesitated Lalla appeared with a telegram which had just been sent over from the palace.

'For *Monsieur le Professeur*,' she announced importantly.

'Hope they're not cancelling the delivery of the seedlings,' John Warrender muttered. 'They're late enough already ... ought to have been planted a week ago.'

But the telegram was from Fiona. 'Arriving Algiers airport March 7 eighteen hours stop. Term ending early because of outbreak of mumps stop Love Fiona.'

'March the seventh!' Alison gasped. 'That's today. And eighteen hours is six o'clock.'

Her father laughed. 'You sound alarmed, my dear. But it couldn't be more convenient, Fiona arriving at the airport the very afternoon I have to pick up those seedlings.'

'Mumps,' Alison mused. 'I remember Fiona having them when she was small—so she won't have had to stay at school in quarantine. It's lucky she'd had her overseas inoculations in good time. I must tell Lalla to get her room ready for her, and she can take a message to Haidie about my change of plan. I'll just say I have to go into Algiers unexpectedly.'

The drive into Algiers was uneventful, the sun blazing down on mile after mile of scrub and sand. Closing her eyes, Alison dozed lightly, having muddled but happy dreams about working with Brett in his clinic. She didn't rouse herself until they were driving through the outskirts of Algiers. And after all there was no time for shopping, just a brief half hour in which to snatch a much needed cup of tea before they went to the airport. The Boeing was just coming in, its great bulk touching down with incredible lightness.

A few minutes later, watching from behind the barrier in the arrival hall, they saw Fiona walking across the tarmac, tall and leggy in a trendy leather coat. Her hair had been done in a new elaborate style, making her look unaccustomedly grown-up. She was not alone. The man at her side, his hand possessively under her elbow, had a familiar air. Paul Everton! Alison felt a quick stab of apprehension. What a coincidence that Fiona should be on the same plane as Paul Everton, and it was even more extraordinary that they had struck up an acquaintance. And how come Paul, who was supposed to be in Paris, had turned up on a London plane?

Fiona, who had by this time spotted them, was waving frantically, her small face alight and beautiful. Paul waved too. Alison waved back, possessing her soul in what patience she could muster while the travellers went to the turn-table to claim their luggage. Paul, hovering over Fiona, was a picture of tender concern and chivalry, the last man in the world she would have let loose on her impressionable sister, Alison mused uneasily.

At last they were all together, the two girls embracing, kissing. Explanations poured forth—the mumps, the lucky escape from school a fortnight early. And Paul had been in London in pursuit of an elusive financier, the man who was mainly responsible for backing *Hills of Sand*. He had found himself seated beside Fiona as they left Heathrow, had introduced himself, and soon learned that she was on her way to Sidi bou Kef and that she was Alison Warrender's sister.

'Wasn't it amazing!' Fiona marvelled, looking up at Paul who was giving her one of his most melting glances.

'We found we had so much in common,' he said.

I bet you did! Alison thought sourly. Poor Fiona, only a few hours in Paul's woman-eating company and already she looked what Alison privately described as 'all dewy-eyed and gooey'.

While the Professor busied himself over the Blida seedlings the three young people had a drink at the airport buffet. Fiona, who seemed intoxicated with excitement, did most of the talking. Going over it all again ... the mumps crisis, the flight, meeting Paul Everton. 'And to end up here in North Africa, with life in an oasis ahead of me! I can't believe it!'

'It's not really our idea of an oasis,' Alison warned her. 'Quite a sizeable town with streets and shops, and of course all these trees Father has come to look after.'

'But it *is* on the edge of the Sahara,' Fiona insisted. 'Paul has promised to take me riding there.' They exchanged another of their long meaningful glances.

Alison was glad when her father rejoined them. But it was only to ask Paul if he would mind giving the two girls a lift back to Sidi.

'I simply haven't got room in my estate car. These seedlings are more bulky than I'd bargained for, and they mustn't be crowded or crushed.'

'Don't give it another thought, Professor!' Paul

broke in enthusiastically. 'I'll be delighted to take your charming daughters back to Sidi. It will make the long drive a pleasure. A great pleasure,' he added softly with another melting glance for Fiona, which Alison noticed had an immediate effect. Poor Fiona! Didn't she realise there were melting glances for her sister too, murmured asides—all going on behind her back? Couldn't she see what a two-timer Paul was? He couldn't help flirting with a pretty girl any more than he could help breathing.

To prove her point Alison began flirting back a little, and manoeuvred herself into the seat beside him when they got into the Cadillac. But Paul, concentrating on his driving, was unresponsive. There was plenty of room on the front seat for the three of them. Fiona, in her corner, exclaimed at everything of interest they passed on their way. She thought the 'real desert' was 'fab' when they skirted it, and Alison recounted once more her early morning adventure on her first day in Sidi bou Kef, and how Paul had come to her aid.

'He has told me about it,' Fiona disclosed, a little absently, her attention taken by a witch-like old woman driving a flock of goats. Paul, skilfully avoiding the excitedly scattering animals, said, 'Fiona knows all about my band of Arab warriors, we had time in the plane to go over the whole plot of *Hills of Sand*.'

'And he's found me a small part in the cast!' Fiona exulted.

Alison wondered if she had heard aright. 'A part in his film!'

'She can stand in for Darienne at one point in the story,' Paul said. 'There's a riding sequence Darienne hates, and she's really not up to it. Fiona, however, from what she tells me, is a crack rider ... over the sticks, point-to-point ... the lot.'

'You make it sound as if I'd been boasting,' Fiona protested. 'I only told you all that so that you'd let me ride in your film. And when you said Miss Chevasse hated the bit in the mock battle...'

'You don't mean Fiona's going to ride with all those screaming, rifle-waving tribesmen!' Alison put in, shocked.

'Oh, it's much safer than it looks,' Paul assured her.

But Alison wasn't convinced. 'I think Fiona ought to get Father's permission before she promises to do this wild ride.'

'Don't be such an old wet blanket,' Fiona grumbled.

'Surely you don't think I would let your adorable little sister come to any harm?' Paul smoothed it all out.

'Anyway,' Fiona exulted, 'I'm to have a mount from the *Hills of Sand* stables, whenever I want it—a real Arab steed. I'm going to start practice rides tomorrow.'

She sounded so elated over the project that Alison hadn't the heart to raise any more objections.

It was dark long before they reached Sidi bou Kef where they headed for the main street and the square.

'I thought you were going to drop us at the Villa,' Alison said a little anxiously. Surely they weren't being let in for a session at the Regence? Fiona would be tired after her long journey ... their father would be expecting them. But they were only calling at the hotel, she was told, so that Fiona could be given a copy of the film script to study.

'Find out what the whole thing is about,' Paul explained. 'Absorb the atmosphere.'

It was just as they were pulling up outside the hotel

that Brett appeared, coming through the swing door of the brilliantly lighted foyer. He couldn't possibly miss seeing the trio in the big American car. His acknowledgement of Alison's startled glance was a curt nod, then turning an adamant back on them he walked over to his shabby little Citröen and drove off.

So what? Alison braced herself. Why should she get all steamed up because Brett Meredith had seen her once more in Paul Everton's company? Brett was a hopeless square, a dedicated medico with no time for girl-friends. He had practically told her so. Why then should he bother his head about the company she kept?

Flustered and off guard, she allowed herself to be persuaded into the bar for a glass of sherry. Fiona was introduced to Darienne and several other members of the cast. It was with the utmost difficulty that Alison evaded Paul's invitation to both of them to stay to dinner. Her father would be expecting them, she pointed out, once more, and Fiona had had a long day. Luckily Fiona did not argue the matter, but before they left it had been arranged that Paul would send a car for her in the morning, so that she could come down to the stables and try out one or two of the horses that might be put at her disposal.

'Isn't it all unbelievable!' she sighed ecstatically some hours later, when she and Alison, on their way to bed, were having a sisterly gossip in Fiona's room. Fiona had duly admired the mosaic floor and exclaimed at the moonlight on the terrace beyond the verandah, and now in a brief frilly nightgown she sat on the edge of her bed brushing her thick curly hair.

'Isn't Paul a dish!' she sighed. 'Imagine my luck in teaming up with him like that on the journey! I knew at once he must be somebody famous; he has such a distinguished air. So I wasn't a bit surprised when he told me he's directing this big film, with Darienne Chevasse in the lead. I've adored her ever since I saw her on the telly in that French historical serial about the Revolution. It was terrific meeting her this evening.'

'Do you think Paul is in love with her?' she asked after a small musing pause.

'Paul is in love with every pretty woman he meets,' Alison pronounced brutally. 'Surely you realise that!'

'You mean the hand-kissing, and melting glances?' Fiona assumed a worldly air. 'That's just his image. The real Paul underneath is a very sweet and serious person.'

Alison groaned. 'Do you mean that you discovered this real Paul on your three-hour flight from London?'

Fiona gazed dreamily into space. 'Yes, I think I did. Time doesn't matter when two people meet and find they're on the same wavelength.'

'Funny old wavelength,' Alison said dryly. 'A school-girl in her teens and a sophisticate like Paul Everton —he must be thirty-five, if he's a day.'

'I know,' Fiona agreed, unmoved. 'We talked about our ages. He says his life is empty in spite of all his successes; that success is an illusion. The only thing that matters in life is ... love.' She brought the word out in a whisper. 'I don't mean I think he's in love with me,' she added hastily. 'But I think he's lost and lonely. It was rather pathetic the hungry way he listened to everything I told him about my home, and school ... and Dora. He said being with me gave him back a sense of his lost youth...'

So that was to be his line, Alison thought wryly. The

world-weary roué, refreshing himself with Fiona's un-spoiled charm.

She said, standing up to go to her own room, 'If I were you I'd take Mr Paul Everton with a very large pinch of salt.'

Fiona gave her a hurt look. 'Paul doesn't need cynic-ism, but understanding.'

It was hopeless at this stage, Alison realised. She'd just have to keep a close eye on her young sister, and trust she didn't come too hard a cropper. And Paul no doubt would sooner or later show himself in his true colours. Chatting up a pretty child on the long flight was one thing, keeping up the act once he was back in Sidi bou Kef quite another. And there was Darienne to be reckoned with, the beautiful Darienne who seemed to have some kind of hold over him. Her quietly possessive manner towards him was very apparent at times.

Fiona would just have to take it as it came, Alison decided. But it was a pity she had got herself mixed up with this film crowd and been offered a part in *Hills of Sand*, however small a part. It meant she would be thrown into Paul's company day after day ... There was nothing to be done about it, however. To forbid her the great adventure would be disastrous.

After a mild objection or two over the dinner table that evening John Warrender, seeing only the hazards of the wild ride in the desert, unaware of the more emotional dangers had succumbed to Fiona's plead-ings. Her sister, Alison concluded, would just have to find her feet in the slippery world of celluloid into which she was straying. She had plenty of sense—surely she would soon realise how little Paul Everton's atten-tions could mean.

Lying in the dark listening to the chanting of the frogs in the lily pond, her last thoughts were of Brett. Odd the way he always turned up when she was with Paul. Did it really annoy him to see them together? That curt nod he had given her, probably because he was thinking of something else. With a sigh she turned over and went to sleep.

She was at the hospital bright and early the next morning, having driven into town in the car Paul sent for Fiona. The morning clinic had not yet started when she walked, unannounced, in at the surgery door. Brett in a white coat was sitting at his desk studying a pile of charts. He looked up sharply as she entered. 'Good of you to bother to come,' he said with such obvious sarcasm that she felt as if she had had a slap in the face.

'Weren't you expecting me?' she faltered. 'I promised I would be here this morning.'

He went over to a filing cabinet and began searching through it for some record he needed. 'I thought maybe you were just being polite. You so obviously didn't want to come back to the hospital yesterday afternoon, and heaven knows there's no reason why you should feel you had to.' He had found the file he was looking for and carried it back to the desk. Sitting down, he looked up at her, his blue gaze very cold and direct— hypnotic eyes. They tore away her defences.

'Old Madame al Raschid had a slight heart attack yesterday afternoon.' He spoke with a sort of ominous deliberation. 'I was called to the palace to see her ... in the harem; where else? I expected to find you there reading to your ladies, but Haidie told me you'd gone into Algiers.'

She stared at him, trying to measure the significance of what he was saying to her. It was dawning on her that he was coldly angry.

'You didn't have to invent English lessons at the al Raschid harem. I quite understand that you prefer running round with your new boy-friend to helping me here in the surgery. It's perfectly natural, and anyway, who am I to object? It's just that I don't much like ... lies.'

Her cheeks blazed. So this was what he had worked up against her! 'I do not tell lies!' she cried, her voice shrill and not quite under control. 'There's a perfectly simple explanation for my change of plan yesterday...'

'I'm sure there is,' he broke in sardonically, as the first patient was ushered in. He must have pressed the bell that summoned the man even while she was speaking, Alison realised indignantly. What an idea of fair play! To accuse her of lying and then give her no chance to clear her name. Her first impulse was to turn and walk out of the hospital, never to return. But something held her back. An irreparable breach with Brett was unthinkable. She couldn't bear it.

So she swallowed her pride with a gulp. 'Do you want me to stay now that I'm here?'

He nodded, not looking up at her, 'I'll be grateful. It's going to be a heavy surgery and Zeena is busy in the wards. There's a spare surgical coat over there on the wall peg.'

When she put it on it was too large for her. She rolled up the sleeves and took her place standing by his side at the desk ... just at she had done in the outpatients department of their London hospital.

They worked for an hour and a half in a curious, impersonal professional harmony. Absorbed in the patients and their history and treatment as they came and went, there were moments when Alison was able to completely forget her emotional involvement with this fair-haired, dogged young man. Quickly, coolly, but kindly he dealt with each case, never faltering, never making a mistake. And the simple people who came to him with their troubles looked at him with awe and gratitude, knowing they could trust him. This was Brett at his best.

When the last patient had been disposed of he stood up and stretched, and then to Alison's astonishment he gave her one of his rare smiles. 'You are good at this job, aren't you, young Warrender? You've been a great help this morning.' Such geniality! She could hardly believe her ears. He walked over to the wash basin and began scrubbing his hands. Alison took off her white coat, hung it back on its peg and waited her turn for the wash basin.

They were drying their hands on the same towel when Brett said, 'And now let's have this explanation. I'm sorry if I was a bit rough with you when you arrived this morning.'

'If this is an apology,' Alison interrupted, 'I'd like to make it perfectly clear that I won't stand for being called a liar.'

The smile widened into what was almost a shame-faced grin. 'All right, I take back the scurrilous word.' He dropped his end of the towel. 'It was just a bit odd, you must admit, that when you were supposed to be reading English books to the al Raschid ladies you were swanning about Algiers with your boy-friend.'

'He is not my boy-friend,' Alison contradicted emphatically. 'And I wasn't "swanning", whatever that may be. A cable came from my sister soon after I got back from the hospital yesterday at lunch time, saying she was arriving unexpectedly at Algiers airport at six o'clock.'

'So you asked glamour boy to take you to meet her...'

'Stop jumping to conclusions!' Alison snapped. 'I drove into Algiers with my father. He was picking up a consignment of seedlings from Blida. As it turned out, there wasn't room for all of us *and* the seedlings in the estate waggon. So my father asked Paul Everton, who happened to arrive on the same plane as my sister, if he would give the two of us a lift back to Sidi. I hope that ties it all up satisfactorily for you?'

'It does,' he agreed, 'and I grovel.'

But it was just a little too flippant to heal the hurt he had made.

'I'll run you back to the Villa,' Brett offered.

'I can walk, thanks,' Alison said shortly, still seething. Brett's apology hadn't really settled anything. He remained convinced she was fooling around with Paul Everton, and despised her for it.

'I'm taking you home in my car,' he said firmly. Putting his hands on her shoulders, he turned her round to face him. 'You're furious with me, aren't you? I suppose you have every right to be. But the truth is I hate to see you tagging along with that theatrical mountebank. You're worth something much better.'

She shrugged herself out of his grasp. 'You're making a lot out of nothing. Paul Everton,' she said with a flick of her fingers, 'doesn't matter that much to me.'

'Yet you kiss him in public, permit him to put his arms around you?'

She gave him a hopeless look. 'You sound like something out of a Victorian novel. Honestly, Brett, you're the end! A goodnight peck coming out of a cinema? What are you trying to make of it?'

He shook his head. 'I know. I'm an impossible old square. It's just that ... I'm fond of you, Alison. I wish you'd found someone worthy of you by this time.'

That was rich, Alison felt, coming from Brett! Tears threatening made her eyes look larger than usual. The sheer despair in them seemed to puzzle Brett. He said, 'I value our friendship, Alison, and your help. It was grand having you with me in the surgery this morning. Let's take it from there ... and forget the rest.'

That halcyon interlude two summers ago. Kisses, that hadn't been in public, words full of imponderables. God knew she wanted to forget it all!

'Now that we've met again in this extraordinary way in the wilderness,' Brett went on, 'let's get what we can out of it.'

The half loaf that's better than no bread, she thought bitterly. But she smiled up at him, forgiving him, saying, 'Let's do just that.'

He said, 'That pottery at Delma I told you about ... I could take you there this afternoon. Ali will see to evening surgery for me. I have a patient to visit some miles beyond Delma right in the desert—a Bedouin encampment. Will you come with me?' He held out his hand to her and she put her own into it.

'I'd like to, Brett.'

CHAPTER SIX

CHANGING her frock for the afternoon outing, Alison felt a twinge of shame at her mood of suppressed elation. Here she was, all worked up at the prospect of her trip with Brett. He only had to lift his little finger and she came running. But he had sounded as if he really wanted to show her Delma with its famous potteries. And that wasn't all. 'I'm fond of you, Alison,' he had said this morning when they were patching up their quarrel. Just what had he meant by that? What he said, and no more. He was fond of her. Fond enough to wish she had found a nice worthy husband by now. Who wanted that sort of 'fondness'? But he had nothing deeper to offer her. Perhaps that was why he had ditched her two years ago? As their friendship developed he had discovered she wasn't really the girl for him. He had liked her, that was all. One day he would find the right person . . . a girl who appealed to him emotionally. He wasn't just cold and calculating, though at times he might appear so. Those compelling blue eyes of his were capable of passion. The thought disturbed her.

She thrust it away from her, turning with relief to Fiona who had come into the bedroom to begin once more about what a fabulous morning she had had riding the Arab horses at the film company's stables. They had had it all through lunch, together with panegyrics about Paul. Their father, Alison could see, was beginning to be a little uneasy about his younger daughter's association with the film director. But she had come through her camera tests that morning with flying colours and was thrilled with her success. It would be cruel at this stage to deny her her small part in *Hills of Sand*. As long as she concentrated on her work and left Paul alone, Alison thought, none too hopefully, as she zipped herself into a frock which had been one of last summer's favourites; a sleeveless sheath of slub rayon in clear turquoise blue.

She was going back on location this afternoon, Fiona announced. 'Paul is sending the car for me.'

'You can give me a lift, then,' Alison suggested. 'I'm meeting Brett Meredith at the hospital. He's taking me to see the pottery at Delma.'

'Brett Meredith?' Fiona enquired.

'A doctor I used to work with at St Clare's. He's turned up here running the Sheik's hospital.'

'How amazing!' Fiona murmured, not really interested. She was far too absorbed in her own affairs.

Brett was waiting outside the hospital when they drove up in the outsize Cadillac.

'This is Fiona,' Alison introduced her sister, and noticed Brett's glance going quickly beyond Fiona to the Arab chauffeur at the wheel. Had he expected to see Paul Everton? He greeted Fiona a little absently. She gave him her dimpled smile and shook back her curls in an innocently provocative way.

'So you have rights in the film company's transport,' Brett said as the car bearing Fiona away went swaying off down the bumpy dusty road. There was a distinct edge to his tone. Poor film company; how he hated everything connected with it!

'It's Fiona who has the rights,' Alison explained. 'Paul Everton has given her a small part in the picture he's making, a short riding sequence. She's very good with horses ... adores riding.'

'Indeed?' Brett had obviously lost interest, and was fixing his attention on Alison in a rather disconcerting way. And when Brett fixed his attention it was a hundred per cent. Had there ever been eyes with a more piercing and penetrating power? That hungry, almost ruthless way they looked right through you, it made Alison want to squirm. But all he said, surprisingly, was, 'I like the blue frock. You look as cool as a crocus on the snowline.'

Alison laughed. 'When did you see crocuses on the snowline?'

'A few years ago when I had a skiing holiday in Switzerland.'

With a light hand on her shoulder he led her over to the waiting Citröen. A quiver of fire ran through her at his touch, for which she despised herself. It was a relief when they were in the car, on their way.

They took a road out of Sidi which she hadn't seen before. It led rapidly away from the planted trees of the oasis to an area of bushes and scrub. Then suddenly it was all great billows of golden sand, stretching to a line of far blue hills. After a while Brett stopped the car and switched off the engine—'So that you can feel the silence,' he said. It was so quiet that they could hear the lizards rustling across the rough sandy track. The sky was a violet blue, pressing down on them in the afternoon heat. They had stopped on a rise, the desert a vast emptiness all around them under the pitiless sun.

'Hard to believe that this was once all forest,' Brett said, 'and that even now there's water in plenty hidden beneath the sand.' As they drove on he talked of the rediscovery of Roman wells and water systems, and of the delving oil companies who frequently probed deep enough to find water in plenty. 'A pity they aren't satisfied with it, instead of concentrating on oil wells, flooding the world with petroleum fumes. Here in this remote place one glimpses primitive societies who seem to get along quite happily without some of the more doubtful blessings of our modern civilisation.'

They passed through a village that was just a hand-ful of whitewashed mud hovels surrounded with scrub, where goats and donkeys grazed. Wild-looking chil-dren in rags ran out of the houses to stare at them. It was all pitifully poverty-stricken and bleak, in spite of the blazing sun.

'If this is your primitive society,' Alison said, 'I think I'd settle for a few of the doubtful blessings of civilisa-tion!'

Brett laughed goodhumouredly. 'You could be right. But poverty on that level crops up in almost every under-developed country. The primitives I mean aren't necessarily poor. It's just that they have a differ-ent set of values from us in the affluent West. Wait until you've seen Delma, and the Bedouin encamp-ment I'm taking you to.'

They were back in the trackless sand again. Alison shivered in spite of the heat. 'Imagine being lost in this wilderness!' she said.

Brett shrugged. 'It wouldn't be much fun. They give a man alone and on foot and without water about twenty-four hours before the vultures take over.'

'Vultures!' She looked round apprehensively. 'Where are they?'

'Invisible for the most part. But they appear out of the sky in the most astonishing fashion when there's carrion to be had.'

Alison shuddered. 'Give me civilisation, petrol

fumes and all!'

Yet a few moments later she uttered an exclamation of delight as they rounded a corner and slid down into a shallow valley, suddenly and miraculously green. 'The beginning of the Delma Oasis,' Brett announced in a tone of personal pride. The grass was studded with hundreds of small bright flowers. Once more he stopped the car so that Alison could see them; narcissus, little mauve gladioli, bright blue iris, cyclamen. She wanted to get out and pick them, but Brett pointed out that they wouldn't live an hour in this heat if taken out of their environment. Driving on, they came to fields of poppies, marigolds and daisies. Here, cupped in a hollow of the barren Sahara, born of the merciful rains, flamed all the beauty of spring. On the rising land at either side of the road, the bushes with their new young leaves, the emerald grass and brightly coloured flowers breathed of new life and hope.

'Oh, Brett, it's fabulous!' Alison said on a long sigh of content. 'All that frightening emptiness we came through, and then ... this!'

He gave her a quick, grateful glance. 'I'm so glad you've seen it. I hoped it would be this way for you. I remembered how lovely it was when I passed this way last March, and I wanted to show it to you. But I wasn't sure the flowers would still be in bloom. They fade so soon after the rains, in this blazing sun.'

He had wanted to show it to her, share it with her. Her heart lay very still. This was a moment that must not be spoiled by looking back, or looking forward. She was with Brett in this enchanted place. Let that be enough.

She said in a voice not quite under control, 'I'll always remember this lovely little valley, Brett.'

> *'O, beauty, are you not enough?*
> *Why am I crying after love?'*

She did not speak the lines aloud, and hardly knew
where they came from—the echo of some poem she had
been reading with Haidie and Kaira the other day. She
couldn't remember what the Arab women had made of
it, nor did it matter. She could only, at that moment,
endure the pain the words evoked.

They drove on in a silence that seemed to throb with
things unsaid ... things inexpressible, perhaps. She was
letting her imagination run away with her.

They came to a small plantation of palm trees clus-
tering about a well. Women who had drawn water
from the well walked before them on the road balancing waterpots on their shoulders.

As they approached the centre of the little pottery
town clouds of wood smoke drifted out to meet them.
It came from the ovens which fired the pots, Brett explained. 'They burn esparto grass, dried palm leaves
and olive branches to heat the kilns.' The odour was
aromatic and pleasant.

Cruising slowly down the main street, Alison was
fascinated by the whiteness of the houses, their doorways decorated with strings of scarlet pimentoes. In the
open-fronted shops craftsmen were making esparto
grass mats, and weaving brightly coloured prayer rugs.
They came to the street of the potters, and, left the car
to watch a potter working with a slab of wet clay, shaping it on the wheel between his hands, until the perfect
curves began to appear. Finished pots and jars were
piled around him, the colour of ochre and rose. Many
of them were beautifully decorated, with patterns of
fishes and leaves. Brett insisted upon buying her a

small delicately shaped pitcher the colour of a ripe apricot, stencilled with geometric designs.

'It will hold the milk for your endless cups of nurses' tea,' he told her.

'Only that I'm not a nurse any longer.'

'Yes, you are,' he urged. 'If you want to be. As from this moment you have a roving commission as my assistant at Sidi bou Kef cottage hospital.'

'If you don't mind it being really "roving",' she said.

He nodded. 'I know. You have other interests. But if you would just show up at my clinic whenever you have a few hours to spare you'll always find a welcome awaiting you ... and plenty of hard work.

'And now,' he ended as he led her back to the car, 'we must speed up a bit. We still have a good twenty miles to cover.'

The road was rough and empty, the scenery, once the valley was left behind, monotonous—just sand and sand and more sand. Brett spoke of the patient he was going to see, an old man suffering from spondulitis, so stiff and crippled with rheumatic pains that he couldn't possibly get into the clinic for treatment. 'Whenever I can make the time I drive out to give him one of the injections that can relieve his condition. He's a wonderful old chap, head of a tribe of nomads. They wander from place to place looking for water for themselves and pasture for their animals, and have an extraordinary instinct for finding both; living the sort of life that was going on when Noah built the Ark. Yet they have a culture and standards that in many ways modern man might envy. Their laws of hospitality, for instance; they will house and feed a wandering traveller for several days, asking for nothing in return—even going without food themselves, so that the guest may have what he needs.'

'Sounds out of this world,' was Alison's comment.

'It is. That's just the point. Right out of the world we've fashioned for ourselves with so-called civilisation.'

It was the second time he had spoken in this way during the afternoon. What was happening to him? Had the desert a siren attraction for him?

As if answering her unspoken questions he said, 'There are things about life out here that are an immense relief after the modern rat race. Not that one can ever quite opt out of the rat race. There's no going back in the scheme of things. If we're making mistakes in the way we live at home we have to work through those mistakes and come out somewhere to find the solution. Meanwhile it's no harm to take a look back at the more primitive and simple values.'

'In other words you're enjoying your spell in the Sahara?'

'Enormously! And you?'

'I haven't been here long enough yet to make judgements. But I'm learning.'

The road, inches deep in sand, topped a small rise, and there some way ahead in a hollow of rock and bushes were the Bedouin tents, looking very small and black against the tawny background of coarse desert grass. But as they drew nearer Alison could see that the tents were surprisingly roomy, stoutly erected square-shaped dwelling places, round which the goats and donkeys grazed; there was even one shabby camel, and a mongrel dog. Brett stopped the car outside the largest of the tents, its front flaps fastened back to reveal a dark but spacious interior.

A middle-aged woman came forward to greet them. She had an air of dignity, quite unruffled by the sudden appearance of the visitors. She wore a loose robe of striped cotton, and though her feet were bare her large earrings and bangles were of solid silver. In her gypsy way she was strikingly handsome, her smile giving her an added beauty as she warmly welcomed the doctor. Ushering them into the tent, she was speaking in a mixture of Arabic and patois French. Alison was surprised when Brett answered her in Arabic. After that the conversation was all in Arabic, and Alison could only guess its drift by the actions of the family around her. There was an old grannie who sat on a low stool in a corner, nodding and smiling, a younger woman who might have been the sister of the woman with the earrings, and presently two stalwart, handsome young men, dressed in short sleeveless belted tunics, came in through a back flap in the tent to greet the strangers. Both of them carried vicious-looking rifles, and there were daggers in the belts round their waists. In the free hand of the first young man dangled what Alison thought were a pair of dead baby rabbits. But later Brett told her they were gerbils, the little hamster-like animals who with lizards and scorpions and the occasional fox are the only living creatures in the desert.

Presently an older man appeared, fondling in his arms a little goat. With a shyly murmured, 'Marhaba', for the visitors he retired into the shadowy background and seated himself on the ground, still fondling the kid. He seemed to be examining one of its hind legs with gentle hands, for the little animal made no protest.

They were to eat, Alison gathered, becoming aware of culinary activities in the adjoining kitchen tent.

Cushions had been placed for their comfort on the magnificent hand-made carpet which entirely covered the tent floor. Other colourful rugs hung from the walls. Everything was spotlessly clean. The water jars standing in the shade of the kitchen corner were covered with white linen cloths.

'You have got to tackle a hot spicy stew,' Brett warned in a whispered aside. 'And you must look as if you like it!'

It was served with the usual flapping pieces of un-leavened bread, and was much more palatable than Alison had feared it would be, when it was handed to her in a deep terra-cotta bowl. There was no spoon with which to eat it, and copying Brett, she scooped up the savoury mess with folded pieces of bread. Then they drank mint tea, and afterwards Brett was taken to his patient in another part of the encampment.

Left alone, Alison glanced around her, feeling a little lost. The woman with the silver earrings, meeting her gaze, smiled and nodded as if in reassurance. 'You are a visitor to our country?' she asked in her strange French.

Alison, in her own schoolgirl version of that language said, 'I am here with my father, who is planting trees for the Sheik Achmed al Raschid.'

The woman turned to the big man who was still nursing the wounded kid, and poured out an animated flood of Arabic. The man's face lit up and he looked at Alison with fresh interest.

'My husband,' the woman told Alison, 'says it is good. You are a thousand times welcome to our dwelling. He has heard of your father, this great man of the trees, and we are proud to receive his daughter.'

'Is the little goat hurt?' Alison asked, smiling across

at the big man, who seemed to understand her question, though he answered her in Arabic.

'The kid's mother was killed by a fox the other night,' the woman translated for her. 'Now my husband feeds the little one and guards it. At night it sleeps by his side.'

It made a pretty picture—which didn't quite match up to the usual image of Bedouin warriors, who carried rifles rather than orphaned goats.

But life in the Sahara, Alison was discovering, was full of contradictions.

Two small faces peered round a corner of the tent's front flap. 'Our children,' the woman explained, holding out her hands to the small boy and girl, who advanced slowly, their dark eyes wide with awe for the stranger.

'They ran away when your car approached,' the mother said. 'Foolish and fearful.' She spoke to them in Arabic and they stood by her side, half hiding behind her skirts, peeping out at Alison. She wished she had sweets or some little gift to offer them and searched in her handbag for inspiration. Money she felt would be an insult in this atmosphere—and anyway, what use would it be out here with the gerbils and foxes and measureless miles of sand? She found a small pocket comb in a pretty case for the girl, and a mother-of-pearl penknife for the boy. The gesture was a terrific success; the entire family crowding round to marvel at the simple objects held proudly in the children's hands.

Just then Brett reappeared—to find her the centre of excited gratitude.

'You seem to have made yourself very popular with my nomads,' he said a few minutes later as they drove away. She told him about the knife and the comb.

He gave her an approving glance. 'You couldn't have thought of anything that would go down with the family better. You'll be remembered by them for years to come as the lady of the comb and the penknife. Won't you miss these things, by the way?'

'I have another pocket comb,' Alison told him. 'And I hardly ever use the knife. Anyway, I just had to find something to give those gorgeous children!'

'Born and brought up without benefit of ante-natal clinics and child guidance pontification,' Brett said. 'Makes you think, doesn't it? Here they are, these people, without as much as a cold water tap to their names, or a drainpipe, to say nothing of a roof over their heads, yet they manage to maintain an existence of some dignity and order. They wake with the sun, and sleep when it sets. Never heard of a nervous breakdown in their entire lives. Maybe this close to Nature stuff has its points.'

Alison gave him a quizzical glance. 'Yet I can't somehow see you living in a rough black tent in the middle of nowhere, wresting a livelihood out of the empty desert.'

'It might do me good,' Brett grimaced. 'But you're right, I'd never have the guts or the inspired insanity to take it on. I'm hooked, for what it's worth, to doctoring.'

'Ending with a Harley Street practice,' Alison suggested.

He shrugged. 'Once I might have thought that was the only goal. Now I could settle for a good deal less—in one sense. And, in another sense,' he added softly, 'a good deal more.' An oblique remark which puzzled her. So did the thoughtful glance that accompanied it.

The sun was beginning to set, rapidly disappearing behind the line of far off hills. Three men on camels loping into view suddenly reined in their beasts and dismounted. The camels, as though the moment contained some ritual with which they were familiar, lay chewing their cuds with a somnolent air. The three men, tall and impressive in their long robes and flowing headdress, walked slowly into the light of the setting sun, and stood facing it, with heads bowed.

'The hour of prayer,' Brett said, and stopping the car, switched off the engine. The silence that fell upon them then was awesome and complete. The three men, their long shadows falling behind them, remained motionless, the camels drowsed. For an instant, like the passing of a ghost, the sand whispered in a passing breeze. Then the utter silence again. Suddenly the sun was gone, the light over the rolling wastes of sand dying as swiftly as though a switch had been turned off. The three men, coming to life, went back to their camels, mounted and rode away. Brett started the car. The rapid twilight fell and the magic moment had gone. Neither of them spoke of it—or of anything else for some time. Alison was glad about that. There were no words just then that would not have been clumsy. But she would treasure the unexpected and moving incident and the fact that she and Brett had shared it.

Quickly it grew dark, the sky above their heads splintered with a million stars, that seemed to dance in their brightness. Brett drove for the most part in silence, concentrating on covering the miles. They had travelled a long way from Sidi bou Kef. 'Lucky you know the road!' Alison couldn't help remarking as they sped over the limitless and at times seemingly unrouted sands.

'I don't really,' Brett returned disconcertingly. 'But as long as I keep to this semblance of a track and head towards the west we're sure to hit Sidi in time.'

Over the horizon a pale glow appeared. 'Moonrise,' Brett said. The great orange globe appeared, slowly at first, then seeming to gather speed until the orange turned to silver and the whole vast plain was bathed in a mysterious greenish-blue light. Lying back in her seat Alison looked up through the open car roof into the starlit infinity.

'It's so vast,' she whispered. 'All this sky and wilderness. It makes me feel small ... and lonely.' Her face was pale, her eyes shadowy as she turned to the man at her side. He stopped the car and putting an arm about her drew her close. It seemed inevitable, as natural as the moonlight, when he kissed her. His lips were cool and firm on her own. She felt her heart beating wildly, her thoughts in chaos.

So soon he released her, his hands going back on to the wheel of the car, flicking the starter. She had fallen back against her seat, confused by her temptuous feelings, not quite daring to believe in that kiss. 'Why?' she asked breathlessly. 'Why did you kiss me, Brett?'

'Why not?' he returned lightly. 'You like being kissed, don't you?' He was taunting her with Paul Everton again.

Her anger flared. 'Why do you bother with me, Brett, if you think I'm so cheap and horrible?'

He threw her a startled glance. They were almost at their journey's end, the lights of the oasis town twinkling on the skyline.

'I don't think you're cheap and horrible, Alison. I like you a lot.'

'I know,' Alison said bitterly, 'you're fond of me.'
Here they were with the half loaf again.

'Of course I'm fond of you. We've always been good friends. But you're right out of my orbit.'

'And what's that supposed to mean?' she asked bitterly.

He shrugged. 'Forget it. If you didn't want me to kiss you just now, I'm sorry.'

Half a dozen retorts flashed into her mind, but she crushed them down. It was too humiliating to go on discussing that poor little kiss—mauling it. Besides, they were stopping at the Villa gates by this time.

'There's nothing to be sorry about,' she said with forced brightness, and got out of the car. 'It's been a lovely trip, Brett. Thank you for taking me.'

With her hand on the latch of the gate, she turned.

'What about coming in and joining the family for supper?'

'I'd love to, but I can't. I've got to get back to the hospital.'

The reply she had been counting on. If he had accepted her invitation she couldn't have borne it.

CHAPTER SEVEN

LIFE settled down into what was an almost humdrum routine during the next two weeks. Every morning, sharp at eight o'clock, the three Warrenders sat round the table on the verandah to a breakfast of coffee, boiled eggs and fruit. The Professor was usually the first to leave, hurrying off in his estate car to one of the new plantations, a briefcase full of plans and diagrams at his side.

A little later the Cadillac would come for Fiona. Alison too would get into it, and it would drop her at the hospital. Invariably it was the Arab chauffeur at the wheel. Alison took comfort that it wasn't Paul. Just what was happening to Fiona's infatuation for him? Perhaps she was a bit too engrossed with her own affairs just then to face up to the occasional pangs of uneasiness which came to her about her young sister. The filming of the riding sequence seemed to be taking a long time. Day after day, Fiona implied, she was busy on location. Did that mean hours of hanging about the bars and lounges of the Regence Hotel? But as long as Fiona was surrounded by the other members of the cast—not alone with Paul—it was surely all right, Alison would argue with herself.

The one time she probed, Fiona was instantly on the defensive.

'Are you still stuck with that riding sequence?' she asked one morning, while they were waiting for the car. 'It seems to be taking ages.'

'Of course it is,' Fiona snapped. 'You don't know the first thing about film-making. To begin with I had to get used to my mount. Riding a spirited Arab stallion isn't like bumbling about on fat old Dora...'

'Of course,' Alison agreed humbly. 'I'd like to see you doing your stuff... it must be terrific.'

'Paul doesn't approve of onlookers when we're working,' Fiona said discouragingly. 'Besides, it's right out in the desert.'

'But surely you're not out in the desert *all* the time? Sometimes you don't come home until quite late in the evening.'

'Because Paul likes me to wait to see the rushes; that's the run through of the film that has been made during the day.'

A disarming reply, but it left Alison unconvinced. Fiona, who usually chattered freely about all her doings, was strangely uncommunicative about these days she was spending working with the cast of *Hills of Sand*.

'How are you getting on with Paul?' Alison asked bluntly at last.

Fiona gave her an odd look. 'I wish you'd stop cross-questioning me! I know you don't like Paul. I haven't forgotten the mean things you said about him the day I travelled with him on the plane. So if you don't mind I'd rather not talk to you about him—only to say that you're completely wrong about him. He's not a bit like you tried to make him out to be.'

Alison's heart sank, but before she could think of anything to say the Cadillac was drawing up at the Villa gate. And it wasn't the Arab chauffeur at the wheel this morning. It was Paul.

With an exclamation of delight, Fiona raced down the garden path, her arms outstretched. Paul, who had got out of the car to meet her, picked her up and gave her a hearty kiss, then putting her down, turned to Alison who had followed at a more leisurely pace.

'Alison! How wonderful! Long, *long* time, no see. Why don't you join us on location sometimes? Watch your baby sister ride. Stop off at the hotel for a drink. You aren't being very friendly, are you? I've sent you messages by Fiona time and again suggesting a get-to-gether.'

Messages Fiona had been careful not to pass on! It looked as if things might be even worse than Alison had suspected. And Fiona was brazening it out, calling from the car impatiently: 'Oh, Paul, come on! You know Alison's all tied up with that stuffy doctor at the hospital. I've *told* you, again and again ...'

'Is that how it is with you? You have no time for old friends?' With his hand on Alison's arm Paul was contriving to look impossibly handsome ... and hurt. Though how he could imagine himself in the role of old friend ...

'I work at the hospital,' Alison said, shaking his hand away. 'Your chauffeur takes me there when he fetches Fiona in the mornings. I hope you don't mind?' she ended, getting into the car.

'I'm delighted I'm even that much use to you,' Paul said nobly, taking his place at the wheel.

Mercifully it was a short ride, with Paul saying, 'What about dinner tonight, Alison?' And Alison answering him stiffly that it was impossible. While Fiona, at her side, looked daggers.

Maybe I ought to have said 'yes' to the dinner invitation, Alison thought. Let her see how fickle Paul can be.

Then they were at the hospital, and she got out, and thanking Paul for the lift hurried inside.

Crossing the crowded courtyard she put Paul and Fiona firmly out of her mind. It looked like being a busy morning, and she was glad of it. Working with Brett day after day wasn't all that easy. In spite of her good resolutions she couldn't help her feelings becoming more and more involved. He treated her as a rule with cool detachment, but there were moments when she had a sense of unity with him, a feeling of companionship that wasn't altogether based on their shared interest in the hospital work. She treasured the mid-morning coffee break—when they could snatch it. As she sat with him in his sunny kitchen, he would talk to her eagerly, swiftly—always about his work, about patients they had seen or were about to see. But she was honoured to think that he confided in her, even asked her opinion from time to time.

Then for the rest of the morning they would be in the operating theatre, working in complete unison. Handing instruments, threading surgical needles, she knew that Brett depended upon her, trusted her—and she would never let him down. If I never have anything more of him, she thought, at least I've had this. The satisfaction of hours of hard work in a hot cramped little theatre. The irony of it did not occur to her. She loved him and she was serving him ... that was enough. Or she tried to make it so. Twice she had invited him to dinner at the Villa, twice he refused, pleading work. So there was to be no social life between them. Gradually she came to accept this. The trip to the nomad camp that halcyon afternoon, that moonlit evening, faded into a past that might never have been.

Most afternoons Alison went to the palace harem. Warmth and gaiety and a hearty welcome awaited her. She couldn't but enjoy the hours she spent with the Al Raschid women. They were so childish, so sweet, and yet in their unworldly way they were very wise. Their quiet acceptance of their lives, their delight in simple pleasures comforted her. Gradually she came to know not only the younger women and the children, but the grandmother and the great-grandmother as well. She had even learned a little more Arabic so that she could talk to them in the tongue with which they were most at home. Haidie and Kaira stuck valiantly to English and were soon reading fluently, stopping again and again to ask questions about the strange English stories. What did they really make of Jane Eyre and her Mr Rochester? Alison sometimes wondered. She had borrowed one or two modern novels and Kipling's *Jungle Book* from Brett's shelves, but the Brontë sisters remained the firm favourites.

'I wish I could see these Yorkshire moors. I can't imagine what they must be like,' Haidie yearned one hot afternoon in March, when the icy spring winds would be blowing up Wharfedale and over Simon's Seat. 'If only I could go to England!'

Kaira looked sorrowfully at her daughter and shook her head. 'You have all you need here, my child. Soon the Sheik will find you a husband.'

Haidie threw Alison a look of despair that was a cry for help. 'I don't want a husband. Not yet. I want to go places ... see the world. Here I am a prisoner, shut up in this house for ever. At school I could ride, play tennis, go swimming. But not here ... here I must sit in the courtyard and sew day after day, until I am old, until I am *dead*!' The last word was a wail, she buried her face in her hands and burst into tears.

There was a shocked silence.

Kaira and Alison exchanged glances of concern. 'The university,' Kaira said at last. 'In Algiers. Perhaps your grandfather would agree to your going there.'

Haidie raised a tear-stained face. 'I am not clever enough for the university. It wouldn't be any good. Besides, I want to go away—right away, travel.' She turned to Alison. 'Isn't there something I could do in England? Care for children, perhaps?'

'You could train to be a hospital nurse,' Alison said on a sudden inspiration. 'I'm sure my old hospital, St

Clare's, would accept you as a student. You got your Bachot at the French school in Algiers, didn't you? That would be the equivalent of the entrance exam at St Clare's.'

It took Haidie a moment or two to absorb this amazing suggestion, then her face lit up. 'Oh, Alison, what a wonderful idea!'

An animated discussion followed. Kaira seemed impressed, and even the older women, when they had been made to understand, indicated their approval. But nothing must be decided in a hurry. The Sheik must be consulted, as befitted his status as head of the household.

'Meanwhile,' Alison said to Haidie, 'why don't you come down to the hospital with me and find out what nursing is all about, and if you're going to like it? That is if Dr Meredith agrees.'

Brett, who encouraged enterprise and ambition, welcomed the prospect of an addition to his staff. So without further delay Haidie was installed as the cottage hospital's most junior trainee, starting work under Alison's guidance. Quickly she learned to take temperatures and pulses, and made copious notes on the memo pad she carried in her apron pocket. 'Ophthalmia: Routine treatment for infants: first swab the eyes with distilled water, then apply half-hourly drops of silver nitrate,' she scribbled industriously.

'I like your little protégée,' Brett told Alison one morning when they were drinking coffee in his kitchen. 'She's got quite a flair for the job. When we had her in the theatre this morning for an hour she didn't turn a hair; handed swabs as though to the manner born. With the Sheik's money behind her she might well think of having a shot at entering St Clare's medical school.'

'Study to become a doctor!' Alison exclaimed with a quick stab of jealousy. Brett had never suggested anything of the kind for *her*.

'Why not?' he demanded. 'She evidently has a good brain, a quick intelligence and plenty of enthusiasm for hospital work. They could do with a woman doctor in Sidi bou Kef. It will be some time before these Muslim mothers take kindly to the idea of a male doctor delivering their offspring. Yet there are times when expert gynaecological help is needed.'

A fact there was no denying. But that young Haidie, skipping the humbler role of nurse, would one day become a qualified gynaecologist was a startling proposition.

'She's supposed to be going to England with us when we return,' Alison said, trying to be glad about Brett's startling suggestion. 'That is if St Clare's accept her application. And there's no reason why they shouldn't.'

'That gives us a little more time to see how she develops,' Brett mused. 'Meanwhile, I could be sounding the Sheik.'

Alison carried the coffee cups over to the sink. It was time for them to be getting back to the hospital.

The next day the much-talked-of festival began, starting with a procession through the town, led by the Sheik Achmed Al Raschid, dressed in flowing robes of scarlet and purple, his headdress bound about his brow with a filet of gold. His horse, a great white stallion, was no less magnificent, its saddle and bridle elaborately decorated, tassels and bells about its neck. The silken saddle-cloth that covered its haunches reached almost to the ground. A great golden canopy sheltered the Sheik from the sun, held aloft by four outriders. Behind him came the town's elders and merchants, the town-band, filling the air with their reedy music. Finally a troupe of male dancers appeared, followed by a lone almost naked figure festooned with snakes—the local snake-charmer.

Alison with Kaira and Haidie watched it all from the latticed upstairs windows of the town's one bank. She had been excused from surgery this morning since Brett expected few patients. Everyone who could stand upright would be at the festival. From her vantage point in the bank window she could see down the street to the market square where the procession had formed and started. Paul Everton was there with his camera team, seizing on this Arab occasion which he had counted on being able to incorporate in his film. Fiona, who had rushed off in his car as usual this morning (though there could be no prospect of serious work), was at his side on the decorated float he had reserved for himself and his staff. These floats, parked round the square, were being used as grandstands by the excited townsfolk. Fiona was standing on one corner of the film company's float, looking a little neglected. She was the only female in the group of cameramen and technicians. If Darienne and the other actresses in the cast were watching the procession it would be from the comfort of the hotel balconies. Only Fiona had elected to spend the morning out in the blazing sun, no doubt in order to be near Paul, who, as far as Alison could see, hadn't a moment to spare for her. Poor silly kid! Wasn't she ever going to get over her infatuation? Surely not even a lovesick schoolgirl could be taken in for ever by Paul Everton's glib insincerities?

Dismissing the worry that was Fiona, Alison saw that the procession had now stopped in the tree-lined *place* outside the bank. The Sheik and his entourage took up a dominating position, the band burst into a frenzied cacophony, and the dancers took up their positions and began to dance. They were all very young, little more than boys, small and slender, but adding to their height by the tall, glittering conical hats they wore. Their tunics were vividly coloured, sleeveless to reveal the arms and hands which were used in the ritual of the dance in slow ballet-like movements. There was little other action. Sometimes the boys made their movements while standing, sometimes they knelt, swaying back and forth; and it was all done with a slow and dreamy grace to the music of the native flutes.

Was it some sort of homage to the Sheik? Alison wondered. But Haidie said no, it was a religious dance.

In the afternoon there were horse-races, mock battles and jumping competitions on a flat plain some way out in the desert. Fiona, who had come home for lunch, persuaded her father to take them to see these events. Paul apparently was not interested. 'Doesn't he want to film the mock battles, and so on?' Alison asked her sister, when they arrived on the scene of action to find the film cameras missing.

'He's got all he wants in the can already,' Fiona answered. 'His own mock battles, and the bit where I do the riding sequence. He's spending this afternoon looking for interesting snippets in the town, snakecharmers and sword-swallowers and so on.'

Alison, who was glad Fiona had managed to tear herself away from him for an hour or two, made no comment. But her peace of mind was short-lived. There was to be a dance at the Regence that evening, and as soon as dinner at the Villa was over, Fiona rushed off to her room to get ready for it. She was going with Paul. Of course! With a sigh of resignation, Alison followed her to her room.

'You can come too,' Fiona told her sister expansively. 'It's an open invitation tonight. The *Hills of Sand* cast are "at home" to anyone who likes to join in the fun. I'm sure you would find the odd partner.' There was condescension in her tone.

'And if Paul dances with you,' she added, 'remember he's *my* property. I haven't forgotten the way you tried to muscle in the other morning when he was driving us both into Sidi ... manoeuvring him into asking you to have dinner with him.'

'Fiona!' Alison burst out, goaded. 'What on earth are you talking about? If I was manoeuvring him, why did I refuse his invitation?'

'Just being devious, I expect, leading him on. And it isn't a difficult thing to do. He's so soft, so kindhearted towards everybody. People ... girls, I mean, are apt to get him wrong.'

'If you call the eternal passes he makes being kind...'

'I do,' Fiona returned equably. 'I understand Paul.'

'*Honestly,* Fiona!' Alison gasped. 'How you can be so dumb!'

'Now you're just being offensive,' Fiona remarked pityingly. Was there no way of piercing her complacency? Going over to the wardrobe she took out the frock she was going to put on. With growing dismay Alison watched her wriggling into it. It was a crude pink satin, skin-tight.

'Where in heaven's name did you get that dress?'

Alison asked. It was cheap, vulgar and looked home-made—as in fact it was.

'I bought the material in the *souk* and made it up myself,' Fiona declared triumphantly. 'The wardrobe mistress of the company let me use her sewing machine.' She was busy applying dark, heavy eye-liner as she spoke. With her curls piled up on her head in a Grecian cascade, her over-done make-up and the daringly low-cut frock, which revealed every line of her young body, she had achieved a sort of mock sophistication that was almost comical. In fact, Alison decided privately, her young sister looked a mess. But she didn't dare to risk the storm there would be if she said so.

'If you're coming to the dance you ought to wear something a little more interesting than that dreary old white frock,' she told Alison.

'I'm not coming to the dance,' Alison answered. 'I'm meeting Brett in the town. They'll be roasting whole sheep there in the open, and having Arab dances and music. Brett says it ought to be interesting.' She couldn't quite keep the elation out of her voice. All day she had been gloating over her evening engagement. The first Brett had suggested since the trip to Delma.

'Oh well, you can come as far as the Hotel with me in the Cadillac,' Fiona offered magnanimously, throwing on a white woollen wrap, so that the Professor, who saw them off, was spared the sight of his younger daughter's lamentable and all too revealing pink satin frock. If he was startled by the amount of make-up she had plastered on her young face, he made no comment.

Brett was waiting on the steps of the Regence where they had agreed to meet. Fiona, acknowledging his presence with a hasty, 'Hullo!', darted through the foyer into the lounge, where an animated crowd had already collected. There was a sound of dance music in the distance.

Gazing after the retreating Fiona, Brett said to Alison, 'I didn't realise they were having a public dance here tonight. Wouldn't you rather we went to that? It might be more amusing for you than a trek round the town.'

'Oh no!' Alison said quickly. 'The Arab festivities will be much more amusing. Let's get out of here before we find ourselves being caught by *Hills of Sand*.'

Brett, seeming in no hurry to move, gave her a quizzical look. 'Don't you like your film world friends any more, then?'

'They aren't my friends, but Fiona's. Even though she's finished her bit in the film she spends most of her time with them.' The note of regret in Alison's tone might have been misleading. 'Paul Everton is taking her to the dance tonight.' Somehow she was glad to be able to add that.

'I should have thought he would have asked you to go with him,' Brett persisted.

'Well, he didn't,' Alison rapped, only anxious to get away from the Hotel precincts. It would be awkward if Paul appeared, gushing all over her, even kissing her, perhaps.

'So you'll have to make do with me,' Brett was saying. 'Come on, young Warrender. Let's see what the *souks* can offer you by way of compensation.'

Compensation for what, in heaven's name! Why did he have to twist everything about her tenuous relationship with Paul Everton, making it so much more important than it was? If it had been a more favourable opportunity she would have asked him outright, but, with his hand on her arm, he was hurrying her along the narrow main street where the crowd surged around them. White robes, purple robes, rainbow-coloured *djellabahs*; the scene was as gay as a workbasket full of embroidery silks. And the noise was overwhelming, excited voices everywhere raised in exclamations and chatter. The beggars, the sellers of soft drinks and sweets, the donkey men crying '*Balak! Balak!*' as they drove their heavily laden beasts before them. From a side street came a sudden rush of bleating, scrambling sheep, being driven from the *souk* where they had been on show all through the hot day. 'Going to be watered, poor beasts, let's hope!' Brett said, edging Alison into a shop doorway while the sheep surged past. They would spend the night, Brett explained, corralled in the scrub outside the town, and be offered for sale again tomorrow. Sheep sales and horse trading were important parts of the festival, when people from all over the area came into the town.

The doorway in which they had taken refuge was occupied by an old man squatting beside a huge pannier of jasmine. Most of the strollers in the street, Alison had noticed, were wearing this flower, clusters of blossom tucked into headdresses and belts. Brett bought a spray and with a murmured, 'May I?' pushed it gently into a fold of hair behind her ear. 'Have you a pin? Will it stay put?'

She made it secure, laughing up at him, her heart light with sudden happiness. The old flower-seller nodded and smiled at the little incident, saying something in Arabic to Brett which brought a wicked twinkle to his blue eyes.'

'What did he say?' Alison demanded unwisely.

Brett's grin widened. 'That I've chosen well and that you'll make me a good wife and give me many sons.'

Alison, furious with herself for doing so, blushed crimson, Brett obviously enjoying her confusion. Then a distant burst of fireworks set him hurrying off again, eager as a small boy for the evening's fun. Alison, who had never seen him in quite so carefree a mood, had a job to keep up with him. The centre of the town when they reached it was a-blaze with torches and flares. A wide space in front of the mosque, its perimeter packed with spectators, had been cleared to accommodate a huge fire of wood, over which a whole sheep was being roasted on a spit. The figures attending to this opera-tion had an Arabian nights look, bending over the leaping, sizzling flames. Succulent odours of roasting meat hung on the air, competing with the pervading jasmine, and the less appealing aroma of packed humanity on a warm evening.

In another part of the arena, floodlit by the head-lamps of a stationary lorry, musicians, sitting on the ground, played their reed instruments and banged on their drums. Motionless before them stood the boy dancers in their conical hats.

'Let's go and watch them,' Brett suggested, and tak-ing Alison's hand, pressed his way through the crowd. Many people recognising him greeted him, and way was made for him with murmured Arabic blessings. The dancing boys were now kneeling, swaying to and fro, their arms undulating, their young faces grave. It went on interminably and seemed a little monotonous to Alison, but Brett said every movement had its sym-bolism, evidently appreciated by the crowd, who watched the performance in breathless silence.

When the boys had retired at last, their places were

taken by an almost naked fakir, who writhed silently on the ground for some minutes. Suddenly, with a cry, he leaped to his feet and an assistant handed him giant needles, which he put through his cheeks, his tongue and his lips. With the needles still in place he executed a wild dance, the assistant pressing swathes of burning straw against the soles of his feet and under his armpits. It was all pretty horrible to watch and when the fakir with a final terrible scream fell to the ground, apparently unconscious, Brett took the shuddering Alison into the shelter of his arm.

'It's all faked,' he assured her, adding a little less certainly, 'It must be! No flesh could have withstood the heat of that burning straw.'

'He could have been in a trance,' Alison suggested. 'He seemed to be working himself up into a hypnotic state when he was writhing on the ground.'

Brett shook his head. 'There are mysteries in this ancient world to which we Westerners have no answer. Those needles, for example. I've seen them before. They really pierce the cheek and tongue, and yet the next day, or even immediately after the show, there's no scar left, no bleeding.'

Alison shuddered again. 'It's scary, Brett! Let's go.'

'I know an outdoor café not far away,' Brett suggested. 'It should be quiet there. I think we've had enough of horrors for one evening.'

'But I wouldn't have missed it,' Alison assured him. 'And the dancing boys were beautiful.'

Pushing their way back through the crowd, Brett led the way down a side street full of excited sightseers; great black Negroes, graceful Bedouin, Arabs by the score, a few veiled women, a group of dancing girls on their way to some rendezvous, their foreheads tattooed, their eyes darkened with kohl. In the distance behind them the plaintive Arab music echoed. Alison felt as if she was moving in a dream.

Brett's outdoor café proved to be situated in an alley well away from the noise and bustle of the festival. They had to climb a short flight of stone steps to reach it and found themselves in a whitewashed patio enclosed by a high wall and dominated by a great central fig tree, under which tables and chairs had been set out. The only lighting came from the brilliant stars overhead, and a dim swathe of illumination from the open doorway of the café. Taking one of the tables under the fig tree, they glanced at the other customers, male exclusively, slouching over the little tables smoking their long pipes. 'Hashish mostly,' Brett said. 'They seem to thrive on it here.'

Alison sniffed the sweet pungent odour, like hay spread to dry in a field on a summer evening.

A waiter in Ali Baba slippers and voluminous trousers brought them thick sweet black coffee and a dish of Turkish delight. There were stars caught in the branches of the fig tree. Inside the café someone began to sing a sad sweet song.

Alison gave a sigh of content. 'I can't really believe I'm here!' she said. 'It's all so "rich and strange" ... so far away from the little café where we used to meet, outside the gates of St Clare's. Remember?' She couldn't help the tremor in her voice.

'I remember.' The blue eyes went dreamy. 'St Clare's certainly does seem very far away.' And after a pause, 'They were good times, Alison.' He reached across the table and took her hand.

'Especially that summer we went for long car rides,'

she ventured, 'picnicking by the river, walking on the Downs.'

'That swan at Marlow, who came tramping up out of the water on big black feet, to march over your nice clean tablecloth and help himself to a Cornish pasty.' He shook his head, laughing. 'And I was too much of a coward to shoo him away. They can be dangerous, those big cobs, especially at nesting time. He was probably taking the pasty back to a family of hungry cygnets.'

She was touched that he had remembered the comical incident. And he was still holding her hand, his fingers warm and firmly closed. It was very quiet in the patio under the fig tree, where the hashish smokers dreamed. Brett's face in the shadows showed the strong bone structure, his eyes deeply hollowed. Meeting their glance, Alison felt her pulses stir. That gently questioning look with a hint of something that could have been tenderness...

'Yes,' he said slowly, 'it was very good that spring and early summer. Even if it did end with a dance to which I couldn't take you.' Releasing her hand, he sat back in his chair. 'Which was perhaps just as well, since I'm sure you found young Simon Frayne more amusing.'

Her heart turned a somersault. 'I was waiting for you,' she began hurriedly. 'Simon happened to turn up...'

As though she had not spoken Brett was continuing: 'And tonight when I could have taken you dancing you didn't want to come.'

'I thought you'd rather see the sheep being roasted,' she said, quickly defending herself, though she didn't know yet what Brett was accusing her of. Dancing with Simon Frayne?

'So you gave up the Regence ballroom and dance band for my sake?'

'I didn't care about the dance.'

'Not even if it meant finding your film star friend waiting for you?'

So that was it! Paul again. 'I only wanted to be with you!' she cried, goaded.

'Very sweet of you, I'm sure.' It was so cynically spoken, so deliberately a snub; breaking the harmonious mood which for a few moments had seemed to hold them. She could have wept. Their lovely evening spoiled! Why had Brett turned on her, taunting her about Paul? And once more he had spoken of Simon Frayne who had partnered her at that unlucky hospital ball. Could it be that he was jealous? That it was jealousy which had made him turn away that summer evening, seeing her in Simon's arms on the steps of the Nurses' Home. And after that he had wanted no more to do with her. But if he had really cared about her he would surely have had it out with her the next day, made a row? Just walking out on her was so strange, so cold a thing to have done.

And now he was always on at her about Paul. And he had seen her in that compromising little scene with Paul outside the cinema here in Sidi bou Kef. Could it be a case of history repeating itself? 'You like kisses', he had mocked her when they were driving back from Delma the other day.

Her thoughts whirled in confusion. If it were jealousy, not indifference which made him hold her at arm's length ... But that was too much to hope for. Jealousy meant love. If only she could talk to him freely, tell him what was going through her mind—or at least try to find out what was going on in *his*. But he was lighting his pipe, his face a mask in the little flame of the match. That knack he had of putting a steel barrier between them, and right at this moment it was well and truly in place. 'I only wanted to be with you,' she had cried unguardedly just now, giving herself away. Was it that which had made him slam the door in her face? Now she only longed for the evening to be over.

As if sensing her mood, he stood up. 'It's getting late. Perhaps we ought to be on our way. I'll drive you home.'

But confused, sick at heart, she didn't want him to drive her back to the Villa. She had had enough of his swift changes of mood, the moments of kindliness, then the coldness, the flashes of scorn. Oh, that blue and golden day at Marlow! And he had remembered the riverside picnic ... the swan stealing the pasty. Tears pricked her eyes. 'You don't have to bother to take me home,' she told him. 'If you'll just see me as far as the hotel I've got to collect Fiona.' Which was true. With the clock close on midnight it was high time she discovered what her young sister was up to in that pathetic pink frock. An amorous journey home with Paul was the last way her evening ought to end.

'I can take you both, then,' Brett was suggesting.

'It's all right,' Alison said unthinkingly. 'Fiona always has the Cadillac.'

'With the dazzling Mr Everton at the wheel. I wouldn't dream of competing.'

'Brett, *please*!' Alison cried, goaded. 'Why are you always taunting me about Paul?'

Brett's spurt of laughter was genuine. 'Honestly, Alison! You have a vivid imagination. I wouldn't dream of taunting you, about Paul, or any other man you might happen to cultivate, I was merely stating the obvious. The Cadillac must be far more comfortable for three than my humble jalopy.'

They did not speak again on the short walk to the hotel. When they reached it she thanked him for an enjoyable evening. 'My pleasure!' he murmured mechanically, and walked away.

The foyer was deserted, the sound of distant dance music throbbing in the air. Feeling bruised and shaken, Alison stood listening to it in a distracted sort of way. If only she understood Brett! But he was an enigma. That he could be jealous of her sketchy associations with chance acquaintances was too simple, too human an explanation. He was fundamentally cold towards her. There were times when she felt he despised her. Was it that he saw her as a good-time girl, shallow, frivolous, incapable of serious emotion? If she could make him see that it was not so, that there was no one in her heart or life but himself. That there never had been. She was glad now that she had cried out to him, I only want to be with you,' because it was true.

Slowly she moved towards the sound of the dance music and came to the ballroom door. A pop session was in progress. Drums and percussion were deafening. Scanning the gyrating, swaying throng, she searched for the pink satin frock, but there was no sign of Fiona. Paul too was noticeably absent. Had she come too late to forestall that dangerous starlit drive home?

'Hullo, Alison!' It was Darienne greeting her, magnificent in a colourful caftan, decked with rows of glittering beads. 'Are you looking for your sister?' Her voice was tight and hard and she was oddly pale, her great eyes flashing. 'She's gone off in the car with Paul.

God knows just where he's taken her; to some low haunt in the town, perhaps, or more likely for a prolonged petting party in the desert. They've been gone most of the evening, if it's of any interest to you!' Her voice had risen hysterically.

Alison gazed at her, dumbfounded. It wasn't only the disturbing news that Fiona had disappeared into the unknown with Paul, but the angry way Darienne had spoken. Nor was it merely concern for Fiona's welfare that was making her so distraught. Paul's defection obviously mattered to her a great deal.

'I'm sorry, Darienne,' Alison offered helplessly. Fiona is such a child; she doesn't think, doesn't mean any harm.'

'No?' The monosyllable was a sneer.

'I ought to have come to the dance with her,' Alison said guiltily. 'But I wanted to see the celebrations in the town.'

They stood staring at one another in a throbbing silence.

'There's nothing you can do about it,' Darienne ended it with a shrug. 'Just go home ... and hope for the best. Paul will bring your baby sister back in his own good time. But if I were you I should keep a closer eye on her in future. She's been seeing far more of Paul Everton than is good for her soul.'

Turning, she walked away, her beads jangling.

CHAPTER EIGHT

GOING through the revolving doors Alison looked absently about her, her thoughts all of Fiona. Where had she gone with Paul? What were they doing? Sick with worry she left the hotel garden and stood hesitant a moment in the square beyond, still thronged with festive crowds. Brett, with his offer of a lift, would long ago have disappeared. She would have to walk home. It was pitch-dark in the narrow sandy lane, the trees shutting out even the dim starlight. A chill breeze was blowing across the desert and the rustle of the palm trees made an eerie sound. But Alison was too preoccupied to be nervous.

The Villa was in darkness when she reached it, her father having already gone to bed. In her own room she undressed, feeling utterly helpless. It was all wrong to be getting ready for sleep while Fiona was heaven knew where ... with the charming, unscrupulous Paul. But standing around in her nightdress wasn't going to help, so she got into bed and lay staring into the darkness, not daring to shut an eye inviting sleep.

It was close on five o'clock when at last she heard a soft rustle in the lounge beyond her open bedroom door. She had left the verandah door open too, so that Fiona could get into the house with the minimum of noise. Simplest to keep this nocturnal adventure from their father—at all events for the moment. Later it might be wise to have a word with him about Fiona's involvement with Paul Everton. Just now Alison could feel only relief that her night's vigil had ended, and that the wanderer had returned—in what state it remained to be seen!

'Is that you, Fiona?' she called softly.

Fiona, slippers in hand, edged into the bedroom, her finger to her lips. When Alison turned on the bedside light she blinked. There were streaks of mascara on her cheeks, as if she had been weeping. But her expression was radiant, her eyes shining. 'Is Pa asleep?' she whispered.

'Naturally,' Alison answered coldly. 'Do you realise it's getting on for breakfast time? Where on earth have you been all night? I've been worried stiff about you.'

'I know. I was afraid you would be.' Fiona gave a little giggle and sat down on the edge of the bed. The home-made dress was draggled and shapeless by now, the piled-up curls drunkenly adrift. 'Paul took me for a run in the car,' she began, 'and we broke down somewhere in the middle of the desert.'

Alison uttered a scornful, 'That hoary old excuse!' Anger and anxiety churned within her. 'Oh, Fiona, what sort of a fool have you been tonight?' she cried.

Once more Fiona giggled. 'Now don't you start on at me, Ally! You're not my maiden aunt. I haven't been any sort of fool. The car really did break down, or Paul said it did, and who was I to contradict him? If it was an excuse for a spot of petting, what of it?'

'Fiona!' Alison breathed helplessly.

'All right, "Auntie", don't get excited. When he began to get rather too intense I put on the brakes. Paul was a bit cross about that and went all sulky for a while. But he didn't start the car. We just sat there in that spooky desert silence until a great shadowy beast loomed up in front of us. Paul said it was only a donkey, but I was sure it was a lion. I was scared to death and begged Paul to take me home. Still sulking, he got out and fiddled with the engine and made it come right, if it had ever been wrong. The noise sent the lion or whatever it was galloping off into the darkness.' Fiona yawned. 'Gosh, I'm tired!'

'Is that the whole story?' Alison asked doubtfully.

Fiona shook her tumbled curls and went into a sort of beatific trance. 'It's only the beginning. After Paul fixed the car we set off, making as we thought for Sidi, still not on very good terms. Then we got really lost in a sandy waste where there was no road. It was terrifying. I realised Paul hadn't a clue where we were heading. Though he tried to put a brave face on it, I could see he was worried stiff. I wondered what would happen if we ran out of petrol, and Paul was thinking the same thing. So he said we'd better stop and wait for a glimmer of daylight. It was horribly cold, but he wrapped his coat around me and took me in his arms. Somehow we forgot all about our little quarrel.' A look of fatuous bliss came over Fiona's tired little face. 'It was all marvellous after that. Paul is so sweet when you really get to know him. The wonderful things he said to me! I think we're going to be married.'

'What!' Alison all but shouted. Then lowering her voice more cautiously, remembering the sleeping Professor the other side of the thin wall: 'Do you mean Paul Everton actually proposed to you?'

'Not in so many words, perhaps,' Fiona returned predictably. 'But everything he said pointed that way. I'm the only girl he's ever really loved. He can't live without me ... he only wants to make me happy, show me what love is really all about ...'

'I bet he does!' Alison said bitterly.

Fiona looked dashed. 'I know it must sound a bit phoney in the cold light of morning ...'

'It certainly does!' Alison agreed.

'Now don't start being horrible, Alison. Paul loves me. I trust him. You don't understand.'

'I understand only too well. Paul Everton is about as much to be trusted as a prowling tiger. Every woman he meets has to fall for him, pander to him, assure him that he's irresistible. He tried it on with me when I first came here.'

'That's what infuriates you,' Fiona put in angrily. 'You're jealous because he's switched his interest to me. It's been obvious since the moment I arrived. If you could have seen the look on your face when you saw me with Paul that day at the airport!'

Alison groaned. 'Paul switches his interest, as you call it, six times a day. Haven't you seen him with Sally the continuity girl ... and Darienne Chevasse? I've an idea there's something pretty serious between him and Darienne.'

'They're just good friends ... he told me.'

'And of course you believed him!' Alison mocked.

Fiona stood up, her face an angry red. 'Oh, it's no use talking to you! All this superior big-sister act. Just because you're a few years older than I am you think you can push me around, jeer at me. I won't tell you any more.'

'So we're to leave you sitting in the desert in the middle of nowhere. How did you get home in the end?'

'Just after first light a camel train turned up, making for the festival,' Fiona conceded grudgingly. 'They put us back on the road again. As it happened we were quite close to the town.'

'How amazing!' Alison couldn't keep the irony out of her tone.

'There you go again,' Fiona accused.

'I'm just trying to *help* you, Fiona,' Alison pleaded, 'trying to make you see sense. You're heading for nothing but trouble if you continue this friendship with Paul, imagining he's in love with you. He isn't capable of love. He only loves himself—has to have admiration from every woman he meets.'

'I'd rather not discuss it any more.' With an air of wounded dignity, Fiona walked towards the door, swaying seductively. It would have been funny if it were not so pathetic. The tumbled curls, the cheap bedraggled satin frock, bursting apart at the ill-sewn seams. A child dressed up, playing at being grown up. 'As long as Pa doesn't realise I was out on the tiles all night...'

'He was in bed and asleep when I came in soon after twelve,' Alison said. 'Having seen us start off together after dinner last night he was possibly under the impression we would be together the rest of the evening.'

'Well, don't tell him we weren't.'

Alison made no promises and Fiona crept away to her belated rest. Switching off the bedside lamp, Alison lay back on her pillows, weary after her sleepless night. But there was no chance of sleeping now. Fiona had given her more than enough to think about. Poor silly Fiona! What was to become of her? How would she face up to the inevitable disillusionment? Alison prayed it would come before any serious harm had been done. At the moment the poor kid would be as wax in Paul's unscrupulous hands.

The cold air of dawn was blowing through the verandah door, which Fiona had left open. Getting up to close it, Alison stood looking out over the shadowy garden. Caught in this moment of mystery between light and dark, flowers and shrubs had a magic unfamiliar air. Like a ghostly presence, the light breeze stirred, ruffling leaves and blossom. But the tranquil scene brought no peace to her troubled heart. What could she do about Fiona? Ought she to tell their father about last night's escapade? He would be embarrassed, at a loss, more familiar with the problems of desert reafforestation than the peccadilloes of a teenage daughter. There was only one practical course open to her, Alison realised with a sinking sensation. She would have to talk to Paul, appeal to his better nature, if he had one! If he persisted in his pursuit of her, Fiona had about as much chance as a baby rabbit with a stoat at its heels.

Shivering in the dawn air, Alison went back to bed and to her surprise slept heavily until nine, when Lalla came in with her breakfast tray.

'You ought to have called me earlier,' Alison reproached the little maid. 'I'm going to be frightfully late at the hospital.'

But things were fairly slack when she got there, the festival still being the predominant interest. Clinic attendance was light, and there were no operations. Brett greeted her coolly. 'I hope you were none the worse for your festival adventures last night,' he said when she apologised for being late to work.

'I overslept,' she confessed, and left it at that, though she longed to tell him of the worries she had run into when he left her at the hotel. Could she some time confide in him about Fiona? Ask his advice? Her motives, she realised, were not wholly disinterested. It would be one way of showing him how clearly she saw through Paul Everton, and what a low opinion she had of him. But it would also make Fiona appear in a pretty sordid role, the silly victim of a would-be seducer. Best, she decided regretfully, to leave Brett out of it.

She could have the morning off, he said, since there was so little going on. He was dressed, unfamiliarly, in open-necked shirt and whipcord breeches, and told her he was going to visit a patient in an outlying village, riding instead of taking the car, as there was no road to speak of.

'I didn't know you were a horseman,' she said.

He grinned, looking pleased with himself. 'An accomplishment I picked up since I came out here. One couldn't very well be in this land of superlative horsemanship and not have a bash. My mount is a well-behaved little mare, named Shani. Come and meet her.'

She followed him out of the hospital and watched him ride away, her pulses quickening, the elemental thrill produced by the sight of a well-set-up man on a superb mount. He rode well; but everything Brett did would be done well. When he had vanished round a corner of the dusty street her thoughts returned with a sick jerk to Fiona, who had been fast asleep when she left the Villa. She would sleep probably until lunch-time after her wild night out.

Would this be a good time to get hold of Paul? Alison wondered. Talking to him about Fiona wasn't going to be very pleasant, and the sooner she got it over the better. Perhaps he was in the town filming bits of the festival. But walking to the main square she found no sign of him or his camera crew. He was probably still in the hotel.

It was there she found him, drinking iced lager with a couple of cameramen.

'Alison, how marvellous of you to drop in!' he greeted her ecstatically. Leaving his companions he hurried over to her and put an arm about her waist. 'The dance was desolate without you last night,' he said softly.

'So you consoled yourself with my little sister.'

Paul laughed smugly. 'Not jealous, are you, sweetie? There's no need to be.'

She could have boxed his ears, but controlling her dislike of him said, with a glance at the beer-drinking cameramen: 'Look, Paul, I've got to talk to you. Can't we go somewhere quiet?'

He gave her a wary glance.

'You kept Fiona out all night,' she went on.

'So I'm to be hauled over the coals,' he shrugged. 'It was all an accident, my dear; pure accident. Oh, very pure!' he giggled fatuously. Once more she longed to hit him.

'Don't look so worried: I can explain it all.' He put an urgent hand on her arm. 'But I can't stop now. We're off to the market-place to take a few shots of a snake-charmer doing things to cobras. What about a quiet little chat tonight? Over a bite of dinner? All right? I could call for you at the Villa about eight. If I've been overdoing it a mite with Fiona this should give her something to think about, make her realise she isn't the only pebble on the beach and so forth.'

It was a cruel suggestion. And how exactly like Paul to make it! But it might just work, Alison mused; give Fiona the jolt back to reality she so sorely needed. Also it seemed to be the only way of achieving that quiet talk with Paul. 'Right,' she agreed. 'I'll be expecting you.'

With impudent assurance he dropped a light kiss on

her brow and went back to the bar. The nerve of the man! And he hadn't even offered her a drink. Not that she would have accepted one, though she was hot and thirsty. She was glad to be out of the hotel, on her way home.

Fiona, who had only just got up, was her usual cheery self at lunch time, chatting away to her father, assuming an interest in his work which pleased him. Her questions were surprisingly knowledgeable and to the point, though she barely listened to the answers.

She's manipulating him, Alison thought bleakly, getting him ready for the moment when she has to disclose her involvement with Paul Everton. She knows he won't approve. For John Warrender had made no secret of his reservations about Fiona's film-world friends, only tolerating the association for her because he thought she was solely interested in the novelty of playing her small part in the making of *Hills of Sand*.

They lingered over dessert, the great bowl of fresh fruit Lalla brought to the table daily. The seedlings were all planted now, John Warrender told them with satisfaction—flat top eucalyptus, ivory and blue leaf acacia, Arizona cypresses ... Now all that remained was to see them established. There was the problem of irrigation. 'Not too much water and not too little,' John Warrender mused. 'Trees, like people, are inclined to be lazy. If you over-water them the roots don't do their work. Keep them a little short and they push down, finding even in this sandy soil supplies of moisture to feed on. However,' he ended, 'another couple of weeks should see us in the clear.'

Did that mean returning to England? Alison wondered with a sickening pang. But of course they would be returning sooner or later. Why did she let herself go drifting on, feeling she was here for ever? Like the trees, putting down roots, even in the sandy soil of Brett's indifference.

When presently John Warrender left in his estate car to return to the scene of his labours Fiona went with him, saying he could drop her off in the town. She was going to the coiffeur's in the Regence to have her hair set, she announced.

More likely she was going in search of Paul, Alison thought uneasily, and could only hope he would still be occupied with his snakes and cobras in the market-place. Fitting companions for him!

Drowsy after her sleepless night, she retired to the verandah after lunch and dozed in one of the long cane chairs. Half asleep and half awake, she watched the gardening boy drifting in a leisurely fashion about his work. How wise these people were, who lived in the sunshine, never hurrying and apparently never worrying. 'Peace'! they called to one another a dozen times a day. 'Peace' they murmured on their knees when they answered the muezzin's call to prayer. And peace it seemed to be. The thought carried her into a dreamless slumber. How long it lasted she did not know, only that a movement at her side aroused her. She opened her eyes to find Brett looking down at her. Her heart jumped.

'I was just about to waken you in the traditional fashion,' he said.

She held up her face to him. 'You don't have to wait till you find me asleep...' She spoke impulsively and instantly regretted the easy invitation, which he ignored. 'You like kisses,' he had once taunted her. Any man's kisses, was the implication. Oh, why did she always in moments of crisis have to say the wrong thing to Brett? And anyway, why was it a moment of crisis? Because he had found her asleep, her defences down, just as he had done that day she had first discovered his presence in Sidi bou Kef.

She said, with a self-conscious little laugh, 'You must think I spend all my spare time snoring the hours away on this verandah.'

He looked a little puzzled. Perhaps he had forgotten that earlier meeting. She patted the chair at her side and he sat down. Why had he come? she wondered. 'Was it a good ride this morning?' she asked.

'All right,' he answered, without enthusiasm, his thoughts obviously otherwise engaged. He was still in riding kit and said he had left his horse tethered in the lane outside the Villa gate. 'Actually, I dropped in to ask if you would like to have dinner with me tonight. Last evening wasn't much of an effort, a cup of sticky black coffee and a lump of Turkish delight. I can do you better than that. There's a small restaurant behind the Medina where they serve excellent native dishes, cous-cous, of course, and another concoction which is a mixture of onions, pimentoes, tomatoes, potatoes and soft-boiled eggs. It may sound revolting, but I assure you it's something you ought to sample before you leave Algeria.'

She could have wept. That Brett should ask her to dinner on the one night she would have to refuse!

She said, 'Oh, Brett, I'd love to come to your wonderful restaurant ... more than anything else in the world I'd adore to have dinner with you. But could you make it some other night? I've got a date I can't very well break. It concerns Fiona . . .' She broke off, baffled by the impossibility of telling him the whole sordid little story. 'I'm terribly sorry,' she blundered on, 'but I just can't make it.'

'I see,' was Brett's terse reception of her refusal. He stood up, his face clouded, his blue eyes steady and cold, looking down at her.

'I'm so disappointed, Brett. Can't we make an arrangement for another evening? I've absolutely nothing on the cards for the rest of the week. If I had I'd cancel it.'

'But you can't cancel tonight?'

She shook her head, her heart beating thickly. 'No, tonight it would be quite out of the question.' She had to act quickly on Fiona's behalf. Paul must be dealt with before it was too late.

'I'm afraid we must leave it for the present,' Brett said. 'It's not easy for me to make dates ahead ... foresee my commitments.'

Alison walked through the garden with him to where Shani had been tied up. She whinnied appealingly at the sight of her master.

'Do you ride very often?' Alison asked.

'Not often enough. It's the only exercise I get. Sometimes I go for an early morning canter in the desert, but most of my peregrinations are made behind the wheel of my hot, smelly little car.' He sounded, disgruntled, put out. It was clear he had been upset by her refusal of his dinner invitation. How upset? Alison asked herself, searching hungrily for some sign of Brett's reviving interest in her. But she mustn't kid herself. His reaction could well be simple chagrin. He had come out here on a generous impulse to invite her to dine, and she had turned him down. A blow to his male vanity ... no more. She ought to have swept that other phantasmal engagement aside, he would think.

She watched him ride away and returned heavy-hearted to the house to face the complications of her evening with Paul. How would she dress? The black filmy frock was too dressy and provocative, the simple white one overdue for a trip to the cleaners. Which left her with a nondescript blue-green affair she had worn through two summers. But the dowdier she was, the better, she told herself. Paul's opinion of her dress sense couldn't matter less.

It was almost seven when Fiona came home with her hair newly set. Alison found her in her room putting on a new frock of violet taffeta. 'I bought it in that snazzy boutique in the Regence,' Fiona explained, turning a slim back to be zipped up. 'Suits me, doesn't it?'

'It's quite a frock,' Alison murmured with little enthusiasm, finding the violet taffeta even less attractive than the pink satin effort of the night before. It was quite the wrong style and colour for Fiona's youthful prettiness. 'You're being a bit lavish with new frocks, aren't you? How come?'

'Can't you guess?' Fiona smiled dreamily into the mirror, as she applied a generous daub of eye-liner. 'There's another dance at the hotel tonight and I know Paul will want to take me to it. Naturally, I'm going to look my best.'

'Has Paul asked you to this dance?'

'No. But it goes without saying that we shall be spending the evening together, now that we're practically engaged.'

'Fiona!' Alison gasped. 'When will you come to your senses! You're not going out with Paul tonight. *I* am. He's coming to fetch me at eight.'

Fiona stared at her as if she didn't believe her ears.

'How do you mean, you're going out with Paul to-night?'

'I met him this morning and he invited me.'

'To join us, you mean?' Fiona suggested. 'It is just like him not to want you to feel left out.'

Alison shook her head. 'That's not how it is, Fiona. He wants me on my own. He made that very clear.'

Fiona sat down on the edge of her bed, her small face bewildered. 'You must be joking, Alison. Unless it's that he feels he has to talk to you about me, tell you the way things are going between us. Ask your permission for my hand, or something,' she ended with a laugh. 'He knows the way you fuss over me, like an old mother hen.'

Help! Alison thought. This whole exercise is going to lose its impact if I don't handle it more brutally.

'Listen, Fiona! You've got to stop taking your friendship with Paul so seriously. He would think nothing of taking you out one night, and me out the next. Just so long as he's got a girl to tote around and say sweet nothings to...'

'I won't listen to you!' Fiona cried, putting her hands over her ears. 'You're just being jealous and horrible, trying to put me off Paul, because you want him yourself. You've been doing it ever since I came. But it's no good. I've spent hours and hours in his company. I know him better than you ever will. If he asked you to have dinner with him tonight, it's because you worked it in some devious fashion. But it doesn't mean a thing. You can't tell me that everything he said about loving me last night was a lie.'

'That's just what I am telling you,' Alison confirmed relentlessly. She glanced at her wrist-watch. 'Gosh! It's just on eight now! I expect Paul is waiting for me in the lane. I told him I would meet him there.'

'So that you could sneak off with him without my knowing,' Fiona accused, following Alison across the verandah. 'But I'm not going to let you get away with this. I'm coming, too. You're just doing this to hurt me, Alison, making Paul take you out. You *worked* it,' she repeated.

'Who worked what?' said Paul, appearing suddenly, walking up the shadowy pathway between the shoulder-high rose bushes. The garden was in darkness, save for the glimmer from the low powered lamps on the verandah. Wearing a white suit, he looked tall and wraith-like, advancing with arms outstretched. Fiona running to him, flung herself into them. 'Paul! Paul!' she began in a tearful voice.

'Now then, honey-baby!' he tilted her face upwards and kissed her lips. 'Alison and I have a little business to discuss tonight, so you be a good girl and stay at home until your Uncle Paul is free to come and fetch you.'

'You mean you'll come for me later on?' Fiona asked breathlessly.

'Uh-huh,' Paul murmured non-committally. Fiona continued to cling to him, and gently he loosed himself from her grasp. 'I'm sorry, sweetie, but I've got this date with your big sister, and there it is. We've got things to discuss ... like I told you. Things that concern you.'

Fiona flashed a triumphant glance at Alison. 'I knew that's how it was!' she exulted.

Paul held out a hand to Alison. Ignoring it, she walked before him through the garden, angry and baffled. Fiona, who had retired to stand under the verandah lights, waved them off imperturbably. 'Be seeing you later, Paul,' she called after them confidently.

In the car as they drove off, Alison maintained a stony silence.

'So we start off with me in the doghouse,' Paul said with an unrepentant grin. 'Maybe you'd condescend to tell me what I'm supposed to have done wrong?'

Alison rounded on him, shaking with indignation. 'What sort of a man are you? Telling Fiona you would be coming back for her. Can't you see what you're doing to that child? She thinks she's the love of your life.'

'She's so cute!' Paul murmured fatuously.

'I thought the whole idea of my having dinner with you this evening was to make her realise you can take me out as easily as you can take her out—and that none of it matters to you a great deal. Then you go and spoil the whole thing...'

'What else could I do when she literally threw herself into my arms?' Paul demanded in a tone of injured innocence. A momentary frown crumpled his untroubled brow. 'You keep out of this, Alison, and let me handle it in my own way. I'll get it across to Fiona that I think you're both swell and that I can enjoy being with either of you. Which is exactly how it is. So why all the fuss?'

They were pulling up outside the Regence as he spoke. Alison made no attempt to get out of the car. 'I think you might as well drive me straight home, for all the good I'm doing in trying to talk to you about Fiona. You're just too stupid to understand.'

Paul opened the car door at her side. 'Now, Alison, *please*! I'm sorry if I sounded frivolous just now. It's just that your schoolmarm manner gets my goat. I don't want to hurt Fiona, I promise you. If you'll come in and have a quiet meal with me, I'll try to explain myself. I'm very fond of the child.'

Did he mean he was serious about her? Alison stared at him in bewilderment.

'I'll do whatever you think best,' he urged. 'Break with her, if you think I should. Only it would have to be done carefully, gradually. A clumsy let-down on my part just now could do her a lot of harm—if she's as involved with me as you say. I didn't realise it. Anyway, let's talk it all out. I've got Fiona's welfare at heart as much as you have.'

Which was a bit much to swallow. But there was truth in Paul's observation about a clumsy handling of the end of the poor little affair. Was he capable of putting into action the tact and wisdom his remarks implied? Still doubtful, Alison got out of the car and followed him into the hotel. The moment they crossed the foyer they were surrounded by the inevitable crowd of film company bar loungers. Alison found herself drinking a dry Martini with Tony Wren, the chief cameraman. Paul, with his elbow on the counter, was more or less wrapping himself round Sally, the continuity girl. The moments flew by. This is hopeless, Alison was beginning to think, when Darienne appeared, squired by Pierre Jamelle, the male lead. She gave Alison a cool nod and her glance went to Paul and Sally. Ignoring Darienne's arrival, he continued his heart-to-heart chat. He couldn't talk to any woman of any age, Alison had noticed, without that air of complete involvement, hanging on his companion's every word, riveting her with a rapturous gaze, as though she was the only woman in the world. Had he forgotten he was supposed to be taking her to dinner?

Alison wondered. Moving away from Tony Wren, she edged herself into his line of vision. The ruse worked and he hailed her with an exaggerated exclamation of delight, abandoning Sally.

A few moments later they were seated in his favourite alcove in the dining-room, two waiters fussing over them. He made a prolonged ceremony of ordering, and it turned out to be the kind of meal which kept the waiters coming and going, cooking things on chafing dishes close to their table—not exactly the atmosphere for the serious conversation they were supposed to be having. Nor did it help when Darienne and Pierre appeared and took a table within earshot. Paul, with an uneasy eye on Darienne, talked impersonally, mostly about, *Hills of Sand*. The picture was just about in the can, he told Alison. In a short while the company would be pulling up stakes and heading back to Paris.

'You can't go too soon for me,' Alison broke in, her patience exhausted, her voice shrill above the hubbub of diners and waiters. 'If you can just keep away from my sister until you leave Sidi perhaps not too much harm will have been done. As for ending the miserable little affair tactfully and gradually, as you suggested just now, I think that's utterly beyond your crude capabilities.'

'Look, sweetie!' Paul stopped her. 'If you're going to give me hell we'd better get out on to the terrace. I'm scared of women when they start bawling me out, and I don't want a scene in here.'

'As long as you know you deserve a scene, that you realise what a heel you are...' She hated him so much that she didn't care how loudly she was shouting at him or who overheard her. And come to that, the more

Darienne picked up of their exchange the better.

Thoroughly alarmed, Paul jumped from his seat, and taking her arm urged her out of the room, leaving their dessert untouched. If it was a somewhat dramatic exit, neither of them was in the mood to care. French windows closing behind them ejected them on to a wide stone terrace. The garden below them was dimly lit by the lights from the dining-room.

'There's an arbour somewhere,' Paul muttered, seeking even greater privacy. It proved to be a vine-clad bower, supported by stone pillars covered with climbing roses. There was a wooden bench, a weatherbeaten table, a smell of damp and roses.

'I haven't told my father of the way you're pestering Fiona,' Alison began, 'but if you don't leave her alone I shall have to urge him to take some action.'

'Pestering?' Paul sounded hurt. 'Look, Alison my dear, how *did* all this get so out of hand? What are you accusing me of? Perhaps it wasn't very wise of me to take Fiona off into the desert last night—but it was so hot and stuffy in the ballroom. I thought a breath of fresh air would do us both good. Then I missed the road—we were lost, genuinely lost for some hours, during which time I treated your sister with the utmost consideration. If she's given you any other impression...'

'She's got it firmly into her head that you proposed to her last night,' Alison broke in.

Paul made an exasperated sound. 'I didn't realise she was that dumb. If she thought it was matrimony I was talking about...'

Then Alison's temper flared and she let herself go. Just what she said she couldn't remember afterwards, only that she had the maddening feeling that none of it was really getting through. Paul just stood there in the dim light, an unruffled expression on his handsome face, letting the tirade roll over him. Gradually it was borne in on her that he wasn't even listening, his eyes smouldering as they raked her face, her hair, her frock. She felt his hands on her shoulders.

'You're so beautiful when you're angry, Alison!' The unruffled look had vanished. His voice was hoarse and shaken. 'If you'd been nicer to me in the first place this silly business with Fiona would never have happened. You don't know how crazy I am about you. I've thought about you constantly since that magic morning I found you in the desert.' He was speaking rapidly, breathlessly, his hands moving over her, caressing her. Strong hands from which there was no escape.

'Please, Paul!' She tried without success to push him away.

'Be nice to me, Alison. You don't know what you mean to me—maybe because right from the start you've been giving me the brush-off. Something that doesn't often happen to me. I find it exciting. You're so lovely, so cool, so unapproachable ... it sends me wild. I've tried to put you out of my mind, fooling around with your little sister. But it's no use. I've got to have you. Marry me, Alison! Come to Paris with me.'

'Are you mad?' She tried once more to twist away from his grasp. 'I wouldn't marry you if you were the last man on earth. I loathe you, despise you ...'

Besottedly he gazed at her. It was as if he had not heard her, an egomaniac with a hide so insensitive that it was impenetrable. He began to kiss her and she was helpless in his strong arms.

It was just at that moment that a French window on the terrace crashed open, and Darienne appeared. Perhaps from past experience, she made straight for the arbour. Paul's arms fell away from Alison with a suddenness that sent her reeling against one of the rose-covered pillars.

'Hullo, sweetie!' he greeted Darienne with such an obvious air of guilt that it was comical. But nobody laughed.

'Sweetie indeed!' Darienne echoed bitterly. 'You and the two Warrender girls—I'm just about sick of it.' She swung round on Alison. 'This isn't what I meant when I told you to get your little sister to lay off my man. For that's what he is, for what he's worth. My man! For the past year I've worked with him, loved him ... if we haven't married yet it's because we haven't had time to get around to it. We'd planned to announce our engagement on the opening night of the film.' Her voice broke on a sob. 'Paul thought it would make good publicity.'

'So it will,' Paul put in imperturbably. After his first startled reaction at Darienne's appearance he had pulled himself together surprisingly quickly. Perched on the edge of the rickety table, he surveyed the two women with an air of kindly condescension. He turned to Alison with a rueful shrug. 'Seems I'm not as free as I thought I was. Perhaps it is just as well you loathe and despise me.'

'You're beneath contempt!' Alison exploded. To Darienne she said, 'I don't suppose you'll believe it, but what you saw as you came out on the terrace just now was none of my seeking. I came here tonight to beg Paul to leave my sister alone, and was answered with a crazy marriage proposal.'

'Oh, I know how he works. And in case you're under any misapprehension all that "will you marry me" routine is just a line he uses when he can't get his girl in any other way.' Darienne covered her face with her hands. 'He's just a cheap womaniser, and I love him!'

Paul said, 'Now, honey!' and heaving himself reluctantly from the rickety arbour table, drew her into his arms. Making no protest, Darienne melted into his embrace. 'You think you can get away with murder!' Alison heard her say. 'You think I'm so sold on you you can do what you like with me...'

Unnoticed, she crept away, leaving them to sort it out as best they could. She would slip out through the garden, avoid going back into the dining-room where curious glances might await her. There was a gate somewhere, leading out into the square. As she approached it she heard a faint rustle of bushes behind her and the muffled cry, 'Alison!'

She turned sharply. 'Fiona! What on earth...!'

With a moan Fiona fell into her arms. She was shaking from head to foot. 'I was waiting and waiting at home, for Paul to come back for me,' she said in a dry stunned tone. 'When he didn't arrive I had to come and find him.' A violent shudder ran through her. 'I thought you were keeping him from me, that you wouldn't let him go.' Alison held her more closely.

'I didn't like to come through the foyer in case you thought I was pursuing you, so I decided I'd just have a peep through the dining-room windows.' The confused little explanation trailed away. She began to cry.

'Don't, darling, he isn't worth one tear,' Alison begged.

For a moment Fiona was too choked with sobs to speak. 'I heard everything,' she managed at last. The sobs shook her thin shoulders. 'First you, and then Darienne. Oh, Alison, what am I going to do?'

CHAPTER NINE

THERE was a crowded surgery the next morning, people tiring of the festival remembering their ailments once more. Most of them were minor ailments, a mother with a baby for vaccination, a toddler with whooping cough, which was very prevalent in Sidi bou Kef, and without the aid of modern drugs often proved to be a killer. Brett produced the classic injection and the wailing toddler was removed, to be replaced by a T.B. suspect, a skin rash and an old man with red weeping eyes who had to be taken by Alison into the little ante-room and given irrigation treatment, after which she took up her sentry stand by the consulting-room desk again, resenting it. Who was it that had decreed that all nurses must stand in awed respect while doctors sat? Some starched old follower of Florence Nightingale in the nineteenth century? It gave swollen-headed young men even more swollen-headed opinions of themselves. And Brett was not in the humblest of moods this morning.

He had greeted her curtly when she arrived, barely looking up from the papers before him on his desk, seemingly absorbed in some abstruse problem, his brow furrowed. It struck Alison as a little bit phoney, and in the brief glance he had conceded her his eyes had been steely, almost colourless—Brett at his most poker-faced.

Was it possible he had seen her at the Regence last night with Paul? She remembered with a sinking heart that when she and Fiona had come out into the little square last night she had thought she saw Brett's

Citröen parked with a bunch of more opulent cars not far from the hotel entrance. But she had been too occupied with Fiona to look closely. Anyway, what did it matter? Only that it might have been better if she had been more open about her evening engagement. But Brett was so unreasonable about her contacts with Paul.

Two little Arab women came into the surgery, heavily veiled and almost too scared to speak. They knew no English and refused to understand Brett's attempts at Arabic, which did not improve his temper. Alison tried to smooth out the situation, talking to the women in French, persuading them that it was all right for the one who was the patient to remove her veil and allow the doctor to examine her chest.

'The doctor,' she assured them, 'is not as other men.'

'Thanks very much, I'm sure!' Brett muttered. It might have been meant humorously, but there was no glimmer of a smile on his set young mouth. Nor did Alison find it funny. She was tired after her second sleepless night in succession, and the scene which had gone on and on after she and Fiona reached the Villa still haunted her. Fiona sobbing with such hysterical abandon that it had brought their father from his room. After that there was the sort of painful family row that can leave scars. Somehow the whole pitiful little story of Fiona's entanglement with Paul Everton came out. 'If only I hadn't hidden in the hotel garden last night!' she wailed unreasonably. 'The way he was going on with Alison ... and the awful things she said to him.'

'At least you know now I wasn't trying to take him away from you,' Alison pointed out.

'I waited all evening here thinking he would come

for me, until I couldn't stand it any longer and just *had* to go to the hotel to find him. It was terrifying going down that dark lane under the trees. There were Arabs creeping about in the shadows.'

'Why didn't you take me into your confidence?' the Professor asked, in bewilderment. 'You knew I was here, in my room.'

Buried in his papers and reports as usual, Alison thought bitterly.

'I couldn't talk to you; you wouldn't have understood,' Fiona was answering him. 'I thought Alison was trying to get Paul away from me. I hated her ... I could have killed her!'

John Warrender said angrily, 'Stop talking such utter nonsense, Fiona. Alison was perfectly right to send the fellow about his business. I can't understand your ever becoming involved with him ... going off for midnight rides with him, making a complete fool of yourself over a man who never for a moment had any serious intentions towards you. In fact it's abundantly clear that what intentions he had were strictly dishonourable.' He paused to give her a despairing look. 'Just what did go on between you and this fellow last night? You'd better tell me the rest of it.'

'He was sweet to me,' Fiona sobbed. 'He couldn't help it if we got lost in the desert. He comforted me when I was scared, didn't even go on kissing me when I said I didn't think he should ...'

'Well, thank God for that!' The Professor mopped his brow. 'But I hope you realise how foolish you've been.'

Accepting the bitter truth at last, Fiona was deeply ashamed of herself, and it didn't help to realise that her father too was ashamed of her. His anger was no balm for her wounds. Alison had tried to provide what comfort she could for both of them. In his way John Warrender was as troubled as his younger daughter. Hysterical young women were not exactly his province.

'I want to go home,' Fiona wept. 'I can't stay here another day. I hate this place and everybody in it. I wish I were back with Dora, poor Dora in strange stables, probably fretting for me. I ought not to have left her.'

This was a point of view Alison felt should be encouraged. If Fiona could think of anything outside herself and her love troubles, even a pony, there was hope for her. This foolish episode with Paul Everton would in time be forgotten.

It had been well into the small hours when she made them all some hot tea and at last got Fiona off to bed. She herself was too strung up to sleep and watched the dawn break over the palm trees and roses.

Now as she showed the last of the patients out and set about clearing up the surgery her eyes felt like orbs of lead set in gritty sand. Brett was noisily banging the drawers of the filing cabinet, his face a thunder-cloud.

He *did* see me with Paul last night, Alison thought with a sinking heart. His car had been outside the hotel—which meant he had probably come into the lounge bar for a drink. It would have been a very natural thing for him to do.

Ferociously he cleared his throat, then turning to her abruptly, said, 'I hope you enjoyed your evening with Everton at the Regence last night.'

'You're good at snooping, aren't you, Brett!' The moment it was out she could have bitten off her tongue.

The look he gave her was one of utter disgust. 'I

think that's a remark best ignored.' And after a pause and some more banging at the filing cabinet: 'Don't think I care whether you go out with theatrical celebrities or not. You're your own mistress. It's just that I feel you might have paid me the very minor compliment of being a little more frank with me. I don't see why you had to make such a mystery of your evening engagement—or why, come to that, if you have any regard for me at all, and knowing how few my free evenings are, you couldn't have postponed your dinner with Everton.'

She said helplessly, 'I couldn't postpone it, Brett. There were *reasons*. I can't tell them to you without betraying somebody else's confidence.'

'For heaven's sake!' Brett growled. 'All this melodrama about betrayal of confidences. You went out with Everton because you like going out with Everton.'

'No!' Alison cried out.

Brett kicked the bottom drawer of the filing cabinet shut with a vicious bang. Alison dropped a noisy handful of instruments into a dish of surgical spirit. The air throbbed with things unspoken.

'Paul Everton is every kind of a heel,' Alison brought out at last. 'I hate him, despise him...'

'And you went out to dinner with him to tell him so?'

'Yes. Roughly, that's the way it was. He's been giving my young sister a terrific run-round ever since she got here, and she's going to be badly hurt.'

'So you decided he could give you a run-round instead.' Brett treated her to his deadliest cold stare and stalked out of the room.

Back at the Villa Alison found Fiona still in bed, weeping.

'Fiona darling, you've *got* to snap out of it!' Alison sat on the edge of the bed and stroked the tousled head. 'Why not wash your face, put some clothes on and come and have lunch?'

'I don't want any lunch,' Fiona wailed, and burst into a fresh spate of sobs. 'I hate him! I hate him! I wish I'd never set eyes on him!'

Alison said bracingly, 'That's the spirit! Now you realise how despicable he is you don't have to go on fretting about him. He isn't worth a single tear. What about a nice bath? I'll turn the water on for you.'

But Fiona only buried her poor little swollen face deeper into the pillows and choked with sobs. John Warrender, who had just come in from a morning's trek in the heat, stood looking in at the bedroom door with a helpless air. 'Tears, tears and more tears,' he sighed. 'If only I could have a little of this precious liquid to irrigate my trees! All this waste of water in a dry and thirsty land.'

The little joke died on the air. Fiona went on gulping, her thin shoulders shaking.

'She'll make herself ill,' Alison said, beginning to be seriously worried.

'I want to die!' moaned Fiona. Suddenly she sat up, turning her ravaged face to them, a wild gleam of hope in her eyes. 'If I could just see Paul once more, hear from his own lips what he feels about me. If everything he said about loving me was a lie, as Alison says, I'll accept it. But I want it from *him*.' There was an odd childish dignity about her in her crumpled nightgown and tangled curls. 'The way he behaved last night doesn't make sense—engaged to Darienne and then rushing at Alison and asking her to marry him. It's as if he's all adrift—just as I thought he was the first time I met him. Even the way he went on with me was because he's lost and lonely. Perhaps I could be the right person for him after all.'

'For heaven's sake, Fiona!' John Warrender broke in impatiently. 'Where's your common sense?'

A useless question, Alison felt. Fiona was in no frame of mind for common sense, which is another word for reality. She was too dangerously lost in her world of fantasy. In this mood she was capable of any foolishness. What was to stop her rushing off to the Regence and confronting Paul? And if she did how would Paul react? He would either be angry with her—which was too much honesty to expect from him; or he would humour her, take her off into the desert again and offer her goodness knew what squalid consolation.

She had said she wanted to go home to England. Perhaps that would be the best thing for her to do. I would have to go back with her, Alison thought, her heart sinking. They could book seats on a plane and be home in a matter of hours. Both of them fleeing with broken hearts from imaginary love affairs!

John Warrender, trying the heavy father touch, was telling Fiona to get up at once and come to lunch. But Fiona only wriggled deeper down in the bed and pulled the covers over her head. She had had nothing to eat since yesterday lunch time. Last night, convinced Paul was coming to collect her, she had refused dinner, and this morning she had been far too upset to think of breakfast. How long would she continue this hysterical fast?

Alison and her father discussed it over the midday dish of the inevitable cous-cous. Fiona was behaving impossibly and would make herself really ill. 'I think

I'll run down to Sidi immediately after lunch and ask your doctor friend to come and have a look at her,' John Warrender suggested. 'Meanwhile, you'd better keep an eye on her. She's distraught enough to do something ... silly.'

Alison nodded. 'The same grim thought had occurred to me.' Yet she shrank from bringing Brett into their poor little domestic drama. Cold-eyed, clever, he wasn't the type to deal with hysteria. Psychiatry, Alison decided, was hardly up his street. Yet in his surgery at times he could be pretty penetrating with his patients, kindly and understanding. With me, she thought sadly, he's at his scornful worst.

'A nuisance there's no telephone,' John Warrender mourned, not for the first time.

'Would you like me to go for Brett?' Alison suggested a little unwillingly.

'No, it's all right, I'll go. It will be on my way to the plantation where I shall be working this afternoon. You stay with Fiona and try to get her to have something to eat.'

But Fiona refused either food or drink. 'I just can't stop crying,' she wailed. 'I don't think it's even Paul any more, that's a pain too deep for tears: it's just that my eyes are running, running and my heart is bleeding, bleeding...' Which sounded so pathetic that she wept more vigorously than ever.

Alison went to the bathroom cupboard and searched for some kind of sedative. There was only a large bottle of aspirin. Something prompted her to take it from its shelf and hide it in one of the drawers in her own bedroom, having first extracted two tablets which she took to Fiona with a glass of water. Fiona obediently swallowed them, and was promptly sick.

It was while Alison was dealing with this rather sordid little crisis that Brett with a doctor's right of way came marching through the living-room and straight through the open bedroom door.

He seemed to take in the situation at a glance. How much had John Warrender told him?

'Leave us,' he ordered Alison. 'Give me that towel.' He took the basin of warm water from her hand and turned back to Fiona, lying exhausted on her pillows, looking as wan as a little ghost. The tears had stopped. The bout of sickness appeared to have done her good.

Alison went out of the room feeling vaguely hurt. But no doubt Brett was right. Fiona would talk to him more freely if they were alone. Perhaps he was a better psychologist than she had thought. She sat herself in one of the wicker lounging chairs at the far end of the verandah, not wanting to eavesdrop. The sound of voices came drifting to her over the quiet afternoon air, Fiona's treble and Brett's deeper tones. They seemed to be having plenty to say to one another in low intimate tones—and there was no more weeping.

After about half an hour Brett emerged, his doctor's bag in his hand. 'I've given your sister an injection,' he said. 'She'll sleep now for some hours and I think you'll find her much better when she wakes up.' He handed over a small bottle of tablets. 'Give her one of these tonight and one in the morning.'

'Did she tell you what was troubling her?' Alison couldn't resist asking.

Brett gave a rueful shrug. 'Yes, poor kid, she did. Mr Paul Everton doesn't come out of it very well.'

'That's putting it mildly,' Alison flared. 'Now you know what I was trying to put right in my muddled way last night when I turned down your dinner date.'

'Quite!' Brett murmured in an uninterested way, his thoughts still apparently with his patient. 'She's of an intense temperament, your young sister. And I think she's pretty lonely.'

'Lonely?' Alison echoed in an astonished voice.

'She spoke to me of her mother. Her death made a deep impression on Fiona. She misses her perhaps more than she has shown. She longs to be important to somebody—in the special way her mother made her important. Longs to be uniquely loved—a natural desire, at her age, indeed at any age.' He gave Alison one of his more inscrutable looks. 'But intensified in Fiona's case by her mother's death, coming at a critical time in her childhood.'

In fascinated silence Alison waited for more. Brett the great analyst, the healer of souls; this was a new facet of his medical skill. Unless it was just plain human sympathy and insight, qualities she had never suspected he possessed.

'Away in boarding school,' he went on, 'she feels herself cut off, not quite a part of the family. It's you who are the important one, in your role of housekeeper. Inevitably you're closer to your father than she is. So when our film-making friend produced his spurious brand of that overworked word "love", she fell for it in a big way.' He broke off, looking suddenly and most uncharacteristically diffident—almost boyish and confused.

'All this must sound like damned cheek, probing into your family affairs. I don't after all set up to be a psychiatrist. But Fiona did seem to find a certain relief in pouring out her heart to me, and this is what I've made of it. If,' he ended hesitantly, 'you could work her into the family circle a bit more, give her some responsibility...'

'I'll try,' Alison agreed, feeling as if she had taken a header into deep breath-catching water. Fiona neglected ... lonely! Lost in the impersonal world of school.

'It was good of you to take so much trouble,' she told Brett. Belatedly she pushed a wicker chair towards him, inviting him to sit down. But inevitably he refused. 'I've got far too much to do than to sit sunning myself on delectable terraces all afternoon.' He made it sound as if he thought Alison shouldn't have the time either. Feeling guilty, she stood up.

'Fiona has actually finished with boarding school this term,' she said. 'She'll be at home for good.'

'Well, let her take her share of the work there.' He turned back, on the point of leaving, and as if on a sudden inspiration added, 'Hand the whole thing over to her for a bit when your father returns to England. And you stay out here and get on with your good work among my sick and suffering.'

She could scarcely believe her ears, and couldn't resist saying, 'I shouldn't have thought you would want me. A featherheaded good-time girl addicted to promiscuous dinner dates and goodnight kisses.'

He said, 'You could have fixed Everton, surely, without spending an entire evening with him. However! ...' He shrugged. 'That's your private life, which concerns me not at all. It's your nursing skills which interest me. You would be good for my hospital. So think it over. I expect the Sheik would gladly take you on the pay-roll.'

Which put the whole thing in its proper perspective. She would be good for his hospital, that was all. There was no glimmer of personal feeling in his invitation.

She watched him stride down the flowery path, past the singing fountain, under the creamy acacia blooms and out through the lane gate. She heard the clatter of his noisy little car; then he was gone and the afternoon silence descended.

She stood still for a few moments, her thoughts chaotic. Brett's suggestion that she should remain in Sidi and work for him—or rather for his sick and suffering ... Characteristically he had made it sound like a command. How much had Fiona told him about the scene in the hotel garden? Did he know now of Paul's wild marriage proposal to herself; and of her refusal of it? If so it seemed to have made no difference in his attitude towards her. She had been wrong in imagining he might be jealous of her association with Paul. And that crack about her dining with him last night—enjoying his infatuation for her, perhaps. Oh, Brett would believe what he wanted to believe. And it would never be to her advantage.

Going into the house, she looked into Fiona's room. She was deeply asleep, looking very young and pathetic. Had they really neglected her? Kept her outside the family circle? It could be true. Father and I have always treated her like a child, Alison mused, never made an equal companion of her. It was clever of Brett to have put his finger on the deeper wound; not so much Paul Everton, but a lifelong loneliness. And how did she herself come out of it? The bossy, insensitive elder sister, hogging the limelight and the lion's share of their father's affection. Added to the good-time girl image it made her into a pretty unattractive person! She seemed fated to give Brett the most unfavourable impressions. No wonder he looked at her with such cold and criticising eyes.

She spent the rest of the afternoon in the harem with Haidie, who was in the seventh heaven, having received an entrance form for her application to enter St Clare's, for the time being as a student nurse. Later, if she continued to show promise, she might go to the Medical School. She was very young and there was plenty of time for weighty decisions.

Brett appeared at the Villa early the next morning, getting his visit to Fiona over before his day's work at the hospital started. Alison and her father were breakfasting on the verandah, and when he had seen his patient Brett joined them for a quick cup of coffee.

Fiona was almost her normal self again, he pronounced. 'One factor which may help to complete her recovery is that the film crowd are pulling up stakes today and getting out of Sidi bou Kef. The august director' (there was a sneer in his voice) 'has, I believe, already left. And good riddance!' he added under his breath, with a barbed glance in Alison's direction. 'I told Fiona, wondering if it would lead to fresh floods of tears, but she took it very calmly. We talked about her pony, Dora, and I've offered to let her ride my mare, Shani, when she's on her feet again. Shani doesn't get enough exercise, so it will do them both good. I've told her she can get up later today.' He turned to Alison. 'She needn't take any more of those pills. What she needs now is plenty to do and lots of attention from her family.'

'Now just what did he mean by that?' John Warrender enquired when he had gone.

Alison gave him an edited version of her conversation with Brett the previous afternoon. John Warrender mulled it over, and then said with a rueful headshake, 'A perceptive young man. He could well be right. Fiona has always been rather the odd one out, now I come to think of it. But I can't see her taking over your duties, or enjoying them; ordering my meals, entertaining my dull academics...'

'There are your students as well,' Alison reminded him. 'I think she'd love arranging "evenings" for them, queening it over them.'

'And what would happen to you?' her father asked.

'Oh, I might go back to nursing for a bit. I ought not to lose my skills and I enjoy the work, especially the theatre. St Clare's might take me back as a theatre sister.' She didn't tell him about Brett's offer of a job in his hospital. An offer she had no intention of accepting. She had more regard for her peace of mind!

'Well, we have still got a couple of weeks in which to sort it all out,' the Professor said. 'Meanwhile it seems as if Fiona is going to be able to make herself happy here a little longer. With lover-boy off the scene and a pony to ride she should soon forget her unfortunate romance.' He sighed. 'The sort of crisis your mother would have been so much better able to deal with. Young women of seventeen are a mystery to me ... rather a terrifying mystery. I don't remember you, Alison, ever going through this hysterical phase of being "crossed in love".'

Maybe I'm still going through it in my quiet, re-pressed fashion, Alison thought wryly.

'You were always the sensible one,' her father continued.

But not to Brett, Alison qualified inwardly. I'm only sensible for him in cap and apron. When I'm off duty I'm the world's butterfly, flitting from fancy to fancy.

Life settled down once more into its quiet routine, Alison spending her mornings at the hospital and many of her afternoons reading and talking with the Sheik's family in the harem. Sometimes she drove round the estate with her father, watching him put the finishing touches to his tree cultivation, giving last instructions to his Arab assistants, two of them with agricultural college degrees. Fiona rode Shani daily and was already a little bit in love with Shani's owner, who treated her with a gentle kindliness Alison found it hard to witness. Brett who could be so understanding with his patients, with Fiona, but for her there was only an increasing coldness, or so she felt. His manner was invariably businesslike and aloof, though they worked harmoniously together. But never once did he suggest a meeting outside their work. He had not forgiven her for refusing his dinner invitation that unfortunate night she had had to go out with Paul.

Then one afternoon he took her to see a patient in Delma, the pottery town. During the long drive there and back he kept the conversation strictly impersonal. Vainly she waited for some glimmer of warmth. Desperately determined to focus his attention on her, she told him her father's work for the Sheik was practically finished. 'We shall be leaving Algeria, next week,' she warned.

'You mean you are going back to England with your family? That you won't consider staying a few weeks longer at the cottage hospital?' His voice was dry and toneless, his gaze fixed on the limitless billows of sand through which they travelled.

I don't think I could bear working with you much longer, she almost blurted. But instead she told him she was thinking of applying for a post as theatre sister at St Clare's.

'Well, don't let me stand in your way.' He sounded

ridiculously hurt—so hurt that for a moment Alison was tempted to relent. But she knew it would be unwise. Brett only wanted her for what he could get out of her in the way of professional assistance.

He said, 'You'll make a darned good theatre sister, Alison. And you'll have much more scope at St Clare's than in my ramshackle set-up. But it's been good having you with me for a time.' He turned to give her what was quite a warm and friendly smile.

'And you're taking young Haidie with you, I suppose. Oh, well,' he shrugged, 'I'll have to get on as well as I can without you both.' (Lumping her in with young Haidie.) 'After all, I managed very well before you came.'

'I'm sure you did.'

The momentary warmth was gone.

With the familiar bleakness in her heart, Alison gazed through the windscreen, shielding her eyes against the glare of the setting sun. A great crimson globe going down in a ragged tatter of black clouds. 'The first clouds I've seen since I came to the Sahara,' she said.

'A wicked sunset,' Brett pronounced. 'Looks as if we may be in for a sand-storm.'

Next morning the clouds had cleared away. But the sky had an oddly metallic look, and small scurries of wind disturbed the air, sending particles of sand flying. They got into Alison's eyes and gritted between her teeth as she made her way to the hospital after breakfast, Fiona in riding kit beside her. Leaving Alison at the hospital door, she went on down the street to the *fonduk* where Shani was stabled.

'Do you think it's wise for her to go riding this morning?' Alison asked Brett, when she reached the surgery. 'The weather doesn't look any too settled.'

'She'll be all right,' Brett returned carelessly. 'As long as she keeps to the pathways between the trees. If the sand begins to blow she'll find it unpleasant, and make her way back. Shani won't like it either and is quite capable of insisting upon a return to her stable.'

It was a busy morning at the little hospital. A minor epidemic of dysentery had filled the wards, so when surgery was at an end Alison went and helped Haidie and the other young nurses with bed-pans and low-diet lunches. Outside the wind was blowing strongly, sending handfuls of gritty sand against the hospital windows. Surely Fiona would have abandoned her riding and gone home by now—leaving Shani safely in her stable. But there was little time for worrying in the rush of work and small emergencies; wailing babies with tummyache, adult patients groaning with Oriental abandon.

At last the rush was over and she was getting ready to leave, hanging up her white overall in the surgery. Just as she was wondering where Brett might be—for she usually reported to him when she was leaving—he came in looking worried. He had been down to the *fonduk* and there was no sign of Shani in her stable. 'If Fiona has been silly enough to get caught in this wind in the desert she may be in difficulties,' he said. 'I think I'll take the car and get on the main road and have a look for her.'

'Shall I come too?' Alison asked, beginning to feel the chill of misgivings.

'No, you go home to lunch; you've had a marathon of a morning. I'll bring Fiona along when I find her. I'm sure she's all right,' he added, almost too confidently, Alison thought, listening to the eerie shrieking of the wind and the rustle of the flying sand.

'You can't possibly walk back to the Villa in this,' Brett declared, as they came out of the hospital entrance. 'I'll run you home in my car before setting out to look for Fiona. We may even come across her on the way.'

But they didn't. Putting Alison down at the Villa gate, Brett swung off south, on one of the rough tracks through the trees. 'Don't worry,' he called over his shoulder as he drove away. 'Fiona and I will be back before you've finished lunch.'

'In which case you'd better eat with us,' Alison called after him, and took comfort from telling Lalla to lay an extra place at the luncheon table.

They were half-way through the meal when Fiona walked in ... alone.

'Isn't Brett coming in with you?' Alison asked, disappointed.

'Brett?' Fiona echoed in obvious mystification. 'Why should Brett be coming in?'

'He went to look for you,' Alison explained. 'He was worried about you being out in the desert in the sandstorm.'

'Oh, it wasn't too bad,' Fiona said lightly. 'I took Shani into a thick grove of cypress trees and we stayed there for a while, but when the wind didn't let up we made a dash for her stable, where I left her with the stable boy as usual. Now,' she ended with a rueful laugh, 'my mouth and my hair are full of sand. I can't possibly eat until I've dug myself out, had a bit of a wash and brush up.'

She hadn't seen anything of Brett, she ended.

There was no sitting on the verandah that afternoon.

Alison, restless and increasingly uneasy about Brett, went over to the harem, where it was hot and stifling with the balcony doors and windows closed against the drifting sand. The storm was getting worse every moment. Haidie hadn't come back from the hospital.

'I expect she has decided to stay until the wind dies down a bit. It usually drops at sunset,' Kaira said.

'Has Dr Meredith came back?' Alison asked Haidie when she returned at last, about tea-time.

Haidie shook her head. 'Dr Ali Ben Hassan is on duty alone. I think he is worried that Dr Meredith should be away all this time in the storm. It is always worse in the open desert.'

That was the beginning of the hours of anxiety. If only there had been telephone communication between the Villa and the hospital! Twice during the endless evening Alison braved the flying sand and the darkness, going down to the hospital to find out if Brett had returned. It was on her second visit that Dr Ali met her in the small entrance hall, his face set and pale beneath its Arab tan.

'Brett hasn't got in yet,' he said, 'But his car has been found abandoned about fifteen miles along the desert road ... half buried in sand.'

CHAPTER TEN

ALISON felt the walls sway about her. For a timeless moment she and the young Arab doctor gazed at one another in horror-struck silence; a silence filled with the moaning of the wind and the rustle of the blown sand. Then Hassan said: 'The police have been alerted. There is a mounted patrol out looking for him.'

'Who found the car?' Alison asked through dry lips.

'A lorry-driver battling his way through the storm to Sidi from Delma, bringing a load of pots. He stopped to examine the stranded car, and noted the particulars on the licence, which he took to the Sidi police. It was the sergeant who came and told me.'

'And now ...' Alison breathed on a shuddering inhalation, 'what next?'

'We wait for the patrol to come back. There is nothing else we can do. They are pretty experienced in this sort of emergency and will know how to set about the search. It looks as if, when sand choked his engine, Brett tried to make his way back here on foot, and missed the way, an easy thing to do when the roads are inches deep under sand. The patrol will spread out; cover all possible routes...' He broke off with a keen look at Alison's stricken face. 'Meanwhile you had better have a cup of coffee; you have had a shock.'

Alison shook her head. 'I don't want anything, thanks. I'd better get on home. My father and sister will be waiting, anxious to know what's happening.'

At the door she turned back. 'If there are any developments during the night could you let us know?'

'Of course I will. But don't worry if you don't hear from me. I'm sure you will find Brett taking surgery as usual when you come to the hospital tomorrow morning.'

It was all just a little too hearty. Pushing her way against the wind, Alison stumbled along the sandy lane in the darkness. When she saw the estate car parked under a thick roof of cypress branches, covered with a tarpaulin to keep out the sand, she longed to get into it and drive off along that fatal fifteen miles of road. But it would be an idiotic thing to do. Brett could be anywhere by this time, heading for what he hoped was Sidi bou Kef. But out in the open desert, in the teeth of this sand-lashed gale, what chance would he have? The road, like his car, would be buried in sand, impossible to negotiate. Which meant he was probably wandering aimlessly through trackless wastes of billowing sand; a landscape that every hour changed its contours, shifted by the force of the wind.

Once adrift in that featureless wilderness how would he ever find direction again? With horrifying force she remembered it was Brett who had told her no man could last more than twenty-four hours if lost in the Sahara. She remembered too the vultures ... and thought she was going to be sick.

Reaching the Villa, she pulled herself together and tried to make her report as hopeful as possible. Brett's car had broken down, and a police patrol had gone out to collect him. But after a few probing questions Fiona was in tears. 'Are you sure the police will find him, Ally? It's all my fault he's lost. If he hadn't gone to look for me ... all those hours ago! Even if he walked the whole fifteen miles he should have been in Sidi by now.'

'The road will have been blotted out by the drifting sand,' Alison pointed out. 'And it's difficult walking through deep sand. He may even have found a sheltered place where he can rest during the night, waiting for daylight.' But somehow it wasn't very convincing.

'At least the storm seems to be easing up a bit,' the Professor said with determined optimism.

After which there was nothing to do but go to bed.

Not that any of them slept very well. For the first part of the night Alison lay listening for the footsteps of Hassan's longed-for message, saying Brett had been found. But no message came, and when she did at last fall into an uneasy doze it was to dream of vultures.

They were at breakfast next morning when Ahmed arrived for his day's work in the garden. He had, he announced importantly, brought news from the hospital. The police patrol had returned to Sidi at dawn without being able to locate Dr Meredith. A fresh patrol was now out in the desert continuing the search.

Fiona buried her face in her hands and said she couldn't bear it. 'If I had brought Shani home earlier yesterday instead of sheltering under the trees he wouldn't have gone looking for me.'

Putting aside her own grinding pain, Alison tried to think of reassuring things to say. There were none that sounded sincere. The Professor's approach was more hopeful. Brett knew the desert round Sidi pretty well, and there were the nomad people whom he had doctored. He might well have taken shelter in some encampment, or he could have been picked up by a camel train making for Algiers.

It was late when Alison managed to get away to the hospital, where Hassan was glad of her help. And at least she was in the front line here, on the spot to receive any news of Brett which might be brought in, or even Brett himself. He could walk in the door at any moment, ready to explain his absence. But as the sun mounted higher and higher in the heavens this wholly unconvincing picture faded. All she could see now was Brett, in the final stages of exhaustion and heat stroke, staggering over the endless dunes. The worst of the sand storm was over now, the sky its usual burning blue.

How she got through her morning's work she did not know, and the general atmosphere of gloom did not help. Everyone knew Dr Meredith was missing and faces in the wards were strained and grave. There was a miserable lunch interval at home, with Fiona tearfully refusing to eat. 'This place has a curse on it!' she wailed. 'There's been nothing but trouble since I came here. First I lose Paul, and now Brett has gone...' Did she mean she had fallen in love with Brett? Alison wondered, and was too distraught to care.

She returned to the hospital as soon as she could, eager for what news there might be. It was not good. The second patrol had come back, Hassan told her, having covered a pretty wide area without finding any trace of Brett apart from the stranded car. The first patrol were on duty again and would continue the search until darkness fell.

Unfortunately he had to go out, Hassan told Alison. 'Madame Dubois has chosen this untimely moment to start labour and I've got to be with her to deliver the child.' The Dubois family were French, the father a painter of some repute. They lived in a village on the outskirts of the oasis; a remnant of the colony of artists and writers who had built houses there during Colonial days.

'I don't anticipate any complications, since this is Madame Dubois' fourth confinement,' Hassan said as he left. 'I should be back here in plenty of time for evening surgery. Zeena will help me with it. I don't suppose you will feel like working this afternoon.' He gave Alison a keen glance. 'You look all washed up. I think you ought to go home and rest. I'll tell Zeena to send you any news of Brett that may come in.'

Zeena, the senior nurse, was used to being left in

charge if both doctors were out, so there was no need for Alison to hang about. But she couldn't bear to leave the hospital. She told Zeena who was busy in the wards that she would clean out the instrument cabinet in the surgery. It was the hottest hour of the day, but Alison's hands were ice-cold as she cleared the glass shelves of the cabinet; a boring job, leaving her thoughts to stray. These endless hours of sickening uncertainty! Why had she ever thought she knew what trouble was? If Brett would only walk in at the surgery door, safe and sound, she would never ask for anything else as long as she lived.

It was three o'clock when she heard footsteps in the little vestibule outside the surgery. Her heart leaped ... but it was probably only one of the patients arriving early for the evening clinic. Some of them had very little sense of time. The footsteps halted uncertainly. Alison opened the ripple glass door to find herself confronted by a tall young Bedouin, his magnificent body only half clad in picturesque rags. He was carrying a dangerous-looking rifle.

'Peace be with you,' he greeted Alison incongruously. 'I come from the Doctor Meredith, who sends messages.'

Alison put a hand to the jamb of the door to steady herself. Had she heard aright? The young man had spoken in a strangely distorted English.

'Doctor Meredith!' she echoed incredulously. 'Where is he? Is he all right?'

The young man bowed his head over clasped hands, which still held the rifle. 'He is sick. Ver' sick. You come to him.'

Alison braced herself, ignoring the wild pounding of her pulses. 'Do you mean he sent you to fetch me?'

'He ask for doctor. His eyes blind with sand. Bring medicines ...'

'Do you speak French?' Alison enquired desperately. The young man shook his head and went into a long spiel in Arabic. Alison led him back to his halting English. Brett, she managed to establish, was being cared for by the Rahoud family, the Bedouins he had taken her to see when he visited the old man with spondulitis. The young man with the rifle was, he claimed, one of the old man's grandsons.

'I have been to this encampment,' Alison said. 'It is many miles away. The doctor has travelled far!'

The young man shook his head. 'Not so far. Now we move nearer to Sidi, find fresh pasture. But the doctor, when his car go "pouf", walk much through the sand going in circles.' He made an eloquent gesture, swinging his rifle dangerously. 'Allah send great storm. Yes? Now the doctor is sick, ver' sick. We go quickly.'

Alison's thoughts raced. Brett was alive, sheltering with the nomads, but gravely in need of help. And Hassan, for whom he had asked, was out of reach. With a pang she remembered the crazy moment when she thought it was to fetch *her* that Brett had sent the young Bedouin. But failing Hassan he would surely be thankful if she turned up instead. But whether he was or not, nothing on earth would keep her from him. Looking back afterwards she was amazed how little sober reflection she gave to this decision. Her only thought was to get to Brett. She could take the estate car which her father was not using this afternoon. At lunch he had planned to walk down the narrow avenues between the newly planted trees to see how much damage the storm had done. Fiona had been persuaded to go with him—an attempt on the Professor's part, Alison supposed, to follow Brett's advice and include his younger daughter in some of his activities. She hadn't really wanted to go, but anything, she said, would be better than sitting alone in the Villa waiting for news of Brett.

So, Alison worked it out now, there would be no one at home to object to her taking the car and making this wild dash into the wilderness.

'How did you get here?' she asked the Bedouin.

'I come with camel,' he answered. 'I leave it tied up in the *fonduk*.'

'Can it remain there for a few hours? I want you to come with me in the car and guide me to the encampment.'

The young Bedouin's face lit up. Riding in a car would be an unusual adventure. 'I go ask friend to guard camel until my return,' he said.

Alison nodded. 'Good. But hurry!' she called after him as he loped off into the blinding light. 'I will be waiting for you with the car outside the hospital.'

'I go with Allah,' the young man called back, beginning to run.

Firmly keeping her emotions under control Alison went to the surgery store cupboard and collected eye lotion, an undine, bandages, drops. If Brett's blindness had been caused by flying sand he would need irrigation. She took glucose tablets for exhaustion, salt tablets for dehydration, some brandy and a large bottle of distilled water, packing all these remedies into a large tin box.

Then, running recklessly through the afternoon heat, she fetched the car. Back at the hospital the Bedouin was waiting for her. At the last minute she remembered she hadn't given Zeena the news of Brett's whereabouts, and hurried through the wards to find her. Zeena listened with Oriental calm. 'Allah be praised that the doctor has been found,' she said.

'I will bring him back in the car,' Alison told her, making light of the whole expedition. 'I don't suppose I shall be long. The encampment where Dr Meredith is sheltering is quite near Sidi bou Kef.' Privately she hoped it was, but had her doubts. The abandoned car had been found fifteen miles away and Brett had obviously walked a good distance since. But it was important not to alarm Zeena, or provoke any arguments about the wisdom of this one-woman rescue operation. Arguments would mean delay. Zeena might even insist on contacting Dr Hassan. Brett was ill and suffering and nothing must hinder her going to his aid. Alison didn't stop to examine her motives, or analyse the surge of hope and elation which came to her as she set out on her journey. Brett needed her and she was going to him, that was all; in the company of a wild-looking Bedouin whom she had never seen before, but who said he was a grandson of Brett's elderly nomad patient.

As they left civilisation behind them she glanced at her companion a little uneasily. He was sitting bolt upright at her side, the murderous-looking rifle standing upright between his bare knees.

'Are you sure you know the way?' she asked him, as they bumped along a rough sandy track that soon lost itself between great hummocks of sand.

'We go with Allah,' was the only assurance the young man could provide. They rattled on. Little eddies of sand blew in what was left of the wind. Like desert ghosts they rose up in a spiral, and danced a moment or two, before falling back on to the ground. Now and then flurries of grit hit the windscreen. What it must have been like out here at the height of the storm, Alison didn't dare imagine. How lonely it was, how vast! She tried not to be too conscious of the motionless figure at her side. If only he wouldn't keep the gun between his knees, swaying dangerously with the motion of the car. Supposing it were to go off accidentally—shattering the windscreen! And the young man was so grimly silent. 'What is your name?' Alison asked, trying to make some small human contact.

'Omar,' he replied. 'I am son of the son of Fuad al Rahoud.'

'I know,' Alison nodded. 'The grandson. You told me. Is the old man's pain any better?'

He stared ahead of him blankly, not apparently understanding the question. Perhaps he was not Fuad al Rahoud's grandson after all, Alison thought. But an armed bandit. She had not seen him around the Rahoud encampment on her visit there, she recalled, with growing apprehension.

'Have we much further to go?' she asked when they had covered some twenty miles.

'It is far,' he answered sullenly.

On and on they travelled. The sun beat down on her uncovered head, perspiration rolled into her eyes. Why had she not brought some kind of head-covering? She began to realise just how impulsively she had rushed into this expedition, crazy to reach Brett. But she wouldn't be much use to him if she arrived with sunstroke—assuming she ever *did* arrive! She stole another nervous glance at the fierce-looking Bedouin, then stopping the car, fished in the back seat for one of the sacks in which her father carried his tree specimens. It was lightly woven and luckily fairly clean, and would give her some protection from the sun. She draped it around her head, Arab fashion, binding it about her brow with the belt of her dress.

'Now you Bedouin girl,' Omar said, giving her a wicked grin. He *is* a bandit, Alison decided desperately. But there was nothing for it but to start the car again and drive on to wherever he was taking her.

The road dipped into a valley. Here the sand had formed into drifts during the night of storm. Driving became more and more difficult until the inevitable happened—the wheels clogged and refused to revolve.

'Camel better than car,' Omar offered uselessly. But he did get out and started pushing the car from behind. Alison ran the engine furiously; the wheels spun fruitlessly in the loose sand. When he had pushed and sweated without result for some minutes, Omar straightened up and wiped his brow. 'Car go pouf!' he said happily. 'Now we walk. I show you. Camp beyond the sandhills over there.' He pointed vaguely into what looked like the limitless Sahara. 'We leave road to make shortness.'

So this, Alison thought, is where I go off into the trackless wilds with this ruffianly-looking character and his gun! Her heart beat furiously as she got out of the car, conscientiously locking it. As if anyone would be able to move it—let alone steal it! Lingeringly she looked back at it, her last contact with civilisation.

They had only gone a few steps when she remembered the box of remedies and had to go back for it. When she rejoined him, Omar took the box from her, tucking it under one arm—a kindly gesture that reassured her a little. But it wasn't easy to keep up with his long loping strides. He seemed to have a knack of skimming over the sand in his goatskin sandals, while she sank ankle-deep at every step. The sun grew hotter and hotter; in spite of the sacking her head ached and her eyes felt like balls of fire. Why had she embarked on this journey so unthinkingly? Too late she realised how much more sensible it would have been to contact the police, the Sheik ... anyone responsible. But no, she had to dash off on her own in a wild romantic fashion which had nothing to do with the grim realities of the situation.

The miles went on and on—or was it that every few yards of this impossible terrain seemed like a mile? And the encampment was apparently as far away as ever. Each step was a labour in the vicious heat, breathing became difficult. In the end she could only put one foot before the other with the dogged resolve to keep going. Until at last she sank to her knees ... beaten.

Omar, striding on ahead, was at first unaware of her collapse, but presently, missing her, he turned back. Putting down his rifle and medicine box, he stood over her, surveying her ruefully. 'You go "pouf"—like the car,' he said sadly. Then kneeling beside her, he took her in his arms, trying to lift her from the sand.

This really is the end, she thought, drunkenly, as her aching head dropped on to his shoulder. In Omar's embrace only rape and murder awaited her. She would be left, when he had finished with her, for the vultures to pick over. But she hardly cared. Omar's naked shoulder was strong to lean upon, and his dark eyes looking down at her were unexpectedly kind. She felt the blessed trickle of water between her parched lips—the precious water she had brought for Brett. 'No,' she whispered, 'we must not use this water. It is for the

Doctor Meredith.' But the few drops she had drunk partly restored her. Sitting up, she saw the open tin box beside her, and groped in it for the brandy bottle, swallowing a fiery sip. Then she made herself eat one of the glucose tablets, forcing it down her dry throat. For a few minutes more she leaned against the hard young body of the Bedouin. Then she struggled to her feet.

'You are better now?' he enquired with such tender concern that she could have wept. He was good, he was wonderful, she had misjudged him.

They set off on their trek once more. The sun was sinking to a red horizon, and a cool breeze began to stir. Alison drew it into her lungs in great gulps, to keep herself going. But by this time she was so exhausted that nothing seemed quite real.

It was dusk when the black tents came into view. 'Praise be to Allah!' cried Omar devoutly. After that everything was very confused. The tents as they approached them seemed to swell and rise up in the air like great black balloons. The sky wheeled in a vast slow circle. Then the world went dark and Alison stumbled and fell.

When she opened her eyes after a timeless interval she found herself lying on a bed of cushions inside one of the black tents with Brett bending over her. He was gazing down at her, his glance as blue and hard and direct as ever.

'You're not blind!' she marvelled.

He held a cup to her lips. It contained something sweetish and cool—a drink he had no doubt contrived from the glucose tablets she had brought. 'You found the medicine box?' she whispered.

He gave a despairing head-shake. 'Humping all that stuff across the desert, struggling through the sand for the best part of thirty miles ... what on earth possessed you, Alison?'

He was angry with her. Tears stung her throat. 'Omar said you were very ill, that you were blind. Someone must come to you at once. Dr Hassan had gone to Madame Dubois to help at her confinement. There was no one available but me...'

'So you set out on foot?'

'No, I'm not quite that mad. I took the estate car ... my father wasn't using it.'

'Did you tell him what you were doing?' Brett interrupted.

Alison shook her head. 'I didn't tell anyone but Zeena. It was all right at first, but after about twenty miles the car packed up in the sand and we had to leave it, and come the rest of the way on foot.'

Brett gave a bitter laugh. 'That makes two of us littering the Sahara with our hardware. Omar will just have to go back to Sidi again and get the garage to send out a breakdown outfit with caterpillar treads, to pick up the stranded cars.'

He sat down on the edge of the bed of cushions, his face set and grim.

'You'd been gone a day and a night,' she began apologetically.

'What about Fiona?' he broke in sharply. 'I've been worried sick about her.'

'She came home yesterday about half an hour after you'd gone haring off to look for her. She'd been sheltering from the storm under some thick cypress trees, but in the end managed to get to the town where she left Shani safely in her stable.'

'Good!' Brett said on a long breath of relief. 'Thank God she's all right!'

Alison struggled to hold back her tears. Here they were talking about Fiona and Shani. She had forgotten how concerned he would be about them. Wasn't he the least bit glad to see her? She knew now she had been counting on his being grateful for her effort to help him—her courage in setting off across the desert to come to his aid. But all that happened was that she had collapsed in a heap on the edge of the encampment.

He said, 'What made you think I was blind?'

'Omar said so, and that you were very sick.'

Brett looked annoyed. 'Omar exaggerates. I was caught in the worst of the sand-storm when my car broke down. By the time I'd struggled here on foot— and how I made it I'll never know—my eyes were rather bunged up with sand. But with the help of Jamilia, who is the mother figure around this pad, I contrived a saline irrigation, and after a few hours with my eyes bandaged I was rested and okay. But I couldn't get back to Sidi without transport, so I sent Omar to ask Hassan to send me a car.'

So that was the whole story. Alison digested it in complete bleak silence. What an anti-climax! She had made a complete fool of herself, believing Omar's highly coloured report, rushing off with him unthinkingly. Now there would be anxiety in the hospital and at the Villa, not only about Brett but about herself. Instead of helping she had made everything a hundred times worse. She closed her eyes, fighting back the tears. 'I shouldn't have come!' she gulped. 'I always do everything wrong.' A sob escaped her.

'Take it easy, young Warrender! Just hold on to yourself for a moment and I'll fix you another drink. I want you to take a couple of these tablets.' Brett was groping in his jacket pocket as he spoke.

Tablets, she thought bitterly. He's a walking pharmacy. I needn't have brought that great box of remedies.

Supporting her with an arm, he held the cup to her lips. When she had swallowed the tablets he laid her gently back on the piled cushions and stood looking down at her. In the shadowy tent, lit by the last gleams of daylight, his face was a mask, his bleached hair very blond and bright.

'You'll sleep now,' he told her. 'Just let go and stop worrying about anything under the cruel Sahara sun. It was sweet of you to come to my rescue. Sweet and crazy ... and just like you.' But already she was drifting off into a light, delicious drowsiness. She must have dreamed that he kissed her, his mouth firm and cool on her poor swollen lips. And it couldn't have been true that he whispered, 'Oh, Alison, Alison! There are times when you break my heart.'

When she woke some hours later it was dark. There was an oil lamp burning on the upturned box that served as a bedside table. She gazed at it, feeling rested and curiously at peace. Sedation, she decided. Brett's miracle pills. The tent flap lifted and a middle-aged woman came in carrying a mug in which some liquid steamed. Jamilia, Alison thought, recognising her as the woman who was the wife of the man who had been tending the little orphaned goat the time she and Brett had visited the Rahoud family. 'The mother figure,' Brett had called her. She looked a very beautiful mother in her colourful dress, her placid face alight with concern for the invalid.

'You are better,' she said. 'Twice I have looked in to find you sleeping. Last time you moved and opened your eyes, so I hastened to make you some tea.'

It was milkless and unsweetened, but Alison drank it thirstily.

'The doctor will come to you,' Jamilia said. 'All evening he has waited for you to waken, sad that you have made yourself so tired walking through the heat and the sand. Omar,' she continued, 'has eaten and is now on his way back to Sidi with the donkey. He will journey all night to reach the garage that will, at his command, send out the big-wheeled desert tractor.'

'I hope he will go first to the hospital and to my father and tell them the doctor and I are safe.'

'Surely he will do so.' Jamilia's earrings tinkled as she nodded her assurance. 'The doctor has written a letter to the hospital doctor, telling him all is well.'

Excepting that I'm the dimwit who muddled the whole rescue operation, Alison thought sadly. Why hadn't it occurred to *her* to go to the garage in Sidi and ask for advice before setting out? She had seen one of those tank-tread tractors used by the film company, the only practical way of dealing with sand-clogged roads. But practical considerations had been far from her mind when she tore off into the blue with Omar.

Jamilia had left the tent flap open and the sweet cool night air came in. Alison could see a triangle of navy blue sky, spangled with outsize stars. Somewhere a goat bleated and a dog barked. Then silence took over again—the eerie silence of the Sahara. A smell of cooking drifted in, mixed with the tang of wood smoke. It made her feel hungry. She sat up in her nest of cushions and saw that her shoulder bag, which had somehow survived the journey, had been placed on the box table beside the bed. Groping in it, she found a comb and mirror. One glance in the mirror told her the worst. Sun-scorched and red-eyed, never had she

looked more of a wreck. And Brett was coming to her,
Jamilia had said. She set about combing her tangled
hair, letting it fall in a curtain over her face, so that she
did not see Brett enter, nor did she hear his footstep on
the carpet-covered mud floor. Startled, she felt his hand
on her head, stroking her hair with a gentle touch.

'Your beautiful hair,' he said softly. 'So often I've
wanted to run a lock of it through my fingers! In this
soft lamp light it is the colour of autumn gold.'

Throwing it back over her shoulders, she gazed up at
him. Had he really said what she thought he said? Or
was it those pills again, producing hallucinations now
as well as sedation? Everything was happening in a
beautiful dream.

He sat down on the bed beside her and picked up
her wrist, counting her pulse rate. She could feel it
racing under his touch, and met his glance of professional concern.

'What do you expect,' she whispered recklessly,
'when you sit so close to me?' She saw his mouth
tighten and his face harden. The beautiful dream deserted her, leaving the old familiar pain. 'Oh, Brett!'
she cried, 'don't you know what you do to me?'

'I've tried not to know.'

'Why, Brett? Why?' She turned her head away, not
waiting for the answer which she already knew. 'It was
something that happened that June, wasn't it?' she
said, greatly daring.

'That wonderful June,' Brett said.

'When you dropped me flat.'

'Because I had nothing to offer you.'

But she had known all along that was why he had
gone from her.

'No love,' she said on a smothered sob, 'only friendship. And when you thought I was becoming rather too involved you took even that away.'

'It wasn't quite like that.' He put a hand under her chin, turning her head towards him. 'Look at me, Alison!'

The tears were stinging her scorched cheeks. 'I'm so awful!' she wept. 'The sun has burned my face and my eyes hurt.'

'Never mind; a little weeping will help them—a natural dose of normal saline.' He laughed softly as he gathered her into his arms. 'I'll give you something to ease your sunburn.'

'And a pat on the head for my broken heart!' she cried bitterly.

He just drew her closer, held her more firmly. 'That night of the hospital ball ...' he began.

'When you saw me kissing Simon Frayne,' she interrupted him. Let it all be cleared up now they were at it. The good-time girl throwing her kisses around.

'Yes,' he remembered, 'that goodnight kiss for Simon Frayne. Naturally I was suitably jealous. But it wasn't that which made me walk away, leaving my note of apology to you for the spoiled evening undelivered. I realised, you see, that it hadn't been a spoiled evening, but that you'd had a jolly good time. And I knew that if I married you I wouldn't be able to bring many such evenings into your life, with me working something like a hundred hours a week for a salary that would never keep a wife—and a home going. Haven't you seen what happened to other young medicos when they marry? The wife, as often as not, having to keep on at her job if they're to get by. This isn't what I wanted for you ... or for our children. I wanted the lot, you see. For both of us. I couldn't have offered you less.'

'You could,' she said. 'I wouldn't have cared.'

'I hoped,' he went on as if she had not spoken, 'that if I got out of the picture you would find someone more satisfactory, a husband able to support you.'

This simple explanation of the mystery which for so long had tormented her! It was all so sensible and practical, and *Brett-like*.

'I didn't want a husband able to support me,' she cried. 'I wanted you. There's never been anyone else in my life—there never will be.'

'Oh, Alison, you defeat me,' he murmured brokenly. 'I can't hold out against you any longer.' When they kissed the whole world dissolved in a crash of glory. Alison's thoughts whirled. Brett loved her after all—in no matter how crazy a fashion. He had loved her all along. Deep in her heart she must have known it. And fate had brought her all the way to Sidi bou Kef to find him again. It was like a beautiful shining pattern falling into place.

But when he laid her back on the pillows she saw that his face was troubled.

'I'm still not quite in the clear, darling, I've my consultant's exam to take, and I've sacrificed a lot of time out here—not that it's all been lost. I've picked up a lot about eye diseases, and I'm not as hard up as I was. On the Sheik's generous salary I've built up quite a decent bank balance ...'

'So what are we waiting for?' she prompted shamelessly.

He gave her a long thoughtful look. 'I came out here for wholly material reasons, Alison; quite selfish reasons, I suppose. But I've become a bit more involved than I meant to be. The Sheik is such a good old chap, working away at his efforts of social reform. I'd like to help him. And I've grown fond of the people and their simple way of life. In this rat-racing modern world there's something very appealing about the peace and sanity one finds in a Sahara oasis.'

'You mean you want to stay out here,' Alison broke in, her heart lifting. If that was all that was worrying Brett…

'Not for good,' he said. 'But at least until I've got this exchange scheme I was telling you about organised. It means finding English doctors and nurses who'll do a stint out here, like the American medical teams are doing in Tunisia.'

'I think it's a marvellous idea,' Alison encouraged him.

'Only that it will take time, still keeping me in the unsatisfactory husband class.'

Alison put out her hands to him. 'Oh, Brett, *honestly* … How many more times do I have to tell you I like unsatisfactory husbands, especially if this particular unsatisfactory husband will let me help him!'

'You mean you would stay in Sidi and go on working with me for a while?'

'As long as it takes to do what you want to do.'

This time there was purpose and passion in their kiss—a question asked and answered. There would be no more barriers between them.

'The time we've wasted!' Brett sighed.

'The time *you've* wasted,' Alison corrected.

'But I was right,' he asserted stubbornly. 'What we have for one another might easily have been spoiled if I'd rushed you two years ago into a difficult, impecunious marriage. I wanted you to be free to look round, find out if there was someone whom you felt would be more suitable for you than myself.'

'Like that heel, Paul Everton,' Alison couldn't resist reminding him.

He had the grace to look abashed. 'I don't think I was ever seriously concerned about Everton as a rival. It's just that I couldn't bear to see that worm laying hands on you. I'm a possessive type, I warn you, darling. I want you all to myself. No more goodnight kisses for personable young men!'

'Not as much as a glance for personable young men,' Alison promised, her head on his shoulder.

'To make sure, I'm not letting you out of my sight again. I'm going back to London with you and your family when you leave Sidi next week.' He was speaking quickly, excitedly, his blue eyes ablaze. 'We can be married by special licence, for I won't be able to take more than a week off.'

Not a, 'Will you?' or a, 'Won't you?' or a 'By your leave.' It was Brett the masterful making the plans now. And she was content that it should be so.

'I bring food,' called the voice of Jamilia outside the tent's entrance. Brett hurried to hold back the flap which made the door, and Jamilia came in carrying a dish of the savoury stew which Alison had smelled cooking.

Omar, Jamilia announced, had returned to the camp with the donkey, having met a lorry bound for Sidi bou Kef. 'He sent message by the lorry-driver to the hospital,' she said. 'And also to the garage, asking them to send transport. That was two hours ago, so help will soon be on the way. The big-wheeled car should be arriving at any moment. It is to pick you up here, Omar arranged, before it starts looking for the two abandoned cars.'

So her strange adventure in the wilderness was nearly

over. Alison reflected, a little regretfully. She had come to look for Brett, and she had found a Brett who loved her, wanted to marry her. It was all so unbelievable that she couldn't yet think of it soberly, or with complete conviction. The eternal miracle of love given and returned. In time she would be able to accept it. Now she could only look into Brett's blue eyes, wondering why she had ever thought them hard and cold, uncompromising eyes. What they held for her at this moment was truth and sincerity—and a love that would never let her down.